ELIZA

The Willow Pool

HarperCollins*Publishers*

For David North

HarperCollins*Publishers*
77–85 Fulham Palace Road,
Hammersmith, London W6 8JB

www.harpercollins.co.uk

This paperback edition 2001
3

First published in Great Britain
by HarperCollins*Publishers* 2000

ISBN 0 00 651430 8

Set in Stempel Garamond

Printed and bound in Great Britain by
Clays Ltd, St Ives plc

One

Two hats. A leghorn straw and a warm winter felt, belonging to a faraway, mist-wrapped happiness. They were all she would keep of her mother; all that mattered. Meg closed her eyes and clamped her jaws tightly against tears. Yesterday she had wept, raged against the Fates for the very last time. Today she arranged her mother's clothes into two piles: one to be discarded, the other to be given to the deserving – except the hats, of course.

She picked them up, spinning one on each forefinger, liking them because Ma had worn them year in, year out; disliking them because they were the badge of her poverty, given in charity. Dolly Blundell would not wear them again. She had laundered her last sheet, ironed her last starched shirt, washed and laid out her last corpse. Ma had gone to a heaven called Candlefold, where all happiness was and is and would be, and only someone selfish as herself, Meg thought sniffily, would want to call her back to Tippet's Yard.

She slid her eyes to the clothes on the tabletop. Not much to show for over forty years of living, and they could go as soon as maybe. All Meg wanted was the hats, and Ma's nine-carat gold wedding ring that hung now on the chain around her neck. Funny about that ring, when there was no man in Ma's life; never had been.

Of course, there must have been really. If only for a brief coupling there had been a man, though who he was and where he was Meg would never know now. He'd never even had a name, which was sad. Bill Blundell was he called, or Richie or Ted – and had he been a seaman, a scholar or a scallywag?

Ma had never let herself be drawn to speak one word about him, good or bad. Nor had Nell Shaw been of any help. If Nell knew anything, she too had been stoically silent and had Meg not discovered at an early age how babies were got, she could have been forgiven for thinking Ma had found her on the doorstep of 1 Tippet's

Yard, and taken her in and worked like a slave to keep her fed and clothed.

'Come in, Nell,' she called, when the door knocker slammed down. But it couldn't be her neighbour, because Nell always walked in uninvited. 'That you, Tommy?' Meg squinted through the inch-open door.

'No it isn't, and let me in, girl, or you'll not get the pressies I've brought you!'

'Kip! Kip Lewis, am I glad to see you!' She nodded towards the table. 'I was trying not to whinge, see. But sit yourself down and I'll make us a brew. And leave the door open, let a bit of air in!'

And let all the misery out, and Ma's unhappiness and that constant, frail cough. Let Dolly Blundell go to her Candlefold and be happy again.

'Sorry about your mother,' he said gently. 'Amy told me. I knew she wasn't all that good, but I hadn't expected – well – not just yet . . .'

'Nor me, Kip. It came quick, at the end. Looking back on things she'd said, I think she'd had enough. I found her there one morning early, sitting against the lavvy wall, arms round her knees; must've been there for hours. You might have thought she was asleep, but I knew straight away she was dead – it had been a bitterly cold night. Promise you won't say anything to your Amy, but I think she meant to do it. She'd got that she couldn't work, because of the coughing. She was just getting thinner and weaker, so in the end I sent for the doctor.'

She set the kettle to boil, closing her eyes tightly, determined there would be no more tears.

'Ma wasn't best pleased; said doctors cost money and, anyway, there was no cure for what she'd got. But the one who came was very decent; said he'd get her into a sanatorium in North Wales; told her there was a charity ward for people like her, without means. Said he could have her in, within a week . . .'

'She had TB?'

'Yes. I think she always knew it. Mind, she had a decent funeral. Always kept her burial club going, no matter what. Said she wasn't letting the parish give her a pauper's funeral. God! She was so cussed proud, even at the end!'

'Don't get upset, Meg. You did your best.'

'I did what I could, once I was working. And I think she'd have gone into that sanatorium if the doctor hadn't mentioned charity. There was something about her, Kip; a sort of – of – *gentility*. Even Nell noticed it. Maybe it was because she'd been in service, you see; housemaid to the gentry.'

'She was different, I'll grant you that. Amy said she always kept herself to herself.'

'Which wasn't hard in a dump like this.'

Apart from the entry and a sign to the left of it marked 'Tippet's Yard', you could pass by and never know it was there.

'It isn't such a bad little place, Meg.' He wanted to take her in his arms and kiss her breathless, but he held back, sensing her need to talk. He loved her, did she but know it, though he'd never dared say so; never gone beyond hugs and goodnight kisses.

'Not bad, but the Corporation would've had it pulled down if the war hadn't come. If it hadn't been for flamin' Hitler, me and Ma would've been in a decent house now, with an inside lavvy and a garden. But where have you been, Kip? It was a long trip this time.'

'Sydney and back by way of Panama. Never been through the canal before. It's amazing. Fifty miles long and about a dozen locks. Australia's a smashin' country. Real warm and no blackout, them being a long way from the war. And when it's Christmas there, it can get up to eighty degrees! The opposite to us, see. Upside down!'

'Kettle's boiled. Tea won't be long.'

She looked up and smiled and it did things to his insides. This was the time to tell her how he felt, ask her to be his girl, but instead he said, 'I've brought you a few things. There's not such a shortage of food down under as there is here.' He emptied the carrier bag he had brought with him.

'Kip! Are they black market?'

'No. All fair and square.'

'Oooh!' A packet of tea, a bag of sugar, tins of butter, corned beef and peaches and – oh my goodness, silk stockings! 'Kip Lewis, you're an old love and you're to come to Sunday tea, and share it. I'll ask Nell and Tommy too.'

'By Sunday I'll be gone again. Got the chance of another trip the same, so I signed on for it before I came ashore. The Panama run is a good one – safer than the Atlantic. And don't look so put out, Meg Blundell! You won't miss me!'

'But I *will*! When I saw you on the doorstep I was real glad to see you, honest I was! It's been awful these last six weeks. I just couldn't believe Ma was gone; not even after the funeral. I've been putting things off, I suppose – y'know, sorting her clothes and going through her papers.'

Papers. That was a laugh. Ma's special things, more like, locked inside a battered attaché case and, since the war started, never far from her side, night or day.

'That's sad, Meg.' He took the mug she offered, then sat on the three-legged stool beside the fireplace. 'And I interrupted you, when you'd made up your mind to tackle it.'

'No, Kip. I wasn't given much choice. Nell said if I didn't shift meself and sort things out, she'd batter me! None of Ma's things fit Nell, so she's goin' to find good homes for the best of them and take the rest to the jumble for me. She's been a brick. I don't know what I'd have done without her that morning I found Ma.'

She closed her eyes, biting her teeth together, swallowing hard on a choke of tears. Then she drew a shuddering breath, forced her lips into a smile and whispered, 'Now you know how glad I was to see you, Kip. There'd have been another crying match if you hadn't come when you did. I'm grateful. Honest.'

'I'd come to ask you out, but I can see you've got other things on your mind. What say I leave you in peace, girl, and take you out tomorrow night? There's a good band at the Rialto. Fancy going to a dance?'

Meg said she did, and would he call for her at seven, so they could get there early before the dance floor got crowded. And could they find a chippy afterwards, and walk to the tram stop, eating fish and chips out of newspaper?

'The only way to eat them, sweetheart,' he smiled. 'I'll be here on the dot. Want me to wear my uniform or civvies?'

'Uniform, please.'

She liked to see him in his walking-out rig, peaked cap tilted cheekily. And besides, uniforms were all the fashion these days, and popular. Men in civilian clothes were not!

'Then I'll leave you to get on with things.' He placed a finger beneath her chin, kissing her lips gently. 'Sure you don't want me to stay?'

'Sure.' This was the last thing she could do for Ma, and she needed to be alone. 'See you tomorrow, Kip, and thanks a lot.'

She watched from the doorway as he crossed the yard, bending his shoulders as he entered the alley that led to the street. When Tippet built his yard in 1820, Meg thought, men must have been a whole lot shorter. She looked to her left to see Nell, arms folded, on the doorstep of number 2, waiting to be told about the visitor.

'There's some tea in the pot,' Meg called. 'It'll take a drop more hot water. Want a cup?'

Nell said she did, ta very much, and wasn't that Kip Lewis who just left?

'It was. And I've done what you wanted, Nell. Just got to put them in bags.'

'And her case? Have you opened it yet? I think you ought to. Dolly told me there was a bankbook in there, and her jewels.'

'Ma had no jewellery, and I don't think there'd be much in the bankbook.' If a bankbook had ever existed, that was. 'And I haven't got around to the case yet. One thing at a time, eh?'

'Then you'd best do it whilst I'm here to give moral support, as they say.'

Dolly Blundell had been a quiet one, Nell thought frowning. Never said two words when one would suffice. She had always chosen not to reply to questions concerning Mr Blundell, and had answered Nell's probings about why the tallyman never called at number 1 with quiet dignity.

'The tallyman doesn't call because I don't borrow. We manage. I've got money in the bank.'

Dignity. She'd learned it in service, Nell had long ago decided. How always to speak slowly and quietly; never to shriek or laugh loudly; always to hold her shoulders straight and her head high. There had been a dignity about her even in death, because who but Doll could fade away so quietly and with so little fuss? And who but Doll could look almost peaceful with her face pinched blue with cold, her shoulders leaning against a lavatory wall?

'Saccharin for me, please.' Nell was not a scrounger of other people's rations, even though she had noticed the bag of sugar the moment she walked through the door. 'An' when we've drunk this, I'll fold the clothes whilst you get on with seein' to that case. I've brought a couple of carrier bags.'

Two bags, she thought, briefly sad. Her neighbour's life stuffed into a couple of paper carriers. It was to be hoped, she thought, all at once her cheerful self again, there'd be more to smile about when Meg got that dratted case opened.

'Cheers, queen!' She lifted her cup in salute.

'Cheers!' Meg arranged her lips into a smile, liking the blowzy, generous-hearted woman, even though she drank gin when she could afford it, and swore often, and took money, some said, from gentlemen. Nell's man had not come back from the last war, and she had remained a widow. Marriageable men were thin on the ground after the Great War, so Nell had become a survivor and laughed when most women would have cried.

'And thank the good Lord the clocks have gone forward, an' we've got the decent weather to come, and light nights.'

To Nell's way of thinking the blackout was the worst thing civilians had to endure; worse even than food rationing. In winter, the blackout was complete and unnatural. Not a chink of light to be seen at windows; streetlamps turned off for the duration and not so much as a match to be struck to light a ciggy outdoors, because Hitler's bombers, when they raided Liverpool, were able to pick out even the glow of a cigarette end. If you had a ciggy to light, that was.

'Think I'll put a match to the fire.' Early April nights could be chilly. 'And I suppose I'd better open Ma's case. I've put it off too long.'

'You have! What are you bothered about?'

'Don't know.' Meg reached into the glass pot on the mantelshelf for the tiny key. 'Nell – did Ma ever tell you about my father? I could get nothing out of her, so in the end I stopped askin'. Was he a scally or somethink?'

'Dunno. Doll made it plain that the subject of your father wasn't open for discussion. I never even knew if her and him was married.'

'But she wore a wedding ring!'

'Weddin' rings come cheap, and ten bob well spent if it buys respectability. Your mother never said he'd been killed in the trenches either.'

'But she wouldn't say that when I was born four years after the war ended. I wish she'd told me, though. Had you ever thought, Nell, that my father could be a millionaire or a murderer? It's awful not knowing, and all the time wondering if you're a bastard or not.'

'Now that's enough of talk like that! Your ma wouldn't have allowed it, and neither will I! Dolly asked me to look out for you, once she got so badly, so it's me as'll be in control, like, till you're twenty-one. Doll wore a wedding ring, so that says you're legitimate, Meg Blundell, and never forget it!'

'OK. I won't. And I'm glad there's someone I can turn to, though I won't be a bother to you.'

'You'd better not be, and you know what I'm gettin' at. No messin' around with fellers; *that* kind of messin', I mean. And where has Kip Lewis been, then?'

'Australia. He brought me those things.' She nodded towards the table. 'You and Tommy are to come to Sunday tea. We'll have corned beef hash, and peaches for pudding. How will that suit you?'

'Very nicely, and thanks for sharin' your luck, girl. Tommy'll be made up too. Poor little bugger. He's that frail he looks as if the next puff of wind'll blow him over. Sad he never wed. But are you going to open that case or aren't you?'

Nell was curious. Any normal girl, she reasoned, would've done it weeks ago. But Meg Blundell was like her mother in a lot of ways: quiet, sometimes, and given to stubbornness. And besides, there really could be a bankbook locked away, and heaven only knew what else!

'I suppose I must.' Meg gazed at the tiny key in the palm of her hand. 'I don't want to, for all that. I don't want to find out – anything . . .'

She and Ma had been all right as they were and all at once she didn't want to know about the man who fathered her. And when she turned that key it might be there, staring her in the face, and she might be very, very sorry.

She fumbled the key into the lock, turning it reluctantly. In the fleeting of a second she imagined she might find a coiled snake there, ready to bite; a spider, big as the palm of her hand. Or nothing of any importance – not even a bankbook.

She lifted the lid, sniffing because she expected the smell of musty papers; closing her eyes when the faint scent of lavender touched her nostrils. She glanced down to see a fat brown envelope, addressed to Dorothy Blundell, 1 Tippet's Yard, Liverpool 3, Lancashire. The name had been crossed through in a different ink and the words *Margaret Mary Blundell* written in her mother's hand. The envelope was tied with tape and the knot secured with red sealing wax. Meg lifted her eyes to those of the older woman.

'You goin' to see what's in it, girl?' Nell ran her tongue round her lips.

'N-no. Not just yet.' The package looked official and best dealt with later. When she was alone.

'There might be money in it!'

'No. Papers, by the feel of it.' Ma's marriage lines? Her own birth certificate? Photographs? Letters, even? 'Ma would've spent it if there'd been money. I – I'll leave it, Nell, if you don't mind.'

'Please yourself, I'm sure.' Nell was put out. 'Nuthin' to do with me, though your ma left a will, I know that for certain. Me an' Tommy was witness to it!'

'But she had nothink to leave.' Meg pulled in her breath.

'Happen not. But to my way of thinking, if all you have to leave is an 'at and an 'atpin and a pound in yer purse, then you should set it down legal who you want it to go to! Dolly wrote that will just after the war started; said all she had was to go to her only child Margaret Mary, and me and Tommy read it, then put our names to it. Like as not it's in that envelope. Best you open it.'

'No. Later.' Quickly Meg took out another envelope. It had *Candlefold Hall* written on it and she knew at once it held photographs. To compensate for her neighbour's disappointment she handed it to her. 'You open it, Nell.'

'Suppose this is her precious Candlefold.' Mollified, Nell squinted at the photograph of a large, very old house surrounded by lawns and flowerbeds.

'There's a lot of trees, Nell.' It really existed, then, Ma's place that was heaven on earth. 'Looks like it's in the country.'

'Hm. If them trees was around here they'd have been chopped down long since, for burnin'! And look at this one; must be the feller that 'ouse belonged to.' She turned over another photograph to read *Mr & Mrs Kenworthy*, in writing she knew to be Dolly Blundell's. 'They look a decent couple. Bet they were worth a bob or two. And who's this then – the old granny?'

A plump, middle-aged lady wearing a cape and black bonnet sat beside an ornamental fountain, holding a baby.

'No. It's the nanny,' Meg smiled. '*Nanny Boag and Master Marcus, 1917*, Ma's written.' Her heart quickened, her cheeks burned. All at once they were looking at her mother's life in another world; at a big, old house in the country; at Ma's employers and their infant son.

Hastily Meg scanned each photograph and snapshot, picking out one of a group of servants arranged either side of a broad flight of steps – and standing a little apart the butler, was it, and the housekeeper? And there stood Ma, all straight and starched, staring ahead as befitted the occasion.

Another snap, faded to sepia now, of three smiling maids in long dresses and pinafores and mobcaps, in a cobbled yard beside a pump trough.

'See, Nell! *Norah, Self & Gladys*. That's Ma, in the middle. And look at this one!'

Tents on Candlefold's front lawn, and stalls and wooden tables and chairs, and Ma and the two other housemaids in pretty flowered frocks and straw hats. Only this time the inscription was in a different hand and read. *Candlefold 1916. Garden Party for wounded soldiers. Dolly Blundell, Norah Bentley, Gladys Tucker*. Her mother, sixteen years old. Dolly *Blundell*! So Ma had never married!

'What do you make of that, Nell?' Her mouth had gone dry. 'Ma's name was –'

'Ar. Seems it's always been Blundell.'

'So whoever my father was, he didn't have the decency to marry her. I *am* illegitimate, Nell!'

Tears filled her eyes. When she hadn't been sure – not absolutely sure – it somehow hadn't mattered that maybe she was born on the wrong side of the sheets. But to see it written down so there was no argument about it – all at once it *did* matter! Someone had got a pretty young housemaid into trouble, then taken off and left her to it. And that girl became old long before her time, with nothing to lean on but her pride!

'There now, queen.' Nell pulled Meg close, hushing her, patting her.

'Your ma wasn't the first to get herself into trouble, and she won't be the last. She took good care of you, now didn't she? Didn't put you into an orphanage, nor nuthin'. And if the little toerag that got you upped and left, then Doll was better off without him, if it's my opinion you're askin'.'

'I'm sorry I opened that case. I never wanted to.'

'Happen not, but at least we've got one thing straight; somethin' your ma chose to keep quiet about. An' don't think I'm blaming her! She brought you up decent and learned you to speak proper. You'd not have got a job in a shop if she hadn't.'

'Edmund and Sons? That dump!' Years behind the times, it was, and people not so keen to part with their clothing coupons for the frumpy fashions old man Edmund stocked. 'I'd set my heart on the Bon Marche, y'know. Classy, the Bon is.'

The Bon Marche had thick carpets all over; the ground floor smelled of free squirts of expensive scent, but you had to talk posh to work there.

'You were glad enough to go to Edmunds, Meg Blundell. Your wages made a difference to your ma.'

'Ten bob a week, and commission! Girls my age are earning fifty times that on munitions!'

'So go and make bombs and bullets.'

'I might have to, Nell. Trade's been bad since clothes rationing started. The old man's going to be sacking staff before so very much longer.'

'Then worry about it when he does! Now are you going to get on with it?' Nell glanced meaningfully at the attaché case. 'Your mother's will is in there somewhere.'

'You're sure?' Meg slid the photographs back into the envelope. 'I know she used to talk about a bankbook; said if we were careful with the pennies we'd go and live in the country one day.'

'That's daydreamin'. We're talkin' about fact – like all that's in this house, for one thing, and the bedding and –'

'There's not a lot of that left. The people from the health department took Ma's mattress and bedding when they came to stove the place out; you know they did!'

'They always do, with TB. You were lucky they didn't take more!

But there it is, girl! It's marked on the envelope, see? *Will*. Told you, didn't I?' Nell clenched her fists, so eager were her fingers to light on it. 'And there's more besides; that bankbook, I shouldn't wonder.'

Nell was right, Meg thought, picking out two smaller envelopes, glancing inside them. Ma's will, and the bankbook! It made her wonder – just briefly, of course – if this was the first time Nell Shaw had seen inside the case.

'So is this what you and Tommy signed?' Meg offered the sheet of paper. '*All I own is for my daughter, Margaret Mary Blundell*. Straight and to the point, wouldn't you say?'

Her words sounded flippant, though she hadn't meant them to. It was just so sad that it made her want to weep again.

'Your ma wasn't one for wasting words. Keep it safe, girl. That's a legal document, properly witnessed and dated. And you'd better open the bankbook!'

'Yes.'

To be told of the existence of a bankbook had always been a comfort in a strange sort of way. Not many in these parts, Meg had been forced to admit, would have one; wouldn't have a magic carpet that might one day take them to a cottage in the country. It had been something to cling to when bad times got worse. To return to the countryside had been Ma's shining dream. She had often talked about how clean the air was; how sweet the washing smelled when you took it from the line. They would have a little garden, one day. Dreams. Ma had had them in plenty.

'You want to know how rich I am, then?'

'Of course I do!' Nell was past pretence.

'Four pounds, eighteen and sixpence.' Meg's whisper broke into a sob. 'Oh, God love you, Ma!' Ma had thought near on five pounds was riches, yet it wouldn't have paid for the funeral tea – if they'd had one; if food hadn't been rationed.

Nell Shaw gazed disbelieving at the figures, then, swallowing on her disappointment, said, 'I told you so, didn't I? Dolly *did* have something put by, though only the good Lord knows how she did it, and her never once in debt to the tallyman. Is there anything else, Meg?'

'Only her jewels.' A string of pearl beads, a marcasite brooch in the shape of a D, a wristwatch and a lavender bag, daintily stitched. Meg held it to her nose. 'Suppose the lavender came from Candlefold garden.' Tears still threatened. 'Would you like the brooch, Nell – a keepsake?'

'No, ta. Best you should have it, girl. I wouldn't mind the lavender bag, though.' A glinty D-brooch wouldn't serve to remind her of Dolly as much as the sweet-smelling sachet. She smiled, seeing in her mind's eye a fair-haired girl hanging stems of lavender to dry in the sun, then sewing them into muslin.

'I suppose that tea's gone cold? Never mind. See if you can squeeze another cup. Think I'll have a ciggy.' She gazed lovingly at the cigarette she took from her pinafore pocket. 'Terrible, innit, when They cut down your fags? This one's my last. Think I'll nip to the pub later on; see if they've got any under the counter. Landlord was saying that his beer supplies are going to be cut; something to do with the breweries not being allowed enough sugar. Things are coming to a pretty pass when They start interferin' with the ale. Bluddy Hitler's got a lot to answer for!'

She took in a deep gulp of smoke, holding it blissfully, blowing it out in little huffs.

'I don't know how you can do that.' For the first time that day Meg laughed. 'Swallow smoke, I mean. I once had a puff at a cigarette and I nearly choked!'

'So don't start. Once you get the taste for them you're hooked, and the scarcer they get in the shops, the more you want one! I never thought I'd live to see the day I'd queue half an hour for five bleedin' ciggies!' Nell threw back her head and laughed, then returned her gaze to the little case. 'Anything else in there?'

'I know what there *isn't*. There doesn't seem to be a rent book, Nell. Will the landlord let me stay on in the house, do you think?'

'Dunno. Best you say nuthin'. If he doesn't find out your ma's passed on, he'll be none the wiser, will he? Where did she usually keep it?'

'I don't know. Come to think of it, I've never actually seen one. All Ma said every Saturday morning was, "That's the rent taken care of and the burial club seen to. What's left in my purse is ours, Meg." I don't even know how much she paid, or who she paid it to.'

'Well, my 'ouse is five shillings. Yours would be a bit more, bein' bigger.'

'I should've asked, I suppose. I just presumed it was paid Saturday mornings, though I never saw anyone call for it. But I'll have to find that book and try to catch up with the arrears. It must be at least six weeks behind.' She didn't like the house in Tippet's Yard, but she didn't want throwing onto the street until she was good and ready to go!

'And that looks like the lot – except for this.' She picked up a blue envelope. Perhaps it was the missing rent book, though she doubted it, even as she pushed a finger inside it.

'Oh! *Look!*' She felt the colour leaving her cheeks and a sick feeling on her tongue. 'It's my birth certificate. I never knew I had one.'

'Everybody's got to have one It's the law!' Nell caught the paper as it slipped from Meg's agitated fingers. 'Oh, my Gawd! *Name of mother, Dorothy Blundell. Name of father – not known. Place of birth, Candlefold Hall, Nether Barton, Lancashire.* Well . . .'

'So I *am* illegitimate, in spite of the wedding ring! Wouldn't you have thought there'd have been a letter from Ma, or something? But not one word of explanation, even at the end!'

'Maybe not, but what was you expectin' – an apology? So your mother and father wasn't wed; does that make it the end of the world? And if it's explanations you're lookin' for, then that birth certificate says it all! You thought you was born here, in Tippet's Yard, but it was at that Candlefold place, so what you've got to ask yourself is why!'

'Exactly! Why, for one thing, didn't *you* tell me, Nell?'

'Because I flamin' didn't know! Your ma had been living at number 1 the best part of a year when I moved into the yard! I just took it you was born in this house.'

'Well I wasn't, it seems, and it doesn't make sense. Why, will you tell me, when she'd got herself into trouble, wasn't Ma thrown out, because that's what usually happened, wasn't it? Unmarried mothers were thrown onto the street with their shame – or into the workhouse! They still are, even today!'

'I've got to admit,' Nell frowned, 'that it's all a bit queer – unless, mind, those toffs she worked for was decent people, and they helped her out.'

'You think that's likely?'

'N-no. But your ma *was* a housemaid at Candlefold Hall, that we do know, and your birth certificate says you was born there, so there's no getting away from that. Seems they didn't show your ma the door – well, not until after she'd had you, Meg.'

'All right. So maybe the Kenworthys were decent – Ma always spoke of the place as if it were – well –'

'Flippin' 'eaven,' Nell supplied bluntly. 'But any place would have seemed like heaven, once you're reduced to livin' in Tippet's Yard!'

'But Ma loved working there; she longed to go back. She once told me that the day she first saw Candlefold was one of the best she would ever know; said she'd never seen so many fields and trees and flowers. I don't think she ever wanted to leave there.'

'Then it's a pity some fly-by-night got her in the family way, 'cause she never knew much happiness in this place. Where was your ma born, by the way?'

'I don't know. All she told me was that she was sent into domestic service as soon as she was old enough. She didn't ever talk about anything before that. Not once. Her life began – and ended, I think – at Candlefold.'

'There must've been a lot of poverty in Liverpool once.' Nell threw a minute cigarette end into the fireplace. 'People had so many kids they was sometimes glad to put them into orphanages, or send them to the nuns. At least Dolly kept you, girl. Happen she knew how shaming charity was.'

'I think she must have, Nell. And I wasn't being nasty when I said Ma should have left a letter. She worked her fingers to the bone for me, and if she didn't want me to know about when she was a little girl, or how I was got, then that's her business, I suppose. It makes you think, though . . .'

'Ar.' Nell got to her feet. 'Don't do to go dwelling on how *exactly* it was, if you get my meanin'.'

'Which dark corner, you mean? Which hedgeback, and with who? And if he told her that if she loved him she would let him – you know . . .'

'Let him have a bit of what he should've waited for till he'd wed her? Ar, men always said that; always will. It's the nature of the beast, see?'

'Kip Lewis hasn't tried it on!'

'Then just wait, girl! Even the best of them are after only one thing!' She paused, red-cheeked, wondering if this was the time to warn Dolly's girl how easy it was to get babies, and how difficult they were to get rid of! 'Anyway, it'll be up to you to put your foot down, Meg Blundell. You'll never get a husband if you're easy. Men don't run after a tram once they've caught it! But I'll be off to find a few ciggies, if you're sure you're all right?' She picked up the carrier bags.

'I'm fine, Nell – or at least I will be when I've weighed things up. Let's face it, I didn't catch Ma's TB, I've got a job and a roof over my head. Things aren't all bad, are they?'

'Not when you look at it like that,' Nell laughed. 'G'night then, girl. God bless.'

Meg watched from the doorway until the neighbour who all at once had become her legal guardian crept on slippered feet into her house. The sky was darkening; best she should close the door, draw the blackout curtains. She ranged her eyes around Tippet's Yard. Opposite, the little houses of Nell Shaw and Tommy Todd, and next to them, where numbers 4 and 5 once stood, an empty area. Ma had tried to dry washing there, but the clothes were covered in chimney smuts in no time at all, so she had given it up as a bad job and dried them indoors.

Beside the empty area was the coalhouse, where the coal rations were stored carefully in three separate corners, never to be borrowed from, nor stolen from. You had to be honest, Meg considered. It wasn't right to steal from your own kind – especially when coal was rationed now to one bag a week for each household.

At the end of the yard were two lavatories and beside them, a washhouse. Once, Ma said, there had been earth closets and a midden, but the landlord was ordered by the Corporation to put in proper sanitation. So now there were water closets and the midden concreted over and a washhouse built – and the rents increased by a shilling a week!

But you got nothing for nothing, Meg shrugged, shutting the door on the miserable yard that had been condemned years ago. And Nell and Tommy were decent folk to have as neighbours.

She thought again about the rent book, then pushed it from her mind. She would worry about it tomorrow. Tonight, there was the sealed package to open, and only heaven knew what she would find inside it. Just to think of cutting the tape and breaking the seal made her uneasy.

'Right then, Meg Blundell!' She squared her shoulders and tilted her chin as her mother had done so often in the past. 'Shift yourself! The blackout, a cup of cocoa and then the fat envelope!'

In that order, and no messing!

Tommy Todd paused beside his coal heap, listening to the sound of Nell Shaw's slippers as they slithered and slapped across the yard.

Nell and Dolly Blundell, he considered, carefully selecting pieces of coal, had been strange stablemates. Nell as rough and common as the milkman's horse; Mrs Blundell softly spoken and ladylike – a filly with a bit of breeding. Yet the two became friends the day Nell moved into number 2, and remained friends in spite of Nell's ways.

There was, he supposed, no accounting for taste, and not for anything would he give voice to his opinions. After all, Nell washed his Sunday shirt every fortnight without asking for payment and he, in turn, swept Nell's doorstep every week, and the cobbles outside; Mrs Blundell's too, since she'd been responsible, till she got badly, for the ironing. He also took it upon himself to keep the yard tidy and free from tomcats. That, he considered, was his duty done and his shirt dues paid.

Through the open door of the coalhouse he heard the door of number 2 being closed, then shrugged and walked to his house with the few lumps of coal that must last until he went to bed. The sooner it was used, the sooner he went to his bed. It was as simple as that.

Only when heavy black curtains had shut out the April night; only when she had slowly sipped saccharin-sweet cocoa and painstakingly washed and dried the cup, did Meg break the seal of the package.

She found only papers and let her breath go with relief. Papers relating to her mother's indentures, set up and signed when young Dorothy Blundell first went to work at Candlefold? Or maybe papers concerning Ma's childhood?

But domestic servants were not apprenticed, and why should Ma's parents give her a bundle of documents when all they had wanted was to be rid of her? Meg focused her eyes reluctantly on the flowing handwriting.

> THIS CONVEYANCE is made the 1st day of October one thousand nine hundred and twenty-two BETWEEN CANDLEFOLD ESTATES NETHER BARTON IN THE COUNTY OF LANCASTER (hereinafter called 'the Vendor') and DOROTHY BLUNDELL SPINSTER DOMICILED AT CANDLEFOLD HALL NETHER BARTON IN THE COUNTY OF LANCASTER (hereinafter called 'the Purchaser').
>
> THE VENDOR is seized of the property hereinafter described and has agreed to sell the same to the Purchaser for the price of one shilling (12d) and that the said property shall be vested in the Purchaser . . .

'Oh, my Gawd!' Breathless almost, Meg read on. It looked like Ma had bought this house from the people at Candlefold for a shilling! But who in his right mind sold a house – even a slum like this – for a bob! More charity! Ma had been given a place to live – damn near *given*, mind you – just five weeks after the birth of her child at Candlefold Hall!

Dry-mouthed, Meg made for the door and Nell, then stopped in her tracks. No! Nell must not know. No one must know yet! Before she said a word to anyone, those pompous words must be read and read again, so there could be no mistaking that the house belonged to Ma, and if what was in that package really meant what she thought it did, then her search for a rent book was over an' all, because people who own a house don't pay rent.

The rent, Ma always said, had *been taken care of.* And so it had, but by the charity of John Kenworthy, Landowner, whose signature appeared with Ma's at the end of the document. And now, Meg thought incredulously, it would seem that this house was truly hers; willed to her by her mother. *Meg Blundell's house!* No landlord to pay six weeks' arrears to; no bailiff to throw her out!

The fingers on the mantel clock, the only really decent thing Ma had owned, pointed to five minutes to midnight before Meg had read and read again the conveyance and deeds; dry, legal phrases so difficult to make sense of. Yet even so, one thing stood out clearly from all the gobbledegook: 1 Tippet's Yard had been sold to her mother for a shilling before she left Candlefold. And, far from throwing her onto the street, the gentleman she worked for had allowed her to remain there to have her baby, then put a roof over her head! It was queer, to say the least, and Meg wanted to know why, because nobody, not even people as decent as Ma made out the Kenworthys to be, gave away a house. Not without good reason.

Then all at once the curiosity, the disbelief and anger gave way to tears, and they flowed hot and unhindered down her cheeks.

'Oh, Ma,' she whispered. 'Why didn't you think to tell me? Couldn't you, before you went out into the freezin' cold and sat down outside the lavvies to die, have told me just who I am?'

They left the Rialto when the floor began to get crowded and the dance hall too warm for comfort.

'You're a smashing dancer.' Meg laced her little finger with Kip's as they walked. 'I can do fancy footwork with you better'n any other bloke.'

'That's because we fit, kind of.' He didn't like to think of her dancing with other men. 'You and me get on well in most things.'

'Mm. And oh, wouldn't you know!' They arrived at the fish and chip shop to read, with dismay, the notice: 'SORRY. NO FAT. OPEN FRIDAY.'

She should have expected it! Chippies ran out of fat all the time, because fat was severely rationed; shops ran out of lipsticks and face creams too. Hardware shops ran out of mops, brushes, floor polish and paint all the time, and wallpaper had ceased to exist long ago!

'Never mind – will this make up for it?' He tilted her chin and kissed her gently.

'No!' she teased.

'Then maybe another . . . ?' He folded her in his arms, this time with lips more demanding, and because she liked him and had had a lovely time dancing with him, she returned his kisses with warmth.

'I'm going to miss you, Kip.' She pulled away from him.

'And I'll miss you, sweetheart; more'n you think. Be my girl, Meg? I love you a lot . . .'

'Kip, I love you too, but you wouldn't want me to be your steady, would you? What I mean is –' she took a deep breath – 'you're the nicest man I know, but I'm not ready for courtin' seriously; not just yet.'

'So there's some other bloke you fancy?'

'No! There's no one! But I don't want to be tied to a promise just yet. I still haven't got myself straight over Ma. There's a lot of things to be sorted – mostly to do with money.'

'But I could make you an allotment out of my pay and the shipping line would send it to you every month. You'd never go short – if we were married, I mean.'

'*Married!*'

Oh, my Lor'! Here was Kip proposing marriage, near as dammit, and her not ready for it! Not by a long chalk she wasn't! Just to think of it made her insides churn, because Nell had put her finger on it only last night! Men were out for one thing, so it was best they wed you first! And the trouble was that she wasn't ready for that sort of thing, because that was how babies happened and she didn't love Kip enough to have his child; not when you had to do *that* to get one! Kip was nice and kind, good to dance with and to kiss, but her and him in a double bed making babies was another matter altogether!

'Don't look so shocked! I'm not askin' you to marry me – not just yet. But I'd like you at least to think about it. Tell you what – why don't I look out for a ring? I know you can't get engagement rings here any more, but I've seen plenty in Sydney. Can't we give it a try, Meg?'

His words were soft and urgent, his eyes tender, and she came near to hating herself when she said, 'Kip – I'm nineteen. I don't know my own mind yet, except that you're one of my best friends and I like being with you. But it wouldn't be fair if I made a promise I wasn't sure I could keep. Don't go spending your money on a ring – not just yet? Give me time?'

'OK. If that's the way you want it, I'll have to take no for an answer. But I'll buy a ring, no matter what, and every time I come ashore I shall ask you to wear it – so be warned!'

He was smiling again, and she sensed an easing of the tension between them and was so relieved that she reached up on tiptoe and kissed him gently.

'I'd like to be your best girl, Kip, if that's all right with you, but

I'm not ready, just yet, to start thinking about – well – *serious* matters. Not with any man, I'm not.'

'Then when you do, sweetheart, be sure that I'll be top of the queue! And don't worry. I'd never ask for anything you weren't willing to give. I'd wait, Meg. I'd respect your feelings.'

'Then what more could a girl ask for?' she said, remembering the way it had been for a housemaid called Dolly Blundell. 'And if we don't get a move on, we're goin' to miss the last tram to Lime Street!' Smiling, she took his hand, hesitating just long enough to whisper, 'And thanks, Kip, for what you've just said. I do care for you – only be patient?'

That night Meg thought a lot about Kip Lewis and about the way he loved her. Yet she, deceitful little faggot, had hemmed and hawed and asked for time, saying she was too young; not over Ma's death; didn't know her own mind. But it was none of those things, because truth was that she was in a muddle still about Ma and the people at Candlefold Hall, and a legal document in which her mother was hereinafter referred to as the Purchaser.

She had told no one about the deeds, yet before much longer Nell Shaw must know, because the enormity of her inheritance must be shared with someone; the mystery of it too. So tomorrow, after she had said goodbye to Kip and wished him Godspeed and a safe landfall, she would show Nell what was inside the bulky packet; would hand it to her casually – 'So what do you make of this, eh?' – then watch her face as the truth dawned.

What was more, Meg fretted, punching her pillow, turning it over, Nell must promise never to say a word about it; especially to Kip. It was bad enough, she sighed, being illegitimate; what would people around here think if it got about that Dolly Blundell hadn't been entitled to the wedding ring she wore and had been given a house into the bargain? Ma's reputation would be in the gutter!

Yet her mother's good name would be safe with Nell. Nell had been her friend and wouldn't blab, though what she would say when she got her hands on the packet of deeds was anybody's guess!

'Well! *Bugger* me!' Nell said. 'It makes you think, dunnit? I mean – givin' her an 'ouse for a silver shillin'. It isn't on, is it . . . ?' She laid the documents on the kitchen table and fished in her pocket for a cigarette. 'Tell you what, girl. How about puttin' the kettle on? A cup of tea is what we need, and sod the rations!'

'A bit of a shock, Nell?'

'Not half! Now don't get me wrong, Meg Blundell, but those Kenworthy folk must have been plaster saints, or sumthin'! I mean *who*, will you tell me, looks after a girl who was nuthin' to them but a paid servant, doesn't show her the door when she's been left high and dry and in the club, then gives her somewhere to live into the bargain?'

She drew hard on her cigarette, sucking smoke through her teeth, shaking her head in bewilderment.

'So now you know how I felt.' Meg stirred the teapot noisily. 'When I'd got over the shock I thought the same as you. Were those people at Candleford saints or sinners? Did someone have a guilty conscience? Was Ma paid off? I went over it and over it, and y'know what, Nell? I decided that they were decent, even if they were toffs, because Ma never spoke of them with anything but respect and she loved Candlefold till her dying day.'

'So we let well alone! Doll's gone, and we don't speak ill of the dead nor think ill either. If your ma had wanted us to know she'd have told us, so we respect her wishes – say nuthin' to nobody! Don't give the gossips bullets to fire – is that understood?'

'Understood.' Gravely Meg nodded. 'And I appreciate you sticking up for Ma.'

'She'd have done the same for me.'

'She would, but for all that, Nell – and strictly between you and me – aren't you just a bit curious? I know I am. I'd give a lot to get to the bottom of it, though where I would start, I don't know.'

'At the beginning, I'd say – if you're really set on knowing. But before you start anything, Meg Blundell, ask yourself if you're goin' to be prepared for what you might find.'

'What d'you mean? Just *what* might I find, will you tell me?'

'Dunno. But if you go poking and prying you might find something you didn't bargain for. When you start turnin' over stones, something nasty might just creep from under one of them – see? And before you go all toffee-nosed on me, remember I'm on Doll's side, no matter what.'

'So if I was to try, Nell, would you be on *my* side, an' all?'

'You know I would, 'cause, let's face it, I'm as curious as you are, truth known.'

'So where, if you were me,' Meg smiled, all at once relieved to have Nell's blessing, 'would you say the beginning is?'

'Can't rightly say.' She took one last, long draw on the cigarette end, then threw it into the hearth. 'The more I think about it, the more baffled I am. Happen by tomorrow I'll have had a bit of time to take it in. But you're not serious, are you?'

'I'm not going to seriously jump in with both feet, if that's what you mean, but I'd like to know more about the house I was born in and the people who looked after Ma, and stood by her. You can't blame me for that, now can you?'

'Suppose not – but be careful. You and your ma got on all right for the best part of twenty years, so ask yourself if raking over the past is what she'd have wanted – bearin' in mind that she leaned over backwards to keep it from you!'

'Yes, and bearing in mind that she must have known things would come into the open when she died, don't you think Ma would've understood how curious I am about her precious Candlefold?'

'So what do you aim to do?'

'Like you said, the best place to begin is at the beginning, Nell. Once, Candlefold was a fairytale place to me. Ma would talk about it like it was all from a storybook, and I never quite knew if she was making it up or not. But suddenly it's real. It's the house I was born in, and the first thing I'm goin' to do is go to the library and have a look in the atlas for Nether Barton!'

'Up to you, I'm sure.' Nell rose to her feet to glare at the pile of offending documents. 'Think I'll get me 'ead down for a couple of hours. What time are you expecting me an' Tommy?'

'Tea is at six,' Meg smiled primly.

'I came by some pickled onions the other day,' Nell said, hand on the door knob. '"I've got something for you, Mrs Shaw," the grocer said, all smarmy. Then he went under the counter and brought out the onions, would you believe? From the look on his face I thought I was in for half a pound of butter – but there you go! You're welcome to them. They'll go down nicely with corned beef hash. Sorry I can't bring a spot of cream for the peaches, girl! See you, then!'

And throwing back her head she laughed until her shoulders shook.

The table was laid with Ma's best cloth, the cutlery placed neatly. Potatoes cooked gently on the stove; the peaches lay in a glass dish on the cold slab in the pantry. Meg sighed with delight. This was her first party ever, thanks to Kip's bounty. Pity he couldn't be here too.

She closed her eyes and sent her good wishes to him wherever he was now. Probably still anchored in the rivermouth, waiting for the convoy to gather. They were, he'd said, going part of the way under escort; stopping at the Azores to take on fresh water, then on to the Canary Islands alone, and across to Panama. SS *Bellis* was a new ship, and fast – could outrun any U-boat, just as the *Queen Mary* and the *Mauretania* did. Once they were free of the slow-moving convoy they could get their revs up, and go like the clappers! Kip had done more sea miles than most young men, Meg thought with pride. Kip loved her and she wished she could love him back; yet love, *real* love, made her afraid, because things could get out of control, Nell said, and then where were you?

'Sorry, Kip,' she whispered to the clock on the mantelshelf. 'Take care of yourself, mind . . .'

She hoped he wouldn't buy a ring in Sydney.

'Now that,' said Tommy Todd, 'was a smashing meal. You didn't tell us you were a good cook, Meg.'

'I'm not. It was something easy, and a tin of peaches doesn't take a lot of opening. But thanks for the compliment, and thanks for coming.'

'It was kindly of you to ask, girl.'

'And kind of Kip to provide it for us! Now would you both like to sit by the fire, whilst I clear away?'

'I'll help wash the dishes,' Nell offered, sinking deeper into the chair that had always been Dolly's.

'Thanks all the same, but I'll see to everything after you've gone. Give me something to do with myself. I miss Ma most in the evenings, y'know.'

'I miss my feller all the time,' Nell sighed, 'for all it's more'n twenty years since he was took, God rest him . . .'

'That was a terrible war.' Tommy gazed into the fireglow. 'The day I got my Blighty wound I was mighty relieved, I can tell you.'

'*Relieved?*' Meg gasped. 'To get wounded?'

'Oh, my word yes! When you was wounded bad they shipped you to Blighty, to England. It was worth a badly leg to get away from those trenches. Thought I was in 'eaven in that 'ospital. Clean beds, no more fighting, meals reg'lar. I was lucky.'

'So how did you get that limp?' Nell demanded.

'Was too small for the infantry, me being a stable lad-cum-apprentice jockey, so they put me in a horse regiment. Horses were used a lot in that war. More reliable than motors. Motors was always getting bogged down in winter. We was hauling a big gun – took six horses – and I was on the lead horse. We started getting shelled, and copped one. Horse was killed – went down on top of me.

'By the time I was fit for active service again the war was over. Kids skit me when I walk past, but I'd rather have a limp and an army pension than what Nell's man got. Life was cheap in that war. I was one of the lucky ones.'

'Ar.' Nell nodded, hooking a tear away with her knuckle. 'Folks made a fuss at Dunkirk; said it was awful our army retreatin' like they did, but if I'd been a feller I'd have been glad to get out of that country. No good to us, France isn't!'

Seeing Nell's trembling bottom lip, Tommy smiled, diving his hand into his jacket pocket, offering five cigarettes. 'I stood in a queue for these! Thank God I don't smoke. I was always a little runt, and folk said that smoking stunted your growth, see. I never growed over five feet, for all that! Go on, Nell. You're welcome to them!'

Tippet's Yard, Meg thought later as she washed dishes and scrubbed pans, was an airless, run-down slum that should have been knocked down years ago. Liverpool was a dump, but Liverpudlians were the salt of the earth, and people like little Limping Tommy and brash, buxom Nell made life worth living in Tippet's Yard. You had to count your blessings, Ma always said, and that, Meg decided, was what she would try to do, because there were a lot of people worse off than she was!

Yet for all that, she knew that this city would never hold her; that somehow, some day, she would find Candlefold. And when she did, she would find Ma's heaven; that special somewhere she must have yearned for, the night she walked out into that cold, mucky yard to die.

Candlefold. Place of dreams.

Two

The first day of May had been like most other days. Ordinary. A postcard from Kip; Nell, who had seen the postman, demanding to know what he had pushed through the letter box; a fatless day, since Meg had used up her butter, lard and margarine, and would have to do without until rations were due again tomorrow. A boring day until a little after the nine o'clock news. Meg had carried out kitchen chairs, and she and Nell sat there, faces to the last of the evening sun, talking about the days when grocers' shelves were piled high with food few could afford, and wasn't it amazing that the minute unemployment dropped and people had money in their pockets for a change, *They* had rationed food!

'Ssssh!' All at once Meg tilted her head. 'Listen . . .'

They heard no sound, yet there was no mistaking what was to be, because each had sensed the strange quiet that hung on the air before an alert sounded. People had come to recognize that silence: a stillness so complete they could sense it, taste it almost. It was like nothing else Meg knew; a void so all-embracing that it was as if the entire city waited with her, breath indrawn, for the stomach-turning wail.

The first siren sounded distantly and she whispered, 'It is! It's a raid, Nell!'

Her mouth had gone dry, fear iced through her. She ran into the kitchen, gathering up her handbag and Ma's attaché case, throwing a coat over her shoulders, grabbing the woolly scarf that hung on the doorpeg. Then she turned the key in the lock and ran to the door of number 3, opening it without preamble.

'Tommy! Be sharp about it!'

'You two go on ahead!' He hobbled across the room, lame leg swinging jerkily, gas mask over his arm.

'We're goin' together!' Nell slammed shut her front door. 'There's nuthin' happenin' yet. No hurry.' It was a matter of principle that unless bombs were actually dropping, she *walked* to the shelter. Not for a big clock would she give bluddy Hitler the satisfaction of knowing how afraid she was; that every time the siren went she had an overwhelming need to pee. 'Just poppin' to the lavvy! Won't be a tick!'

'By the heck,' said Tommy, as they hurried up Lyra Street towards St Joseph's church, 'that lot know when to come!' He glared vindictively at a near-full moon rising low in the sky.

Father O'Flaherty stood at the church door, gathering in his flock. The crypt was deep and solid, and safe against anything save a direct hit. There were worse places to be when bombs were dropping than the crypt of St Joseph's.

'Evenin', Father,' Nell smiled. 'God luv yer.'

'Down ye go!' None who lived in Tippet's Yard were of the faith of Rome, yet they were always made welcome by the elderly priest.

'Father.' Tommy nodded, tipping his cap; Meg smiled her relief and thanks.

Already the crypt smelled of damp and body sweat, but it made no matter. They were safer than most, Meg thought thankfully, making for a corner seat, spreading her belongings either side of her, reserving places for Nell and Tommy.

A woman with three small children and a baby in her arms was helped down the twisting stone steps by an elderly nun; children, wakened from sleep, began to fret, only to be told to shurrup their whingeing, or big fat Goering would come and get them!

'As quiet as the grave up there!'

The blackout curtain covering the door swished aside and Father O'Flaherty beamed reassuringly at all present, who smiled back, even though they knew it was only a matter of time before the bombs fell. Perhaps though, Tommy thought, it was all part of a war of nerves. Perhaps those bombers had flown in low up the river, just to make sure the sirens would send most of Liverpool to the shelters. After which, perversely, they turned south-east to drop their bombs on Manchester, instead. Them Krauts didn't change.

'Looks like they're not coming.' Nell's whisper sounded loud in the strained, listening silence.

The flock turned, seeking out the optimist, warning her, unspeaking, not to tempt Fate.

The eyes of the pretty young nun found those of the priest, and she raised her eyebrows questioningly. Father O'Flaherty nodded, and she bent down to turn up the flame beneath the tea urn.

'Soon be ready,' she smiled, dropping a small calico bag in which tea had been carefully tied into the steaming water. 'Dear sweet Lord, what was that?'

Accusing eyes turned once more to the tempter of Fate, then opened wide with fear as the company listened for the second bomb to fall, and the third, because bombs usually fell three at a time.

Indrawn breaths were let go noisily. The explosions were far enough away. Seemed like the docks were getting it, poor sods; the north-end docks, that was, and maybe too on the other side of the river, Birkenhead way. As long as they didn't come any nearer it would be all right.

Feet shuffled; bottoms wriggled; the flock settled down to await the tea that would soon be passed round in thick, earthenware mugs. Mothers shifted sleeping babies to a more comfortable position; small, grubby thumbs slid into small, pink mouths; old men folded their arms and closed their eyes. Almost certainly the docks were the target, and the city centre. Again.

The all clear came with the dawn. It sounded high and steady; a promise that the skies above Liverpool were clear, the danger over. Now people could shuffle stiffly into the real world, get on with their lives as best they could; men wondering if there would be a tram to take them to a place of work which might not now be there, women to resume the task of looking after children, searching shops for off-the-ration food – if the bombers had left any shops standing, that was.

'No damage up top that I can see!' The priest's booming voice filled the crypt. 'They gave us a miss last night! Away to your homes now, and I'll want volunteers for a bit of cleaning up down here after eight o'clock Mass!'

Heads lifted, shoulders straightened. No damage done to the streets around St Joseph's. They still had homes to go to! Sad about the docks, mind, but a sup of tea was the first thing that came to mind, then washing away the stink of the crypt.

There was a brightening in the sky behind the crowd of warehouses at the distant dockside. A faint breeze blew in from the river, bringing with it the smells of destruction: the acrid stink of blazing timber doused with water, the stench of sewage, mingling with whiffs of escaping coal gas. All around them, the dust of bomb rubble was beginning to settle, reminding them that the danger had not been so very far away, and that next time . . .

'You'll be gettin' a bit of a wash, then, and going to work?' Nell said, matter-of-factly.

'Suppose so . . .' Meg's eyes seemed full of grit and she smelled of sweat, but a night spent in the shelter was no excuse for being late for work.

'I'll be getting me head down for a couple of hours,' Tommy said, calculating that the bombers would just about now be landing on aerodromes in Holland or France. 'I hate Jairmans,' he grumbled, still not able to forgive them for the last war, let alone for starting another. 'One of these days, they'll get what's coming to them, and I hope I'll still be alive to see it! Ta-ra well, each.'

'I'll make a brew.' Nell unlocked her door. 'Come to mine when you're ready, queen.' She had bread and jam; best see that Dolly's girl had something inside her before she went to work, because God only knew how long it might take her to get there. It needed only one unexploded bomb or a few yards of mangled tram track to bring the city centre to a standstill. But ill winds, and all that. There'd be shovelling and clearing up to do; put a few quid into the pockets of the poor sods still on the dole, like as not. Funny that it should take a war to bring work. Liverpool folk had benefited from the war, even the prostitutes on Lime Street. Yet given a choice, they'd all have voted for poverty and peace. 'And you'd better leave your ma's case with me, in case bluddy Hitler sends them bombers back whilst you're out!'

'I'll do that, Nell. And it'll be early to bed for me tonight!'

She closed the door, slid home the bolt, then, drawing the kitchen curtains, turned on the tap above the sink to make sure there was water still in it. Then she took off her clothes and began to wash the stink from her body.

The cold water did little to revive her and she thought achingly of her bed in the slant-roofed bedroom. Tonight she would sleep and sleep.

Sleep was not to be. As the May-blue sky began to shade to apricot, the air-raid sirens wailed again.

'Oh, *no*!' Meg gasped. 'Not two nights on the trot!' She flung wide the door to find Tommy on the doorstep.

'Come on, girl! They're back!'

'Where's Nell?'

'Said she was off out to see if she could find a few ciggies and a drop of the hard stuff. Reckon she'll be at the pub . . .'

'She'll have heard the sirens, won't she? She'll make her way to the crypt?'

'Happen. Mind, the pub has good cellars – she'll find somewhere. And we'd best be off. You got everything, then?'

'Think so.' Ma's case, a coat and scarf, her handbag and gas mask. 'God, Tommy, but I'm tired.'

'Aye.' At least he and Nell had managed a few hours' sleep. 'Not like them to come two nights runnin'. They've never done it before. Maybe this one's a false alarm.'

False alarms sometimes happened. Once it had been a V-formation of geese flying up the Mersey; another time it was fighters which turned out to be ours. Tonight might be another cockup, Tommy decided, and before the little nun had time to light the gas under the tea urn, the all clear would go and they'd shove off to their beds.

As Meg and Tommy walked carefully down the worn, twisting steps, they saw Nell sitting in the corner, waving, and beside her Kip's sister, Amy.

'Was just outside the church when the sirens went,' Nell beamed. 'Sit yourselves down.'

Her breath smelled of gin and there would be cigarettes in her pinafore pocket, Meg was sure.

'I take it the pub came up with five,' she smiled, relieved to see her neighbour.

'No. Not the pub.' Nell dipped into her pocket and brought out a packet – a *twenty* packet, would you believe – of Senior Service such as no civilian had seen these twelve months past. 'I ran into a gentleman friend, just docked from the USA.'

'Ah.' Tommy nodded.

'A friend,' Meg said, then closed her eyes and leaned her shoulders against the rough stone of the wall, willing the all clear to sound by the time she had counted to a hundred and one.

Seconds later, bombs began to fall, and nearer to St Joseph's tonight. Those who sheltered there felt the awful crunch as the first landed – slamming into the earth just a second before the explosion roared and raged directly above them – sensed the shock waves through the thick, rough stones of the crypt, as the bombs went to earth.

'*Jaysus*, but that one was near!' Father O'Flaherty gasped as years of gathered dust and flakes of plaster fell from the vaulted roof. Eyes widened in silent terror, fingertips fondled rosary beads; children, too afraid to cry, whimpered softly. 'Ah, well, a miss is as good as a mile,' the old priest roared defiantly. 'And will you move yourself, sister, and light that tea urn? Aren't we all just about choked with bliddy dust?'

Nell wrapped an arm around the shoulders of the girl who sat beside her, crossing her legs tightly, wondering if there was a lavvy in the crypt.

'Bluddy Hitler,' she muttered, wanting desperately to light a cigarette, knowing that if she took out the packet and broke the Cellophane wrapping, she would be expected to offer it round. 'Want to get a bit of shuteye, girl? Ar, well, I suppose not,' she shrugged when Meg shook her head, because who could sleep with all that lot going on above? 'Bluddy Hitler,' she said again.

Yet when the all clear sounded, those who had spent five fear-filled hours longing for it were all at once reluctant to climb the crypt steps; shrank from reality, because last night's raid had been too near to home.

Meg rose to her feet, rotating her head painfully. There was a crick in her neck and every bone in her body ached.

'What do you suppose it'll be like?' She offered her arm to Nell, needing her comforting closeness. 'What if –'

'If Tippet's Yard has copped one, d'you mean?'

Meg nodded mutely. Through the open doors ahead she could see a square of pink and grey morning sky, though what she would find when they stepped into the world beyond, she did not know.

'Well! Will you look at that!' Clutching the gatepost for support because her legs had all at once gone peculiar, Nell gazed down Lyra Street.

'Oh my God!' Kip's sister, her husband away at sea, lived in Lyra Street.

'Looks like Amy's is all right,' Meg whispered, eyes scanning the rubble-piled street. Three houses had been bombed; one stood broken and jagged, with wallpaper flapping in the breeze and what was left of a chimney stack looking as if were ready to fall if someone sneezed. Of the other two houses, nothing remained. It was as if, Meg thought, some giant hand had scooped them out so cleanly and thoroughly that they might never have stood there. She turned to see Kip's sister standing beside her, a baby over her shoulder, a small girl at her side.

'It's all right, Amy. They didn't get yours . . .'

'No, thank God,' she breathed, her face crumpling into tears of relief. 'What about Tippet's?'

'Dunno. Haven't had a look yet, though it seems all right.' Ahead, Meg could see slate roofs, gleaming black in the morning light. 'I'll push off, if you're sure you're OK?'

'I'm fine . . .'

Tippet's Yard was undamaged; not so much as a broken window pane to be seen.

'Thanks be for small mercies,' Nell muttered, her eyes ranging the roofs for missing slates, glad that the small, soot-caked huddle of buildings seemed not to have been worth a German bomb. It wasn't much of a house, but it was hers and she called it home. She had even, she admitted, been glad when Liverpool Corporation had declared it a slum and placed a demolition order on it. Yet the Corpie was entitled to knock it down if the mood took them, Nell thought mutinously; the German Air Force was not! 'You'll not be goin' in to work, Meg? You look like you're asleep on your feet!'

'Not this morning.' She'd had to walk the best part of two miles yesterday to get to the store, only to find half the staff missing. 'I'll get a few hours' sleep; maybe I'll go in this afternoon.' When she could think straight, that was; when she had washed away the smell of the crypt and had a couple of hours in bed.

Nell unlocked her door, calling down hell and the pox on Hitler, muttering that at least the Kaiser had been a gentleman and not a pesky corporal! 'And if that lot come again tonight, I'm stoppin' here!'

She couldn't take another night of hard benches and air that almost choked you to breathe it. And she couldn't stand one more night of whingeing kids, poor little sods, and the stink of pee and unchanged nappies. Tonight, Nell Shaw would sleep in her own bed, and Hitler could go to hell!

Tommy and Meg – and Nell, too – spent five more nights in the shelter of St Joseph's church. Five nights more the sirens wailed. Liverpool was cut off from the rest of the country, railway stations out of action – no trains out, or in. Buses were thin on the ground; tram tracks lay in grotesquely twisted shapes, fires still burned on the docks either side of the river.

Poor old Liverpool, Nell sighed. How much more could it take? As much as bluddy Hitler could dish out, she decided, and then some, though what Meg would do now that Edmund and Sons had been flattened was another worry on her mind.

The girl had been lucky, for all that; had been given her pay packet only the day before, and the commission she had earned during the previous month. Meg wasn't penniless, exactly; not for a couple of weeks.

'What'll you do – about a job, I mean?' Nell asked a week and a day after that first raid. 'I suppose you could sign on the dole . . .' If the dole office was still standing, that was.

'Suppose I could, though I don't much care. All I know is that I've had just as much of this as I can take! Seven nights of it!'

'Haven't we all, queen? But there's nuthin' we can do about it! And you an' me an' Tommy are still alive and a roof over our heads!'

'For how much longer?' It was against the odds, Meg thought despairingly, for Tippet's Yard to survive many more nights of bombing. Sooner or later it would be hit, and then they would join the homeless in makeshift rest centres and live from night to night, wondering when it would all end.

It was very soon to end, though those who waited wearily that Friday night with bags packed ready for the shelters did not know it. The moon was waning, Tommy had said cautiously, gazing into the sky. Soon the German bombers would be without the benefit of a city laid beneath them as clear as day, almost.

Not that they'd had it all their own way. Anti-aircraft guns blazed shells into the night sky and naval ships in the Mersey had elevated their guns and joined in the barrage too. Many Luftwaffe planes had crashed or been blown up in mid-air; it hadn't been as easy as Fat Hermann thought.

'They're late.' It was past the time they usually came; what trickery did they have in mind tonight, then?

'Whisht what you say,' Nell snapped. Like most of the people of Liverpool, she was tired and afraid, and wished she had relations in the country she could go to – if there had been a bus to take her there, that was. 'Don't do to go tempting fate, girl.'

At eleven that night, the sirens had still not sounded; at midnight Nell said cautiously that she was going to have one last ciggy, then be damned if she wasn't going to bed.

'Looks like you were right, Meg Blundell. Maybe they aren't coming,' Tommy ventured. Happen tonight some other city was to get Liverpool's bombs. London perhaps, or Birmingham or Clydeside. 'Think I'll chance my luck and go to bed, an' all!'

They weren't coming, said the people of Liverpool in disbelief. To those who waited it seemed there was to be a reprieve. Watchers on rooftops searched an empty sky; fire crews and ambulance crews remained uncalled. In rest centres volunteers counted off another hour and said that maybe, perhaps for just one night, Liverpool was to be allowed to lick its wounds – and sleep.

This was the time, Meg thought, dizzy from so many hours of sleep, to take stock of her life. Of course, the bombers might return tonight and she would be back to square one again; but if they didn't come, then top of the list was finding a job. Rumour had it that the city centre was in a mess, with roads blocked and ARP men still digging in the rubble for bodies, dead or alive. So maybe – if the Labour Exchange was still standing, that was – she could offer to help the rescuers. She was young and strong and could learn to handle a shovel. Or maybe they could do with help at the rest centres or at one of the hospitals. Just as long as the job paid money she wasn't particular, and besides, she thought, it would be her way of giving a two-fingers-up to Hitler's lot.

But first she would make her way to the city centre and see for herself exactly what the Luftwaffe had done. She'd heard that the city gaol had had a direct hit and twenty prisoners killed in locked cells, and that a match factory had been hit and blazed so brilliantly that it attracted still more bombers to flatten still more streets.

Rumour had it too that no cars were allowed in the city centre; that unidentified dead were laid in rows in makeshift mortuaries and that no one knew what was to be done with them. And where, she wanted to know, did you put the people from the seven thousand homes that had been bombed to the ground?

If she were honest, mind, she'd had no great love for Liverpool; Liverpool had been where she and Ma lived until they could go to the little house in the country. Yet now when it had suffered a terrible blitzkrieg, she pitied it with all her heart; felt in tune with the roistering, bawdy city because she had been a part of its terror. And Liverpool was, if you looked facts straight in the face, the only home she had ever known, dump though it was. In Liverpool lived people like Nell and Tommy, and others ever ready to offer a smile to strangers, or a shoulder to cry on.

What she could not believe was that there had been rioting in the streets and the military called in to put a stop to it. Nor could she believe that looting was rife and the homes of those who fled the bombing had been broken in to by angry mobs.

Yet she was to find when she reached the heart of the city that things were even worse than she had imagined. True, there were soldiers in the streets, but digging in the rubble and setting up a field telephone system, because so many telephone exchanges had been bombed. Of rioters and looters she saw none; only acres of emptiness that once had been streets, with here and there a shop still standing with 'BUSINESS AS USUAL', defiantly daubed on its boarded-up windows.

She lifted her head and smiled with pride that she was a part of it; had endured seven nights of bombing and come out of it with her life. She was ready now to get on with that life and do whatever she could to help. Ready, that was, until she turned a corner to where ARP workers and soldiers were digging, and wished she had heeded the cry of the man who told her to go back; to stay away.

But it was too late, and she stood stock-still to gaze at bodies laid almost reverently side by side, some with staring eyes and open mouths as though they had died of suffocation; others with blood-caked, mangled limbs. And all of them covered in the dust of destruction. It matted their hair, their eyes, their clothes.

Yet even as the kindly soldier led her away, she looked back in disbelief, not just at wanton, stinking death, but at the small body of a baby that could almost have been asleep on the pavement were it not for the dust of death that covered it.

'Away to your home, lassie,' said the soldier. 'Away and make yourself a cup of tea.'

'A baby!' she gasped as she flung open Nell's door. 'A little thing with no one to own it! Just laid there, all mucky on the pavement, as if it meant nothing to nobody!'

The tears came then as the motherly arms folded her close and hushed her and scolded her for going out looking for trouble.

'I told you, Meg Blundell; said there'd be nothing gained by goin' into town, but you would go, see it with your own eyes, you said! Not a pretty sight, by all accounts.'

'It wasn't, Nell. It wasn't Liverpool any more. Just streets and streets flattened, and people with lost looks on their faces. And would you believe it – in the middle of all that mess there was that statue with not a mark on it! All that – that *shambles*, yet Queen Victoria looking down on it all with a right gob on her, as if it wasn't her Albert's bluddy lot that done it! The world's gone mad!'

Her sobs were wild, as if all the bottled-up grief of the past months had burst out and was not to be silenced. Her body shook with anger and loathing for what she had seen. She wanted to run, but had no place to run to; only Tippet's Yard to come home to. She fished for a handkerchief, dabbing her eyes, blowing her nose noisily. Then she took a deep breath and held it until her head pounded.

'You finished then?' Nell said sternly.

'Yes. An' I'm sorry if I upset you. I know I'm better off than a lot and I should be saving my tears for that little baby. But I'll tell you something for nothing, if you're in the mood to listen. I'm gettin' out of this place! I've had enough. I'm off, Nell!'

'Oh, ar. And where to, then? Your auntie's place in the Lake District will it be, or yer posh cousin's 'ouse in Llandudno?' Nell asked with a sarcasm she didn't really mean. 'Oh, grow up, girl. Tippet's Yard isn't exactly the Adelphi, but it wasn't bombed like Lyra Street. At least we're sleepin' in our own beds, and not on the floor of some drill hall. And where is there for the likes of us to go, will you tell me? And who'd pay our fares, even supposin' the trains and buses was normal?'

'She's right,' said Tommy, who had heard the commotion and come to see what was to do. 'We sit tight and count our blessings and stick together. And hope them bombers don't come back again for another seven nights!'

'Sorry Tommy, Nell. It was just that I couldn't believe what I saw. And the baby . . . It was so little, and lonely. What right have they to kill babies?'

'We send bombers out too,' Nell said mildly, nodding to Tommy to fill the kettle. 'Wars are no respecters of innocence.'

'I'm a selfish little cat, aren't I?' Contritely Meg shaped her lips into a smile. 'And Ma would be glad to be alive, wouldn't she – bombs and all?'

'I'm not so sure about that.' Tommy lit the gas with a plop. 'Your mother had a hard life. She's better off where she is, in heaven.'

'Ma never talked about heaven, nor God. Don't think she believed in all that, Tommy.'

'Oh, my word, but she did! Not your religious 'eaven, mind, but if poor Doll's soul is anywhere it's at that Candlefold of hers. Her face'd light up when she talked about it,' Nell said softly. 'So don't go wishing her alive, girl. She was a sick woman and she's happy now. Heaven is where you make it, don't forget! Now, who's for a sup of tea, then?'

The May evening was warm, and what they could see of the sky a bright blue, still. They sat on wooden chairs in the little cobbled yard, wondering at the silence; trying not to think of those seven nights past, nor allow themselves to wonder if the blitz would happen again.

'It's true, then. He really did come,' Nell murmured. 'Was on the nine o'clock news.' If it was on the wireless, you had to believe it.

'Hess, you mean? Fishy, if you ask me. Will they shoot him, d'you think?'

'Hope so.' Nell gazed longingly at a cigarette, then placed it tenderly back in her pocket. 'Suppose they'll lock him in the Tower, though.'

'I'd lock him in a house in the East End of London,' Meg offered with narrowed eyes. 'Then when his lot bomb London, he'll get a bit of his own back. He must be mad, though, coming here. Maybe Hitler's sent him to offer peace terms.'

'Well, we don't want peace with that lot. And won't bluddy Hitler be annoyed when he finds out that his deputy was taken prisoner by a ploughman with a pitchfork?' Nell laughed heartily. 'Ah, well, it takes all sorts . . .'

The capture of Rudolf Hess was of no interest to Nell Shaw. Of more importance was where she would find her next five cigarettes and if the butcher – whose shop had survived the bombing – would have off-the-ration sausages for sale tomorrow.

'I did hear,' said Tommy, 'that there's an office been opened in Scotty Road – a sort of help place for bombed-outs. Seems a lot of folk have lost their identity cards and their ration books – just blown to smithereens. Got nuthin' but what they stand up in. Mind, I'd have thought they'd have taken things like that with them to the shelter.'

'Folk only think of finding somewhere safe when that siren goes,' Nell defended.

'Mm . . .' Meg was thinking about the baby still, and about the cardboard coffins they were putting the dead in – those no one had claimed, that was – and burying them in mass graves. At least Ma had had a decent funeral. It made Meg wonder, since she was almost sure her mother had never been a one for religion, what she would have made of it all, and the vicar who didn't even know her saying kind things at the graveside. And was heaven where you made it, and hell too? There was a lot of sense in what Nell said, because Meg already knew that hell was a blitzed city and a baby lying on the pavement. This morning, she had looked hell in the face.

'A penny for them!' A hand broke Meg's line of vision. 'You were miles away, girl. Thinking about Doll, were you?'

'Yes. And about the baby . . .'

'Now see here, Meg Blundell! Isn't no use gettin' maudlin'. What's done is done. Nuthin' any of us can do about it. And maybe you'd better try to find that place in Scotty Road – ask them where you can sign on, for a start, and if they've got any jobs. Did you pay your stamps? They'll have to give you dole if you did! First thing tomorrow you'll have to snap out of it and get on with your life, 'cause if you don't, bluddy Hitler'll have won, won't he? Can't you see that that's what he wants to do; knock the stuffing out of us so that when he invades we'll throw up our hands without a fight?'

'Do you think he'll come, then?' Since Nazi Germany had occupied France, it seemed only a matter of time before an invasion fleet set out for England.

'Nah! He'll have to get here first! Don't forget we've got the sea all around us, girl, and a navy to protect us. Oh, it was easy for them stormtroopers to walk through Belgium and sneak round the end of the Maginot Line into France, but even Hitler can't walk on water, don't forget!'

'But do you think that if it happened, we'd make a fight of it, like Churchill says? Would we fight on the beaches and in the streets?'

'I think you should worry about that,' Tommy said firmly, '*if* it happens. As far as I'm concerned, them Jairmans are taking their time making their minds up. Nearly a year since Dunkirk, don't forget.'

'So where'll he go next?' Meg persisted. 'Hitler's been very quiet lately, you've got to admit it. Hasn't invaded anywhere . . .'

'I wouldn't say quiet exactly,' Nell sniffed, thinking of the nights of bombing, 'but I'm inclined to agree with you, girl. Hasn't taken over anywhere this last year. Mind, there's precious few countries left for him to grab.'

'Except ours . . .'

'And Sweden and Spain and Switzerland,' Tommy offered. 'Mind, them three's neutral. Maybe it suits him to leave them alone – for diplomatic purposes, like. So that only leaves America and Russia.'

'America's too far away,' Meg reasoned, 'and Russia's got a pact with Germany.'

'Hitler don't trust Stalin, for all that.' Nell gave into temptation and placed the cigarette between her lips. 'But forget about 'im. I'm goin' to put the kettle on – make us a cup of cocoa. You got any dried milk, Meg?'

Nell Shaw had had enough of war talk, and she was tired. She would, therefore, have a cup of cocoa, her last cigarette, then take herself off to bed. Tomorrow, was another day. Time enough to worry about it when it came.

Meg snuggled into her mattress, pulled the sheet up to her chin, then stared unblinking at the ceiling. She had still not made up the sleep lost during the bombing but she could not forget the baby, wondering where it was now, and if someone had claimed it. But maybe its mother was dead too.

A tear trickled out of the corner of her eye and ran into her ear; a tear for a dead baby, not for herself, because Meg Blundell was alive, and that, in this city, was something to be thankful for. And tomorrow she really would start looking for a job because nobody could live on fresh air, and the money in her purse wasn't going to last for ever. There was the money in Ma's bankbook, of course, if things got really bad. It shouldn't be too difficult to go to the post office, copy the simple, rounded writing of her mother's signature.

'Tsk!' She groped for the matchbox and lit the candle at her bedside, looking at her watch with dismay. Half-past one in the morning and wide awake still!

'Ma?' she whispered.

But she heard no answer, nor felt one in her heart. Ma was back at Candlefold where she'd been happy, and was bonny again, with pale blonde curls and a wide smile, and standing in the sunshine beside the pump trough in the stableyard, waiting for Norah Bentley and Gladys Tucker. Or was she bobbing a curtsey as Nanny Boag sailed past with baby and perambulator? That little boy would be going on twenty-four now, and called up into the armed forces; married, perhaps, with a baby of his own.

She wished she could forget babies. Had that German pilot stopped to think, just for one second, what his bombs would do, or had he been as afraid, perhaps, as the people in the city he dropped them on? She hoped fervently he would never know peace of mind again, but she was as sure as she could be that he would sleep soundly when he got back to his aerodrome, thankful he was still alive. And anyway, wars were about killing, weren't they? Our lot did it too.

The rattling of the letter box awoke her and she stretched and breathed in the acrid smell of a burned-out candle.

Dammit! Nine in the morning and Nell on the doorstep! Meg pulled back the curtains and opened the window to see the postman, holding a parcel.

'Miss M. M. Blundell, is it?' he called, squinting up.

'That's me! Hang on a minute!'

'Fewd parcel,' said the postman laconically. 'All right for some, innit?'

But Meg only smiled and thought warm thoughts about Kip, who loved her, then read the green label in Kip's handwriting, declaring the contents to be unsolicited food.

'Well, then, and who's the lucky one?' Nell beamed from the doorway. 'That young man of yours looks after you all right. Goin' to see what's inside, then?'

'You open it, Nell. I'll put the kettle on and do a slice of toast. Lovely day, isn't it?'

'Glorious. If you didn't step outside this yard you'd never know there'd been any bombing. Pity the roads are in a mess still. We could've gone to Sevvy Park.'

Sefton Park was as near to being the countryside as Nell could want: trees and flowers and wide expanses of grass for sitting on. She'd had many a canoodle there in her courting days.

'We'll go there, Nell, just as soon as the trams get back to normal. We'll take some sarnies and sit in the sun.' The park was on the posh side of Liverpool, on the outskirts; the bombs wouldn't have reached that far out. 'But I'm going to see about finding a job or getting some dole to tide me over. And I'm going to try to get Ma's money. I – I thought I could sign her name – it wouldn't be dishonest, would it? When Ma died I didn't give back her identity card. I could show them that . . .'

'Then you shouldn't have a lot of bother getting it. And it wouldn't be as if it was hundreds of pounds you'd be askin' for.'

'No.' That five pounds had been a fortune to Ma, though, and saved shilling by shilling. 'But what has Kip sent?' Her eyes ranged the array on the tabletop. 'Ciggies? Think he must have meant them for you, Nell. And you'd better take the mints to Tommy; tell him he's invited to Sunday tea.'

'You're a good girl, Meg Blundell. Give me your ration book. I'll take it with Tommy's and try to get half a dozen sausages out of the butcher.'

'Ask him if he's got a piece of off-the-ration suet, will you? Then we can have meat pie,' Meg smiled, holding up a tin of steak.

She felt near contentment as she ate her breakfast. Mind, Nell wouldn't approve of what she planned to do, but she had thought things over during the wakeful night. A job in a shop, perhaps; go the whole hog and sign up for the Army? There had been ATS girls at the Rialto dance, looking great in their uniforms. Bed and board and all provided, and leave four times a year – when there would be Tippet's Yard to come back to, and Tommy and Nell.

All very well, but she had decided on neither, because until the Government told her to register for war work she was footloose, could go where she wanted and already she knew where that place was. Approximately, of course. You went to Ormskirk, took the train to Preston, then somewhere between there and a place called Whalley was a dot on the map so small she'd had difficulty finding it. And likely she would have difficulty getting there, an' all, but she was as sure as she could be it was to Nether Barton she must go; find the house where Ma was now. It wasn't until she did that she would know what to do with her life.

Candlefold had rarely been out of her thoughts since the night she discovered she had been born there, and now her roots were calling her back – just to take a look at the place and maybe hear Ma's voice with her heart, telling her she wasn't to fret and to straighten her back and hold her head high and get on with her life. The only bother, she knew, would be telling Nell, because Nell Shaw was going to take a lot of convincing!

Yet go there she must, because she knew in her heart that Candlefold – or Ma, was it? – had something to tell her.

She sighed, arranged the tins and packets in a straight line on the tabletop, deciding that for Sunday tea they would have steak pie –

suet permitting, that was – and tinned fruit salad and tinned cream. And on Sunday, when they had eaten and were less likely to argue, she would tell Nell and Tommy what she intended to do.

Relieved that for the time being at least she had got her life sorted, she picked up Kip's letter.

Darling Meg,

I wish you were here with me. It isn't as hot as before but I have spent time on the beach in the sun. This is like a different world. Some things are in short supply, but there is fruit and plenty of tomatoes in the shops – no standing in a queue for two apples – and at the weekend whole families were on the beach with picnics. The girls here are beautiful and brown from the sun, but I haven't seen one as lovely as you, Meg.

By the time you get this – if it doesn't go to the bottom – I should be under way again and counting off the days till I see you.

Take care,

Love from Kip

She glanced at the date at the top of the letter, realizing it had been written long before the bombing. Would Kip know about it now, and be worrying about her and Amy? Dear, kind Kip, who thought she was lovely.

She rose to gaze into the mirror. Not lovely at all, Kip Lewis; perhaps pretty in parts – blue eyes that didn't go with black hair; a good complexion, though pale. And she was slim, she supposed, but so were most people these days, thanks to rationing. And Nell had said she had good legs and should shorten her skirts a bit – but lovely? Not really.

She took the sixpenny airmail letter from the mantel, and pen and ink from the drawer.

Dear, kind Kip,

The parcel arrived safely this morning and you are very popular with the people in Tippet's Yard, who will be having a luxurious tea on Sunday at number 1.

I saw Amy and the children yesterday, and they are all very well.

She stopped, frowning. Best not mention the bombing; just that they were all right and, anyway, if she did, the Censor's Office would slice it out and the folded letter card would arrive looking like a paper doily!

> Today is lovely and warm and the light nights a blessing. Nell has suggested a picnic in Sefton Park. (She says many thanks for the ciggies, by the way.)

She stopped again, reading what she had written. Not much of a letter to send to a man all those miles from home and planning to buy an engagement ring in Sydney.

> I think of you often, Kip, and look forward to seeing you again, and wish you a safe journey home.
>
> Take care, Kip.
>
> All my love,
>
> Meg

All my love. That sounded better than the rest of the letter, and a nice bit to end up with. She wished she could love Kip and want him *that* way. He was a good, kind man, and anyone with half a brain would jump at the chance to be his girl and wear his ring. And to marry him, and have an allowance every month from the shipping line he sailed for.

But that would not be enough, and she wasn't able to love Kip as he deserved; not yet, anyway. And she *had* to love him – or any man she married – with all her heart and soul, and want him *that* way.

Once, twenty years ago, Ma had wanted a man *that* way; hadn't thought of the consequences, only about being in love. And the fact that his name did not appear on her birth certificate was neither here nor there, Meg brooded, because Ma would have been deeply in love *that* way the night her daughter was conceived.

It was a point in her favour, Meg frowned, that she was really a love child, which sounded better than illegitimate and much, much better than bastard. Who was he, Ma? Why did he leave you? Did he know about me? Would he have married you, if he had?

Meg had already worked out when she'd been conceived. Babies born at the end of August were got round about Christmastime, she'd decided. Or had it been New Year? Had there been holly and ivy and a Christmas tree and dancing and fun? Was her conceiving a happy one?

In which room at Candlefold had she been born, and had Nanny Boag delivered her? And why hadn't she been called Carol or Holly or Noelle? Why two saints' names?

Oh, there were so many questions, so much still to discover. And all the answers were at a house called Candlefold Hall, if only she knew how to get there. And whilst she was daydreaming about bonny housemaids and sunny summer days, did the Kenworthy family still live there, or had it been taken by the Government as an Army billet, or a hospital or convalescent home for wounded soldiers.

Candlefold 1916. Garden Party for wounded soldiers, and Ma in a long cotton frock and a pretty straw hat.

Oh, Candlefold, why are you bothering me like this? Or is it you, Ma? Is there something you want me to know, like who my father is? Do you want to tell me you are happy again, and waiting at the pump trough in the cobbled courtyard? And if I stand there, will I hear your voice with my heart, and be glad?

And had you thought, girl, demanded her common sense in Margaret Mary Blundell's most scathing voice, that the flamin' pump trough might not be there; that the house, even, might have gone, an' all?

But if she found the house unchanged, did she march up to the front door and say, 'Excuse me, missis, but can I sit on yer pump trough for a couple of minutes; have a word with Ma?'

She clucked with annoyance, because what she intended to do was so ridiculous and stupid that Nell would give her the length of her tongue and tell her to grow up and get herself down to the dole office like most folk else with one iota of sense in their heads would do!

Yet it didn't matter what Nell would say, nor Tommy, because Ma did have something to tell her and Candlefold hadn't fallen down, nor the Kenworthys left it, or why did she feel so strongly about going there? Why had an old house called to her, all sunlit and shining, and why, ever since she'd opened Ma's little attaché case, had she felt so curious and excited?

Was she bomb happy? Had the seven fearful nights got to her, and the desolation that had once been a city, and the baby on the pavement? Or was it simpler than that: did she want to get out of this place and had she latched on to Ma's dreams and made them her excuse?

Only one thing was certain. She would never know until she found a house called Candleford. And Ma.

Three

Getting to Preston had been easier than Meg had ever dared hope. Liverpool city centre was still choked with the debris of shops and offices and warehouses, but once she had skirted streets closed by 'DANGER. UNEXPLODED BOMB' signs and taken heed of 'NO NAKED LIGHTS' warnings, and tried not to look at piles of rubble under which might still be bodies, she had seen a red bus going to Ormskirk, and any time now, the conductor told her.

'So get yerself on sharpish. There's a war on, or had you forgot?'

As if she were likely to! Meg selected a seat, settling herself, arms folded, to think about what was to come, and what had been.

'You're goin' *where*?' Last night, Nell had drawn sharply on her cigarette, then blown smoke out fiercely through her nose. 'You're goin' to a place you don't know exists, on the off chance? What if it's been bombed, then, or them Kenworthys have upped and offed? Goin' to look a right wet nelly, aren't you, and wasted time and money into the bargain? What do you expect to find there? *Who* do you expect is goin' to be there?'

'Ma.' Meg had whispered so quietly that Nell had stopped for breath and appealed to Tommy to tell the girl she was round the bend and God only knew where she would end up if she went on with such foolishness.

'But what harm can it do? She knows right from wrong,' Tommy had reasoned, 'and not to take lifts from men. Can you blame her for wantin' out of this hole, even if it's only for a day? Wasn't you young once, Nell Shaw? Didn't you do daft things, an' all?'

'I was, and yes, I did daft things and lived to regret some of them. But I promised Dolly I'd look out for Meg and that's what I'm tryin' to do! She's getting as bad as her Ma! That Candlefold was like some magic place Doll dreamed up!'

'You can't photograph dreams, Nell. That house is real and it's there still, an' I'm goin' to find it! If I leave early in the morning I can be there by noon – with luck, that is.'

'So what'll you do for food?' Nell was wavering.

'I'll take cheese sarnies, and a bottle of water.'

'You're determined, aren't you? If only you'd tell me *why*.'

'I don't know why. I only know there'll be no peace for me till I find the place. You said Ma thought it was heaven on earth, and you said that heaven was where you made it! Well, if I'm to find Ma, she'll be at Candlefold. I've got to know she's all right before I decide what I'm goin' to do.'

'Oh, Meg Blundell, why can't you let Doll rest in peace? She was sick and fed up with life, went the way she wanted to. Why can't you accept it and act your age? And if you want to know what you're goin' to do with your life, wait till August! All the twenties are goin' to have to register for war work soon. Why don't you just wait and see?'

'Because till I'm twenty, my life is my own, and until *They* tell me what to do and where to go, I'll do what I want. I'm goin' to find that house, just to look at it. I've got to, can't you understand?'

'I'm trying! But what's going to happen if you can't get there and back in a day? Where are you goin' to sleep and what'll you use for money? And how will you let me know if you end up in trouble? Ring me up on me telephone, will you?'

'Nell, I'll be all right! It's somewhere I've got to go. Then I'll do what the Government tells me, and go where they tell me come August. But, just this once, don't try to stop me, Nell?'

'Is there anything I can say that would?'

'No, there isn't. And I *will* be all right!'

Of course she would be all right. She was going to Candlefold, wasn't she? What harm could come to her there?

With Aintree Racecourse behind her she could almost forget those nights of bombing, Meg thought, relaxing a little. There were fields ahead and to each side; she was in the country now and, apart from the houses in villages they drove through having criss-crosses of brown paper on the windows, you could be forgiven for thinking those nights had never happened.

Dear, kind Nell. Meg smiled, recalling that Nell had been up at the crack of dawn to see her off and taken Ma's attaché case to put inside her gas oven, which was made of cast iron, and solid as any safe, she said.

Then she hugged Meg and told her to take care, demanding to know what poor Doll would say if she knew what her daughter was up to. And Meg smiled and hugged her back, and kissed her cheek, and almost said that Ma did know; was waiting for her at the pump trough.

She hadn't said it, though, because if she had Nell would have said the bombing had driven her out of her mind, and had her locked up!

'Ta-ra, well,' she had said instead. 'See you as soon as maybe, Nell.'

'Never mind maybe! You'll get yourself back tonight before it's dark!' Nell called after her, but Meg had waved her hand without turning round – bad luck to turn round, Kip said – and made for Lyra Street and Scotland Road at the bottom of it. Her heart had thumped something awful, she remembered, though she was calm enough now she was on her way.

She looked at her watch. It was nearly eight, and once she was on the Preston train she would be halfway there; halfway to Nether Barton and an old house called Candlefold. And to Ma.

She had come too far too quickly, Meg realized when told at Preston station there were no trains to Nether Barton. Never had been, and that if she wanted to get to a place like that, then she had better try her luck at the bus depot.

Luck was with her. There was a bus service, though sadly she had missed the eleven o'clock, and there wouldn't be another until two. Fuel rationing, see? Bus services had been cut by half.

'Then I'll have to try to hitch,' she said disconsolately, asking to be pointed in the direction of the Whalley road, along which she walked, right arm swinging, thumb jutting, half an hour later. She had just decided to accept *any* vehicle that stopped, men or not, when, with a clatter and a clang a milk lorry drew in a few yards ahead of her.

'Going anywhere near Nether Barton?' she called to the driver.

'Sure. Got three farms to collect around that area. Get in, and don't slam the door! And what are you staring at, then?'

'Since you're askin' – *you*.' Meg closed the door carefully. 'I've never seen a lady lorry driver before. What made you want to drive a lorry?'

'Money. And the Army, who gives me damn all for taking my husband off me, never mind enough to keep my kids on. Got three. Mum looks after them for me. But why is a young girl like yourself going to a dead hole like Nether Barton?'

'Relations. Ma died, see, three months ago. I'm trying to trace her family.' Not lies, exactly. 'I'll be twenty in August and my age group'll have to register for war work, so I'm making the most of me time till then. And taking a bit of a break, after the bombing.'

'You're from Liverpool? Nasty, that blitz. Your home all right?'

'Yes, thanks be. But all of a sudden I wanted to get out of the place. Them Germans have left it in a hell of a mess.'

'Well, you'll get plenty of peace and quiet where you're going!' Again, the hearty laugh. 'Now I'm turning left at the next crossroads; got a collection at Smithies Farm, then it's full speed ahead to Nether Barton, and your auntie.'

'Cousin,' she supplied, choosing to forget the lies that slipped off her tongue with no bother at all. 'Honest to God, I can't get over a woman drivin' a lorryload of milk churns!'

All at once she was enjoying herself, and very soon she would be at Candlefold, though what she would do then was wide open to debate!

'Where did you say you were going?' the driver asked.

'Candlefold.' The word came lovingly.

'No Candlefold Farm around these parts. Leastways, if there is it hasn't got a milk herd.'

'It isn't a farm. How am I goin' to set about finding it, do you suppose?'

'I'll drop you off at the shop in the village when we get there. It's a post office too, and the lady behind the counter delivers the local letters. She'll be able to tell you. Now, hang on. This lane's a bit bumpy!'

The lady in the post office at Nether Barton did indeed know where Candlefold was.

'Going after the job?' she asked.

'Job?'

'In the window, on a postcard. Thought you'd come in to ask for directions.'

'Oh, er, yes!' Heaven help her, a *job*! 'Any idea what it's about?'

'Just general help around the place, I imagine. Hours to suit, Polly said, or live in. They're pretty desperate, if you ask me. Mrs John's got a lot on her plate.'

'It's a big house, isn't it?'

'Not any more, so to speak. The powers-that-be took Candlefold – left the Kenworthys only the very old part of the house that used to be the servants' quarters in the old days. But there's no help to be had now for love nor money, and the Kenworthys such nice people. Real gentry, you know!'

'Ar.' She did know. Ma had said much the same thing. Often. 'So how will I get there?'

'Straight down the road you'll see the gates. They're locked, so carry on a couple of hundred yards till you come to a stile. From there, cross the field to the far corner and you'll come out at the back of the house – the part they're living in now. It's the way I go to deliver the letters. You'll see a stone archway that opens on to the courtyard – the door is straight ahead of you. Are you used to housework, then?'

'Yes. And I nursed Ma when she was sick. I'm not afraid to roll my sleeves up.'

'Then you'll be more than welcome, if you suit. Old Mrs Kenworthy is bedridden, poor lady. In pain a lot of the time. Would be a mercy if she was to slip away. But I'm not one to gossip, you'll understand.'

'Oh, of course not! And thanks for your help.'

'Be sure to let me know how things go,' called the postmistress as Meg left, and she turned to smile, and said she would, then took a deep breath because her heart was thudding so.

A job at Candlefold! Ma had known about it all along! Must have, or why was her daughter here now, flush-cheeked and hardly able to believe her luck, because all she had ever thought to do was get a look, somehow, at that pump trough.

She picked up her bag, straightened her shoulders and lifted her chin, walking head high as Ma had always done, no matter how bad things had been.

'This is it, Meg!' And oh, if there really was a heaven and a God in it, she could do with a bit of help right this minute because she needed – no, *wanted* – that job; wanted to live and work in the middle of fields and trees and be happy like Ma had been. She'd had enough of Tippet's Yard and rows of little houses and mucky streets and bombs, and here, on a plate, was her chance to get out of it!

The gates, when Meg reached them, were chained and padlocked. They were wide and tall, and patterned in scrolls and swirls, and far more beautiful than the gates to Sefton Park taken away by the iron collectors. She was glad *They* hadn't melted down Candlefold's gates. She gazed down the long, straight drive to a red-brick, two-storeyed house with little gabled windows in the roof. Even from a distance, she could see that the downstairs windows were shuttered from the inside; that the drive was weed-choked, the grass either side of it in need of cutting.

She remembered Ma's faded photographs and the trees and lawns and flowerbeds and the garden party for wounded soldiers. For whatever reason the Government had taken the house, they'd got it well shut up! And why could those men in London just take what they wanted because there was a war on; your house, your car and, at the time of Dunkirk, your little boat, even!

Meg wondered what Ma would have made of the neglect, then turned abruptly away. That part of Candlefold was of little interest to her. It was a pump trough she needed to find!

The stile looked over a field of sheep and lambs. Meg hoped sheep weren't fierce, then decided it was only bulls she needed to look out for! Carefully, at first, looking to either side, she began to walk.

The lambs were pretty little things; the old mothers just looked at her with stupid faces, then went on with their chewing. Braver now, she made for the corner of the field and the far stile that would lead to an archway and a courtyard.

The archway was in the centre of an old, thick wall. The stones were uneven and plants with tiny purple flowers grew between the cracks. There was a safeness about that wall, as if it had stood for hundreds of years and seen things you would never dream of. Dry-mouthed, she stepped beneath it to see the cobbled courtyard of the long-ago photograph.

Her heart began to thud, her cheeks flushed red. She was looking at Ma's heaven on earth and a trough Dolly Blundell once stood beside to be photographed. Ma had sat on that old granite trough often, and had laughed beside it and been happy.

All at once Meg knew she had done the right thing, because there was nothing foolish in following a dream. Head high, she made for the wide, low, nail-studded door, because it was no use just standing there, wallowing in sentimentality! Ma had got her here and now it was up to herself. Chin jutting, she knocked hard with bare knuckles.

'It isn't any use doing that!'

Meg spun round to see a fair-haired girl wearing a short cotton dress.

'Beg pardon?' It was all she could think of to say.

'That door's so thick they wouldn't hear you knocking on the other side. You've got to ring.'

She took the chain that dangled from a bell hanging beside the door, shaking it to make the most terrible din.

'See what you mean,' Meg grinned. 'They'll hear that half a mile away!'

'They once did. Years and years ago, when this was a farmhouse, they rung that bell so the workers in the fields could hear it. Now, we shouldn't really use it. Bells aren't supposed to be rung, except if the invasion starts, but we are so far from civilization, it doesn't matter. I'm Polly Kenworthy, by the way, and I hope you've come about the job. Come in, won't you?'

She lifted the heavy iron latch, pushing on the door with a shoulder. It opened slowly, creaking protest.

'Hecky!' Meg gazed at the huge, high room. Its walls were wood-panelled, the roof rounded and high. Despite the warmth of the day and the brightness outside, it was dim and cool.

'Mm. Like the inside of a church, isn't it? Come into the kitchen and sit down whilst I find Mummy. You *have* come about the job?' she asked anxiously.

'I have, though I haven't got any references. Worked in a shop that got bombed, see?'

'Look – we're so desperate for help I don't suppose references will be asked for. Mummy's a pretty fair judge of people. I'm sure she'll like you. What's your name, by the way?'

'Meg Blundell.' For no reason she could think of she offered her hand, which was taken without hesitation and shaken warmly.

'Take a pew. I think Mummy will be with Gran – or Nanny.'

'No she isn't. She heard the bell!' The voice from the doorway caused Meg to turn. 'Gran is comfortable for the time being, and Nanny is asleep. I'm Mary Kenworthy. Have you come about the job? If you have, you'll be the first! Girls don't want to bury themselves in the middle of nowhere these days. Be a dear, Polly, and put the kettle on? You'll join us, Miss – er . . . ?'

'Blundell. Meg. And I wouldn't mind living here. When you come from Liverpool that's been bombed something terrible, a bit of peace and quiet is just what the doctor ordered!'

She stopped, embarrassed, wondering if she had gone too far; been just a little bit forward.

'Then you're welcome, Meg, if you won't mind helping out sometimes with two elderly ladies. I'd better tell you right from the start that Mrs Kenworthy senior is an invalid. She has chronic arthritis and we have to do everything for her – sometimes even feed her. And Nanny is still with us. She is fit of body, but her mind has gone. She's very childlike now, and can be rather – well, mischievous, you know, if we don't watch her. There would be quite a bit of running up and down stairs, I'm afraid.'

Her eyes were anxious – pleading almost, Meg thought; looked as if a good night's sleep would do her no harm. And she was straight, an' all, looked you in the eyes, which was to be expected of a Kenworthy.

'Then right from the start, I'd better tell you I haven't got references, but if you'll give me a try, I don't mind giving a hand with naughty nannies,' she grinned, 'and I know a bit about nursing sick people. Ma died of TB, you see, so I know what it's like.'

'Tuberculosis? Oh, my dear, I hope you –'

'No. I haven't got it,' Meg interrupted. 'When Ma died, the people from the Health came and stoved out the house – sent me to hospital for tests. I'm all right. I didn't catch it. I'm only pale because that's the way I always am!'

'Please – forgive me. But it's natural to ask, you'll understand?' Nervously, she brushed her hair from her face. 'And I'm not too worried about references. You've got an open face, and I'm not often wrong about people. Will you give it a try for a couple of weeks? The wages would be a pound a week, all found, and there would be time off, which we could arrange between us. Shall we give it a go?'

'I'd have to live in . . .' Meg warned.

'That would be no problem.'

'Then when would you want me to start? I'd have to go home first, see to one or two things and collect a ration card for two weeks. I could start the day after tomorrow, if that's all right with you – and if you're sure about me, 'cause you don't know the first thing about me, do you? I might be a Liverpool scally!'

'Scally?' Polly set down a tray.

'Scallywag. A wrong 'un, a thief. Somebody what's light-fingered.'

'And are you a scally?'

'Course not – though youse people aren't to know that. But I'd like to give it a try, and the wages are quite satisfactory,' she added primly.

'So let's have that cup of tea.' Relief showed plainly on Mary Kenworthy's face. 'Then Polly can show you the house and where you'll be sleeping. We have three empty bedrooms; you can choose the one you like best. The bus to Preston leaves the village at five – that gives us a couple of hours, doesn't it? Will you be very late getting back, my dear?'

'About ten o'clock, but it'll still be light. No bother!'

Meg took the china cup and saucer with a hand that shook. There was so much she wanted to say, to ask – like why, all of a sudden, should she be so lucky and what would go wrong to spoil it? She had come here on a whim to find a welcome she had not expected. But maybe it was all a dream; maybe she was going to wake up in the slant-roofed bedroom and draw back the curtains to see rooftops and Tippet's Yard.

Yet it wasn't a dream. All this was honest-to-God real, and if she didn't grab the chance with both hands she was a fool, because Ma must have gone to a lot of trouble to get her here! It was the only explanation that made any sense. She had Ma to thank for this!

* * *

'And where have you been till now?' Nell Shaw demanded. 'Coming in at this hour! Tommy and me was sick with worry!'

'You know where I've been. It's only eleven, and I'm ravenous, Nell. There's a tin of Spam Kip sent in the cupboard. What say we open it and make ourselves some sarnies? Then I'll tell you all about it!'

'There's something to tell, then? You found the place?'

'I did! And a job too! A pound a week; live in! We're giving it a go for two weeks, see if I suit – and if they suit me. Remember the photo of Ma and two maids standing by a stone trough? Well, it's still there. It was like stepping back more'n twenty years!'

'What sort of a job? Skivvying?'

'People like the Kenworthys don't employ skivvies! But let's make a brew, Nell, and a plate of sarnies, then I'll tell you about it all, right from when the milk lorry picked me up.'

'You've been hitching lifts, then?'

'The driver was a lady. Look, Nell, let me tell it? Don't be saying I've done something I shouldn't till you've got the whole story?'

'All right, then. I'll provide the tea; you supply the sarnies. Then we'll have a good natter.'

'Where's Tommy?'

'Gone to bed ages ago. Said I was bothering over nothing!'

'You said he was worried sick.'

'Now see here, Meg Blundell, you get on with them sarnies and I'll go fetch me tea caddy! All right?'

They talked long into the night about how it had been; about the lady at the post office and the job on a card in the window; about Polly Kenworthy and Mrs John and the elderly ladies and the pump trough; talked about peace and quiet and the little white-walled bedroom with matching curtains and bedspread, and the washstand with a blue and white china bowl and jug on it.

'And you'll be expected to help clean the place and run up and down the stairs and fetch and carry; all for a pound a week!'

'A pound a week and Candlefold, Nell!'

'So Doll was right?'

'Ma's heaven on earth, and I want to give it a try. It might only be for two weeks, but I want to go there.'

'Tommy and me'll miss you.'

'I'm not going to Australia! Once the buses and trains get back to normal I can be here and back easy in a day – if I take on the job permanently, that is.'

'You will. That house has got you charmed like it charmed your ma. What's to do with the place? Even after she'd got herself into trouble, not one bad word did Doll say about it!'

'And now I've seen it I know why.' Though there weren't words to tell about the brightness of the air; about the trees and the sky, all high and wide around them. And the old part of Candlefold, with its huge entrance hall and walls covered from floor to ceiling in carved wooden panels. And the big bell beside the door, and birdsong.

'Ar, hey. I suppose there'll be no living with you till you've given it a try. And it won't be for long.'

'Two weeks, Nell.'

Only it wouldn't be for two weeks. Candlefold had called her, and as far as Meg Blundell was concerned she was staying for ever!

'Did you tell them who you was?' Nell asked, spooning tea.

'Decided not to. Said nuthink about Ma, or that I was born there. I'm going to wait and see what I can find out first. As far as they're concerned I'm someone who went there for a job. I never said nuthink about Ma getting this house for a shillin', and anyway, the man who gave it to her is dead now – Mr John Kenworthy. He died when Polly was quite young. The old lady who is sick is his mother, Mrs Kenworthy, and the other one – Polly's mother – is called Mrs John so as not to get them mixed up.'

'And the name Blundell – didn't it ring any bells? After all, it wasn't all that long ago. Surely Mrs John would remember a housemaid called Dolly Blundell who got herself into trouble? That lady would be there when you was born, don't forget. It was her husband who let Doll stay there to have you, then gave her this house.'

'Nothing was said, Nell. After all, Blundell is a fairly common name around these parts. There's Ince Blundell and Blundellsands, the posh areas. And I don't look anything like Ma did. Why should Mrs John get suspicious?'

'OK, then – why should she?' Nell shrugged, and wondered instead about the flush to Meg's cheeks and the brightness of her eyes.

'Is there a son?' she asked bluntly.

'I believe so. He's a soldier and Polly is engaged to his best friend. Want mustard on yours, Nell?'

Although they had talked late into the night, Meg awoke early, lying very still for a little while to hug her joy to her.

There was much to do today. She must take her ration book to the Ministry of Food office, get a temporary card for two weeks; and she must draw out the money from Ma's bankbook and write to Kip and make arrangements for Tommy and Nell to take in her coal ration when it came, and for them both to keep an eye on number 1 for a couple of weeks, after which she would be back. Back to visit, she hoped, on her first day off, though there was no need to say that, yet.

'I did hear the buses are gettin' through again to Skelhorne Street,' Nell said. 'You'll be able to get a bus from Lime Street through to Ormskirk tomorrow, no messin'.'

'Yes, and maybe catch the eleven o'clock bus to Nether Barton.' Allowing for the walk, carrying her case, she could be ringing that bell tomorrow by one o'clock. 'You're not mad at me, Nell?'

'No. More mad at myself at realizing I'm goin' to miss you! But Doll would want you to give it a try, and if heaven gets to be too much for you, girl, there's always Tippet's Yard to come home to! Reckon I'd do the same if I was your age!'

The post office in Scotland Road was open again for business, its windows boarded up, the inside gloomy. There was a queue in front of Meg and a longer one behind her.

'Gotyeridentitycard?' The lady behind the counter was too busy to go into minute details over a few pounds. Meg handed over the withdrawal form and her mother's identity card.

'Four pounds, ten shillings you want?'

'Yes, please. Leave the eight and six in, will you?'

Meg signed D. Blundell with the exaggerated looped D and a rounded B. It might, she thought, have been her mother's own signature, so well had she done it.

'Next, please!

The clerk pushed the book, in which she had folded three pound notes, three ten-shilling notes and the identity card, under the grille.

Meg walked out into the road, relief shuddering through her. Though why she should feel like this she didn't know, because it was her money, left to her in Ma's will, and if she had signed – or was it forged? – Ma's name, she hadn't done anything illegal; not *really* illegal!

The branch office of the Ministry of Food, next door but one, which had been damaged by the same bomb that had closed the post office, was now open too.

'Gotyeridentitycard?'

If there was a phrase that would go down in history when this war was over, Meg decided, it was the time-after-time requests for identity cards!

Meg offered her ration book and watched as two weeks' food was obliterated by a purple stamp and two one-week emergency cards filled in with her name and identity number.

Now there was only a letter to write to Kip, the floors at number 1 to be swept and mopped, and the last of the bomb dust shifted from the furniture. Then she would pack enough for two weeks, collect Ma's case from Nell, and all would be ready for an early start in the morning.

She wouldn't sleep tonight, but who cared?

Four

Meg was surprised and pleased to find Polly Kenworthy waiting at the bus stop.

'How did you know when I'd be getting here?' she beamed.

'I didn't. I was posting a parcel to Davie and Mrs Potter asked me if the young lady had managed to find Candlefold – about the job, she meant – and I told her you had. And that you'd be coming today. The bus was about due, so I hung around just in case.'

'Did you think I wouldn't come?'

'I hoped you would. My bike is outside the post office. We can put your case on the seat – save you carrying it.'

'That's very kind of you,' Meg said slowly, remembering how her mother had spoken, feeling that now was her chance to knock the edges off her Liverpool accent; talk proper, like Ma had done.

'So how often do you write to your young man,' Meg asked as they walked.

'Every day. Sometimes more than that – even if it's only I love you and miss you – oh, you know what it's like when you'd give anything to be with them for just a couple of minutes.'

'No. I don't. There's someone I write to; he's in the Merchant Navy. He'd like us to go steady – even said he'd buy me a ring in Sydney, but I hope he won't. I – I'm not ready to be in love with anybody yet.'

'Not ready, Meg? But falling in love just happens, whether you're ready for it or not! You see a man and that's it! The minute I laid eyes on Davie everything went *boing!* inside me. He's in Mark's regiment – Mark is my brother, did I tell you? – and he got a crafty thirty-six-hour pass and brought Davie along. They were walking across the courtyard, Mark said something, and Davie threw back his head and laughed. That was the exact moment I fell in love with him. I didn't know who he was and it never occurred to me to wonder if he had a girl or might even be married. He was the man I wanted; simple as that! And don't tell me I'm too young to know my own mind, that I haven't been around enough. I met Davie, so I don't want to gad around now. I just want us to be married.'

'And will you be, or must you wait till you're twenty-one?'

'Mummy would like me to wait. She agreed to our being engaged but she wants us to give it time, so we're both sure. Mind, if Davie gets posted overseas she might let us get married on his embarkation leave, which wouldn't be very satisfactory, really.'

'See what you mean. It would be lovely bein' married, but it might only be for a week.'

'Yes. I'd be a lonely young wife for the rest of the war, probably. I wish I were twenty-one.'

'How old are you, Polly?'

'Twenty, almost.'

'Ar. You'll have to register when you're twenty, for war work.'

'Don't I know it! If Davie and me were married, *They* couldn't send me into the armed forces – only make me find a job. I'd like to stay at Candlefold. When I'm not helping in the house, I work in the kitchen garden, digging for victory, sort of. We grow a lot of vegetables and saladings and soft fruits – apples and pears too. Once, when fuel wasn't rationed, we could heat the greenhouses and get early crops, but not any more.

'When the Government took the brick house, they left us the kitchen garden, and the Home Farm, which Mrs Potter's brother-in-law rents from us. I suppose it was a good thing really that *They* wanted the brick part of the house. It saves us heating it, because one bag of coal a week doesn't go far, does it? Thank goodness we have the woods. We go scavenging if there's been a gale, and bring in branches that have come down and saw them into logs. Every little helps.'

'So what do we do here?' They had come to the stile. 'Shall I give you a lift over with the bike?'

'No. We'll carry on to the crossroads. A lane leads to the house from there. It's a bit further to walk but it's better than pushing the bike through the grass.'

'Tell me, please.' Meg decided it was time to sort out the way things were to be. 'I've never worked as a servant before. In the shop, we had to call ladies madam and men sir. Is that what I call your mother? And do I call you Miss Polly?'

'Good heavens, no! You're not a servant, Meg. You're a home help and we're glad to have you! I'm Polly; Mummy is Mrs John, Gran is Mrs Kenworthy, so there's no mixing them up. My real name is Mary, like Mummy's, so I get called Polly, which I like. With two Marys and two Mrs Kenworthys, you'll see what I mean. Oh, and there's Nanny Boag!'

'Boag!' Meg gasped, remembering the lady on the photograph.

'Mm. An unusual name, isn't it? Scottish, I believe. She came to Gran when my pa was born, then stayed on, and when Mark and me arrived she was our nanny too. She's part of the family really, when she remembers who she is. Mostly, these days, she's in love with the Prince of Wales!'

'But we haven't got a Prince of Wales! He shoved off with Mrs Simpson.'

'Nanny chooses to ignore that, poor thing. She was such a love. Now, she's in a world of her own most times!'

'And you go along with it?'

'We-e-ll, she's no trouble, really. You'll soon get used to her ways.'

'And Mrs Kenworthy?'

'Darling Gran. She doesn't have much of a time of it. You'll be kind to her, won't you, Meg? Often, especially when the weather is cold, she's in pain; sometimes her hands are so bad she can't hold a cup. She doesn't complain, though, and she'll be so pleased if you pop in from time to time, ask her if she's comfy – maybe have a little chat. She hasn't been downstairs for ages, poor love.'

'Then wouldn't it be better if she was?' Meg reasoned. 'When Ma got real bad, I made her a bed on the living-room sofa.'

'We've thought about that, but someone would have to sleep downstairs, then, and there isn't room. It's one of the reasons we need you, Meg. Mummy gets tired sometimes.'

'Then it's a good job you'll be getting an extra pair of feet,' Meg smiled as they came into the courtyard from the far end. 'And doesn't the house look lovely, all covered in flowers?' Her mother might once have stood at this very spot and felt as she did, Meg marvelled.

Ma? She sent out her thoughts as they passed the pump trough. *Do you know I'm here?*

There was no reply; she hadn't really expected one. But a red rose that trailed over the doorway blew in the breeze as if it were nodding to her, telling her what she needed to know.

'Here we are, then!' Polly pushed open the door. 'Welcome to Candlefold, Meg Blundell, and I do hope you'll stay.'

'I hope so too.' Meg returned the smile, and contentment washed over her.

Oh, but she would! She had come home to Candlefold and to Ma, and no doubt about it, she was stoppin'!

'So you've come, Meg!' Mary Kenworthy – Mrs John – stood at the door, drying her hands. 'I'm so glad. Be a dear, Polly; pop and tell Nanny I'll be up in five minutes! She's been ringing her bell for ages and I was determined not to answer it until I'd peeled the potatoes!'

'OK,' Polly sighed, disappearing.

'Well, now that I'm here, peelin' potatoes will be my job, and once I've met Nanny, I'll run up and down when she rings. But should you be waitin' on her, Mrs John? Why can't she come down once in a while? Is she bad on her feet, or somethin'?'

'No. It's just her mind that's sick – muddled. Nanny lives in the past, you see, and the nursery is her domain still. She sleeps in the night nursery and the day nursery is her sitting room. She insists the stairs are too much for her, but it could be because she doesn't want to leave her rooms. Yet there must still be some semblance of reason in her head, because I think she's unwilling to come downstairs in case the present catches up with her! She knows that Mark has joined the Army. She just wants to pretend she has children in the nursery still, and the war hasn't happened. My husband was severely wounded in the last one – his abdomen and chest. He died when Polly was four. Nanny never forgave the Kaiser!'

'So when this war started she decided to ignore it?'

'She was already getting a little vague; when she found we were at war again it seemed to be the last straw. And when Mark left, that was it! She just lapsed into her long-ago world. She's eighty, you know. Best we go along with her little moods, I suppose. She was so good to me when John died. I don't know how I'd have pulled myself together if it hadn't been for Nanny.'

'But she rings her bell to call you like a servant, Mrs John – surely, that can't be right?'

'No, but understandable. She's back in the days when we had a staff to run the house – we never called them servants, Meg – and she still thinks she's only got to ring.'

'Well, she won't be ringing till she finds her bell,' Polly grinned from the kitchen doorway. 'I've hidden it behind the curtain. I'll take you to meet her after lunch, Meg. You'll learn to humour her. She's no trouble really. If she gets a bit bossy you just walk away!'

'But why do you have to put up with such a carry-on? I mean, she isn't family.'

'No, but she's Nanny,' Mary Kenworthy smiled gently, 'which is pretty much the same thing. And she stayed with us through good times and bad. *Almost* family, Meg.'

'Ar. I see,' Meg nodded, though she didn't see at all! That Nanny seemed a right old faggot! In the photograph she'd had a mouth on her like a steel trap! *Nanny Boag and Master Mark* her mother had written on the back of the picture of Polly's brother in his christening gown.

But no one here knew about the photographs of Candlefold and no one would get to know until she was good and ready to tell them. Good-hearted though they were, and decent to a servant who'd got into trouble, Meg wanted to find out for herself how it had really been, and not be told kindly and gently about it by an embarrassed Mrs John. Because that was how it would be if ever she admitted being Dorothy Blundell's daughter, and herself born at Candlefold!

'By the way,' Polly giggled, 'Nanny is busy at the moment sticking pins into a newspaper picture of Mrs Simpson. I'll leave her to it and take you up there, Meg, when she's back to more normal, sort of. Seeing a strange face in her present mood might be a bit too much for her!'

'Oooh! She isn't a witch, is she? Sticking pins, I mean!' Meg gasped.

'Don't worry, my dear. Nanny, even at her most troublesome, is no worse than a child having a fit of the sulks. I'm sure she doesn't know the first thing about witchcraft, even though it's supposed to be witch country around these parts! Now, shall Polly take you to your room, then show you round the house and what is left to us of the gardens and outbuildings? And the kitchen garden, of course. And when you do, Polly, can you ask Mr Potter if we can have a couple of spring cabbages?'

'Potter? That's the name of the lady at the post office, isn't it?'

'That's right. Our gardener is her husband. We are such a tiny community that everyone seems connected in some way or another. It's Mrs Potter's sister and her husband – Armitage – who rent Home Farm from us. Everybody knows everybody. And by the time you've had two weeks with us, Meg, you'll know if you want to be a part of it or not. There are no picture houses or dance halls in Nether Barton. Only hops, sometimes, in the parish hall. Will you miss things like that?'

She said it anxiously, Meg thought, as if to think that her home help might leave at the end of the fortnight troubled her.

'I might, Mrs John, but I don't think I will. After that bombing it's safer here! And anyway, Ma and me always wanted to live in the country, so I hope I suit.'

'I think you will. And by the way,' Polly smiled at her mother, 'is it omelettes for lunch? I can get some saladings from Potter if it is.'

'Omelettes!' Meg gasped. 'You need eggs for them, don't you?'

'Yes, but we have our own hens, you see, and we're very lucky to have our own cow too. A little Jersey. We keep her at Home Farm with the herd there, and Armitage milks her for us. So you can have plenty of milk on your porridge at breakfast, and an egg as well.

'At night we have a big mug of Ovaltine – if we've been able to get any in the shops, that is – or milky cocoa. We sit round the table here, and call it our quiet time; think of the day ahead. We Kenworthys are optimists. Tomorrow is a day to look forward to, not the day that never comes! Are you an optimist, Meg Blundell?'

'Yes, I am,' she said firmly, because who in her right mind wouldn't be an optimist in a house like this, with all the milk she could drink, and a fresh egg for breakfast?

The afternoon sun warmed the stones of the old house to honey, and bees buzzed around roses and clematis that climbed the walls and peeped into upstairs windows.

'I like this bit of Candlefold best.' Polly waved an embracing hand. 'Oh, the newer, red-brick part of the house is very elegant, but this old greystone bit is solid and safe, somehow. The walls are two feet thick, which makes it cooler in summer and warmer in winter. The very first Kenworthy built this in 1320; look over the door, you can still make out the date. It was chiselled there when a yeoman farmer brought his bride here and fathered eight children on her, though only two lived.

'Children died in medieval times. I suppose my early ancestors thought themselves lucky to rear two sons to manhood. The elder took the farm, as it was then; the younger went to London to seek his fortune, so maybe there is another line of Kenworthys running parallel to ours. Fortunately, the one who lived here was taught to read and write by the monks at the abbey, so he could count his money, and read his Bible – in Latin, of course!'

'And I bet he gave plenty to the Church, an' all!' Meg remembered from history lessons at school how large the Church had loomed in long-ago England.

'Yes. Mummy says they gave their tithe, always – a tenth of all the crops they grew and a fair bit of the cash in hand, so to speak. I don't know when our lot stopped being Catholics. A lot of the families around this part of Lancashire never gave up the old religion – held secret Masses. But it seems the sixteenth-century Kenworthys thought it politic to be Anglo-Catholic. It's common knowledge they sat on the fence during the Civil War too, paying lip service to Cromwell, yet all the time helping royalists or hiding them if they were on the run from Roundhead soldiers! I suppose we got very good at surviving; that's why we're still here!'

There had been a Kenworthy at Waterloo and one fought in the Crimea. 'Our lot have lived here for six hundred years, Meg. No one else but a direct-line Kenworthy. God, wouldn't it be awful if something happened and the line ended? Hell! I hate wars!'

Tears filled her eyes and Meg was in no doubt she was thinking of Davie, and thought herself lucky she wasn't in love – not properly in love – with Kip Lewis. Loving someone so desperately took over your whole life; she knew that already from the way Polly went from smiles to tears in seconds. Mind, Polly Kenworthy was lucky knowing who she was, Meg had to admit; knew all about her ancestors way back to 1320, whilst Margaret Mary Blundell didn't even know her grandparents, nor even who had fathered her. Polly was twice lucky because she had background *and* a pedigree.

It was all because of Candlefold, which wasn't just a very old house, but a way of life. Candlefold had become Ma's happy place because before she had come here to work, the life she'd led hadn't been worth mentioning. Where Ma was born and reared Meg would never know now; sufficient only to accept that Ma's life began here, as a fourteen-year-old girl sent into domestic service.

Small wonder Dolly Blundell had loved the place, and the kindness and happiness and the belonging; no prizes for guessing where Ma had blossomed into a pretty girl who laughed a lot, for hadn't she always been laughing or smiling on those photographs?

Who were you, Ma? Who am I? And why does this house have a hold over you and me? Why did you tell me with your thoughts that I must come here?

'Hey! A penny for them! I asked if you'd like to see the other part of the house, but you were miles away.'

'I was thinkin' that you know so much about your family and I know nuthink at all about mine.'

'But you must know *something* – your mother and father and your grandparents – unless you were a foundling.'

'What's a foundling?' Meg scowled, sorry she had said what she had.

'An orphan of the storm, an abandoned child . . .'

'Well, I wasn't! You know I had a mother! But I never knew my father. He was a seaman and died at sea of plague, or something. Anyway, they sewed his body in sailcloth and weighted it and buried him at sea. That's all I know. Never knew my grandparents'

She told stinking lies too. Her father dying at sea, indeed! Mind, if he had, that was the way he'd have gone, because Kip once told her that was how it was. One of Kip's crew had died of yellow fever and they'd got him overboard pretty quick, he'd said, so it wouldn't spread.

'I never knew my grandpa; can hardly remember my father either. Sometimes bits come back, but they are very hazy. But I've got a gran, and you can share her with me, Meg. So are we going to have a look at the brick house, then?'

'Won't we get into trouble? Won't there be guards?'

'Not a bod in sight. Oh, someone comes about once a month to check the place over, and sometimes a van arrives and things are taken in. Mummy says she thinks that either documents or records or works of art are stored there. Well, they couldn't leave all the stuff in London for the Luftwaffe to bomb, could they? Museums and art galleries were emptied as soon as war started, don't forget. Maybe some of it is here, snug and safe – who knows?'

'But don't you care, Polly, about them nicking your house?'

'No! Why should I? All I care about is that this war is over as soon as maybe, and that Davie and Mark will come through it safely – and all the servicemen and women. Wars are wrong and stupid. Look what happened to my father. His war wounds slowly killed him!' Tears came once more, and Meg knew she was thinking about Davie again.

'Ar hey, girl! Nuthink's going to happen to your feller! How could it, when he's never out of your thoughts? And your brother's goin' to be all right too, so how about you and me doin' a tour of the place? Then you can take me to meet your gran, eh?'

'Yes, of course!' Polly pulled her hand across her eyes. 'And Nanny too.'

'Y-yes . . .' Daft old Nanny, who lived in a pretend world and stuck pins in pictures and had tantrums you walked away from. No harm in her at all! Childlike, Mrs John said. So why, all at once, did Meg not want to visit the nursery? Why did just thinking about it make her uneasy, even though she would be meeting an old lady who had brought up two generations of Kenworthys and who Polly obviously loved; Mrs John too! Why should she feel peculiar about meeting someone she had only before seen on a photograph as a nanny in long skirts, a baby boy in her arms?

She did not know what gave her the creepy feeling. Sufficient to say she would know soon enough if her fears held substance. This very afternoon, in fact, when they climbed the stairs to the nursery.

The wide, cushioned windowsill in her bedroom made a comfortable seat and Meg sat, arms around knees, looking out over fields and trees to the distant evening sky. It was past ten and the light was beginning to fade, blurring the outlines of trees and hedges, rounding them with mist. Twilight here was gentler than at Tippet's Yard, where the fading of the light made outlines of buildings sharp and dark against the skyline. Here at Candlefold a bird sang to warn against the ending of the day, and all about was soft and hushed.

The white-painted walls of the room reflected the light from the window and softened into palest apricot; over the weathercock atop the stables, the first star appeared, low in the sky. Did you wish on first stars? *Starlight star bright, first star I've seen tonight . . .* Did you close your eyes and cross your fingers and wish to stay here for ever and sleep always in this blue-flowered room?

Meg closed her eyes to call back the day that had been: she and Polly pushing through a gap in the hedge and into the garden of the house the faceless ones had taken, to gaze at its shuttered windows, neglected lawns, the broad sweep of weed-choked steps. She had seen it all before in a photograph. . . . *1916. Garden Party . . . wounded soldiers.* The tussocked grass was fine-trimmed then, and roses that ran wild over the front of the house were once trained into obedience. Afterwards, they had climbed the stairs to the nursery.

'Can I come in? Polly pushed open the door. 'I've brought someone to see you.'

Nanny Boag in a rocking chair, knitted slippers on her feet. She wore a printed cotton dress, and an embroidered pinafore tied at the waist. She looked younger than the long-skirted, black-bonneted lady in the photograph. Her cheeks were plump, her eyes wide as she turned eagerly.

'Polly, dear! How nice of you to bring your little friend! What is your name, child?'

'Meg.'

'Meg who? Cat got your tongue? Did your nanny bring you? Where is she?'

'In the kitchen, talking to Cook,' Polly hastened, pink-cheeked.

'Doesn't Nanny get a kiss then, or have we forgotten our manners?' The elderly woman offered her cheek; dutifully Polly kissed it.

'Were you having a little sleep? Did we wake you? Shall we come back later?'

'Sleep? Goodness me, no! Nanny hasn't time to sleep! I was just thinking about Scotland and all the packing to be done! August already, and the year flown by! Go and play with your friend, dear, and don't get into mischief! And put your bonnet on, or you'll get freckles! Close the door quietly!'

Her eyelids drooped, her chin fell on her chest.

'Heaven help us! What's to do with the old girl?' Meg gasped as they tiptoed away. 'August? Goin' to Scotland? It's May!'

'We stopped going to Scotland before Pa died. We used always to go in August, I believe.'

'So we are both little girls, and my nanny is talking to Cook – only there isn't a cook!'

'Not any more.'

'I thought she'd be – well – sterner.'

'She was once. Now she seems to have got smaller and more frail.'

'And if I take her tea up tomorrow, will she remember me?'

'I doubt it,' Polly smiled. 'I'll introduce you again, in the morning.'

Childlike, Meg frowned. Frail? Oh, she might be that, but her eyes had been sharp and beady; had taken in every detail of Polly's little friend.

They had met Polly's mother then, closing the door of Mrs Kenworthy's room, a finger to her lips.

'Mother-in-law is sleeping. Perhaps you could look in on her later?'

Meg picked up the tray from the floor outside the door, asking if there was anything she could do. 'I came to help, Mrs John, and I've hardly done a thing.'

'Then you can make tea. Use the small pot. We'll count today as your settling-in day. And when we've had tea, will you go with Polly to feed the hens and collect the eggs? I could do with a few for a baked custard for supper.'

'It isn't right your mother should work so hard,' Meg protested as they crossed the courtyard, making for the henhouse. 'I mean – she once had people to do the housework for her, and a cook, an' all! Now, she's got your gran and Nanny Boag to worry about, as well as the war and food rationing. And she's such a lovely lady.'

'She is, Meg. I adore her. And things will get easier once you're into the swing of it. By the way, hens drink a lot of water when they are in the lay; could you fill a bucket at the pump whilst I get the feed?'

There was an iron pump at the trough. Meg lifted the handle up and down; water splashed into the bucket.

'Ma?' she whispered, thinking how it had once been for Dorothy Blundell and how her life had ended in the cold and dark of a mucky yard. 'Oh, Ma.' She sucked in her breath sharply, then arranged her mouth into a smile as Polly waved from the far archway. 'Coming!' she called.

Twelve fat brown hens had run to greet them; drank long at the water trough, then pecked up the wheat Polly threw, feathered bottoms bobbing as they scratched.

'Oh, they're lovely!'

'Don't get fond of them, Meg. They aren't pets! Would you like to collect the eggs?'

Collecting eight brown eggs, Meg thought, had been just about the nicest, most countrified thing she had ever done. She had laid them carefully in the empty feed bucket, then placed them in the wooden egg rack in the pantry.

Mind, meeting Polly's gran had been something altogether different. It might even, Meg thought as she watched big black birds settling in the far trees, have been a disaster, but for the lies. *More* lies!

'Meg Blundell, is it?' asked the old lady whose gnarled hands rested unmoving on the counterpane. 'How strange. We once had a housemaid called Blundell – Dorothy, her name was. Would you perhaps know of her?'

Her eyes were troubled as she said it, Meg thought, a look of apprehension in them, as if she had needed the stranger who stood at her bedside to deny it.

'Dorothy? Oh no. Ma was called Hilda.' Clever of her to have it all worked out – just in case! 'An' she wasn't never a servant; worked in a tobacco factory. She died three months ago.'

'Ah, yes.' A small smile – almost of relief, Meg thought – moved the comers of Mrs Kenworthy's mouth. 'Just that the name brought it back . . .'

'Blundell's a common enough name around where I was born,' Meg was quick to answer. 'There's even districts of Liverpool with Blundell in them. And me da died at sea,' she added, to take care of the nameless scallywag. How glib a liar she was becoming – she who'd always prided herself in telling the truth and shaming the devil!

'I'm very glad to meet you, Meg Blundell, for all that.'

'And I'm very glad to meet you, Mrs Kenworthy.' Meg took the offered hand carefully in her own, knowing that hands so swollen hurt a great deal and must not be shaken. 'And I'm glad I've come here to work. It's so beautiful. You can't imagine how different it is from Liverpool.'

'Where, in Liverpool?'

'Lyra Street.' And that took care of Tippet's Yard, Meg thought as she offered the road where Kip's sister lived. 'A lot of houses got bombed around there, but I was lucky.'

'Poor Liverpool,' the old lady sighed. 'We had relatives there once. One of them – a cousin – died without issue and left some of his property to my son. John, that is; Polly's pa. But he got rid of it very quickly; sold it off. I don't think it brought a lot at auction . . .'

Sold? But he'd given one – as near as dammit, that was – to her ma, hadn't he? But for all that, 'Ar,' was all she said, because it was best Mrs Kenworthy shouldn't be reminded about a place called Tippet's Yard, or about the name signed beside that of Dorothy Blundell. She wouldn't learn the truth by admitting whose daughter she was, because people like the Kenworthys wouldn't tell it to her if they thought it would be hurtful. Their sort never did things that hurt.

'Do you want us to stay for a while, Gran?'

So they talked about Davie, and how many more days it would be until he came on long leave, and Mark too. And Meg told of the thrill of collecting eggs and how lovely it was to live at Candlefold and how awful that That Lot in London could just take your house!

'But it might have been worse, Meg. We could have had an army unit who would be marching up and down all the time, and sergeants shouting orders and men doing target practice! And those people could have thrown us out completely, don't forget! I'm grateful they let us keep this old part, and the kitchen garden and the acres. At least we are still here. One caring owner, as they say, for six hundred years. At least we've been able to hold on, unbroken. And I'm slipping down in bed! Could you prop me up again – save Mary having to do it?'

So one either side of the high single bed, Polly and Meg lifted her gently, placing pillows at her back and beneath each arm for support.

'Thank you.' Mrs Kenworthy opened her eyes. She had closed them in anticipation of pain to come, and there had been none. 'That's much better. Awful of me to be so helpless . . .'

'No it isn't,' Meg defended. 'An' I'm used to lifting 'cause Ma was sick for a long time with TB – and I didn't take it,' she supplied to save any bother. 'I'll come up again – see if you want anything doin', Mrs Kenworthy.'

She had taken a liking straight away to the woman who lay so still in the lace-covered, old-fashioned bed. So softly spoken, and thanking them gratefully for comfying her in bed. Not like the old girl up the stairs, and her able to walk about and do things for herself had she wanted to! And ringing her bell to summon a long-ago housemaid to do her skivvying!

Had she once, Meg thought now, as the distant trees began to fade into the night, rung her bell and had Dorothy Blundell hurried up the stairs to do the nanny's bidding? Had Ma carried up nursery meals when the baby in the christening gown was growing up? Mind, Ma wouldn't have known Polly who, Meg calculated, must have been born after she left. Ma's replacement would have answered the ringing then!

Poor Ma. Did she leave Candlefold in tears, even though they had cared for her and put a roof over her head? Had she turned for just one last look? And had she longed, even as she left, for the man who was the cause of it all to make an honest woman of her?

Well, Ma had managed without him, Meg thought defiantly. In spite of the shame and having to wear a cheap wedding ring, Ma had kept her end up till she caught TB from a woman she helped nurse, Nell said; probably when she had washed her and laid her out and got her ready for the undertaker. Ma needn't have died if she hadn't had to do things like that.

Yet she came up trumps in the end, God love her! Ma it had been who'd enticed her to this place where there were eggs for breakfast and fields and trees and flowers and kindness. And Dorothy Blundell's daughter was stoppin' here, no matter how many lies she told! And what was more, she would keep her mouth shut until she found out what she wanted to know and was good and ready to tell them who she really was. *And* where she had been born!

'Come in,' Meg answered the gentle tap on the door.

'Thought you might be asleep . . .'

'Nah, Polly. Been sittin' at the window, thinking about today, watching it get dark. It's like another world after Tip – after Lyra Street. Wasn't I lucky, chancing on Mrs Potter?' She swung her legs to the floor.

'But we were lucky, too. Did you ever find the relations you were looking for, by the way?'

'Weren't any relations.' My, but news travelled fast in Nether Barton! 'Don't know why I said that. As a matter of fact, I'd just got sick of Liverpool – the mess after the blitz, and so many killed, I mean – that I jumped on the first bus I saw and ended up here. Just a day away from it all, it was supposed to be.'

How many more lies?

'And you saw the card in the post office window, and asked directions to Candlefold?'

'Well, the store I worked in had been bombed. I needed a job and, like I said, Ma and me used to talk a lot about livin' in the country. One day. There was this little place – all in our imagination, mind – with a garden where you didn't get smuts all over the washing when you hung it out to dry. Only Ma didn't make it.' Her bottom lip trembled and she straightened it into a smile. 'But I made it, Polly! And I'm sure Ma knows I did!'

'And will you like it here?'

'You bet I will!'

She would be stoppin' till they threw her out or, come August, the Government told her to find war work. And she was moving on nowhere without a fight!

'Mind if I stay and talk? I've been writing to Davie, and I always feel so lonely afterwards. Are you very tired, Meg?'

'No. I'm all keyed up, 's a matter of fact. Just can't get over my luck, if you want to know. Been telling myself I'll wake up in L-Lyra Street, and find it's all been a dream. Let's sit on the bed and talk?'

She closed the door; *her* door! It was giddy-making. Then she carefully folded back the valanced bedspread, kicked off her slippers and offered a pillow to Polly.

'What's them flowers called on the bedspread and curtains? They're ever so bonny. You'll have to teach me the names of flowers.'

'Well, those particular ones are delphiniums. They once grew in the garden of the brick house – all shades of blue – but they've been overgrown. Potter says it's going to take him for ever to lick it all into shape when he gets it back again; says Armitage ought to be allowed to take the reaper to the lawns. Says it's the finest crop of hay he's seen in a long time! Potter took it badly, losing the main garden, but like I pointed out to him, he had an undergardener then, and an apprentice. They were both called up into the Army, so he couldn't have coped on his own.'

'But you help in the kitchen garden? And feed the hens?'

'And go to the farm for the milk. That's the first thing I do, mornings. Then I wait for Mrs Potter and Davie's letter.'

'You spend your life waiting for letters, or writing them. How long since you saw your feller?'

'Six weeks. He and Mark got a crafty forty-eight, as they call it – hours, I mean, not days!'

'Your brother is a real good-looker, isn't he?' Meg called back a photograph she'd noticed in the drawing room of a soldier, a small smile on his lips and mischief in his eyes. 'I'll bet your Mark can get any girl he wants. Can he dance?'

'Loves it. Davie, too. When he was last here we went to Preston to a dance, then hitched a lift back as far as Nether Barton. There was a moon, and we walked home the long way round – took us ages and ages.' She sighed yearningly.

'Mark wasn't with you?'

'No. He said he wasn't playing gooseberry. He got into civvies as soon as he arrived and said he was going to have a lazy couple of days. Actually, he spent most of the time sawing logs and barrowing manure for Potter! D'you know, it's lovely sitting here, chatting. Almost like having a sister!'

'Mm. You're a good bit younger than your brother, aren't you?'

'Four years. It took a bit of time to get me, I suppose. I'm adopted, actually.'

'*Adopted!*' Meg's eyes opened wide. 'B-but you don't seem to mind about it.'

'Why should I? I've known about it since I was old enough to be told. I actually remember when they told me – suppose it was such momentous news it stayed in my mind. Hand-picked, Mummy said I was. A little fair-haired girl.'

'But aren't you ever curious, Polly, about where you came from and who your mother is? And you are so like your brother it's amazing!'

'Mummy's my mother. The one who had me is my other mother, but I don't think about her – we-e-ll, hardly ever. They got me through an adoption society – hope it didn't upset my natural mother too much, handing me over. A young girl who couldn't keep me, I think it must have been. No one has ever told me.'

'And don't you wonder just a little bit who your father was?' Meg demanded. 'I'd want to know.' By the heck, didn't she just!

'Why should I? As far as I'm concerned, the one I look on as my father died when I was little. I'm lucky, being adopted into all this, and I never forget it. After all, my other mother must have been unmarried, and you know what a rumpus that causes! Maybe she knew that the finger would have pointed at me too. Illegitimate babies always suffer, you know. I think that if ever I was to meet her, I'd tell her I was very happy, and thank her for being brave enough to give me up. It must have hurt her a lot.'

'Oooh, Polly Kenworthy! You aren't half cool about it. Doesn't it bother you at all?' Meg was still taken aback.

'No. What bothers me is that my parents might have walked on to the next cot and decided on the baby in that one! Don't you understand? I'm lucky being who I am and having a lovely family. Just think of it – I might never have met Davie. Now that would have been a tragedy! And I'll tell you something, Meg. If ever I were in the same position – with Davie's baby, I mean – I wouldn't let anyone take it from me for adoption!'

'And could you ever wonder if you might be pregnant?' Imagine that happening to a Kenworthy, Meg thought wildly. 'What I mean is – well, have you ever . . . ?'

'No. Have you?'

'Heck, no! Mind, I've never wanted to, as a matter of fact.'

'I have, Meg. Oh, we've done some pretty heavy petting and there have been times when I've thought, what the hell!, but either me or him have managed to count to ten in time!'

'But what if it does happen? What'll you do, then?'

'Hope and pray and count! Oh heck, I'm hungry! Just to even think about me and Davie doing it always makes me want to eat. Shall we go downstairs for a glass of milk, and some bread and jam?'

'Let's! And shall we bring it back up here, eh?'

Laughing, they tiptoed to the kitchen.

It was a queer carry-on, Meg thought as she lay awake still, counting as the grandfather clock downstairs struck twice. Her and Polly eating jam and bread sitting crossed-legged on the bed; Polly telling her about the way it was, being in love and about being adopted. Funny, it hadn't seemed to worry her, but she'd fallen on her feet, she admitted it! Maybe, if Ma had given her up for adoption, Meg frowned, she could have ended up at a place like this too. And even more peculiar was the fact that Polly could be so matter-of-fact about her natural father, though she'd had a long time to get used to being adopted. And who in her right mind would worry about an absent father when she'd ended up a Kenworthy? Meg sighed and turned over her pillow, closing her eyes, breathing deeply and slowly.

Her last thought, before sleep took her, was to wonder yet again which sneaky little sod had fathered *her*, then shoved off without a scrap of regret. But she would never know now the name of Father Unknown – and was it all that important when Polly was technically in the same boat, sort of. After all, a sneaky little sod must have fathered her too, yet it didn't seem to bother her! So best she forget it and, like Polly, count her blessings!

Meg surveyed the drawing room she had just cleaned, sniffing the scent that was a mixing of beeswax polish and freshly picked flowers.

The drawing room had been in need of a good clean, come to think of it, but with two old ladies to fetch and carry for, and Polly working all the time she could spare in the kitchen garden, Mrs John had little time for cleaning and it would please her to see what the new home help had done to the white-walled, slate-floored, cosily-old room. Now mirrors and windows shone, woodwork gleamed. She had even polished the copper jugs before she'd crept into the forbidden garden of the brick house and gathered flowers with which to fill them. Smugly pleased with her work, she picked up the photograph of Mark Kenworthy, clucking with annoyance that any man that handsome should be heart-whole and fancy-free.

'You like my brother, then?' Polly smiled from the doorway. 'And it's drinkings-time in the kitchen. Mummy's just made tea.'

'Like him? He's not a bad-looker, I'll give you that!' Hastily Meg replaced the likeness. 'I don't suppose you could blame any girl for falling for him.'

'They do. In droves. Yet he just loves them and leaves them, even though he knows Mummy would like him to marry. After all, he's twenty-four.'

'Suppose your ma wants a grandson so the Kenworthys can carry on here. Why did you never grab him for yourself, Polly?'

'Never gave it a thought – after all, he *is* my brother . . .'

'Yes, but only by adoption, so him and you aren't blood kin. Hadn't you ever thought it would be lawful if you had fallen for him?'

'N-no. All I ever wanted was for him to be my big brother. Falling in love with him never entered my head. And thank heaven it didn't! Davie is the one I want!'

'Can see what you mean. Reckon if you had fallen for him, there'd always have been a kind of – of – What's the word I'm looking for?'

'Incest?' Polly raised a surprised eyebrow.

'That's it! Would've smacked of incest, wouldn't it, in a roundabout way?'

'It could have. But he seemed ages older than me when I was growing up. His friends treated me like a little girl – which I was, to them. And Mark always treated me as his kid sister, so the awful situation didn't arise.'

'You were waiting for Davie,' Meg nodded, 'though you didn't know it.'

'Waiting for Davie. It just about sums it up. Waiting for letters, for phone calls if he's lucky enough to get through, waiting for his next leave; waiting to be twenty-one, then Mummy will know we aren't going to change our minds about each other. One long wait . . .'

'Ar, cheer up, queen! One of these days, when you're least expectin' him, he'll be there on the doorstep!'

'And if that happens, Meg, I wouldn't know whether to be glad or sorry. You see, unexpected leave is often embarkation leave! But we'll take the tea upstairs before we have our own. About time you met Nanny Boag – properly, I mean!'

'Ar. Prop'ly.' And hope, Meg thought, that the daft old girl had come back to earth again; hope she wasn't still Polly's little friend, whose nanny was in the kitchen gossiping with Candlefold's cook!

'Tea for upstairs.' Mary Kenworthy was arranging cups and saucers on two small trays.

'So sit yourself down, Mrs John. Me and Polly will take it. Don't forget I haven't met Nanny yet – not properly, that is.'

'Well, she's fine, today – or she was when I took her breakfast up. Mind, her mood changes can come on without warning, so fingers crossed.'

'You take Gran's first,' Polly said as they crossed the great echoing hall, making for the stone arch in the corner of the room and the stone stairs that rose from it, 'and I'll take Nanny's – prepare her for a surprise, and your second coming! Let's hope she isn't in – in –'

'Cloud cuckoo land again,' Meg grinned.

'Fingers crossed!' Polly smiled back, thinking yet again how lovely it was to have someone her own age about the place.

Nanny Boag had not been in cloud cuckoo land, and anyone, Meg thought as she sipped tea at the kitchen table, could have been forgiven for thinking she ever had!

'Meg Blundell, is it?' Emily Boag's eyes had swept Meg from head to toes. 'So why haven't I met you before, miss? You arrived yesterday, at lunchtime. Where have you been until now?'

'I – I – we-e-ll, we came, and –'

'Yes! We came yesterday, but you were so busy planning the Scotland trip that Meg and I thought we'd better leave you to it!' Polly had hastened.

'Scotland, for goodness' sake! We haven't been to Scotland these twenty years past! What on earth are you thinking about, Polly

Kenworthy? Is it your time of the month, or are you so head-in-the-clouds over your young man that you can't think straight? But I'm glad you have come, Meg Blundell. Mrs John could do with some help. My, but I remember when there was a cook and kitchenmaid here, and two housemaids and a parlour maid as well as myself in the nursery. Things have changed since that man Hitler started the war! When it's all over, I hope they hang him! Maybe, if we hadn't been so gentlemanly with the Germans at the end of the last war things might have been very different. I shall never forgive the Kaiser for what happened to John. Such a good child; such a gentle young man. It wasn't right to make a soldier of him, send him to the trenches!'

Shuddering, she had closed her eyes and hugged her cardigan round her, setting her chair rocking in agitation.

'Oh, thump!' Polly had gasped. 'She's pulled up the drawbridge again!'

For a moment the old woman sat, shoulders hunched. Then she'd opened her eyes, straightened her back and smiled fondly.

'Off you go then, whilst I drink my tea! Take your little friend with you, Polly dear, and don't forget to tell her nanny you are going out to play. And remember your bonnets!'

'Wouldn't you know it?' Meg had whispered. 'Back to square one again! Never mind! Third time lucky. Next time she sees me she might just remember I'm Meg! And don't look so miserable. Give and take, eh? After all, the old girl doesn't know she's doing it!'

'I'm not so sure,' Polly had flung as they closed the door behind them. 'Sure, I mean, that she doesn't know she's doing it!'

'But you said, and your mother too, that you –'

'That we have to humour her because she doesn't know where she is or what time of the day it is, most times? Well, sometimes I'm not convinced! Sometimes I think she does know what she's doing!'

'But your mother said her mind has gone; that mostly she had shut the world out.'

'Yes, but is she as senile as she'd have us believe, Meg? Sometimes I think it's all an act and that she's putting on Mummy's good nature so she can still have people running after her like it was the old days! She's got Mummy fooled and even I accept it, most of the time! But like you saw, she can be as bright as a button one minute, then just go back into her other world as the mood suits her!' Her eyes had filled with tears and she'd shaken her head impatiently. 'Oh, don't take any notice of me! I'm in one of my miserable moods, I suppose, because there wasn't a letter from Davie this morning! I always get fratchy if he doesn't write and do peevish things like taking it out on Nanny – who really *is* senile!'

'Like you said, Polly girl – sixpence short of a shilling. She can't help it, I suppose, for wanting to put the clock back. I often wished I could have done the same after Ma died; wished I'd made her go to that sanatorium, charity ward or not!'

'Meg! Please don't upset yourself. We're both of us getting in a tizzy, wishing we'd done something – or hadn't done or said something. I shouldn't have said things about Nanny, who can't help being –'

'Nutty as a fruitcake!' Meg had sucked in a deep breath then forced her lips into a smile. 'Cheer up, queen! There'll be two letters tomorrow! There might even be a phone call tonight!'

'Yes. And even if there isn't, at least I'm young and fit and not in pain like Gran.'

'Or daft as a brush like Nanny Boag. Now let's get our tea. Then I think I'll give the outside steps a good scrub!'

Stone steps leading to the thick, nail-studded door, worn into hollows by generations of Kenworthy feet. Safe and enduring, those steps, and four hundred years old.

Now, as she drank her tea, Meg wondered how many times Dolly Blundell had scrubbed them. It was a sobering thought.

Five

The first few days in June, Meg was to consider as the end of her fortnight's probabion drew close, had been interesting, especially with regard to Nanny Boag. Indeed, the more she thought about it, the more sure Meg became that her uneasiness seemed justified.

Take Sunday, for instance. Meg had insisted that collection of the Sunday papers would henceforth be her responsibility.

'Fair's fair, Polly. After all, you collect the milk.'

Daily papers were delivered as an act of kindness by Mrs Potter, together with the letters. Sunday papers, however, were left for collection in an outhouse at the back of the post office because, like anyone else, the postmistress needed a day off.

'Will I take the papers upstairs, Mrs John?' Meg asked on her return.

'Later, perhaps. Think I'll take a quick look at them myself first. After all, it *is* Sunday,' she added almost apologetically.

'OK by me.' Polly Kenworthy hardly ever read newspapers; did not want to know that the war was not going as well for the Allies as it might. Nor did she want to see the obituary columns and lists of the names of men who were missing or believed killed in action. True, Davie wasn't in action, but every one of those men who would never come home could have been the soldier she loved, and it hurt her to think that some other unknown woman had received one of the dreaded telegrams. Regretting.

'Want porridge, Meg, or just an egg?'

Meg had been about to opt for an egg, when, 'Oh, no! Would you believe it?' Mary Kenworthy gasped. 'I mean, it's bad enough doing a thing like that, but to announce it on a Sunday when all the shops are shut so no one can buy in a few things is just – well – *sneaky*! Coupons for clothes! It just won't work!'

'Let me see!' Polly shook open the second paper. It consisted of only four pages, so news of the rationing of clothes and footwear was not hard to find.

'Well! If that isn't just the last straw! No more luxury goods to be made and everything else to be manufactured under the utility mark. Shoddy, I shouldn't wonder. And *fourteen* coupons must be given up for a winter coat, it says, and five for a pair of shoes! What on earth are *They* thinking about? How can anyone last for a year on sixty-six clothing coupons.'

'If we're to have utility clothes they're bound to be cheap,' Meg hesitated. 'At least more people will be able to afford them – poor people, I mean . . .'

'But no more luxury goods nor even wedding dresses!' Polly pouted. 'And I did so want a long white dress for my wedding! By the time Davie and me get around to it, though, they'll be a thing of the past!'

'Then why don't you go to the shops tomorrow, good and early?' Meg soothed. 'Grab one while you can.'

'But *how*, when I don't have any clothing coupons? They haven't given them out yet, and it doesn't say when they will!'

Her eyes filled with tears, and she blew her nose noisily.

'Hush, Polly. It isn't the end of the world!' There was a hint of admonition in Mary Kenworthy's voice. 'If you read what it says, you can give up your margarine coupons instead – till the proper ones are issued.'

'But how can anyone do that? We need the margarine to eat! What a stupid idea!'

'So how about waiting like we'll all have to do? Then the minute you get your hands on the coupons you can nip off to town and hunt down a wedding dress – though how many coupons you'll have to give up to get one, heaven only knows! There's a lot of material in a wedding dress,' Meg cautioned. 'It seems that a dress is going to take seven coupons, but I don't think it applies to long wedding dresses.'

'I think what Meg says makes sense.' Mary Kenworthy stared pointedly over the top of her reading glasses. 'And if the worst comes to the worst, do you have to have a white dress?'

'But every bride has one! It wouldn't be like a wedding without one!'

'Then it would seem to me, Polly, that you are more in love with the idea of walking down the aisle in white than you are with Davie!'

'*Mummy!*'

With a scraping of chair legs Polly flung from the table, to run sobbing across the courtyard.

'I'd better go –'

'No, Meg. Leave her. If she loves Davie as much as I'm sure she does, then she'll see how unimportant it is. Come to think of it, there'll be a lot of shattered dreams, this morning . . .'

Polly returned ten minutes later, tears still wet on her cheeks, her expression contrite.

'I'm sorry – I truly am. Forgive me? I acted like a spoiled brat. As if it matters what I wear! When I thought about it, I realized that if Davie turned up tomorrow on a week's embarkation leave, I'd marry him in my best cotton frock and Sunday hat!'

'You'd marry him, girl, in an old sack with a pan on yer 'ead,' Meg grinned.

'Yes, I would. It isn't what you wear at a wedding, but how you say the words.'

'And never forget, darling girl, that I know what it is like to have the man you love away at war. So don't worry, you *will* wear white when you marry Davie – how ever many clothing coupons it takes. I promise.'

'That's settled, then,' Meg beamed. 'And we'd better listen to all the news broadcasts so we won't miss bein' told how we get the dratted coupons. And when we do, you can be off to the shops for a weddin' dress – if they haven't all disappeared under the counter, that is! An' you must go with her, Mrs John. I'm not taking no for an answer. No excuses. I'm here now, and a day out at the shops will do you both good – even if there won't be a lot to buy. Now what do you say to that, eh?'

'I'd say,' Polly smiled, tears gone, 'that if I'd been lucky enough to have a sister – well, I wish she'd have been exactly like you!'

Indeed, it had been the matter of the unfairness of clothes rationing that gave strength to Meg's suspicions about the true state of Nanny Boag's mind the next day.

'Awful, isn't it, Nanny, and Polly so wantin' a white dress and white shoes and some pretty nighties and things for when she gets married?'

'That, I suggest, is Polly's worry and not yours! For my own part, I have worked it out that I can manage quite well for the rest of my days on what is in my wardrobe and drawers. I don't go out, so I won't need new shoes nor a winter coat – that's nineteen coupons saved already,' she smiled smugly. 'And I have enough knitting wool put by for the odd cardigan and slippers. Oh no, clothes rationing won't worry me at all!'

'Then you can give them nineteen coupons to Polly! If she can't get a proper weddin' dress she'll have to have one made for her. At two coupons for a yard of white satin, that would be nine and a half yards – more than enough!'

'*Them* nineteen coupons? Don't you mean *those* nineteen coupons? You speak so badly, child. And if you have come to play with Polly, then she'll be at church with the family, so I suggest you collect your nanny from the kitchen and go back to where you came from!'

'Polly isn't at church. You know they went yesterday – Sunday.'

'Don't argue! What Nanny says in the nursery is never to be contradicted. Now be off with you, little girl!'

Strewth! At it again! Meg closed the door behind her. When something didn't please her, that one could change from sane to silly at the drop of a hat!

And wasn't that it? Nanny had read about clothing coupons in the paper; was even able to calculate how many she would be saving. Yet the moment it was suggested she give some to Polly, the daft look had come back on her face and she was in another world again.

Yet the truth was as plain as the nose on your face, Meg thought triumphantly as everything clicked into place. Nanny Boag was as sane as most folk, given her age, and it was only when something didn't suit her did she start her gaga act! She didn't need her coupons, but no one else was getting their hands on them, so pull down the shutters and act stupid!

'Gotcher, you crafty old biddy!' Meg gloated. That one was as normal and nimble as need be, all things considered, but she'd got the Kenworthys fooled! From now on, though, she would have her work cut out pulling the wool over Margaret Mary Blundell's eyes!

Though something Nanny had said *was* right, Meg sighed. No denying it: she didn't speak properly! She got her thems and thoses wrong, and dropped aitches and spoke with a thick Liverpool accent – which was all right for Liverpool where most people she knew spoke the same and understood each other perfectly well, but it wasn't right for Candlefold. She must ask Polly to help her. It was the only way she would ever learn to talk proper like Ma!

The second incident to give strength to Meg's suspicions was two days later when the death of Kaiser Wilhelm II was reported, taking only four lines in the daily paper, which was all he deserved, come to think of it. She had been on her way to collect Mrs Kenworthy's breakfast tray when dreadful wailing came to her from the floor above.

'Oh, my goodness!' Meg had taken the narrow nursery stairs two at a time to stop, breathless, outside the open door.

'And thank God you are dead, you pig! It was you caused my John to be wounded! If you hadn't started that war he'd be alive today! You should have died in those filthy trenches and not lived another twenty years! But I hope you died in pain, you evil bastard, and I wish I'd been there to see it! I'd have stood and cheered!'

'Nanny! What's to do?' Meg pushed the door wider. 'You'll do yourself an upset, carryin' on like that!'

'Like what?' The old women turned, eyes wide, lips relaxed in a smile, looking so cherubic that it was hardly possible to believe the venom in her words, nor the swearing either.

'The Kaiser, I mean. Him bein' dead.'

'Dead, is he? Well, fancy that, now. I once heard it said he had a funny left arm – withered, you know. Must have been a great trial to him!'

'It must have.' Yet that same Kaiser with whom Nanny now sympathized had, only seconds ago, been loudly cursed by that apple-cheeked, smiling old lady! 'Is there anything I can get you, Nanny?' she said quietly.

'No, thank you. Pop off and play. I'll ring for one of the maids if I want anything.'

She had beamed again, the two-faced old cat, Meg fumed; changed from her cursing and swearing to a soft-voiced, gentle old woman and all because she had realized she might have been heard!

My, but she was going to take some watching, though how she was going to convince Mrs John and Polly about Nanny's deceiving ways Meg sighed, was altogether another matter!

Meg had brushed the worn stone floor of the entrance hall and was dusting the panelling when Mary Kenworthy said, 'Do you wonder as I do, Meg, how many people have dusted and polished and touched those panels?'

'Thousands, I reckon. I like touching them. Silly, isn't it, liking the feel of wood under your fingertips . . .'

'Not at all. I feel the same way myself. And be sure that the long-ago woodcarver would be pleased to hear you say it.'

'*How* long ago?'

'About five hundred years, I would say. It was the third Kenworthy who had this hall panelled – to proclaim his growing wealth, I suppose. When the Lancastrians ruled England, it would be. Y'know,' she smiled, 'hand-me-down talk has it that Richard Kenworthy – he was known as Dickon – wanted his great hall embellished with linenfold carving, but the artisan who did it didn't please Master Dickon. It's said that he told the woodcarver it looked more like drips of tallow down the side of a candle and that he would be the laughing stock of the Riding, with such a shoddy job! Whereupon the crafty carver told him that he would be the envy of all, being the first gentleman to benefit from the new *candle*fold panelling. And Dickon believed him, and paid him well for his pains. I think that is how the house got its name.'

'You're lucky, Mrs John – bein' able to tell family jokes about all them – *those* – years ago. Don't you feel proud – special, sort of?'

'I'm not a Kenworthy, Meg, though I married into it and helped carry on the line and the Kenworthy pride too. And Polly – who is adopted as you will know – is the most devout Kenworthy of us all!'

'It must be something about this place,' Meg said softly. 'It takes you over.'

'So you like being with us, Meg? Your two weeks are almost up. Are you going to stay?'

'Are you askin'?' Meg smiled.

'I most certainly am!'

'Then if it's all right with you, Mrs John, I'm stoppin'.' She held out her hand. 'And I hope I give satisfaction, I'm sure.'

'I know you will. I've got used to having you around. But you haven't taken the time off due to you. Why don't you go home for a couple of days? There must be things you need to see to?'

'We-e-ll, I'll have to get my new address put on my ration book and identity card. And there's the house, an' all. I'll have to ask next door to keep an eye on it; send on any letters that come.'

Letters. From Kip. They might be there, waiting for her. Yet she had hardly thought about him, so charmed had she been with her new life! Nor had she sent him so much as a picture postcard of Nether Barton, which, despite the shortage of such things, could still be bought at the pre-war price of tuppence at the post office.

'Then shall we say you are on a forty-eight-hour pass, as Mark would call it. Will that suit, Meg?'

'It'll suit very nicely indeed.'

A pound a week, and all this? Oh my word yes, it would suit!

Meg stripped her bed of sheets and pillowcases, folding them neatly, ready to be taken to the wash house for Mrs Seed, who always came Thursdays. Before her marriage she had worked at Candlefold as a housemaid and now came each week to see to the laundry and, on Friday mornings, to do the ironing. It seemed to Meg that Mrs Seed was another who had come under the spell of this house, and still looked on it as a part of her way of life.

Mr Potter – you always called him Mister – was exactly the same, caring for the garden as if it were his own, he having arrived there as an apprentice thirty years ago and not inclined to go elsewhere, in spite of tempting offers. Ma had been the same, loyal to it in memory, a place never to be forgotten. And now her daughter was equally besotted. Even to think of visiting Tippet's Yard did not please her as it should, for wasn't Candleford to be her home now? But she was looking forward to seeing Nell and Tommy again; telling them about her new life and what it was really like living deep in the countryside. If she missed anything about Liverpool, she admitted, it was the two people who shared the shut-away little yard with her.

But first to catch the Preston bus. A good three hours it would take her with all the chopping and changing, and each mile taking her back to a place she would really rather not be. Yet Nell and Tommy deserved to be told about her good fortune, because up until now they had shared her troubles – them, and Kip.

Kip Lewis. She wished she could love him as Polly loved Davie, but she wanted to be really in love – which girl didn't? – wanted to know the highs and lows of it and the needing and the giving. She would accept, even, the absolute misery when a letter did not arrive and the brief hours spent together to balance out weeks of separation. If she loved as Polly loved, that was. If it happened to her as suddenly and completely as it had happened to Polly, and her stomach went *boing!* as Polly's had done, then she would be glad to be in love for ever.

And until it happened she must wait, because couldn't she next month, next week, *tomorrow* even, turn a corner and see him there and know he was the one? She thought again of Kip, and sadness took her.

'I'm sorry, Kip, that it can't be you . . .'

At Preston station she was able to buy a return ticket to Liverpool, which meant that at least the trains were back on the lines. But Liverpool, when she arrived there, seemed still to be reeling from the vicious bombing. The stink of blitzkrieg still hung on the air, a dusty, musty smell mingling with the acrid odour of burned timber and the stench of escaped sewage.

Yet she saw no danger signs as the bus made towards Scotland Road; at least ruptured gas and water mains seemed to have been taken care of, and bombs that had lain there unexploded and dangerous. Gangs still shifted rubble, though, and shovelled and heaved the heart of what had once been a proud seaport onto the backs of lorries.

Where would they take all the debris? Would it be dumped in bomb craters or tipped into the Mersey? Did anyone give a damn? Meg thought dully, because inside her she had the grace to care; not because it was Liverpool and people's homes and jobs and way of life, but because there were places, not so very far away, that knew nothing of destruction and death; places surrounded by fields and trees and flowers, and where old, old stones stood untouched by time or destruction, would go on for six hundred years more. Could she ever, during those terror-filled nights, have thought such peace existed? And wasn't she the lucky one to have left the nightmare behind her?

She gazed fixedly at her hands because she did not want to look out on the destruction either side of her and because she felt guilty it was no longer her concern. She lived in the country now; must learn to forget Scotland Road and Lyra Street and Tippet's Yard!

Yet despite her resolve, the feeling of unease was still with her when she walked beneath the low alleyway and stood to gaze into the airless little court, taking in the wash house, the lavatories and three little houses packed together as if clinging for support. Nor did the feeling leave her when her eyes lit on her neighbour, sitting on a wooden chair, arms folded, eyes closed, outside number 2.

'Hi there, Nell!'

The head jerked up and, all at once wide-eyed, Nell Shaw straightened her shoulders and ran her tongue round her lips.

'Well, if it isn't Meg Blundell, come home from the wilds and the kettle not on! Come here, girl, and let's be lookin' at you. My, but you look as if you've been on yer 'olidays!'

Her cheeks had filled out and pinked, Nell thought; her eyes shone, her hair too. Real bonny, she looked. No, by the heck, two weeks in the country had turned her into a little beauty.

'I have been – leastways, it seems like it. Compared to this place, it's another world. You wouldn't believe it!'

'So come inside and try tellin' me whilst I'm brewing up.'

'These are for you.' Meg laid the carefully carried sheaf of flowers on the kitchen table.

'Lord help us, you shouldn't have! What did they cost you, and how many vases do you think I've got, girl?'

'They cost nuthink. I got them from the garden of the brick house. But you'll never guess what I've got in me bag. Eggs! Fresh, an' all. Two each for you and Tommy. Polly sent them and, oh, there's so much to tell you, Nell!'

'So first things first. Are you stoppin'?'

'At Tippet's? No. I'm going back on Saturday. Just came to see you both and sort out a few things, then I'm off back. Mrs John wants me to stop and I want to, Nell. 'Fraid I haven't brought any food with me, but I'll nip out and buy a loaf, and there's jam in the cupboard. And tonight I'll go to the chippy and treat us all to a fish supper.'

'Then you'll have to be in the queue good and early, girl – half an hour before they open. But let's have your news, though I'm sorry you are off back there. Me an' Tommy have missed you. Met a young man, have you?'

'Heck, no! There's only Mr Potter, who's the gardener, and Mr Armitage at Home Farm, and they're old. Polly is engaged, though – to Davie, who's in the Service Corps – lorries and transports and things – and Polly's brother is in the same regiment. And, would you believe it, Polly is adopted and it doesn't bother her one bit! But I'll tell you all about it right from the start, eh?' She plopped a saccharin tablet into her cup and watched it rise fizzing to the top of her tea.

'By the way, you didn't stop your milk, so I took it. That all right, Meg? I paid for it.'

'Then don't cancel it. No need for the milkie to know I'm away. They've got their own cow at Candlefold, so they don't need my milk coupons. You're welcome to my ration, Nell. An' I hope you took my coal, an' all – get a bit stocked up for the winter.'

And Nell said of course she had, since Meg had told her to, then lit a cigarette, glad that Doll's girl was back, if only for a little time.

'Tell me, Meg, before you start, do they know who you are? Did you tell them you was born there?'

'No, and I won't till I'm good and ready, though the old lady remembered Ma. Said they'd once had a housemaid called Dorothy Blundell, but I told her it was a common enough name around Liverpool and she hasn't mentioned it since. But let me tell you . . .'

And the words tumbled breathlessly out, about the old part of the house, and the newer brick part that *They* had taken over, though no one quite knew why. And how the garden had got overgrown so you wouldn't recognize it from Ma's photo, and how she had nipped through the hedge and gathered the flowers she had brought with her; told how Polly was a love and treated her like an equal; how they all did, except batty old Nanny who lived in another world, when it suited her. And about sunrises and sunsets and that it hadn't rained one day since she had been there, and feeding hens and running up and down the stone stairs and Mrs John being grateful for another pair of hands to help out with the old ladies.

'Polly works almost every day in the kitchen garden. They send vegetables an' things to the local shops. And next time I come, there'll be strawberries ripe, I shouldn't wonder, and I'll be able to bring you some. And there'll be raspberries and plums and apples, and Mr Armitage told me that if I let him know next time I'm over, he'll make sure I have a rabbit to bring with me.'

She talked on, eyes shining, about how right Ma had been about Candlefold, and how it was a place hidden from the war; a place where there was milk to spare and vegetables so fresh you wouldn't believe it; talked on and on till Nell took a hand.

'Written to Kip, have you, since you've been away?' she interrupted, eyes narrowed.

'Kip? Well – no, Nell. But I've been so busy there didn't seem time. I've brought a postcard with me, though, of the village. I'll send him that.'

'There's a letter with a New Zealand stamp on it behind your clock, and a parcel I put in the pantry. Arrived yesterday, so mind you write and thank him for it.' She fixed Meg with a no-nonsense stare. 'What kind of a way is that to treat your young man!'

'He isn't my young man, Nell; not my steady. We don't have an understandin'. You know we don't!'

'Then more's the pity. Kip Lewis is as good a lad as you're likely to meet, and think on that I've told you so!'

'I know he's decent and I'm not leading him on, honest I'm not. I'm fond of him, though, and grateful for what he sends – and I'll not need to go to the chippy now. I'll open the parcel and we'll all have a slap-up meal tonight!'

'So is that all he means to you – the food he sends?'

'I said I was fond of him, Nell, but I'm not rushing into anything. You said men are out for the main chance – I'm living proof of it, aren't I? Have there been any more raids, by the way?' Best talk of other things.

'No, thanks be.' She took Meg's keys from the sideboard. 'Now off you go and open the windows and get the house aired, and see that the parcel's all right and that nothing's leaked. And give Tommy a knock on your way out. Tell him there's tea left in the pot.'

'She looks well on it,' Tommy said. 'The fresh air suits the girl.'

'Aye. And just like her mother, God rest her, used to be! Was always goin' on about that place, yet we both know what happened to her in the end! Just let's hope it doesn't happen to her daughter! And Meg doesn't know I've told you about – well – the way it was, and what was in Doll's case. Keep it to yourself, don't forget!'

'I will. But why should it happen to Meg?' Tommy frowned. 'History doesn't repeat itself, don't they say?'

'You're thinking about lightning not striking twice in the same place, Tommy Todd! History *does* repeat itself, or why has bluddy Hitler started another war?'

'Give the girl credit! She knows right from wrong!'

'So did her mother, and much good it did her! And it isn't Meg I don't trust, it's all them fellers, out for what they can get 'cause there's a war on! But I suppose she'll have to make her own mistakes. Only way she'll learn, come to think of it!'

'So who says Meg's going to end up in trouble? A nasty tongue you've got at times, Nell Shaw!'

So Nell said if that was what he thought she wouldn't say another word on the subject; said it indignantly, then closed her mouth into a tight round button and glared across the table, narrow-eyed.

'Not one more word!' she hissed.

Kip's letter bore no address, so he was able to write, without risking the censor's scissors, that by the time Meg got it he would have reached you-know-where and was looking forward to a few days ashore. . . . *And by the way. I'll be posting you a parcel. Fingers crossed that it won't go to the bottom.*

The carefully packed parcel had indeed arrived, Meg thought uneasily, and before she went back to Candlefold she must write him a long chatty letter, post it at once so there was a chance it would be waiting at Panama on the way home. But first she took the postcard, a pretty view of Nether Barton's only street, showing the post office, the pub and the church next to it, and a row of cottages.

On the back she wrote her new address, that all was well and that a letter followed. Then she took it at once to the post office, asking for an airmail sticker and a sixpenny stamp. 'There now!' Feeling a little less guilty, she slid it into the pillar box.

'Just been to post one to Kip,' she said to Nell on her return. 'Thought you'd like to know. And I'll send him another before I go back. There's a tin of meat in the parcel; would you and Tommy like to come to supper tonight? And Kip sent these for you.'

As if it were a peace offering, she passed a packet of cigarettes to the older woman.

'Ar. Tell him thanks a lot when you write back. He's a good lad, Meg, and you'll have to go a long way to find better. But it's none of my business and you're old enough to know your own mind. And yes, ta, I'll come to supper.'

The smile was back on Nell's face. All was well again in Tippet's Yard.

The house swept and aired, Meg made for the Ministry of Food office in Scotland Road. Its windows were still boarded up, the inside gloomy.

'Change of address, please.' When her turn came, Meg offered her ration book and identity card. 'And where do I go for my clothing coupons?'

'Board of Trade office, four doors down.' The overworked clerk had no time to chat.

'Thanks.' Meg felt relief that her Tippet's Yard address was now secret beneath a white sticky label; that another part of her past had been officially hidden. Half an hour later her identity card had been changed and *Clothing coupons issued* written on the front cover of her ration book, together with a Board of Trade stamp and a scribbled initial.

By the time she had queued for potatoes and bought a cabbage Mr Potter would have been ashamed to offer, it was time to put the kettle on. Kip's parcel had included a packet of tea, and tomorrow she really would write a letter, telling him about Polly and Mrs John, and how she was learning the names of flowers and to recognize a thrush and a blackbird, and that soon she would be helping with the fruit picking.

But first she would prepare supper; peel potatoes and do what she could with the sickly cabbage. And since Kip had sent biscuits – real, pre-war chocolate biscuits the likes of which were only a memory now – she would arrange them daintily on a plate instead of a pudding. Such a treat they would be, and she, Nell and Tommy would eat the lot and toast the sender's health in a cup of strong Billy tea from Australia!

Meg wished she could be in love with Kip – *really* in love – but he wasn't the one and she hoped he hadn't wasted his money on a ring when he got to Sydney, because that was what it would be. A waste.

'Sorry, Kip,' she whispered, over the potatoes. 'Take care of yourself, eh?'

As the train pulled shuddering and heaving out of the station, Meg could feel only relief at leaving Liverpool behind her. Yet she still felt guilty at being so lucky when most other Liverpool folk, many of whom still had family missing, even yet, had no choice but to remain amongst the devastation. And guilty about the killing and injuries, and about the baby covered with rubble dust. She would never forget the little one, nor forgive either. She felt guilty, too, about Kip, who sent her letters and food parcels, and who would hope for letters from her at ports of call.

Mind, she had written the letter, telling him about her new job and her bedroom window that looked out onto such a view that it brought tears to her eyes; told him about the hens and the Jersey cow, and that she thought about him often and remembered him every night in her prayers, both of which were downright lies.

Polly prayed every night for Davie and Mark and for all servicemen and women – ours, of course – and a speedy end to the war. Took a bit of understanding, come to think of it, since German women would be praying for much the same thing, so if there really was a God, how did He know which side to listen to? Us, or them? Tossed a penny, did He?

They were nearing the outskirts of Liverpool now, and Meg knew they were passing through Aintree, even though station names had been removed; part of a grand scheme to bewilder invading parachutists by not providing any clues as to where they had dropped!

Aintree, where the most famous horserace in the world was run, and rich men in top hats, with their wives dressed up to the nines, came from all over the world with their horses and jockeys and grooms, and had a real good time afterwards at the luxurious Adelphi Hotel.

She pulled her thoughts back to Kip, because he was the one she felt most guilty about. Mind, she hadn't asked for the parcels he'd sent, though she had been glad enough to get them. Nor was it her fault that he liked her a lot whilst she could only feel sisterly affection. It made her think of Amy, Kip's sister who lived in Lyra Street. Meg had had the good sense to visit her so she was able to tell Kip he must not worry about her and her children, and that there had been no more bombing.

Thank you for the parcel. Nell and Tommy came to supper to share my luck and have a real tuck in, she had written, *and Nell says thanks a lot for the ciggies and sends her best regards, as does Tommy.*

Take care of yourself. She had ended the letter tongue in cheek: *I think about you every night before I go to sleep. With love and kisses . . .*

She had placed a lipsticky kiss beside her name, thinking that love and kisses was the least she could do for a parcel not only containing food, but a tablet of soap, a jar of cold cream and a carefully wrapped bottle of shampoo, all of which were in very short supply and could only be got by being in the right place at the right time, then standing in a queue!

Conscience almost cleared, she had propped the airmail envelope beside the mantel clock, then set the kettle to boil for hot water in which to wash. She missed the bathroom at Candlefold, but would make up for the all-over wash by using the sweet-smelling soap. She had sniffed it greedily, for toilet soap – when you were lucky enough to get it – had long ago ceased to be scented. It made her think enviously of a country where the sun almost always shone, where there were warm beaches and scented soap in the shops and no blackout.

And oh, damn the war and the stupid men who had let it happen again! And damn Hitler, who was probably sniggering into his champagne, knowing the British still expected to be invaded, and only he knowing exactly when it would be! It didn't bear thinking about, so she closed her eyes and pushed the war from her mind.

And thought about Candlefold instead, just two hours away.

Six

She was back, and never before had two days taken so long to run. Meg blinked up into the sky, breathing deeply, because even the air here was special; golden-coloured and scented with green things growing, and hay and honeysuckle.

She smiled at Mrs Potter, who always peeked through the post office window whenever a bus arrived, checking in those she knew, making a mental note of those she did not, and who, two weeks ago, had drawn the attention of a stranger to a printed postcard.

'Candlefold,' Meg whispered, lips hardly moving. 'Where I live; where I was born; where I am meant to be.' And where she would stay till Fate – or the Ministry of Labour and National Service – decided differently.

At the stile she stood quite still, listening to the safe stillness: a bird singing, leaves rustling green above her. Even the lambs were still, laying close to the ewes who stared steadily ahead, mouths rotating cud, like the blank-faced tarts who stood on every street corner the length of Lime Street, chewing gum.

But Lime Street was a long way away and in just a few more seconds she would see the old house, the worn stone steps, the thick, squat door and the pump trough. In just a few more seconds, she would be home.

'You're back!' Mary Kenworthy smiled. 'And just as I was thinking I'd have to go all the way to the garden to tell Polly that lunch is ready!'

'What's to do with that thing, then?' Meg nodded in the direction of the bell that hung outside the door.

'They're both asleep, upstairs – thought we'd get our lunch before they're awake.' She broke two more eggs into the bowl. 'Omelette and salad and stewed apples,' she answered the question in Meg's eyes. 'Be a love, and tell Polly it's on the table in three minutes, will you?'

The walk to the kitchen garden took Meg across the courtyard, beneath the far arch, past the henrun and across the drying green to the tall, narrow gate in the eight-feet-high wall. Mr Potter's little kingdom where the war was shut out every morning at eight o'clock sharp and not confronted again until work was over for the day and the gate clanged shut behind him.

Meg saw Polly on her knees beside the strawberry bed and whistled through her fingers.

'Hey! Ready in three minutes!' she called, then ran down the path, delight at her heels. 'What are you doing?' Everything that happened at Candlefold delighted her.

'Strawing up,' Polly grinned, linking her arm in Meg's. 'The berries are starting to swell so we put straw beneath them to keep them clean and to keep the slugs away. Then when we've done that we'll net them over, and that'll take care of the thieving blackbirds too. But I'm so glad you are home. Yesterday there wasn't a letter. I felt so miserable I got to wondering what else could go wrong, and you not coming back was high on the list. But this morning –'

'This morning there were two letters and I *am* back. And if you thought I wouldn't be, then you're dafter than Nanny Boag – who is asleep, by the way!'

Home again, and omelettes for lunch, stewed apples for pudding, and the sky high and blue and bright. Life was all at once so good that it almost took her breath away.

'Pull out any weeds, and tuck the straw around the roots,' Polly instructed later that afternoon, initiating Meg into the mysteries of Mr Potter's garden.

'I don't know which is weeds and which isn't . . .'

'Anything that isn't a strawberry plant, just yank it out before you shove the straw in. We'll be having strawberries and cream in two or three weeks.'

'Creeeeeam!' Wasn't cream illegal, Meg demanded.

'We-e-ll, yes, but once every Preston Guild, Mummy pours the morning milk into a large bowl and skims off the cream that rises to the top. It's illegal to sell it in the shops, but nobody can stop you skimming your own milk. And, like I said, she doesn't do it often.

Davie and Mark are due leave at the end of June, so I hope there'll be plenty of sun to ripen the berries. When that happens, we have to be up good and early to do the picking and have them ready for the van that calls. I often think how pleased some lady will be to get some – even though she probably won't have sugar to spare to sprinkle on them.'

'Nor cream,' Meg grinned. 'And I wonder how long she'll have to queue for them, an' all. That's when your Davie will be on leave, then – three weeks from now?'

'Twenty days. I've started crossing them off on my calendar. Mind, the bods in the armed forces are always told that leave is a privilege and not their due, but most times nothing happens to stop it.' She crossed her fingers. 'We're having two days here, then spending the rest of his leave with his parents. They live a few miles from Oxford where Davie ought by rights to be, studying engineering. Oh, damn this war!'

'What d'you mean! It was because of the war youse two met!'

'Mm. That Davie met Mark and Mark brought him home for a weekend. Funny, isn't it?'

'Nah! Just meant to be.' Meg removed a weed then manoeuvred straw beneath the berry plant. 'Ma always said that what was to be would be; that the minute you are born there's this feller who knows what'll happen to you an' he writes it all down. Your Book of Life, it's called, and there's no gettin' away from it.'

'And you believe that, Meg?'

'Makes as much sense as anythink else.'

'More sense than believing in God?'

''Fraid I'm not a God person. I mean – what about when Ma was bad and I'd believed, and prayed for her to live? Well, where would I be now, eh? He'd have let me down stinkin', wouldn't He?'

'We don't always get everything we want.'

'Then why bother?'

'Meg, you really don't believe, do you?'

'Reckon not. Ma didn't either; only in the Book of Life thing.'

'But what about Christmas and Easter?'

'We never bothered. Christmas trees and Easter eggs cost money, she said, an' it was all a big con by shopkeepers to get cash out of you, and by the Church, so you'd go and put money on the plate. All down to pounds, shillin's and pence!'

'So you don't say your prayers or go to church?' Polly whispered. 'Nor ask God to take care of your young man?'

'Told you, I haven't got a young man. Kip's only a friend.'

'He sent you shampoo and scented soap you told us at lunchtime!'

'A friend,' Meg said firmly. 'And we'd better stop nattering and get on with this strawing, or Mr Potter isn't goin' to let me work in the garden again!' And she liked working in Mr Potter's garden. It was better than running upstairs every time Nanny rang her bell. Anything was better than being near the old biddy, who'd been in a right mood, earlier on.

'You're back,' she had grumbled. 'I thought you'd gone, Meg Blundell!'

A fine way to greet someone you hadn't seen for two days and who'd brought up your lunch, an' all!

'Bad penny, that's me!' she'd said saucily. 'And if you aren't hungry I'll take this tray downstairs again!' She was starting the way she meant to go on, turning away to show she meant what she said! And the old girl had jumped to her feet like a two-year-old and grabbed hold of her lunch with a look like thunder on her face.

'Give it to me, girl, and get out! And never, ever, give me backchat again! Remember your place here and that a word from me will get you dismissed instantly, and without a reference too!'

So Meg had got out of the nursery and drew in her breath and held it all the way down two flights of stairs and into the courtyard.

'*Ten!*' she'd gasped, thankful she had kept a hold on her temper, rubbing her hands on the roughness of the pump trough, remembering Ma, who knew all about Nanny Boag too. But maybe when Mark had been little, Nanny had been a nicer person, or why did Mrs John put up with her?

And so, remembering how desperately she wanted to stay at Candlefold, she had determined never again to let the old woman upset her, and no matter how much she might long to give her a piece of her mind, she would do as Polly said she should: turn her back, and walk away!

She tugged fiercely on an offending weed and wished with all her heart it could have been Nanny Boag's nose!

* * *

Days were ticked off on Polly's calendar; the strawberries swelled and Mr Armitage had thrown caution out of the window and taken a scythe to the grass on the brick house lawns because it was eighteen inches high and as good a crop of hay as he had seen this year. And wasn't every forkful of hay needed for the war effort? And whose hay was it, anyway?

'Now you're supposed to leave that grass three clear Sundays,' he told Meg, who had watched the sweeping strokes of his arm with fascination. 'And it's got to be turned every day so it'll dry. Any good with a hayfork, young Meg?'

She had been obliged to admit she was not, but was very willing to learn if he would show her how. And so haymaking became another delight, with she and Polly turning an acre of grass twice a day. At first, her arms ached with the effort, then she began to look forward to their stealthy visits to the brick house lawns, each time wondering if they would be caught by the faceless ones on one of their visits.

'So if *They* catch us at it, what can *They* do?' Meg reasoned. 'I mean – *They* only requisitioned the house, now, didn't they? Surely nobody's goin' to make a fuss over a bit of grass?'

'An acre of hay, actually. And I think that requisition covered the whole shebang, with the exception of the kitchen garden, Meg. But it's drying beautifully. I reckon we'll get it cocked and carted away before anyone from London finds out. Armitage says it's good hay, and nice and herby; says a bit of neglect has done it the power of good, but don't repeat that to Mr Potter, will you?'

'I won't. And had you thought, Polly, that by the time the hay is ready, Davie will be here on leave?'

'I've hardly thought about anything else! Ten more days to go. And we mustn't forget, Meg, that when the hay is loaded and carted off to the farm, we must wish very seriously as it goes by.'

'Whatever for?'

'Because you always wish on the first load of hay you see every year. Hay wishes are good ones, like first-swallow wishes. Hay and swallows have never let me down, so keep an eye open for your first swallow. They'll be arriving any day now!'

'Wouldn't know a swallow if I saw one, Polly. You'll have to show me.'

Mind, she was getting good with robins and tits and thrushes and blackbirds; especially with blackbirds since now she knew the difference between cocks and hens! Only give her a little more time and she would know as much about the countryside as Polly!

'Bet I know what you'll be wishin' for,' she teased, so happy that all at once she felt peculiar – like someone had walked over her grave – if she'd been dead and buried, that was. 'And it's OK! I know you can't tell me, and I won't tell you what I wish either!'

But her wish was there in her mind already, so that when she saw her first swallow of the summer and when the hay wagon trundled past, she would close her eyes, cross her fingers and say in her mind, 'I wish to stay at Candlefold for ever, and live here till I die . . .'

They saw their first swallow next day as they fed and watered the hens. It came swooping and diving out of the sky above the drying green.

'There you are, Meg. Wish!'

Eyes closed they wished tremulously, smiling secretly.

'You're sure it'll come true?'

'Always has, Meg, though now I always wish for the same thing – y'know, pile them all up so in the end it's *got* to come true.'

'A sort of long-term wish, like mine. An' maybe when we load the hay there'll be another one of the same, eh?'

'Oh, *yes*! I do so miss Davie. There wasn't a letter this morning, y'know . . .'

Meg had noticed. It was always the same, the no-letter look: sad and yearny, sort of.

'There'll be two tomorrow. Maybe he's on manoeuvres.'

'Maybe.'

'An' he's out in the wilds with no pillar box.'

'Probably.'

'An' I'll tell you something else. This isn't our lucky day, Polly.' She nodded in the direction of two camouflaged trucks that swooped in from the lane to stop outside the far archway. 'Wouldn't you know it? That lot from London, on the snoop! What'll they say when they see our hay? Just a few more days, an' we'd have got away with it!'

'No! It can't be!' Polly, face flushed with disbelief, gasped. 'But it is! It *is*! Davie Sumner! *Darling!*'

Then she was running, laughing, to where two soldiers stood, dressed in battledress tops, khaki trouser bottoms bound by puttees, their brown boots shining. And the two of them grinning with delight at the upset they had caused.

With a cry of joy, Polly went into Davie's arms, to stand close, cheek on cheek, not kissing, just glad to touch and hold, to fondle the back of his neck with her fingertips.

'You weren't expected yet!' She closed her eyes and offered her mouth. 'Davie – nothing is wrong . . . ?'

'No.' He kissed her lips gently. 'Leave next week.'

'Then what? *Why?*' She turned to hug her brother. 'Meg, this is Mark.'

'Mark,' Meg whispered, offering her hand, feeling it tremble as Mark Kenworthy folded his own around it. And if he was good to look at in a silver-framed photograph, then standing there, warm and real, he was altogether too much to take in. And he looking down at her with eyes bluer than Polly's, even; eyes that swept her from head to toes – slowly and deliberately so there could be no mistaking his approval.

'Glad to meet you at last, Meg.' He let go her hand to raise his cap in salute, all the time smiling as if he really meant it.

'And this is Davie, my fiancé.'

Polly's voice seemed far away and strange, like an echo, because something had hit Margaret Mary Blundell with such force that she recognized it as a very real *boing!* and knew that unless she held her breath and counted slowly to ten, she was going to do something very stupid, like falling in a delicious, disbelieving faint.

'Davie . . .' Meg murmured, knowing she should be liking what she saw – a happy grin, a fresh, freckled face, thick, untidy hair the colour of a ripe conker. But she was incapable of doing anything because the *boing!* was reverberating unchecked around her stomach and slipping and slicing to her fingertips and toes.

'Well – come on, then – tell. Why are you here, and are you sure it's nothing sinister?'

'Nothing more than a thirty-mile detour on the way down to Burford Camp – in Wiltshire.'

'You're both being posted somewhere new, then?'

'No. Going to collect a convoy of trucks and lorries, actually –

escort them north,' Mark supplied. 'Fifty-three to be exact and all newly passed-out drivers. First time any of them will have done a long-distance convoy. And to add to the confusion, there are ATS drivers amongst them – women . . .'

'And what is wrong with women?' Huffily, Meg found her voice, stung to defend her own sex, and because she wasn't going to let him get away with being so gorgeous nor play havoc with her insides without some show of protest, she glared as she said it.

'Nothing at all. In their right and proper place ATS girls are a delight. But I don't appreciate them in a long-haul convoy, Meg Merrilees. They're just not built for driving heavy army lorries!'

'No. I reckon they'd all rather be in their proper place at home, but a lot of them didn't have much of a choice!' Meg flung.

'Now stop it, Mark! C'mon – let's find Mummy!'

Polly took Davie's hand, her happiness a delight to see.

'Shall we?' Mark indicated the archway with an exaggerated sweep of his hand.

'Er – no, ta. I've got things to do – the hens, for a start.' This was a family thing and she wasn't pushing in. 'And why did you call me Merrilees? My name is Blundell!'

'You haven't heard of Meg Merrilees?' He was looking at her as if she were stupid.

'No. Should I have?'

'I'd have thought so. She was a gypsy, who lived upon the moors. It's a poem!'

'Oh. I see.' She didn't see, of course, because no one had taught her poems about gypsies. 'Er – well – got to go. Nice meetin' you,' she added, remembering her manners.

'Nice meeting you too. See you around. Bye, Merrilees!'

And he was gone, boots clattering on the courtyard cobbles, back straight as a ramrod. So sure of himself, she thought angrily; sure of his charm, the certain knowledge that his smiling gaze could charm the ducks off a pond! Likely he did that to all the girls he met, but it wasn't goin' to work with Meg Blundell – too right it wasn't! Her insides were back to normal again. She was in charge of her emotions though she knew now exactly what Polly had meant about that *boing!* It had really been something – till she'd got the better of it, that was!

But for all that, her hand was just a little unsteady as she laid eggs as carefully as she was able in the bottom of the bucket. Meg Merrilees, for Pete's sake! A gypsy, was she, because she couldn't talk proper! Skittin' her, was he?

Well, sod Mark Kenworthy, because he wasn't gettin' the chance to throw her into a tizzy again, she would see to that! Nell had been right. Likely he was no better than the rest of them, and out for one thing!

Well, she wouldn't let him make a fool of her like some scally had made a fool of Ma! And anyway, would a feller like him, who could have any girl he took a fancy to, be interested in someone from a slum like Tippet's Yard and who was illegitimate, an' all? Bet your life he wouldn't, so forget him, Meg Blundell; stick to your own kind!

Yet, for all that, she wondered if he could dance and remembered that Polly had said he could. Oh, heck! Imagine dancing with him. Close. It didn't bear thinking about!

'There you are! Where on earth did you get to, Meg? They've gone now, and you weren't there to say goodbye! Mark asked especially; said I was to say so long to you – Davie, too.'

'Ar, well, that was nice of them both, but I reckoned it was family, so I went to see Mr Potter, ask if he wanted anything doing. I heard them go.' Such a hooting and laughing and crunching of tyres on the gravel drive, and she breathing a sigh of relief – or was it regret? – that they'd gone. 'Less than two hours! Talk about a flying visit!'

'Mm. They only had time for a sandwich. Mark looked in on Nanny, then went to sit with Gran, and Davie and I went to look at the hay at the brick house. Then we sat on the front steps as if we'd every right to be there, and talked and talked.

'And I forgot to tell you! Mummy had a letter from a school friend this morning – they've kept in touch for years and years – and would you believe it, her daughter got married about a month ago. She sent a photo of the bride. Such a beautiful white dress with a full skirt and train.'

'Don't tell me. Bet she's offered the lend of it!'

'She has! Isn't that lovely of her? And we are about the same height and build. She's even offered her wedding shoes, which are size five, like I take.'

'And will you mind being married secondhand, then?'

'Of course not. And think of the coupons I'll save. Davie and I were talking about it, and when he comes on leave we're going to ask if we can get married before I'm twenty-one. It's so awful, waiting, when we both know there'll never be anyone else.'

'I'll agree with you there. You and him look good together. Made me a bit envious, wishin' I was close to someone. But I haven't met him, yet . . .'

'So you didn't like Mark? Surely you found him just a little bit attractive?'

'Listen, Polly, your brother isn't for the likes of me. I'd be a right fool, wouldn't I, to let myself fall for him?'

'Why would you? And I've told you before, you don't *let* yourself fall in love; it just happens. Seems pretty obvious that you just didn't like him. A pity, that, when I'd thought we could make up a foursome when they're home and go to a dance somewhere.'

'I didn't say I didn't like him, and I certainly wouldn't mind going dancin' with him – in a foursome. But I wouldn't let it go any further than that!'

'You're a strange girl.' Polly frowned. 'You seem so set against being in love. Why, will you tell me?'

'I'm not against it!' Meg coloured hotly, because she *had* fallen for Polly's brother, if that *boing!* had been anything to go by. But his sort would take advantage of her sort. Stood to reason that any feller as good-looking as he was would think girls were there for the taking. 'I – I'll know when I've fallen in love, and when I do you'll be the first to know. I wonder where they are now.'

'Going like the clappers to make up the lost time, I shouldn't wonder,' Polly smiled dreamily. 'Such a lovely surprise. And by the way, what did you do with today's eggs?'

'Left them in the wash house – didn't want to come to the house, like I said. I'll get them for you.'

She hurried off, glad to be away from Polly's questioning and from her own downright lies, because to think of Mark kissing her made her go very peculiar.

But thinking about it was all she would do, because kissing and all that was what got girls into trouble, and she was living proof of it!

Yet mightn't it be nice to give it a whirl? Just the once? For the heck of it?

'Especially not for the heck of it, Meg Blundell, if you know what's good for you,' hissed a voice in her ear that sounded remarkably like Nell Shaw's.

'Oh, damn and blast!'

She shook the voice away, gazing intently at ten brown eggs, wondering why all of a sudden life seemed to have become so very complicated.

It was Sunday – six days more to cross off on the calendar – and they worked for the best part of the day on the hay on the brick house lawns, gathering it into lines with three-foot-wide wooden hay rakes. The better the day, the better the deed, Armitage said, and since the war didn't stop on Sundays, he could see no reason why they shouldn't get it cocked and loaded and safe in the barn by evening.

'Right! Are you ready?' They stood side by side, eyes closed, fingers crossed as the load of hay bumped past them. 'Wish, Meg . . .'

And though she had never felt so tired in her life before, and there was a blister on her hand, Meg knew she had never been so happy, and hoped with all her heart that her wish to stay at Candlefold for ever and ever would be granted. Oh, please it would!

'Tomorrow, if anyone asks, I'll be able to say that Davie will be home this week. Think of it, Meg; *this week*. Seven whole days to spend together.'

'I'm goin' to miss you when you go off to Oxford.'

'No you won't. There'll be Mark around.'

'So there will. But I'm here to work, remember, an' I'll be busier than ever when you're away.'

'So you won't be going out with my brother, if he asks you – which he will!'

'You think so? Oh, I don't think he will – me bein' a servant, I mean.'

'You're *not* a servant. You're Candlefold's home help, and I'd miss you if you left. It's my guess he'll ask you out once Davie and I have gone to Oxford. Don't be so prim, Meg. Say you'll go!'

'He hasn't asked, yet.' Mind, it might be fun for the heck of it, whispered a voice in her ear nothing at all like Nell Shaw's. 'Let's wait and see, shall we, Polly?'

It was then they heard the bell and ran laughing down the lane to the far archway, then across the yard to arrive breathless in the kitchen.

'All safely gathered in. Armitage says there's the best part of a ton, and all good stuff for the war effort, and I'm *starving*!' Polly gasped.

'Then off upstairs, the pair of you, for a wash. It'll be on the table in two minutes. Roast rabbit, and gooseberries and custard for pudding. Away with you now!' Mary Kenworthy smiled, feeling almost contented. Mind, there was always the war out there, ready to take all your waking thoughts if you let it, but on the credit side was a wagonload of good hay, and Mark and Davie coming home on Friday.

It was because of her relaxed mood that they decided to play gramophone records in Mrs Kenworthy's room instead of listening to the nine o'clock news. Had they listened, maybe the shock of what Mrs Potter was to push through the letter box next morning might have been less acute. And since Polly always waited for the morning mail it was she who burst into the kitchen, eyes wide.

'My God! Hitler's invaded Russia! Go on – read it!'

'*Russia!*' Mary Kenworthy reached for her reading glasses. 'Oh my goodness, let me see!'

The headlines in the *Telegraph* were large and unmistakable: 'RUSSIA ATTACKED ON 1,800 MILE FRONT'. Agitated, she spread the paper on the kitchen table so they might read it together. 'Yesterday, it was. Early in the morning. More than three million soldiers! And Mr Churchill was on the wireless last night. The one time we miss the evening news, and he's on!'

'It says he said we'd give Russia all the help we can; said he'd warned Stalin about it. Will our troops be sent there to fight?'

'I – I wouldn't think so, Polly. After all, we've never got on very well with the Communists, have we?'

'But they are fighting Hitler now, so that makes them our ally!'

'It says,' Meg jabbed a finger, 'that Mr Churchill offered any technical or economic assistance. There's nuthink about sending troops.'

'Oh, I hope not. And had you thought – Davie and Mark's leave might be cancelled now?'

'Darling, don't upset yourself before we know what it's all about,' Mary Kenworthy soothed, 'and I think we should spare a thought for the Russian people. It seems they've been terribly bombed and weren't able to put up much resistance.'

'Then Stalin should've listened to what Mr Churchill told him,' Meg said matter-of-factly. 'An' if all Hitler's soldiers and bombers are attacking Russia, they'll maybe leave us alone.' She remembered the seven-night bombing of Liverpool and was instantly contrite. 'Mind, it isn't very nice for them, gettin' bombed.'

'What shall we tell Gran and Nanny?'

'I think we'd better switch on for the eight o'clock news, hear what the BBC has to say about it, then when we take up the breakfasts we'll know better what to say.'

'Gran'll be all right, but how Nanny is going to take it is anybody's guess,' Polly shrugged.

'Then it's my guess that she'll pull up the drawbridge and pretend none of it is happening,' Meg offered.

'So how about we get ourselves a cup of tea and a slice of toast and jam,' Mary Kenworthy smiled brightly, 'and listen to the news? Switch on, will you, Meg? Polly, cut the bread, please. And let's all think how lucky we are safe here at Candlefold.'

'And let's hope them – *those* – Russians'll give Hitler the shock of his life, 'cause he's invaded whichever country he thought fit,' Meg muttered. 'About time someone stood up to him!'

Then she wondered what Nell and Tommy were thinking and saying about it back in Tippet's Yard, and all at once she missed them and wished she could be with them – just for a little while . . .

Next morning low clouds blotted out the sun and not long afterwards it began to rain; drops the size of halfpennies making dark circles on the flags and cobbles of the yard.

'*Rain!*' Meg was dismayed, because it shouldn't rain at Candlefold! Since she'd come here the sky had been blue, the sun constant. Now, all was gloomy and rain fell steadily. 'It looks as if it's set in for the day!'

'We did need it, Meg. The ground was getting very dry.' Mrs John said. 'Armitage said that once the farmers had got their hay in, it could rain as soon as it liked.'

'There'll be no work done in the garden now,' Polly shrugged, 'so tell me what needs doing inside.'

'If you wouldn't mind, you and Meg can make up the beds ready for Mark and Davie, and give the rooms a clean – put out towels.'

'*If* they come,' Polly sighed, taking sheets from the linen cupboard.

'Of course they'll come. Give me one good reason why they shouldn't!'

'We-e-ll, Russia, for a start.'

'Them Russians can look after themselves. Mr Churchill as good as said we wouldn't be sending troops. But how about Nanny – sayin' the Tsar would send the Cossacks in and soon put paid to the Germans?'

'Nanny's in another world. She just doesn't want to know!'

'So what would happen if everybody did the same, then? What if our lads in the Forces acted like she did? "Stick yer 'eads in the sand, lads! Pretend it isn't happening!"'

'Meg – don't. It isn't like you to be vindictive!'

'All right! I'll say no more! Let's talk about Davie. Had you thought that when you wake up in the morning, there'll only be three days to go?'

'Go-to-beds, I used to call them. Y'know – how many more go-to-beds before Father Christmas comes.'

'Then it's four go-to-beds, and your Davie'll be here and you'll be wondering why you worried! Now chuck them pillows over, will you?'

'Meg – don't ever leave, will you?'

'I won't. And that's a promise!' A promise, she thought as she stuffed pillows into cases, she would do her utmost to keep. 'Had you thought,' she smiled, 'that this rain will do the strawberries a whole lot of good – make them swell?'

'So it will. You're getting to be quite a country girl, Meg Blundell! Mind, enough is enough. If it rains too much they'll rot, then Mr Potter will hit the roof. All our work wasted. Now, let's get these rooms seen to, then we'll have a chat with Gran. Being in bed watching it rain must be awful, and cold wet weather makes her joints ache more.'

'Then we'll try to cheer her up a bit.' Meg liked Mrs Kenworthy, who was so grateful for even the smallest attention and hardly ever tugged on the bell pull at her bedside. And the old lady had remembered Ma, so it was almost certain she knew what had happened to her and even, Meg brooded, who the feller was. Yet Meg had insisted her mother's name was Hilda and that her father died at sea, because she'd known instinctively the time had not been right for questions. Nor for answers either, because the Kenworthys might want to forget what had happened under their own roof twenty years ago, and all the upset it must have caused. 'We've neglected her these last few days, what with the haymakin', an' all.'

'Mm. But I enjoyed it, Meg. It was great stealing our own hay, and getting away with it, didn't you think?'

'Yes, an' serve London right for nicking your 'ouse without a by-your-leave. We'll do it again next year, eh?'

If she were still here, that was. If National Service didn't catch up with her. If *They* said that helping to look after two old ladies and working sometimes in the kitchen garden to dig for victory wasn't enough, and she had to go into the armed forces or get herself back to Liverpool to work in munitions. Big money to be earned there, but she didn't want big money. A pound a week suited her very nicely and she wanted nothing to change.

'Hey! You were miles away! Bet you were thinking about Mark!'

'No, I wasn't! I was thinkin' about when I'm twenty and have to register. I don't want to, you know.'

'Nor me. When is your birthday, Meg?'

'August the twenty-ninth.'

'Goodness! And mine's on the twenty-eighth, would you believe! Sometimes I wish I knew where I was born, but Mummy always says she was never told, that they got me from the Church of England Adoption Society, and they wouldn't say. They don't, you know. Where were you born, Meg?'

'Lyra Street, Liverpool 3.' The lie came easily to her tongue. 'Mrs Shaw – the neighbour I've told you about – was there, helping the midwife, I believe.'

Lies, which led to more lies, and all the time wanting to say she had been born here at Candlefold.

'It isn't allowed to try to find your natural mother, is it? Not that I want to, mind. Mummy said she got me when I was two months old and that from then on I was a Kenworthy, as far as she was concerned. Though what is so amazing is that she got a baby who looks as if she really was one – Mark and me, I mean, being so alike. Still, that's life, as they say, and I'm very lucky.'

'Me too, findin' this job, and I'll tell you something, Polly. When the times comes for me to register for war work, I'm goin' to try to get out of it. After all, who's to know that I wasn't killed in the blitz? There are hundreds of Liverpool people still missing.'

'And you'd really do that? Don't you think it's a bit unpatriotic?'

'Maybe it is, but they're not getting me without a fight! When Ma died it was up to me to get along as best I could, and that's what I'm goin' to do! I like it here and as far as I'm concerned, if that lot want me they can come lookin' for me. So what do you think to that?'

'I – I don't know what to say.' Polly had no answer to such forthrightness. 'Mind, I'm going to try to stay here too. Mummy couldn't manage without me and I do help grow food for the war effort.'

'An' you reckon helpin' in the garden counts as war work?'

'Not really, if I'm honest. I think *They'll* make me leave home and it worries me sick. The only way out of it is if Mummy lets Davie and me get married. A married woman still has to work, unless she has small children, but she can't be sent away from her home. Maybe if I were married, working in the kitchen garden would count. So I'm going to be sneaky, and convince Mummy it would be better if I were married. Do you think that's awful?'

'No. Anyway, who am I to judge after what I've just said?'

'Oh, dear. We shouldn't be talking like this, Meg, when there's a war on.'

'Suppose not. But let's worry about it when it happens, eh? Perhaps *They* won't get round to our age group for a month or two. I don't think we'll be expected to register on the very day we're twenty. And it's funny, innit, you and me bein' born on the same day, almost?'

'It's maybe why we get on so well together. But let's finish these rooms, then if Mr Potter doesn't want anything done in the tomato house, we'll go and sit with Gran for a while. And, Meg, I can understand you not wanting to leave Candlefold because I don't want to either.'

Seven

The Thursday morning sunshine had been a delight to awaken to. Meg opened wide the bedroom window, sniffing in a rain-washed new day, thinking that yesterday's gloom was gone, just as surely as Wednesday was now no more than a cross on the calendar.

'Just one more go-to-bed,' Polly had sighed blissfully at breakfast-time, 'then they'll be here. Today will drag, just see if it doesn't!'

Yet for her the days never dragged, Meg thought later, setting down the trugs she carried, to stand beside the kitchen-garden gate and gaze at the view that never failed to please her; the length of the drying green, the wire-netted henrun and, beyond it, the far stone archway, opening on to the quadrangle of old stone buildings that was the original Candlefold. And if she cared to split hairs, she pondered, she had almost as much right to be here as Polly, given that even though Polly was the daughter of the house, she had probably been born in a home for unmarried mothers, address unknown, whereas she, Meg, had actually been born at Candlefold, though in which part she had no idea. She would like it to have been in the old part of the house, which was once the servants' quarters, though it didn't much matter where. She could ask, of course. Mrs John would know, as would Mrs Kenworthy and Nanny Boag, but she wasn't ready, yet, to tell them. Only when the time was right would she show them what was inside Ma's little case, ask of them how it had really been. Later. When she was more sure of herself.

She picked up the trugs which Mr Potter had filled with potatoes, fresh-dug from the earth, and carrots and a crisp pointed cabbage. And given one more day of sunshine, he had said, there would be the first picking of strawberries, which couldn't have come at a better time, young Mark being very fond of them.

Tomorrow, that would be. When Davie and Mark began their leave and when she, if she had one iota of sense left in her head, would take herself off to Liverpool. Best she should, because she would feel out of place amongst so intimate a family gathering; wouldn't know whether she was a part of it or merely the hired help. And what made a lot more sense was that for two days at least she would be out of sight and sound of Mark, who was too handsome for his own good and who wasn't for the likes of Meg Blundell!

She had discussed the matter with Polly, who disagreed with her very firmly, telling her she would be needed more than ever with two hefty soldiers cluttering up the place, extra beds to be made, extra food to prepare. And as for not being a part of the family – well, that simply wasn't the case, and she knew it!

So there would be no getting out of Mark Kenworthy's disturbing way, even for two days! Stupid of her even to have thought about it because, truth known, she still felt uneasy just to think of those too-blue eyes that were capable of undressing her at a glance. Felt delightfully uneasy, if she were brutally honest!

But no man was using his charm on her to get what he wanted. Ma had given in and look what happened to her! Trouble with a capital T, and left high and dry and dependent on the charity of the Kenworthy family! A foolish young woman who had offended against the rules of respectability; had loved too much and given away something that would best have been kept for her wedding night! Mind, Ma had been unlucky. Pregnant girls mostly got married 'in a hurry', and were usually forgiven when the baby was presented at church for baptism. It was a queer old world if you let yourself think too deeply about it!

'Hello, Mrs Seed,' she called through the wash-house door to the woman who rotated the peggy-legs in a large tub of blue rinsing water. 'Nice day for it!'

'Oh, aye! They'll dry all right today!'

'If you're ready for the mangling I'll give you a hand. Did it for Ma as soon as I was big enough to turn the handle.' She set down the vegetables and gazed at the old-fashioned mangle, green and red painted, with large wooden rollers and a large screw at the top to tighten them, make them squeeze out the very last drop of water. 'That old thing you've got there is exactly like Ma's.'

'So your mother was a laundrymaid?'

'No, she worked in a factory, but after I was born and she got her own 'ouse, she took in washing to help out.'

'I believe both your parents are dead?' Mrs Seed wiped her hands dry on her pinafore and pulled out a stool.

'Mm. Me da died at sea; Ma died of TB last winter, an' I haven't got it,' she hastened.

'Of course you haven't! You look far too bonny and healthy! Got a young man, have you?'

'Nah! I write to a seaman, but we're only friends. Haven't met nobody I'd care to get wed to. I'm not in any hurry,' she said airily. 'Polly told me you once worked here.'

'Oh, my word, yes, and I was right pleased when Mrs John asked me back to help out Thursdays and Fridays. And since I'd always done the washing – laundrymaid I'd been, really – it came as second nature to start again where I'd left off twelve years ago. Got two boys now, and since the war has made it respectable for a married woman to go out to work, I enjoy coming here. It's as if I'd never been away.'

'I know how you feel, though I suppose it's the family makes Candlefold what it is. I haven't been here long but I don't want to leave, not ever. My, but it must have been some place, Mrs Seed.'

'Afore the Government decided to take most of it, you mean? When they had both houses – the stone house and the brick house we always called them, even though they were joined together – there were three housemaids, a parlourmaid, a cook and a kitchenmaid. And me, of course, and a sewing lady who came one day a week. There was a butler, an' all, and a housekeeper, once. Mrs Kenworthy did away with the butler and the housekeeper after Mr John died but we were a happy lot, always. I'll be thirty-six, next, and when I come here I'm a young lass again, and thinking about how it used to be.' Smiling, she got to her feet. 'Ah, well – this and better may do, young Meg, but this and worse won't get the washing out to dry!'

'Then let me help with the mangling, Mrs Seed. With two of us, we'll be able to put the clothes through twice and Ma always said that twice through the mangle saved half an hour's drying.'

'Then I'll be glad of your help. This contraption is past its best, the old brute. Should've been thrown out ages ago. Mrs John said we should have a new one, but we never got round to it. Now, of course, you can't get a mangle for love nor money in the shops, and I'd been so looking forward to a modern wringer with rubber rollers.'

She fished in the tub up to her elbows and brought out a towel, folding it expertly, gently easing it into the wooden rollers, nodding to Meg to start turning.

'I've never been inside the brick part of the house, Mrs Seed. Is it – well – *stately*, sort of?'

'Oh, my word, yes! The staircase is so big and grand it took ages to sweep the treads and dust and polish it. And a long gallery goes the length of the house, on the south side. In the old days, the ladies of the house used to take their exercise there when it was too cold and muddy to go out. And there was the staircase hall – massive, it was – and a dining room and servery and a drawing room and a library and, oh, so many bedrooms! Twenty, if you counted the attics. Mind, it's a mercy the people from London took it, because it would have been terrible for Mrs John, trying to keep up with a place that size, and domestic staff all gone on war work to make more money!'

'Polly took me round the outside of it, but all the shutters were closed across the downstairs windows and you couldn't see nuthink!'

'Well, I've got some photographs at home and they show the brick house when it was in its prime and there were three gardeners. I can point out the rooms for you so you'll get a better idea of things. Shall I bring them tomorrow, when I come to do the ironing?'

'Please. Mind, I like the old house; it's so solid and safe, but it might be nice to know which room was where in the brick part. Havin' been brought up in a diddy little house, y'see, great big places always get me thinking about what it must have been like to be gentry, and have servants, and more rooms than you knew what to do with. But let's get these clothes seen to, then I'll help you fold them and we'll give them a second turn. Like I said, I'm good when it comes to mangling clothes!'

And they laughed, and Meg knew that here was another who had come under Candlefold's spell, just as Ma had done. Strange it should have such a hold over people. Was there magic in its old, rough stones or was it bewitched, or haunted? By a good, kind ghost, of course!

'Sorry to be so long.' Breathless from hurrying, Meg put the trugs on the draining board. 'Stopped by to give Mrs Seed a hand with the mangling.'

'That was thoughtful, dear . . .'

'An' Mr Potter said there'll be strawberries tomorrow, if this sun keeps up.'

'Good.' Mary Kenworthy beamed. 'That's tomorrow's pudding taken care of! Remind Polly to ask at the farm for extra milk tomorrow, for skimming.'

'Strawberries and cream,' Meg sighed. 'Seems sinful, really, with food so scarce.'

'I feel the same way, truth known. Then I ease my conscience by telling myself that as long as the odd little luxury hasn't had to be brought here at risk to our merchant seamen, then it's all right – especially if we have produced it ourselves.'

'Ar. Home grown.' These days the Government made a fuss about growing vegetables for the war effort and not using gas or electricity unless you had to, and not using trains or buses unless your journey was really necessary! And being careful with tap water and not wasting even a piece of string or the wrapping paper from a parcel, and though it was said there were people who never seemed to go short – people who bought food and petrol on the black market – most housewives made do with rations that weren't half enough, really.

Mind, bread wasn't rationed, nor vegetables, when you could get them, and many a rumbling stomach was eased with butterless toast or a vegetable pie with a crust made from unrationed suet. If the butcher was in a good mood, that was, and let you have a lump from under the counter, Meg thought, remembering the terrible food queues in Liverpool after the May blitz.

Managing to feed a family was hard for women in cities and towns. Here in the country they had milk, and could feed hens on kitchen scraps and potato peelings and gleanings from the fields when the wheat and barley had been harvested. Everyone gleaned, Polly said; even branches blown down in a gale were gathered and sawed into logs to eke out the coal ration. And here there were wild rabbits to be got and wood pigeons for pies and stews. Make no mistake about it, country life suited Margaret Mary Blundell and when the time came, that lot at the Ministry of National Service would have to come lookin' for her, unpatriotic or not!

'What are you thinking about, Meg? You look quite fierce,' Mary Kenworthy laughed.

'Well, if you want the truth, Mrs John, I was thinkin' about havin' to register when I'm twenty. I don't want to leave here, see.'

'Neither does Polly. But there's a war on. We have to do as we're told.'

'Ar. Soft in the 'ead, aren't we? Like sheep. Ma said that in the last war, young men fell over themselves to join up, an' look what happened to them. And then the daft Government let it happen again!'

'That's what is so terrible about it. When Mark was a baby I'd think he would never go through what his father did. The war to end all wars, we said.' Her eyes held a sad, remembering look, then all at once she tilted her chin and formed her lips into a smile. 'But our soldiers are coming home tomorrow – let's be glad. And here's my daughter with the milk and the mail.'

A beaming Polly set down the white enamelled can with a clatter, laid the newspaper beside it, then held aloft a postcard.

'That's it! He's really coming. No more waiting for letters for seven lovely days! Just a postcard with *See you. Very very soon. D.* He can send me one like that every other week!'

Her cheeks were flushed pink, her eyes bright with excitement as she offered the card for Meg's inspection.

'There you are, then. So no more worrying the Army's goin' to cancel their leave. But it's a bit straight and to the point, isn't it – not one I love you nor nuthink? In a hurry, was he?'

'You don't put personal things on a postcard. No salutations, nor names.'

'Salutations, Pol? What's them?'

'Well, you wouldn't put Dear Polly, or Darling Polly. And you use initials in place of a signature. Postcards aren't considered private, so that's the way they are written.'

'Ar.' You'd have thought he'd have slipped in a few Xs, for all that. 'Not even kisses?'

'Especially not kisses.'

'I see.' Something else for her how-to-improve-yourself store of knowledge. She was a quick learner, mind. Nowadays she was getting most of her thems and thoses right, and using her knife proper and not holding it like it was a pencil. Given time, Meg thought, she would be as ladylike as Ma, and nobody would be able to skit her for being a Scouser!

'Oh dear.' Mary Kenworthy folded the newspaper.

'Russia, Mummy?'

'Yes, poor things. They aren't putting up much of a fight. The Germans seem to be advancing pretty much as they please, and burning everything as they go. It was so sudden and savage. You don't expect to be attacked by a country you have a peace pact with, do you?'

'Since when has Hitler bothered about things like that?' Meg scowled, recalling the bombing of Liverpool. 'That man's so crooked he couldn't lie straight in bed!'

'Oh, Meg – you say such funny things! But we must remember the Russians in our prayers, especially the old and the very young.'

'Meg doesn't believe in praying,' Polly offered.

'Maybe I don't. But I'll tell you sumthink I do believe in. Every time I think of that Hitler, I wish somethink nasty on him, like an 'eadache or a dose of the runs! I ill-wish him all the time.'

'That's a bit – well, *pagan*, isn't it?'

'Not if it works, it isn't. Anyway, you do it your way, Polly, and I'll do it mine!'

'Then between you both I think that odious man is in for a bad time, especially with Nanny's pinsticking too! Now would you collect the breakfast trays from upstairs, Polly, before you go to the garden, and don't forget to tell mother-in-law you've had a card from Davie? And will you do the vegetables, Meg, whilst I see to the dishes? And, Polly, do please put the milk on the cold slab! Goodness, there's so much to do, they'll be here before we know it!'

'Yes. Tomorrow!' Lovely, lovely tomorrow! Polly closed her eyes and sighed ecstatically. 'And has anyone remembered that I'll be going to Oxford on Monday and Mr Potter is going to need a hand with the strawberry picking?'

'Then either Meg or Mark – or both – will help. I'm sure the garden won't grind to a halt without you, dear. We'll manage somehow,' Mary laughed.

Laughter came easily to Mrs John when tomorrow her son would be home for a week, Meg thought, but there'd be an awful gloom over the place when he went back. Oh, damn and blast the war, and Hitler too!

Meg closed her eyes and sent a headache darting through space. Mind, she was pretty sure that ill-wishing didn't work, but she enjoyed trying! For good measure she closed her eyes again, and sent a nasty bellyache in the same direction – just to make sure!

Friday, at last! Meg let go a small sigh of contentment, because today would be all rush and bustle and hugs and kisses, and Army gear cluttering up the kitchen floor. And strawberries and cream!

She swung her legs out of bed, pulled on her slippers, then drew back the curtains. Her favourite moment of each day, if she really had to choose, was to look down on the early morning courtyard and know that Candlefold was not in her dreamings, but real and solid, with another new day hers for the living.

'Flipping heck!'

Her eyes were drawn to the granite trough and Polly, who leaned over it, pumping water and manoeuvring her head beneath the spout at one and the same time, gasping as each gush of water hit her. Then she groped for the towel and began to rub her hair vigorously.

'What are you doing?' Meg called.

'Come down. It's called washing your hair!'

'In a pump trough? With *cold* water?' Meg demanded half a minute later. 'Have you gone bonkers, or somethin?'

'No. I often wash it out here in summer. Pump water is good for your hair; every bit as good as rainwater. And it'll be dry in no time at all!'

'I wish,' Meg grumbled, 'that all I had to do with my hair was to wash it and shake it dry – like a dog that's been in the river! Wish I was fair and curly, like you are.'

'And I have always longed,' Polly sighed, 'for dark hair exactly like yours. We always want what we can't have but oh, Meg, today's the day! I woke far too early, so I decided to wash my hair before I went for the milk; anything to make the time go more quickly.'

'When will they be arriving?'

'Haven't a clue. It'll all depend on the buses, when they've got to Preston. They'll probably hitch a lift from there. People are very good at stopping for uniforms. They'll be leaving Richmond about eight, so I think they could be here around twelve, given luck – and provided the train isn't late. Oh, I feel quite sick!'

'No you don't. You just feel peculiar from stickin' your head under the pump on an empty stomach. I'll put the kettle on and you can take your ma a cup up, and tell her she's to drink it in bed. Then you an' me will get our breakfast good and early before you go for the milk. Being busy helps pass the time.'

'It won't. The morning will drag. And I couldn't eat a thing. My stomach is churning something awful!'

'You'll do as you're told and have toast and jam and a cup of tea, so don't argue! And your hair is almost dry already, and it looks lovely. You're the only girl I know, Polly Kenworthy, who can wash her hair with carbolic soap and rinse it in a pump trough and look beautiful; just like you'd been to the hairdresser's!'

'Carbolic was all I could lay my hands on. You know it's ages since there was shampoo in the shops. And I'm not beautiful, Meg. I'm pink-and-white pretty, but I don't care. Davie likes me the way I am, and that's all that matters.' She picked up her towel and soap and made for the house. 'And there is still almost five hours to go before we can even *think* of them arriving. Don't ever fall in love, Meg, because it's all either down in a pit or up in the clouds, and I don't recommend it.'

'You know you do! But I won't fall in love. How many more times have I got to tell you? And next time you wash your hair, don't forget that I got a big bottle of shampoo from Australia and it's there for the sharing. Now, let's get the kettle on. And you're not to forget to ask for extra milk, today. It's strawberries *and cream* for pudding tonight!'

Meg sighed blissfully. Life was good, and if anyone had told her a year ago she would be this happy, she would have laughed in their face.

It wasn't until ten o'clock that Meg was able to get to the wash house and only then because Mary Kenworthy said, 'Goodness! We've forgotten Mrs Seed! Be a love, Meg, and take her a cup of tea, will you?'

And Meg was glad to, because didn't Mrs Seed have something to show her: long-ago photographs of Candlefold the way it used to be when life was back to normal after the last war, and everyone sure there would never be another?

'Goodness! Thought I'd never get away!' Meg laid down the tea tray 'It's all rush over there, and Polly going round in circles and no more use than a chocolate teapot! Did you bring the photos, Mrs Seed?'

'That I did.' She reached to switch off the iron. 'And I'll take five minutes off while I explain the layout of the place to you.' She fished in her shopping bag for a large brown envelope. 'Now this one here is when you are looking at the brick house from the far side – away from the lawns where you and Polly were haymaking, that is. That row of shuttered windows is the drawing room, the library and what used to be Mrs Kenworthy's little boudoir. She used to write her letters there, and talk to Cook about the menus for the day. Such a pretty little room, with chintzy chairs and a long bookcase and her desk under the window. And plants and flowers everywhere. And now it's all dark and full of dust and clutter, I shouldn't wonder. And above those rooms is the gallery – I told you about it – and above that were six guest rooms and two bathrooms. Such a view from those windows; stretches for miles.'

'I've never seen the south side.' Meg gazed intently at the photograph, trying to imagine rooms with windows open to the sun and people living in them and having guests to dinner. 'I got a good look at the other side, though, when Polly and me turned the hay every day. We did well for the war effort, didn't we? Almost a ton of hay, Mr Armitage said; it'll be for our own little Jersey cow in winter. So what do the windows on the right-hand side of the front door belong to?'

'Ah, now, the hay side was the gentlemen's preserve, kind of. There was a smoking room – all leather sofas and chairs and fat red cushions – and beyond it was the billiards room. When the entertaining was on a grand scale, there would be dancing in the gallery, but mostly dinner parties were small, and the ladies settled themselves with coffee in the little drawing room and the men took themselves off and played snooker or billiards, or bridge, if the mood was on them.'

'Hm.' Meg thought of her mother. 'When the ladies had their coffee, would one of the housemaids take it in?'

'Oh no, my dear. The parlour maid did that. A cut above we housemaids, she was; was trained up by the butler to help wait at table and wore a very smart uniform when there were guests, though she would come down to the kitchens and tell us what the ladies were wearing, and little bits of gossip she'd managed to hear – in strictest confidence, mind. She'd have been shown the door without a reference if she'd been caught talking about above stairs!'

'And the other windows?'

'Well, those to the left of the door belong to the great hall; a huge place, though no use for dancing in because of the uneven stone floor, you see. A very lofty room, that was, and off it was the little drawing room and the estate office and the gun room and the lamp room, though when electricity came, lamps were only used in an emergency, and candles only on the dining table.'

'It must have been marvellous, Mrs Seed.'

'Oh, there were good days and bad, but mostly things ran very smoothly. Now here,' she smiled, dipping into the envelope, 'is one very special photograph I want you to see. It shows how lovely it once was. It's from 1916; taken at a garden party for wounded soldiers in the last war.'

'Ooooh!' It took Meg a great deal of effort to bite on her tongue and not cry out that she had the very photograph too. 'Ooooh, aren't the gardens nice? Wouldn't think them lovely lawns was a hayfield now.'

'Yes, but look carefully, girl, because there is someone on that photo that you know, isn't there?'

There was! Meg drew in a deep breath and remembered *Candlefold 1916. Dolly Blundell, Norah Bentley, Gladys Tucker*. Three pretty housemaids in flower-sprigged frocks and straw hats.

'I – Is there? *Who?*' Oh, no! Mrs Seed knew about Ma!

'Well, of course there is! Look again! The one with the white pinny and the Union Jack! *Me*, you duffer, when I was ten! My dad was undergardener here. I was born in an estate house! Part and parcel of it all my life, I was, till I got wed and moved down into the village!'

'But of course!' Not Ma! Not Dolly Blundell! The finger pointed to a little girl with a beaming smile proudly waving her flag for the photographer. Flaming 'eck, Mrs Seed, never do a thing like that to me again! 'You were a pretty little thing,' was all she could think of to say.

'Proud as Punch, more like. I had a new hat and shoes especially for the occasion. I remember that day as if were yesterday, and Mr John on leave from the trenches, and young Mark a bit of a bairn. And look at him now!' Her eyes misted with tears. 'A grown man and fighting for his country!'

'Yes, and him home today on leave, don't forget.' Meg's heart made little pitipats in her throat. 'But drink your tea, it's getting cold.'

'So it is. But best get on! You'll be busy today, young Meg, but if you want to see the rest of the photographs, or if there's ever anything you want to know about the Kenworthys or Candlefold, you pop along to the wash house Thursdays or Fridays. And just to make you curious, I'll tell you something that very few folk know. Now, those people from London think they've got the brick house all locked and bolted and secure, like, but they haven't!'

'You're kiddin',' Meg gasped, wide-eyed.

'Oh, but I'm not, and what's more I could take you inside that brick house and show you round if I wasn't sworn to secrecy, that is! And don't you go saying anything about what I've told you, Meg, or you and me both will be in trouble! Now off you go, and don't forget the tray.'

'Oh, *please*? Give me just a clue?'

But Mrs Seed said her lips were sealed and that Meg had better watch her own, an' all and not say one word to anyone! And especially not to Nanny Boag, who blabbed!

'Away with you, now, and say nowt, or I'll never tell you another thing as long as I live!'

And with that, Meg had to be content, and wished Mrs Seed hadn't told her about the secret way in that even the people from London didn't know about, for now she wouldn't rest until she knew where it was, because she really, really wanted to see inside the brick house, shuttered and desolate though it was. Oh my goodness, what a day this was turning out to be!

Meg was closing the kitchen-garden gate when a cry from Polly as she ran beneath the far archway told her that Davie had arrived. She had been sent for news of the strawberry situation as it wasn't any use asking Polly, Mrs John had said, because since half-past eleven she had disappeared every ten minutes beneath the small archway to gaze across the field, or beneath the far archway to peer anxiously up the lane towards the road.

And Meg had laughed and said, 'Remind me never to fall in love with a soldier, because it seems to get you in an awful tizzy.'

'Oh, it does, Meg; it really does. I know exactly how Polly feels. My John was a soldier, don't forget. It was almost unbearable when he had to go back to the trenches, though at least I had his son for comfort. I wish Mark would find a nice girl . . .'

'Don't worry. He will. He'll marry and there'll be another Kenworthy to carry on here. That's what you're worried about, isn't it – that after more'n six hundred years there might not –' She stopped, shame-faced, fearing she had gone too far. 'I'm sorry! Really I am! Nothing awful is goin' to happen here. Not after all those years it isn't!'

'It's all right. I know you didn't mean – well, you know. And if I'm honest, Meg, my greatest fear is not that the line will be broken if Mark doesn't have a son, but that something will happen to him – something too awful to say!'

'Then don't say it! Them Kenworthy fellers have been good at hanging on to what they've got and lookin' after number one. You said so yourself. Sittin' on the fence, careful like, since the year dot! Your Mark is goin' to be all right – Davie, too. I know it!'

'Well, if hoping and wishing and praying counts for anything then yes, they'll both come safely home. That matters more to me than keeping up the line. Only let Mark get through this war, and I'll not care if he presents me with half a dozen granddaughters! But off with you, child, and get those berries, and if you run into Polly, tell her to calm down or she'll disappear in a puff of smoke!'

Mr Potter had said that yes indeed there were a fair few big red ripe ones, and lined the bowl Meg carried with cabbage leaves, since that was the way it had always been done. And as always, he said very seriously, it was his privilege and prerogative to pick the first of any crop, be it early potatoes or peaches or strawberries, like now!

So contented, Meg had waited as the bowl was carefully filled, sniffing in the strawberry scent, knowing that never before had she eaten one fresher than the one offered to her with a flourish.

'There you are, young Meg. First fruit's to you!'

'Is there a wish on a first strawberry, Mr Potter,' she had asked huskily, 'like on a first swallow?'

And he had laughed and said the only thing that should come into your head when you bit into your first strawberry was to wish for more!

So here she stood, the precious bowl in her hands, watching as Mark and Davie were hugged and kissed, though she was forced to admit that Davie got the best of it. What she was unwilling to admit, though, was the way she felt when Mark saw her beside the gate, and waved to her and smiled, as he disappeared beneath the archway.

She had prepared herself for that first sight of him, schooled her insides not to dare give way to another *boing!* She had instinctively tightened her buttocks and pulled in her stomach against such a thing happening again; had got that particular part of her anatomy well under control. But she was not prepared for the flush that burned her cheeks, nor the strange dryness in her mouth. Nor was she prepared to accept the sudden dull thumping of her heart so that she felt its wanton pulse beats at the back of her nose and the hollow of her throat. And she was completely mystified by the lovely shiver-making urge to close her eyes and part her lips for his kiss, because she knew perfectly well that kissing was the start of you know what, and though for the first time she understood a little of how Ma might well have felt, there was going to be no messing as far as Mark Kenworthy was concerned. Because he was all of the things a girl should watch out for and say 'No!' to. He had eyes that said 'I dare you!' and the height of him, the perfection of his sudden grin and the broad, lovely shoulders any girl would gladly lay her head on made him dangerous to be near.

'No!' She said it out loud and with such determination that she almost dropped the bowl, seeing in a split second the lush red fruits squashed and scattered on the dry-as-dust lane. 'Oh, my word, *no*!' she said again more quietly but with equal determination. No, no and *no* to falling in love and saying 'Yes!' and giving in, and getting herself into trouble, which was what giving in was all about! Like Nell said, all men were the same, and especially in wartime when they wanted to know what life was all about before they maybe got themselves killed! And oh, please God don't let anything happen to Mark? Don't let that beautiful body end up shattered and bleeding on some battlefield!

And why she was bothering with God and praying like someone demented she didn't know, because hadn't she said time and time again that praying wasn't for Meg Blundell? Hadn't she insisted that you left it to Fate and took whatever had been written in your Book of Life on the day you were born?

Bewildered, she stopped beside the henrun. Not the kind of place at which you were all at once prepared to admit that there just might be a God in heaven and that sometimes, when a prayer was as heartfelt and sincere as hers had been, that the old feller up there might listen, and nod wisely, and say to the duty angel who sat beside him, 'All right! Grant that one for Meg Blundell!'

It was at so unlikely a place, for all that, she was forced to admit that given half a chance she could, if she wasn't careful, let herself fall in love for the first and only time. And the thought scared her half to death.

'You've been avoiding me, Merrilees! Tell me why!'

This time there had been no avoiding him, Meg thought, since they had bumped into each other, literally, as she entered the courtyard through the far archway.

'N-no, I haven't. I've been busy, what with Polly with her head in the clouds and two extra to look after. Don't forget I'm the hired help around here!' She tossed her head haughtily as if his nearness didn't bother her one bit.

'I hate to contradict a lady, but from the moment I got here you've been placing yourself out of my reach! You scuttled into the kitchen with a bowl of strawberries then scuttled out again; you sat as far away from me as you could at supper and hardly looked in my direction and then, just to make sure I got the message, you took yourself off to the village without even having the decency to ask me if I'd care for a stroll there myself!'

'Like I said, I work here, and when it's a family gathering I don't stick my nose in! And as for shoving off to the village, I was doin' your mother a favour by takin' a knitting pattern to Mrs Potter, and two ounces of khaki wool!'

Her voice shook with the effort of denying what she knew to be the complete and utter truth, and her mouth had gone dry again so her voice came clickily, sort of, and didn't sound a bit like her own. And as for raising her eyes and meeting his with a defiant Liverpudlian glare – well, it just wasn't on. And tomorrow, no matter how selfish it seemed or how inconvenient it might be, she would ask Mrs John if she might possibly take the two days off due to her so she could go to Liverpool on a bit of urgent business. The business of getting out of Mark Kenworthy's way!

'Family gathering? But Mother said you fitted in right from the start; one of the family, she said you were. So don't go all uppity on me, Meg, because I'm here with a request, and you're going to be very unpopular with Poll and Davie if you say no to me! They – me, too – want you to make up a foursome for tomorrow night. I managed to get hold of a petrol coupon and I'm borrowing the car so we can all go to the dance in town. Say you'll come? Please?'

That was when she looked up and met the full force of his pleading and realized that nothing on earth could keep her away from that dance; that she wanted him to hold her in his arms and, when the lights were turned low for the last waltz, she wanted to be held so close that their cheeks touched.

Yet for all that, she tilted her chin and said in her best, couldn't-care-less voice, 'All right! I'm not one for spoilin' anybody's fun, but don't start any messing, Mark Kenworthy, 'cause if you do, I'll land you a fourpenny one, and I mean it!'

And, would you believe, instead of contritely promising that she would be as safe as houses with him and that he would keep his hands in his pockets and behave like the gentleman he was, he threw back his head and laughed.

'Oh, Merrilees, you really are one heck of a girl! And what's more, I think a fourpenny one would be well worth it for the chance to mess with you! But since you seem determined to hold on to your virtue, I won't ask you to come to the pub with me, where I could ply you with gin so you were putty in my hands! Instead, I'll say good night to you. Sleep well, Miss Blundell, and dream of me!'

He reached for her hand, then slowly and deliberately laid a lingering kiss in its palm. Then he closed her fingers over it and whispered huskily, 'That's one you owe me. I'll redeem it – with a bit of luck – tomorrow night. See you!'

And with that, he stuck his hands in his pockets and sauntered up the lane, so sure of himself, she thought angrily, making it so obvious that like all the rest he was after you-know-what that she opened her mouth to give him a piece of her mind. Trouble was, the words wouldn't come, because every part of her seemed to be shaking with something akin to a mixing of fright and delight!

'Go to hell, Mark Kenworthy,' she had intended to say, but instead she just stood there and whispered, 'Oh God, what do I do now, will You tell me?'

Oh, good heavens to Murgatroyd! Praying twice in one day! Best not tell Polly about it!

Meg tapped on Nanny's door, pushed it open with her bottom, then backed into the room.

'Here we are! Afternoon tea for one,' she said cheerfully, determined that nothing, not even Nanny, would upset her on this beautiful Saturday afternoon. 'Cucumber sandwiches, Nanny, and I've put a few strawberries in a little dish – knowing how much you like them.'

'Can't abide cucumber. Gives me wind!'

'Well, all I can say is that there won't be many having sandwiches like them for afternoon tea! Most folk have to queue half an hour and are well pleased if they get a couple of tomatoes and a diddy piece of cucumber at the end of it! We're lucky, here, to grow our own,' Meg retorted mildly.

'And what have you got on your head, girl?' Nanny Boag changed tack without warning. 'How dare you walk around with a scarf tied round your head?'

'Because I've just washed my hair and put it into pin curls, and I thought my head looked tidier covered up.'

'Servants are expected to wash their hair in their own time! Couldn't it have waited until tonight?'

'No, 'cause I'm going dancing tonight and I want it to be dry in time! We're all goin' in the car,' she smiled, still trying to be friendly.

'*All*? And who gave you permission to use the car? Servants usually take the pony and trap!'

'Mrs John said it was all right, specially since Mark got hold of a petrol coupon.'

'But it *isn't* right! You simply can't go out with your betters, Meg Blundell! If Mr John got wind of it, you'd be dismissed at once!'

'Mr John is dead,' Meg said softly. 'It's Mark that owns Candlefold now – has done since he was a little boy. And Polly an' Davie an' me an' Mark are going dancing 'cause there's a war on and people aren't snotty any more!'

'*Snotty!* Such talk in the nursery!' With hands that shook, Nanny lifted the teapot. 'What kind of a word is snotty? And it's Mark and *I*! Why must I always have to correct you? I really don't know how someone like you got a position here. Be off with you, and take that thing off your head. Why you can't cover your hair with a mobcap like the other housemaids do is beyond me!'

Meg closed her eyes tightly, took a deep, steadying breath, then closed the door quietly behind her. My, but she really was getting good at walking away from Nanny's tantrums and imaginings, yet one of these days she would give the old biddy a real telling-off, just see if she didn't! And why was she getting herself all het up when it was obvious that Nanny had deliberately lapsed into the past, just to get a dig at her? She did it all the time; pretended to be nuts so she could be bitchy and get away with it!

So let her, and see if Meg Blundell was goin' to get upset. For six more days it would be a happy time at Candlefold and Nanny Boag could choke on her cucumber sandwiches if she wanted to.

Then she thought of her silver dancing shoes and her best summer dress, newly pressed, and going in Mrs John's little car to a dance with Davie and Polly – and Mark.

Happy again, she returned to the kitchen and Mrs John, who smiled and said, 'There now! Polly has taken her gran's tray up and she and Davie are sitting with her for a while. That leaves just you and me, Meg. I'm dying for a cup, and isn't it a beautiful day?'

'Beautiful-sunny or beautiful-happy?' Meg beamed, adding more water to the teapot.

'Beautiful-*both*! I wish this week could last for ever!'

'Me, too. It's lovely to see Polly so happy.'

'And you, Meg? Are you looking forward to the dance tonight?'

'You bet! I'm really excited about gettin' dressed up. Hope my hair is dry in time!'

'Then take that scarf off your head and give it a chance! And when we've had our tea, will you see to the hens and collect the eggs? Sorry if you've got to do some of Polly's jobs.'

'Then don't be! Helpin' out is what I'm here for!'

Smiling contentment, she took off her scarf, then stepped outside, lifting her face to the sun. Mrs John hadn't been one bit bothered about her gaudy scarf and it didn't matter if her head looked like a hedgehog, all stuck with little pins, because Mark was taking his uniform to be dry cleaned, so he wouldn't see her.

Mark! She shook him out of her head. Mind, no matter how hard Mrs John wished, the week wouldn't last for ever. Soon they would be off; back to the North Riding, to their camp. And Mark would be taking some other girl dancing, she shouldn't wonder.

It was why she had got it all sorted in her mind, had decided it was all right to go dancing with him and flirt back if he flirted with her. She had even gone so far as to admit it might be all right, even, if she let him kiss her, because in a week they would go their separate ways and each forget the other until his next leave came round. Her candid common sense had helped her to see the situation for what it was; helped establish that men like Mark Kenworthy didn't get serious over girls who came from Liverpool 3, but it was all right to go dancing with a man who was fighting for King and country, and her patriotic duty to help make his leave as pleasant as possible. Then it would be 'Ta-ra, Mark. Nice meeting you. Take care, soldier – see you.'

That was how it would be, and no messin'!

'Goodness, don't you both look nice?'

They had gone, at Polly's suggestion, to say good night to Mrs Kenworthy and to let her see them dressed up for the dance.

'Will we do, Gran?'

'*Do*? You'll be the prettiest girls there! That cornflower-blue suits you so much, Polly.'

'It's special. I wore it the first time Davie took me dancing.'

'It matches your eyes. Now, Meg, do a turn for me. Let me see your frock too.'

Meg spun round, laughing, sending her skirt swirling above her knees.

'All right, Mrs Kenworthy?'

'You'll do very nicely, Meg Blundell. Your hair looks lovely! Now off with you both and have a splendid time. And tell that grandson of mine to drive carefully coming home in the blackout!'

'He's a soldier in the Service Corps, Gran. He's used to driving in the blackout. But it will be light tonight till eleven o'clock. It'll be lovely at the dance. They'll be able to have the windows open till ever so late so the place won't get like an oven.' She bent to kiss her grandmother's cheek. 'I'll come in early tomorrow to see you – tell you all about it. Night, darling.'

'Good night, Mrs Kenworthy,' Meg smiled. 'We'll both come in and tell you . . .'

'So don't I get a kiss from you too, Meg, on this very special occasion?' the old lady smiled.

'I – er – well, if you don't mind, I'd be glad to!' Pink with pleasure, she gently kissed the pale cheek and in that moment she was embracing Candlefold and an old lady who had given a son to it and had once been mistress of a great house. But much, much more than that, she was kissing her mother, whose cheek had been pale and paper-thin too. 'Night-night. Sleep well . . .'

She felt choked with emotion. Never before had she been so completely, dizzily happy. It was such a warm, wonderful feeling that if she had allowed herself to, she could have stood there and wept buckets!

Eight

'Well, that's them off to church!' Meg settled herself at Mrs Kenworthy's bedside. 'Thought they'd never get away!'

'What held them up?'

'Polly. Got a ladder in her very last pair of stockings and it was panic stations. Of course, she had to change legs so the run was on the inside and didn't show too much. Said she couldn't go to church without stockings, though I reckon we'll all be bare-legged if this war goes on much longer.'

'Poor child. She's trying hard to save her clothing coupons so she can have a few pretty things for her trousseau. It's hard on brides these days. Soon it will be considered unpatriotic to marry in white.'

'Ar, but Polly's all right in that department, her having got the lend – the *loan* – of a white dress, if ever they get round to naming the day. My, but it's hot already. It's goin' to be a stinker today. Want me to stay for a few minutes?'

'If you can spare the time.'

'Well, the vegetables are done and the dinner is cooking nice and slow in the bottom of the oven, an' I've laid the table, so I reckon I can give myself a bit of a break. Anything you want me to do?'

'I feel rather warm . . .'

'Of course you must! Let's get some air through the room!' Meg propped open the door, then threw wide the windows. 'And let's get rid of this eiderdown, an' all! Shall I prop you up a bit?' With gentle hands, she lifted the frail, aching body. 'There now, how's that?'

'Much, much better – and cooler. You're a good girl, Meg. You aren't going to leave us, are you?'

'That I'm not! His Majesty can whistle for me when the time comes. Reckon I'm doin' more good here than I would be making shells and bullets. There's this great big munitions factory in the country, outside Liverpool, and the money you can earn there you just wouldn't believe! But my war work will be at Candlefold, if I've got any say in it!'

'So tell me about the dance. Did you all have a good time?'

'We did!' A good time – was that the way you described heaven, because heaven it had been, dancing with Mark. 'We got there good and early so we'd get a few dances in before the floor got too crowded and it was a real giggle, us four squeezin' into Mrs John's diddy car!'

'I don't think baby Austins were designed with such a load in mind. Did you manage all right?'

'Well, me an' Polly had our knees up to our chins in the back, but it was real funny with Davie an' Mark in the front. Them little cars wasn't intended for strapping great soldiers with long legs either. Anyway, Mark took it slowly – especially going up hills – and we made it. It was lovely in the dance hall, being able to have the windows open. We danced every dance – well, except the silly ones.'

'Silly dances, Meg?'

'Ar – you know. "The Chestnut Tree", and "Boomps a Daisy". Proper silly, that one. You've got to sing the words, see, and every time it comes to boomps, you bump bottoms with your partner!'

'Oh dear. That wouldn't have been allowed in my day,' Eleanor Kenworthy smiled. 'Young ladies were strictly chaperoned at dances when I was growing up, though we still flirted outrageously when we thought we weren't being watched! But bumping bottoms in public? Oh, no!'

'Well, we gave it a miss, and watched them all making a show of themselves! But you do daft things, I suppose, when there's a war on.'

Gave it a miss? She and Mark had found a corner near an open window and he had reached for her hand, smiling down at her so that the little pulses began all over again. She'd been glad when the dancing got back to normal, though being so close to him was just as unsettling as hand-holding nearness. And when the band played the last waltz, the pressure of his hand between her shoulder blades left her with no alternative but to dance closer. So close that their cheeks had touched!

'A war on! That phrase covers so many things!' From far away, a voice brought Meg back to the bedside. 'I think you like my grandson. Have you fallen for him?'

She was teasing, Meg knew, but it didn't stop her telltale cheeks from blushing bright pink.

'Nah! I know my place, Mrs Kenworthy. The likes of me and the likes of your Mark don't fall for each other.'

Oh, but they did, if she told the God's honest truth! Almost the minute she'd set eyes on him when he and Davie had breezed in on the way south to pick up the convoy, her thoughts had never been far away from Mark Kenworthy, drat the man!

'What on earth to you mean, child? You are a very pretty young woman and Mark would have to be half blind not to notice it.'

'N-no. I didn't mean that, exactly. What I should've said was that his sort don't marry my sort, so falling in love with him doesn't come into it!'

'Meg! Don't tell me you don't find him attractive, because every time you say his name, your eyes light up! And you blush too!'

'I didn't say I didn't like him!' *Like* him! That was a laugh! Just being in his arms had made her realize exactly how Ma must have felt about that Father Unknown. Ma must have gone limp and her legs gone all peculiar, an' all. You couldn't blame Ma for getting pregnant; not if she felt as helpless as her daughter had done. 'In fact, I like him a lot, but you don't marry beneath you, and that's what Mark'd be doing.'

'So you've got to be madly in love to marry?'

'Of course! Weren't you in love, Mrs Kenworthy?'

'To be truthful – no. My marriage was arranged, you see. I was happy enough to be off the shelf, I think you call it now, and be mistress of Candlefold. But we quickly fell in love and it was delightful! We were so happy!'

'And was your son's marriage arranged to Mrs John?'

'Goodness, no! Those two fell in love at a birthday party, when she was five and he was eight! And Polly fell in love with Davie the minute they met!'

'Ar, yes. But you lot fall in love with the right people, don't you? That's what I meant when I said I know my place. People like Mark don't go slumming in Tip – in Lyra Street, do they? If there hadn't been a war on, you'd have only mixed with your own class, so everything would have been all right!'

Oh, my goodness! Polly's gran had hit the nail right on the head, because stupid Meg Blundell *had* fallen head over heels and though it was all right for one week, it would not do for her and Mark – not marriage. Not even to think of it!

'But, Meg, there *is* a war on, and feelings run high! There's a sense of urgency about – well, *things*. It's perfectly understandable.'

'Yes. When we were gettin' bombed night after night in Liverpool, I thought it wasn't fair – me gettin' killed, I mean – and not knowing what life was all about! I can understand how soldiers feel, and I wish Polly and Davie could get married. I'm not criticizing Mrs John, mind, but they love each other so much. Where's the sense in waiting when they'll neither of them want anyone else?'

'Maybe there'll be a way round it before so very much longer. And I think if Davie were to be posted overseas, Mary would give her permission. I hope so. I would like Candlefold to have another bride before my time comes.'

'You'll see Polly married, I promise you, Mrs Kenworthy. It's a feeling I've got. Watching them together last night made me real sure about it. You'd have thought there was no one else but them on that dance floor.'

'I hope you're right. Now, tell me what was on the wireless this morning.'

'Reckon the news isn't worth repeating, though there's a couple of good bits.'

'Then the bad bits first, please!'

'Well, them Germans have advanced to Leningrad and Smolensk. There was a map in this morning's paper, and it showed them almost halfway to Moscow! Isn't there anything can stop that man?'

'We-e-ll, Napoleon Bonaparte had designs on Russia but they settled his hash, in the end!'

'Ar. Napoleon.' She would take Mrs Kenworthy's word for him. 'Anyway, the Germans have taken six hundred thousand prisoners, the man on the news said. Now where are they goin' to put them all, will you tell me? And how are they goin' to feed them?'

'With great difficulty, I would say.'

'An' it said on the news that people in Russia who are Jewish are gettin' murdered. Seems if you're a Jew they don't take you prisoner. Mind, on the good side, President Roosevelt has given it out that America is more or less with us.'

'Mr Roosevelt, Meg, will get his fingers burned before so very much longer. He sails so close to the wind, bless the man. The things he does for Britain, the food and armaments he sends, must really annoy Hitler! Something will happen, just as it did in the last war, to tip the balance and drag America into it.'

'But it would help us if they came in, though you can't blame them for not wanting to. After all, they've got the Atlantic between them and Hitler. But there's more good news. The RAF had a go at Cologne last night. A lot of damage done, the announcer said.'

'That's sad, Meg – for the very old and the very young, I mean.'

'No it isn't, not really, if you'll pardon me for sayin' so!' She remembered the baby pulled out of the rubble, and laid on a Liverpool pavement. 'It was Hitler started the war. We warned him, didn't we, but there was no stoppin' him! And now, I suppose, it looks like there'll be no stoppin' him in Russia either! Oh, let's talk about something else? It's too nice a day to have it spoiled by Hitler! Tell me about Candlefold and the way it was when you had a butler and a housekeeper?'

'Who told you about them?'

'Mrs Seed. She brought photographs for me to look at. I wanted to know, see, what it was like in the days when there was loads of servants – before the Great War, I mean.'

'Candlefold will keep for another day, Meg. What I would really like is a cup of tea. Do you think Mary would notice if we stole a spoonful out of the rations?'

'Not if I count the tea leaves real careful, she won't,' Meg laughed. 'I'll use the little pot, an' I'll make it stretch to three, so Nanny can have a cup an' all.'

'You're a girl, Meg.'

Eleanor Kenworthy smiled fondly at the retreating back, shaking her head. Not head over heels in love with Mark? Just who did she think she was fooling?

Then the smile left her lips as she thought of her grandson.

Was he head over heels too, or was he just a soldier home from the war and in need of a pretty girl to dance with and to kiss, maybe?

She closed her eyes as if to shut down her thoughts, and didn't open them again until Meg stood in the doorway with a tea tray.

'And I forgot to tell you! Something else good! Our lads have kicked them Italians out of Abyssinia, so that's another one up to us, innit? Oh, we'll win this war.'

'Of course we will!' Eleanor Kenworthy had never doubted it; not even after Dunkirk, when all that stood between Britain and defeat had been a narrow strip of water – called the *English* Channel, naturally! No doubt about it, though when was an altogether different matter.

'Y'know, it's a pity Nanny is up there and you are down here,' Meg said when tea had been sipped and cups collected. 'There she was, fast asleep and her tea beside her, cold in the cup. It's all she seems to do – sleep, and remember the way things were.'

'That's the way it is for me too; remembering and sometimes sitting at the window, wanting to be out there to walk like I used to . . .'

'Oh, but I wasn't meaning you, Mrs Kenworthy – it's Nanny. She can move about, can get to the nursery bathroom. She isn't like you who can't move without help, and she isn't in pain either.'

'What are you trying to say, Meg?'

'Well, I know it's none of my business, but don't you think that if Polly and me helped her she could get down here, sometimes, to see you. It would be quite an outing for her and there's heaps you could talk about.'

She stopped, embarrassed, thinking she had said too much; that being left in charge whilst the family were at church had gone to her head.

'But Nanny couldn't make it. Mary says her balance is not at all good, and the nursery stairs are narrow and very steep.'

'She could get down on her bottom, if she had a mind to!'

'Oh dear! Nanny would never consider that! It would be far too undignified.' A small, mischievous smile tilted the corners of her mouth. 'But even if you got her down here, I very much doubt she would know who I am. She's been in another world since the war started. It was the shock of it, you see. She only feels safe in the nursery.'

'I suppose you could be right,' Meg said softly, knowing that she had let Nanny Boag get to her again, biting hard on the words she had wanted to say.

'But don't you see, she's got you all fooled! She's as sane as you and me! Crafty, for all that, and she ought to be ashamed of herself, having people at her beck and call!'

Yet she did not say it, because Mrs Kenworthy was a lovely lady who never complained, even though she was almost always in pain and her fingers gnarled and useless. No point in adding to her troubles. And anyway, what right did the hired help have to an opinion?

'Yes. You're right, and it was wrong of me to suggest it,' Meg said instead. 'I'll get used to Nanny, I suppose.'

Only she wouldn't, because she had already got the measure of that one upstairs! Nanny was mischievous through and through, and needed watching. And watch her she would!

'Meg! Do you think it would run to a cup of tea? I'm absolutely gasping for one!'

'Kettle's on the boil, Mrs John. My, but it's hot!'

'Just about the hottest I've known it for a very long time!' Mary Kenworthy peeled off her gloves, removed her hat, then kicked her shoes beneath the table. 'Aaaah! Stone floors are not the height of modernity, but they are so cool. And thanks for looking after things here. We haven't been to church as a family for ages. Is everything all right?'

'Right as rain. Nanny is dozing and I took Mrs Kenworthy a little pot of tea, and now she's having a sleep too. I've kept an eye on the stew and it's just about ready for the dumplings. And Mr Potter says this sun is ripening the strawberries like mad, and there'll have to be a picking this afternoon, Sunday or not, or they'll get overripe and be no use at all. Says he'll need volunteers.'

'I suppose the war doesn't stop on Sundays, so we'll have to give a hand. The strawberry crop fetches a good price, apart from being classed as food for the war effort.'

'Well, I'm game, for one.' Meg placed the cosy on the teapot and took cups and saucers from the dresser. 'What about Polly and Davie?'

'Gone to the vicarage for a sherry. They promised to be back for one, for dinner, but I'm sure they'll help.'

Dinner was taken at one o'clock sharp at Candlefold on Sundays and at seven during the week. Always had been.

'The batter for the Yorkshires is nice and cold in the pantry, Mrs John.'

Yorkshire puddings, Meg had quickly learned, required the batter to be made the night before use, then a little cold water added and a final beating given to it before being placed to bake. They were also served separately before the meat course, with hot, thick gravy and pickled shallots or some other spicy accompaniment. It harked back to the old days, Mrs John said, when farm workers lived in the house and ate their meals in this very kitchen, and a serving of batter pudding took the edge of a hungry man's appetite and made him more inclined to accept the smaller portion of meat that followed.

'You're kiddin'!' Meg had gasped. 'That's proper mean!'

'Probably why the Kenworthys got rich. A bit of Yorkshire parsimony adopted by we Lancastrians in the old days. But meat isn't such a luxury now – well, not until rationing started.'

Meg had gone straight to the dictionary and looked up the word she had never before heard. *Parsimony. Being sparing in the spending of money; economy; niggardliness*, she had learned. Mean, really, like she had said, but it was another word to be stored in her head as part of the improving of Margaret Mary Blundell!

Mind, it wasn't so much the words as the way they should be said, she had quickly found. Take the word *learned*. Would she ever say it properly, and not *lained* like Liverpudlians did? And when would she ever learn to say *anything* instead of *anythink*, and *nothing* instead of *nothink*? That ink-ing didn't half mark you out for a Scouser!

Not that she was ashamed to come from Liverpool. It was just that it might be nice to talk like Ma, because talking proper was expected of a young woman in service. Not ashamed to be called a Scouser, Meg insisted, because Liverpool people were kind, and stuck together when there was trouble, even though they were a bit direct in their manner of speaking and blunt – so outsiders thought – to the point of rudeness!

But just being able to speak as nicely as Polly and Mrs John would be lovely. And Mark, she was sure, would like her a lot more and not call her Merrilees, which was skitting, to her way of thinking. Mark, who was dead gorgeous, who danced better than anybody she'd danced with before and was soon going to claim the kiss he'd put in her palm. She would know, then, just how well he kissed.

'Er – sorry! What was that you said, Mrs John?'

'I said you were miles away and I offered you a penny for your thoughts. Or were they worth more than a penny?'

'Nah. You can have 'em for free! I was thinkin' that I'll never talk proper like youse lot – and I know I've just said sumthin' wrong because it ought to be *like you lot*. I'm not ashamed of coming from Liverpool, or anythink, but I just wish I didn't talk the way I do!'

'What a silly thing to say! We all love you. You came to Candlefold when we desperately needed you, like a breath of fresh air, and Polly said that you and she get on so well that if she had ever wished for a sister, it would have been one like you. So please don't say anything like that again. We love you for what you are and wouldn't change a thing about you!'

'*Love* me?'

'Yes. Very much,' Mary smiled, and gently kissed her cheek. 'Just be your dear self is all I – *we* – ask.'

Love you. If only Mark would say it too! But best he shouldn't, because if ever he did, heaven only knew what it would lead to!

They picked slowly and searchingly, basking in the sunshine, strong even for July, discovering that the reddest, fattest strawberries lay hidden beneath leaves.

Mr Potter fetched and carried, lining flat wooden trays with cabbage leaves to keep the berries cool, carrying them, when full, to the icehouse. Since the coming of electricity, the icehouse had ceased to be in regular use, but neglected though it had become, it was still the coolest building on the entire estate, he said.

Backs bent, Davie and Polly were never far apart; Meg, on the other hand, kept her distance from Mark, who wore nothing but shorts and sandals and was altogether too disturbing to be near. In his uniform he had been toe-curling attractive; now, near-naked, his body slim and muscled, she could, Meg thought as calmly as she was able, have taken a bite out of him he was so good to look at.

'Now what am I offered for this most beautiful thing?' Davie straightened his back, holding high a very large, very ripe strawberry.

'A kiss, perhaps? Two kisses?'

'Done!' Polly twined her arms around his neck, closing her eyes, offering her lips. 'I'll settle for a kiss, but you can keep the berry – I've had enough of those for one day.'

'Oh, for Pete's sake!' Mark flung. 'If you two can't keep your hands off each other for five minutes, you'd better push off and do your canoodling round the back of the potting shed!'

'Is that an order, sir?' Davie, whose rank was junior to Mark's, grinned.

'It is! Or you could both do something useful for a change. Nip and get water and glasses, if you would, and ask Mother if she can lay her hands on a straw hat. The back of my neck is feeling the heat a bit.'

'Granted soon as asked, sir!' Davie gave a comic salute, then taking Polly's hand ran with her, laughing, towards the drying green.

'Those two,' Mark flung, 'are like a pair of undisciplined puppies!'

'Oh, leave them alone, can't you? They're head over heels about each other,' Meg defended hotly. 'What's so wrong with kissing – especially when they're engaged?'

'Nothing wrong with it at all, Merrilees! I'm rather partial to it, in fact!' He looked at her, eyes narrowed.

'Are you now? Well, just in case you'd forgotten, we're here pickin' frewt for the war effort, not for snoggin'!'

'Now who mentioned snogging?' He was looking her full in the eyes, and it unnerved her.

'We-e-ll, I did, but I was only saying it was all right for those two to kiss, if they want to, without snide remarks from you!' Attack, she was quickly learning, was the best form of defence against such blatant masculinity. 'And you can stop calling me Merrilees! Common I may be, but I'm no gypsy!'

'Gypsy girls are attractive and exciting. It was meant as a compliment! And talking of kisses – you owe me one and I think I'd like to redeem it now!'

'Well! How two-faced can you get? You skit Polly and Davie for kissing, and now you want to stand snogging in the middle of the strawberry bed!'

'I don't *snog*, Merrilees. I kiss, as you are about to find out!'

'The heck I am! You think I'm cheap, don't you – easy! Well, I'm neither, because I know what kissing leads to. It ends up with a feller gettin' his own way with a girl, and it's not on!'

'Oh, for God's sake! Seduction was the furthest thing from my mind. Obviously, though, it's the first thing that springs to yours!'

His mouth was set tightly now, and the teasing had left his eyes. The easiness was gone, and something very disturbing darted between them.

'Well, now! Have we lost half our pickers, then?'

Saved by Mr Potter, carrying an empty tray, Meg thought with sudden gratitude, from giving Mark Kenworthy the dressing-down of his life, using words she had hitherto only heard from the gutter and never yet had cause to utter!

'Hello, Mr Potter! Not lost. Just gone for water and straw hats,' Meg called croakily. 'How are we doing?'

'Three trays, which is about fifteen pounds, and as many again to come, if you can abide this sun! The man from the market is going to be real pleased with them in the morning! Have a queue half a mile long, I shouldn't wonder!' Mr Potter, impervious to the atmosphere around him, chuckled. 'And I wouldn't say no to a nice long drink of water, unless there was beer instead, Mr Mark, from a cold stone jug!'

Mark had laughed heartily at that, mopping his forehead as if everything was normal. But it wasn't normal, Meg thought worriedly, because Mark Kenworthy was running true to form and she, stupid little fool, was in a right tizzy over him and would have to count to ten times ten, if she were to keep a jump ahead of him. Mind, it was all very fine knowing what she must not do, but she had to admit that she really wanted him to claim the kiss he had folded, so sure of himself, in the palm of her hand, two days ago.

Hell! Oh, *bloody* hell!

The little breeze that pointed the weathercock on the coach-house roof to the south-east, was welcome after Sunday's searing heat.

Feet wide apart in the strawberry bed, Meg picked methodically with red-stained fingers. She supposed that if she had to choose her very favourite place at Candlefold – apart from the pump trough, of course – it would have to be here, shut away behind high walls. The vast kitchen garden with its rows of vegetables and potatoes fascinated her; the fruit trees that grew on its walls and the strawberry bed and the raspberry canes that were doing nicely, Mr Potter said. And before you knew it, they'd be picking rasps, and after that plums and apples and pears! She had little experience of vegetables actually growing, was more used to seeing them in boxes in shops or laid on stalls in the market, in town. There was so much a city child missed; so many delights Polly had grown up with and took for granted. Yet for herself, Meg thought, every waking morning was a delight, with something new to learn and see and touch. And Candlefold, it seemed, had come to accept her for what she was, and love her in spite of it.

Take this morning, when she had suggested they might, between them, carry Mrs Kenworthy to the chair beside her bedroom window – a little treat.

'You like Mother-in-law, don't you?' Mary Kenworthy had smiled.

'Yes, I do. I like everyone at Candlefold.' Except Nanny Boag, of course, though it didn't do to say so. 'Working here isn't like work at all!' More one lovely long holiday in the country, she supposed.

'Then I'm sure she would like half an hour by the window. You're very good with her, she says, and gentle. Had you ever thought of taking up nursing?'

'Nah. For one thing, I'm not bright enough. You have to pass exams and things, and for another, I don't think I would like seein' people suffer. I had enough with Ma, when she was so poorly.'

'I think you must have been very good to your mother, Meg.'

'She had no one else but me.'

'And your father. Do you remember him?'

'No. Only know he died at sea when I was two and was buried over the side.'

Lies! She hated herself every time one slithered off her tongue.

'Tell me, Meg – was your mother a Catholic?'

'A *Cathlick*?' What a queer thing to ask, all of a sudden. 'Ma wasn't anythink. Never knew her to go to church at all. We never talked about God, nor nothink, and I never said my prayers every night, like Polly does. What made you ask?' she demanded warily.

'I really don't know. Something that just came into my mind out of the blue about someone I once knew. Forgive me for asking, Meg?'

'Course I will – just as long as it doesn't upset you, me not believing in the things you do.'

'I wish you could, dear. I've always found it such a comfort to believe. But like you say, this and worse will get us nowhere! Do you suppose you could give Mr Potter a hand until Mark gets back from the station? You do know, don't you, how much I appreciate all the help you give me?'

'And I'm glad to be here,' Meg had beamed, 'so think no more of it.'

She'd looked at the kitchen clock. Half-past nine. Mark should be back in a couple of hours. In no time at all it would be half-past eleven and she would see the little black car on its way to the coach house that was now a garage. She was, she thought, getting as bad as Polly, counting hours and minutes and seconds; impatient to see the man she loved again.

But she, Meg, was not in love with Mark, nor could she ever be. The very best she could hope for was to dance with him, and laugh and talk with him, and hope that when his leave was over he would think of her sometimes – maybe even write. A post card would do!

She had let go a *'Tcha!'* of exasperation, then headed for the garden. A postcard indeed. She should be so lucky!

Mark arrived in the kitchen garden a little before eleven. He was stripped to the waist again, and his fair skin glowed apricot from yesterday's sun.

'Hi, Merrilees!'

'They got off all right, then?'

'I presume so! I dropped them off at Preston station and left them to it. Reckon Davie's got the sense to get on the Oxford train.'

'Hope they aren't too late getting there – the trains, I mean. I shall miss Polly.'

'Well, she won't miss you, nor any of us! I'm away to the woodyard. There's still a fair bit of timber needs sawing and chopping into logs. And, by the way, Mother says you haven't had your drinkings. You're to go at once, whilst the tea is hot!' He smiled, lifted a hand, then strode away without a backward glance.

Meg watched him go. Not only did she find his sun-warmed back attractive, but his legs too were worth a second glance; long, straight, with well-muscled calves; the legs of an athlete. Altogether too perfect, she thought dismissively, and too sure of himself by far!

She sucked in a deep breath and headed for the cool of the kitchen. A cup of tea whilst it was still hot? A glass of icy water, she thought, would be more to the point. Or better still, she might try sticking her head under the pump!

Now that would cool down her overheated thoughts!

At three o'clock that afternoon Meg, who had turned her efforts to the picking of beans, heard the clamour of the courtyard bell and knew it was time for tea break.

'Won't be too long, Mr Potter.'

'Fifteen minutes, same as Polly takes. Call by the woodyard on your way, and tell Mark, will you? He mightn't have heard the bell.'

'It's time for drinkings,' Meg whispered when she had had her fill of watching unseen the rise and fall of his arms, and the logs that splintered into halves and quarters as the axe hit true. He was still wearing only shorts, and just to look at him made her want to close her eyes and wish desperately for that kiss.

'Hi there, Merrilees.' He wiped his face and neck. 'Know what I'd like to do, right now?'

'N-no.' Oh Lor'! Not here, with Mr Potter not twenty feet away!

'I'd like to swim stark naked in the river. There's a little still pool beneath the willows where the water is shallow and warm. Did you know there was a swimming place? And can you swim, Meg?'

'Yes, I know about the pool – and I can swim.' That was one thing they *had* taught her well at school! 'But I don't go swimming with men with nothink on!'

'OK. I'll wear trunks if you'll come with me tonight.' He took her elbow, guiding her towards the house.

'I didn't bring a bathing costume with me.'

'No matter! Polly has loads, and she's about your size.'

'I couldn't! It wouldn't be right to take things from her drawers without askin'. And besides, she mightn't like other people wearing her clothes.'

'She'd lend you a cossie, no problem. We'll ask Mother if you're bothered about it, and I know she'll say of course you can!' He stopped, taking her arm, pulling her to face him. 'Be a devil, Merrilees! Or are you afraid, or something?'

'No!' Dammit, he was always skitting her! 'OK, then! If Mrs John says it's all right, I'll show you who's afraid of gettin' wet!'

And with that she lifted her chin and strode ahead because one confrontation at a time was enough!

'Oh, Miss Hoity-Toity Blundell,' he said softly when she was out of his hearing. 'Do you know what a lovely little bottom you've got?'

Then he grinned, because she was one heck of a girl and he was going to make the most of the four-and-a-bit days left to him. With a bit of luck, that was!

The evening was still very warm. They walked without speaking across the drying green towards the cow pasture gate on their left.

'Are you afraid of cows, Merrilees?'

'No.' She had been at first, though now she knew that, unless the bull was in the pasture, a field of grazing cows was safe enough.

'I told you it would be OK to use one of Poll's cossies – seems she has a drawer full of them!'

'Three,' Meg said scathingly, not knowing why she did not want to talk. Worried, was she, that swimming with Mark was far more unnerving than dancing with him? The dance floor had been crowded and he'd had his clothes on; tonight there would be no one to hear her if she yelled for help, and they would be near-naked too!

Oh, for Pete's sake, girl, what's to do with you? she thought snappily. What makes you think he fancies you as much as you fancy him? And even if he did, hadn't she got it all straight in her mind that as far as she was concerned, he was only someone to go out with whilst he was on leave; someone who would forget her the minute a pretty ATS girl marched past him when he got back to camp?

'Penny for them, Merrilees?'

'I – I was just wondering how well you can swim.'

'Very well.'

'Modest with it, aren't you? Bet it was you taught Tarzan all them high dives!'

'Hey! Hold on! Why the sarcasm?'

'Ah! Don't like it, then, when I skit *you*?'

'Look, woman! Getting cold feet, are you? Said you could swim, and you can't – is that it? If that's the case, I'll gladly teach you.'

'I can swim,' she insisted softly. She was probably every bit as good as he was, so teaching her was out, thank heaven, because he'd have had to hold her and the cool, water-soft feel of his nearness would start the pulses throbbing again! 'And don't call me *woman* in that tone! I'm not tuppence short of a shillin', you know!'

'Then don't be so prickly. Hell, you must be thinking I want to ravish you, or something – and I don't!'

'That's all right, then.'

'Good! All I want is to go swimming with a pretty girl and maybe, when I say good night to her, ask for the kiss she owes me. Now what's wrong with a goodnight kiss on the doorstep?'

'Nothing! But I wouldn't want it to develop into a snoggin' session!'

'Now would I?'

Too right he would, if she was daft enough to let him! 'You're a man, aren't you?' she said, as if being a man explained it all.

'OK! The minute my hot, wandering hands start feeling your bottom, you can belt me a fourpenny one – OK?'

'Like I said, Mark, as long as you understand the way it is and how far you can go, it's all right.'

'Merrilees!' He stood stock-still in the middle of the field and shouted with laughter. 'How did we get on to this subject? You really don't have anything to worry about. As far as I am concerned you are a girl I like being with. Nothing more sinister than that, I promise you. So can we stop all this sniping and have a swim like two civilized people? Please?'

'Oh, all right. You're on.' She offered her hand. 'No more rubbing each other the wrong way.' We-e-ll, not until the next time, she supposed!

They hurried then to the riverbank, neither of them speaking, because Meg was thinking about that goodnight kiss and Mark was telling himself what a damn awful liar he was, because he would have liked nothing better than to kiss the living daylights out of her, and that was only for starters! Because she was the most exciting, provoking, beautiful girl he had ever met; a girl who seemed completely unaware of how attractive she was, at that!

The pool, caused by an erosion in the willow-grown bank where the river looped back on itself, shone glassily beneath a canopy of trailing branches. Generations of Kenworthys had swam and splashed in its summer safeness, though in winter heavy rains and falls of snow caused the river that fed it to swell to the tops of its banks and overflow into the soft, secret place and make it a part of itself again. Now, though, its cool serenity called them and they stood gazing at the early evening sunlight that dappled through the graceful, trailing willows to speckle the water with motes of gold.

'It's lovely,' Meg breathed.

'One of my special places,' Mark smiled, 'and all the more special if that lot send me to Egypt, or some place that's barren and too hot. The willow pool will be a magic place then to think back on.'

'They aren't sending you abroad?' Her stomach contracted. 'Is this your embarkation leave?'

'No! But sooner or later I'll be posted. I don't expect to spend the war in England, especially now it's pretty certain we won't be invaded.'

'You're sure, Mark?'

'Almost sure – or that's what soldiers more experienced than I are getting around to thinking.'

'Even though Hitler's winning hands down in Russia?'

'Even though, Merrilees. He can't keep up that pace for much longer. And there'll be the Russian winter to contend with. But no more war talk! I've been looking forward to this swim all day.' He took off his shorts, then grinned as relief showed on Meg's face. 'Said I wouldn't swim starkers, didn't I?'

Laughing, he ran down the grassy bank, taking a jump to land waist deep in the centre.

'Watch out for the willow roots under the water, Merrilees. Not safe, until you know where they are.'

This was it, then. She walked a little way along the bank, out of his gaze, then pulled her frock over her head, hanging it on a willow branch.

The swimsuit she wore underneath it was black, and low-cut at the back. She looked down at her breasts and wished she had chosen one a little more modest, but it was too late now.

She walked back to the pool, then slowly entered the water, wading deeper until it touched her ribcage and caused her to draw in her breath. Then she sucked air into her lungs, held her nose, and ducked beneath the surface.

'Aaaagh!' She shook back her hair and wiped the water from her face to sink again, chin deep, paddling slowly with her hands. 'It's so cool . . .'

'Come to me.' Mark trod water, holding out his hands. 'Just till you get an idea of the depth.'

Depth? She was all right, he'd known it at once; wouldn't panic if her toes couldn't feel the bottom. But she was sleek and slim and her breasts tantalized. He wanted to touch her, truth known; cup her shoulders with his hands, run them down her arms to her fingertips.

'OK!' They were equals now, she thought triumphantly. Two people in a pool and all that mattered was who was the best swimmer.

She took a breath, bent her face into the water, then, moving her feet slowly, was beside him in two sweeping circles of her arms.

'Give me your hands, Meg.'

'Why? I'm all right.'

'Because you are too far away. I want my kiss now, you see, not on the doorstep.'

'Ha!' She dived deeply to surface behind him. 'You'll have to catch me first,' she gasped, swimming to an overhanging willow branch, grabbing it, circling it with her arms.

He was at her side in an instant, reaching up for the branch so their bodies touched beneath the water.

'I told you to watch out for roots!' he said sharply. 'They're all over the place. Keep to the middle of the pool till you get your bearings.'

Then he slipped his hold on the branch, taking her waist tightly in his hands, searching for her lips with his own.

It was a brief kiss, a gentle touching of cold lips, that was all. She pushed him from her and swam away.

'What a fuss over nothing!' she yelled, making for the bank, pulling herself out of the water.

She was angry; had thought often of that kiss and all it had been was a schoolboy peck, and her with her arms tight-clasped round the willow branch!

She got to her feet, making for the shelter of the bushes, towelling her shoulders, her hair, raging inside for being such a fool. Men!

'Meg.' She turned to see him standing there. 'I'm sorry.'

He dripped water, his hair pushed back from his forehead. His trunks clung wet to his thighs and she dare not look.

'What for? And would you mind shoving off till I get dressed?' Only give her a minute to pull herself together, then she could stare him in the face and tell him she'd had better kisses in the school playground!

He shrugged and walked away and when they came face to face again she was dressed, her hair knotted on the top of her head. She held her sandals in one hand and a rolled-up towel in the other. Mark, too, was barefoot and wore shorts and a blue, baggy sweater. He sat down, patting the grass at his side, and she sank to join him.

'I said I was sorry,' he resumed, staring over the pool, 'because I was only teasing – the kiss, I mean.'

'I see,' she said primly, looking at her toes, thinking what funny things feet were. 'So you've had your bit of fun, Mark, and we're all square.'

'No, Meg. I'd like that kiss now, please. A proper one.'

He pulled her closer, tilting her chin so she had to look into his face. She closed her eyes and parted her lips because she wanted him to kiss her. Properly.

It lasted until she was forced to jerk back her head, breathless. It was a kiss that began on her lips then squirmed right through her, disturbing the telltale, wayward pulses.

She did not speak, nor look at him. Instead, she lowered her head so her forehead rested on his shoulder, relaxing in his arms, trying not to think how mind-shattering it had been, wondering if he would feel the thudding of her heart against him.

'Was that better?' he whispered.

'Much better.' Her lips could hardly form the words. Then common sense took her and she pushed away from him, not knowing if she wanted to laugh or cry, feeling capable of neither.

'Then shall we do it again? It gets better with practice.'

So she reached to clasp her arms around his neck and closed her eyes and offered her mouth. And all Nell Shaw had ever told her was forgotten as their lips met again.

She had reason to be glad, she thought as they walked home, that someone had rowed past in a boat and called a greeting, and waved. Mark had got to his feet, then, pulling her up beside him, waving back, calling, 'Hi, there!'

'Someone you know?' Meg whispered.

'The water bailiff,' he supplied, absolutely in command of his feelings.

'Oh Lor'. It'll be all round the village by morning!'

'So who cares?'

'I do! I don't want to be the talk of the place!'

'But, Merrilees, all he saw was a soldier kissing a girl! I'd bet you anything he's seen worse than that on this riverbank.'

'We'd best be getting back,' she whispered. 'Mustn't stay too long or your mother won't let me come here again.' She ran her tongue round lips gone all at once dry.

'But you're entitled to time off! Do you want to swim here again?'

'Yes, I do,' she heard herself saying, when she should have shrugged instead, and said, 'Dunno. Maybe we can find time for another dip before you go back.'

'Tomorrow night, Merrilees?'

'Yes. Tomorrow night is fine . . .'

But for all that, she had gone to bed that night and given way to tears, because he shouldn't have kissed her like he did and because she was glad that he had.

Trouble was, the way Mark Kenworthy kissed was frightening and toe-curling and giddy-making too, and Meg Blundell was a little fool, because now she knew how very easy it must have been for a housemaid called Dolly and an unknown man to get a love child.

The willow pool. Mark said he would remember it if ever he needed to recall greenness and cool and home. She would remember it too, because there, she who should know better had fallen helplessly, hopelessly and wantonly in love.

'Oh, Ma,' she whispered into her pillow as tears flowed afresh.

Nine

'You're late!' Nanny Boag stared pointedly at the breakfast tray Meg carried, then at the clock.

'Sorry.' She was in no mood for a tantrum this morning. 'I had to go to the farm for the milk, see, Polly bein' away.'

'And what were you doing last night, girl?'

'Doing? Nuthink!'

'There you go again! How many times do you need telling! It's nothing! Noth*ing*,' she emphasized. 'And don't lie about last night, because I saw you with Mark! Walking across the courtyard, holding hands as if you had every right to! He's only amusing himself, you know! Men in his position always take advantage of girls of your class!'

'What do you mean?' Meg banged down the tray so angrily that the china rattled and milk slopped from the jug. 'You think I'm a Liverpool tart, don't you?' she flung.

'Yes. I always have, and after the main chance, if I'm not mistaken. But you're wasting your time, Blundell. Mark will marry – but one of his own class!'

'Now who said anythin' about me wanting to marry him? All we did was go swimmin', and holding hands means nuthink, these days! There's a war on, had you forgotten? Or do you just use it as an excuse to sit up here, bein' waited on?'

'Goodness me!' The old woman had seen the fury on Meg's face and took her cue from it. 'Polly's little friend come to play again. How kind of you to carry my tray up for me! Do you think you could pour me a cup, child?'

'Pour it your flaming self!' Meg turned in the doorway. 'And I'm watchin' you, Nanny, so don't try to come it with me! It won't work!'

She closed the door quietly behind her, because banging doors got you nowhere, except to let old biddies know they'd got you upset! And Nanny seeing them last night proved only one thing: that not only could she walk to the dormer window set high with the safety of young children in mind, but could get herself onto a chair to look out of it, an' all! Afraid of her balance on the steep nursery stairs! That one had managed to climb on a chair last night!

She drew in a deep breath because no one, especially Nanny Boag, was going to spoil something that all at once had become very precious – and, with less than four days to run, fleeting too.

She would have been shaken, for all that, had she turned to poke her head round the door again, because had she done so she would have seen the round-eyed, innocent look to have gone; would have heard, too, words hissed like a curse.

'And don't *you* try to come it either, my girl, because there is something about you that isn't above board, and I shall find out what it is, be sure of that!'

Calm again, Meg placed the tray on the table at the head of the main staircase, then tapped gently on Mrs Kenworthy's door.

'Can I come in? Is there anything you want?'

'Nothing I want, Meg, but do come in. District nurse is arriving soon to give me my injection – and a thorough bed bath, I hope. It's been so hot and sticky these last few days.'

'District nurse only comes twice a week, Mrs Kenworthy, so what do you say if I offer to help her this morning, then I can bed-bath you any time you want in this hot weather. I'd be ever so gentle. I always washed Ma.'

'Oh, would you? It would be one thing less for Mary to do. I'll have a word about it with her. *Sure* you wouldn't mind?'

'You know I wouldn't.' Gently Meg smoothed back the undressed hair. 'Now, I'll just take your tray down, an' I'll have a word about it too with Mrs John. It was only the other day she said she wondered why I hadn't taken up nursing, so if *you* don't mind, I'm sure she won't.'

She blew a kiss as she left, comparing the two old ladies. Chalk and cheese! Nanny, an angry wasp, annoying people, getting in a jab wherever she could and always demanding as if it were her due. Mrs

Kenworthy, so gentle and grateful for anything that was done for her – a lady right down to her poor, hurting fingertips.

Meg smiled, because after the district nurse had been, and if she hurried through her housework, she would be able to go to the kitchen garden again, where she hoped she might find Mark.

Mark. This morning, suddenly shy, she had avoided being where he might be, but he had found her and smiled and said, 'Good morning, Meg. Will you be in the garden, later?'

Meg, he had called her as he had done last night when they'd kissed; said it tenderly and softly. Merrilees was only a teasing name, she knew it now; a bit-of-fun name. The *Meg* of last night had been a love word, almost.

Housework done and lunch cleared from the table, Meg walked to the garden by way of the woodyard. She knew Mark was there because she had heard sounds of sawing and wood-chopping He was sitting in the shade, eating sandwiches.

'Hi,' she said when he looked up and saw her. 'I've brought a jug of water. Sorry it can't be beer.'

'Thanks.' He looked down at his blistered hands. 'Afraid manual work isn't for me!'

'But you do manual work in the Army.' If working on heavy engines wasn't hard work, she didn't know what was.

'Suppose so, but I know where I am in the workshops. I'm an engineer, don't forget. But logging in a heatwave is heavy going. Will we go to the willow pool tonight?'

'Yes,' she nodded, feeling her cheeks redden, wishing – but only briefly – that she was having her period so she could tell him not for a few days with complete honesty. 'Er – will you be having your drinkings at the house at three?'

When Mrs John clanged the outside bell, that was; when she, Meg, would stand barefoot on the cold kitchen floor and laugh and joke as if she had every right to, she being almost a part of it all.

But being natural and normal as it was before Mark and Davie came on leave couldn't happen again; not even when the two of them went back to their unit, and she and Polly were best friends like before, and talked and giggled, sitting cross-legged on beds.

It couldn't ever be the same because something had happened to Meg Blundell, who once was proof against all masculine wiles and tricks. Now she was in love – *no*! Not in love! Loving – the real loving Polly and Davie knew – was gentle and sure, and they were easy together. What she, Meg, experienced last night had been an awakening to her feelings. An awful needing had shivered through her and made her want to be even closer, eyes shut tight and lips clinging. And it felt right and proper for Mark's hand to gentle her breasts. Abandoned, she had felt, and relaxed, even as the exquisite little pulses throbbed out a warning.

It had been Mark who had first realized the danger; he who said huskily, 'Which one of us is going to count to ten? Because someone had better!'

Neither! The word had stuck on her tongue and stayed there, unsaid. She was glad about it now, though last night had been a near thing, because even though she felt dizzy and bewildered, a small voice uncommonly like Ma's had whispered, *This is how it starts. You count to ten or something happens, and when it does it could be the making of a baby.*

Last night beside the willow pool, the decision had been taken out of their hands by a man in a rowing boat. Tonight she wondered who would be the first to start counting.

'Hey! Merrilees!' Fingers snapped beneath her nose. 'You were miles away. Tell me?'

'Tell – er – tell you what?'

'Exactly what put that look on your face!'

'And what kind of a look was that?'

Her head was clear now. No more abandoned thoughts; no more remembering how it might have been! She looked him straight in the eyes.

'I don't know. Brooding, perhaps? Or bewildered? And your cheeks were very red.'

'Well, that's because it's hot and if you must know . . . oh, I – I can't tell you!' She couldn't. She really couldn't!

'And why not, Meg?' He stepped closer.

'Because I – well, I promised I wouldn't. Promised Mrs Seed, you see!' It was the first thing that came into her head; the first thing that had nothing to do with last night, that was!

'You can tell me, Merrilees. Village scandal?'

'No! I promised I wouldn't tell, and that's it. And it wasn't scandal, so you can stop grinning!'

'You weren't thinking about Mrs Seed at all! I'll bet she didn't tell you anything! You were thinking about tonight, weren't you, and the willow pool?'

'No! Oh Lor'! He'd read her thoughts, knew he had her just where he wanted her. 'And don't flatter yourself, Lieutenant Kenworthy! I can take the willow pool, or leave it! And Mrs Seed did tell me something,' she rushed on, 'and I *did* promise I wouldn't blab. About Candlefold, it was. Not the people, but about the house.'

'Is that all? And did she tell you where it is?'

'Where *what* is?' she demanded, relieved to have wriggled out of a nasty situation.

'The hide – the priest's hole. Where the Candlefold ancestors kept their money before banks existed. That's what we're talking about, isn't it?'

'N-no. All she said was that the London lot who took the brick house off Candlefold didn't know there was still a way in. You won't tell her, will you, or she'll think I talk. And she didn't tell me where, honest; just that there is one!'

'There is. The people who commandeered the brick part thought they had sealed it off completely. We were lucky, really, that they didn't take the stone house as well, but because they seemed satisfied the two parts could be easily separated and because we had two elderly invalids, I suppose they let us keep part of it.'

'Oh, I've found where they did the bricking up. Three places, aren't there?'

'Three. They took out a doorway on the nursery floor and sealed it up, and the archway at the top of the stone stairs was blocked up too. And I suppose you've opened the green baize door next to the pantry, and come up against a brick wall?'

'I have. And it isn't too noticeable really. With curtains over the other places, it doesn't look bad at all.'

'Oh, there were plenty of curtains! Mother took them all down from the brick house and had the carpets taken up too, and put into storage with the furniture. But there's another place that Mother – who is usually too honest for her own good – didn't tell them about. Actually, she had thought it all out and decided that if ever fire broke out there – incendiary bombs, I mean – at least we'd be able to get to it more quickly. And a fire in there would spread like mad, because I reckon – we all do – that's it's full of old papers and things.'

'And you don't know? You've never been in through your secret entrance to see what's there?'

'No. For some reason, none of us has.'

'Well, all I can say is that I would have. Like a shot!' It was all right – they were on an even keel again.

'Then I shall take you in, Merrilees! We'll have a quick swim, first and –'

'And no hanging about afterwards!' She stared him full in the face.

'All right. No kisses at the willow pool. Then, when we get back here, Mother will have gone out, which is very convenient. Tuesday is the night she goes to Mrs Potter's. Most of the village will be there – the ladies, of course. But you'll know about it?'

'Mm. The make-over thing? They unpick old clothes and unwind jumpers to save clothing coupons.' Mrs Potter sold savings stamps, Tuesday nights, for the war effort, and everyone caught up with the gossip. 'It's a bit of a change for your mother. Polly and me don't go, though. Not our style!'

'And you really want to get inside the brick part of the house?'

'Didn't I just say so?' With Polly in Oxford and Mrs John out, there would never be a better chance.

'It's only a house, and full of clutter now, I shouldn't wonder.'

'Maybe it is, but you know the layout, I don't. And I like big houses.'

'Why, Merrilees?'

'Because I lived in a diddy little place, I suppose.'

'Ah, yes. In *Liverpewl*!'

'You're skittin' me again! And I'll have to go. Mr Potter needs a hand, with Polly away.'

'I'll have finished the logs by tonight, then I'll be able to put in more time there.' He looked at his hands. 'Give these blisters a chance to heal!'

'You should have said. I could have put ointment on them for you, and lint.'

'They'll be fine. Think I'm a sissy, or something? The water will clean them tonight.'

'I've really got to go.' They were back to the willow pool again. 'See you at three, perhaps? Ta-ra!'

And she was off for the safety of the high brick wall as fast as her feet were able.

'Shift yourself, Merrilees!' Mark waited beside the open door.

'Sorry! Been to tell your gran we're off for a swim; see if there was anything she wanted.'

'And was there?'

'Only the wireless tuned in to some music. And I left water by the bed. Said I'd look in again when we get back.'

'And Nanny?'

'She's fine.' She hadn't looked in on Nanny Boag; was not prepared to face narrowed eyes and the vinegar look when she told her she was going to the pool. With Mark. Nanny had two looks; wide-eyed and slitty-eyed, and both dangerous. 'She knows where we are.'

Or would do when she heard the door close and the sound of their voices in the courtyard. She'd have that chair under the high window in five seconds flat, and climb on it and glare down. And there would be slitty-eyed ructions in the morning!

Then mischief took Meg. Be blowed if she wouldn't be hanged for a sheep! Banging the door loudly she stood on the top step, slowly rolling her towel, tucking it under her arm. The face would be at the window now, and she'd give the old girl value for her efforts! Taking Mark's arm she smiled brilliantly into his eyes.

OK, Nanny?

Meg slid into the pool, sighing pleasure as the water lapped cool against her body. Face down, she made for the overhanging willow branch, then grasped it, letting go her breath, shaking back her hair, watching Mark, who swam with slow, even strokes, making hardly a ripple, his body good to look at.

That's enough, Meg Blundell! There was to be no messing about tonight, no kisses that took her breath away. Tonight she must be completely in charge of her feelings.

She drew in air, then slid beneath the water, feeling with her toes for the tangle of roots, sending up a stream of bubbles. Then she surfaced, gasping, to find Mark beside her, so close that briefly their bodies touched, silkily smooth limb to limb, flesh sensuously cool. She laid her hands on his shoulders to distance herself from him, then swam for the bank, pulling herself onto grass dry as a bone, to stand dripping water.

'Won't be long!' She made for the shelter of the bushes. Slipping down her straps she wrapped herself round, pulling down the costume, kicking it aside. Quickly she secured the towel, tucking it firmly over her breasts.

She was covered up now, and safe; safe from his eyes and from herself. She rubbed her hair vigorously and by the time Mark left the pool she was dressed and her hair pinned into a twist on the top of her head.

'What's the hurry, Merrilees?' He towelled his shoulders and she tried not to look at his hips.

'No hurry at all.' She sat down, rubbing dry her feet, pulling on her sandals. 'But if we're to get inside the brick house we'd best be sharp about it. Mrs John is usually back by half-nine.'

'Which gives us loads of time. And don't look so prim, woman! I'm not about to ravish you!'

'The heck you're not and anyway, it takes two to tango!'

'OK. Pax. One kiss, and then we'll be off.'

One kiss, a quick one, would do no harm. She rose to her feet, tilting her chin, parting her lips. Then he laughed and she opened her eyes to see him kiss a fingertip and lay it against her mouth.

'That's one you owe me, Merrilees!' he grinned, taking her arm, making for the field gate.

'We'll see about that,' she said firmly, feeling her cheeks flush hotly. My, but he knew how to tease, to play with her feelings. She'd bet anything he did it to every girl he met. Davie was happy with Polly, had given her a ring and had eyes for no one else, but Mark Kenworthy played the field, she knew it, loving and leaving, sure of his charm, his masculinity, his film-star good looks. There would be more notches on his bedpost than Soft Mick had had hot dinners. 'And let's get a move on. I really do want to see inside the brick house!'

'I've just thought,' Meg said as she pegged towels and costumes on the drying green line. 'We won't be able to see anything. It's all shuttered up.'

'We can take torches.' Mark smiled at the disappointment in her voice. 'And the upstairs windows are all right – no shutters there.'

'I've been trying to figure out,' she said as they walked towards the courtyard, 'just where the secret place is.'

'Behind the panelling, actually.'

'That the third Kenworthy had put in?'

'The same. Our lot were getting a bit of loot together by then, and there were no banks in those days. People kept valuables beneath the hearthstone – deep down – and since the kitchen fire rarely went out, it was reasonably safe. Then Kenworthy Three had the great hall tarted up, and one panel, to the right of the fireplace, was made to open and shut – a sort of medieval safe for his gold and things.'

'Yes, but that was only a hidey-hole.'

'Had to be. The brick part wasn't built then.'

'So the secret passage was made when it was added on to the stone house?'

'Not at the actual time of building. Later.'

They were standing in the lofty hall now, and Meg's eyes slid to the right of the stone fireplace. She had dusted and polished that wood many times, yet there hadn't been a crack or any sign of a hinge to be found.

'I'll go and tell Mrs Kenworthy we're back – OK?' She was excited now; needed to make the most of the time left to them.

She wouldn't look in on Nanny Boag, who would know they were back. Nanny she would confront in the morning, Meg decided, and by morning she would be so pleased about getting into the brick house that nothing the old woman might say would upset her.

'Everything OK upstairs,' she said breathlessly, a few minutes later. 'And I'll be blowed if I know where that panel is.'

'No one would, unless they were told. Nicholas Owen was too good at his job, for that.'

'And who was he, then?'

'Well, if you want the whole history, Merrilees, there was originally the hidey-hole and then, when Henry the Eighth fell out with the Pope and established the Church of England with himself at the head of it, a lot of people around these parts decided they were going to stick with the Church of Rome, and the old faith.'

'But how could they?'

'It wasn't too hard in the wild north. There were few roads in those days. London was a long way away, and though dissenters were fined fivepence for not going to Sunday services, many thought it was well worth it. Fivepence for each member of the household was a tidy sum in Tudor times. In the end, my lot saved their money and said their prayers in English. Outwardly, that was.'

'So your lot joined the Church of England?'

'On the surface, yes. They saved their money and conformed. Mind, they were great fence-sitters, so when Catholic priests came secretly to these parts to say Mass, the Kenworthys confessed, received absolution and everything was all right.'

'Yes, but what about that secret passage?'

'Well, the medieval safe was where Nicholas Owen, a travelling carpenter, began. He built priests' holes into a lot of the bigger houses around here. Catholic priests had prices on their heads, and often had to be hidden. Master Owen rehinged the panel and when he had finished – but you'll see for yourself.'

'Fence-sitters, you said. So Candlefold turned C. of E. in the end.'

'*Expert* fence-sitters. During the Civil War, they fed Cromwell's troops and hid the King's men in the priest's hole at the same time. They had to hang on to Candlefold, you see. Nothing was more important. Conscience didn't come into it.'

'Six hundred years in the same house. It takes a bit of beating. But show me, Mark?'

'Right! Let's see if it still works.' He dropped to his knees, fingering the candlewax drips in the carving, pointing to a larger than average blob. 'There – see? Push hard on it, so . . .'

Meg heard a click to her left, then saw the panel move a fraction of an inch.

'But I could have done that accidentally when I was polishing the wood!'

'I doubt it, Merrilees. You've got to know just where to push, and which way to turn it at the same time. Smells a bit, doesn't it?'

'Musty? Yes. What happens now?'

'Got the torches?'

'Here.' She had already unscrewed the tops, taking out the circle of brown paper which, as regulations demanded, let only a half-inch diameter of light through. 'Hadn't we better bolt the front door? Someone might come in.' It was a habit of locals to knock and walk in.

'No. We'll be all right. Here we go, then.' Easing a knife blade into the crack, pushing with the flat of his hand on the side opposite, the panel swung open and outward. 'Good. Master Owen knew what he was about.' Mark shone his torch on slim brass hinges, then into a cavity large enough to take a man either standing up, or sitting down, Meg calculated, knees drawn up to his chin.

'But how did the feller breathe? And how did he stop himself from sneezing,' she demanded as fine dust danced on the air.

'They got their air from the other side – through a crafty piece of carving on the brick house side. 'I'll show you.' He swung the torch again, then slipped into the hole. 'This next bit you've got to feel for – a little lever, that's all it is, cleverly disguised as a thin lathe. 'Got it! Now – just a little push and we're in, Merrilees! Hang on a second, then I'll light you through.' There was a sliding sound, then she was looking at his pumps and his shorts, up to knee height. 'Careful. Keep your head down. There's plenty of room – just take it slowly.'

He was shining both torches into the cavity and she lowered her eyes to the floor.

'Right. You can stand up now.' He gave her his hand and in the torchlight she could see that they had come through the side of a wooden archway. Fond of archways, those Kenworthys.

'See, Merrilees. Looking at it from this side, it's just a carved arch at the end of a passage. The wall behind it was too thick to break through and besides, it would have spoiled the panelling in the stone house hall. Once, there was an oil painting hanging there and shelves below it with photographs and ornaments on them. And why are we whispering?'

'Dunno,' she whispered back. 'Think it's because we're excited.'

'Speak for yourself. I've been through loads of times. And if there is time, I'll oil those hinges – keep them up to scratch. Now, step back, and you'll see how clever it all is. We never lost a priest, nor a King's man – and you are privileged, Miss Blundell, because I'm as sure as I can be that you're the first outsider to be shown this.'

'Then thanks a lot, and I won't split that I've been in – not even to Polly.'

'Good girl. Now, can you get an idea of the layout? This passage we're in leads to the grand hall – you'll be able to get a rough idea of the way it is. The room on our right is the dining room, and to the left is the small drawing room and the servery. The servery used to lead into the kitchen through the green baize door – blocked up now.' He took her hand in his, shining the way ahead. 'There now! What do you think?' He handed her a torch and they sent beams of light around and above them.

'Hey up! Imagine sweeping down that in a ball gown!' Oh, she had seen it so many times in films; beautiful ladies lifting their hems ever so slightly and gliding downstairs, watched by an admiring, always handsome, young man! And this staircase was just like something out of a film, an' all! Wide and carved real lovely. Just made for gliding down!

'Are we going upstairs?' She shone her light up to the half-landing.

'Of course. You'll be able to see more up there. Come on, then!'

She took the hand he offered, swinging her torch to light up half-panelled walls and faded, dull red wallpaper.

'That paper could do with coming down,' she said more loudly.

'Old it may be, but that *paper* is silk! Once up, it stays!' he laughed. 'Here's the long gallery. At least that lot had the sense not to clutter it up with too much rubbish.'

Packing cases were stacked to window height; a narrow walkway had been left down the entire length. They stood on a wooden floor, its boards of uneven widths. The windows were closed and in need of cleaning but even so, they could look out to the south, over an ornamental, tree-lined walk that led to a wood.

'That's Pygons Wood.' He followed her gaze, 'And nearer, you can see the river.'

'And the willows, hiding the pool!'

'And look! There's Armitage, inspecting his bullocks – beef cattle, Merrilees, being fattened up for the meat ration!'

Meg hoped the farmer wouldn't look up and see them at the window, and said so.

'He wouldn't say anything if he did! He'd just think he'd seen the ghost, and keep his mouth shut! There's a ghost here, I forgot to tell you,' he said offhandedly.

'Ghost! Honest, Mark?'

'Mm. A young serving wench. One of the Kenworthys got her pregnant, and she jumped off the roof with her shame. Happened in 1810, I believe. Pity it wasn't earlier by a couple of hundred years. In the sixteen hundreds a man acknowledged his by-blows; saw the mother all right and had the child – if it was a male – educated, after a fashion. But in the early nineteenth century, the poor girl didn't have a chance. Our ghost jumped. Better, I suppose, than being shown the door – the *back* door!'

'An' I suppose you think that's funny?' She sucked in her breath, wanting to tell him that his father at least had dealt decently with Dolly Blundell, not shown her to the door. And he not even responsible!

'Don't get uppity, Merrilees! I was only kidding! There isn't a ghost. Never was!'

'Then why say such a bluddy stupid thing?' She glared, red-cheeked.

'To be perfectly honest, you seem so besotted with the place I thought I'd invent a ghost for you. Anyone would think you'd been born here like the rest of us! Funny, y'know, but Polly wasn't born here either, yet she's the most devout Kenworthy of us all!'

'Well, you don't have to patronize me – remind me I'm only the hired help!' She was so furious she had to bite on the words that sprung triumphantly to her tongue – *Who says I wasn't born here, then?* But instead she said, 'I want to back, please. Don't want to see any more, if you don't mind.'

'Merrilees! I *was* kidding! Don't get so uppity about a badly done to serving girl! She was an invention. Just for a bit of fun. You're quite a little Bolshie, aren't you?'

'An' wouldn't you be if you lived where I did in a tatty yard – *street* –

that should've been knocked down years ago? The lavvy outside across the cobbles and one tap – *cold* – inside the house. No bathroom! You should try it, Mark Kenworthy!'

'I have. Soldiers have to live rough too!'

'Yes, but you've got Candlefold to come home to! Yours, it is. Worth fighting for!'

'Merrilees! Sorry! Sorry! *Sorry!* People used to ask, sometimes, if we had a ghost. Being such an old house, I suppose a ghost or two was to be expected. So I invented one for you – your own special one! Sorry it backfired!'

'And so you should be! Condescending, that's what!' She was still angry, though whether it was because he had teased her, or whether because she couldn't tell him that she really had been born at Candlefold, she didn't know.

'I will never patronize nor condescend again, I give you my word!'

He looked at her, eyes pleading, a small smile on his lips, so that she had to whisper, 'We-e-ll, all right, then. But let's get back now, if you don't mind. I – I think I've seen enough.'

She hadn't. Not only did she want to see every bit of the brick house, but she'd had it in her mind to ask him to bring her again – if it could be managed, that was! And she had been looking forward to the claiming of that kiss too; probably upstairs, as they looked out towards the hills – romantic, sort of. Yet the magic had gone. Only a joke, really, but his teasing words had been like clogged feet, stamping on her private, precious dreamings.

'Then that being the case, can I have my kiss – or two?'

'OK.' She stepped nearer, then raising the forefinger of her right hand to her lips she kissed it, placing it on his mouth. Then she walked towards the head of the staircase, lighting the way ahead, walking down the wide, shallow trends, hurrying towards the opening at the bottom of the archway. 'Give me a hand through, please. And thank you for showing me.'

That last sentence she had said carefully and slowly without a trace of accent, she thought wonderingly.

Indeed, she thought, as she lay wide awake that night, she had done very well, all things considered. For one thing, she had slapped Mark down in her best blunt Liverpool manner – for being snide about serving wenches, that was – but by far the best were the words she had used.

Condescending. Patronizing. Mind, she'd got a bit hot around the collar, but by the heck, she was learning! Ma would have been proud of her.

Yet for all that, she had been a fool. Stupid of her to give him a finger-kiss when she had wanted to be kissed breathless.

Fretfully, she threw back the blanket, then, ballooning the sheet so that cool air billowed soothingly over her, she closed her eyes against tears that threatened.

It wasn't fair, because she knew that this was only a flirtation on Mark's part; something like a holiday romance that would be forgotten the minute he put on his uniform again and left to join his regiment, Somewhere in Yorkshire. And she didn't want him to go back, ever. She wanted him to be here always, just as Polly wanted nothing more than to be married to Davie, and never have to say goodbye to him again. But Davie loved Polly, didn't he, every bit as much as she loved him? It shone between them like candleglow, and everyone who saw them together was the better for it.

But Mark, Meg brooded, did not love her. Oh, she was good for the odd kiss, and to dance with and swim with, and to tease and call Merrilees, but he never would love her the way she wanted him to; would never feel for her the way she felt for him.

'Head over heels,' she whispered into the lonely darkness. 'That's what you are, Meg Blundell, if only you'd admit it!'

That was when she gave way to tears, big and salty – and silent, pillow-muffled sobs that shook her body.

'Ma! Now I can understand how you got me,' she choked. Oh, too true she could!

Next morning, when Meg took the breakfast trays upstairs, she found Nanny Boag neither slit-eyed nor round-eyed. For once, the old nurse was distant and haughty, her mouth rounded in disapproval, her jaws tight. It was as if, Meg thought, she had weighed up the situation but was unable, as yet, to deal with it. Last evening, perched on a chair, she must have seen the two of them walk laughing across the courtyard, been angered by what she saw, and was powerless to do anything about it – yet!

'Thank you. Put it on the table. And close the door behind you,' was all she said, and Meg, who had almost come to terms with moods and mischief, could make neither head nor tail of stony disapproval.

'Anything you want?' she ventured.

'Nothing, I thank you. Be off with you!'

So Meg closed the door quietly and walked slowly down the stone stairs and into the hall. For just a moment she hesitated, eyes fixed on the bottom panel next to the fireplace, then shrugged, shutting last night out of her thoughts.

'Just going for the milk, Mrs John,' she called to Mary Kenworthy's back. 'Won't be long.'

She trailed her hand over the granite pump trough, making for the far archway carrying the four-pint, white-enamelled milk can. She was missing Polly more than she thought.

Today was Wednesday; tomorrow, late, Polly and Davie would be back. On Friday afternoon two soldiers would return to their unit and seven days would have passed in no time at all. On Friday night, Polly would be either tearfully quiet or would sit cross-legged on the delphinium-covered bed, pouring out her loneliness, telling of how it had been in Oxford, already accepting thirteen weeks apart from her man.

That was what being in love did to you, Meg thought, passing the drying green, making a note to take down the towels, black costume and swimming trunks she had pegged there the night before.

Last night had not gone well, but then Meg Blundell was her own worst enemy. Why, when Mark had asked for the kiss she owed him, had she not wrapped her arms around his neck, there in the brick house gallery? Why did some imp inside her make her act as she did, when all the time she wanted nothing more than to be kissed and kissed and be damned to where breathtaking kisses might lead!

Because, supplied her common sense, she was the illegitimate child of an unmarried housemaid and Mark Kenworthy was gentry and had a pedigree going back six hundred years. Her own pedigree was short; Father Unknown had seen to that!

Oh, why had she come here and why had she not come here sooner? Why did she feel right at Candlefold, and happy, as Ma had done? Why was Mark so good to look at? Why did he dance so well and kiss so well? And why did she find him so attractive that common sense had left her the minute he had walked beneath the far stone arch on a two-hour visit?

She stood beside the field gate that led on the one hand to the farm and on the other to the riverbank. She was not going there again; not with Mark. Not if she had any sense. Men like Mark Kenworthy should be given a wide berth, she knew it. What she didn't know was why she hadn't listened to the warning in her head; had let the thudding of her heart drown out all reason the minute she'd set eyes on him?

She was leaving the wash house after bringing sheets for Mrs Seed to find tomorrow, just as Mark passed the door. He was pushing a wheelbarrow piled high with logs and said, 'Hi, Merrilees! Lovely day for it!' without even stopping.

'Oh – hi,' she whispered to his retreating back; his bare, broad, brown back. She closed her eyes and imagined them beside the willow pool, half hidden by trees and twilight, making love. And her hands fondling that back and his waist, his hips. And oh, what hips! Slim and hard and . . .

Aaaaaagh!

She shook her head, trying to control the squirming inside her when a voice called. 'Meg! Meg *darling*! We're back!' Polly, at the far archway, waving.

'Well, I never did!' Her voice didn't sound like her own, because the squirming had reached her throat now, and was threatening to choke her. 'But youse two aren't expected till tomorrow!'

'No, but we've got to see Mummy. It's urgent, you see. We got the overnight train – made good time, actually. Davie's following with the cases.'

'Mark is in the stable – stacking logs. Shall I tell him you're back?'

'No. He knows what it's about, has done for a while, but Davie didn't tell me until yesterday! That's why we've got to see about getting married! But I'll tell you when we've told Gran and Mummy – or, rather, *asked* them. I'm still only nineteen, you see!' she called over her shoulder as she ran towards the house.

Got to see about getting married! Yet that wasn't the same, Meg frowned, as *having* to get married. She turned to see Davie, a case in either hand, smiling at the top of the yard. No. He and Polly weren't *having* to get married, she was sure of that. Davie was a virgin, she'd bet a week's wages on it, as was Polly. As was Meg Blundell come to think of it, though she, Meg, just might not have been if she hadn't walked away from Mark last night, because when he kissed her, when he looked at her, eyes half closed, when even she thought of them lying together doing it – lovely *It* – there was a squirming, squeezing, don't-give-a-damn feeling that made her entire body ache for him.

'Hi, Davie! Good to see you!' She was speaking normally; was actually making words come out whilst she was shaking all over with need. 'Had a good time in Oxford?'

'Smashing – what little time we had there. Oh, Polly will explain everything later. There wouldn't be a kettle on the boil, Meg? My mouth tastes like it's full of blotting paper.'

'Well, it looks like there isn't going to be a lot of sense out of Polly, 'cause she wants to talk to her mother and gran. So I'll give it five minutes, then I'll make a cuppa.'

Mark emerged from the stable, held up his hand to Davie, who disappeared through the open door and into the cool gloom of the hall.

'Ah! So Poll knows? He's dropped his bombshell!'

'What bombshell?' Meg demanded. 'What's to do with them, coming back early, travelling overnight? They've only been gone five minutes!'

'Nothing that wasn't to be expected, really, but Polly will tell you. I'm going back for another load.'

'And I'm going to give them a couple of minutes then make a brew. I'll ring the bell when it's ready.'

'You're an angel, Merrilees!'

And with that he was gone, whistling so cheerfully that Meg was sure that nothing – nothing awful that was – could be wrong.

She shrugged, then made her way to the kitchen – which was completely deserted.

'Well, now! Take a deep breath, Polly, and tell us. Slowly! And don't you think we might first have a cup of tea? Good for shock, don't they say?' Mary Kenworthy settled herself at the bedside; Davie and Polly sat, fingers linked, on the window seat.

'It isn't a shocking shock, Mummy.'

'No. And Meg is going to make tea. She told me so,' Davie added.

'Then hadn't you better tell us your news, child?' the old lady smiled.

'I – er, *we* – aren't telling you both anything. We're asking, actually.'

'Asking if we can be married, if I get posted. Because if I do, it's almost certain it will be overseas. Mark thinks so too,' Davie offered anxiously.

'Mark knows?' Mary frowned.

'Yes. He was bound to, it being Army business and he being Davie's immediate superior, sort of. But I didn't know. Davie only told me yesterday afternoon.'

'I hadn't intended telling you until tonight, sweetheart. It just slipped out that I've been made up to full lieutenant – it's in the pipeline, actually,' Davie smiled at Polly's mother by way of explanation. 'I'm only a second lieutenant now, but I'm getting another pip on my shoulder, and that will make me Mark's equal! Trouble is that with promotion comes a posting. I didn't want to say anything to spoil our leave for Polly, but like I said, it just slipped out.'

'Yes, and thank heaven it did! You see, it made me remember that you promised – *almost* promised – that if Davie went abroad you'd let us get married. So we decided to come back straight away and try to get things settled. I want you to say yes, Mummy, so I can go to the vicarage today – arrange to have the first calling of the banns on Sunday, even if Davie won't be able to hear them with me!'

'I see. But Davie wouldn't be sent overseas without leave?'

'It isn't usual, Mummy. They're pretty good about such things,' Polly supplied breathlessly. 'But we aren't using the promotion as an excuse to make you let us get married before I'm twenty-one. I just want you to let us have the banns read so that if Davie comes home suddenly on embarkation leave, we won't have to waste two or three precious days getting a special licence from the Bishop. If the banns have been read we can get married straight away!'

'Then congratulations on your promotion, Davie,' Eleanor Kenworthy smiled. 'And I, for one, will be very happy to give my blessing, though it is really up to your mother, Polly.'

'Yes, it is. And your mother, Miss Polly, is happy to agree with Gran. We'll see to the banns, then once they've been read on three Sundays we can have a wedding at Candlefold – if the worst happens, that is. And goodness, I'll have to try to get through to Shelagh – you remember, Mother-in-law – her daughter Maudie offered the loan of her wedding dress.'

'Oh, darling! Thank you, thank you, thank you!' Cheeks flushed, eyes bright, Polly hugged her mother, then gently kissed her grandmother's cheek, just as there was a tap on the door and Meg called, 'It's outside!'

But Polly flung wide the door, calling Meg back, demanding she come in and hear the news.

'Isn't it wonderful? Davie's been recommended for promotion and when it comes through, and if he's sent overseas as a result, we can be married! I'm pretty sure we can get the first reading of the banns for Sunday, and you're to come and hear them, Meg!'

'Well, first – I'll pour, 'cause a cup of tea is what you need, Polly my girl! And second – congratulations, Davie, and last but not least, all happiness to you both. Now then, will you just take a deep breath, drink your tea, then get yourself off to bed, Polly? You've been on that train all night, don't forget!'

'Yes, but we're fine. We both slept quite well.' Best not mention that they had pushed up the dividing arm and snuggled together under Davie's greatcoat to sleep close, just as if they were married. *Almost* as if they were married. She had been thankful, Polly thought, that there were six others in the dark compartment, or heaven only knew what might have happened! 'No! What I want is a cup of tea, then I'm away to the pool. A good swim will wake me up, and save wasting bath water. You coming, Davie?'

'Oh, what it is to be young and in love,' Mary smiled when the two of them had run laughing in search of towels and costumes. 'And what it is to have someone like Meg Blundell, who brought tea exactly when it was needed!'

'Ar, well, I'll just make you a bit more comfortable, Mrs Kenworthy, after your shock – prop you up a bit, eh, – then how about having your tea out of a nice rosebud china cup for a change? I'll help you, Gran, and be blowed to that daft little feeding cup 'cause I know you don't think much to it – and oh, I'm sorry!' Her cheeks flushed red. 'I shouldn't have called you Gran. It just slipped out. Suppose I'm as shocked as youse two, underneath. Sorry. I won't do it again.'

She offered the cup, gently wrapping the frail hands that held it with her own, guiding it to the old lady's mouth.

'And why,' Mrs Kenworthy asked when she had sipped her fill, 'should you not do it again, Meg? Gran sounds far less formal than Mrs Kenworthy, don't you think, Mary? And it might be rather nice to have two granddaughters.'

'But I couldn't! Honest to God, I *couldn't*!' Meg gasped. 'I wouldn't presume, me bein' a servant here. Just because I love Candlefold doesn't mean I'm goin' to take liberties, thanking you kindly for all that, Mrs Kenworthy!'

'Oh, for goodness' sake, Meg – and why not?' Mary laughed. 'You and Polly are most times together, you chatter like sisters and act, sometimes, as if you were. Why can't Mother-in-law have another granddaughter?'

'You mean it?'

'We both mean it,' the elderly woman said softly. 'You are kind to me, and so gentle, Meg. I want you to call me Gran just as Polly does, because if I'd been lucky enough to have another granddaughter, she would have been exactly like you, I'm sure.'

'Oh! Oh, my goodness!' Meg put down the teapot with a not-too-steady hand. 'I mean – ooooh, you're such lovely, lovely people, all of you. And I've never had a gran!'

Eyes brimming with tears, she ran from the room. Such happy, happy tears. But then they would be, she reasoned as she closed her bedroom door behind her, because she had never, in the whole of her life, been so happy!

'Did you hear that, Ma?' she whispered sobbily. 'Gran. Now what do you think to that, eh?'

Ten

The Reverend Hugh Rushton, parish priest of All Saints, Nether Barton, stood at his study window from which he had a splendid view of the drive – even though there were still four minutes to go before Polly and her young man were due to arrive.

Polly of the sunny smile; pretty Polly who had short, fair, inclined-to-be-curly hair and the most amiable disposition. She had smiled and waved her small pink fists right through her baptism with not so much as a whimper of protest when he'd poured holy water onto her head, and signed her with the cross and named her Mary Eleanor.

Four months old, Polly had been. Late, for a christening. Something to do with her adoption, and the time it took for her to become a Kenworthy.

In her fourteenth year he had prepared her for confirmation into the Church of England, and now she was coming to see him to talk about the calling of her banns of marriage. All very satisfactory, he thought, since it would all come full circle when he baptized her firstborn. And it was a peculiar thing, he frowned, that since this war began, he had baptized twelve babies in the two parishes of Nether Barton and Upper Barton, and instead of the six of each which could averagely be expected, there had been eight boys and four girls. It was ever thus in wartime, the old ones said. Mother Nature not up to her tricks, exactly, but compensating, for all that. Making sure. He sighed, raised his eyes heavenwards and sent up a hasty prayer.

Don't let those eight be soldiers in another twenty years' time? Two wars already in less than half a century. Lord – isn't it a bit much?

He dropped his eyes to the scuffed, faded red Turkey carpet. Sad, these wartime weddings – not the nuptials, of course – but sad about the *till death us do part* bit.

A crunching of the gravel on the drive made him look up. Polly and her young man were coming. Two minutes before time. Always punctual, the Kenworthys – was only to be expected for people like them.

Another wedding he hoped, and within the year another baptism. Smiling, he went to open the front door.

The market van had collected cabbages, carrots, tomatoes and cucumbers – and potatoes so fresh you could rub the skin off them with your fingers, Mr Potter thought fondly.

The strawberries were all finished; the raspberries needed rain to swell them, then two weeks more of sun. And after the rasps and loganberries would come plums and pears and apples and fat, juicy cultivated brambles. Pity there was little or no sugar for jamming and bottling and pickling; pity Hitler had ever been born, come to think of it. Because he was the cause of it all; he and his U-boats sinking food ships in the Atlantic. Hadn't been able to bomb us into submission, so now he was trying to starve us out, instead.

But Hitler was reckoning without the Mr Potters of these islands, and gardeners everywhere who were sowing and planting and digging for victory, though when victory would be, no one in his right mind was prepared to hazard even the wildest guess.

Sufficient to say that on this mid-July afternoon, with Mark gone to the village and Polly and Davie away to the vicarage and Meg helping Mrs John in the kitchen, Candlefold kitchen garden was a mite too quiet for his liking. And it was more than a mite too hot and sultry. The garden was dust-dry and in need of rain, though there would be a storm before so very much longer.

He gazed with satisfaction at the low, yellow clouds gathering to the west; rain clouds without a doubt, though whether the rain would come in a vicious downpour or whether it would be gentle and steady and last for a full twenty-four hours, he didn't know. The latter, if they were lucky. His garden needed water, then after that a week at least of sun. Not a lot to ask, really, especially when there was a war on – a war Candlefold's soldiers would be going back to on Friday.

Polly would be quiet for a few days – that was what war did to the young ones – but at least things would be back to normal in his garden once again, and a whole lot quieter! Yet you couldn't have it both ways, he supposed; not these days!

* * *

'If your mother were a gambling woman, she would have wagered the housekeeping money that the minute the cosy was on the pot, you would appear,' Mary Kenworthy said to her son. 'I should have known you'd be back early.'

'I hitched a lift, Mother, and I'm dying for a cup of tea! Poll not back from her banns yet?'

'Any time now, I shouldn't wonder. Will you take up the trays, Meg? Currant scones today, for tea!'

Scones, because they took little fat and little sugar and because the fire-oven had been at scone temperature and the heat was too precious to waste. And because Mary had gone into her secret, ever-dwindling stock of prunes and taken two and cut them into tiny pieces to resemble currants.

Currants, raisins, sultanas, candied peel and all things good to bake with were in such short supply in the shops that they were almost non-existent. Christmas cakes were a thing of the past, as were christening cakes and wedding cakes. Davie and Polly would not be able to have one.

'Why the sigh, Mrs John?'

'Oh dear, I must stop it. They do say that every sigh takes away a minute of your life. I was thinking, though, that Polly won't have a wedding cake.'

'I don't think she'll mind overmuch. All she'll want is Davie's ring, and to wear a white dress for him.'

'Yes, and it will be such a lovely day. A wedding in the family will be beautiful, except that it will mean Davie is going to war – *really* going to war – when it happens. And at least Polly will have a twenty-four-carat ring. Isn't it awful that you can only get nine-carat rings in the shops now, and a waiting list for them, would you believe?'

'Polly said she will have her gran's ring.'

'Yes. Mother-in-law took it off when her hands got bad. It upset her at the time, but now she's very happy for Polly to have it. Something old, I suppose . . .'

'And the wedding dress borrowed, so that takes care of two of the things. But I'll see to the tea trays.' Meg glanced down as she passed Mark because she knew his eyes were on her, willing her to look at him, and she wasn't giving him the satisfaction of seeing her cheeks blush scarlet. 'Won't be a tick – and hasn't it gone dark, all of a sudden?'

'We're in for a storm,' Mark said, but still she wouldn't look at him.

The rain came just as Polly and Davie crossed the courtyard; spots the size of halfpennies at first, dark on the dry cobbles. Then it fell faster and more fiercely and cascaded down roofs and gurgled down drains and spilled over from gutters. And then the ferocity lessened and the drops became smaller and more gentle. Mr Potter sat in the cucumber house, watching it with pleasure, willing it to continue for twenty-four hours. No more, and no less!

'Well, that's put paid to another swim tonight,' Polly sighed, 'and it was so lovely in the pool this morning.'

Maybe as well, Meg thought, though with four of them there it would have been all right – safer, sort of.

'I'll collect the trays,' Meg said, 'and see if there's anything Mrs Kenworthy wants.'

She made for the hall, her eyes lighting on the panel as she passed it, knowing that every time she looked at it, dusted or polished it, she would think of Mark and the kisses that hadn't been – never would be now, except maybe a goodbye kiss on her cheek tomorrow. When she came downstairs he was waiting in the hall beside the stair door, and this time she had to look at him.

'Tonight, Meg?'

'It'll probably be raining still.' He had called her Meg; said her name gently.

'So don't you like walking in the rain? There are oilskins and sou'westers in the garage. It'll be our last night . . .'

'Then shouldn't you be spending it with your mother and gran?'

'There's tomorrow morning for that. Are you afraid of getting wet?'

'No. And I suppose I wouldn't mind a walk, for an hour or so. Do me good.'

'Never mind about doing good! You and I have got to talk!'

'Talk, Mark?' Oh God, the pulses again! 'What about?'

'You know damn well, Merrilees, so don't go all coy on me. You want to, don't you?'

'Want to *what*?' Her mouth was all at once dry, her tongue made little clicking sounds as she spoke.

'Go for a walk, for Pete's sake! Didn't I just say so! And for us to talk.'

'I see. You want me to write to you, sometimes?'

'That, as well. After supper tonight, then?'

'When I've helped with the washing-up. I – I mean, I can't just get up from the table and walk out!'

'As soon as you can, then – OK?'

He said it, she thought, like he was back in camp, and giving orders. Yet for all that she whispered, 'As soon as . . .' then made for the kitchen, the china on the trays clinking as if her hands were shaking. Which they were, of course.

'Did you say you two are going walking?' Mary Kenworthy asked of her son after supper, when all was shipshape in the kitchen.

'We are – if we can find gumboots for Meg, that is.'

'There are all shapes and sizes in the garage – you'll find something.' Nothing was thrown away at Candleford. Keep a thing for seven years, it was said, and be sure you'll find a use for it. 'I shall be upstairs with Gran. Why don't you light a fire in the sitting room, Polly?'

'But can we spare the coal?'

'Not coal, but Mark has chopped enough logs to last out a siege and there is plenty of dry kindling. It would air the chimney out too.'

Candlefold's flues were wide, and smelled of soot in wet weather. Once, it had been the practice to tie a holly sapling to a pole twice a year, and push it up each flue as far as it would go. A messy business, but the Kenworthys of old had not believed in paying a sweep when there were holly saplings aplenty, and good stout arms to do the pushing.

'That will be lovely, Mummy. We've got a lot of things to talk about.'

And sit in the firelight and dream about too, and pretend the war was a million miles away and everything was as easy and uncomplicated as it had once been but never could be again.

'That's everyone settled, then! It's Tommy Handley and his ITMA crew tonight. He makes Mother-in-law laugh. And then we'll listen to the news, and see how things are in Russia . . .'

* * *

'Comfortable, Mother-in-law? Warm enough?' Mary took up the khaki sock she was knitting, settling herself beside the bed.

'Yes to both, thank you. The rain has cooled things down nicely, and I'm sure we needed it.'

'According to Mr Potter, and now that the strawberries are all gathered, not a moment too soon! Mark and Meg are going for a walk in it, brave souls, and Davie is lighting a fire in the sitting room.'

'Sad, isn't it, that tomorrow they leave us? And we said never again, after John's war . . .'

'Darling, don't be sad.' Gently Mary cupped the lined face in her hands. 'Mark and Davie will come home to us, I know it. And I think Polly would like to have a baby as soon as they can. Just think – a great-grandchild for you!'

'And for Candlefold. And why is Mark being so cavalier about things? He should be thinking about getting married too!'

'Mark, I am sure, thinks often about marriage,' Mary smiled. 'Trouble is he doesn't think hard enough or long enough! He flits from romance to romance without a care in the world! It would please me so much if he brought a nice girl home.'

'But there's one right under his nose, did he but know it! Haven't you noticed that Meg blushes every time she sees him, or speaks his name, even. I think she's very fond of him. I hope he isn't trifling with her feelings.'

'I don't know what he's up to, Mother-in-law, and that's a fact. I think, you see, that he's attracted to her too. She's rather a challenge to him – he's never met anyone quite like her before. She's so direct and uncompromising. I only hope he isn't going to hurt her. I'd even thought of talking to him about it, but I can't. He's a grown man now – one simply can't interfere – and I'm sure Meg is too level-headed to fall for his blarney.'

'But, my dear, like I said, I think she's already fallen for it!'

'She has? Oh, my goodness!' Mary gasped, and promptly dropped a stitch.

'How do you think the Russians are doing?' Meg ventured, pushing her feet into gumboots, determined to be matter-of-fact, thinking at the same time that maybe she should be glad the grass was so wet underfoot.

'Russia? It seems there's no stopping Hitler's lot. I reckon he'll be trying to get to Moscow before the bad weather sets in.'

'But if he takes Moscow, then he'll have beaten them!' Dismayed, Meg pulled on a sou'wester. 'And then what? Us, will it be?'

'Merrilees, I'm an engineer and know little about military tactics, but anyone with half an ounce of gumption in their head must think that he's going too far too fast.'

'What do you mean?'

'I mean he's forging ahead like wildfire, but what about his back-up – supplies and things? And it's going to be interesting to see if the Wehrmacht is properly kitted out for a Russian winter.'

'So it's not all gloom and doom, Mark?'

'Tonight gloom and doom is strictly forbidden! And you owe me a kiss!'

'I know. You can have it tomorrow, when you leave.'

'Leaving is forbidden too!'

'I think it's easing off a bit.' She stepped into the courtyard, holding out her hand for raindrops, looking up at the sky.

'It better hadn't just yet, or Potter won't like it. Oh, let's go, then, since you seem determined to be provocative!'

'I'm not trying to be anythink, Mark. All I want is to go for a walk, and us have a chat, maybe. What about Polly and Davie, then?'

'Careful. The cobbles can be slippy.' He took her hand as they crossed the yard. 'And as for those two wanting to get hitched – don't they know there's a war on?'

'Of course they do!' She pulled her hand away and stuck it in her pocket. 'It's why they want to get married! They're in love, Mark. L-O-V-E.' She spelled out the word. 'Well, just wait till you fall for somebody like Davie's fallen for Polly! See if you're so sarcastic when it happens to you! And when it does, I hope she'll ditch you!'

'My word, Merrilees! I thought you were a sensible girl.'

'Of course I'm sensible, but it wouldn't stop me falling in love – if I met the right feller, that is! And for goodness' sake, can't we go for a bit of a walk without you skitting all the time. Leave your sister alone, 'cause I'm on her side!'

'My most abject apologies, ma'am! So what's news, then, and where shall we walk?'

'Up to you, I'm sure,' she shrugged, nose in air.

'The riverbank?'

'OK by me. And news is – oh, you'll never guess!' She couldn't be uppity with him when there was such news for the telling. 'I made a slip of the tongue yesterday; called Mrs Kenworthy Gran. So I said I was sorry and wouldn't do it again, but she said she would like me to call her Gran; said Polly and me were like sisters, and why shouldn't she have another granddaughter? And your mother agreed. I've never had a gran, Mark. I'm real chuffed.'

'I'll agree with my grandmother there. You and Poll get on very well, don't you? But maybe if you were real sisters, you wouldn't. I've heard it said that sisters fight and fratch all the time. And I don't think I much care for the idea of you being Poll's sister.'

'And why not? Aren't I good enough to be a Kenworthy, or sumthin'!'

'Don't be a bloody little Bolshie – of course you are. And anyway, you'd only be my adopted sister like Poll is. What I meant was that if you were my *real* sister, I'd be up to the neck in trouble.' He opened the field gate, handing her through.

'What trouble?'

'Simply that I want to make love to you, Meg, and if you were my sister – well, it wouldn't be on.

'N-no, it wouldn't . . .' Oh, my Lor'! All at once she felt dizzy.

'Well, now you know, darling.'

'Now see here, Mark! You can't just come it like that!' Everthing inside her was going haywire; the pulses, her thudding heart and shivers darting through her body. 'All at once you're saying you want to – to –'

'Make love,' he said softly, leaning his back on the gate.

'And how are we to do that, will you tell me, even if I wanted to? The grass is wet and it's raining and we're wearing oilskins and gumboots!' she said wildly.

'Merrilees! Take it easy! I've put my cards on the table, so it's up to you! And you don't just grab a girl. There's got to be all sorts of things besides.'

'Like?' she glared, holding tight to the gate because she was shaking so much, though she knew the danger was past – he was calling her Merrilees again.

'Like us both wanting to at the same time, for instance. I didn't say I wanted you this very minute!'

'Well – that's all right, then! And you can stop your skitting!'

'I like getting you angry!'

'Well, don't get too fond of it, Lieutenant! And I've had enough walking. I want to go back.'

'Spoil sport. Just when Polly and Davie are snuggled up in front of the fire, you want to play gooseberry.'

'There's the kitchen! And I do have my own room, you know! You an' me don't have to be in each other's company.'

'Yes, we do.' He took her arm and swung her to face him. 'Oh, but we do, Meg. Because I'm serious about us. I *do* want to make love to you – when the time is right! And you want me to, don't you?'

'I – I don't know. If I'm honest, I'm not sure. I haven't – well, I don't know how to, and that's the God's-honest truth.'

'Then I'm glad, because it's going to be wonderful showing you.'

'Wonderful doing it? Making love? But you've never said you love me. Do you *love* me as well, Mark, or will I be just another notch on your bedpost?'

Oh, but his last night shouldn't be like this – them all soaking wet and her hair in rats tails and water dripping off her sou'wester and down her neck!

'No, Meg. What I feel for you has nothing to do with bedposts. OK – so I've been around? So what? I've found *you*, so now I don't want anyone else.'

'You can't mean it, Mark.'

'I can. I do. From tonight on. Look – let's go to the woodyard; it'll be drier there.' He took her hand and they ran to the open-fronted wood store to sit, gasping, on a comfortingly dry tree trunk. He took out a handkerchief, gently wiping dry her face, and then his own. 'Now, for Pete's sake, woman, will you take off that stupid rain hat so I can get near enough to kiss you?'

Obediently, gladly, she did as he asked.

* * *

'I want tonight to go on and on. I want us to turn on the wireless and hear them tell us it's all over. I want us to be married, yet when we are you'll be leaving me . . .'

Polly sat on the hearthrug, her back against the chair in which Davie sat. Her arms rested on his knees either side of her and he leaned forward from time to time, and kissed the top of her head, or her ear.

'It'll work out just fine, darling. I don't want to leave you, but at least when I do you'll be my wife. I've wanted you so much that it'll be almost worth going overseas, just to sleep with you for a week.'

'But one week, Davie – then how long will you be away?'

'Lord knows! How long will the war go on for?'

'As long as the last one, some say.'

'Then we're halfway through it, Mary Eleanor! Y'know, it's going to sound funny marrying Mary Eleanor when all the time I'm in love with Polly!'

'I'm called for Mummy and Gran. We can't have two Marys in the house. And, anyway, I like Polly better.'

'I'd adore every inch of you no matter what you were called.'

'Would you love me if I were called Dolly Mixtures?' she giggled.

'I'm afraid not. If you were dolly mixtures I'd have eaten you up long ago. I do love you, sweetheart. I always did, from the first time I saw you. And I always will.'

'That's all that matters then, isn't it? And, darling, when we are married can we make love a lot so we'll be sure to start a baby on our honeymoon?'

'Polly! Do you think that would be a good thing?'

'Making love a lot? I can't think of anything I want more.'

'I was talking about starting a baby. It's going to be hard enough when the war is over, keeping you in the manner to which you were born, without having a baby too. Do you realize I'll be three years at university – at least – before I earn a penny! I suppose, when you think about it, I've got a cheek wanting to marry you and not being able to support you. And I don't think it's about the number of times you make love, but doing it – maybe only once – at the right moment. I read it's the time of a woman's cycle – when she's fertile for a few days – that's important.'

'Where did you read that, Davie?'

'Oh – I got this book about how things happen, sort of.'

'About doing it?'

'That came into it too.'

'Was it a dirty book,?'

'It was not! And I only read it because . . . because . . .'

'Because you've never done it before? Then that's two of us virgins, because I haven't either.'

'I've never for one minute thought you had, sweetheart. It's just that a man is supposed to know all about it, and I don't.'

'Then I'm glad, my darling, because I'd hate not to be the first.'

'Would you? Even if it's a bit of a fumble to start with?'

'We'll learn how together, Davie. If we both want to – and we will – then it'll come wonderfully right for us. And I do so love you. Do you know how much?'

'I think so, Miss Mary Eleanor Kenworthy. It's like a lovely pain inside me. You're always in my thoughts and beside me when we're apart. I can't seem to get away from you.'

'Then don't ever try, because you belong to me and I shall never let you go. Now, budge up, will you? I want to sit on your knee and be kissed. And kissed and kissed!'

'Oh, isn't it awful?' Polly sat on Meg's bed, legs crossed, hands clasping toes. 'It's still raining, and Davie and Mark have gone! Why do the months between leaves grind on and on into for ever, yet seven days are gone in a flash? I don't know how I kept from crying this morning, when they got on the Preston bus.'

'You didn't cry because that's the way it has to be. You wish them goodbye an' you smile, then do your weeping afterwards. It was the same for me too,' she whispered almost as an afterthought, then wished she could suck back the words.

'*You*, Meg?'

'Yes. We all had a smashing week, didn't we? I mean – well – I've liked being with Mark.'

'Only *liked*?'

'No. Truth known, I never thought I'd find a man so smashing to be with, if you want to know!' There now. The cat was out of the bag!

'And . . . ?'

'And we're goin' to write to each other. And maybe he'll ring me up, if he can get through.'

Maybe he would ring? Mark had said he would call her just as soon as he could and ask her if she still loved him. And wanted him. And she knew she would answer him truthfully; say it was yes, to both!

'He'll ring *and* write. I know my brother, and he's smitten, Meg, he truly is!'

'He can't be! We've only known each other a week.'

'He can be! I fell in love with Davie in the space of ten seconds.'

'But Mark's different,' Meg hedged, desperately wanting reassurance. 'I mean, he loves 'em and leaves 'em, you said so yourself.'

'Yes, I did, but in your case I know it's different. Like I said, I know Mark. Surely you like him? Just a little . . . ?'

'I – I like him a lot! And what's more, if it hadn't been raining – if we'd gone to the willow pool – heaven only knows what might have happened. So now you know!'

'Good! So now *you* know how it feels! Now you know how miserable I am right now.'

'Yes, and I know, an' all, how easy it would've been to – to . . . Oh heck, Polly – have you ever felt like that?'

'All the time, even when Davie's not with me. I just hurt all over I want him so much. If he wasn't so decent – he's always the one who puts a stop to it, counts to ten – I'd have lost my virginity ages ago!'

'Mm. You've got a good man there, Polly Kenworthy.' Not demanding, like Mark had been.

'Next time I'm home, Meg?' he'd said, leaving the words hanging on the air, eyes fixed on hers, his mouth set tight. And she had nodded and whispered. 'Yes. Next time – I promise . . .'

'Davie is the very best! And tonight, instead of crying my eyes out, I told him I would think of Sunday, and pretend he's there beside me, to hear the first calling. And I know you don't go a lot on church, Meg, but won't you come with me and Mummy, just once, to hear the banns?'

'No. And I don't think your mother will be with you, either! She won't be able to leave Gran and Nanny Boag, 'cause I won't be here to keep an eye on them. I should've gone to Liverpool last weekend, but

I didn't, 'cause I knew you'd want time with Davie. But I've written to tell Nell and Tommy that I'll be there, tomorrow. Sorry, Polly.'

'Oh, well. Can't be helped. Only right you should take the time due to you. But will you come for the second calling? *Please?*'

'Oh, all right, then. And give us a hug, girl, then get yourself off to bed. You're tired out. Whatever time did you stay up till last night?'

'Two o'clock. We didn't want to leave each other.'

'Then into bed, quick! I'll give your mother a hand with the supper drinks. Want me to bring you a cup?'

'Would you? Hot milk?' She swung her feet to the floor, then paused in the doorway. 'And Meg – I'm so glad you and Mark are in love.'

Meg smiled, and for once didn't bluster nor contradict. Because she *was* in love with Mark Kenworthy and as far as she dare hope, he was in love with her too.

'Next time. Meg?'

Oh, yes! Next time he came home on leave they would be lovers.

Eleven

Meg straightened her shoulders as she neared Tippet's Yard, trying to shake off the black mood that had wrapped round her as she stood at the tram stop in Lime Street; a mood she could only describe as tearing, despairing sadness. Poor Liverpool, so battered and burned and blasted, yet people were going about their Saturday business as if everything around them was normal, and shattered buildings and boarded-up shop fronts were the fashion of the day.

True, it seemed that tram tracks had been relaid, sewers repaired; electricity cables and gas mains had been sorted too. Yet although the streets were now passable again, bomb rubble lay in huge heaps where buildings once stood and it would be a long time, she supposed, before those sickening heaps grew over with grass, or bedded themselves down so that every time a wind blew in from the Mersey, everything and everyone was not covered with dust.

She drew in a deep breath, arranged a smile on her lips and pushed all else out of her mind. She was back in the yard again, and Monday morning could not come soon enough! But until it did, Candlefold and memories of it and daydreams about it, were forbidden!

'Well, will you look who's here!' Nell Shaw stood on her doorstep, arms folded. 'We're honoured!'

'Hello, Nell. Nice to see you too!' The smile left Meg's face. 'And don't look so toffee-nosed. I wrote to say I was coming!'

'So you did, girl. Don't take any notice of her.' Tommy joined them. 'She was real chuffed to get your letter.'

'And she'll be more chuffed when she sees what I've brought with me!' The smile was back. 'You're both invited to Sunday dinner 'cause I've got enough for us all!'

'I've kept your place aired – opened the windows every day,' Nell conceded, reaching for the key to number 1 that hung behind her front door. 'An' since you bothered to let me know you was coming,

I had a bit of a dust round for you. And there are letters on your kitchen table.'

'From Kip?'

'One of them is. But Kip's home. He wanted to go over there to see you, so I told him to hold on – that you'd be home.'

'How is he?' Meg unlocked her front door. 'How long is he stoppin'?'

'He didn't say and I didn't ask.' Nell pulled out a chair, looking pointedly at the tea caddy. 'Kettle's full.'

'Then I'll make a pot of tea. Kip will be staying at Amy's?'

'Where else?'

'Give Tommy a call, will you? Tell him I'm brewin'.' Meg was aware of the hostility in the older woman's voice. 'And what's eating you, Nell? Run out of ciggies, have you?'

'No. Got five, as a matter of fact. And if you must know what's botherin' me – well, it's Kip. He's real gone on you, girl, yet it seems he's hardly heard from you at all.'

'Letters overseas get lost all the time, you know that. And what Kip feels about me is his business; nuthin' to do with anybody else. I like him too. He's a good friend.'

'To my way of thinking, the way Kip feels has nuthin' to do with friendship. But I'll say no more,' Nell sniffed as she heard the closing of Tommy Todd's front door. 'So what did you bring with you, then?

'A rabbit. I said I would. It's been skinned and cut into pieces, ready for the pot. An' Mr Potter gave me carrots and onions and potatoes to go with it. And I've brought you both a fresh egg. Polly sent them.'

'Decent of her, I'm sure.' Nell took a cigarette from her pinafore pocket and laid it on the table to await the mug of tea, trying not to dwell too much on the way it had once been when all the ciggies anyone could want were there for the asking – and a ha'penny change out of a silver shilling when you bought twenty! Oh, bluddy Hitler had a lot to answer for!

'How's the job going, then? Still like working for them toffs?'

'Yes, I do. Y'know, Nell, I went to the village to see Mrs Potter – her at the post office – and she opened a bankbook for me. I can save money, see; put away half my wages every time I'm paid. And I must remember to take my swimming costume back with me. There's this place where you can swim. It's a sort of loop in the river, but it's great for a dip. They call it the willow pool. But Kip is calling round, didn't you say?'

She pushed her other life to the back of her mind; to talk of Kip Lewis was the best way to do it. Her other life was sunshine and fields and trees – and Mark. Kip was Lyra Street and Tippet's Yard, Liverpool 3; a place of bombed streets and smuts on the washing and things best forgotten – like Father Unknown. And Kip loved her, which was more awful than before because now she loved Mark, even though he had never actually said he loved her. And she would never, ever want any other man.

Yet how was she to tell Kip he had no chance at all? How did you find words kind enough so someone as decent as Kip wasn't hurt and his dignity offended? And why did she want Mark – with or without marriage – when Kip had probably bought her a ring in Sydney? Men like Kip took no for an answer, were willing to wait for the Church to make it decent before they asked for something that was better kept until after the priest's blessing.

And that was another thing. Kip was Catholic; she, Meg, was neither Protty nor Pape, had rarely been in a church. All she believed in was the Book of Life, and that what was written there wasn't open to chance nor change. And if she married a Catholic, she frowned, she'd have a string of kids and they'd all have to be Catholics, even though their mother wasn't one. And –

'Hey, miss!' A hand passed before Meg's eyes. 'What was you thinkin' about? You had a right old gob on you! And what's to do with that tea? It'll be stewed black!'

Nell's shout of laughter shut down all Meg's thoughts except how to keep out of Kip's way as much as she was able.

'I was thinkin', if you must know, that I'd decided to go into town. There's sometimes a lipstick queue at Lewis's on a Saturday, and I want to do a bit of personal shopping.'

Knickers, actually, though she knew better than to mention so intimate a garment in front of Tommy.

'I see. So what do I tell Kip when he comes lookin' for you?'

'Tell him I'll be back sharpish – all right?' Hastily she took the rabbit from its layers of newspaper, laying the pieces on a large plate, placing it on the cold slate slab in the pantry, covering it with a tea towel. 'And next time I come there should be windfall apples and the first of the early plums. We'll be able to have stewed fruit with our dinner.'

'Then let's hope you bring sugar with you to sweeten it,' Nell said sourly.

'I'm sure if I asked Mrs John she would give me some. After all, there are five ration books at Candlefold and no one takes sugar in drinks. That means there are two pounds every week just for cooking with, and half a pound saved up for things like Christmas and jam making.'

'Yes, well, ordinary folk that live in Tippet's Yard like sweet tea and a spot of sugar on their porridge, and we'll have less of Doll's precious Candlefold and a bit more tea pouring, 'cause I'm sick of waitin' to light my ciggie!'

She would be glad, Meg decided as she handed the last cup out of the pot – the strongest – to Tommy, who liked a decent cup of tea and couldn't manage it, these days, rationing being what it was. She gave him a smile, saying she was sorry there wasn't a slice of rich fruit cake to go with it, or a strawberry cream tartlet or even a buttered scone.

Then she said, 'I'll leave you two with the pot – saccharins in the little brown bottle, if you want them. The tea leaves'll take a drop more boiling water – be my guest. I'm nipping off to town, if you don't mind. Won't be long!'

It was not until she was aboard the green tram that clanged and swayed into Liverpool that she felt safe – safe from Kip, that was. And before she returned to face him, she would have her story off pat; nicely rehearsed so as not to hurt him, because Kip was a decent sort who deserved to marry a nice girl from a good Catholic family and live with her happily for the rest of his days.

She fished in her pocket for two pennies, then offered them to the lady conductor with a brilliant smile.

'All the way into town, please!'

And the conductress, who liked working on the trams and was grateful to the war for making it possible, said, 'All the way it is, queen!' and smiled back.

It was seven in the evening when Meg returned from Liverpool. Nell was waiting on her doorstep, arms folded, to demand where the 'ell she had been and hadn't Kip been twice, and her not there. And to tell her that he would be up at the Tarleton if she cared to join him for a drink and a chat.

'And if you don't want to go in the pub, he says, then he'll be back here at ten. All right?'

'Of course I'll pop up and see him!'

It would be better in the pub. For one thing, he wouldn't try to kiss her in there – not passionately, anyway – and for another, when they closed at ten – or even earlier, if the beer allocation had all been sold – she could plead tiredness and could he, perhaps, meet her tomorrow? Or maybe he wouldn't want to meet her tomorrow when she had told him that friendship was all she could offer. If she had the chance to tell him, that was!

'Good.' Nell said it snappily because she liked Kip. Kip could be relied upon to give her cigarettes every time he was ashore. Hadn't he only this afternoon given her a packet of twenty – and them all sealed lovely in crackly Cellophane? Twenty, all at once, not doled out in miserable fives after standing in the heat – or the cold – for ages to get them.

'Meant to give them to you yesterday, Nell,' he'd smiled. Kip didn't smoke, but he collected cigarettes in various ports of call to give to his friends who did.

'So have you had something to eat, girl?'

'No. I got a loaf of bread, though, and there's jam in the cupboard. I'll make do till tomorrow, Nell. We'll have a good old rabbit stew, then. And besides, it won't harm me to miss a meal. We eat far too well at Candlefold.'

And Nell had snorted 'Candlefold!' as if the place were the devil's invention, and stalked off to the pub – and maybe a tot of gin, if the landlord was so inclined. If the landlord had gin to sell, that was.

Meg saw Kip the moment she pushed open the snug door at the Tarleton. He was easy to see. His fair skin was tanned golden and his hair looked even fairer. He was wearing grey flannel trousers, and a white shirt open at the neck, sleeves rolled up to his elbows. He smiled when he saw her; a deep, wide smile that showed in his eyes.

'Meg!' He crossed to her side and kissed the cheek she offered him. 'You look great.'

'Country living. You look good, an' all, Kip!'

He *did* look good. Anybody would notice him in a crowd – any good Catholic girl, that was.

'So – you're on a crafty weekend?'

'Mm.' She lowered her voice. 'How much longer have you got, Kip?'

'Tuesday.' He said it with only the slightest moving of his lips. Liverpool public houses were not the places for careless talk. 'What are you drinking, then?'

'What's on offer?' she smiled, relieved the first hurdle was over.

'Beer or shandy,' he grinned back. 'They're out of shorts.'

'Then I'd like a half of shandy, please.'

He settled her at a corner table, placed his glass on it, then returned to the bar counter. She looked at him dispassionately, having to admit that he was tall, slim and good to look at. He had a regular berth with the shipping line – didn't need to go to the pool to get signed on at the start of every trip. She might – given time and patience on his part, that was – have got closer to him.

But not now. Now, there was Mark, who had offered her nothing. Neither a ring, nor his love. You took men like Mark Kenworthy the way they were and on their terms: I want you, Meg Blundell, and there's a war on so next time I'm on leave . . . ?

And she would let him because she loved him and was in love with him too, and besotted by him. *His* terms? OK. Any way he wanted.

She smiled up at Kip as he placed her glass on the table; smiled as a mother would smile at a child who was about to be refused something it desperately longed for.

'Cheers, Kip.' She lifted her glass and drank deeply and slowly before saying, 'There's something we have to talk about.'

'You and me, Meg?'

'Yes. Did you buy that ring in Sydney?'

'I did, as a matter of fact.' He took a small red box from his pocket, opening it. 'The middle one's a sapphire. Blue, to match your eyes. Will you wear it for me, Meg – be my girl?'

She looked down at the ring because it was a hundred times easier than looking into his eyes. It was very beautiful; a sapphire with a diamond either side. It must have cost every penny he had earned this last trip. There wouldn't be one like it in any Liverpool jeweller's shop; rings like that had vanished with twenty-four-carat wedding rings.

'I'm sorry, Kip.' She forced her chin up so her eyes met his. 'I asked you not to; told you I wasn't ready to go steady yet. I'm sorry,' she said again, then dropped her eyes once more to the red box.

'Give me one good reason why not?' He asked it softly of her.

'I don't want to be tied down yet. And you are a Catholic and I don't think I believe in God.'

'So, we don't get married in front of the altar? Does it matter as long as the priest says the words and the Registrar is in the vestry? You haven't got anything against Catholics, have you? You aren't Orange?'

'No, Kip. I respect your beliefs, just as you accept that I haven't got any.'

'Well, that's one problem solved. And I don't want to tie you down, Meg love. If you want us to be married that's all I could ask, but if you want to wait I'll understand. There's a war on. I might not make the end of it, I know that. Maybe I won't always be lucky gettin' the Panama run to Down Under; one day I might end up on the Atlantic run – or even the Russian convoys. But wear the ring, eh? I'd never force myself on you . . .'

Unspeaking, Meg took the box and snapped it shut. Then she placed on his palm, gently folding his fingers over it.

'I'm sorry. I'm tryin' to say that I want more from life than Ma had. I don't want to risk being a widow, Kip, with maybe a couple of kids to rear in a crummy little house in Tippet's Yard. When I get married, I want to be normal – live in the country and never have to see a mucky street again. I'm sorry . . .'

She kept saying sorry, but was she *really* sorry? Or was she sorry she hadn't the guts to tell him straight out that she was in love with Mark Kenworthy and even though his sort didn't marry her sort, that was the way it was and always would be. For her, anyway.

'There's someone else, Meg? You've met another man?'

'No! Haven't I just told you I don't want to marry any man. Not till the war's over.'

'So if I said I'd pack in the sea, would you marry me then? When it's all over, I mean.'

'No, Kip. I can't promise anything to any man!' And oh, may God help her, she was the most awful, bare-faced liar and ought to be punished for it. 'Sorry, Kip,' she whispered as tears filled her eyes, then ran down her cheeks.

He reached across and dabbed her eyes, then, without speaking, took her hands in his and held them tightly until the shaking in them began to lessen.

Then he said, 'Don't be, Meg. Only remember that I won't change. If ever you're in need of a shoulder, I'll come to you, if I can. Want to go home?'

'Please.'

She couldn't bear to look at him for the shame that writhed inside her. She only knew that from this minute on she could expect no luck at all. And it would be her own selfish fault, because she'd have asked for it.

They walked past St Joseph's church and down Lyra Street, to turn left at the bottom and follow the wall that led to the Tippet's Yard sign and the archway beside it.

'This is far enough, Kip.' Meg stopped and leaned against the wall. 'Will I see you tomorrow?'

'Tomorrow I'm taking Amy's two to Birkenhead to see their nan. Be a break for Amy and they'll enjoy the ferry over.'

'Busman's holiday for you . . .'

'What time are you leaving on Monday?'

'Early, Kip. I want to get there before twelve.'

'And I have to be at Gladstone Dock by midnight, Monday. Reckon we'll sail on the early tide. We won't have a convoy to wait for, this trip; the pilot'll want to get us out of the river pretty quick.'

'The *Bellis* again, is it?'

'Mm. Same ship, same run. What I've seen of Australia I like a lot. Wouldn't mind settling down there – if I give up the sea, that is. A good place for kids to grow up in.'

'Yes.' They were back to kids again – one every year till she was tattered. 'If we don't see each other again, Kip, will you and me write, still? If I don't see you tomorrow night, that is, when you get back from Birkenhead?'

'I'd like us to keep writing, but I'd like more than one from you – and a postcard.'

She heard the teasing in his voice and longed to hug him as she would hug a best friend. But Kip wanted more than friendship, so she dug her hands in her pockets.

'You've got my address? And I'll write every week care of the shipping line, I give you my word.'

She let her shoulders go in the smallest of shrugs. Her word. And dammit, she'd been back here less than a day and she was sayin' *waid* instead of word! Nanny Boag would have been on to it like a terrier on a rat! She felt with her hand for Kip's. That at least she owed him.

'There's this old girl at Candlefold – Nanny Boag. Been there years and years. Family, sort of. She brought up Polly's dad and stayed on and looked after Polly and Mark. She makes out she's an invalid now, and they all go along with it when she goes off into the past and imagines things. She pulls me up when I talk Scouse, an' all.'

'Then tell her to shurrup, Meg. When she goes off, like, is it because she's been at the gin?'

'Nah! Nothing stronger than Communion wine.' She laughed and some of the tension left her. 'She never leaves the nursery. The vicar comes every two weeks to give Communion to her and old Mrs Kenworthy. I like the old lady. She's crippled with arthritis, but Boag is an old biddy.'

'So why do you put up with her, girl?'

'Because everybody does. Mrs John told me that when Nanny had a tantrum I was to walk away from it.'

'It's a queer going-on at that place, if you ask me.'

'No. It's Candlefold. There are so many good things there, Kip, they far outweigh Nanny. They're lovely people to work for. Ma worked there, when she was a girl – I told you – but I haven't told them I'm Dolly Blundell's daughter. Not yet.'

'But why not? They'd be real chuffed.'

'No. I shan't tell them yet.' Kip didn't know about her being born there, nor about Ma being given the house in Tippet's Yard for a shilling. Only Nell knew that.

'Up to you, Meg. You've obviously got your reasons. Are you going to ask me in for a cup of tea, then?'

'If you don't mind, Kip – no. I'm tired. But see you tomorrow night, maybe?' She owed him a friendly goodbye.

'Maybe. I'd thought to nip up to the Tarleton again. Happen I'll see you there?'

'Yes. I'd like that.' She let go of his hand and half turned from him, but he took her shoulder so they were standing close, toe to toe.

'See you then, Meg. Take care of yourself, eh?'

'And you, Kip.' No use saying she would pray for him. 'I'll think of you every day, and wish you well and I'll write a proper letter every week. Promise I will.'

'Right, then.' It was as if he was reluctant to go; as if he needed her to give him a push in the direction of the street outside.

'Ta-ra, well.' She reached up, hands on his shoulders and kissed his mouth softly, briefly. She felt his body stiffen, then he stepped back and in the half-light, she knew there was a small smile on his lips. 'Look after yourself, sailor.'

Then she turned and ran, fumbling her key into the lock, banging the door behind her, leaning against it because her whole body shook.

'Bitch, Meg Blundell! That's what you are! *Bitch!*'

'Are you seeing Kip Lewis tonight?

Nell sat back in her chair, swallowing hard on a belch because she was in number 1 and you didn't do that in Doll's house – even though she was dead and gone, God rest her.

'Maybe. He's taking Amy's kids out today, then he's goin' to the Tarleton. Likely I'll see him there tonight.'

'Only likely? If you want my advice, Meg Blundell, I'd get in there pretty sharpish, or there's plenty will. Since you've been at that Candlefold place you're getting too picky. Just like your ma.'

'Now see here, Nell, it's –'

'Hey up! We've all had a good dinner, courtesy of Meg, and we wouldn't want to bite the hand that's just fed us, now would we?' Tommy wasn't given to saying two words when one would suffice, but when he offered an opinion it usually made sense. 'And this gravy's too good to waste – can I beg a slice of bread, girl, to mop it up?'

'You can, and welcome.' Meg threw him a look of gratitude as she cut a thick slice.

'Now hang on – I wasn't bein' ungrateful,' Nell persisted. 'That was a fine meal and I haven't eaten so well in ages. All I was trying to say is that Kip Lewis is a decent young feller, and –'

'And it's up to him and Meg to sort things out between them – all right?' Tommy said it quietly and firmly, and Nell knew she was beaten.

'I'm sorry there's nuthin' for pudding,' Meg said, wanting to kiss Tommy soundly. 'I'll make us a cup of tea, if you like.'

There was Australian tea in the caddy, still, from Kip's previous visit. *Kip. I'm sorry it couldn't have been you . . .*

'We wasn't expecting afters, girl. Mind if I light up? And you haven't told us the latest from Candlefold yet. When is the Kenworthy girl gettin' married?'

Nell was offering the olive branch and Meg took it thankfully, telling them about Davie's promotion and the banns being read this very day at All Saints and Mrs John's friend offering the loan of a long white dress.

'Mm. There'll be a lot of that goin' on now, what with clothes on the ration, an' all. But I reckon she won't care, that Polly.'

'No. As long as she and Davie get married is all she wants – and a honeymoon baby, she says.'

'Aye, but babies aren't all that easily got. I was never blessed. Wouldn't have minded one of my own before my man was took.' Nell drew deeply on her cigarette. 'Ar, hey. It's a funny old world . . .'

Later, Meg thought deeply about whether or not to go to the Tarleton, then decided that if she were careful what she said, it would do no harm. Kip had accepted, she was sure of it, that all she was prepared to offer was friendship; maybe a drink and a chat would smooth the way ahead, because she really did like him and what Nell had said was true. Kip was a good catch for any girl who wanted a decent man with steady money coming in; would be glad to land a feller like Kip Lewis. All things considered, she reasoned, she could have done a lot worse than say yes; that she would wear his ring. Once, she may well have done, but not now; not when she was spoken for; not when Mark wanted her, even though he had never said he loved her. Mark was a part of the magic that was Candlefold; sunny days and trees and fields and flowers, and being treated like she was a part of the family and her being Mrs Kenworthy's other granddaughter. She did not, she argued silently, belong in Tippet's Yard. Candlefold was where she had been born and now she looked on it as her home. Ma had been right. To live in the country had been a beautiful dream. Pity it hadn't come true, for Ma.

Meg combed her hair, deciding against lipstick. Then she locked the door behind her, calling to Nell that she was going up the road for a few minutes. A few minutes, she stressed; just to show willing and friendly and to ask Kip how his trip over the water had gone.

This morning she had looked out of her bedroom window – the only one in the house that didn't face on to the yard. From it she could see the length of Lyra Street and the steps of St Joseph's church. This morning she had seen Kip, a small child on his hip, another at his side. Kip liked children – wanted some of his own to bring up decent, he once said, and not be put in a home because a widowed father couldn't cope.

Amy, his sister, was expecting again. It was probably why Kip was taking the kids off her hands for the day. That would make three confinements in five years. All right, so maybe it suited Amy and maybe Kip wanted children of his own, but it wasn't for Meg Blundell. Oh, no way was it!

She looked into the bar parlour of the Tarleton, but Kip was not there. He was easy to spot – bronzed and fair, and head and shoulders above most men. She walked through into the snug, but he wasn't there either.

'Kip Lewis been in?' she asked the landlord's wife.

'Been and gone, queen. Just had a quick half then said ta-ra. He'll be at their Amy's now. You missed him by ten minutes.'

Meg thanked her, saying she would catch him at Lyra Street, but she would not. She had looked in at the Tarleton as she said she would and had missed him. No point in going to Amy's. She wouldn't be welcome there. Kip's sister was all right, but Meg was not one of them. Amy was devoutly Catholic and wanted a good Catholic wife for her brother.

When Meg returned to the yard, her neighbour's door was closed, and top and bottom windows curtained. Nell, she supposed, had gone to bed early, doubtless to read the *News of the World*. Mind, newspapers these days were soon read – eight pages, if you were lucky, and very few pictures. Magazines, too, were not as thick nor as well illustrated as they used to be. Paper – newsprint – was now a munition of war, like everything else that once made life worth living. Food rationed. Go careful on electricity and gas! Coal rationed and clothes rationed; decent soap a rarity and perfume a thing of the past. Toothpaste you bought when you could, and face cream and powder you got only if you were lucky and after half an hour in a queue. And fingers crossed that you would get the right shade or colour at the end of it!

On Saturday Meg had bought a brassiere and one pair of pale pink, bias-cut French knickers; bought them defiantly because they were in no way sensible nor promised to be long-wearing, and which claimed three of her clothing coupons. But a nice pair of knickers made you feel good underneath, she had told herself, and to hell with cotton drawers!

She had got a lipstick, too, though not in a colour she would ever have dreamed of wearing. English Rose it was, and pink; exactly right for Polly. And Polly would get it too, on her birthday next month.

She switched on the wireless to listen to the end of the news; after which she would turn over to the Forces programme. At half-past nine it would be *Music Hall*, and tonight Anne Ziegler and Webster Booth would be on. She felt in the mood for love songs, because she was in love.

It was too light yet to draw the curtains; blackout was not until 10.32 and darkness wouldn't come for half an hour after that. So she would sit in Ma's chair in the quiet of Ma's kitchen, and listen and think and wish for it to be tomorrow morning, early, when she could decently lock the door of number 1 behind her, slip the key through Nell's letter box and make for Scotland Road and a tram to the station.

Nell knew she was going back early; all that remained to be done was to write a note saying *Ta-ra. See you in a fortnight*, and push it through the letter box with the key. Then, if the train ran to time, she would be at Candlefold by noon. Back home.

The train into Preston was as near on time as made no matter; the bus to Nether Barton stood there, with ten minutes to go, as if it were waiting for her. She had stepped off it at the post office stop and Mrs Potter was at the window; not to wave, but to note who had alighted from the 11.40 bus.

Meg made for the stile then walked diagonally across the field. The lambs were grown now, almost as big as the ewes, though they were suckling still; had the ewes' back legs in the air in their eagerness to drink.

She climbed the field gate, then saw the bottom archway. She was home again and still ten minutes to go before noon. She began to run because she had been away too long; too long apart from the old stone house and fields and trees and roses that climbed the walls and the granite pump trough, and Polly and everyone. And tonight, when her work was done, she would walk beneath the far archway, past the drying green and the henrun and turn left into the cow pasture through which the river ran. And she would sit beside the willow pool, and send her love and longing to Mark.

'Where did you get to after supper?' Polly sat cross-legged on Meg's bed, hands clasping her toes.

'I – oh, just went for a bit of a walk – made sure nothing had changed, glad to be back.'

'I missed you.'

'Missed you too, Polly. Two days is too long to be away.'

'How was Liverpool, then?'

'Getting over the blitz, I suppose. The air smelled still of bombing – you know, rubble dust and – and things. Central Station is back in business, after a fashion, and the trams seem OK again. The demolition lads are busy still. Walls standing there – four or five storeys high; windows gone, no doors. And you think that if you sneeze they'll come tumbling down on you. There's still a lot of clearing up to do.'

'What did you do, though?'

'Went to Liverpool, bought some pink knickers and a bra; I'll show you later.' She was careful not to mention the English Rose lipstick. 'And I went to the Tarleton for a drink with Kip.'

'The one who goes to sea?'

'Yup. He sails tonight. Same run, Down Under. I wasn't lucky this time. Reckon his sister got the shampoo and cold cream instead of me. I promised to write to him.'

'I had a letter from Davie this morning.' Polly's cheeks pinked. 'Wish he'd been with me yesterday. It was so lovely in church – everyone asking me afterwards when the wedding was going to be. Two more to go. Mummy's coming with me next Sunday, if you don't mind, to hear the second reading.'

'You know I don't mind. Maybe I'll come to hear the third.'

'I wish you would, Meg. If you'd only go just once, I'm sure you'd like church. I find it a great comfort really. I think about Davie all the time he's away from me, and he's in my prayers every night, but in the end it's got to go into God's hands – taking care of him, I mean. But I'm not trying to convert you from the Book of Life,' she added hastily.

'So what's been happening here, Polly?'

'Just the banns, and Mummy managed to get through on the phone to her friend. It's OK about the wedding dress. And her daughter is expecting!'

'Heck! That was quick!'

'It was very good indeed, considering they only had seven days' leave together, and a quick forty-eight-hour pass. Hope me and Davie can do the same. If he's got to go abroad, then a baby would be the next best thing.'

'Keep you out of mischief – and from having to do war work!'

'Suppose so. I'm trying not to think about being twenty and having to register.'

'Me, too, but it's less than six weeks away, though I don't suppose we'll have to register on the very day. So has Davie heard yet about his promotion?'

'No. Seems it's still in the pipeline. I don't want him home just yet – not until we've got the banns done and dusted. Oh, Meg, I have so missed you. I wanted to come and sit on your bed and whinge after Davie went, but you'd deserted me.'

'I had to see to things in Liverpool, but I won't go again till you've had your third reading. I went as far as the willow pool tonight,' she confided reluctantly. 'Suppose I wanted it to be last week again and us all together, and picking strawberries and Mark chopping logs.'

'Are you like me, Meg – storing memories, I mean? I do it all the time; put all the nice things on hold. Then when I'm miserable I can close my eyes and let them come out. It helps a lot.'

'Suppose it must. But I don't have memories – not like you. Oh, last week was great, but – well – me and Mark aren't like you and Davie. It wouldn't surprise me if Mark wasn't out with an ATS girl at this very minute.'

'Well, it would surprise *me*! Can't you get it into your head that Mark is really gone on you? I was talking to Gran about it, and she agrees with me.'

'Polly! He isn't gone on me, you daft ha'porth. Your brother could have any girl he wanted, and you know it.'

'Well, he wants you, now, and I'm glad, because you'll give him a run for his money!'

'Polly Kenworthy! Will you shurrup? Mark and I won't be havin' our banns read – ever. Don't be saying things like that – it's how rumours start!'

And oh, Polly, I tell lies too. It happened the same for me as it did for you – the very minute I saw him. But he isn't in love with me, though I'll be grateful for any crumbs he drops my way . . .

'OK. Not another word. But I'll bet you anything you like he'll write to you; bet you a bob there'll be a letter in the morning.'

'You're on! It'll be the easiest shillin' I've ever made,' Meg laughed.

And the best way of losing a shilling, an' all! A letter tomorrow from Mark would be marvellous – and worth a week's wages!

When they had crept downstairs to the kitchen and heated milk in a copper pan and sprinkled it with Ovaltine, they whispered good night at the top of the stone stairs.

'Night-night. I'm glad you're home,' Polly whispered.

'Glad to be home,' Meg choked, her entire body aching with relief and gladness and her heart vowing never, ever, to leave Candlefold again – not even to spend one night at Tippet's Yard.

She closed the door quietly behind her, then opened the wardrobe to take her dressing gown from its hanger. And she would wrap its pink fluffiness around her, then switch off the light, pull back the curtains and sit at the open window, listening to night sounds and a stillness and peace you could reach out and touch, almost.

But her dressing gown was not on its hanger. It had slipped off to lie on top of the case – Ma's little attaché case in which she had kept her important papers; that same case she had reluctantly opened to discover, oh, so many things she would rather not have known. It lay there on the wardrobe floor, still, exactly where she had left it on Saturday morning when she turned the key in the door. Only now she realized the wardrobe door had been unlocked, and one of the little hasp fasteners on the case was open. And she was sure both had been closed, which could only mean that the case had been moved! Someone had been into her room, and they had no right!

But *someone* had every right! This wasn't her house and someone had probably been in to check the blackout or to leave clean towels – of course they had the right! Yet no one had the right to unlock her wardrobe and rummage inside and no one, especially, had the right to open Ma's little case!

She bent to take it out, lay it on the bed, snapping open the other hasp, carefully lifting the lid, unwilling to look down. Because she would know if anything had been touched; knew exactly how she had left everything.

She pulled in her breath sharply. The big fat packet of deeds tied with pink tape should have been on top – and so it was. But underneath had been the photographs and Ma's will and her own birth certificate. Only now the photographs were beneath Ma's will and the envelope containing her birth certificate, and whoever had opened that envelope, would know exactly where she had been born – and exactly who she *wasn't*; would read that her father's name was unknown!

Her mouth had gone all at once dry and she reached for the mug, gulping on its hotness, trying to think clearly, because someone *had* unlocked her wardrobe door and someone *had* opened the case and looked inside it!

But who? Not Mrs Kenworthy, who couldn't move without help; not Mrs John, who was too much of a lady even to think of such a thing, and certainly not Polly. So that left –

'Nanny Boag!' That was who! Never left the nursery because the steep staircase was too much for her, even with help! Emily Boag, troublemaker, who could see out of the high window of her sitting room because she could climb on a chair! Oh, it had been Nanny, all right, but how was she to prove it?

Then all at once Meg's blood ran cold, because of all the people in this house, Nanny Boag was the last person she would have told about how it had once been for Ma at Candlefold, because the old woman was mad and bad and full of wickedness and jealousy.

'Oh, Ma,' Meg closed her eyes, her lips barely moving, 'what am I to do now, will you tell me?'

She switched off the light, then flung back the curtains to gaze down into the courtyard and the dim outline of the black iron pump and the granite trough.

But no one was there: no laughing housemaids in long cotton dresses and starched white pinafores. It was no use asking Ma! She was on her own now; only herself to defend Ma's past against an old woman who would stop at nothing to get Dorothy Blundell's daughter out of this house.

Because now Nanny knew who Meg Blundell was; had been there, most likely, on that late August night when the child of Father Unknown had been born into the charity of the Kenworthy family.

'Damn you!' Meg hissed, then flung herself face down on her bed, and wept.

Twelve

Meg reached out sleepily to silence the sudden, strident jangling at her bedside, shaking her head, wondering why it had been necessary to set the alarm when almost always she had no trouble awakening early. Then she recalled the sleepless tossing, mind shocked and angry, and the fingers of the clock pointing to two. And Nanny was the cause of it. Last night, over and over again, Meg had come to the same conclusion. It had to be Nanny Boag!

Mrs Seed? She came upstairs every Friday to lay ironing in the airing cupboard, but it was not she who had looked inside the little attaché case. The lady who did Candlefold's laundry had not not remarked upon Dorothy Blundell in the photograph she'd shown Meg; had no reason to connect the home help with that long-ago housemaid.

So had Polly unlocked the case? No! Of course not! Polly would have remembered to close the case properly – both hasps – and to turn the key again in the wardrobe door! And besides, Polly was a Kenworthy and wouldn't stoop to such sneakiness! She had, Meg brooded, decided long before midnight that Polly was not to blame.

Mrs Kenworthy, then? She had asked, Meg remembered, if she had any connections with Dorothy Blundell; must have remembered, even twenty years on, the birth of a baby one August night. But Mrs Kenworthy accepted that Meg's mother was called Hilda, and that her father was a sailor, buried at sea. And it was stupid even to think that an old crippled lady, who couldn't move without help, could have done such a thing.

Which left only Mrs John and Nanny – and there was no contest! Mrs John was a lady right down to the tips of her fingers and wouldn't pry into a servant's locked wardrobe. Even though she was mistress of the house, she wouldn't even think of doing such a thing.

Yet Nanny dare not leave her rooms high in Candlefold's roofspace, nor dare she, Meg had been assured, brave the steep and narrow nursery stairs for fear of turning giddy and falling.

But Nanny was no invalid; moved freely about the rooms that once were the nursery, and Meg was as sure as she could be that Nanny was able to balance herself on a chair at the high dormer window. Nanny Boag was a fraud; even Polly had once had doubts about the old woman's state of mind.

It was only then, when it was almost two in the morning, that Meg had set her alarm clock for six and fallen asleep, almost sure she had found the culprit.

But what could Emily Boag do about it, she thought, reluctantly swinging her feet to the floor. Could she announce triumphantly that Meg Blundell was a cheat and a liar into the bargain? Of course she couldn't! 'I went down the stairs to her room, unlocked her wardrobe, then opened a case with private papers in it!' would she say? She wouldn't, couldn't, because it would make Mrs John very angry, and Nanny knew better than to admit to a thing like that. Nanny was sly, and would keep what she knew to herself until such times as it suited her to tell it!

Yet from now on, Meg sighed, there would be a lot of hints and digs and funny looks whenever she went into the little sitting room at the top of the stairs, and Nanny's eyes shining with malice because they held a secret still to be told. The old biddy must have been over the moon to discover who the home help really was; she who couldn't talk proper – *speak properly* – and had the cheek to flirt with Mark Kenworthy, who wouldn't have looked twice at a girl from Tippet's Yard if there hadn't been a war on.

Now Nanny knew exactly where she came from, even though her ration book and identity card gave nothing away. Nanny had seen the proof of it, then crept back up the steep stairs to gloat.

Yet hadn't Nell Shaw always said that there were more ways than one of skinning a cat? Couldn't there be some way to make sure Nanny kept her mouth shut? And wasn't attack the best form of defence? Should Meg fling wide the nursery, then say, 'All right – so you know who my mother was and that she had me here, at Candlefold! So what are you going to do about it? Tell Mrs John, will you, that you got downstairs with no trouble at all, and went through my things whilst I was away?

Afraid to leave your room, are you, because the stairs make you dizzy even to think of getting down them without someone to help you? OK – so I'm a fraud, but so are you, Nanny, and you can't split on me, can you? You'll have to be content with climbing on a chair and snooping out of your window!'

Meg let go her indrawn breath then slowly took in another, closing her eyes to shut out the old nurse and her mischief, opening them again to see the courtyard and the far archway and, beneath her, the iron pump and granite trough; Ma's trough. And she could see a morning sky of pale blue and yellow, and the sun, big and bright and low, coming up behind Pygons Wood; a sun that would soon shine down on the willow pool and scatter pieces of sunbeam to glitter on the water.

The sun knew about her and Mark, had shone unblinking from an early evening sky on two lovers – two who would have been lovers, but for the water bailiff. Mark wanted her; Mark owned Candlefold and everything in and around it; Mark's generosity kept a sly old woman in her make-believe world and provided her with shelter and warmth and food. So how could that old woman harm her? Meg fretted. How could she, when she and Mark would be lovers?

So she didn't have to go in feet first. More ways than one, weren't there? Oh my word yes, and the best way would be to match slyness with slyness!

'Ma?' she whispered softly, aching for reassurance.

But she heard no words of comfort, either with her ears or silently in her heart, because that long-ago housemaid knew about the needs of men and could she have spoken from the past she would have said, 'Take care, Meg. Tell it to your conscience, not to me! And when you have, take notice of what it tells you.'

'But, Ma,' she called with her heart, 'I love him!' Even though, she didn't add, he doesn't love me.

'Oh, damn, damn, *damn*!' It was all such a mess now. Suddenly her lovely world was tainted and it was Nanny Boag's doing! Yet nobody – not anyone on the face of this earth – was going to take that world from her!

* * *

At eight o'clock Meg walked carefully up the steep stairs then knocked firmly on the nursery door.

'Mornin'!' Her voice was as near normal as she could make it; there was even a smile on her lips. 'Brought your breakfast. Missed me, did you?'

'Not one bit! Pity you came back!' Sharp and narrow, Nanny's eyes met Meg's, the eyes of a woman who had all her wits about her; a malicious woman who seemed sure of herself now, because she held all the trump cards.

'Well! That's not very nice, is it?' Meg's words dripped honey. 'You know you don't mean it! Now eat up your toast. It's raspberry jam, this mornin'. Shall I pour for you?'

'No you shall not! I can lift a teapot!'

Yes, and walk down those stairs and go nosing into my wardrobe, an' all! Meg longed to fling defiantly into the shrewish face. But she bit on the words and said them instead with her eyes, gazing unflinching, holding that gaze so her silence said more than words ever could.

'Of course you can lift a teapot,' she said eventually; said it softly and clearly and exactly as Ma would have done. 'You can do a lot of things, can't you, Nanny? Well, if you don't want anythin' else, I'll leave you to it.'

Head high, she left the room, closing the door quietly behind her, taking a deep, calming breath because she was shaking so much. But she had confronted the old woman with dignity, and Dolly Blundell would have been proud of her daughter!

When she got back to the safety and sanity of the kitchen, both Polly and her mother were smiling as if they knew a lovely secret and were about to share it with her.

'Well – go on, then! On your plate!' Polly laughed.

On her plate. An envelope with Mark's writing on it. Meg recognized it at once, though never before had one of his letters been addressed to Miss M. M. Blundell!

'Mark?' she whispered, picking it up. 'Oooh! He said he would write, but I never thought –'

'I know! You said he wouldn't and I bet you a bob he would! So give!' Gleefully, Polly held out a hand.

'I-I'll owe you. My purse is upstairs . . .'

'Polly! You didn't bet money on it?' Mary Kenworthy laughed. 'You're not to give it to her, Meg.'

'Oh, but she must, and I'll put it in the charity box!'

'A Blundell always pays her gambling debts!' Meg said croakily. 'I'll read it later,' she added laying it beside her plate. 'In private, if you don't mind, Polly!'

'Good for you, Meg! Now – porridge or flakes is it to be?'

'Just toast, Mrs John,' Meg cut a slice of bread, spearing it on a toasting fork, holding it to the bottom of the firegrate where the coals glowed redly. 'An' some of that lovely raspberry jam, if you don't mind.'

She gazed steadily into the fire, trying hard to compose herself, to stop the lovely shaking inside her, and breathe evenly and slowly, as if a letter from Mark was quite the normal thing; that he wrote one every day, just as Davie did to Polly.

'You're blushing!' Polly was determined to get value with her shilling. 'You *are*!'

'I have just,' Meg said in her new, quietly dignified manner, 'been toasting bread at the fire, Polly Kenworthy! And now I would like to eat it, if you don't mind, an' no more of your teasing!'

'I told you, didn't I, Mummy? Didn't I say there would be a letter from Mark because he's gone on Meg! Does no one ever listen to me?'

'What is between your brother and Meg is their business entirely, so I suggest you let Meg get on with her breakfast,' Mary Kenworthy said primly. 'Although I must say,' she added with ever such a slight wink in Meg's direction, 'that my son doesn't usually keep the promises he makes to young ladies. Perhaps Polly is right. Maybe he is – er – gone on you!'

'Now don't you start, Mrs John!' Meg's cheeks flamed even redder. 'It's only a letter!'

'Well, what that letter says is completely between you and Mark, but might I suggest,' she whispered, 'that you give him a run for his money, Meg? He's had it altogether too easy in the past with girlfriends.'

'Mrs John! You mean to say you don't mind?' Meg gasped, dignity gone. 'Him writing to me, I mean – me that can't talk proper!'

'Of course I don't mind! Talking – er – properly doesn't come into it! And might I just say, before we let the matter drop, that I'm glad Mark has written to you, and I hope you'll write back? Now can we please,' she shifted her gaze to her daughter, 'eat our breakfasts and might I, just for five minutes, have a look at the morning paper in peace and quiet?'

'You might, darling,' Polly smiled, trickling honey onto her porridge, taking out her own letter for a second reading.

But Meg said nothing, because all she could think was that happiness – soaring, sun-kissed happiness – was a slice of raspberry toast and an unopened letter. From Mark.

The postman who delivered parcels in his red GPO van said that the large registered parcel required a signature, and Polly, knowing what was inside it, signed with pleasure, rewarding him with a beaming smile and enquiring of him if he didn't think this was the most beautiful day.

'It's come! It's the dress!' she gasped. 'Do let's get it unpacked!'

'Carefully now, child. Take it upstairs in case there's any grease about here. I'll ring the exchange – see if there's any chance of getting a quick three minutes to Shelagh, let her know we've got it.'

The dress was draped on Polly's bed when Mary arrived to say she hadn't been able to get through, but the minute a line to trunks was available, the exchange would ring her. And wasn't it awful that even the telephones seemed to have been taken over by the war, and military calls given priority over civilians!

'Isn't it *lovely*?' Meg whispered.

'It's beautiful, and though I'm not one to look a gift horse in the mouth, I'm so glad it isn't stark white,' Mary smiled. 'White does so rob you of your colour, Polly.'

The dress, in oyster satin, had a pearly gleam to it and was just the most beautiful thing Meg had ever seen, with a softly draped cowl neckline and a train – oh, *yards* long! And beneath it, side by side on the floor, were shoes in matching satin, their toes stuffed with tissue paper.

'Are you goin' to try it on – see if it fits?'

'You bet I am, and aren't I the lucky one? Just think how many clothing coupons are in the train alone! And weren't they lucky to have bought it before clothes were rationed? Wonder how many more brides are going to wear it before this war is over.'

The dress could have been made with Polly in mind; a perfect fit and exactly the right length.

'Would you believe it?' Meg gasped. 'It's perfect on you, colour an' all. I think that Maudie must be your twin. Oh, drat!' She closed her eyes in horror. 'My big, stupid mouth! Polly, I'm sorry! I wasn't meanin' – you know I wasn't! You bein' adopted, I mean . . .'

'I know you weren't meaning anything. Don't be sorry, Meg. This is such a lovely wedding-dress day that nothing can upset me!' She gathered the train over her arm and turned to face her mother. 'But it's a thought, isn't it? Could I have had a twin – or brothers or sisters?'

'I – I don't know, child. You know the adoption people don't go into details like that – wouldn't tell us, even if we asked them. And – and I think, Polly, that twins were kept together wherever possible. But don't talk about such things. You've never mentioned it before – why now?'

'I don't know. Must be because I'm so happy, seeing my wedding dress. And I haven't mentioned it before because it doesn't bother me, being adopted. Maybe it was what Meg said that made me think of it. But it doesn't matter, honest it doesn't!'

'Then in that case, how about trying on the shoes – just to be sure.' Mary smiled. 'And put on a stocking before you do! Your feet smell of gardening boots, Polly Kenworthy!'

'Flowers,' Polly said dreamily to her satin slippers. 'What will my bouquet be?'

'It will depend on what flowers are around when the time comes. It may be roses or it may be chrysanths – all depending on what's in season. But don't worry about it. Potter will come up with something beautiful, you know that. Had you thought of bridesmaids?'

'Only vaguely. Really, I want it to be just Davie and me and the families; a quiet, wartime wedding, like most other couples these days. No wedding cake, no champagne – but who cares?'

Just to be Davie's wife, she thought yearningly, was all that really mattered.

Only when lunch had been served and eaten and washed-up after, and potatoes peeled and cabbages chopped and a suet-crusted Woolton pie set in the bottom of the fire-oven to cook slowly for supper, did Meg open her letter. She did it carefully with her nail file, then sat at the bedroom window to read it. There were two pages, neatly and firmly written in black ink. It began *My dear Meg*, and ended *Yours, Mark*. And every word between she would remember, so that if her letter was lost – or stolen, even – she would know to her dying day what Mark had writen in his first letter.

My dear Meg,

So you see, I am writing to you though you said I would not, doubting Thomasina that you are! Already I miss you. It was good that you were at Candlefold and so comfortably at home that it was as if you were meant to be there.

Dear Merrilees, I teased you shamefully, I know. Truth was that I didn't quite know how to treat someone like you. I couldn't believe you were real, the girl I had always wanted to meet yet never thought I would. You knocked me sideways and for a couple of days I vented my bewilderment on the logs, and chopped for dear life!

Then we went to the willow pool, and everything came clear to me. I knew there that you were the one, and no one else would do. So there you are – my soul laid bare at your feet. Don't trample on it, Meg Merrilees? Write and tell me that you meant what you said – that you want me too?

There is little here that is different. We eat, we sleep, we drill and salute our betters. I would rather be at home with you. Will this war never end?

I am lonely and sorry for myself. Write to me with all news of Candlefold: all news, even if it seems of no importance to you. Tell me, so I can be there with you.

Once, I couldn't understand Polly because she counted the days between, but now I find that in ninety days I will see you again unless Davie and I can manage another crafty forty-eight – or even just two hours, en route to some place in England.

Take care of yourself – for me.

Yours, Mark

'Who,' Meg asked of Polly as they sat at the kitchen table, 'is or was Thomasina?'

'Thomasina *Who*?'

'Doubting Thomasina.'

'Ah. Thomas doubted, so now a doubting Thomas is someone who won't believe anything until he can see it or touch it. A Thomasina, I suppose, is the female counterpart.

'Ar.' Now it began to make sense. 'But what did Thomas doubt?'

'He was one of Christ's disciples and couldn't believe in life after death. It wasn't until Jesus appeared to him that he believed. But I won't preach religion to you. Was it Mark, by the way, who called you a doubting Thomasina?'

'Mm. Suppose he knew I didn't expect a letter from him.'

'And you got one. I hope you'll write back – quickly. Does he still love you?'

'He never said . . .'

'Hell! What a waste of a stamp!'

'Not *love* me, exactly. But he wants me, so maybe that's the same thing.'

'But it isn't, Meg. And if I were you, I'd ask him outright: do you love me, or do you merely want to make love to me? There's a difference, you know, and you'll have to hang on to your virginity like mad if you want to get Mark to the altar. I love him to bits, but he just expects the whole lot from a girl, then loses interest.'

'Ye-e-s – but maybe it's just that he doesn't want to say he loves me – not on paper, that is.'

'If he loved you,' Polly said angrily, 'he should be willing to write it on a postcard and put it in Mrs Potter's window for all to see! And you should ask him for a ring!'

'Polly! I *couldn't*! You didn't ask Davie for a ring, did you?'

'No, because he offered one. He loves me and he's in love with me, too!'

'Poll! You haven't? I mean, you said you –'

'Counted to ten? Yes, we both have, scores of times, and as yet we haven't done anything, though it's a miracle we haven't. But I don't mind so much hanging on now, because we'll be married soon.'

'Only if he goes abroad. What are you going to do if he gets a forty-eight-hour pass, and it isn't embarkation leave? Start counting again, will you?'

'I don't know.' Polly lifted the lid of the teapot. 'Want another cup? Think it'll take a drop more hot water.'

'N-no, thanks. Tell me – what will you do? Would you let it happen before you got married, Poll?'

'Sometimes I think I would. When we get ourselves into a twist, I often wish he wouldn't listen to me when I say, 'No, Davie! We mustn't!' I really mean that sometimes.'

'I know what you mean, because Mark wants me. He said so. Next time he's home.' There now! She'd said it!

'So you tell him no way! Not without *at least* an engagement ring! But best of all is that you learn to count to ten, Meg. Pass your mug, will you? Believe me, I know my brother. It's the only way you'll land him. OK?'

'OK. Message received.' Meg pushed her mug across the tabletop. 'And anyway, he'll have gone off me, bet you anything you like, by the time his next long leave comes round.'

'You still want to bet? You lost the last one, don't forget. I've got five bob that says Mark won't have gone off you – OK?'

But Meg shook her head and stirred her tea, staring down at it miserably.

'I'm not betting, Polly, because Mark and me aren't like you and Davie. Mark is way above me and I know that he'll marry – one day – one of his own class. So till that happens there's no way I'll be counting to ten. If it's the only way I can have him, then so what?'

'You mean it, don't you?' Polly gasped.

'I mean it, and there's nothing I can do about it.'

'Well, that's it, then,' Polly said flatly. 'That's the end of the matter!'

'It is!' Meg's cheeks blazed red. 'And can we shurrup about it? I've got work to do!'

'Right! I'll say no more!'

But she would, Polly vowed. Tonight she would write to her brother and ask him what he was doing to Meg and why, for the life of him, did he find it so hard to tell her he loved her? And he wasn't to think she was interfering, but she was as sure as anyone could be that all Meg wanted to hear was that he loved her. And if he didn't, would he stop his messing about with her affections and find some other poor girl to torment – and seduce? Because that, if his past record was anything to go by, Polly was forced to admit, was what he had in mind!

Meg dusted the Candlefold panels in the great hall, reaching up with a feather duster to the high bits, glad it wasn't the week for waxing and polishing them. She ran her hand over the panel to the right of the fireplace; the place where Mark's fingers had pushed and turned, longing for him to be beside her so they could creep into the darkness of the priest's hole again.

She was, she thought, her own worst enemy because last Tuesday night hadn't she stuck her nose in the air and said she'd had enough of the brick house, when she really wanted to stay there all night, had it been possible, and be kissed and kissed till she was dizzy? But it was no use bothering over what might have been, and maybe it was best they had left well alone, because had they stayed there, anything might have happened. And if it had, there would have been no letter from Mark, and Meg Blundell would be just another notch on a bedpost and worrying like mad, now, about the period that was due in three days' time!

She began to sweep the floor, working the bristles of the birch broom into the gaps between the flagstones, trying hard not to think of Mark; wondering why she loved him so much that she was willing to risk getting herself into trouble to prove it.

'You're a fool, girl,' she whispered. 'What are you?' And her conscience told her that for once she'd got it spot on – though wasn't it a pity she had every intention of going on being a fool – as far as Mark was concerned? Half a loaf was better than no bread at all, didn't the saying go? Well, fool that she was she would be glad of *crumbs*!

An engagement ring, Polly? And who do you think you're kiddin', eh? What makes you think that people like your brother give rings to people like me?

She turned to gaze at the secret panel; gazed so hard and with such longing, that if there had been any justice in the world, there'd have been a click and a creak and Mark would have stepped out of it and taken her in his arms and whispered, 'I love you, love you, love you, Meg. Marry me? Tomorrow?'

And wasn't that a purple pig she could see through the open doorway, flyin' past and laughing fit to bust?

Polly thought better of it and did not write angrily to her brother. Instead, she wrote an extra long, extra loving letter to Davie, whom she trusted implicitly and who would never, ever look twice at another woman.

She had paused during the writing, to think of Meg, then less kindly of her brother, whom she was sure was leading her friend up the garden path and would leave her there without a qualm as soon as another took his fancy; would leave Meg, that was, if she were stupid enough to say yes to him instead of no, no, *no*!

But when calmer, she had decided that her brother's wanton ways with women was none of her business, even when he intended having his wanton way with dear, lovely Meg, who would be very unhappy when he abandoned her. Trouble was, she loved her brother too. It was the reason she had decided to let things take their course and not interfere in something both he and Meg seemed to want and were prepared to take – and be damned to the consequences.

She had just finished Davie's letter when Meg called out at the door.

'Meg – come in, love. And no, you're not disturbing me. Just got to write the envelope. Something's bothering you, isn't it?'

' 'Fraid it is. I've never written a letter – not a love letter – before and I'm not sure what to say . . .'

'Say! If you can't think of anything, you fill every line with I love you, I love you, I love you. It's what they want to hear really.'

'N-no. Thing is, Poll, that I'm not very good at spellin' and I wondered if you'd take a look at this and tell me where the mistakes are. Wouldn't want Mark to think I was thick, would I?'

'You aren't thick, Meg – but should I be reading a private letter?'

'Oh, there's nuthin' to make you blush in it. Mark wanted me to tell him everything that's happening here – so he could imagine himself back home, sort of. I've written it in pencil, then when you've had a look at it, I'll put my own private bit at the end, if that's all right with you. Polly? But I want it to be a good letter, because he seemed really cheesed off with Army life. An' will you read it out loud, so I can imagine Mark readin' it?'

'OK, But only if you're sure. And then we'll walk down to the village and post them. That way, they'll make the early collection in the morning and get there half a day sooner. So let's see . . .

'My dear Mark.

'It was lovely to get your letter and I am sorry you feel lonely and fed up. Here's a bit of news that should help cheer you up because you said you wanted to know every little thing about Candlefold that I could think about.

'Well. Candlefold is still here, safe and sound and waiting for your return like it has waited for soldiers to return safely from a lot of wars.

'I didn't read your letter until this afternoon. I sat at my bedroom window and read it and read it. Then I read it again in a whisper, so the room could hear it and down below, in the courtyard, all the people who have walked across it in six hundred years could hear it too. Adding my own little bit of history to Candlefold I suppose I was doing, because it was my very first love letter and I had to tell it to someone, even to the ghosts.

'I went then to the willow pool. I walked under the far archway and past the hens, scratching away, and the kitchen-garden gate. It was golden-sunny, and I could see Mr Potter and Polly working there. And the cows just looked at me, then went on with their chewing as if nothing in particular had happened.

'But when I got to the pool it was very quite. Nothing moved, not even the willow branches. It was as if I was looking at a picture and trying to wish you and me back into it. Not even the water bailif rowed past, and it was all so sad. Polly is sad, too. She misses Davie so much.

'Your mother is well and cheerful as always, and your gran too. I told her you had written to me and that I would send her love to you. As for Nanny – well, she's still queening it in the nursery, though she's having one of her quite moods and has a queer look on her face – stern, sort of. I think it is because she had suddenly realized that the Prince of Wales has gone off with Mrs Simpson!

'Nothing changes here, Mark, but then Candlefold will never change. Think of it when you get fed up and all of us here, wanting you home, and if you sometimes wonder what the heck you are doing in the Army, remember that this old house is worth fighting for, and coming home to, like all the other Kenworthys have come safely home to it.

'But that's a smashing letter, Meg; you've got a lovely way with words. Just add one or two I love yous and an I miss you, and he'll be very pleased to get it.'

'Any spellin's?'

'Yes. You've put quite instead of q-u-i-e-t, and bailiff has two fs, but that's all. And what's with the water bailiff? Some joke between you and Mark?'

'Not a joke, Poll, though if he hadn't rowed past and called to us and waved – well, it was a count-to-ten situation, sort of. I don't know whether I should've been grateful to him or not . . .'

'On the riverbank, Meg, where everyone could see you!' Polly gasped.

'No, just the feller in the boat could see us.'

'I'll ask no more,' Polly grinned. 'None of my business. So write the letter again in ink and finish it with a whole lot of love, then we'll take a walk down to the village. And, Meg – why did you think Nanny was strange? She's always a bit funny – well, *isn't* she?'

'No. Last time I was up there, she was very quiet and a bit snappy – not one bit wide-eyed and gaga like she sometimes is. This mornin', when I took her breakfast, it was as if she was as sane as you and me. I don't trust her, Polly.'

'But she's harmless enough. She's old, and this world frightens her. Be kind to her?'

Kind! Be kind to an old witch who isn't to be trusted, Meg thought. Be kind to someone who goes into wardrobes without permission and who could, if she felt that way, spill the beans to Mrs John just the minute the mood took her?

'Harmless,' Meg echoed, then forced her lips into a smile as she said, 'Won't be long, Poll – writin' the letter, I mean. And I'll put sumthin' loving at the end of it, promise I will!'

This letter comes with my love and to let you know you are never far from my thoughts, it would be, when all the time she longed to write, *I love you, Mark. I love you so much and I want you too, as much as you want me*.

She hoped that when he wrote back he would say that he loved her too. But she knew he wouldn't . . .

Thirteen

'Gran?' Meg pushed open the bedroom door.

'Come in. I'm not asleep . . .'

'Then I can give your room a bit of a clean? And isn't it awful? Raining, I mean!'

'It rains in the country too, and could you give me a hand, Meg? I'm slipping down the bed.'

'Course I can.' She adored Mrs Kenworthy, who was not only nice to her, but was now her more-or-less grandmother. She bent low so the elderly woman could fold an arm round her neck.

'There, now. My arm under your knees, and we'll soon have you comfy.'

'I'm not too heavy? Awkward . . . ?'

'Bless you, no!' She always asked it, Lord love her, and there was nothing of her. 'There now – just lean on my arm whilst I sort your pillows.'

'You are so gentle, Meg. You know I appreciate it.'

'And I,' Meg cupped the pale, thin face in her hands, 'appreciate you bein' my gran. Never had a nan like the other kids did. Mind, I must have had two somewhere – stands to reason, I suppose – but Ma never mentioned them.'

'Did she never talk about her own mother?'

'No. Ma was good at not answering. I gave up in the end and told the kids at school my grandparents had gone down on the *Titanic*. They didn't believe me, but I didn't care. There were quite a few in our school in the same situation, and at least I didn't get free milk and cod liver oil 'cause I was undernourished. I'd have hated that! You could smell the cod liver oil kids, all fishy, and besides, it was charity, and charity was a dirty word in our house. But I'll get on with the dusting whilst we talk. Any news in the paper, Gran?'

'No. I wish I hadn't read it – Russia, I mean. Those Nazis are almost to the outskirts of Leningrad. Once, it was called St Petersburg, and the capital of Russia. The Tsar had his palace there, and a summer palace too, outside the city. I went to Petersburg once, with my parents. We did a Baltic cruise and St Petersburg was such a lovely city, though we were only there for a day. And now Hitler is going to destroy it like he's trying to destroy London.'

'Ma once said she remembered the Tsar and his family gettin' murdered. Ever so dreadful she said it was. Said King George should've sent the Royal Navy in and rescued them, the Tsar being family, sort of.'

'He was cousin to our king – 1917, I'm talking about – but then, most of the crowned heads of Europe were first cousins.'

'So tell me, Gran, what was it like when you were young?' Meg leaned out of the window to shake the duster with a snap. 'What would your folks have thought if the Government said you had to register for war work on your twentieth birthday, and maybe be sent into the forces?'

'Goodness! Women in uniform? There'd have been an uproar! Girls didn't leave home, except as brides.'

'Not even workin'-class girls?'

'Not even – unless it was to go into nursing, or into service. Nursing was a very ladylike profession and warranted leaving home. And if a young girl went into domestic service with a good employer, she was set up for life. A girl who had been trained up from under-housemaid to parlour maid, or one who had started as a kitchenmaid and ended up as cook, were much in demand as wives, you know. Was your mother in service, Meg?'

The question, though innocently asked, almost caught Meg off guard, and she was forced to be extra careful with the china ornament she dusted to give herself time to think.

'I told you, Gran. She worked in a tobacco factory in Liverpool.' She let go a little breath of gratitude for a good memory, which was one thing liars should always have.

'Of course. Did you like Polly's wedding dress?

'Oh, *yes*. Ever so romantic.'

'I thought she looked beautiful. Brought quite a lump to my throat – the way the years have slipped away. Mary is going to get out the veil she and I wore. Last time we checked, it was fine – Brussels lace, you know. All the Kenworthy brides have worn it since Queen Victoria's time, and the beauty of it is that it isn't too long to be a nuisance. After all, Polly will have a train to contend with, too.'

'It's all lovely, isn't it, Gran? Weddings are, oh, so *romantic*, especially in wartime. Can't wait for Polly and Davie to get themselves to church!'

'And you, Meg – wouldn't you like to get married?'

'Yes, I would – but only when the right man asks me,' she added hastily, blinking the stars out of her eyes. 'And if you're sure there's nothin' else you want, I'd better be off. It'll soon be time for elevenses, so I'll bring yours up.'

She gathered up mop and dusters, eager to be away from questions she dare not answer, making for the door.

'Meg, dear – before you go and whilst I remember – something I was keeping for Polly. Would you get it for me, please? In the top left-hand drawer of the chest, beneath my handkerchiefs. Vinolia soap. Got it long before soap was rationed . . .'

'Ooooh.' The soap was wrapped in lavender-coloured paper, its scent heavy and delicious. 'It smells lovely! There's no scented soap in the shops now – not for love nor money, there isn't!'

'Then it'll be something nice for her honeymoon. I'll give it to her later. Not a word, mind . . .'

'Not a word. And there's Nanny's bell! I'd better pop up and see what she wants.' Smiling, she closed the door then let go a huff of annoyance.

'What is it, Nanny?' Meg asked from the nursery doorway.

'My word! You were quick!'

'I was in Gran's room. Is there something you want?'

'*Gran's* room? You mean Mrs Kenworthy's room! Don't you know that it's rude and common to be so forward!'

'Yes, I do, but Mrs Kenworthy asked me to, see? Might as well have two granddaughters as one, she said. So you can stop telling me what I can and can't do! I know my place in this house!'

'Do you? Your position, Blundell, is that of a servant, and don't think you can ever rise above it! I had my doubts about you the minute you set foot in this room, and nothing has happened to change that opinion! And I'm warning you – stop getting ideas above your station or you'll end up like – like –'

'Like what – or who?' Meg flung, red-cheeked.

'Like most girls who get big ideas – *in trouble*! Oh, I know what you're up to! You're after Mark – as if he'd ever marry the likes of you! Just who do you think you are?'

'I know who I am, Nanny!' Dear heaven, if only she did!

'Yes, and so do I! You're a scheming little hussy who wants taking down a peg! Mark Kenworthy isn't for the likes of you! Mark is doing what most young men in his walk of life do: he's sowing his wild oats! Then he'll settle down with one of his own class and forget you ever existed! Now be off with you, and don't say you haven't been warned!'

'Very well, Nanny.' She said it softly, Ma's way; did it when for two pins she'd have used the rough side of her tongue, Tippet's Yard fashion, an' all! 'And I'll take this, if you don't mind!'

Chin set at defiance, she picked up the little brass bell, putting it in her pinafore pocket.

'Give it back! Give it back *at once*. It's *my* bell! How dare you?'

'Oh, I *do* dare, and what's more, if you want it you'll have to come downstairs to get it!'

She stood, eyes closed, at the top of the staircase, taking deep, calming breaths, letting them go in little puffs, all the while telling herself that Nanny Boag couldn't hurt her if she kept her temper, refused to be goaded by taunts. She had known there would be hints and digs, and hadn't she decided that digs and hints would be as far as it went because what that old woman knew, she must keep to herself.

'She *can't* hurt me,' she whispered in a voice so like Ma's that all at once the anger left her and the shaking inside her stopped. And she knew that as long as she kept her head, it was Meg Blundell who held all the aces; not the bitter old woman in the nursery upstairs.

She paused at the foot of the stone stairs, taking the bell from her pocket, placing it on the chest that stood beside the staircase archway. Then she lifted her chin, straightened her shoulders and pushed open the kitchen door.

'What did Nanny say when you took her bell back?' Meg asked of Polly as they drank elevenses.

'Nothing at all, except she hadn't noticed it was gone. Why do you ask, Meg?'

'Dunno! Thought maybe she'd have decided I took it on purpose.' Slyness with slyness!

'Well, she didn't, and before I forget, how about us going into town tonight? It's *Target for Tonight* at the flicks – everybody's talking about it. If we shift ourselves, we can be there for first house.'

'Not tonight. It's Tuesday.'

'So it is. The saving-coupons class at Mrs Potter's. Mummy enjoys it – not the make-and-mend bit so much as the company. And it gives her a break from the house. Gran has given her a crochet shawl she doesn't like the colour of, so it'll be interesting to see how many ounces of wool she gets out of it – and what she knits with it. Somehow, I can't see Mummy wearing bright red!'

'Me neither. She'll probably give it to you.'

'Mm. I'll have to wind the wool into skeins round a thick book, then tie it and wash it carefully so it doesn't get in a tangle. Amazing, isn't it, the trouble you've got to go to these days, to save a few clothing coupons?'

'Common sense, though – every little helps. And if there isn't enough for a jumper, you can always knit a scarf and gloves for the winter. So shall we try to make it to the pictures tomorrow night – if your ma can spare the two of us at the same time?'

'I'm sure she will if we get the supper cleared away early. I heard that the film was shot on an actual raid over Germany with the real crew members – not actors. I'm glad Davie isn't flying. At least I don't have to worry too much at the moment, though it's only a question of time till the two of them get overseas postings. Just as long as they don't get sent to Russia – now that we're all at once friends with the Communists.'

'They won't be. We need all our troops to look after this country and Egypt and Malta. I think the help Mr Churchill was talking about was sending tanks and things by sea.'

'Hope you're right. Well – suppose I'd better get back to the garden or Mr Potter'll be looking at his watch very meaningfully. Did I tell you – we've started on the rasps? With a bit of luck it'll be raspberries and cream for Sunday pudding. By the way – was there a letter?'

'From Mark? Course not! He'll probably not have got mine yet. We aren't like you and Davie!'

Yet she wished they were, she yearned. Wouldn't she give anything, anything at all, to be like those two?

They were sitting on cushions on the front steps, enjoying the evening sun, which was still warm, Polly with a writing pad on her lap; Meg knitting laboriously, wishing she hadn't opted for two-ply wool.

'This is so fine,' she grumbled. 'Like knitting with cobwebs. Doesn't half need a lot of stitches. I'll never get it finished!'

'Well, it's the best way. Knit a jumper in three-ply and it'll take four coupons for the wool; knit it in two-ply and it goes so much further it only uses two coupons. On the other hand, you can save yourself the trouble and buy one in the shops and you'll part with *seven* coupons!'

'I know, but if I get this thing finished by Christmas, I'll be lucky!'

'But it's such a beautiful blue, Meg – matches your eyes. And you'll have saved enough coupons, don't forget, for two pairs of silk stockings.'

Few wore stockings now, in summer, and many of the young ones declared their intention to rub their legs with gravy-browning, come winter. After all, a careless snag and *ping!* – a ladder from top to toe and one clothing coupon wasted. All the women's magazines enthused about gravy-browning, which, when applied carefully and evenly, they said, looked exactly like American Tan, the most popular stocking shade.

'I'll have better things to do with my coupons than buy stockings. An' that's something we'll have to remember, Poll – to get a stock of gravy-browning in, 'cause everybody'll be after it – there'll be none left!' Neither for legs nor for gravy; something else that would very soon be going under the counter. 'And what's your ma doin' home so early?'

But Polly only shrugged and said she didn't have a clue, but they'd doubtless soon find out. Then they saw the expression on Mary Kenworthy's face, and knew something was very wrong.

'What is it?' Polly ran across the courtyard. 'Not bad news?'

'I'm afraid it is. Luckily she hadn't got there – Mrs Keating, I mean. Mrs Potter was putting the kettle on when the phone rang – the post office phone. At first she took no notice. "Let it ring. Do they think I'm on duty twenty-four hours a day?" she said. But it went on ringing, so she went through to answer it.'

'And it was bad news for the Keatings?'

'A telegram, phoned through. Mrs Potter said we'd best all of us go home and she would deliver the awful thing. No one wanted to stay, so I said I'd go with her – she shouldn't have to do things like that – but she said she would manage; that it was much worse for Emmie Keating than for her. And I know what it's like. It happened to me – one of those yellow envelopes just three months before the end of the Great War – your father wounded.'

'And Bill is their only child. How bad is it, Mummy?'

'Missing at sea, believed killed in action.' She sat down wearily at the kitchen table, fighting tears, telling herself that the telegram might have been delivered to Candlefold. 'Oh, damn this war!'

'Did it say if there was any hope?' Meg whispered.

'No. Just the bald news and that no information was to be given to the press – and that a letter followed.'

'Dear God! The press, indeed! As if the Keatings are going to want to shout it out from the rooftop! They won't want to speak to anyone about it, and surely the press wouldn't be so cruel as to go knocking on their door – not our local paper?'

'I don't think they will, Polly. Newspapers know they shouldn't ask. It's to do with security, I think. Bill was on a destroyer and though she couldn't be sure, Mrs Potter thought his ship was escorting a convoy to Archangel – that's Russia. Mention in the local paper that his ship was in action – maybe lost – would let the Germans know their submarines were doing a good job in the Arctic. And what can one say? What words are there, to give comfort? Wars are – are *obscene*!'

'I know, darling. I know,' Polly whispered. 'I should feel guilty that Davie is safe, yet all I can feel is relief that he's not in danger – Mark, too.' Her eyes filled with tears, her cheeks flushed angrily. 'Oh, I wish Hitler was dead! I wish he'd been killed in Daddy's war! I wish he'd never been born and I hope he dies horribly! And I don't feel one bit wicked, saying that!'

'No. Not about someone as evil as Hitler. And we'll remember the Keatings in our prayers tonight – that their boy is alive, still . . .'

* * *

Mrs Potter, who usually made her delivery with a cheerful, 'Morning, each!' left the morning paper and three letters at Candlefold's open door with never a word.

'Poor love. Bet she feels awful,' Polly whispered, 'having to deliver that telegram. This war is horrible. The only good thing I can say about it is that I met Davie.'

'You'd have met him, anyway, one way or the other – Book of Life, don't forget. Now, who's them letters for?'

Not one for her, Meg knew it. Even if Mark had replied the minute he got hers, today wasn't the day for letters. Mark wasn't like Davie, wouldn't pour out his love each day. Mark had written, Meg realised, to lay claim to her. Love just didn't come into it. And that letter, and what he had said in it, would suffice – according to Mark's way of thinking. *I want you. You are mine!* Straight and to the point and downright arrogant, if she dare admit to the truth. But arrogant or not, she wanted him and loved him as well, so there was no changing it.

But wouldn't it have been marvellous if there had been one for her, this morning? And wouldn't it have been mind-blowing and unbelievably out of this world, if it had only consisted of a few lines.

I miss you. Meg. I think of you and dream of you and I want you desperately. How much I love you you'll never believe.

That was all she wanted to read, and that he was safe and well. For those three small words he could have her, body and soul; could have her, come to think of it, whether he said them or not!

And Meg Blundell was a fool – but so what?

Picking raspberries allowed time for thought, especially since Polly was at one end of the long row, and Meg was at the other, and chattering and time-wasting impossible. Mr Potter was nobody's fool, telling them that one was to pick one side of the bushes – canes, he called them – and Polly the other, and that Polly should start at the bottom end and Meg at the top, so that only when they met, mid-ways on, could they whisper and talk.

So Meg picked and thought about Mark, and about the letters she would like to get from him every day of the week, except Sunday, and what he would say in them and how often he'd say he loved her. And then she daydreamed about Mark turning up completely unexpected –

just as he and Davie had done when they had been going south to pick up a convoy of lorries, and made a sneaky detour.

How would it be, next time? Where would she be? What would she be wearing and would her hair be freshly washed, and shining? Would they walk, arms linked, thighs touching, to the cow pasture gate and would he demand a kiss before helping her over? And would they go to the willow pool and undress slowly then slide, clinging tightly, into the water . . . ?

No! For one thing that pool was cold, even in summer, and would soon clear all thoughts of you know what out of their heads. And for another, she thought, laughing at her own stupidity, things like that didn't happen to people like Meg Blundell, who didn't believe in miracles.

So shove another rasp in yer gob, girl, and get on with the pickin'!

'What's so funny, will you tell me?' Polly demanded, peering through the canes in the middle of the row.

'I couldn't tell you, Poll. You're much too young!'

'I'm not! I'm older than you, if you want to be picky.'

'By one day! Anyway, I suppose you do it, an' all – invent lovely things between you and Davie – daydreamin', sort of.'

'I do it all the time, only they aren't always lovely. Most times they are passionate, very shocking and toe-curlingly sexual, if you want to know!'

'So join the club,' Meg grinned in passing. 'Reckon it'll soon be time for the tea-bell. See you at three.'

And oh, she thought as she wished herself back to a seductively warm willow pool, wasn't life good? Just what had Meg Blundell done to deserve such contentment, and a billet at Candlefold into the bargain? What had been written in her Book of Life to cause such giddy happiness?

Oh, ar, what the heck! Have another raspberry, girl, and count your blessings!

They sat in the one-and-sixpenny seats in the picture house, not really interested in the adverts; wishing instead that things could be as they once were when usherettes walked up and down during the interval, carrying lit-up trays of ice cream in tubs and packets of sweets, and chocolate bars and bags of nuts, and soft drinks. Now, most of those usherettes had gone to war and the wonderful things they once sold were no longer available. Most of them needed sugar, which was severely rationed, and besides, all of them had needed packaging, and paper was in short supply too.

The lights dimmed, the beam of light from the projection room at the back of the cinema whitened the screen and cut through swirls of cigarette smoke that rolled blue-grey beneath the vaulted ceiling.

'It's the news!'

To everyone, the newsreels shown at cinemas – even though heavily censored and almost always a week out of date because of national security – were of utmost importance and vividly alive after the unemotional voice required of a wireless newsreader. For each piece of awful news came several pictures of servicemen and women, smiling, giving the thumbs-up sign so that Hitler should know that the British weren't beaten yet.

That night, after the announcement of the mauling of yet another convoy of ships trying to reach Malta, came something entirely different to lift hearts and minds and to remind that V stood for Victory; that henceforth it would be pinged out over airwaves so people in occupied Europe should hear it, and take heart: Dit dit dit dah. Boo boo boo boom. And not only would it be heard everywhere, but the letter V would appear everywhere too – especially in countries overrun by Hitler's armies. V would be secretly scrawled on walls and windows; any and every place for the Nazis to see until they hated the sight and sound of it! The V-sign, from this time on, would be paramount. V was for nothing less than total victory!

'An' who thought that one up?' Meg whispered as the image of Winston Churchill, one hand making the Victory-sign with his first and second fingers, the other holding a cigar, and heaven only knew how he managed to get so many when most folk were hard put to it to get the odd ciggy!

'Haven't a clue. Some of the Government's back-room boys, I suppose. It's a good idea, though.' Polly smiled as the sound of the Royal Air Force march past filled the cinema with blasts of triumph, and searchlights swept the screen to meet and touch and herald the start of *Target for Tonight*.

Bottoms shuffled on seats, lovers clasped hands and arms stole round seat backs in the intimate darkness. Meg and Polly sat, ankles crossed, hands primly folded, gazing at the screen. The Wellington bomber *F-Freddie* was preparing for take-off from an aerodrome Somewhere in England, though everyone knew it was based in Suffolk. And after tonight's showing, Polly thought, young men would volunteer to fly just such another bomber. The film had been a dangerous one to make, but it was the best recruiting job she had ever seen. Well, thank everything holy that Davie drove lorries and repaired them, and nothing more dangerous than that. The Brylcreem Boys were tops for glamour, but give her a soldier in the Royal Army Service Corps, whose hands got so dirty, sometimes, that nothing would shift the grease and grime completely! And oh, how she loved him and missed him and wanted him beside her now, his hand holding hers, thighs and knees touching, and a kiss only the bending of his head away.

But that was war for you, and few of the armed forces could hold a candle to RAF aircrews and fighter pilots when it came to glamour – or to losses in action. Unless it was the Royal Navy, she was forced to admit, who fought so desperately to get convoys to Malta – and now to Archangel.

A tear of pride trickled down her nose and plopped onto her bottom lip; a tear, too, of loneliness and of need. She closed her eyes tightly, grateful that Davie was not flying on a raid over Germany, nor at sea being stalked by U-boats. She sniffed into her handkerchief and thought instead about Sunday, and the second reading of their banns, then gave her entire attention to the crew of *F-Freddie*.

It was still light when they stood in the queue for the Nether Barton bus; would be light, even, when they got home. Blackout tonight was not until 10.57, or 22.57 hours, as people now called it. And even after curtains were drawn and outside lights doused, the July twilight would linger until almost midnight, to gentle sharp outlines and mist over trees and hedges. In summer there was hardly any blackout at all, which made up for the drear months of winter, when darkness was official at four in the afternoon, and lasted for sixteen hours.

'Did you like the flick?' Polly asked.

'Mm. But that newsreel was an eye-opener all right! Who'd have thought them Germans would bomb Moscow?'

It was as if, Meg brooded, Hitler had bombers and to spare, because he hadn't let up on London, though Liverpool had been left alone since May.

'I said,' Meg hissed, 'that even Moscow is copping it now.'

'Y-yes. Sorry. Miles away . . .'

'With Davie.'

'No. As a matter of fact I was thinking about Bill Keating, and being glad, I suppose, that Davie isn't in the Navy. And what's the matter with me? Why am I so weepy?'

Which prompted Meg to look in front and behind her, then lean close to whisper, 'Time of the month, love. It happens to us all – thank heaven!'

Which profound remark made her think of Mark Kenworthy, though for the life of her, she didn't know why.

Sunday morning. Eucharist at eleven and the second reading of the banns of marriage between David Sumner, bachelor, and Mary Eleanor Kenworthy, spinster of this parish.

Sounded strange, Meg thought; almost as strange as sitting here, trying to look as if she went to church every Sunday, keeping one eye on Polly, so she wasn't left standing up when everybody else was kneeling and the other way round!

But the singing, she had to admit, was nice, with 'Onward Christian Soldiers' remembered from her schooldays to make her feel more at home in these unfamiliar, uncomfortable surroundings. And, fair play, she sighed, it was all worth it just to see the lit-up expression on Polly's face and the look of love that changed her from pretty into absolutely beautiful.

'One more to go,' Hugh Rushton beamed as he shook hands at the church porch, 'and then we won't need a special licence.' The Reverend did not entirely agree with the quickly got licences for hasty marriages, even though the Bishop granted them.

'Just one,' Polly beamed. 'And this is Meg.'

'I'm so glad you have come.' The vicar took Meg's hand firmly. 'I've been hoping you would.'

'Ar. We-e-ll – it was really to hear Polly's callin'.' She had to be fair. 'I don't have religion, see? Was brought up more on the Book of Life, though I enjoyed the singin'. Maybe I'll come again,' she smiled, though not just yet, of course. One laddered silk stocking – it was the hassocks that did it! – was enough to be going on with, because you simply couldn't go into church, Polly had said, bare-headed nor bare-legged either!

'I felt very sad,' Polly said softly as they climbed the stile, 'when the vicar asked prayers for Bill Keating, and his poor mother kneeling there. I just hope it was God's day for listening to prayers from Nether Barton.'

'So you really believe in all that stuff – miracles? 'Cause it'll be a miracle if anyone survives for long in them seas; even in summer it's cold up the north of Russia.' She knew that as fact – hadn't Kip told her so?

'All right – so we were asking for a miracle! Maybe it's God's day for dispensing miracles too. You can only try, Meg. Do you think you might go to church again, now you've broken your duck, sort of?'

'No, Poll. It isn't for me, all that bowing and scraping. If it's for you you'll get it, and any punishments due, an' all – that's the way I see things. But I hope Bill makes it. Liverpool's a port, see, an' we care a lot about sailors and seamen.'

'Of course – Kip. Are you still writing to him – well, in view of the fact that you're in love with Mark, I mean?'

'Course I'm writin'. Why shouldn't I? Kip's a good friend, and anyway, it's our duty to write to men away from home. We don't have to be in love with them!'

'Of course not,' Polly sounded convinced. 'I wonder why Mark has only sent the one letter. Perhaps it's because he's away on manoeuvres.'

'Is Davie manoeuvring?'

'Er – no.'

'Then why should Mark be? Don't make excuses for him, Polly. Your brother isn't the best of letter writers, and let's leave it at that!'

Meg refused, absolutely refused, even to consider that Mark's passion was cooling and that already he was out on the town again – with ATS girls who looked just gorgeous in their uniforms.

'Mm. He doesn't write a lot. Even Mummy considers herself lucky to get one a week.'

'Polly! I'm not Mark's *mother!* I'm the girl he says he wants; the stupid ha'porth who'll *give* him what he wants, whether he loves her or not! So let's drop it, shall we?'

'Dropped, soon as asked! And oh, I feel quite bereft – of letters, I mean. Sunday is a sod, isn't it – no deliveries? Ah, well – maybe two tomorrow!'

She waved, smiling, to her mother who sat on the wide worn steps, cutting beans and squinting into the sun. And Meg waved too, because she was a part of it; a part of Candlefold, and everything lovely that went with it. Yet what would happen, she thought, frowning at the pump trough, if Mark went off her and she became an embarrassment? What if Mark went the whole hog, and brought some other girl home to meet his mother? How would she bear it? How could she stay another day at Candlefold?

It was exactly then that a voice inside her head – a voice very like Ma's – seemed to whisper, *The Book of Life, remember? What is to be, will be. Live for today and leave tomorrow to the pages of The Book . . .*

'Hello, Mrs John.' She smiled down. 'I enjoyed church – the singing was lovely, and hearing Polly's banns called, though Mary Eleanor didn't seem like her. Want anythin' doing? I felt guilty going off and leaving everything to you.'

'You didn't go off! You went because of *The Banns*! Polly was prepared to drag you there to hear them, so don't feel guilty. And would you do two things for me? Can you first answer Nanny – she's been ringing for ages – and then could you scrape the potatoes? And after that, will you tell me just what I'd do without you, Meg?'

Oh, my! For praise like that, Meg though warmly, she would answer Nanny's aggravating little bell every hour on the hour! And if tomorrow there was a letter from Mark, she would just burst with happiness and go spinning off like a rocket, never to be seen again!

The very next Sunday – the 27th – and the day that followed were to be very special, had they known it; two golden days for ringing round on calendars. It had started at 10.45 in the morning when Polly

Kenworthy was putting on her hat, frowning with concentration into the hall mirror.

'Wouldn't you know it, I'm going to be late! And I've lost a glove!'

'Have you, now?' Two arms wrapped her waist; behind her in the mirror was Davie, face alight with pleasure, kissing the back of her neck.

'Davie! What, just *what* are you doing here! Not bad news?'

'Only if I'm caught!' He turned her to face him and kissed her. 'I've gone AWOL. Just had to hear the third calling. Mark's covering for me.'

'Ooh! Kiss me again, then we'll have to run. We're late.'

'I know. I passed your mother in the lane. I love you, by the way.'

'I love you too – but absent without leave – isn't that serious?'

'Not unless some bod asks for me by name or in person. I'm duty officer this morning in the workshop, so Mark is covering for me. Then he'll do his own stint, too. He says if I'm not back in camp by six, then I *am* in trouble!'

'And will you be – back, I mean?' Polly took his hand as she climbed the stile. 'Will you be able to hitch a lift?'

'Course I will. It'll be all right!'

'I can't believe it! I've wanted you there so much and now you're here! And Davie! What are you going to tell people when they ask if you're on leave?'

'The truth – that I've gone AWOL for a couple of hours to hear my banns read with my girl.'

'Darling, I *adore* you! Now, *run* . . .'

Morning service had begun when they crept into the back of the church. The lifting of the iron door sneck had sounded like a pistol shot and all had turned to see their arrival. From the front pew, Mary Kenworthy smiled and Polly smiled back radiantly, then gave her attention to the singing of the first hymn, 'Eternal Father, strong to save' – a prayer and a hymn in one, for sailors everywhere. Polly's eyes searched the pews for Emmie Keating, seeing a head held high and shoulders unnaturally straight, and sent a warm wave of love and hope, and when it was time for prayers, she vowed she would pray extra hard for the sailor believed dead. If only to atone for her radiant, pulsating happiness she would do it, then beg that Davie's parents might never get that small, yellow envelope.

She stepped to her left so they might briefly touch, then sang the remaining verses with tear-filled eyes, knowing those tears were part pity, part gratitude because Davie was beside her.

Then, when Confession had been whispered and Absolution given and the Collect read and the Gospel and the Creed chanted, The Reverend Hugh Rushton slowly mounted the pulpit steps to say, 'I publish the Banns of Marriage between David Sumner, bachelor, of the Parish of St Mary, Litchby and Mary Eleanor Kenworthy, spinster of this parish.'

He paused to peer meaningfully over the tops of his spectacles to the latecomers in the back pew.

'If any of you know cause or just impediment why these two persons should not be joined together in holy Matrimony, you are to declare it. This is the third time of asking . . .'

There was the slightest pause, a shuffling of feet, then the congregation turned, smiling briefly, to let them know they had no objections at all to the two of them being wed in this very church as soon as the war allowed, and a pink-cheeked Polly linked her little finger with Davie's and felt so happy that she wanted the moment to last for a very long time.

And then she thought about Bill Keating, whose banns would never be read in this church, and wanted to weep because she was so very lucky and because she could not help but wonder just how long that luck could last.

Davie said he might as well be hanged for a sheep, and why not stay for a bite of lunch, if it would run to it, and he and Polly took trays upstairs to say a quick hello and so long, then sat side by side at the big old table, looking so right together and so thankful for the few stolen hours that it made Meg feel happy and sad at one and the same time. Happy for Polly and Davie, sad that her own banns would never be read from All Saints' pulpit; not in a million years they wouldn't, though dreams cost nothing.

Then Polly said she was going as far as the main road with Davie, and would Meg mind? And Meg said of course she wouldn't, and be off, the pair of them, or Davie would land up in trouble. And to give her best regards to Mark when he saw him, if he would be so kind?

It was almost four when Polly returned, bright-eyed and pink-cheeked, to demand of them all if they had ever known such a lovely third-reading of anybody's banns, and had Davie really been beside her in church, and wasn't she the lucky one?

'Luck aside, Polly – is Davie going to make it back to camp all right?'

'I think so, Mummy. We waited for about twenty minutes. There was nothing on the road at all and I started to get a bit worried. And then an RAF lorry stopped. A Waaf was driving it and she said, "Where to, sir?" and Davie said he was aiming at somewhere near Catterick Camp. And, would you believe it, she said she was going to Leeming, which is most of the way there! She was such a pretty girl and it was so sad; she wore a wedding ring. I wonder where her husband is now. Davie kissed me goodbye and she looked so – well, not sad, exactly – more, perhaps, wishing it could be her. I said, "Thanks a lot," to her and she just winked and held up her hand. Aren't people good, and hasn't today been wonderful – thanks to Mark?'

And her mother said yes, hadn't it and wasn't Polly the lucky one to have such an understanding brother and you never knew the day, did you, when something special was going to happen, and could she have a volunteer, please, to make cucumber sandwiches for afternoon tea? And there was such contentment in Candlefold kitchen that not one of them gave a thought to tomorrow, and what was to come.

It had the makings of an ordinary Monday morning, if you could call a sunny Candlefold morning ordinary, Meg was to think afterwards. Better to say it was a bright, bird-songed morning, with Polly gone off to the village to post the gloves Davie had left on the chest in the hall and she, Meg, popping off to the garden to tell Mr Potter Polly would be a couple of minutes late and could Mrs John have a couple of cabbages, please?

Then collecting breakfast trays and stacking plates and cups and saucers ready for washing; waiting for the kettle to boil. An ordinary enough morning, until Polly had come bumping across the cobbles on her bicycle, bell ringing, cheeks flushed.

'You're never going to believe it; not in a month of Sundays are you!' Her breath came in gasps, and she held on to the back of a chair, gulping in air, blowing it out again, cheeks puffing.

'Believe what? Somebody killed Hitler, then?'

'No, Meg. And where's Mummy? Go and get her,' she gasped. 'She's got to hear this, too!'

The pantry door banged and a voice said, 'She's here and why are you in such a state?'

'Because – because . . .' Polly sat down, shoulders still heaving. 'And let me get my breath back before I tell it, because you'll never believe it!'

'Ar. You said,' Meg remarked. 'So what is it we won't believe?'

'You want it from the beginning or straight to the point?'

'I think, child, it had better be from the beginning – draw it out a bit, because it's something worth the telling, isn't it?'

'It is, and you'll never believe one word of it!'

'For the third time, we will – if only you'd tell us,' Meg urged.

'OK – well – I was going to the post office –'

'With Davie's gloves.'

'Yes, Meg, but let me tell it? Well, Mrs Potter had weighed them and just stuck on the stamps when the phone went. The post office phone, I mean.'

'Ye-e-s . . .' Mary Kenworthy was becoming impatient.

'So Mrs P. gave it one of her I'm-seeing-to-a-customer looks and let it go on ringing for ages and ages – well, for at least half a minute – then picked it up and said, "Yes?" quite snappily.

'Then her eyes opened wide and after a while she said, "Would you mind repeating the name and address, please? Just to be sure." And then she said, "Thank you very much, my dear," and got a form out and wrote on it without saying so much as a word to me. So I had to ask what it was and she said, "You'll see," then pushed it under the grille and told me to read it!'

'And what was it?' Meg hissed. 'Just *say* it!'

'It said, *Keating, Smithy Cottage, Main Street, Nether Barton. The Admiralty is now able to inform you that D/WRX 805 Seaman Keating W. has been admitted to hospital with wounds sustained in action. Condition satisfactory. Address HMS St Angelo, c/o GPO London. Letter follows in due course.* That's exactly what it said! I remember every word!'

'And . . . ?'

'And then Mrs Potter said, "Come you behind this counter, Polly my girl. You'm in charge of this post office till I've been to Smithy Cottage! And if anybody comes in, tell them the postmistress is on urgent business and tell them to wait. And if they don't like it, ask them if they've forgotten there's a war on!'

'And with that she was off – no hat, not even taking off her pinny. I've never seen anyone move so fast! I called after her could I tell anyone who came in and did she know where HMS *St Angelo* was, and she said be buggered if she knew, but of course I could tell people – the more the merrier! Oh, it was so lovely being almost the first to know!

'And then the vicar came in for six stamps and would you believe it – he knew where *St Angelo* is because of his brother once being with the Mediterranean Fleet. It's Malta, and HMS *St Angelo* isn't a ship, but the naval HQ there. Bill Keating is in hospital in Malta. He must have been in that last convoy that took such a lot of flack. And we all thought he was on the Russian convoys!'

And because she was Polly, her eyes filled with tears and she began to cry softly, and Meg reached out and hugged her and said, 'Oh, be buggered to rationing! Let's splash out on a cup of tea to celebrate!' because if Mrs Potter could say it and Polly could say it in Candlefold kitchen and get away with it, then be buggered if Meg Blundell couldn't say it an' all!

And Mrs John said why not indeed and what a pity they didn't have a snifter of Scotch to put in it too! And to get the kettle on, if they pleased, whilst she went upstairs to tell Mother-in-law and Nanny!

There were days you never forgot, Meg thought that night as she sat at the open window waiting for Polly to bring mugs of Ovaltine, watching the high-swooping swallows, listening to the singing of a blackbird. Days that were magic and precious and had to be stored away and taken out and lived again when times were bad. And yesterday and today were magic, storing-away days.

'*Ma. If only you knew how happy I am!*'

But Ma had known all along, hadn't she, that happiness was Candlefold and now her daughter knew it too.

She crossed to open the door which Polly had kicked with her toe, and sighed, 'Oh, Poll, isn't life good?'

And Polly replied dreamily that it was, and weren't they the lucky ones?

1/2

Fourteen

Instead of thrusting the blue airmail envelope through the front door letter box and bringing the knocker smartly down, Mrs Potter called at Smithy Cottage back door instead, and with a beaming smile offered the censored letter which bore no postmark.

'Could be from your Bill, though it's not his writing.' Mrs Potter recognized the handwriting of all her regulars and stood there, waiting for news to be passed round Nether Barton – and Upper Barton too, if it was good enough for the telling.

'It *is* from our Bill, though it seems someone else has written it. Yes! *My nurse is writing this for me as my right arm copped some shrapnel and is in a sling at the moment* – that's what it says,' Emmie Keating beamed, cheeks pink with pleasure. 'He's well and has a good billet ashore on a very little island and not in any danger. And how he can say that I don't know, with Malta getting more bombs than London, if the papers are to be believed. The nurse has underlined very. I wonder why.'

'Think I'll have a word at the vicarage. The Reverend might be able to help,' Mrs Potter nodded. 'And I'm pleased your lad'll be out of the fighting for a while, Emmie.'

Mrs Keating retired to her kitchen rocker to read the letter again, and Mrs Potter headed for the vicarage, even though it should have been her last delivery, apart from Candlefold.

'Would you say, Vicar, there was anything to be gained by saying Bill was on a *very* small island and not in any danger. I mean – we all know how little Malta is, don't we?'

'Ah, yes. But according to my brother, there are three islands in that area. Malta – the biggest – and Gozo, and another very, very small one. So a *very* little island could be his way of telling his parents without naming names for the censors to cut out. And I don't think Gozo is getting as much attention from the bombers either. A better place for a hospital, I would say. Mind, it's only a guess.'

A guess was enough for the postmistress, who hurried back to Smithy Cottage with the news that Bill was as safe as houses on an island called Gozo, but not to say a word about it as even the walls around Nether Barton had ears!

She arrived at Candlefold half an hour late, but expected to be forgiven since she'd had to deliver Emmie Keating's good news with every letter and newspaper. And Mary Kenworthy was delighted to hear it and didn't mind at all about the lateness.

'One for me, one for Miss Polly Kenworthy and *two* for Miss M. M. Blundell!' she called over her shoulder. 'And Mrs P. says there has been a letter from Bill Keating and he's fine!'

'Which only goes to show,' said Polly smugly, 'that the White Rabbits thing works!' You had to, she told Meg most earnestly, say 'White Rabbits' on the first morning of a new month, crossing your fingers, closing your eyes, and wishing. 'And I'll bet you anything you wished for one from Mark, and it's come!'

'Yes, but only a postcard,' Meg whispered, turning it over. 'A view of Salisbury Cathedral. The letter is from Kip.'

'Makes sense. We knew Mark and Davie were going down south for a week. What does he say?'

'*M. See you soon, M.* That's all.'

'So don't look so down in the mouth. My brother isn't one to waste words. See you soon, he said. Maybe they'll call in on the way back to Catterick. Mark is full of tricks like that. Bet you anything you like they'll do another detour. You agree with me, Mummy?'

And Mary Kenworthy said, 'Yes, dear,' without taking her head from the morning paper.

'I'll read the letter later.' Meg stuffed the envelope into her pocket, wishing it could have been from Mark, who didn't love her, instead of from Kip, who did. 'Gran said she would like a few minutes at the window. Care to give me a hand, Poll?'

And Polly said yes, of course she would, provided it didn't take more than five minutes, since the Preston van was calling for the vegetables early, and she didn't want a look from Mr Potter, even though it was his wife's fault the late mail had thrown them all out of kilter. 'We'll tell Gran and Nanny about the letter from Bill,' she called to her mother, who smiled without taking her attention from the morning paper, thanking heaven there was a shortage of newsprint, which meant, indirectly, that there was less room for bad news. And the news *was* bad: Nazi armies pushing deeper into Russia with a hundred thousand of their soldiers killed, which she couldn't be glad about because they all had mothers, she reasoned, and there would be a hundred thousand telegrams to German mothers. So senseless, all the taking of young lives.

And Mr Roosevelt was going to get his fingers burned, she sighed, affection for him washing her warmly. Now warships of the United States Navy were joining with Canadian ships, sailing out from Iceland, to give protection to convoys heading to and from Britain. Just one incident and America could be in the war, whether they wanted it or not. Which wouldn't be a bad thing for our side, she pondered, but did American mothers want their sons at war again, little more than twenty years after the last one?

Mind, somewhere amongst all the miserable news was a blessing to be counted. She searched for it every day, and almost always found something to be glad about. And today's gladness was that shipping losses in the Atlantic had actually dropped for the first time since war began.

She smiled, straightened her shoulders and decided to make wartime jam. Only one jar, of course, and with the last of the raspberries she had managed to coax out of Potter – just half a pound. But it would be a birthday treat, and only took half a pound of sugar – which she could just afford from her precious hoard. And when Meg had finished upstairs, she would show her how to make economy jam which would keep for a month in a cold pantry – if allowed to do so, that was!

She turned on the wireless for a programme of light music and counted her blessings as she always did at the beginning of each day. It helped her to survive – and was a patriotic thing to do.

So, blessing number one: Bill Keating was safe in hospital when only ten days ago he had been believed killed in action. Blessing number two: letters from Candlefold's soldiers and home-made jam for the birthday girls.

She did not allow herself to think that this month both Polly and Meg would leave their teen years behind and would, as soon as the

Government decided, have to register for war work. No! One definitely did not think of such things on a bright and sunny August morning!

'Are you going to tell Nanny about Mrs Keating's good news, or am I?' Meg asked Polly when Eleanor Kenworthy had been settled at the window of her bedroom.

'You tell her, there's a love. Today's a busy one, in the garden.'

So Meg climbed the nursery stairs with reluctance, determined not to mention the postcard from Mark.

'I'll take your tray, if I may, Nanny,' she said with a smile, determined not to invite trouble. 'And what do you know! Mrs Keating has had a letter from her Bill and he's got shrapnel wounds but is safe in hospital. Now isn't that something to be glad about? I'll bet she's made up, eh?'

'Made up? What kind of expression is that? Don't you mean that Mrs Keating will be pleased and relieved?'

'Suppose I do. But made up is what we say in Liverpool, and it means the same thing.'

'Ah, well, I don't suppose one can make a silk purse out of a sow's ear. Take the tray and get out, girl! It's come to something when Mrs John is reduced to hiring servants who can't speak the King's English.'

'Suppose it has, Nanny. But when there's a war on you can't be too particular, can you?'

She longed to fling a retort about people who poked into private wardrobes which was a far worse thing than being common. But she did not, because it was something Ma would not have done, her being refined and quietly spoken.

She sent love to a mother not so very far away, she was sure of it, and it was good to know that Dolly Blundell, who had never said two words when one would suffice, would approve of her daughter's tongue-biting. She closed the door quietly behind her, then peeped round the door of Mrs Kenworthy's room.

'Comfy, Gran? I'll be up in half an hour to get you back in bed.'

Then she took the postcard from her pocket and, unlocking the wardrobe door, placed it inside. Everything personal she now locked in her wardrobe before hiding the key beneath her pillow.

Insults dismissed, Meg walked beaming into the kitchen to be initiated into the making of wartime raspberry jam – the recipe taken from the monthly bulletin issued by the Ministry of Food.

'Why do you think, Mrs John, that the Army likes sending soldiers on courses? Those two seem always to be goin' on a course.'

'I suppose because there is always something new for them to learn, though I often think that they welcome a change from the wilds of Yorkshire. Mind,' she added hastily, 'it's a whole lot better than being in Egypt, all sun and sand and danger.'

'Do you think it's because they'll both have to go abroad, sooner or later?'

'Not especially, though I accept that both Mark and Davie will go overseas, and sooner rather than later. We have been lucky, at Candlefold – our men still based in England and it nearly two years since war broke out. Just five weeks, Meg, then we'll be into the third year. Awful, isn't it?'

'And how long do you think it's goin' to last, Mrs John?'

'God alone knows . . .'

'And He isn't goin' to tell, is He?'

'He isn't, Meg, so how about this jam? Take eight ounces of raspberries, it says, and eight ounces of sugar, and mix together until liquified. A squeeze of lemon juice would help it set, but will you tell me the last time we saw a lemon in the shops? So would you like to try your hand?'

'You bet,' Meg beamed, pleased Mrs John trusted her with a precious half-pound of sugar. 'And then what?'

'Then we cover the bowl, place overnight in a cool place and tomorrow we bring it to boiling point and simmer for two minutes. It should, or so the recipe says, give one pound of delicious, off-the-ration jam and we'll save it for a treat for the birthdays.'

The birthdays, Meg brooded. Hers and Polly's. And after the 29th, neither could call their lives their own, though they had both agreed their registrations would not be required on the very day they reached twenty. It could be as much as two months before they were ordered to report to the Ministry of Labour offices. With a bit of luck, it could be even longer, by which time Polly might be a married woman and would not be sent away from her home, provided she found work of national importance locally. And what was more important than digging for victory and growing food?

Only what, Meg fretted, was to become of herself, who only did housework and helped care for two elderly ladies? Housework, if you were a single woman aged twenty, was not considered important, and would almost certainly mean she would be sent to the far north to work, or the even further south and never see Candleford again for the duration. Nor Mark.

Meg sat, hands round knees beside the pool, watching the fronds of willow that trailed in the water, longing to turn back time, live again that brief, blazing passion. Yet thoughts of Kip disturbed her. This morning's letter, still unread, had seen to that. Reluctantly, she slit open the envelope.

There was no address, no ship's name for the censor to cut out; just *You know where*, and the date at the head of the sheet of paper.

My darling Meg,

I am sitting in the sun, even though it is winter here, and wishing you could be with me. I miss you, especially when I see couples hand in hand. You are not far from me, though, because the ring – your ring – hangs for safety with my disc and medallion around my neck. I need only touch it to bring you closer.

This is a good country and the more times I dock, the more sure I am that I could pack in the sea and settle here, emigrate and bring up my kids in a better place. Liverpool doesn't figure in my plans any more. You and I could make a fresh start. I only wish you could see this country and feel the freedom we seem to have lost in England. And here there is no Them and Us, no toffs looking down on people like you and me. And no mucky streets – none that I have come across, anyway.

Would you take the plunge, lovely girl? Would you marry me and make a new life on the other side of the world? Next time we meet I shall ask you again to wear my ring. I shall go on asking until you say yes. And you will marry me, Meg. One day you will be my wife, I know it.

I miss you so much. Take care of your dear self. I love you more than I can find words to say. God bless and keep you.

Ever. Kip

'No, Kip! Not you and me. It *can't* be,' she whispered to the darkening gleam of water. Not now. Not since Mark had claimed her. Oh, a Kenworthy would never ask her to marry him, nor wear his ring, but she had long ago decided to settle for crumbs, so besotted was she. Right from the start it had been like that; not love; not like it was for Polly and Davie. It had been attraction, really. The need to touch and kiss and give and take and belong, utterly. And unconditionally.

'Kip, I'm so sorry . . .'

She dipped into her handbag for pad and pen. She had intended writing tonight, but not with such urgency, because now she knew there must be a letter waiting at Panama when the *Bellis* collected mail on the homeward journey. Kip was too decent, too straight to be made a fool of any longer. And too good for a girl who had thrown away a ring and marriage and yes, real love, because she hadn't the sense she had been born with! Mark would marry one who could trace her family way back, as the Kenworthys could. People with breeding didn't look in the back streets of Liverpool for a woman to carry on their line. Toffs who owned land and fine houses only went slumming in such places with wild oats to sow before they settled down to respectability. So it came back to crumbs, didn't it? And for crumbs, Meg Blundell would be grateful.

Dear Kip, *she wrote,*

Your letter has just reached me and I am glad you arrived safely. There is something, though. I must tell you. I've got to come clean, even though this letter will hurt you. There is no chance for you and me. Kip. You are everything a girl could want in a partner for life, but there is someone else. I fell head over heels the first time I met him and I shall never change. I should have told you last time you and I met. It would have been kinder than words on paper, but I couldn't find the courage to say them. I love this man so much I would give my all to him, and pride and common sense don't come into it. I just want him and no other man will do. It is as simple as that.

I ask you to forgive me. Kip, for hurting you in this way and for letting you hope. You deserve better than me: a good Catholic girl who will love you the way you should be loved and give you children and settle with you in another country. And if it is any comfort to you, Kip,

I know I will be punished, because the man I want does not know how much I love him, nor will he ever. But foolish and stupid I am and I know I will pay, in the end.

Please forgive the hurt I have caused you. Forget me, Kip, and get on with your life and dream your dreams without me. And may God take care of you and bring you safely through this war.

There! She had written it! And she had even asked a god she didn't believe in to watch over him, and people didn't come more wicked than that! And if, as she had written, there was a price to be paid for loving Mark, then that was the way it must be. Only time would tell; only the god Kip believed in knew how it would be. And that god never told.

She had sealed and addressed the envelope when Polly came running, calling, across the field, cheeks flushed.

'Meg! Such news! Davie's just phoned and he's getting leave at the end of the course. They both are! A seventy-two-hour pass and it *isn't* embarkation leave either. So what do you think to that?' Breathless, she sank to the grass. 'I'm to go to Oxford, Davie said – meet him at his folk's place. We didn't stay there long on his last leave because of the banns and us rushing back to see the vicar. So it's only fair we go to his folks, this time. Isn't it *wonderful*?'

'But are you sure – that Mark has leave, too. Did he ring?'

'No! Of course not. He told Davie to tell us – you know what he's like. And will you come to the village with me? I've dashed off a few lines to Davie's mother to let her know, just in case the trunk lines to Oxford are busy and I can't get through.'

'Course I'll come. I've one for the post too – to Kip. I've just done something awful, Polly. I didn't mean to be so cruel, but it's obvious that Kip is still keen on me – even though I hardly ever write to him. He said Australia is a fine country and he'd like him and me to settle there after the war, and bring up children there. So I told him I couldn't marry him, and that was final. I've hurt him, but what else could I do?'

'Nothing else. And I agree he'll be hurt when he gets your letter – one you should have written ages ago, if you want my opinion. After all, you're in love with Mark, aren't you?'

'No use trying to hide it.'

'Well, you aren't going to land my brother by letting him treat you like a doormat! He only wants what he thinks he can't have, so square up to him, like I told you. Play hard to get or you'll never get a ring out of him.'

'Polly! Listen! I don't expect Mark to marry me. I've accepted that he wouldn't want to, either. People with my background are just a bit on the side to the likes of him. Mark is only amusing himself – think I don't know?'

'Then more fool you, for letting him! But you know what I feel about things. Oh, if only you'd listen to me!'

They had reached the stile that led to the village road and Meg was saved the futility of a reply by climbing it with extra care and attention.

Only when they had posted their letters did Meg say, 'I'll be punished, Polly, I know it – because of Kip, I mean.'

'Karma, you're talking about? Take what you will. Take it – and pay?'

'Something like that.'

'And will it have been worth the bother and soul-searching?'

'Yes. I reckon so.'

'That's it, then! No more to be said!' Polly flung huffily, and it was not until they were in sight of the house that she added, 'Sorry, Meg. I went too far. Did I upset you?'

'No. What you said makes sense, but I love the man. Mad, aren't I?'

'We-e-ll, I still think you should –'

'Play hard to get? Yes, but there's a war on. We don't have time for messing around, playin' at anything, do we?'

And to that, Polly had to admit, there was very little to be said, except, 'Oh, roll on Friday, though the next few days are going to crawl, I just know it.'

With which Meg was bound to agree and began to count the hours in her mind. And in her heart.

Blackout was at 22.20 hours. Meg sat on the delphinium-covered window seat to watch the sky dim streakily in yellows and pinks, and listen to the flat, crawky calling of homeward-flying rooks. She always felt contentment at this window. If she had to choose some place, she pondered, some very specially happy place at which Margaret Mary Blundell's soul could rest happily immortal, then it would be here on this window seat, with the courtyard below her with its far arch leading to the lane and the riverbank and the woods. The riverbank was very special, of course, but it was a turbulent, passionate spot and in no way restful for an immortal soul. No! Here was the place of her complete happiness and peace, just as the pump trough was Ma's.

And what would this window be like when winter came and stripped bare the trees and silenced the birdsong and when blackout curtains must be drawn in the late afternoon? Where would Meg Merrilees dream then?

Merrilees. Mark's teasing name for her. Only when his eyes were dark with love – *want* – or when they danced close, cheek on cheek, did he call her Meg. And soon, his eyes would find hers and because she wanted him too, her gaze would be unflinching and soft. *I want you too*, her eyes would tell him. And how would it be? Gentle and sweet, that first giving, or hot with storm and passion?

But how much passion had there been in his one letter? And how ordinary that postcard from Salisbury – except that he had touched it and written on it. And since he went back to his unit, had there been others? Pretty ATS girls or special dancing partners? Had he remembered Meg when a silk-stockinged leg or a small rounded bottom caught his eye . . . ?

Kip. Kipling Lewis, seaman. Born just as the last war ended to a mother who died and a father who couldn't keep him and gave him and his sister into the care of nuns. So why was she all at once thinking about him? He was gone from her life, surely? Hadn't she told him so in a letter that was on its way to him now?

'Sorry, Kip,' she whispered into the twilight, but for all that, his words were clear in her head, or was she hearing a whisper from far away?

One day you will be my wife. I know it . . .

'No! It's over. It's Mark I want!'

She said it softly into the night, then latched the window and pulled thick black curtains over it. Then with a swish and a shake, she drew across the delphinium curtains just as a thud on the door told her that Polly was on the other side of it with hot milky drinks; safe and sane, good old Ovaltine.

She wished her own life was as uncomplicated, then opened the door with a smile and said, 'Hi!' because everything was right and normal – and wonderful too.

Or was it? Must she pay? Karma, was it to be?

Friday. It was really Friday. Yesterday Polly had left in a dither of delight and Meg had helped her onto the Preston bus with her case, then stood and waved as it drew away from the stop opposite the post office.

'You'll be in good time for the train –' the bus stopped obligingly outside the railway station – 'and Davie's Mum will be at Oxford to meet you,' she had soothed.

'Yes, but Davie won't be there for ages and ages . . .'

'I know. But best you travel today, then you can be at the station to meet him tomorrow and not waste one minute of his leave. And you're to have a lovely time and give my love to Davie, don't forget. Take care. Ta-ra, well!'

Yesterday, that had been, with Polly waving all smiles and Mrs Potter squinting through the window. Mrs Potter would make a very good spy if ever she gave up the post office!

Now Meg worked beside Mr Potter, because as soon as breakfast was over she had taken Polly's place in the garden and was picking up windfall apples ready to be taken to the post office with a notice, 'Free. Help yourself' on them. And lucky the housewife who had sugar to spare for an apple pie. And lard, for that matter, to make into a pie crust! And why was she thinking about apple pies when any minute now Mark could walk down the lane and beneath the far archway and into the courtyard, his boots clattering on the cobbles?

Not yet, her common sense told her, because it was a long way from Salisbury, and trains were maddingly slow and most often late, and if he arrived in time for supper, then it was the very most she could expect.

'Will I take these to Mrs Potter?' Meg asked when the wheelbarrow was full of fallen apples.

'Aye. But pick out about a dozen good 'uns for the house. Mrs John is sure to want to make a pie for Mark. Be strange, won't it, him coming without young Davie?'

And Meg said it would, though it was only fair Davie and Polly should spend the weekend with Davie's folks, and because she couldn't talk about Mark without her telltale cheeks flushing hotly she said, 'Right! I'll be off with these, and then what, Mr Potter?'

'Then there'll just be time to pick the tomatoes afore dinnertime. I'll show you how to lay 'em out, all tidy, for the greengrocer. And when you leave the apples at the house, be sure to ask Mrs John what she wants in the way of saladings. Now chop chop, young Meg. There's a war on, don't forget!'

Only at suppertime could she hope to see him, Meg had thought, yet Marcus John Kenworthy had never been one to bow to the expected and at three, just as she walked towards the far archway in answer to the clanging of the drinkings bell, she saw him.

He was walking down the lane, case in hand, respirator swinging loose from his left shoulder, and the sight of him rooted her feet to the ground so she stood there stupified instead of running to him, arms wide; stood as he approached, straight and smiling and so very good to look at. Then he set down his case and looked her up and down as he had done the first time they met.

'Meg,' he said softly.

Meg, not Merrilees. And happiness burst all over her because Meg was his love name for her and all at once she knew it would be all right.

'Mark . . .' She closed her eyes and offered her lips and he took off his cap and drew her close, locking her in his arms. And when they drew apart she smiled tremulously and picked up his respirator and walked with him across the courtyard.

This was, she thought, another golden moment; one to remember and store away in the deeps of her heart and mind and brought out and lived again when golden moments were few and far between.

And soon, her heart exulted, they would be lovers.

Fifteen

Throughout supper Meg said little as mother and son talked easily. Mark sat in the chair directly opposite and raised his eyes to hers from time to time, challenging her uneasy gaze.

'Will you be an angel, Mark, and go to the farm? I'm running short of milk. Ask Armitage for a couple more pints, will you?'

'Sure. Coming with me, Merrilees?'

'I – well, there's the supper things to see to.'

She was all at once reluctant to be alone with him, especially to take the path to the farm, which ran very near the riverbank.

'Then I'll help! You wash, I'll dry and Mother can put away. How would that be?'

'Extremely interesting to watch,' Mary laughed, 'especially as I can never remember you volunteering to help with the washing-up before!'

'There is, my dear Mama,' he took her face in gentle hands and kissed the tip of her nose, 'a first time for everything – don't you agree, Merrilees?'

'Er – of course.' Meg gave her attention to the stacking of plates, turning away so neither should see the blush that seemed never far from her cheeks. Nor did she look up from the bowl of suds nor allow her eyes to meet Mark's until they had crossed the drying green and were standing at the pasture gate.

'Merrilees – why are you going coy on me, all of a sudden?'

'I'm not – at least, I don't mean to. But it's us, I suppose – and me being a bit nervous.'

'About us being lovers?'

'Yes,' she whispered, wincing at his directness.

'But why? You want to, I want to, so where's the problem?'

'The problem is that for me it'll be the first time.'

'Hell! Sorry.'

'I thought you knew – I'll probably make a mess of it.'

'You won't. I promise. What do you take me for? Think I'm going to trample all over your virginity in my Army boots, or something?'

'No – oh, I don't know! Sometimes at work the girls talked about it – the ones who *had*, I mean – and I'd got to thinking it was a bit complicated.'

'Did you now?' He tilted her chin so she was forced to look at him. 'Then I can assure you it isn't. And I can promise you'll remember tonight for always.'

'Tonight, Mark – but where?'

'Where else but the place I'd intended it to happen – if you hadn't gone all uptight on me!'

'The willow pool, you mean?'

'No. You were anything but uptight then! I'd thought about the brick house, actually; no one rowing past in a boat, if we were in there. And do you realize we haven't kissed for almost four hours?'

'Yes, I do. I've been wanting to. I tried not to look at you at supper because I knew it would show – how much I needed you to kiss me, I mean.'

'So let's get the milk, then I'll show you the secret door into the brick house – take you on a conducted tour.'

'But I've seen it – we-e-ll, most of it . . .'

'Of course you have, but Mother doesn't know, does she? And don't look so anxious. Leave it to me? Trust me?'

He kissed her gently, smiling softly, but her heart still thudded because she wanted Mark to remember tonight for always too.

'All right. You're in charge.' She smiled into his eyes, wishing she could be as matter-of-fact about it as he was. But relaxing didn't come easily when she knew that if she spoiled tonight for them, she could lose Mark for ever.

'The milk is on the cold slab,' Mark called to his mother. 'Is there anything else you want doing?'

'No, dear. I'm going to sit with Gran. Why don't you and Meg go for a walk – it's such a lovely evening?'

'Got a better idea. Why don't I show Meg the brick house? Might be a good thing if I took a look around. Would you like to see our secret passage, Merrilees – have a look at the bit the Government pinched off us?'

'We-e-ll, yes, I would.' Her cheeks flushed at the deceit of it. 'If it's allowed, that is?'

'It isn't really, but who's to know? And I'm sure you'll find it interesting. And whilst you're in there, have a look at the upstairs ceilings, will you, Mark – make sure the roof isn't leaking?'

'I'll do that. Come on then, Merrilees!'

'And when you go in, will you close the panel behind you? I don't want someone to come to the door and see it wide open; wouldn't want anyone to know we've been trespassing.'

'In our own house? But I'll do that, and close the front door too. Satisfied, Mother?'

'There now. Front door closed – we'll be doubly safe. So let's see if you can open it, Merrilees. Remember how we did it?'

'Yes.' Of course she did – every time she polished the woodwork! She laid a forefinger on a piece of carving slightly more raised than the rest. 'You press in and turn left till you hear a click – then ease it open.'

'Clever girl. Go on then. Try it!'

He was still teasing, still calling her Merrilees. And he shouldn't be, because she wanted tonight to be special and wonderful and serious.

She pushed with her fingers on the one larger-than-average candlewax trail, manoeuvring it to the left, hearing a click that revealed the most minute opening.

'Got it!' Mark eased the blade of his penknife into the crack. 'Now push with your right hand, and we're in!' He squeezed in sideways, groping for the thin, lathe-like handle. 'One more turn and we're through. Mind your head, Merrilees. Stand still till I slide back the inside panel.'

Carefully she followed him towards the gleam of light, taking his outstretched hand, stepping out through the side of the wooden archway.

Nothing had changed. The walls were still empty of pictures, dusty shelves bare of ornaments. No one had visited from the government department in London, she knew that. It was as if the house slept reluctantly, wanting people in it again, and noise and light and air.

'I know where I am now. Straight ahead to the grand staircase, isn't it?'

They linked hands and walked past the dining room and the servery; past the double doors of the drawing room on their left. Halfway up the wide, shallow stairs they could see the walls of the long gallery, peachy from the reflected evening sky.

'Penny for them, Merrilees.'

'I was thinking that this place would go up like a tinderbox if the Germans dropped firebombs on it. Well, it's stuffed with wooden crates and old papers an' things, and the nearest fire brigade ten miles away!'

'I agree with you, but I didn't come here to assess the fire risk. I came here to –'

'Show me the parts I didn't see last time we were in and – and –'

'Yes, Merrilees?'

'Oh! Do you want me to spell it out!'

There were staircases at either end of the gallery leading to the bedrooms above and she hurried towards the one on her left, clattering up the stairs to stand beside a landing window through which she could look down on the farm and Pygons Wood and everything that was normal and ordinary and sane.

'Merrilees – you're making a big production out of this thing between us. Simmer down, why don't you?' He stood behind her, hands on her shoulders. 'It's you and me, sweetheart. We want each other – it's as simple as that. Don't worry. I promised it would be all right, didn't I?'

His lips whispered against the back of her neck, his hands cupped her shoulders, gentling them softly. She should, she thought as panic took her, take a deep breath, lean her head back until it touched his shoulder and leave everything to him, because he knew what to do and how it would be. This wouldn't be the first time for Mark – he had never denied it – but it was the first time for her, she thought resentfully, and she didn't want to be told – yes, *told* – when it would be and where it would be as if it were part of some prearranged contract; as if she had stood on a street corner in Lime Street, with her wares set out for any man with a pound in his pocket! She had always imagined that the act of love was something that happened naturally; that you kissed and touched and when it was right, the little pulses would tell you so. And you would want to do it so much that when you ended up naked and flesh against flesh, you wouldn't feel any embarrassment at all – just the need to give and love until there was nothing left inside you but happiness and contentment.

'Mark! No! It isn't right!' She turned to face him. 'Not here on the floor on the top landing; not this way . . .'

'Right! Fine by me, Merrilees.' He dug his hands into his trouser pockets, shrugging as if it didn't matter at all. 'So where shall it be? A dirty weekend, do you want? Mr and Mrs Smith creeping into a cheap London hotel or a seaside boarding house? Is that how the girls at work did it, then?'

'Mark! Stop it!' Her voice was harsh with disbelief. 'You know I want to, but I'm afraid; not afraid to do it but afraid I'll make a mess of it and you'll chuck me for some other woman. And even though I don't know how, I do know that here, tonight, isn't the time nor the place! You can't just grab me!'

'OK! Listen, will you? I don't just *grab* a woman. That, in my book, is tantamount to rape! I find you attractive and I thought it was the same for you too. Leading a man on then crying "No further!" isn't on, you know. Why can't you trust me?'

'I do trust you, Mark, but this way it seems I'm just being –'

'Being led like a virgin to the sacrificial altar, is that it?'

'Sumthin' like that.' She was shaking now, and her limbs were cold. She had thought of little else but how much she wanted him; how she would be content with crumbs just sometimes, and happy for them to be lovers with no strings attached, no promises or pledges asked or given. Yet now the time had come she had clammed up and gone back on her word. She was what men called a tease and if Mark never spoke to her again, it was no more than she deserved.

'Oh, Meg Merrilees, there's more to lovemaking than that. I wish you'd take my word for it. OK, so there have been other women; I've never denied it. There's a war on and things seem to become more urgent. I've enjoyed it and I think my partners enjoyed it too. But I can honestly tell you that not one of them excited me as you do. Have you any idea how attractive you are, darling girl?'

'Mark! Flattery isn't going to get you anywhere – not tonight it isn't!'

'Too right it isn't! As far as I'm concerned, that's it. Hell, woman, you can't promise it, offer it, almost, then get cold feet and leave a fellow high and dry!'

'I'm sorry, Mark.' She was near to tears now; tears of despair and bewilderment. 'I was tryin' to tell you how afraid I was – even though you'd said it would be all right. But I think I'd like it to be in a better place and not to have to think it's got to happen this minute because that's what we sneaked in here to do. Oh, I may be common, but I'm not a tart! And I've got feelings, an' all! Can't you understand?' The tears began to fall, and she pulled the back of her hand impatiently across her eyes. 'And can't you try to understand how sorry I am and how much I want you to love me?'

'Ssssh. I do understand, I really do.' He reached for her, cradling her close, kissing away her tears. 'Silly, silly girl to even think I'd treat you like a tart. You're lovely and kissable and very wantable too, and if we can start again – bearing in mind that we've only got two more days left – then shall we give it a try?'

'So you still want to – even after my dramatics?' She blew her nose inelegantly.

'Yes, but tomorrow. Mood's over now, old love. But can I tell you how very beautiful you are right now, and how your lashes cling together and how big and shiny your eyes are? Not many women can weep as beautifully as you, Merrilees.'

'So I'm forgiven?'

'Forgiven. But be warned. Next time there'll be no warning. I'll teach you how to make love and you'll want me so much that it'll be easy and natural and it'll just happen. Exactly the way you want, it'll be, and that's a promise. So let's take a look at these bedrooms, shall we, and you can see the lovely views and try to imagine big, old-fashioned beds in them and curtains at the windows, and flowers in vases, just the way it used to be. And then you can tell Mother how much you enjoyed it – and that everything seems in good order and she's not to worry about it.'

'But I haven't enjoyed it, not really, Mark – spoiling it for you, I mean. Are you sure you're not mad at me?'

'Not any more. And I've got to admit that maybe I was just a little direct. I'll tread softly next time; so softly you'll be surprised how easy it can be between two people who want each other.'

Want each other, she thought dully as she followed him into the first of the bedrooms. *Want* not love. But maybe, she thought as she joined him at the wide, high window and slipped her hand into his, that when they had been lovers, when it had happened and it was as wonderful as Mark promised it would be, then he would say it; say, 'I love you, Meg.'

'Will you kiss me, please?' she whispered. 'Just to tell me I'm forgiven and that we still want each other and that it's going to come right for us?'

'It'll come right for us, Merrilees; it will.'

He kissed her long and hard, his hands on her buttocks, pulling her close and it sent a thrill of need through her and made her sad and sorry she had been so foolish.

'And it will come right soon?'

'Soon. So do you want to see which was my room – after I was considered old enough to leave Nanny and the nursery?'

And she said she would like to very much, yet wondered why she felt all at once apprehensive at the mention of Nanny Boag's name. Was it because the old woman knew things, was a ticking time bomb that could explode without warning, telling all?

She closed her mind to the malicious face, then smiled tremulously. 'Let's go,' she said softly.

There were poppies and harebells and ragwort along the lane that led to the farm; Meg knew all the flowers now; recognized the hovering kestrel as it hunted to feed its nestlings. She carried two lidded milk cans – 'Four pints today,' Mrs John had said – yet in Tippet's Yard milk was strictly rationed to half a pint a day for each person. Mind, with Candlefold's own Jersey cow at the farm they could order a gallon of milk every day if the fancy took them.

Because Polly was away, the task of collecting the morning milk was Meg's, though she couldn't call it a task to walk down a country lane when the dew was still on the grass, and mellow August mistiness moist on the air.

Liverpool. Tippet's Yard. So different, so far away, yet soon she must visit again. It was a long time since she had seen Nell and Tommy; Kip had been home, then, yet by now he must be nearing the Panama Canal, heading into the Atlantic and the south-western approaches. Kip, who would be looking forward to a letter from her; who soon would get one.

She shook her head clear of all guilt. It wasn't her fault, she insisted, if Kip had read too much into their friendship. She had never given him reason to hope he could be any more than a good friend, had she? And she couldn't be blamed if she had fallen in love – deeply in love – with another man, though when she told Nell about Mark she knew what her reaction would be. Nell would take Kip's side and tell her she was a little fool to let a firm offer of marriage slip by.

'Now then, Meg. You the milk monitor today?' Mr Armitage, looking pleased with himself, called from across the yard. 'Just been to take a look at yon' field of wheat; reckon it's ready for the reaper. Weather looks set fair for a day's cutting. Ask young Mark if he fancies a stint with the stooking, will you? Can do with all the help we can get.'

'Stooking?'

'Aye! The reaper cuts and binds the corn into sheaves and we take 'em and lean 'em into stooks – make a little tent, sort of, so the air can blow through and dry them – eight sheaves to a stook. Happen you can't be spared to give a hand, lass – and it's a hot, dusty old job at the best of times. But Polly always comes and rakes up gleanings for Candlefold's hens. You'd be welcome to gleanings when the field has been cleared at the beginning of next week.'

She had never gleaned corn, Meg thought tremulously, but there were a lot of lovely things here that she had never done in Tippet's Yard – like falling in love.

'I'll tell Polly. She'll be back on Monday.' Mark would be leaving on Monday too, and doubtless glad to be rid of a girl who promised all and gave nothing. 'I'll come with her, and learn how to glean.'

She smiled and made for the dairy to leave the empty cans and collect two filled after early milking. She closed her eyes briefly, thankful it had been written in her Book of Life that she would come to this enchanted place and love it as Ma had done.

Mark returned at seven that evening, refusing supper, saying that not even for the war effort would he spend another day in a choking, dusty wheatfield.

'No supper, thanks. Mrs Armitage fed us well. All I want now is a wash down. I'm away to the pool. Coming, Merrilees?'

'If I'm not wanted here . . . ?' She glanced in Mary Kenworthy's direction.

'But of course you must go – though won't it be a little cold?'

'I need something cool on my back. The sun was hot this afternoon. Coming, Merrilees?'

'I'll get my things.' Of course she was coming. She had hardly seen Mark today; a whole day with not even a glimpse of him.

She was careful as they crossed the courtyard not to walk too near for fear of who might be watching from the high-up window of the day nursery: Nanny, who missed nothing. An old woman, afraid of steep stairs, yet who must have climbed down and up them again; who was stupid enough not to leave things as she found them, nor lock the wardrobe door afterwards.

'You're quiet, Merrilees.' They had passed beneath the far arch and out of view of the house. 'Have you missed me?'

'You know I have. Were you punishing me?'

'No. I usually give a hand at harvest if I'm at home. Tell me – why is it that harvesting is always depicted to be an idyllic scene when really it's a dusty, sweaty job, and dangerous too if you don't keep an eye on the reaper blades?'

'I – I don't know.' At this moment she was more interested in the man who walked, stripped to the waist, beside her. 'So if I'm forgiven, do I get a kiss?'

'Of course. But later. Right now I'm in no fit state to come anywhere near a lady. I've brought some soap. Remind me again, when I've swilled the muck off me.'

So this was how it was to be. She *was* being punished for last night. This time it was Mark's turn to call the tune and she had no one to blame but herself. She had thought and thought about it last night as sleep escaped her. Why had she been such an idiot? Why had she panicked? How stupid, when all she had ever thought about was *that*. How would it be? Where would it be? And would it be so marvellous, so heartachingly wonderful, she had daydreamed, that she would lie in his arms afterwards to hear the words that must surely follow. To say he loved her would be enough; a ring, much less marriage, never entered into her dreamings. 'I love you, Meg,' was all in the world she wanted to hear and know. Nothing else mattered.

She smiled her thanks as he opened the field gate, then closed it meticulously behind them. She walked an arm's length away, unsure of herself and of him.

'I'll just get changed,' she hesitated, making for the tangle of low-growing branches beside the pool, then ducked out of sight, hanging her clothes on a branch.

She was shaking. Not from cold but from apprehension and the fear she had spoiled what should have been her first loving; turned something precious into a farce because she was a girl from a mucky alley, who knew nothing of the way things were done; who had no *savoir-faire*, as Polly would put it, or nous, as it was called in Liverpool.

She rubbed her goose-pimpled arms. She was cold and miserable and the last thing she wanted was to swim in a cold river.

'Come in. It's lovely and warm!'

Mark, soaping and lathering his hair and body; Marcus John Kenworthy, who was altogether too handsome and self-assured for his own good! Mark, whom she loved till it was like an ache inside her. She walked into the water until it covered her knees, then waded to the horizontal willow trunk to heave herself onto it.

'Come here, Merrilees.' He threw his soap onto the riverbank in an overarm toss.

'No.' She set her mouth stubbornly. 'I'm all right where I am.'

'It's better here.' He laughed as he said it and it angered her.

'Then come and get me – if you're all that interested!'

She was throwing it away again; she who loved him so much that she –

'Ouch!' she yelled as he pulled her from the branch and into the water. 'That hurt!'

'Scratched your bottom, Merrilees?'

'No. The tops of my legs. Why did you do that!'

'Because you told me to come and get you. Shall I rub it better?'

His hands smoothed the tops of her legs, then inched higher until his palms cupped her bottom. His hair was straight and wet and he looked like Tarzan only more handsome.

She looked into his eyes and said huskily, 'No thanks.' In spite of her blazing cheeks, she was shaking.

'Cold, darling?' He pulled her to him.

They were in deep water now, and her toes left the bottom of the pool. Now she must cling to him for support or swim to where it was shallower.

He was very close. His body against hers was cold and hard as marble. He reached for the straps of her costume, pulling them down and down until she felt it slip over her feet, watching bemused as he wrapped it into a ball then threw it onto the bank, to be followed by his trunks.

She shook her hair into her hands, pulling it away from her face, then clasped her arms around his neck.

His hands gentled her buttocks, her waist, then cupped her breasts, and all the time gazing into her eyes so she was unable to do anything save lay against him, arms floating relaxed on the surface of the water. She smiled into his eyes to let him know she did not want the gentling and touching to stop.

'Is this how it is?' she said softly, closing her eyes because it was all too much to bear.

'This is how, sweetheart . . .'

'I feel funny and wonderful. I want to cling and be close.'

'You want me to make love to you, Meg – is that it?'

'Yes.' She whispered her lips around his face in little teasing kisses.

'Ask me, then. Ask me to love you!'

'Yes! Please, Mark? Please love me?'

'Get out, then.' He swam with powerful strokes to the bank, then bent to help her out. For a little while they clung together then he said, 'Is it to be now, Meg? Here?' They hurried to the sheltered place and spread towels on the ground. Then he took her in his arms again and she strained towards him as he straddled her.

'I love you,' she whispered as he entered her gently. 'I love you so much . . .'

She heard only the lapping of water, as if the willow pool approved and was giving them shelter. She pulled in her breath harshly as he kissed her nipples, teasing them with his tongue.

Then all at once, it came right for them.

They loved twice. Once fiercely, hastily, then less urgently, with time to kiss and kiss again before passion took them once more and fused them into a whole. They moved together, straining ever closer until it ended in a crash of stars.

For a long time they clung, unwilling to part, to let the wonder of it go.

Then Mark said, 'You're cold, darling.' He rolled from her, wrapping her in a towel, telling her to sit up so he might dry her hair. He did it gently, kissing her neck, her ear, her closed eyelids. 'So, Meg . . . ?'

'Are you askin'?' she smiled, very sure of herself. And he said that yes, he was asking, and how had it been?

To which she smiled enigmatically and said she wasn't at all sure, so could they do it all over again tomorrow – just so she might be certain it was wonderful and marvellous and like nothing she had ever dreamed of, or hoped it might be?

'I love you,' she whispered, lips close to his ear, but he kissed her instead of saying that he loved her too. Yet she was content to belong, because belonging to him had set her amongst the angels, and for that alone she was grateful.

'We'd best be getting back,' he said. 'And Merrilees – try not to look too Mona Lisa, will you?'

'You mean I'm not to grin or smirk, or sumthin'?'

'Not exactly, dear girl, but could you try not to look like a cat that's been at the cream? Well, not unless you want to give the game away!'

'I'll be very ordinary – promise I will – and say the water was cold and would it be all right if I made us a hot drink, and that I won't be going there again tomorrow night. Will that suit?'

'Oh, but we will, Merrilees.' He buttoned her blouse possessively. 'Not to swim, though . . .'

He held out his hand and they began to walk, arms around each other, thighs touching. And from time to time they stopped to kiss, because all her doubts and fears were gone now. And when they got to the far archway, she did not pull away from him in case Nanny was perched on her chair, waiting for them to come back, because after tonight, not even she could spoil their loving. Now, she was Mark's and nothing, she thought, could harm her ever again.

She was glad, that evening, that Polly was not there to come to her room with mugs of hot milk. Tonight she wanted to sit alone by the window, wonder at the change in her, recall the words she and Mark had whispered and the unbelievable joy of their coupling.

She sighed into the twilight, wondering if, three doors down, Mark was thinking about her, and hoped with all her stupidly thudding heart that he was.

'Good night, my love,' she whispered, and blew him a kiss into the night. Then she squinted into the gloom, just able to make out the iron pump that stood beside the trough.

'Night-night, Ma,' she whispered. And she knew that never again would she wonder how Dolly Blundell had got pregnant; only that she was glad with all her heart she knew how a love child was made. 'Wherever you are, don't worry about me, will you – never again . . . ?'

Sixteen

'That's them off to church, Gran,' Meg smiled from the bedroom window. 'Mark didn't want to wear his uniform, but Mrs John said he'd got to; says he looks handsome in it and she wanted to show him off. Mind, she's right.'

'So you think him handsome, Meg?'

'Suppose so. It's easy to see why all the girls fall for him.'

'But do *you* find him attractive?'

'I – yes, I do, Gran, but you're not to tell. Polly knows I think he's wonderful, but she says I should play hard to get.'

'But playing hard to get – we used to call it flirting, in my young days – isn't a lot of use, is it, when a girl is in love? And you love Mark, don't you?'

'Does it show?' Taken off guard by such directness Meg went to sit at the bedside, taking the frail, knotted hand in her own. 'Oh, if you want the whole truth, I've loved him since I first saw him – when he an' Davie did a crafty one on the way south. It was like someone had hit me a fourpenny one. Polly said it was the same for her and Davie, but . . .' She shrugged, looking down at the bed covers.

'But you know it isn't the same – for you and Mark, I mean.'

'Yes, I do. It's different with him and me. I'll never love anyone but him, Gran, and you won't say a word to anyone, will you – especially Mrs John?'

'I won't, but whyever not? Mary likes you very much and she's often said she would like Mark to settle down, war or no war. I know she wants grandchildren.'

'And she will have. Polly wants to start a baby as soon as they're married.'

'But Polly's children won't inherit unless Mark has none of his own. And we were talking about you and Mark. Why can't I tell Mary you are in love with her son?'

'Because Mark will marry one of his own kind. Oh, he might enjoy being with me – dancin' and kissin' me good night, but he'd never marry a girl who hasn't got a fancy address and didn't go to a posh school. And I really came in to collect your tray and make you comfy. I don't want Mrs John to come back and me up here nattering!' She had said too much! 'I'll have to go, Gran.'

'Of course you must. And I won't pry. But don't undervalue yourself, because Mary isn't a snob. If Mark wanted you she would welcome you into the family if your father were a duke or a dustman. And before you scuttle off, all pink-cheeked, can I just say one thing? If Mark were to ask you to marry him, it would make *me* very happy, so I'm on your side, you see.'

'Gran! Oh, I don't know what to say!' Tears filled her eyes and she swallowed hard. 'I really don't know!'

She fled the room with such gratitude in her heart that she began to shake, and the china on the tray shook with her and clinked all the way down the stairs and across the hall to the kitchen.

'Oh, Gran, if only I could tell you how much I love him, how close we are,' she whispered, eyes closed tightly against a flood of happy tears.

When she had dabbed her cheeks and taken a deep breath and was herself again, Meg tapped on the door of the day nursery.

'Finished with your tray, Nanny? And sorry I can't stop for a chat, but I'm in a bit of a rush, Mrs John bein' at early church and me with a lot to do.'

Swiftly she collected the breakfast tray, eager to be out of the room, out of sight of the malicious eyes of Emily Boag, who disliked her so.

'Not so fast! I haven't finished with you yet.'

'Sumthin' you want?' Meg paused in the doorway.

'Indeed there is! I want to warn you, Meg Blundell; tell you that not all your simpering and hand-holding will make any difference at all. You're setting your cap at Mark – it's all too obvious – but you won't get him!'

'Why, Nanny,' she whispered as the full force of the old woman's enmity hit her.

'Because I *know* you won't. Not even if he asks you to marry him!'

'Well, you'll be pleased to know that I don't think he will, so you needn't get your bloomers in a twist! But if ever he did, what makes you think I wouldn't say yes?' Her words were whispered and rough with fear, yet she held her head high and sent out a challenge with her eyes. 'Go on! Tell me!'

'Oh, no. Think I'm stupid, do you? But just you wait and see, Miss Uppity, for I'm telling you nothing more – just warning you not to get ideas!'

'Then thank you for your concern, Nanny Boag. And if you don't mind I'm afraid I must go. Like I said, there is a lot to do.'

And with that she walked, straight-backed downstairs, because that was what Ma would have done; even though she might have felt like throwing the tray, crockery and all, at the old witch!

Slowly she counted to ten, then went to stand at the open door to gaze into the courtyard.

'Did I do it right, Ma, or should I have given the old biddy down-the-banks and told her to keep her nose out of my wardrobe?'

She stood unmoving, drawing in steadying breaths, and was as sure as she could be that from little more than a cock's-stride away came the softly spoken words, *You did it right, and I'm proud of you . . .*

'Thanks, Ma,' Meg smiled, 'but it took a lorrer doin' – *a lot of doing* – I can tell you.'

And she was still smiling when the dishes were washed and dried and put away because she had so much to smile about, come to think of it. She was so happy she felt she could go off like a firework in a burst of stars – in spite of Nanny Boag, who was nuts, anyway.

She tried not to think too much about what she had said, and her so sure Mark would never marry someone like Meg Blundell. And why was she so against it when Gran, Lor' love her, had been quite taken with the idea?

But Nanny was a silly old woman – sly, but silly for all that – who took delight in reminding her, Meg frowned, about her class, and being a servant. But wasn't that exactly what Nanny Boag was? Quite high up in the pecking order as servants go, but a servant, for all that. And if Mark ever did ask her to marry him, then no one would stop her saying yes; not even the old biddy upstairs! And barring stops for chats and allowing for the walk back, Mrs John and Mark would be home in fifteen minutes, and her with the tray for morning tea not set, nor even the kettle put to boil!

She pulled her breath in, then let it go in little huffs of contentment, because in fifteen minutes she would see Mark again, and tonight . . .

Tonight, she sighed, was all that was left to them because there was a war on and Mark would be going back to join it, and after Monday, she would not touch him nor kiss him nor love him for weeks and weeks! Yet she couldn't be at odds with the war, because it had given Mark to her, and Candlefold, and she wouldn't think about tomorrow until she had to!

'No harvesting today?' Meg asked of Mark when he had changed into old trousers tied up with a necktie, and a shirt, sleeves rolled up to the elbows, buttons unfastened to three down.

'Armitage doesn't work Sundays – except for the milking – even if there's a war on. And I doubt it will rain, so another day won't make a lot of difference to the harvest.'

'Armitage is right. Sunday should be a rest day, so I suggest we do no more than is necessary today, and enjoy the lovely sunshine,' Mary Kenworthy said. 'What will you do, Mark?'

'Haven't the foggiest. I might walk the riverbank or I might split a few logs and carry them in to dry. Won't be long before it's cold enough for a fire, nights, in the sitting room. Or I might take the gun and pot a rabbit or two. Armitage was saying they're a damned nuisance. Can't make up my mind, actually. I only know it's nice having a choice and not being told what to do. Think I'll spend the morning chopping, though, then nip down to the village for a pint before lunch. And can Meg be spared this afternoon? There are red squirrels in Pygons Wood – ever seen one, Merrilees?'

And Meg was bound to admit she had never been to the wood, let alone seen a squirrel, though if it was all right with Mrs John, she would very much like to.

So Mark made for the woodyard, Mary Kenworthy took morning tea to the upstairs ladies and Meg prepared vegetables for Sunday dinner at one, thinking she had never been happier in the whole of her life and that in just a few more days there would be the birthdays to look forward to, and being twenty, and almost grown up.

Pygons Wood was mostly beech and oaks, and shaded green cool from the afternoon sun. They saw no squirrels, but what could you expect, Mark said, when the entire wood was full of courting couples.

'The place is like Piccadilly Circus,' he grumbled. 'Damn it – whose wood is it anyway?'

'Candlefold's? Yours?' Meg teased, realizing the reason for their visit was not entirely to see red squirrels, then all at once remembering the little mark in her diary set against August 22 she said, 'Talking about *that*, we-e-ll, we were a little bit careless last night, weren't we?'

'Careless, Merilees?' He stared at her huffily, still annoyed about trespassing couples.

'You and me, and watching it, I'm talking about. It never struck me till it was too late.'

'Nor should it have! Didn't I ask you to trust me?'

'Y-yes.' She looked down, all at once ashamed, at the mossy path.

'And didn't you say you would?'

'Y-yes, I did. And I know there are ways and means, though no one has ever told me what they are – not even Nell.'

'Nell? The one who's keeping an eye on your place, you mean?'

'Mm. She sort of took over from Ma and is all the time warning me, but never tells me about things.'

'Then take notice of the warning and leave *things* to me, Merrilees. Actually, they give us lectures about it in the Army – lessons in hygiene, they're called, but useful for all sorts of things.'

'Like how not to get babies?'

'Sort of. Y'know, for a city girl you're quite an innocent, aren't you?'

'Well of course I am! Think that all Liverpool girls are tarts, then?' she flung indignantly, all at once embarrassed by her lack of worldliness and for bringing up the matter in the first place.

'Merrilees, what a delight you are! For Pete's sake, let's shove off out of here. And don't worry! Trust me – OK?'

She nodded and placed her hand trustingly in his, wondering why a voice, amazingly like Nell Shaw's, should whisper in her ear, *Ha! Famous last words, Meg Blundell . . .*

Yet words she chose to ignore, because she was happy and in love, and good advice had no part in it.

'There's no need for you to run me to the station, Mother. It'll play havoc with your petrol coupons and I can just as easily get the bus from the village.'

'And leave a lot earlier than you need? I can spare the petrol. I've been saving it, anyway, for a trip into town. I want to get a wedding hat, you see, just to be on the safe side because you never know the day when hats will be rationed, too. Some bright spark at the Board of Trade is going to realize they were never put on coupons, and that'll be that!'

A hat was the only item of clothing which could be freely bought now, though women lived in fear of the day when hats would require clothing coupons, and become as dispensable as silk stockings, and women would go not only bare-legged, but hatless too!

'If you're sure?'

'Quite sure. And Meg says I'm to take my time and have a look round the shops. She's such a blessing. It'll be awful if she has to go away to do war work – she and Polly both. You won't forget your sister's birthday, will you, Mark – and Meg's is the day after.'

'I'll remember. And where is Merrilees, by the way?'

'In the garden, helping Potter. Mind, I think he'll be glad to have Polly back tomorrow. Meg is very willing. I understand, but she asks so many questions about planting and pruning and propagating, and –'

'Maybe so. But what Potter doesn't understand is that Meg has never lived in the country before, and everything is new to her, and a delight.'

'You like her, don't you, Mark?'

'Yes, I do. She's great to be with and like no other girl I've ever met, if you want the truth. She's so direct and open – and funny, too.'

'You aren't leading her on, Mark? Because I wouldn't want you to do that – not if she's only someone to have fun with when you're home on leave. I wouldn't want you to hurt her.'

'Mother! Stop matchmaking. And I think Merrilees understands the position – that there's a war on, and all that.'

'War or no war, let her down lightly if you aren't serious, because she's serious about you!'

'She told you?' he demanded warily.

'Of course she didn't. I'm a woman, I don't have to be told.'

'Then would you mind very much, Mother, if it was Merrilees I asked to marry me – when the war is over,' he hastened. 'When I'm back in civvy street, I mean.' He looked away, fastening his case with studied care.

'No, I wouldn't. It would make me very happy, in fact. Are you really serious about after the war? Might you ask her one day?'

'If I come through it in one piece, I just might, though don't say a word to a soul – and especially not to Merrilees or she might get like Poll, and demand a ring!'

'So marriage in wartime is out?'

'For me, it is. I don't think it's fair on the woman, actually.'

'And had you thought to ask Meg for her opinion?'

'My dearest Mama! Meg is one heck of a girl, but I've got a thing about wartime weddings, though if she's still around when it's over I might chance my luck and drop down on the old bended! But till I do, not a word to anyone – especially not to Polly – promise?'

'Promise. But don't leave it too late? Don't lose her, will you, because I'd like another daughter and Meg fits the bill nicely, as far as I'm concerned. Your gran adores her.'

'And so do I, truth known.'

'Then would it be such a bad thing to tell her so, Mark?'

'I'll tell her, when the time is right! And it's ten o'clock and time for drinkings. Shall I ring the bell?'

'No. Why don't you go to the garden, tell Meg yourself?' she smiled, mischievously, noting the speed at which he crossed the courtyard.

'And please don't leave it too long, Mark,' she whispered to the empty room, 'or you'll lose her and that would be such a shame.'

Yet all things considered, and knowing her son as she did, Mary Kenworthy was content – or would be if only a way could be found to keep Meg at Candlefold, once she was twenty.

* * *

Meg stood on the topmost step, arms hugged tightly around her, watching as the small, black car on its tiny spoked wheels disappeared beneath the far arch, and she had only once, she thought miserably, felt so desolate in her life. It was exactly as she felt the February morning she had stood at her mother's graveside, alone and bewildered. She had known she would never see her lovely Ma again because death was very final, yet why should she feel exactly the same this morning? Was she never to see Mark again – was that the reason for the hurt that throbbed through her? Or on his next leave, would there be some other woman with him, one whose pedigree matched his own? Why the feeling of doomed certainty that last night had been too wonderful ever to happen again between them?

Last evening they had returned to the green, sheltered place beside the willow pool and loved passionately, all inhibitions gone, fusing into one exquisite, pulsating whole. Then, just before ten this morning, Mark had come to the garden in search of her and to ask Mr Potter if she could be spared for fifteen minutes.

They'd walked hand in hand, speaking little, kissing often on the way back, letting go their clasped hands as they walked beneath the far archway.

'Don't want mother to get any ideas,' Mark had grinned. 'She wants me married, did you know?'

'And don't you want to be?' The words had come in a whisper.

'Not until the shooting is over.'

'But it might last as long as the Great War did – *four* years!'

'If you want my opinion, Merrilees, it's going to last a whole lot longer – miracles excepted, that is.'

'Miracles like what – Hitler getting killed?'

'Something like that.'

'Do we have to talk about him? Can't we talk about writing to each other when you've gone back, and – well – other things?'

'Things like you and me?' They'd been at the pump trough by then, and in sight and sound of the house. 'You and I, dearest girl, are the best of friends and I care for you very much. But there *is* a war on, like I said. And I will write, I promise, on your birthday. And there's Mother, making a noise like a teapot! We'll talk after, Merrilees.'

Yet they had not talked afterwards about anything, because there were goodbyes to be said to Nanny and Gran, and Mr Potter had been to wish Mark all the best, and if he hadn't been busy with the harvest, it was likely that Mr Armitage would have called an' all, Meg thought miserably.

'Bye then, Merrilees. And don't look so downhearted! My little sister will be home any time now, full of wedding talk, and Davie!'

He had grinned cheerfully from the wheel of the car, though just for a moment their eyes had met gently before he had drawn away, waving from the window. And yes, Polly would be home very soon and no, she would not tell her about the sheltered place at the willow pool nor that she loved Mark even more, now it had happened. Yet it would be good to see her and to sit in the bedroom and talk of weddings and Davie and how wonderful the three unexpected days together had been. They would talk about birthdays, too, and how good it had been working in the garden with Mr Potter, who knew everything there was to know about vegetables and flowers and seedlings and pruning and propagating . . .

They would talk about everything save how much she loved Mark, and how wonderful it had been to be loved by him.

On Friday, just as she had fervently hoped it would, her period began, and though she had been certain – *almost* certain – that it would, Meg was nevertheless relieved that a loving so passionate had not resulted in a baby, though whether wanted or unwanted she had yet to be sure.

'Soon be autumn,' Polly shivered, closing the bedroom window as a gust of cold, un-August-like air blew in at it. 'But had you thought, Meg, that even if Davie doesn't get his second pip up just yet – if he isn't given embarkation leave, I mean – he and Mark should be home on long leave again, in less than six weeks?'

To which she replied that she hadn't thought, but talking about weddings, wasn't Mrs John's new hat smashing?

'Mm. Mummy isn't splashing out on a mother-of-the-bride outfit, coupons being what they are and given it'll be a quiet wedding. But she's got a lovely rose-pink silk two-piece she's only worn twice and the hat will go nicely with it. There's a place in Preston you can still get silk flowers and hat decorations, and she says she's going to try to find some full-blown silk roses to put on the new hat so it matches up. Oh, isn't it all exciting and are you getting a new wedding hat, Meg?'

'I don't know. I've got one at home – a very good straw that was Ma's – but it's a bit dated, so maybe your mother will help me decide. And by the way, I'm going to Liverpool tomorrow – haven't been for ages. Just for the night, to make sure everything's all right.'

'And to see your friends, too?'

'Them, an' all.'

'Pity I can't come with you. I'd love to meet them. But it wouldn't be right, would it, to leave Mummy on her own to do everything?'

And Meg hastily agreed that it would not, especially since Polly knew nothing about the house in Tippet's Yard, nor could she ever. It was what happened, Meg supposed, when you started telling lies about where you lived, because something inside you had said it would be better that way – or at least it would until she had discovered who she really was – and the name, maybe, of Father Unknown. Perhaps then she would tell them that her birth certificate showed she had actually been born here at Candlefold, though she had done precious little, this far, about it.

Would she ever? After all the lies she had told and the deceit, wouldn't it be better never to talk about the deeds of Tippet's Yard, or a housemaid called Dorothy Blundell, and leave the man who had fathered her in obscurity as Ma had chosen to do?

'Penny for them!' Fingers clicked beneath her nose. 'You were miles away. With a soldier somewhere in Yorkshire, were you?'

And Meg smiled, and said Polly could be right at that, and pushed Tippet's Yard and Lyra Street to the back of her mind and thought instead about tomorrow and if there would be a letter from Mark. Yet were letters all that important when they had been lovers? *More important*, answered her heart.

August 28 came in mistily with the scent of autumn-to-come on hedges, fields and trees. But the sun broke through as Polly returned with the morning milk, declaring it was going to be a marvellous day and why didn't she and Meg make it a communal birthday? And Mrs John said why not indeed, since the rations would only run to one sponge cake and lucky they were to have eggs to spare and six ounces of carefully hoarded sugar for the making of it.

And when Mrs Potter had delivered letters and one parcel and wished them both a happy birthday, Polly laughed and said, 'Y'know, if you believed the stork thing you could be forgiven for thinking that but for the whim of Fate, you could have been dropped on Candlefold, Meg, and me on Liverpool!'

And though Meg laughed heartily at the idea, she knew that nothing could be nearer the truth. But she said not one word because today was magic and anyway, what Polly didn't know couldn't hurt her!

'Well now, since we are going to make one big happy day of it, what say we open the cards and presents in Gran's room? She would love it, and I know she has presents for both of you.'

'Let's! And you are right, Mummy. We shall have a lovely day, and both of us will try like mad to pretend there isn't a war on and that we won't have to register ever!'

Strange, thought Mary Kenworthy, that no matter how determined they were to forget the war even for a day, it was impossible when behind every smile and peal of laughter would loom the awful prospect of the war reaching out and taking Polly and Meg away – young girls, not yet of age, but old enough to go to war. Yet she had come through an earlier war, and though it had caused the death of a beloved husband she had sense enough to whisper yet again in her heart, *Nothing lasts: neither bad times nor good, so live one day at a time.*

'Register!' she said severely. 'Anyone who says that dreadful word will go without sponge cake – is that understood?'

And they all laughed and said it was, and how about collecting everything together to carry up to Gran's room, and being very, very happy?

Eleanor Kenworthy was wearing her best, lace-trimmed bedjacket and a smile that made a lie of her pain.

'A happy birthday to you both,' she said softly, lifting a cheek to be kissed. 'And you are to open your cards and presents so I can enjoy them too, then you shall have your presents from me! You first, Meg!'

So Meg showed her posted-early card from Nell and Tommy, jointly signed, and the one bearing an English stamp, though the sender was thousands of miles away.

'From Kip. He's my friend and we sometimes went dancing when he was home from sea. He must have left it with Nell to be posted, last time his ship was in dock,' she explained. And because she felt so awful about what she had written to him, she pushed Mark's letter into her pocket to be opened tomorrow on her real birthday, the long wait a punishment for treating Kip so badly. 'An' I'll leave Mark's to read later, if you don't mind, it feeling like it's a letter . . .'

'So now, Miss Mary Eleanor Kenworthy, open your presents,' her grandmother prompted.

From Davie, carefully packed, was an elegant studio photograph of himself in uniform signed, *Darling Polly. Always, David*, which brought tears to her eyes as she held it close and whispered chokily that wasn't he just about the most handsome soldier in the entire Service Corps?

Then she hugged her mother with delight, for tucked inside her birthday card was a crisp, black and white five-pound note and – would you ever believe it? – *five* clothing coupons pinned to it!

'For the special blouse you saw, darling,' Mary smiled. 'For your honeymoon. Now, Meg – it's your turn!'

'Ar hey!' Meg gasped with pleasure to unwrap a small china cupid with a bow and arrow in gold, which made her blush furiously and to wonder if Mrs John knew more than she was letting on about. 'Oh, it's beautiful,' she whispered.

From Polly was a card showing a country cottage so like the one Meg and her mother had dreamed about, with a garden bright with flowers, and roses round the door. Inside was tucked a pair of silk stockings which was no end of a pressie, Meg whispered, since you had to like someone a lot to give them your clothing coupons and silk stockings cost two! Smiling she took her card for Polly from her pocket.

'It's only a lippy, Poll, but it's the colour you like – English Rose. I got it last time I was in Liverpool.'

'But you must have stood ages in a queue for this!' Polly's eyes opened wide at so unexpected – and rare – a gift. 'I shall put it away with Gran's scented soap and keep it for my honeymoon.'

'Well, then – are you ready for my presents?' Eleanor Kenworthy smiled, feeling beneath her pillows for a slim, red leather case. 'This is for you, Polly, because you have been my granddaughter for twenty years. It comes with dearest love.'

'But Gran – they're *real*!' Polly gazed, pink-cheeked at the single strand of pearls. 'Oh, are you sure?'

'I'm sure, my darling. Your mother already has a pearl necklace, so these are for you to wear on your wedding day. I had intended waiting for your coming-of-age, but decided they will look lovely on a bride. They were your grandpa's wedding gift to me. Put them on, child. Pearls are the better for being worn.'

'Gran, they are so beautiful,' Polly gazed into the dressing-table mirror. 'Just how do I begin to say thank you for something like this?'

'By being as happy with your Davie as I was with your grandpa. They look even more beautiful on a young neck. I haven't worn them in years, Polly. Leave them on for the rest of the day and you'll find the warmth of your skin will make them glow. Now for my other granddaughter, recently acquired,' she smiled, offering another smaller box, bidding Meg to open it.

'Oh, Gran. It's the most beautiful brooch I've ever seen!'

'A lover's knot, in seed pearls,' came the soft reply. 'From me to you because you are so good to me, and gentle, and because I hope you will never leave us.'

'Just as if, Gran.' Who in her right mind would want to leave Candlefold? 'When did you get it?' Meg wanted her present to have a memory with it, too.

'It was given to me on our honeymoon. We spent it in Paris, and Paris is the city for lovers. My darling husband pinned it to my gown as I dressed for dinner. I drank my first champagne, that night . . .'

'You shouldn't have given me something so precious,' Meg whispered huskily.

'Oh, but I should! Jewels are no use to an old woman.'

'But you are giving away your memories.'

'Perhaps. But to two very lovely girls who will keep them fresh, long after I am gone. Now, no more thanks from either of you. Surely it's time for elevenses? Oh, do let's make this a special time? Let's forget the war for two whole days and be very, very happy.'

Try to forget, she thought achingly, that on this morning's news bulletin, she'd heard of the vicious deaths by guillotining of three young men of the French Resistance Army, and that in Lithuania, two thousand Jews had been driven into ditches, and shot dead.

'Let's! And we'll have afternoon tea here in your room, Gran. Mummy is making a sponge and we're to have home-made raspberry jam in it! Now, how will that suit you?'

You couldn't, Meg thought as she pushed Mark's unopened letter beneath her pillow to tantalize her until morning, be anything else but happy at Candlefold. And you could, if you tried very hard, forget there was a war on. Yet what she could not forget was the letter she had written to Kip, and wonder if she had any right to such happiness when she had done such an awful thing to him.

Happy birthday to my darling Meg with all my love, he had written. Yet she wasn't his darling Meg, nor could she ever be.

'Sorry, Kip,' she whispered to the words inside the card. 'I truly am sorry.'

And just about now, she thought miserably, his ship could well have taken on mail at Panama, and he would know . . .

Seventeen

'That was a smashin' supper,' Nell Shaw said after eating rabbit stew and fresh Candlefold vegetables. 'Pity you don't come home more often, Meg Blundell.'

'Couldn't get away before this. I've been really busy. And I didn't thank you an' Tommy for the card,' Meg murmured, needing to soothe Nell's pique. 'It had a lovely verse in it.'

'Ar,' Nell sniffed, mollified, because she never read verses in greetings cards, being more concerned with the picture on the front and the price on the back. 'An' you'd get Kip's, an' all. He left it for me to post last time he was ashore. Shouldn't wonder if he doesn't turn up any day now.'

'Hardly, Nell. His last letter from Sydney was written less than three weeks ago so he won't be here yet.' Please, not whilst she was here to see the hurt in his eyes?

'His sister's had another, did you know? That's three in four years. Got a boy, this time, so happen she'll call it a day now. If I was her I'd give that husband down-the-banks, him coming home from sea, gettin' her in the family way, then signing on for another long voyage and her left on her own to cope. Wouldn't do for me. So when do you expect Kip'll be home?'

'Wouldn't know. He's real taken with Australia, though. Says he wouldn't mind giving up the sea and settling down there. Says it's a fine country for bringing up kids in. He – he wants me to marry him, Nell, but I wrote and told him no.'

'You could do a lot worse,' Tommy offered.

'And be like his sister? No thanks!'

'So you don't want kids, then?'

'Hey up, Nell, I'm only just twenty. Do I have to settle down yet? There's a big world out there and I want to take a good look at it!'

'Well, happen now you're twenty you'll be seein' a bit more of it, courtesy of the Ministry of Labour. When do you register, then?'

'Give me a chance! They mightn't send for my age group right away. They don't know what to do with you, anyway, once they've got you!'

'They'll soon find something,' Tommy murmured morosely. 'I did hear it said that some high-ups had soldiers whitewashing a heap of coal because some bigwig was visiting. Oh, they'll know what to do with you all right. What you should get straight in your mind when the time comes, girl, is what *you* want to do. Talk has it that most young women are gettin' sent to work on munitions, at the place out at Kirkby. They get big pay packets, but I wouldn't like to think of you havin' to go there. Very risky, on munitions. Accidents all the time!'

'Don't suppose I'd be sent there, Tommy. I'll have to register at Preston, so it'll be around there I'll work, when the time comes, that is.'

'Ar. Then if there's no munitions factories in that part of the world, you'll get sent into the forces. Fancy marching up an' down, do you, and saluting?'

'No, I don't!' All she wanted was to stay at Candlefold, with its thick walls around her to keep the war out.

'Then I think you should tell them that you'd like to go nursing,' Nell offered. 'A nice ladylike profession, nursin' is.'

'No thanks. I had enough of that when Ma was poorly!'

'That's it, then! Tell them you've had experience. Better nursin' than blowing yourself up or getting bawled at by army sergeants.'

'Leave it, Nell? I'm only a day into twenty, so let's worry about having to register when the time comes. Now – would either of you like a cup of tea? Sorry there isn't a pudding. Mr Potter offered me plums, but I haven't got the sugar to stew them with.'

To which Nell replied it was no problem, that plums always gave her an acid stomach, anyway.

'I'll have a ciggie, though,' she smiled,' and you can tell us about your birthday, and what presents you got.'

'We-e-ll, I got a pair of silk stockings, an ornament and a brooch, as a matter of fact – from Polly, her Ma and her Gran.' No need to mention the ornament was an antique, nor that the brooch was so valuable she had locked it in her wardrobe before leaving, and slipped the key in her purse!

'An' what about that brother of Polly's – did he send you a card?'

'No. He sent a letter, though.'

She turned from the table, concentrating on pouring boiling water into the teapot so they should not see the flush that seemed to fly to her cheeks whenever Mark's name was mentioned.

'So you write to him?'

'Sometimes. I've had two letters from him, and a postcard. And by the way, I'm going back tomorrow.'

'Not stoppin' till Monday? Why ever not?' Tommy stirred his tea.

'Oh, there's a lot to be done at Candlefold. They'll be picking apples and pears any time now, and there's the harvest.'

'Didn't know they was farmers, an' all.'

'They aren't. But Mr Armitage is busy with cutting wheat and barley, and everybody helps – the war effort, sort of . . .'

And I tell lies, Nell, because the harvest is in, and Polly and Mr Potter can manage the fruit picking without any help from me.

'If you want my opinion,' Nell drew hard on her cigarette then blew out smoke in little puffs, 'you're getting far too taken up with that Candlefold. Like your mother, God rest her. What is it about the place – or have you fallen for a feller out that way, then?'

'No, I haven't! I don't want to be tied down. Didn't I just tell you I said no to Kip?'

'Ar well, we'll see,' Nell said complacently. 'He'll go on asking, y'know. An' if you have any sense you'll tell him yes, next time he does.'

'I won't. I'll go on saying no. I'm twenty, that's all, though I know that if you haven't a ring on your finger by the time you're twenty-one, people think you're on the shelf. Well, I don't care! When the right man asks me, I'll know, Nell – and Kip Lewis isn't the right one for me. Now, does either of you want another cup?' she said firmly in her subject-closed voice, and Nell had the sense to heed the warning.

'I did hear,' she said off-handedly, 'that Lewis's are having make-up on sale on Monday morning. Thought you an' me could have gone to town; seen if there was a queue, Meg.'

'I'm going back tomorrow – sorry, Nell. But I won't leave it so long between visits another time.'

And with that, Nell had to be satisfied, though she missed Dolly's girl more than she cared to admit. And anyone as mad keen to get away as she was *must* have a young man in the offing – or she was Betty Grable!

Sleep did not come easily to Meg that night; she had forgotten how the iron bed creaked and that the mattress was lumpy and sagged in the middle. And it wasn't a lot of use opening her bedroom window to watch the coming of night, because all there was to look out on here was a brick wall and a soot-caked window with cracked panes.

Sighing, she groped for the candle at the bedside, lighting it, reaching for her handbag because just supposing Nanny had a duplicate key to her wardrobe, she had thought, and just supposing she read Mark's birthday letter – which she would do without a second thought – then that letter was safer by far in her handbag. Oh, my word, yes!

Dearest Meg, *she read yet again,*

The birthday cards I looked at had silly words and verses in them, and what I feel for you is above such banality. I miss you, Merrilees. Last night I awoke for no reason at all and couldn't get to sleep again for thinking about you. We have not spent a whole night together yet. Shall we try to, next time I am home? There must be a way of kissing you good night and awakening next morning to find you still beside me. I had never thought to miss any woman as I miss you. You seem always in my thoughts . . .

Together all night. She would like nothing more than to smile a dreamy good morning and lift her lips to be kissed. But how could they manage it; how could they even begin to think of getting away with it?

She blew out the candle and walked in the darkness to the window, pulling aside the thick black curtains, willing the pump trough to be there and the outline of the far archway and beyond it in a dark purple haze, the treetops of Pygons Wood.

But instead, dimly in the starlight, she saw only a wall and in it a window that stared at her with dead eyes and she knew that as soon as it was light she would be off! Back home to Candlefold because she didn't belong here in Tippet's Yard. Nor would she, could she, ever again.

Monday, the first day of September and in just two more days the war would begin its third year, Meg thought despairingly, and them no further forward at all, save that Hitler had not invaded like everyone said he would last year after Dunkirk. Mind, he was so taken up in Russia, Mrs John said, that invading Britain must surely be the least thing on his mind.

Russia, that vast secretive country, had proved no match for the German armies, though Leningrad was prepared for a long seige, the papers said; Moscow, too. Maybe when winter came, Meg frowned, the Russians would be better at fighting than the Germans, they being more used to the terrible cold. Soon winter would be here too, and when it came, where would she be? Working on munitions; wearing a uniform? Or would some small miracle keep her here, at Candlefold?

She tutted impatiently, because who was Meg Blundell to think she was in any way different to the thousands of twenty-year-old women who didn't want to be called up? Who was she to expect a miracle when she didn't even believe in the God who worked them?

'Ar – what the heck?' It was a long time to winter, though this morning she had felt the chill of autumn in the air, and noticed that the green-again lawns around the brick house, cut short for their secret haymaking in full summer, were covered with heavy dew and wreathed in mistiness.

But whatever the season, Candlefold would be beautiful. Soon, the leaves would yellow and fall, and the creeper that clung to the walls of the house would turn vivid red, Polly had told her. And in winter, what more beautiful than the courtyard silvered by frost, or laid with snow – clean snow, like they never had in Liverpool?

Meg had learned so much since she came here and so much more, still, to be explored and remarked upon. Indeed, there were times when she thought she might just get away with not registering, because weren't bodies still being found in Liverpool? Not long ago, Nell said, a surface shelter was being demolished, and there was no end of people in it; gassed, it was thought, because a main beneath it had ruptured. So might not Meg Blundell be one of those people, dead and half decomposed now? And had she not already changed her address from Tippet's Yard to Lyra Street – and to number 6, which had been bombed the third night of the blitz? Couldn't many like herself be buried in the mass graves around the city, unidentified and unclaimed?

Then she set her mouth to its most stubborn, pulled back her shoulders and asked herself, very pointedly, where this beautiful old house would have been if, over the centuries, people like himself refused to fight for it? Or might she, on the other hand, just try sitting on the fence as Mark said the Kenworthys were very good at, and see what came of it?

Mark. She had read and read again his letter. True, he had sent no card, but wasn't the promise of twenty kisses – one for each year of her life – better by far than a fancy card and a sloppy verse: *Hold this letter to your cheek and know, Merrilees, that I have magicked twenty kisses inside it, to be redeemed in full and with passion, next time we meet.*

How she adored him, and in all aspects. Her love for him was a mixing of tenderness, laughter and passion, with a sprinkling of jealousy, too, whenever she thought of the ATS girls at his camp. Perhaps being in uniform just might have its benefits if she were stationed near Mark.

On the other hand, of course, *They* might call her up into the RAF, give her an airforce-blue uniform and send her to a bomber station in the wilds of Scotland! Yet she knew that when the time came, she would register. Polly would do it without a second thought, because that was what people like the Kenworthys did. Toffs, Nell called them; people with breeding and background who didn't know how lucky they were!

But Nell had been a bit Bolshie ever since her husband was killed in the last war, and nothing would change her. Nell concentrated on keeping alive and only the basic things of life interested her. She lived each day as it came, with a kind of fatalistic acceptance that was all people who lived in places like Tippet's Yard could do. Nell was Liverpool through and through, with the blunt aggression associated with all Liverpudlians and the warm, open heart that went with it. And if that was what Nell wanted, bless her, then that was fine by Meg Blundell, who had left the mucky streets behind her and was going to fight tooth and nail to stay away from them!

And that being established, and coming down to earth with a bump, what was Mrs Potter doing at the back door at this time of the morning? Meg frowned. Was she bringing a telegram and was someone coming on leave? Davie or Mark – or both?

She covered the distance from archway to door in no time at all, to hear Mrs Potter say, 'For Polly – and not bad news, Mrs John.' And her smiling because she already knew what was in it

'Then would you fly to the garden, Meg, and get Polly? And do you suppose,' she whispered, 'we are going to have a September wedding?'

It had been, Polly was to remark that night, a queer old day that began with Davie's telegram announcing seven days' embarkation leave and ending, as it so often did, with mugs of Ovaltine in Meg's bedroom.

'And even the phones have been peculiar, today. I mean – have you ever, since the war started, got a trunk call straight through, because that was all Mummy did – asked for Mrs Sumner's number in Oxford and was told to hold on, that they actually had a line to trunks! Then Davie phones long distance from Yorkshire and says he hadn't waited at all! What do you suppose it is?'

'Maybe a lovely gremlin on the line that's giving out trunk calls to people gettin' married.' Meg smiled dreamily, because hadn't Mark been given a forty-eight-hour pass and would be able to give the bride away! 'Anyway, you're getting your wish, Polly. You'll be Mrs Sumner the day after tomorrow.'

'I know.' Her sigh was one of pure ecstasy. 'But after that we'll probably never see each other again for the duration – and when you come to think of it, a duration can last an awful long time.'

'So what's the position this far?' Meg smiled again, thinking that since Mrs Potter delivered the telegram that morning, she hadn't stopped smiling, even though there had not been one quiet moment.

'Now tomorrow I must go to town,' Mrs John had said, 'and get the extra rations from the Ministry of Food.'

Authority had a sympathetic side, sometimes, granting food coupons for weddings; a mere half-pound of butter and half a pound of margarine, two pounds of sugar and a quarter-pound packet of tea. And food points too, to be used for the purchase of a tin of Spam or anything with which to fill the sandwiches that would be the sum total of the wedding feast.

No wedding cake, nor tables piled with food. No champagne. Just tea and sandwiches, and that only because bread was not rationed, nor ever would be, Mr Churchill had declared, in spite of U-boats sinking more than could be spared of precious wheat brought in convoy from Canada and America.

'Thank goodness for the hens. I'll be able to do plenty of egg and cress sandwiches, and I think the ration will run to two sponge cakes. Goodness! And I had dreamed of a four-tier wedding cake,' she laughed.

But two sponges it would be, using the very last of her sugar hoard and sandwiched together with the remainder of the birthday jam.

'There must be something for Davie and Polly to cut, after all. And I suppose I can sift icing sugar over it and make it look a bit more bridal.'

'But, Mrs John, when was there last any icing sugar in the shops?' Meg felt bound to point out.

'Heaven only knows, but we'll get round it. I'll have to spare some sugar and grind it in the mortar until the grittiness has gone and it becomes floury.' There was a way around everything in wartime. Polly would have her cake, she had promised, so two sponge cakes it would be!

'Davie's parents are staying two nights,' Polly said, placing a pillow behind her head. 'They're to have Mark's bedroom and he'll sleep in the night nursery. Davie is to spend the night at the vicarage and Mummy's friend Shelagh can't come because her daughter is getting near her time.'

'Maudie? The one whose dress you're wearing? My, but she must've fallen for that baby on her wedding night! I'd watch it, Polly – the dress might be smittled!'

'Hope it is, Meg. If Davie is going overseas, I want a baby as soon as possible.'

'Babies aren't all that easy got,' Meg cautioned, 'but I hope you're lucky and it'll be smashing trying, won't it? But aren't you just a little bit sorry it isn't going to be a big do? I bet if things were normal, there'd be half Lancashire here at Candlefold for your wedding.'

'But things aren't normal. I'm marrying Davie in a borrowed dress and borrowed shoes and there'll be no wedding breakfast nor champagne toasts. And no little attendants because there are no coupons to spare for dresses only to be worn once. But I don't care, Meg. All I want is to be Davie's wife, and for him to come home to me when it's all over. But perhaps the Kenworthys have paid in advance, and I'll be lucky.'

'Your father, you mean?'

'Mm. I don't remember him at all, would you believe? I know from his photographs he was handsome – I suppose Mark takes after him – but I can't call back his voice or his ever being there. I wish I could. And I wish he were giving me away on Thursday. He and Mummy had so little time together.'

'Hey! Chin up! He'll be with you in spirit and with your ma, too.'

'Yes, and I'll put my bouquet on his grave, afterwards. Potter says he's going to pick the best of the apricot roses from the brick house. He reckons there'll be enough left for a bouquet.'

'The rose that climbs up the front walls?'

'That's the one. He said there'll be about a dozen half-open flowers, still, on Thursday morning. He'll get up early to pick them. I did think to carry just my white prayer book – the one I got when I was confirmed – but Mr P. insists it's a bouquet or nothing. Isn't it exciting, Meg?'

'Exciting.' And Mark home for two days and two nights and it would be near unbearable them not being able to –

She shut down her thoughts. The next few days would belong to Polly. 'It going to be wonderful.' Reluctantly, she pushed all thoughts of Mark to the back of her mind. 'Have you decided, yet, about the honeymoon?'

'No. I'm leaving it to Davie, actually. Going abroad is out, though it's traditional for Candlefold honeymoons to be spent in Paris. And the east coast is out, because most of it is a restricted area and the beaches all barbed-wired. Same with the south coast, too. And we neither of us want to spend two days of his leave travelling to and from Scotland, so I think it might be somewhere not too far away – around Lancaster, maybe, or Bowland. Davie won't be going back to Catterick. He's to join a new unit, down south, so he and Mark will have to say goodbye for the duration after the wedding. Sad, isn't it?'

'Yes, but how smashing that Mark just happened to bring home an army friend, and he so right for you!'

'Fate, Meg. And isn't it wonderful to be able to say I'm getting married in two days? I'm not a bit sleepy – too wound up, I suppose. Fancy another hot drink?'

So they sat at the kitchen table and talked of weddings until very late and Polly sighed and said, 'I suppose we'd better hit the hay. But before we do, will you give me a hug and a kiss and tell me you're happy for Davie and me?'

'Of course I will! But what brought that on, will you tell me?'

'Because we've only known each other four months, yet it feels as if we've always known each other – been sisters, sort of, in a past life. But you don't believe in past lives, do you – or life after death?'

'No. Only that if it's for you – good or bad – you'll get it in the goodness of time.' She smiled, holding wide her arms. 'But come here, you daft ha'porth. Of course I'll give you a hug and a kiss, and of course you and Davie will be happy together. Tell you sumthink. If you aren't, then the pair of youse'll have me to answer to!'

They stood there, cheek on cheek, and Meg wished she could believe they had once shared a past life or that she had faith in the hereafter, where they might share another.

Yet all she could be sure of was that moments of happiness like this came rarely and were to be treasured and kept safe and golden-bright in her memory to set against dark days, when they came, to ease the pain.

Mark and Davie arrived at Candleford a little before noon. Meg saw them from her bedroom window and didn't know whether to stand there, aching with love for the tall, fair soldier who crossed the courtyard, or sit on the bed because her legs seemed all at once to have gone very wobbly.

He saw her, and waved, then Polly was running across the cobbles, arms wide, to fling herself into Davie's arms, and everything became wonderful and exciting, and not for anything would Meg let herself so much as think that on this day, two years gone, an old man with a weary voice had told them they were at war again. No! Today and tomorrow would be happy days and on Friday morning early, when Mark returned to his unit, she would lift her chin and smile and tell herself that the past two days had been a beautiful bonus, and that in little more than a month, Mark would be home again on long leave. If the war allowed, that was.

'You're a full lieutenant, now!' Polly pointed to Davie's shoulder epaulette. 'You don't have to call my brother Sir any more!'

And Davie's face had flushed with pride, his smile one of pure joy, even though they knew that his new rank meant an overseas posting into danger. 'So where's your kit?' Polly asked.

'I dumped it in the lane. I had to bring all my stuff with me since I'll be moving on. Do you suppose we can borrow a wheelbarrow? Didn't realise I had so much clobber.'

So they ran hand in hand to the kitchen garden and Mark, who had travelled light, kissed his mother and said, 'Hi, Merrilees,' as if it were only yesterday they had last met and spoken and loved.

'I hope you've got your best uniform with you,' Mary smiled. 'This is going to be a real wartime wedding. Potter and Armitage will be wearing their Home Guard uniforms, and Davie's father, too.'

'Suits me,' Mark shrugged. 'The less fuss, the better. As long as they tie the knot – if tie it they must! – who cares?'

'Now, Mark!' His mother put on her serious face. 'There will be no more sarcastic remarks about wartime weddings. Just because you seem determined to stay single doesn't mean it is wrong for Polly and David. Promise you'll try to feel pleased about it, and make a nice speech afterwards?'

'Hell! I'd forgotten the speech!'

'Then as acting father of the bride you'd better remember it! And since Davie isn't going to have a best man, then I shall expect you to keep the ring safe in your pocket, too.'

'Does it have to be a long speech? What must I say?'

'What her father would have said, had he been with us today. Think about it, Mark.'

And Mark, chastened, said he supposed he would come up with something, and would Merrilees be an angel and check over his best uniform? And polish the buttons, if she wouldn't mind?

'Will you be coming to the church, Merrilees, or will you be holding the fort here?'

'No,' Mary answered for her, 'Mrs Seed has volunteered to stay with your grandmother and Nanny and to have the kettles on the boil for when we all get back. We've got everything organized, Mark. All you have to do is give your sister away and wish her and Davie well at the reception – if you can call sandwiches and tea and sponge cake a reception!'

She raised her eyes in mock horror and hurried away to check there were enough vegetables for two extra to lunch.

'She's loving every minute of it,' Meg smiled fondly.

'Don't all women – go scatty over weddings, I mean? And can you come to my room in a couple of minutes? I want to kiss you, Merrilees.'

'But should I?' The nursery bedroom was much, much too near to Nanny.

'Of course. Haven't you just said you'll give my uniform the once-over?'

'Oh, all right . . .'

'Then see you in two minutes!'

Oh, Marcus John Kenworthy, Meg thought as she watched him take the stone stairs two at a time, what an irritating, bossy, gorgeous man you are! And why was he so intent on staying single when she would give all she owned and ten years of her life to be in Polly's shoes – in Polly's pretty white wedding shoes – tomorrow?

Meg sat at Eleanor Kenworthy's bedside, and the old lady talked of tomorrow's wedding and weddings past but not of weddings to come – for which Meg was truly grateful, since she had been kissed breathless in the small nursery bedroom, then deposited at the top of the steep stairs with Mark's best uniform over her arm and her head in a delightful whirl.

'It's a pity you can't go to the church, Gran. It's goin' to be such a lovely wedding with just about the entire village there – except you.'

'And Nanny,' came the prompt reply. 'Remember it was she who brought up my son and who was with Mary and me at his bedside when he died. And Nanny reared Mark and Polly, has been at Candlefold almost as long as I have. But that's life. Polly will make sure we both see her before she goes to the church. And though Nanny and I can't be downstairs for the celebration afterwards, I'm sure there will be many from the village who will pop up to see us. I'm quite looking forward to a few visitors – and all the village gossip. I found Davie's parents such nice people. He is so like his mother, don't you think?

'So tell me what is happening, Meg, and what everyone is doing. And tell me how Mary is going to cater for the guests, and how the preparations are going. And where is Mary now – having a rest, I hope?'

'She's with Davie's ma in the parlour. It's ever so cosy in there with the fire lit. And they're talking as if they've known each other all their lives, instead of today being the first time they've met. She's a nice little body and real happy about the wedding. And Davie's dad has gone out with Mark to have a look round, though they'll end up at the pub, I wouldn't mind betting.' She laughed, taking a long deep breath. 'And Mrs Seed will be here early in the morning and the farm knows we'll want extra milk and I shall go instead of Polly to collect it. Now – have I missed anything?'

'Yes. You and Mark. You won't see a lot of each other, will you, this time around?'

'No. But these two days belong to Polly and Davie, and Mark will get long leave in a few weeks. It'll be strange, him coming home alone. Polly's going to feel it, Davie being down south – maybe overseas.'

'Mm. I have told her that once Davie is settled in new quarters, and if he isn't sent abroad at once, she must go down there and spend all the time she can with him. After all, once he's abroad heaven only knows how long it will be before they are together again.'

'Then I'll help out in the garden and do all I can in the house. We'll make sure there's nothing to stop her being with him. I think it's a smashin' idea, Gran. Even a few extra days would be good. And had you thought – once Polly is married, the Government can't make her leave home to do war work, so I reckon they'll let her stay with Mr Potter, growing food.'

'I think they well might. But had you thought, Meg, that if Polly starts a baby – and she told me she doesn't mind how soon that is – she won't be required to do war work at all? Maybe then we'll be able to convince the people at the Ministry of Labour that you are the right person to step into her shoes.'

'Work with Mr Potter, you mean? I'd like that, though there's a lot I don't know.'

'And there are land girls who lived all their lives in cities and are now milking cows as if they'd been brought up to it! You could learn, Meg. Think how good it would be if we could find a way to keep you here.'

'And you think I don't want to stay here? I couldn't ask for anything better, though it'll all depend on Polly, won't it?'

'And Davie,' the old lady chuckled. 'But you'll come up too, before you go to the church – let me see how nice you look?'

'I'll come with Polly – give her a hand with her train up the stairs. She's going to be a beautiful bride.'

And Eleanor Kenworthy nodded, smiling softly, then wondered how much longer it would be before there was another wedding at Candlefold – her grandson's perhaps?

But Mark did not agree with wartime weddings when everything was in turmoil. And how could they have been so stupid as to let another war happen twenty years after the one the world had agreed was to end all wars. How wrong that the older generation should have been deaf to the rantings of a madman . . .

'What were you thinking, Gran?' Meg laid a gentle hand to the old cheek. 'You looked so sad.'

'If you must know, child, I was thinking that this war should never have happened, and what an awful world it has become for the young to grow up in.'

'You could be right, but let's not think about it till after Polly and Davie are married, and Mark has gone back to his regiment. And on Saturday, when everything is back to normal, let's you and me stick pins in Hitler's picture, like Nanny does, eh?'

'Nanny? She sticks pins in people she doesn't like? Are you sure, Meg? Sticking pins is witchcraft, you know.'

'Well, she does it, for all that. Sometimes it's when she sees a picture of Hitler in the paper – or Mrs Simpson. She really doesn't like her. Says she got her hooks into the Prince of Wales, and her not half good enough for him! Tell you sumthink – you've got to feel sorry for Mrs Simpson, at times!'

And they laughed, because Meg knew that Eleanor Kenworthy did not believe that Nanny would do such witchy things. But then, Gran was so lovely that she wouldn't believe a wrong word about anybody – Hitler and his lot excepted, that was. Come to think of it, there were a lot of things Gran didn't know and wouldn't believe – especially that Nanny Boag was a spiteful old biddy who did worse things than pin-sticking!

So instead she murmured, 'I wonder what Polly and Davie are up to right now?' Which was a very stupid thing to say, come to think of it!

Polly parted her lips from Davie's just long enough to whisper, 'Tomorrow at this time I'll be Mrs Mary Eleanor Sumner and we'll be in bed at – *where* will it be, darling? Have you decided yet?'

'Yes, but it's a surprise. One thing I will tell you, though, is that your mother is letting us have her car and all she has saved of last month's petrol ration in the tank. And since I came by a petrol coupon too, we'll get there and back in style!'

'Oh, Davie – *style* in a baby Austin! Mind, if we'd waited till after the war, I could have gone to church in a Rolls and you and I would spend our honeymoon in Paris – had you ever thought?'

'No. Because I don't want to wait till the war is over, though sometimes I think I've got a cheek. I mean – how am I to support you when I'm back in civvy street? I shall try for a scholarship to university, but all I'll have is my army gratuity – and that isn't going to keep us for long!'

'Then shall we worry about that when we've got to, and live each day as it comes. All I shall want, after tomorrow, is for you to come safely home – and perhaps a baby to keep me company when you are away from me. Would you mind if I got pregnant right away, Davie?'

'Not if that's what you really want, though how I can afford a family when I can't afford a wife, I don't know.'

'Nor do I, but I couldn't care less. Right now, all I can think about is sleeping with you. Does that make me common, darling?'

'Not a bit, Polly love, because it's all I've ever thought about since you and I first met! But we're on our way to the vicarage, so I think we should put all carnal thoughts from our minds for the time being.'

'I suppose we must.' Sighing, she offered her lips to be kissed again. 'If we try very hard, it's just possible that we can!'

Eighteen

Mrs Seed arrived at eight o'clock exactly, explaining she had taken it upon herself to collect the milk.

'Mornin', Mrs Kenworthy, ma'am. Four pints of last night's milking and I'm to go in an hour for four more of this morning's – when it's been through the cooler.'

She deposited the white enamelled cans on the pantry cold slab, took a pinafore and mobcap from the brown paper carrier bag she carried. Then, rolling up her sleeves to elbow length, she smiled and said, 'There now. Just like old times again, isn't it. Do you remember it was always my job to collect the milk when I was under-housemaid, here?'

And Mary Kenworthy said of course she remembered, then asked anxiously what she thought of the weather.

'A little bit misty, but it's September now, and to be expected. But it's my considered opinion that the sun is going to break through that old mist, and by ten o'clock we'll have weather fit for a bride! Now, tell me what needs doing, ma'am.'

'Do you suppose you could take tea up to Davie's parents? They are in Mark's room and it would be such a treat for them. Then would you take breakfasts for the ladies – just tea and toast – whilst I see to breakfasts here?'

'I saw Mr Potter this mornin' from my bedroom window. He was climbing the fence into the garden of the brick house and I thought he was going for flowers for the church.'

'Actually, no. He did the church last night. Nothing ostentatious – just Michaelmas daisies and a vase of Madonna lilies for the altar from our own kitchen garden. What he was going for – taking what is rightly ours, he said – was for roses from the brick house wall. He is making Polly's bouquet, and doing buttonholes for the guests, you see. Now I think I'll take up a tray for the bride. I insisted she sleep in, but she's sure to be awake and eager to be up. I told her, though, that morning tea in bed is traditional for brides, so she agreed to indulge me.'

'And where is young Meg? Asking questions, I shouldn't wonder. Always asking about Candlefold and the old days. Loves this place, doesn't she?'

'Mm. Actually she's doing the beds – Thursday is bedroom day, remember,' she smiled.

'Oh, my word yes! Washing done on Thursday; ironing on Fridays, but not today! Meg can fold those sheets and pillowslips and put them in the wash house. Happen they'll get done tomorrow. So go you upstairs, Ma'am and I'll set another cup and saucer on it so the mother of the bride can have a cup, too. Just leave everything to me! I haven't forgotten my way around, you know!'

'Mrs Seed is enjoying herself,' Mary smiled, handing out tea. 'I think she would have been deeply offended if I hadn't asked her to help in the house today. So many people are going to have a lovely time, you know. I think there should be more weddings in wartime – chase away the gloom and doom. So how do you feel, darling girl, now that the big day has come?'

'Just peculiar all over, Mummy. I'll be a married lady, soon. Y'know, ever since I met Davie I've wanted to marry him, yet now the day has come I feel as if I'm abandoning all the years of being your daughter and taking one huge leap into another life. Am I being silly? Is it wedding nerves? Am I doing the right thing?'

'No, yes and yes! Of course you aren't being silly! I imagine all brides think like you – for just a little while. Wedding nerves, as you say. But I think you are doing the right thing. Davie is so right for you, darling. And getting married can seem like taking a leap into another life, but Davie will be waiting to catch you when you jump – metaphorically, of course – don't forget. And Candlefold will be here always for you to come home to.'

'And you aren't sad, Mummy – losing a daughter, I mean?'

'Oh, Polly, didn't you know? Women never lose their daughters. I've heard it said that they grow even closer, after marriage, so stop worrying! More tea?'

'No thanks. Think I'll get up. I'd rather be busy – help the time along until two thirty. And, darling – I don't have any doubts; not really. It's just that my tummy's making awful noises.'

'Then down you go, and Mrs Seed shall make you toast and marmalade. And call Meg down, too. She's been up since it was light, dashing about all over the place. I think you'll find her in my bedroom. Tell her tea and toast in five minutes – all right?'

And Polly, all at once more calm, said it was.

'Meg!' She poked her nose round the bedroom door. 'You're to come downstairs for toast! Mummy says you've been at it since the crack of dawn! I do believe you're as nervous as I am!'

'Not nervous, Polly. Just jumpy and excited and happy all over. D'you know, this is the first wedding I've been to. Oh, I've stopped at church gates to watch the bride go in – or come out – but I've never been an honest-to-God guest. We-e-ll, not having any family that I know about, I wouldn't get asked.'

'Well, you've got family now and you're coming to my wedding as a very dear friend! And suddenly I'm desperate for toast and marmalade. Oh, Meg, we're going to enjoy every minute of this day, starting from right now!'

And they ran downstairs, laughing, just as the sun broke through the mist to shine the promise of a lovely day through the landing window.

'Will you see what Mrs Armitage sent?' Mary demanded the minute they entered the kitchen. 'So kind. Save me cooking, and me with extra mouths to feed.' On the table stood an enormous pie, barely cold from the oven, the crusty top shining as if demanding to be eaten at once. 'If I want to be posh, it's a game pie, she says, but it's pigeon breasts and rabbit and onion, and the crust is suet, so at least I don't have to feel guilty about taking her rations.'

Mrs Armitage was never short of unrationed suet to make into pie crusts, truth known, because Mr Armitage supplied the local butcher with rabbits and pigeons, gratefully received to sell as off-the-ration, under-the-counter goodies and gratefully bought by customers whose meat ration had run out. In return, therefore, Mrs Armstrong was regularly given a lump of off-the-ration under-the-counter suet, which made both parties happy, and which today had made Mary Kenworthy very happy indeed!

'Aren't people good, Mummy? And will you look! The sun is out! This is going to be a lovely day! And is speaking to the bridegroom unlucky? Do you suppose I could ring Davie up?'

'Of course you can, but not until you've eaten. And if I were you I'd leave it for another hour, just in case he's having a lie-in. And that, if I'm not mistaken, is the baker with the bread.'

'Then I hope it isn't too fresh,' Mrs Seed went to open the door. 'If it is, it's going to be the very devil slicing it. Did you tell him yesterday's baking, Mrs John?'

And Mary said not to worry, she had told him and, goodness gracious, how they were going to be at the church on time with all that was to be done last minute, she did not know!

But done it was, and by two o'clock everyone was ready and waiting for the local taxi, the owner of which could claim sufficient petrol for fifteen miles from the Board of Trade for weddings or the transporting of expectant mothers to the maternity hospital. If given one month's notice, that was! And fifteen miles would allow for plenty of journeys from Candlefold to the church and back, so no one need worry!

'There now! Mother-in-law and Nanny have seen us all – so parents of the bride and groom will go first.' Mary smiled at Davie's mother, who looked elegant in a lime-green dress and coat with a matching hat that had used up half a year's clothing coupons, but who cared! 'Then Mark and Polly will follow, and will you, Meg, sit in front with the driver and help Polly out – see that the train doesn't get caught in anything? Then after that –'

'After that,' Mrs Seed smiled, 'you will leave everything to me, ma'am, and not worry your head about a thing. All will be ready for when you get back and the kettles on the boil. And I'm used to those great teapots . . .' They had borrowed two-gallon teapots from the church hall and Mrs Seed knew exactly how to get four gallons of tea – and some to spare – from a quarter-pound packet of tea! 'And its beautiful and sunny outside, so I'll put a few chairs on the flags in the courtyard so we won't get too crowded in the hall.'

Two trestle tables – also borrowed – had been covered with starched cloths and were already set with cups and saucers and plates. In the pantry, covered with damp cloths, were three trays of sandwiches and beside them, awaiting a sifting of improvised icing sugar stood the bridal sponge cakes.

Not what you would call a Kenworthy do, the once-housemaid thought sadly, remembering the magnificent parties of old on which she had waited, all stiff and well starched. But there was a war on, and today the entire village would gather to see another Kenworthy married at All Saints, as they had been for hundreds of years.

So who cared, when Miss Polly was the loveliest of brides, who had grown overnight from a bit of a lass to a beautiful woman in white, eyes bright with love?

'Chairs outside, I said,' Mrs Seed repeated to no one in particular and to which no one answered, because walking across the courtyard was the taxi driver in a long white coat, a white cover to his cap and a yellow chrysanthemum in his buttonhole, to tell them that the car was waiting at the far arch and that he would be back at two twenty precisely to collect the bride.

'This is it, then? Are we all ready? Three of us for the church.' Mary beamed at Davie's parents. 'The groom – he *is* there?'

'Delivered him myself, madam, not five minutes ago – him and the vicar's wife.'

'Then what are we waiting for? See you in church, Polly darling – and hold your head high and don't walk too quickly down the aisle – remember, Mark, you aren't on a route march. Give everyone a chance to see her.'

'I will, Mother. Now off you go or the bride is going to be late!'

So Polly kissed her mother and Davie's mother, then she and Meg stood on the top step to wave them goodbye.

'I could do,' Mark said, looking at his watch, 'with a stiff Scotch!'

'And smell of booze in church! Don't even think about it,' Polly admonished. 'And anyway, we haven't got any whisky. Civilians can't get hold of it, you know.'

'Sorry. Didn't mean it, Sis. And might I say you both look extremely elegant?'

'You might,' Meg giggled, 'because we do.'

'Pity Mr Potter didn't make a bouquet for you, Meg girl,' Mrs Seed sighed. 'You'd have made a bonny bridesmaid. You should wear a hat more often. Hats suit you.'

'Well, this is the first and last time I shall wear this one. Got to give it back to Mrs John, see. Borrowed. My own hat has seen better days!'

'So who cares?' Polly beamed. 'And I feel we are about to spend the longest five minutes of my life!'

'One minute, then we go!' They stood in the church porch, Mark look- ing at his watch again. 'You all right, Poll – and why are you sniffing?'

'It hits you, doesn't it?' she grinned. 'The church smell, I mean – all dustiness, mustiness and holiness!'

Mark grinned back, then said, 'Ready? It's time . . .'

'Hang on!' Meg gathered the train onto her arm. 'I'll see you as far as the top of the aisle, Poll, then I'll let this go. If you walk nice and slow like your ma said, it'll look lovely, all flowing behind you. OK?'

And Polly said it was just fine, and as they stood beside a font filled with Michaelmas daisies, Meg arranged the train into folds and whispered, 'Good luck, then.'

She stood to watch them, Polly seeming to glide on a wave of satin, Mark straight and soldierly, smiling down at his sister. Then she crept quietly into the nearest pew, and began to sing the words of the first hymn, 'All things bright and beautiful'. Not, as Polly admitted, exactly a wedding hymn, but her very favourite none the less, and Meg was glad because she remembered the words from school, and the tune, though the creatures great and small around Tippet's Yard had been only dogs and cats and little caged birds, hanging at open front doors.

She moved so she could see Davie, who was smiling down at Polly, and Mark, ready to offer his sister's hand when the Reverend asked who gave this woman in matrimony. She knew the wedding service by heart, almost, having read it secretly and often from Polly's prayer book.

I Marcus John take thee Margaret Mary . . . She had said the words so many times in her heart, though she would never say them aloud. And whilst she was dwelling on the impossible, she thought about tonight and knew they would have little time together because Mark was the master of the house and would have to be at his mother's side – and more so once Polly and Davie had gone off on their honeymoon and Mrs John feeling weepy, maybe.

And surely it was wrong when in a church to think of Mark and herself at the willow pool, bodies silky and cool from the water and the joy of loving and being loved, and taking and giving.

She snapped shut her hymn book, banished such thoughts from her mind, and gave all her attention to the vicar, who was saying. 'Dearly beloved, we are gathered together here . . .'

Aah. Lovely. Weddings were lovely and this day was lovely and everything so lovely she wanted to weep she was so happy. The sun was shining and everyone in the village was here, joining in. And another Candlefold bride was saying, 'I will . . .'

She brushed away a silly little tear and took a deep, shuddering breath, because nobody had the right to be this happy; especially not Margaret Mary Blundell, who was so high-as-a-kite happy it just couldn't be true. And please, if there really was a God, and since she was in church, could she please keep her giddy happiness, if He wouldn't mind?

'Are you enjoying yourself, Merrilees?'

It was the first time they had spoken since the church porch; an age ago, really, though she understood that as father of the bride and master of Candlefold, he had little time to call his own.

'Oh *yes*! Wasn't it lovely in the church and didn't Polly look beautiful and you did as Mrs John asked, and walked down the aisle real slow? And wasn't it just beautiful when Davie turned and smiled as she walked towards him? My, but they're going to be happy, them two. It's on the cards and in the stars, they are!'

'And are you happy, Meg?'

'Course I am. This is the best weddin' I've been to – the *only* weddin' I've been to, truth known. Everybody's enjoying themselves. Didn't know people could be so happy; not when there's a war on.'

'And is it only the wedding makes you happy, Merrilees?' He looked at her keenly, his eyes finding and holding hers, asking an answer.

'No. I'm happy 'cause you're here, Mark – is that what you wanted me to say?'

'It is. And if I'm a bit taken up with other things, will you bear with me? We can make up for lost time tonight.'

'Tonight! But, Mark, it wouldn't be right, us takin' off. People would notice.'

'Not later on they wouldn't. I can't talk now, though, but when Polly has gone I'll tell you – OK?'

'Yes, but, Mark –'

'No buts, Merrilees. See you!'

And with that he was gone, smiling at guests; the host, the master of Candlefold who, on one day out of a war, had come into his own – given away his sister in marriage and welcomed everyone from Nether Barton – and the tiny hamlet of Upper Barton – to his home to celebrate. It sounded very swanky, Meg thought, yet every house in those two villages belonged to Mark – with the exception of the vicarage, Mr Potter had told her. Mark was a soldier, now, because the war had said he must be, but he was a rich man too; a landowner with centuries of breeding behind him.

So why did he bother with someone like herself; a girl who had no background? Or had Nell been right? Did toffs like Mark amuse themselves with a girl from the back streets? A bit of rough, wasn't it called? He hadn't once said he loved her; not even when they were clasped close, loving. And in all the months she had known him, he had sent her two letters and a hastily written postcard. Yet now he wanted them to be together tonight and they couldn't – could they? *How* could they?

She shook all thoughts from her head, seeking out Mrs Seed to ask where Polly was and to be told that she was upstairs, changing for the off.

'Pity about those dratted clothing coupons. By rights she should have had a going-away costume, but there was a cotton dress and straw hat laid out on the bed. Not right. Not for a Candlefold bride.'

'And Candlefold brides usually go to Paris, Mrs John said, but Paris isn't available at the moment,' Meg laughed.

'Sad, isn't it? Wonder how we'd have felt if those Nazis were goose-stepping all over London.'

'But they aren't and they won't be, Mrs Seed. Mark said if Hitler had invaded us instead of Russia, it might have been a very different matter. The King and Queen and the princesses away in Canada, or Australia, and poor old Churchill shot at dawn for all the awful things he said about Hitler! But I know we're going to win, and when Polly and me register for war work it'll be over in six months when her and me get stuck in!'

And they both laughed, because this was a day for laughter. Then Mrs Seed became all at once serious and said such things as young girls having to go to war were not even to be *thought* about on Polly's wedding day, and was Meg sure there wasn't a way for the two of them to get out of it?

'For Polly there is – she's married, now – but there's nothing I can do about it.'

'And they really could make you leave Candlefold?'

'They could. That lot can do what they want. I shall probably end up in the far north of Scotland and never see Candlefold again!'

Her eyes filled with tears of self-pity and her lip trembled even to think of something so awful, and the sight of her prompted Mrs Seed to say sternly that tears on this sunny September afternoon were not permitted and that she was to go and sit on the pump trough.

'I'll bring you a cup of tea, lass, though the food is all gone. Won't be a tick – I'll squeeze the pot for you!'

So Meg did as she was told and sat on the rough, sun-warmed stone and tried her hardest to forget the smiling housemaid at the pump trough who'd had to leave Candlefold, never to return.

'Now then, Meg! Aren't we all having a grand time, then?'

Mrs Keating sitting beside her, treating her like one of themselves – which she was, really, though she could never tell a soul why. So instead she smiled, and asked how Bill was getting along in hospital in Malta.

'Doing fine, by all accounts. And his wounds must be mending 'cause he's writing his own letters now.'

The war, Meg supposed, did sometimes throw up something good – like Bill not being killed, after all, and herself finding Mark.

'Just about managed it, lass, though it's well stewed!' Mrs Seed, with tea. 'But it's wet and warm so drink it down. She's bothered, Mrs Keating, about having to go away to the war.'

'And I don't blame her! Bad enough them taking the young men, but calling up lasses shouldn't be allowed. That Hitler ought to be hanged when this war is over!'

Then there was a murmur that went all around the courtyard and ended up in a burst of clapping. Polly was standing at the top of the stone steps, wearing a cotton dress, a straw hat trimmed with daisies and well-worn, well-polished sandals. A bare-legged bride so beautiful in her happiness that Meg gulped down her tea lest tears came again, then joined the guests making their way to the far archway to wave bride and groom goodbye as they chuffed and bounced away in Mrs John's baby Austin.

'I know where they're going, Meg,' Mrs Seed whispered importantly. 'I heard Davie tell his mother and that she wasn't to tell a soul till they were gone. It's York. The Station Hotel! And I happen to know there's confetti in Polly's case, 'cause Davie's mother put it there. Oh, won't there be some blushes when she unpacks, and hasn't this been a beautiful day?'

And Meg agreed it had, and decided it was another day to secret away, golden, to be brought out and lived again when times were bad.

Bad times? Why should she think of bad times? She returned to the pump trough and sat there alone, fingers gripping the rough stone in search of comfort, and it was there Mark found her.

'Merrilees! Thank heaven they got away all right. They're going to York, did you know?'

'Yes. Mrs Seed heard Davie tell his mother. Suppose everyone will know by now. I've never been to York . . .'

'Nor me. But both Gran and Mother spent their wedding night there, then took the train to Dover – and Paris, eventually. Poor Sis will miss Paris.'

'She won't care. It isn't all that important where you go; what matters is who you are with. If it was the Adelphi Hotel in old bombed Liverpool it would seem like Paris to Polly.'

'You could be right, Merrilees. And thank goodness people seem to be leaving, now. I've had enough oh-ing and ah-ing for one day. Wish I could shove off down to the village for a pint.'

'They won't be open yet. And those people are your guests, Mark – yours and Mrs John's – so hadn't you better wish them goodbye and thank them for coming, just as your mother is doing?'

'Well, Hoity-toity! Just what is upsetting Meg Merrilees, then?'

'You are, if you want to know!' It was out before she had time even to think. 'This has been a lovely day an' Polly so happy it would make you want to weep. Yet you go all snotty about it and act bored. Why, Mark? What is so awful about falling in love and getting married? Or don't your sort bother? Do you expect it as your right – that fools like me are easy? I mean, why get married when it's there for the askin'?'

Unshed tears hurt her throat because it was unfair of him to be so scathing about other people getting married and being happy – unashamedly happy – and vowing in church that it was for always – till death parted them. Why was he so sarcastic about two people being so in love that they said sod the war and took a chance, and neither of them knowing for sure they would come through it alive?

'Suppose I was being a bit blasé about today. Sorry, Meg.'

'Sorry my foot! And what's blasé, anyway?'

'Bored. Indifferent. And I'm not, really. I wish them every happiness. They are doing what they want to do and I suppose it is no business of mine. And before you get on your high horse again, I am not against marriage, even in wartime. I just think they are both a bit young, that's all.'

'Well, I don't, Mark! They are right for each other, so why wait? Hadn't you thought that the few days they are together might be the only ones they ever have?' Tears, so near to surfacing all afternoon, ran unhindered down her cheeks. 'Oh! Now see what you've done!'

She jumped to her feet, making for the house, but he took her arm and held it so she was forced to tell him he was hurting her and to let her go, if he didn't mind!

'I'm not letting you go! I want to talk to you. Where shall we go? Fancy a walk down to the river?'

'To the willow pool, you mean? Just how can I slope off, will you tell me, when there is work to be done? Mrs Seed can't do it on her own and it isn't right your mother should have to pitch in! Oh, you are so selfish, Mark Kenworthy!'

'All right! All right! So we can't leave. It isn't important, actually. I just wanted a few words with you, that's all.'

'Well, you're gettin' them! What about, anyway?'

'About tonight – if I'm not in the doghouse, that is . . .'

'You an' me, you mean? *Tonight?* How can we?'

'Easily. Your room. When everything is quiet, I'll come to your room.'

'You'll *what*?' she gasped.

'Well, I'm sleeping next to Nanny, so mine wouldn't be a lot of good. Yours, on the other hand, is right at the end of the corridor and Polly's room next to it is empty.'

'You've got it all thought out, haven't you, Mark?'

'Actually – yes.'

'All sneaky, sort of! And in your mother's house, an' all!'

'My house, if push comes to shove, Merrilees. I just don't happen to be living in it at the moment, that's all. And sneaky – yes. But wasn't it just that at the willow pool?'

'N-no! We were outside and – and it just happened, sort of, all natural and lovely.'

'Yes. Very natural and lovely. Y'know, I often close my eyes and bring it all back: the scent of the grass and the willows around us and above us and –'

'Mark! Stop it! You're embarrassin' me!'

'Sorry. Thought you'd enjoyed it too.'

'I did. I still do. I think about it a lot and it makes me go all funny inside. But are you sure it'll be all right – in my room, I mean?'

'Once I'm there, it will be as right as ever it was – and will be. Making love is what matters, not that I'll be sneaking down to your room, as you put it. I can do it easily, anyway. I used to sleep up there, don't forget. I know which stairs creak. It *will* be all right, I promise you.'

'I'll have to go, Mark. Mrs Seed really does need help. And there's supper to see to, don't forget.'

'So see you at suppertime, Merrilees.' He smiled right into her eyes, and it did things to her insides.

'Suppertime . . .'

'The vicarage will be extra afterwards – did Mother tell you? I think they want to play cards. So if I get caught up in a game, I'll see you . . . ?'

'All right. Later.' She said it reluctantly, because all at once she felt like one of the tarts in Lime Street, arguing not about how much, but where.

'As soon as I can, after everything has settled down – OK?'

And without waiting for an answer he was gone, striding out towards the far arch, and she wondered if he was going to the garden or the farm. Or maybe to the willow pool, where first they loved.

And tonight they would love again, in her room, in her bed. And afterwards, would he stay with her or would he kiss her good night and go back to his bed in the nursery, as furtively as he had come?

She hoped he would stay. It would be wonderful to awake to find him beside her, something she had dreamed about more times than she cared to admit. So did it matter where, or how secretive their coming together would be? Surely all that mattered was that they should love, and that forever after her room would be a part of it. And every night she would sleep in a bed in which he, too, had slept.

'Now then, Mrs Seed – what do you want me to do?' she asked, tying on an apron.

'You tell me, Meg girl. Where to start is the priority, at the moment. I suggest we take trays and collect crockery, then get the tables dismantled ready for when Armitage calls to collect them. Said he would take them behind the tractor – and the crockery too, if we pack it careful. So let's get that job out of the way, eh, then it'll be time to start on the supper. You game to do the veggies?'

Meg said of course she was; that there were only two extra because the vicarage wasn't coming till after supper, the vicar's wife being most particular about other people's rations.

'You seem a bit more cheerful, lass,' the older woman remarked as they folded tablecloths. 'You were a bit tearful, before.'

'Mm. Sorry. But it was so lovely, and Polly and Davie so happy that it stuck in my throat – happiness, I mean – and came out as tears.'

'Everybody is allowed a little weep at weddings, Meg! I alus feel choked up, an' all. But let's be glad young Polly is so happy. Davie's a grand lad. He'll look after her, all right – if this dratted war allows. Be nice to think, wouldn't it, that we could do all this again next year for Mark, though when he gets wed it'll be in his bride's parish, won't it? Pity . . .'

'Pity. An' I'll take these tablecloths to the wash house, shall I?'

'If you wouldn't mind. The washing'll be done a day late, this week and the ironing I'll do on Saturday. Then it'll be back to normal, with Polly back all pink-cheeked and pretty. Poor lass. We'll have to see she doesn't get too downhearted with her man gone back to the war. And I'll get out of these daft shoes and put something more comfortable on my feet, then you an' me'll soon have things straight!'

'It was all so lovely, Gran. That wedding dress looked as if it had been made for Polly. An' her pearls were the finishing touch.' Meg settled herself beside Eleanor Kenworthy's bed.

'Thank you for coming up, child.'

'But I said I would – tell you all about it. They're all in the drawing room, round the fire. They'll be playing cards, afterwards, but I think Mrs John will be glad of a sit-down.'

'And what is my grandson doing?'

'He said if he wasn't wanted to make up a four, him an' Davie's dad will take a stroll to the pub. Said Mr Sumner should taste northern beer. He gave Polly away real gentle, like – smiled at her when he walked her down the aisle and they took it nice and slow like Mrs John told him they must.'

'And did anyone manage to get any snaps? It's such a pity these days, people not being able to buy films for cameras.'

'Yes. Two people had films in their cameras and Mrs John had three snaps left in hers. Where she's goin' to get another one for the christening, goodness only knows, but there'll be a few pictures for you to see, Gran.'

'Good. So tell me, Meg, right from the start, how it was. Did Polly speak up clearly and was the singing good, in church?'

So Meg took the old hand in hers and said she'd be glad to, but she would have to be forgiven if she got a bit choked up at times, because it had been such a lovely, sunny, unbelievably wonderful day that she still got a bit weepy, just to think of it.

And Eleanor Kenworthy said of course she would understand, and wondered why her grandson, stubborn young fool that he could be at times, had not snapped up the treasure that Meg was.

'Right! I'll just make you comfy, Gran, then I'll begin at the beginnin', as they say!'

Meg shone her torch on the clock at her bedside. Everyone had been late going to bed, as if they never wanted the day to end. But now it was half-past midnight, and goodnights said and doors closed. All was quiet save for the sounds an old house makes when it is settling its timbers for the night.

She lay, hands clasped behind her head, wondering if Mark would come; if he was waiting for Nanny's snores to start or if, like herself, he was listening to the silence and making sure all was well. Or would he fall asleep accidentally, and would she wait and wait until it was light?

She turned as the door opened with a small, swishing sound as it slid over the carpet, wondering why she had never before noticed what a noise it made. Then the door closed, and she heard the slow sliding home of the bolt.

'Meg? You awake?'

'Yes.' Her voice sounded breathless as she sat up in bed. 'Don't put the light on. The curtains aren't drawn . . .'

Outside, a half-waxed moon outlined the square of the window and dimly touched angles of furniture. The stars were bright too, and through the open window there was no sound; not even the cry of a hunting owl.

She watched, not wanting to speak, to whisper even, as he threw off his dressing gown. Dimly she saw the outline of his body, naked like her own. She drew aside the bedclothes and he slipped in beside her, taking her in his arms, kissing her mouth gently.

'You're cold.' He pulled the blankets over their shoulders and for a while they clung tightly, then he said, 'Hello, you.'

She did not speak, but whispered a kiss on his chin, his cheek, the tip of his nose, turning on her side to face him.

'This is better than the willow pool.'

'No, Mark. Nowhere is better than there.'

'Our first time, you mean?'

'Mm. Special . . .' They had pulled the blankets still higher, muffling their voices, making is safer to speak. 'No one heard you?'

'No, but if they did, I could have been going to the bathroom. Kiss me?'

She offered her lips, closing her eyes as he gentled the rounds of her shoulders, searching with his mouth for her breasts. She felt his hardness against her and relaxed her body, lifting her arms above her head in a gesture of surrender.

'Now, Mark? Please?'

It was a silent, whispered loving. They moved gently, mouth on mouth and she tried not to cry out as they reached the heights together then lay back, limp and fulfilled, panting softly.

'Meg,' he whispered huskily. 'Darling girl . . .'

She reached for his hand and they lay shoulder to shoulder, bodies moist from loving.

'I love you, Mark Kenworthy,' she whispered.

'And I love you.'

He said it softly, reluctantly almost, and her heart thudded with sudden joy.

'You – you mean it?'

'Yes. I should have said it long ago.'

'You should. I wanted you to. I thought you never would.'

'Well, I just did – so where do we go from here?

'Ssssh, darling. I'll think about it,' she said softly, indulgently, 'when you've loved me again . . .'

She awoke urgently, reaching for him with an outflung arm, but he was not there, the space where he had lain, cold.

The room was light enough for her to see the clock. It was almost seven and she threw back the bedclothes, pulling on slippers, wrapping her dressing gown round her nakedness, making for the door.

It was then she saw the envelope, and stooped to pick it up and read the note inside.

Darling Meg,

Didn't want to spoil last night by telling you I've got to be on my way very early. Back in camp by nine, so let's hope I can hitch lifts.

This is a kind of goodbye, yet it's a hello, really, to love – our love. I will try to phone tonight and tell you again, but I will write too, and tell you I love you and want to be with you always.

Take care of yourself, sweetheart.

Always, Mark

Oh, dear sweet heaven, he'd said it last night and she had hardly believed it, yet now it was there, written bold on the page. He loved her. He loved *her*, wanted to be with her always.

She sat heavily on the bed, hugging herself with a mixing of joy and disbelief, needing to tell Polly. But Polly wouldn't be back for days. Who, then? Gran? Of course it must be Gran but first, when she went for the milk, she would go to the willow pool and whisper their love to the trailing branches and to the river, so it might know, and tell all it touched that Mark and Meg would be lovers for ever.

Tears – lovely, silly, happy little tears – came to her eyes and she picked up the pillow they had shared, burying her face in it. Today, Mrs Seed would do the weekly wash and she must take off the pillow case and carry it – as if it were something ordinary and everyday – to the wash house to be possed and boiled and rinsed and mangled.

She sniffed, smiling, knowing she must strip her bed of the sheets they had lain in, telling herself it was all right – that no amount of Mrs Seed's zeal could ever quite wash away something so precious, and anyway, you couldn't, just *couldn't,* try to keep inviolate everything he had touched and sat on or eaten from, because now she had his love to keep safe in her heart. For ever.

She tiptoed along the passage to the bathroom, strangely reluctant to wash Mark's nearness from her body, chiding herself for being so foolish, so utterly light-headed.

Then, smiling at the bright-eyed girl in the mirror above the wash-basin, she whispered, 'He loves you!' On Friday, 5 September he had said it and written it, and she was so crazily happy she would take off like a firework and be lost in the clouds!

'Mark Kenworthy, wherever you are this very minute,' she whispered into the towel, 'please take care because you are so precious and so loved and so very wanted.'

She had told it to the willow pool, whispered it deliciously to the lazily flowing river, then stopped at the hen run on her way back from the farm and told it to the hens, who took not a bit of notice. She said it, silently from her heart, as she passed the pump trough so that Ma might know, then said it again to the rose that climbed the walls above the front door, so complete was her happiness, so golden had been the moment he whispered his love for her.

All that remained was to tell Gran, who had been on her side all along; say, 'Last night, Mark said he loved me, and this morning there was a letter pushed beneath my door and he said it again . . .'

And Gran would be very, very happy for her and would share with her the wonder of it, and loving and now of being loved. Gran had given her a lovers' knot brooch, had known all along that one day Mark would say the words.

But first she would take up Nanny's tray; offer it with a polite good morning, then leave at once. Get the moment over with, Meg decided, then spend more time in Gran's room, telling her.

Nanny was the last person she would tell, Meg thought, arranging the two trays prettily. Nanny was at best a foolish, possessive old woman, and at worst, deceitful, bad-minded and a thorough snob, and such wonderful news must be kept for as long as possible from Emily Boag, whose face would be vinegar-sour when eventually she found out!

'I'll take the nursery tray first,' she called to Mrs John. 'And I'll strip Mark's bed whilst I'm up there, ready for Mrs Seed. Then I'll take Gran's, so you can see to Mr and Mrs Sumner. Pity they've got to go back today.'

Pity anyone had to leave Candlefold, which was a place of love and magic and giddy happiness.

'Can I come in?' Deliberately she made her voice as friendly as talking to Nanny would allow. 'Porridge, this morning, and toast. On your little table, shall I put it?'

'You usually do! As a matter of fact, girl, it's of little consequence to me where you put the tray. And close the door. I have things to say to you that no one else must hear.'

'What things, Nanny?' What new malice was there to be?

'I said shut the door! Are you deaf as well as wanton? And a wanton you are, miss! A slut, a trollop!'

'Now listen here!' Meg flushed hotly. 'Just mind your tongue!'

'No! Now it's *you* who will listen! Last night Mark came to your room, and don't deny it because I heard you at it! God, it was sickening!'

Panic washed over Meg from head to toe, leaving her cold and speechless, then she lifted her head and gasped, 'I don't believe you! You're making it up, Nanny Boag! Is there nothing you won't stop at to part Mark an' me?'

'I am not making it up! And stop denying it. There's guilt written all over your face. And anyway, I heard Mark go downstairs.'

'So you thought he was coming to my room? Couldn't he have been going to the bathroom?'

'He could have, but the bathroom door creaks. Yours doesn't.'

'So you came downstairs, and listened outside. You're dirty-minded and you're sick!'

'Yes. I listened. And don't think I liked what I heard. You were whimpering like a bitch on heat!'

'Aagh!' That did it! No one, but no one, was going to dirty something so precious, not even if she was an old woman! She lifted her hand and swung it into the triumphant face, catching Nanny's cheek a stinging slap. 'You are disgusting! Only someone with a twisted mind would listen at doors!'

'So you admit it then?' she said calmly, ignoring the slap.

'Only if you'll admit you can get about better than you'd have Mrs John know! You queen it upstairs whilst the likes of a real lady used to wait on you – before I came! And it isn't the first time you've been down those stairs, is it? You went into my wardrobe and opened my little case!'

'Yes. And if I never leave this room again, that trip was worth it, because I found out who your mother *really* was! Hilda, you said she was called. Worked in a tobacco factory and your father a sailor buried at sea. Lies! All lies! You came here to deceive, but I found you out! You're Dolly Blundell's girl. A tart she was, an' all, and it's come out in you!'

'Stop it! I won't listen to you! Ma wasn't a tart! She couldn't help it if she was let down!'

'Ah, Father Unknown on your birth certificate!' The wrinkled mouth twisted itself into a sneer. 'That's what the fathers of all bastards are called. Unknown! But Dolly Blundell knew who did it, and so do I!'

'You can't know. Ma wouldn't have let you know! She kept it a secret. She didn't even tell me!'

'Maybe she didn't, but I knew! And if you'd come here admitting who you really are, you'd have got short shrift and been shown the door instead of being taken in and given big ideas about yourself!'

'So what are you going to do about it?' Meg's mouth was dry; her tongue made little hissing sounds as she spoke. 'Tell Mrs John, will you? Well, I'll get to her first. I'll tell her *everything* about me – yes, and that I love Mark, an' all. And whilst I'm at it, I'll tell her about you; that you've lived a lie for years, pretending you couldn't tackle stairs and making out you could only walk with difficulty!

'But you're not only good at stairs, you can balance on a chair, can't you, Nanny, and look out of the window at everything that's going on? How's Mrs John going to take your deceivin' her? Is she goin' to count the number of times she's toiled up those stairs, waitin' on you! And when she does, is she goin' to think well of your bare-faced lying?

'Oh, no! You tell on me, Nanny, and as sure as I'm standing here, I'll tell on you! You aren't going to get away with it! Not without a fight, you're not. And if Mrs John is willing to forgive a couple of white lies – and told so's I could stay here and work – I shall be in the clear. But you – I don't think she'll take too kindly to all the lying you've done, over the years! So go on, then! Tell her! I dare you to!'

Her cheeks an angry red, her breath coming in painful gasps, Meg made for the door, unable to look into the evil face a moment longer. And she didn't have to look at her, because she had called her bluff and Mrs John would never be told about her deception, nor about last night either! So sod the old witch! See if Meg Blundell cared!

'Come back! I haven't finished!'

'Oh! You haven't?' Meg turned slowly in the doorway, sure she had won. 'So you're goin' to tell me who my father was?'

'Yes. And more besides! So shut that door and listen! You will *not* tell Mrs John what has been said between us, and what is more, you'll get yourself out of this house just as soon as you can pack your bags!'

'Oh, I see! And who says so, Nanny?' It was so ludicrous she wanted to laugh. 'You think I'm going to take one blind bit of notice of what you say! Only Mrs John can fire me, and she won't do that! It's you who'll be in trouble, not me!'

'No, Meg Blundell! It's entirely up to me. I saw what was in your case, and your birth certificate and the deeds to the Tippet's Yard house – even though you said you lived in a different street! And when I tell Mrs John, she'll have no option but to ask you to go!'

'What! For a couple of innocent lies! The heck she will, Nanny!'

'Maybe not for lies, but when she knows, you'll be on your way, so are you going to go quietly – slip away without making any trouble either for yourself or for Mrs John, who doesn't deserve it, anyway!'

'I'm not goin'. I'm calling your bluff, Nanny Boag!'

'Then I shall tell you! What you did last night is unforgivable.'

'No. More understandable – when there's a war on, especially! Mrs John might be shocked, but she'd understand.'

'But you'd still have to go, Blundell! There would be no way you could stay, once she knew!'

'Knew *what*, will you tell me?' Meg was afraid again. Nanny was too calm, too sure. '*Tell me!* Tell me what Mrs John won't be able to forgive!'

'Very well. Since you seem set upon making trouble for yourself and everyone else in this house, you shall know.'

For a moment she was silent, as though reluctant to say what must be said, then her face twisted with malice and her eyes narrowed in hatred.

'You asked for it and now it is my duty – and pleasure, I might add – to tell you why you will leave Candlefold and never, *ever* come back to it. And why you will leave secretly and without one word of explanation to a soul. Because last night, you dirty little slut, you bedded your own brother!'

Nineteen

'*No!*' Meg let out a gasp as though a great, vicious fist had slammed into her abdomen, knocking the breath from her body. Her *brother*? She felt for the chair beside her, sitting down heavily, trying to suck air into her lungs.

'How can you tell such lies? What did I ever do to you, Nanny, that makes you hate me so?'

Tears brimmed in her eyes and she blinked them away. She wouldn't weep! Not in front of *her*!

'Hate you, dear? Of course I don't hate you.' The voice was gentle now, and slightly surprised. 'I'm only telling you for your own good. After all, it's against the law to do *that* with a close relative. Incest, it's called, and frowned upon . . .'

Meg raised her head to look into the apple-cheeked face and eyes that were round with concern. Oh, but she was clever. Clever, and mad!

'Nanny, you have just said a very bad thing.' It surprised Meg that her voice should sound so calm when the world had gone mad around her and the screaming in her head made it difficult to speak. 'Mark is *not* my brother!'

'No. I got it wrong. You and he had different mothers, which makes him your half-brother. But he's still blood kin and you can't marry kin!'

'I don't believe you!' Her insides were crawling again because the look of triumph was back on the old face; a look that said there was more to tell!

'Then you must believe me! I'll spell it out for you, so there'll be no misunderstanding. After you were born, your mother was given a house in Tippet's Yard by Mr John. It was a slum property inherited from a cousin and it meant nothing to him. But your mother needed shelter, so he sold it to her for a few pence. She was well treated, you know; wasn't shown the door and pointed in the direction of the workhouse as she should have been. She was allowed to remain at Candleford and was confined in one of the rooms in the brick house. I know, because I was there when you were born. Yes, she was treated very well, all things considered.'

'What do you mean, *all things considered*? You talk as if she was a slut and she wasn't! And since you seem to know it all, and since you know I can't deny what you're saying, will you tell me who *really* got my mother into trouble, then abandoned her?'

'You mean you *still* don't know; the penny hasn't dropped?'

'I'm trying not to believe you, Nanny Boag, because what you're hintin' at is nasty and dirty and it can't be true.'

'Oh, but it is. Threw herself at him, Dolly Blundell did, and in spite of everything, Mrs John had compassion on her and cared for her during her pregnancy, when I would have thrown her out, bag and baggage!'

'Mr John – Mark's father – the one who died not long after Polly was adopted – is my father too? Is that what you are saying?' It hurt to ask the question and the words came out in a shocked whisper.

'That is exactly what I am saying and you know it is true because you have your birth certificate to prove you were born here, and you have the deeds of the house in Tippet's Yard to add substance to what I say. So hadn't you better go before you cause any more trouble? Don't you think Mrs John had enough to put up with, twenty years ago, when you were born? And do you want Mrs Kenworthy, ill as she is, to have to be reminded of dirt that should have been swept out of the door long ago? Just who do you think you are, Meg Blundell, to act as if you have a perfect right to be here?'

'I've never thought that.' She shook her head wearily. 'When Ma died it was the first time I'd ever seen those papers in the little case. But she'd spoken so lovingly about Candlefold and how happy she had been, working here, that I thought I'd take a look at it. That was all. Just a look. But then I saw the card in the post office window, and I asked for the job. There was no deceit in it. I was in need of work and I wanted to find out why Ma loved Candlefold so. And I'll admit I hoped that I might find out who Father Unknown was, though I never did, because suddenly it didn't seem important. But I didn't come here to make trouble, you've got to believe that. I swear I didn't know who my father was.'

'Well, now you do, so what are you going to do about it?'

'Nuthin'. What is there to do, though it seems awful I've just got to leave without saying goodbye.'

'And have them ask why you're going? Of course you can't say goodbye!'

'I could make sumthink up . . .'

'Oh, no! You go, disappear, like I said! Because if you don't I'll tell Mrs John this very minute who you are and what you and Mark were up to last night. Do you want her to have her tell you to go, then?'

'Seems I don't have much of a choice.'

'You have no choice at all, so why don't you have a little respect for the people who have been so good to you – and were undeniably good to your mother, too – and take yourself off without any fuss?'

'Without any fuss,' Meg repeated woodenly, holding the back of the chair for support as she got unsteadily to her feet. 'Yes. Seems I'll have to.'

Do it with dignity, as Ma would have done. Pack her things and hide her case until she could get away unseen. Say nothing, not even a goodbye or a thank you. Just go from this place and never come back, as Ma had done, because as sure as anything, Ma would have done it the right way – head high!

At the door she turned. 'I can't just walk out. Give me time?'

She shouldn't be pleading with Nanny Boag, but there was no fight left in her. It was as if, she thought, a telegram had come to Candlefold, just as it had come to Smithy Cottage, telling them Mark had been killed. Because she had lost him just as surely as if he had been.

'No. I know what I'm talking about! And you'd better be careful about it, like I said. Take your things to the wash house – they'll be safe enough there.'

'No, they won't. Mrs Seed is working in there today; she would ask me –'

'Then find somewhere else, only *go*! Don't make any more trouble than you need!'

Unspeaking, Meg closed the door, walking slowly down the narrow stairs, clinging to the rail for support because her legs seemed not to belong to her. With difficulty she made for the kitchen, then sat down heavily at the table, head in hands, too numb to think or reason or accept.

'Meg! What is it? Are you not well?' Mrs John was at her side, face filled with concern. 'My dear, you look dreadful.'

'Sorry. I – I don't feel too good . . .'

'Then you must have an aspirin and a cup of tea. Are you in pain, Meg? You look so pale.'

'No. Not pain. I just feel ill all over. I'm sorry.'

'Don't be. Off you go to bed and I'll bring up the tea and tablets. And if you aren't feeling better by lunchtime I shall call the doctor.'

'No! I'll be all right. Just tea and a couple of aspirins. They usually work. I – I think it's the usual . . .'

'Your period? Oh, you poor thing. And you've been working so hard.'

'It's all right. I'll be fine. Just a little lie down and I'll be as right as rain. But Mrs Kenworthy hasn't had her breakfast yet.'

Meg wanted to take up Gran's tray; see her for just one last time.

'Then I shall take it. Now, up you go and I'll be with you in a minute.'

Wearily Meg rose to her feet, whispering her thanks, grateful for Mary Kenworthy's concern because she needed time alone; time to think. Her bed was unmade and she lay on the crumpled sheets, eyes closed, arm over her eyes to shut out the world.

Nanny was wrong. She had to be. Mrs John's husband wasn't the sort to get a servant pregnant under his wife's nose! And what was more, Ma wasn't the sort to let him, either! Yet pregnancies didn't just happen, and Ma had loved someone enough to get a child.

Someone? John Kenworthy, Nanny said, and why should she lie? Why, when she had pried into the little attaché case and discovered who exactly the home help was, should she invent such a terrible untruth? What couldn't speak couldn't lie. Nell was always saying it, and the papers Emily Boag found established beyond doubt that there was no such person as Hilda Blundell who once worked in a tobacco factory in Liverpool and no husband who had been buried at sea.

Meg's father – Nanny insisted – had been John Kenworthy, who settled a house on Dolly Blundell and whose wife had allowed her to stay at Candlefold until she was safely delivered of her sin.

Because a sin she was, Meg thought despairingly. The result of goings-on between master and servant. Had he crept to Ma's bedroom just as Mark had crept last night to hers? And where did Mrs John stand in all this? Why had she not insisted that the sly housemaid be dismissed at once? Was any woman so good and forgiving that she allowed her husband's mistress to remain at Candlefold until her child was born?

Oh, Mary Kenworthy was a good woman – but which woman was *that* good? Which woman, in the circumstances, could have stopped herself pulling her fingernails down Ma's face when she discovered her husband had been cheating on her? And apart from Nanny who else knew? Gran, maybe? What part had Eleanor Kenworthy played in it? Did the other housemaids know? Gladys Tucker and Norah Bentley on the photograph must surely have been a party to it all. And what about Mrs Potter and Mrs Armitage? Did they remember, from twenty years ago, the young housemaid who had got herself into trouble and did they know who had been responsible? Had Ma been sworn to secrecy, then bought off with a house in a Liverpool slum?

Meg jumped to her feet, throwing wide the window, taking in gulps of air, letting them out slowly in little huffs. She was shaking still, and hurting inside. Nanny had called her a trollop, which made Ma a trollop, too.

Bedded your own brother! God, how crude, yet maybe how true! Perhaps she really had slept with her half-brother. Perhaps Nanny wasn't lying. And anyway, who in this world, unless she were insane or bad to the core, would invent such a story? Nanny hadn't the wit to do it. Nanny could only recognise and remember the truth when she read the papers in the attaché case. That much she was capable of – and of storing it triumphantly in her mind until the time came to use it.

Meg covered her face with her hands, needing to weep the shock out of her and to think carefully what she was to do. Call Nanny's bluff, should she? Tell Mrs John all and swear on her honour she had not meant to deceive her; that she had seen Candlefold and loved it at once and wanted to remain there to work. Would it be too painful for Mary Kenworthy to have twenty years of forgetting raked up and thrown at her again? Was it too much even to hope that Nanny had been wrong?

Much too much. Nanny had been right, had taken delight in flinging the truth in her face, and all because she didn't want Mark to marry out of his class. Would she have kept the secret of the attaché case had Mark not come to this room last night? Was their lovemaking too much for Nanny to bear as she listened at the door? And because Nanny hated her so much, had she enjoyed every minute of it and would she gloat in secret at ridding Candlefold of Dolly Blundell's brat, yet be all consternation and mystification on the face of it? '. . . But how could she go like that? Such ingratitude, Mrs John, and after all your kindness! What could have prompted her to do such a thing?'

And Gran? Dear, lovely Gran. How hurt she would be. What would she think of the girl who had slipped away without a goodbye and told so many lies? Because it wouldn't be very long before Nanny allowed them to drag the truth out of her – the so-reluctantly told truth!

And Mark. What would he make of it all? Would he ever be told that he and the girl he loved had the same father? Would Mrs John, for the sake of decency and a husband held dear, ever tell him the truth of the girl born to a servant in the brick house?

There was a tap on the door, then Mary Kenworthy walked in, a cup in her hand.

'Here you are, Meg.' She placed the tea on the window sill then laid her hand to the flushed cheek. 'Child! You are hot, but your hands are like ice! Take off your clothes and get into bed this instant! Davie's parents are getting the noon bus to Preston station and if you aren't any better by then, I shall phone the doctor!'

'I'm all right, really I am. Just a couple of aspirins and a drink of tea. Honest, Mrs John, I'll be fine. Got myself a bit overexcited about the wedding. Just give me a couple of hours? I'll draw the curtains and lie down, maybe sleep . . .'

Lies! Lies to Mrs John, who didn't deserve them; John Kenworthy's wife, who had been so decent to Ma! And now another Blundell was pulling the wool over her eyes an' all!

'Very well, Meg. I'll look in on you when I've seen the Sumners on their way. You could be sickening for something.' She drew the curtains, then plumped up the pillows, straightening the sheets.

'You're very kind, Mrs John,' Meg whispered, stifling the need to throw her arms around Polly's mother and weep on her shoulder at the injustice of it all. 'Do you realise how happy I've been at Candlefold?'

She looked appealingly into the gentle eyes, wanting her words to be a goodbye message to a woman she had come to love and respect so much; and an apology too, for all the upset her going would cause.

'Kind, Meg? You are very easy to be kind to, and if you are happy with us, then that's just fine, isn't it? Because I – and Gran, too – are very happy to have you. Now, no more to be said. Into that bed and I'll look in later.'

She bent to place a kiss on her forehead and it made Meg want to cry out not to touch her; that when she knew the truth she would recoil from all memory of that kiss. Yet all she said was, 'I'll be fine. Don't ever worry about me, Mrs John.'

Then she closed her eyes tightly, not only to stop the threatening tears but to shut out a world that had become almost too cruel to accept.

'And I loved you so much, Mark,' she whispered into the pillow on which their heads had lain. 'Love you, will always love you and only you . . .'

Yet still she could not weep for her loss and lay there, accepting in her mind that she had just a few more hours to remain at Candlefold. Soon Mrs John would return and when she did she must find Meg Blundell gone.

As if suddenly motivated by the urgency of it, Meg threw back the bedclothes, reaching for her case from the top of the wardrobe, pushing, stuffing her clothes into it, thankful she had so few possessions to pack away.

But possessions were as nothing compared to the memories she would take with her. Polly, cross-legged on the bed; her almost-sister who, in three more days, would be home and missing Davie. Polly, who now that they must part, had become the most loved person in her life – apart from Mark

Mark. Marcus John Kenworthy, whom she loved with all her heart and soul and body; Mark, whom she must never see again, nor kiss nor give herself in love to, nor touch nor smile at.

They would never again lie secretly in the green beside the willow pool, yet the river would always be there, and the trees that draped graceful branches into the water where they had swum naked, bodies cool as marble.

No! No more thoughts of Mark or what had been or might still be. Mark was forbidden. You did not bed your brother and stay unforgiven. Somewhere, sometime soon in the outside world she was about to join, she would have to make retribution. The Fates would demand it. *Take what you will. Take it – and pay!* So she must turn her back on Candlefold and shut away all memories of it, then take what was coming to her. And if she were lucky, if there were more air raids on Liverpool, then it could already be written in her Book of Life that a German bomb would have Meg Blundell's name on it and she would quickly leave an existence that all at once had become unbearable and unacceptable.

And then she thought of the dead baby on the cold, uncaring pavement, and wished she had been able to trade her life in exchange for its own; that she could have hooked a finger inside that tiny, rubble-filled mouth, helped it to breathe again and cry angrily, then left it there for someone to love whilst Meg Blundell wraithed away into a place called Nowhere.

But the baby was dead and Meg Blundell was alive, had taken what she would, and now must begin to pay for it. She had bedded her own brother and she was a harlot. At least Ma hadn't been that!

When her case was packed and every drawer opened and checked and when she had gone on her knees and pulled slippers from beneath the bed, she folded the blankets into neat squares, folded the sheets and pillowcases as if they were ordinary sheets and pillowcases, and covered them with the delphinium bedspread. Then she took a piece of notepaper and wrote,

> I want to thank you all for the kindness you have shown me, and the love, and I need you all to know I will never forget a minute of the happiness I have had in this precious place. I will keep the lovely summer I spent with you in my heart for ever.
>
> Goodbye, and forgive me for what I have done.

She did not sign her name; instead she pinned the lovers' knot of tiny pearls to it, then placed it in the dressing-table drawer with the china cupid, because she could take nothing with her but memories, nothing she could touch, or hold to her cheek; nothing to bring back the past. All she would allow of the magic was Mark's three letters and the postcard from Salisbury and she would, she vowed, put them in Ma's tiny attaché case with all the things that belonged to her past and never, ever read them again.

She went to stand at the window, then, to peer through the chink in the curtains so she might know when Mrs John and Davie's parents left for the village. Only then could she take her case, hide it in the woodyard, then go to the willow pool to whisper her goodbyes to the river, so it would carry them away for all time. And she would pray that no one would see her go and that when she got to the village, no one would be looking out of the post office window.

It was a lot to ask. She wondered how she would bear the pain of it.

She hid her case behind the woodshed door, then put her handbag and Ma's little attaché case beside it, knowing they would be safe, that no one would come here and find them. Then she walked past the tall iron gates of the kitchen garden, past the hen run and on towards the gate of the cow pasture.

No more walking across it for milk; no more feeding hens, nor collecting windfall apples nor picking strawberries, eating the ripest and squashiest. It was over, and all that remained was to walk, head high, to the river, whisper her secret to it. And if she could, walk past the place where first they had been lovers.

She found, when she got there, that nothing had changed. The willows still trailed the water, the undressing place was still greenly hidden and the river ran slowly, low beneath the banks still, waiting for winter rains and melted snow from the hills to swell it and make it run brown. But on this September day, it was that same clear river that swirled the pool, then ran on again, uncaring, to the sea.

Meg sank to her knees, but her mind was too numbed to collect her thoughts and whisper them to the flowing water. Instead, she let the hurt and bewilderment drain from her into the ground beneath her, wondering if she would ever come to this place again to redeem her sorrow.

She kneeled there until her body was cold and stiff, then rose to her feet, wondering why she had come, when nothing could undo the past, nor change nor forgive it. From now on she must get on with life as best she could and not once allow herself the comfort of tears.

She tried to whisper a goodbye, but her lips were stiff. Reluctantly she glanced to her left as she passed the undressing place, then jerked her eyes away and made towards the gate of the cow pasture.

Mrs John would be back, now; probably would have gone upstairs, found the note she'd left. So now she must creep down the lane, hoping not to be seen, take the road to the village then, head high, walk through it to the Nether Barton crossroads where the next bus into town would pick her up.

She did not stop to glance through the far archway at the granite pump trough but hurried towards the road, walking quickly, eyes downcast. Nor was she, when she turned left towards Upper Barton, brave enough to look back on the ages-old house.

'Goodbye, my lovely world,' she whispered.

She had been lucky, Meg thought as the train took her ever nearer to Liverpool, to get through the village without being recognized or seen, because just as she was about to pass the post office, two customers had gone in, making the doorbell tinkle and ensuring that Mrs Potter would not be peering through the window. She was lucky, too, that when the two o'clock bus stopped at the crossroads half a mile outside the village, no one she knew, or who knew her, was on it. If luck you would call it, she shrugged. Yet in spite of her misery and shock she had remembered her ration book, kept always in the dresser drawer. When they discovered her book of food coupons had been taken, they would know she was gone for ever.

She glanced through the window of the crowded compartment, seeing rows of houses with bomb gaps in them; seeing factories with sandbagged doors, and lorries camouflaged in black and green and khaki on the road beside the track. Soon, the train would slow, and the points would set it rocking and the wheels clanking beneath them and they would judder into the station, half an hour late. Soon Candlefold would become a dream that would never leave her, a memory that would not fade, and Tippet's Yard would claim her once more. She was glad she did not believe in God, because now there was no one to blame for the mess her life had become but herself.

She wished her body did not ache so with hurt; hoped she would find the strength to rise to her feet, drag her case from the rack, walk to the tram stop outside the station. And once aboard, the clanging, clanking contraption would bear her to Scotland Road and she would have no option but to walk the length of Lyra Street and beneath the entry into hidden Tippet's Yard.

The train began to judder and slow as they rocked over the points, then lurched left towards the station platform. She rose to her feet, reaching for the luggage rack, clinging to it until they finally came to a stop. Then, in a daze of despair, she tugged at the case.

'Liverpool Exchange,' called the woman porter from the platform. 'End of the line!'

Meg Blundell had come to the end of the line too, and there was nowhere now to go but to the house in Tippet's Yard; face Tommy's curiosity and Nell, who would say she had told her so! And she would tell herself that Candlefold was all in her despairing dreamings and that if she tried long enough and hard enough, she might one day be able to think about it without screaming inside her for something precious and golden, and gone for ever.

So this was it. She nodded her thanks to the driver, who waited until she had got her case off the tram, and to the lady conductor who gave her a hand with it. Then she walked up the rise of Lyra Street with St Joseph's church at the top, towards the rusted iron sign that said 'Tippet's Yard'.

She stopped to gaze around the small square of damp, soot-stained buildings, and ached for Candlefold's cobbled courtyard, the pump trough, the roses and wisteria that clung to the old stones.

There was no evening sunlight in the yard because taller buildings and a warehouse kept it out. At Candlefold, the sun would be slanting now over the far archway, and mellowing the old stones from grey to palest gold. But Candlefold was in the past now, in another world and part of another life and she must try her hardest to wipe it from her memory, because to think of it would lead to the willow pool and to Mark, whom she could not love.

'Good grief!' Nell Shaw, who missed nothing, was out of her door the minute Meg walked into the yard. 'What's to do with you, girl?' She eyed the suitcase obliquely.

'What does it look like?'

'Looks like you've come home. What happened, then? Got the push, did you?'

'No. I left. Just walked out, and I'm back, as you see. And if you don't mind, Nell, I don't want an inquest, not tonight nor any other night. All I want is a cup of tea.'

She marched, head high, arm aching, to her front door, then turned as Nell said, 'You'll be wanting this, then.'

'Thanks.' Meg held out her hand for the key to her house. 'And I've no milk. Can you spare a drop?'

'Course I can – if you'll provide the tea.'

'Fine, then. Be ready in ten minutes.'

She stepped into the kitchen, closing the door behind her, leaving Nell on the step, none the wiser. Then she took a shilling from her purse and slotted it into the gas meter, filling the kettle, setting it to boil. She did it automatically and all the time wondering what she should say to Nell – if she said anything at all, that was.

Yet Nell deserved to know the bare bones of it: that she had decided to leave Candlefold because it were best, now that she was twenty and would soon have to go on war work, to be here in Liverpool where there were more options and choices. Nell wouldn't believe it, of course, but it would serve until an excuse could be found that would satisfy her curiosity.

'Oh God!' she whispered to the empty room, taking in the firegrate, dusty with ashes, the white-topped table in need of a scrub and curtains in need of washing. At Candlefold, now they would be –

No! No more of the benign old house, the stone-flagged hall that seemed tall as a church, the wood she had so lovingly polished and the larger-than-average spill of candlewax to press and slide to the left. No more of it, Meg Blundell!

She took the caddy from the mantelshelf. There was still tea in it; tea brought by Kip from Australia months ago – Kip, who loved her and wanted to marry her. She wiped three cups and set them on the table with one spoon and the small brown bottle of saccharin tablets, then stood arms folded, eyes closed, to await the whistling of the kettle.

'Brewed up, have you?' Nell, eager for tea and more eager for news.

'Ar. I'll sit and wait. Give it a good stir, girl. Can't abide it weak. An' here's the milk.'

She placed a jug on the table, debating whether or not to have a cigarette, deciding against it.

'Did you give Tommy a knock?'

'No. He's gone to the pub. The landlord has ciggies in tonight so he's gone to get some.'

'He doesn't smoke, Nell.'

'No. He'll give them to me. I gave him the money for a half. So is it the son, then?'

The question was so direct, so unexpected, that Meg was shocked into answering, 'I suppose so. But like you said, his sort don't marry my sort.'

'You fell for him?'

'Yes. So best I got out, Nell.'

'Ar. You turned Kip Lewis down 'cause you fancied your chances with the young lord and master?'

'With Mark. I loved him, you see – couldn't marry Kip. Couldn't marry anyone when I was in love with Mark. It's the way it is, Nell. And before you say it – yes, I *am* a silly little bitch, but at least I'm back here and out of harm's way.'

'Harm's way? He wanted it, then?'

'No. He was a perfect gentleman. But I saw the red light and decided to quit.'

'Ar.' Nell watched the shaking hand that held the teapot. 'Oh, well, Kip'll soon make port. He'll be pleased you're back . . .'

'Won't make any difference. I don't want to marry him and settle in Australia. I don't want to marry him, full stop. And I've told you now, Nell, so can we leave it be, please? I'm not proud of myself, walking out like I did, but it had to be done, and that's the end of it!'

'The end. And I think I'll have a ciggie, if you don't mind. So you'll have brought your ration book with you – permanent, like?'

'Yes. And my clothing coupons, and I'll go to the food office tomorrow, get them all changed back. I'll have to, or I'll be on dry bread and fish and chips till Monday.'

'You'll be wantin' a job, won't you?'

'Yes.' Thinking about finding work had not entered her head. 'I suppose I'll go to the Labour on Monday, though there won't be many who want to employ a twenty-year-old.'

'Then get yourself into a reserved occupation before you've got to register. Hospital work counts, I believe, or you could get yourself taken on by the fire service and no, I don't mean puttin' out fires. That's a man's job. But the fire service needs cleaners or clerks or cooks – and there's always Air Raid Precautions. That'd keep you out of the call-up.'

'Yes. On Monday, like I said. And would you mind if I went to bed, soon? It feels like I've dragged that case halfway across the country. I'm tired, Nell.'

'Ar. You will be. Am I to tell Tommy what you told me – that there was a feller behind it?'

'No, Nell – if you don't mind. Tell him I came home 'cause I'll have more of a choice of war work when I register – or make sumthin' up.'

A feller behind it. Last night, they had loved and loved again, then fallen asleep, bodies close. Tonight, she would sleep in the sagging bed and try not to weep for Mark, who would perhaps have been able to phone Candlefold. And if he had, what would Mrs John have told him?

'Hey!' A hand passed in front of her eyes. 'Where was you girl? Miles away, at that Candlefold, eh?'

'No, Nell. I was thinking about war work. They have women conductors on the trams, now . . .'

'Oh, I don't think I'd fancy that – early hours, late hours. Not a job for a woman, if you ask me. But it takes all sorts, I suppose.' She rose to her feet, dusting cigarette ash from her skirt. 'See you in the mornin', Meg. An' you've done the right thing, leaving that place, though I reckon you'll be feelin' it, you being gone on the son. But you'll get over it! G'night, girl.'

'Yes, Nell. Night-night.'

Get over Mark? Get over him, like he was measles or whooping cough? But she did not want to get over him. She wanted to go to bed and think about the golden day that was yesterday; think about Polly and Davie and the happiness around them. Was it really only yesterday? And why couldn't she weep? Was it what people called shock, and was she in it? Or was she asleep still, and would she wake up and it all have been a nightmare?

'No, Meg Blundell.' She said it out loud to get the feel of it. 'There's no waking from this nightmare.'

What upset had she left behind her – Gran and Mrs John, and Polly, when she got back? And oh, imagine Nanny's face, all shocked sympathy, and her trying not to smile. But could Nanny have been wrong? *Could* she?

No. She hadn't been wrong. Too many things added up. The only good thing to come out of it was that no one at Candlefold would ever knew the truth of it, because Nanny would never tell. She couldn't!

Like an automaton, Meg locked and bolted the front door and pulled the blackout curtains over the window, even though it was not yet dark. Then she picked up attaché case and handbag, and walked reluctantly upstairs.

This was not her white-painted, delphinium-flowered bedroom. From this window she would see no pump trough, nor far stone arch, nor Pygons Wood, misty in the early autumn evening.

Deliberately she opened wide the bedroom curtains so she might awaken to the grime-stained wall and the uncaring window; remind her of what she had lost. She pushed case and handbag beneath the bed, then lay on it, hands behind head, hating the room, hating Tippet's Yard, hating herself.

But could Nanny have been wrong – about Mrs John's husband, that was?

No, she sighed. She was a Kenworthy, and Candlefold born. There was no getting away from it, nor from Father Unknown, though she knew now who he was.

But why had Mrs John been so good to Ma? Where was the woman who not only forgave, but who gave shelter to her husband's mistress and was there, at the birth? With Nanny, of course. Meg remembered the story of the christening of a little princess with a good fairy and a bad fairy there. And at Meg Blundell's birth there had been a good woman – Mary Kenworthy – and a bad one called Emily Boag, and the bad one had ill-wished the new-born babe.

You will find love at this house and you will lose it too, because you are a bastard . . .

But had Mrs John really been good about it all? What if Mrs John had never known? What if the house in Tippet's Yard had been a part of the bargain? Keep quiet about it, Dolly Blundell, and you'll come out of it all right! Had that been the way it was?

She turned on her side away from the window, hugging her dry-eyed misery to her, her body aching from the pain of her loss. She wanted to lie here and never move again; wanted to die of that pain.

Why couldn't she weep; scream her dismay and bewilderment so the whole of Lyra Street heard her? Why couldn't she kick out, slam doors, batter the walls with her fists? Why was she so stupid? Why didn't she go back to Candlefold and insist on the truth? Why had she accepted Nanny's evil and not challenged one word of it? Why had she not asked questions and demanded answers?

Because she already knew Nanny Boag had spoken the truth, though why it had been flung at her with such malice she would never know. Sufficient that her father was a war hero, and because of it had been adored by women – his wife included. His wife had forgiven his adultery, hadn't she; shown kindness to the housemaid Dolly Blundell? No use challenging anything.

Meg turned on her back to squint at the ceiling, trying to make out familiar cracks and the peeling whitewash; anything to take away even a little of the pain.

But she could see nothing. It was almost dark. Blackout time was at twenty-past eight. The days were shortening now, and before long, blackouts would be in place at half-past four in the afternoon. In November that would be, and right through most of December, until the shortest day. A winter of drear and despair, when small animals curled themselves into a ball and slept until spring coaxed them to life again. Meg wished she could do that; she wanted, *needed* to curl into a ball and sleep out the dark days and never awaken.

Her eyes hurt. It was as if they were full of gritty dust that only tears could wash clean. But tears would not come. This misery could not be wept out of her. Instead, she must keep it inside her, and the pain of it going on and on would always remind her of Mark. Even if she wanted to forget him, she would not be able to.

And she did not want to forget him. She would accept the constant pain, because loving and being loved by him was worth more than anything in the world she could think of. And the awfulness of it would be magnified each time she remembered that he had whispered that he loved her, then written it again, in a letter. And remembering that he had truly loved her would bring still more pain.

She wondered how long she could bear it before madness took her.

No one had written; no one from Candlefold had come looking for her. She was sad about it, but glad too. Now, four days after, she had done all the necessary things in order to survive: had changed the address on her ration book and identity card, registered with the grocer who had supplied her food before she left for Candlefold; gone back to her butcher of old. And she had stood in line at the Labour Exchange, to be told there was little work for young women of her age – not casual, that was – and why didn't she wait until her age group was called on to register for real war work? Shouldn't be long, now. Meantime, she could sign on and next Monday would receive a dole payment of seven and sixpence.

'Seven and six, that's all they're going to pay me. How am I expected to manage on that, will you tell me?'

'Only just,' Nell grinned, herself being in receipt of an Army widow's pension that was a few shillings more. 'But you'll 'ave saved a bit when you was at that house, surely?'

'Yes. A bit.' Seventeen pounds, ten shillings, to be exact. It would have bought her a whole winter outfit – coat, gloves, and a couple of nightgowns – if she'd had the coupons, of course. Which she hadn't. Only five left until the next issue, and they were needed for winter shoes.

'They're alus lookin' for help at the pub – collecting glasses, wiping tables. But women don't stay there long on account of the pay being bad, and dirty old men treatin' them like they was tarts – pinchin' their bottoms, and worse.'

'Any feller who took liberties with me would get the flat of my hand in his face, the mood I'm in now,' Meg hissed.

'Why? What's to do with you, girl?'

'Oh, I don't know. Missing Candlefold, I suppose.' And hurting inside because Mark had almost certainly written to her and if they forwarded his letter on – to the address she had given them, that was – it would have been returned by the GPO marked, *Address not available owing to enemy action*. And they would think that number 6 Lyra Street had had a bomb on it, so where did they start looking for her? If they really wanted to find her, that was. And anyway, who was there to come looking? Mark was back with his regiment and Polly away with Davie still; only Mrs John there alone, to take care of Gran and Nanny. Nanny, who could take care of herself, truth known.

Meg had spent the past days wandering the streets of Liverpool, always seeming to end up at the Pierhead, gazing across the river to Wallasey and New Brighton, watching the ferries that crossed the grey water or gazing down river where merchant ships, half an inch small, waited for a river pilot to take them through the swept channel and edge them into port.

Perhaps one of those ships was the *Bellis*, bringing Kip home. She had called on Amy in Lyra Street, but her reception had been cool, and no mention of her brother had been made. Amy did not approve of Kip's friendship with Meg; her manner made it clear as she stood at the open door and said she was busy with the children, and could Meg call later?

'I'm home now – for good,' Meg offered, but that had not prevented the firm closing of the door in her face. No Protties in that holier-than-thou house. Meg had shrugged, resolving not to call again, which was a pity really, because the object of her visit was to ask Amy not to say anything if a stranger should come to number 6, next door, looking for her.

So she had made her way to the tram stop again, surprised that Amy's coolness had not hurt her. But then, nothing could hurt someone who was only half alive; someone who felt constantly cold and hungry, yet did not want to eat. Because eating needed effort, so why bother?

'All the way, please.' She handed two pennies to the conductress. Today, she would probably take the overhead railway either south or north, whichever train came first. She liked the Overhead. When she was little, she and Ma had taken it south to the Dingle terminus, then walked from there to Sefton Park, first admiring the gentlemen's houses on The Drive, though Ma had said not one of them was anywhere near as big as Candlefold, where once she had worked for the gentry. And on warm summer days, they had sat on the grass in the park, and drank water from a screw-top bottle, eaten jam sandwiches and dreamed their dreams of the country where one day they would live. A little cottage it would be, with a garden and fruit trees and where washing hung out to dry never got smuts on it. Soon, Ma said. When there was enough money in her bankbook.

Meg left the tram at the Liver Buildings, then crossed the road, making automatically for the Overhead Railway.

'Dingle,' she said to the ticket clerk, then climbed the wooden steps to the platform, because this was a Sefton Park day – probably the last anyone would see this year – and she wanted to be near Ma, remember their dreams of a country cottage, pretend she was little again and Ma was straight-backed and clear-eyed. Before she got TB, that was.

And she would sit again on the grass and try to imagine, as she had done as a child, that she was in the country, and that when they left Tippet's Yard they would go to a place far better than this park, where the trees were taller and grew more thickly, and the grass was greener and so many wild flowers you wouldn't believe. She would go back to her childhood and for a little while forget the ache of being alone and the torment of wanting Candlefold and the despair that coursed through her even to think of Mark. She would sit, hands round knees and remind herself that Tippet's Yard was only somewhere she and Ma stayed until it was time to leave for the country. She would blot out all else, hugging Ma's memory to her; recalling the softness of her voice, the sadness in her eyes and hands always red from washing and scrubbing. And she would not think of Mark nor Candlefold nor how she was to manage on seven and six a week until she could find a job; would blot it out because when she was little, Ma had always made everything come right.

So she would sit on the grass in the park and pretend that Ma was beside her and not worry about a thing – except perhaps that today was Friday and this morning her period should have come. And it hadn't.

Twenty

October 1941 and the first convoy of arms and munitions to hard-pressed Russia, and codenamed PQ1, arrived in Archangel. Also in that month, a newspaper announcement took the eye of Tommy Todd, who was reading in the library – it being pleasantly warm and quiet there, and saved him not only buying a newspaper, but lighting his fire earlier than he need. Taking a stub of pencil from his pocket and tearing off a corner of paper he wrote A – F Monday, 27 October, then hastened to give the news to his neighbour.

'It's official,' he beamed. 'King and Country need you, girl. Register on the twenty-seventh! You'll soon have a job for the duration!'

'How did you know? It wasn't on the wireless.' Nell Shaw folded her arms belligerently.

'Well, it was in the paper, so you'd better put the one o'clock news on then!'

'Fact, is it, Tommy?' Meg drew her tongue round her lips. She had known for a long time the Government would want her, yet still the news brought a dryness to her mouth 'You saw it?'

'Took special note cause it concerned the Bs. But if you don't believe me –'

'Course I do. Just came as a bit of a shock, that's all. An' I've just made a brew. Reckon I can make it run to three cups, though I think this tea's gone off a bit.' The smell from the pot made her insides squirm. 'Some that Kip sent, ages ago . . .'

'Nuthin' wrong with it.' Nell closed her eyes and sipped. 'But then, nothing Kip Lewis brings or does is right for you, is it?'

'We were talking,' Meg said very quietly, 'about me and the call-up. Suppose I knew it would happen, sooner or later,' she shrugged.

'Ar. Shall you go for a uniform, girl, or go on munitions?'

'Dunno, Tommy. Haven't given it a lot of thought, lately.' She hadn't. There had been more important things to bother her. 'I'll do as I'm ordered, I suppose, like most folks else.'

'It's come to sumthin',' Nell said, 'when innocent girls are snatched from their mothers and ordered into uniform.'

Innocent? Meg thought. And she really hadn't given the matter a great deal of attention, though it seemed as if it had been taken out of her hands, now. Not that she cared, mind. Nothing that happened now had the power to jolt her from her awful lethargy. Truth known, she had eaten little and slept less these last six weeks, slipping further and further into depression with never a day passing without thinking about Mark, and telling herself she would never see him again. A life without Mark was a terrible thing, she thought, lifting the cup to her lips.

The tea smell hit her nostrils and went right down to her stomach. She was going to be sick! She took a deep breath, put a hand over her mouth then made across the yard to sink on her knees on the cold floor of the lavatory.

'Well, what's to do with her?' Tommy demanded, mystified. 'There's nuthin' wrong with this tea!'

'Nuthin',' Nell agreed. Mind, she'd heard it said that some women went off tea the minute they caught for a baby. Couldn't abide it, yet the first thing they wanted when it was all over was a cup of strong, sweet tea and oh, my Lord! Meg couldn't be in trouble, could she? She hadn't copped for one?

'Listen, Tommy, can you make yourself scarce – there's a decent feller? I've got a feeling me an' Meg are goin' to have words!'

'What about? The girl can't help bein' sick!'

'Push off, you stupid little sod!' Through the open door she saw Meg, pulling her hand over her mouth. 'It's women's talk!'

'So! Want to talk about it?' Nell asked when Tommy's front door had slammed.

'I want a drink of water.' Meg made for the tap. 'Talk about what?'

'About tea makin' you sick. It's very often tea. First signs, really, though sometimes it's cigarette smoke. Does my smoking bother you, girl'

'I've never liked cigarette smoke, and you know it.'

'All right. Keep yer hair on! Was only askin'.'

'It's none of your business, Nell Shaw!'

'Oh, isn't it? Doll's girl goes and gets herself in the family way, and it isn't my business. Then whose business is it, will you tell me? Young Kenworthy's, eh?'

Meg opened her mouth to protest, then thought better of it, because being sick into an outside lavatory was a humbling experience.

'I asked you a question, girl. Are you, and whose is it?'

'I think I might be, Nell.'

'But you told me that Mark feller was a gentleman, and he isn't, is he? Took advantage like men the whole world over! And there's always some stupid little bitch who'll give them what they want. Oh, I could take the back of my hand to you, Meg Blundell! After what happened to your mother, I never thought you'd be so stupid! It *is* him, isn't it?'

'Yes.'

'You're sure?'

'Of course I'm sure! Mark's the only one.'

'Well, I don't know why you left that place, but you'd better get yourself back there pretty damn quick! Something's got to be done about it! He should be made to marry you!'

'But he won't, Nell. And I'm not going back. I can't.'

'Why can't yer? Did some thieving, eh?'

'No. But I just left, Nell. Crept out while Mrs John was at the village – hid my case in the woodyard. And Mark can't marry me because . . .'

All at once, tears came; tears denied for too long ran down her cheeks to taste salt on her lips. She covered her face with her hands and stood, shoulders shaking.

''Cause he's wed – or spoken for? He's still responsible, no matter what. You must tell him, girl. He should be made to pay.'

'I want *nothing*! And don't ask me to go back there or even to write. I can't, Nell!'

'But why bluddy not?'

'Because – oh, I suppose I've got to tell someone. But can I tell it from the beginning? Can I tell it so I can sort it out in my own head, an' all? 'Cause maybe then I'll find a way out – what to do for the best . . .'

'All right, Meg girl. Sit yourself down. Dry your eyes, eh, and have another drink of water?'

So Meg dabbed her eyes, blew her nose loudly, then took the offered glass. And when she was more composed she took a long, shuddering breath and whispered, 'It all started with Nanny Boag.'

'What? Her that's the invalid? That one's a mite queer, if you ask me.'

'Well, it was her told me. Remember Ma's little attaché case? Remember the night we went through it and found all sorts of things out? Well, Nanny wasn't such an invalid that she couldn't get herself downstairs and go through my papers. But let me tell it?' she hastened when Nell's mouth opened indignantly. 'Just listen, will you, then you'll understand why I can't go back to Candlefold and why Mark must never know.'

And so, punctuated by wiped-away tears, she told Nell all that had happened, and when all was said, she whispered, 'There, now. That's the lot, Nell. No holds barred. So what am I to do, will you tell me? It's my own fault. I deceived them – told them lies about Ma – that her name was Hilda and she'd never been a domestic. Maybe if I'd been straight I wouldn't have been given the job, in the first place. Like you said, I've been a silly little bitch! Oh God! Talk about history repeating itself!'

'Yes – we-e-ll. Must run in families. Shall you have it, then?'

'Got no option it seems. Mind, I haven't seen a doctor but I reckon I don't need to – not now I've been sick.'

'But you'll have to get it all straightened out. For one thing, who's goin' to help you financially? Your ma got a house out of it, but you just walk away without a word.'

'I didn't know I was expecting when I left. Even so, they mustn't know. Like Nanny Boag said, I bedded my own brother! Disgusting, isn't it, put that way? She said it was – incest.'

'Yes it is, but you weren't to know, nor – give him his due – was he. But the fact is you're in the club, girl. How many have you missed?'

'Two.'

'And you'll keep it? Suppose you'll have to, really. Isn't right, offerin' a baby of that sort for adoption.'

'*That* sort, Nell . . . ?'

'We-e-ll, brother and sister, I mean.' Nell looked down at her hands. 'Mind, I'm not sure, but I've heard it said that – well –

interbreeding, sort of . . . the same with animals. All sorts of things can throw back.'

'*Animals!* God, Nell, we made love! Does that make us animals and will the baby suffer because of it? I didn't know he was my half-brother! Honest to God, I didn't!'

'No, girl. No, of course. But what's to be done? You'll have to make your mind up pretty quick. Whether you're goin' to have it, I mean.'

'*Have it?* It's there. It's a fact. I've got no choice, Nell. Well – have I?' All at once she remembered a girl at work who had got rid. The married man who'd been the cause of it had paid. 'Hell! What a mess this is!'

'You can say that again, Meg Blundell! But you aren't the first, and sure as God made little green apples, you won't be the last!'

'That's no consolation. I only know I'm on my own. Ma brought me up, and I'll have to do the same. I've got a roof over my head, which is more than some have.'

'Yes, but babies cost money. They're to feed and clothe. Are you goin' to end up like poor Doll – takin' in washing and scrubbing steps for a living? And washing bodies for the undertaker? Is that what you want?'

'No, Nell. Not for me nor for the baby. And I certainly wouldn't want to have the life Ma had. How she reared me, I don't know. I'll say this for her – she had backbone!'

'So will you get rid?'

'*Nell!*'

'Don't say you haven't thought about it?'

'I have. But only for a few seconds. Besides,' she looked down at her agitated fingers, 'where would I go? There was a girl at work – but it might only have been a rumour. Anyway, it's illegal . . .'

'So is getting pregnant by your half-brother!'

'Oh, Nell Shaw – you know how to hurt!'

'Sorry. But it's got to be said. And since you ask, I don't know where exactly you could go. What I do know is someone who does.'

'What! Some backstreet biddy with a knitting needle and mucky fingernails!'

'No. I think I'd be right in saying he's a struck-off doctor. But he charges. Plenty, so I was told.'

'Well, that rules me out. All I've got in the bank, now, is fifteen quid!'

'There's always the tallyman.'

'Borrow, you mean, to get rid of a child!' Mark's child!

'It's up to you, girl. And I'm not saying I can help. All I'm saying is that I just might know someone who *might* know someone. People don't talk about such things, y'know, it bein' against the law to get rid of a baby. Fifteen years inside, it can get you, if you're caught. But in the end, it'll have to be up to you. Maybe I'll be able to put you in touch, but after that, that's me out! And Gawd, I need a ciggy!' She dipped in her pinafore pocket, opening the door, blowing the smoke outside.

Nell was upset, Meg thought, watching the trembling hand. More than she was prepared to admit. Dear Nell, whose rough tongue hid a kind heart.

'I'm sorry. I never thought it would end up like this. And I've no right to burden you with my problems, Nell.'

'You didn't burden me. I stuck my nose in, didn't I? And who flamin' else would you go to – if you're not prepared to tell them Kenworthys about it?'

'Well, they can't ever know at Candlefold, so there's only you. You'll be my friend, still? I'll try my hardest, but if there are times the going gets a bit rough, you'll be there for me, Nell?'

'Of course I will. Your ma once said to me that she wasn't long for this world, and would I keep an eye out for you. And I will, girl, because I promised Doll I would.'

'Thanks,' Meg whispered chokily. 'So now I've got to think things out – seriously think, I mean.'

'About what you'll do? Well, you've lost your chance with Kip Lewis now, so you can count him out. He'll not want another feller's kid. Stands to reason, dunnit?'

'It does. Even Kip wouldn't be such a fool. Oh, Nell, what would Ma make of it if she were here now? The awful thing is that I've done exactly what she did. I loved a man and trusted him when he said it would be all right – that nothing would happen.'

'They all say that. But yer ma wouldn't judge. Doll was too dignified to let fly, anyway. She'd have understood, Meg. But none of this would have happened, would it, if poor Doll was here today? You wouldn't have opened her little case and you wouldn't have got a bee in your bonnet about goin' to that Candlefold place. She wouldn't have let you.'

'No. Like you say, if I hadn't opened that case . . .'

'Too right, girl. Oh, flamin' bluddy Norah! We're in a right mess, aren't we? You mightn't have fallen for a baby, yet here we are, wonderin' if you should have it.'

'I'm pregnant, Nell. I've known it since last time I was due, really. Now, the curse is due again an' it hasn't come, and when I was sick this morning – we-e-ll . . .'

'That put the tin hat on it, like? First time, was it? Ar, well,' she smiled sympathetically. 'They say it doesn't last long. Three months, I did hear, and you're into your second stage. An' here's me talking as if I know all about it!'

'Would you have liked a baby, Nell?'

'Suppose I would. Wasn't given the option. When I was wed, more'n twenty years ago, you expected to have babies. But the last war took care of that. Maybe, if I'd fallen for one, it would've been a comfort to me. Mind, they do say that if you have no kids to laugh over you've none to cry over either, so it cuts both ways. So since you're pretty sure you've caught, Meg, what are your feelings, really?'

'My feelings are that I'd have been made up, if it'd been possible for me and Mark to get married. Because he would have married me, I know it.' She shrugged, sucking in her breath and holding it against tears. 'But since that isn't possible, not even with a shotgun in his back, then I wish it hadn't happened. But never mind me – what about the baby's feelings?'

'Ar. I see what you mean. Here's you an' me talking about getting rid as if it's up to us. Who's goin' to speak for that baby? Mind, it isn't a baby yet, is it? Not really.'

'I don't know, Nell. I don't know nuthin' about it, 'cept how they get there. I did hear, though, that it isn't a baby till it's half-way. Someone told me that once you feel movements, then it's a real baby, turning and kicking. I suppose that when that happens to me, I'll look on it as a real little person – and my responsibility.'

'Even so,' Nell regarded the tip of her cigarette off-handedly, 'are you ready for that responsibility? You have a choice, remember, to do what you think best.'

'Even if I decided – well, not to have it – it could be dangerous?'

'There's danger in everything, girl, even crossin' the road in the blackout. You pays your money and you takes your chances. In the end, it's up to you. You've got to think it over real hard. And once you've made your mind up, if you don't want to have the baby, I'll make enquiries. I mightn't be able to find out where you go. You realize that, don't you?'

'Yes, I do. But let's put it this way, Nell. If I decide to, and you can find out where, then I suppose it'll be all right for me to go ahead. Fate, you might say. Written in my Book of Life. And if you can't find out, then I'll tell myself it's written I should have the baby – Mark's baby. But you're right. There's some hard thinking to be done, first, and thanks for listening. I know it's been a shock to you – it was to me, those first couple of days when the curse didn't come. But I've had time to get used to it. And you'll not say anything to Tommy just yet?'

'My lips are sealed. S'trewth, I could do with a good stiff brandy, though there's fat chance of that these days, with them Jairmans supping all the brandy the French make. Bluddy Hitler's fault, it is!'

'Bloody Hitler's!' Meg smiled for the first time in many days. And it was good to smile, maybe because a trouble shared was a trouble halved. 'Never mind, Nell. I swear on Ma's grave that when this war is over, I'll buy you a bottle of the stuff!'

And Nell said she would hold her to that, and smiled with her.

Three days later, when Meg had almost made up her mind to ask Nell to see if she could find the address of the doctor, the door knocker came down three times, which wasn't usual, since most people didn't knock; just opened the door with, 'It's only me! All right if I come in?'

But no one came in, so she made for the door, opening it wide, then gasping, 'Kip Lewis! You don't usually knock . . .' Blood rushed to her cheeks and she stood there, not knowing what to say.

'Meg. Hello. Am I welcome, then?'

'You know you are. Always.' The agitation was lessening and she saw not a man she had turned down, but a friend.

'Then mind if we have a few words – I won't make any trouble, Meg. Just wanted you to know that I got your letter, and –'

'Kip! I'm sorry. You're a real nice man and I'm sorry things couldn't have been different, but –'

'There's someone else. Yes. I gathered that. But Amy says you told her you're home.'

'I've left Candlefold, though I didn't know whether she'd heard me or not, she was in so much of a hurry to shut the door on me.'

'Well, she must've. And don't let her upset you. She has her hands full these days. What with wind, and teething and now one of them with chicken pox, she's up to her eyes. Three young ones take a lot of looking after alone. She didn't mean to seem abrupt, Meg.'

'I suppose not.'

Dear, decent Kip. Always with a good word, even for his bad-tempered sister. Pity she couldn't have liked him enough to say yes, Meg thought. But saying yes was out of the question now. No point telling him about the baby because Nell was right: no man wanted another man's by-blows.

'Then can I ask, Meg, if your leaving that place makes any difference to you and me?'

'Look – you'd better come in. And I'm out of tea, sorry I can't –'

No need to tell him there was tea and to spare in the caddy, but tea was taboo.

'No bother! Just came for a chat. I'd appreciate that, Meg – if only for the sake of friendship past. All I wanted to ask is if the man you told me about in the letter lived around Candlefold. I mean – if you've left, is there a chance that –'

'That it's over, between us – is that what you mean?' There was no anger in her words, only sadness. 'It's over between us.' Over. The first time she had said it out loud. 'And I was the one who walked out. But it doesn't mean there's a chance that you and me will ever get together, Kip. Right now, I feel badly hurt by what's gone on. I can't explain it to you, but –' Tears trembled in a knot in her throat and she shut her eyes tightly against them.

'He's upset you, hasn't he? What did he do, Meg? Just say the word and I'll sort him out. Seems to me he's asked for it!'

'No, Kip. Don't concern yourself. It wouldn't have worked between us. It couldn't have. Marriage is the last thing in my plans at the moment.'

'You're sure? I'd be willing to take a chance on you and me still.'

'Knowing there'd been someone else? Would you honestly, Kip?'

'Knowing I was second best – yes, I would. And I wouldn't ask for anything you weren't willing to give, wouldn't force myself on you. And if that makes me sound like a big Jessie, well, hard luck. Just take it as a measure of how much I want to marry you, Meg.'

'Then one day, some girl is going to be very lucky, when she walks up the aisle with you, Kip Lewis. And happen, if I see that day, I'll envy her a lot. But it's got to be no, and if you wouldn't ask me to tell you why, I'd be grateful.' She took his face in her hands and laid her lips on his forehead. 'Just be my friend, Kip?'

'All right, though being your friend isn't what I had in mind. And I know something's wrong somewhere and I know you can't tell me what it is. But if ever there is anything I can do, just let me know, because I'll wait as long as it takes.'

'Then can I just say that you're too good for me, Kip; that I don't deserve you?'

The tears were back, writhing in her throat, and she closed her eyes and swallowed hard on them.

'Deserve, Meg? Wish I knew who the man was. He'd get what he deserves all right!'

'No, Kip. It wasn't him ended it. It was me, and I really can't tell you why. I can't ever tell you. But be my friend – always? Come and see me when you're in port? And next time you're in Sydney, find yourself a nice girl? You know you like it there.'

'Ha! Talking about Australia – afraid the next trip will only be a short one. I won't sail under Sydney Harbour bridge for a good few weeks. Between you an' me, we're doing a quick one to Panama – picking up urgent cargo. Sailing on the evening tide, tomorrow. With our speed, and given a quick turn-round, I should be back in three weeks, or thereabouts. And I'll call, if you don't mind – just for friendship's sake. And maybe we can do a flick, or go dancing?'

'Yes, Kip. I'd like that. And say all the best to Amy for me? Tell her if there's anything I can do – any shopping, or whatever – I'd be glad to.'

'I'll tell her. And chin up! It isn't the end of the world! See you soon.'

'See you, Kip. Safe journey . . .'

She stood there after he had gone, hating herself for what she was doing to him, because no man but Mark would do, and she couldn't have him. Not even by a small miracle could she. And what made it even worse was that just for a moment, when the knocker had banged, she had needed, oh, how desperately she had needed for it to be someone from Candlefold. Polly, perhaps, determined to find her. Or if Mark had stood there, demanding to know why she had left him, then she would have shown him what was inside Ma's little case, and told him she loved him; would always love him, then say goodbye.

Crazy. It couldn't have been anyone from Candlefold. After what she had done, they'd have washed their hands of her, and she'd be forgotten already.

Except by Nanny, that was. Nanny would remember – always – how clever she had been in ridding Candlefold of the dreadful Blundell girl. And when time hung heavily for the old woman, she would recall her triumph and gloat over it, and laugh. Secretly, of course, because it would have to remain untold – that was the only good thing about it, because not even Nanny Boag would tell the truth of it to Mrs John, not if she had one iota of compassion in her wicked old heart, would she.

'Mark, my darling, if only you knew. If only there was some way of telling you the truth . . .' she whispered.

Yet supposing there was – what would she do then? Marry Kip? Oh, no. For much as he loved her now, Kip would not want a wife who had bedded her brother and fallen for his child.

She slammed shut the outside door and pushed home the bolt, then took the stairs, two at a time to throw herself face down on the bed, setting it creaking with the force of her despair.

'Listen! If there *is* a God in heaven,' she cried to the shabby, uncaring room, 'will You tell me what I'm to do? And since I don't often ask a favour, will you tell me how I'm to bear this life I'm living?'

She gave way to tears, then; sobbed as if her heart had shattered into small, hurtful pieces, and would never be whole again.

* * *

Monday, 27 October. The days were shortening and leaves slipping from the trees in the Liverpool parks. Blackout was at 7.28 p.m. now. No more long days and short nights. The city prepared for its winter drabness; cold, wet pavements, bomb-damaged buildings with corrugated iron sheets nailed over windows and doors, and litter everywhere, because there were few unemployed now, to set to street-sweeping.

Meg made her way to the Ministry of Labour office in Water Street, deciding not to take a tram, because trams got you there quicker than two feet and she did not want to get there at all. Registering for national service was a nonsense when you were having a baby; she didn't know why she was bothering.

She was sick every morning now; on each awakening the daily rush to the water closet with the scrubbed-white seat. Down on her knees on the cold, concrete floor, hand on her abdomen. Nell had said that a dry biscuit and a cup of cocoa should help. The midwife from Juvenal Street swore by it, and that a sick pregnancy was a safe one. Old-midwives' tales! Meg crossed the road to the temporary offices. And they'd have to be temporary, she thought scathingly, because the top two floors had been burned out by fire bombs and a week of wet weather would flood out the rooms at street level.

She pushed through the ornately glassed doors, which were miraculously untouched by shrapnel or bomb-blast, to find a large, hall-type room with a row of desks along one side and six queues already forming in front of each.

Meg found queue B. There were ten young women in front of her; she had counted them meticulously, and before so very much longer there would be another ten behind her. All of them twenty years old; some looking miserable; some with mothers in tow; one or two looking as if they were queuing up for the New Brighton Ferry and a Sunday outing. The smiling minority, Meg thought, seemed eager to be registered, to have a legitimate excuse to leave the nest and fly into the big blue sky of call-up. Did they come from unhappy homes; did they have bossy mothers or tyrannical fathers who did not allow them out on dates? Was registration another name for freedom? But the majority, like herself, waited resignedly, sometimes speaking to the girl in front or behind but standing, ears straining for the most part, to hear what was being said at the large desk marked B.

When finally she stood at the line chalked on the floor three feet away from the desk, she felt relief it might allow some small privacy. And you couldn't blame anyone for listening. What else was there to do in this cold, draughty place where few of them wanted to be?

When she stepped over the chalkline she stood for a moment whilst the clerk placed carbon paper between the sheets of a pad, then retrieved a pencil from the floor. A pretty young woman, hair fair and curly, like Polly's. On her blouse was pinned the regimental brooch of the Liverpool-Scottish regiment; on her left hand, a wedding ring.

'Got your identity card, please?'

She said it without looking up. It was the most repeated phrase in the entire country, and Meg had hers ready and placed it, open, on the desk.

'Margaret Mary Blundell, 1 Tippet's Yard, Liverpool 3. That correct? Identity number KRMA 127/2? Date of birth 29 August 1922?'

'Yes. That's right,' Meg said softly; softly because she was really testing to see how quietly she might speak without being heard by the listening queue behind her.

'And do you have any conscientious objection to being drafted into HM Forces?'

'None at all.'

'Are you still residing at the above address?'

'Yes, I am.'

'Well, then.' The young woman looked up and, smiling, handed back the identity card, 'that's the preliminaries over. So have you any preferences? Have you any compassionate reason for remaining at your address – domestic, perhaps?'

'No. No parents. Only me. Nothing to keep me there except – well –' she drew in her breath, lowering her voice – 'I – I think I'm expecting . . .'

'I see. Think?' The clerk lowered her voice too. 'Have you seen a doctor? Do you have a doctor's note?'

'N-no. But I am . . .'

'Then I think we had better proceed as normal. I will register you for national service in the usual way, but meantime, I suggest you see a doctor.'

'Y-yes . . .' Doctors cost money and anyway, she didn't need one to tell her she had fallen for a baby. But she *did* need a doctor's note. 'I – I suppose I'll have to.'

'Think it's best; make sure – one way or the other. Now – is it to be munitions or would you have preferred a uniform?'

'Uniform?' There was a lot of Royal Navy in Liverpool and a great many Wrens. 'The Wrens, perhaps?' If things had been normal, that was. And things weren't normal, so it didn't matter what she volunteered for.

'Sorry. A waiting list for the WRNS. Everyone seems to want to get in on that mob. For my part, I can't stand those hats. Just like the school velours we wore,' the clerk laughed.

'Well, then, how about the Army? How about –' she took a deep breath then said – 'the Royal Army Service Corps?'

'You got someone in that regiment?'

'N-no. But I'm sure they have lady drivers. I'd like to learn to drive.' What a farce this all was!

'Then I'll put you down for the ATS, with a preference for driving. How's that?'

'Very nice, though I don't like them khaki stockings.' Meg managed a smile.

'Perhaps not. The Air Force girls, I think, have the nicest uniform, but they aren't recruiting drivers at the moment,' she smiled.

'Right, then. The ATS it is. And then what?' Now, they must get down to brass tacks.

'Well, first you'll have a medical and I have to tell you that your – er – condition will be picked up right away. It's one of the things they test for. So don't you think it better if you saw a doctor very soon? Then, when you get notification of your medical, you can send them the doctor's note right away and that will be the end of it, don't you agree?'

Meg was grateful for the clerk's kindness and tact, and for not being toffee-nosed; she had made sure the waiting queue was left in no doubt she had volunteered for the ATS. A decent woman, whose husband was a soldier. There was, it seemed, a lot of kindness this bomb-blasted port she had been so eager to see the back of. And just as well, because she was here for the duration now, and wouldn't be joining anything except the dismal list of unmarried mothers, there to be looked down on by society in general and by smug-faced matrons in particular, who thought that lovemaking was something to be endured to keep husbands from straying.

She left the hall, walking aimlessly, smelling the salt of the river as she neared the Pierhead, making for the landing stage to watch the approach of the ferry from the Cheshire side. Soon the gangway would clatter down and people walk purposefully off it, neither knowing nor caring that a young woman with troubled blue eyes and dark, windblown hair had decisions to make.

She had options, of course. The choice was her own. She could board the ferry and, when it was halfway across, jump over the side. People did. Sometimes they were pulled out; most times they were caught by the propellers and it was a quick end.

But for her, jumping was out. She was too strong a swimmer and the sudden clout of cold water would make her want to strike out and swim. And anyway, she wasn't brave enough nor unbalanced enough. Most people who did something like that were ill in their minds, and Meg Blundell was not.

But she was weary, and tired of being sick, and she didn't want a future like Ma had endured. Nor did she want to bring up a child with a Father Unknown, because Mark's name could not appear on its birth certificate.

Where are you, Mark? She closed her eyes despairingly. *Are you hating me for what I have done and the upset my leaving must have caused?*

The ferry came alongside, hitting the landing-stage with a bump, causing the planking beneath her feet to shudder. She shivered as the wind blew cold from the Atlantic. Where was Kip now? In warmer, gentler waters, making for Panama? Kip had sailed half round the world many times; was not bounded by narrow streets and back-to-back houses. Kip had set his sights on a better life. But he wouldn't be taking Meg Blundell with him, not when he knew, because a child of incest was worse than a rape child. No one wanted to adopt such a child for fear of what might be bred in it. Which left one sure way out for her and she must acknowledge it now; make up her mind by the time the ferry walkway was heaved back on board and the rails secured by the seaman in charge of it. Little more than a minute was left to her.

The seaman at the gangway gave a warning shout, last-minute passengers began to run down the incline. Then the gangway was heaved inboard, the railings slid in place, and secured. There was a churning as the propellers began to rotate and the ferry went astern into deeper water to swing into a turn and point its bows at the far shore and the returning boat it would meet mid-river, then pass port side to port side. And her minute had run.

She turned abruptly, pulling up her coat collar against the wind that whipped the back of her neck, digging her hands deep into her pockets. Tonight she would ask Nell to make enquiries about the struck-off doctor and how much he charged. And from this time on she would not allow herself to think it would be Mark's precious child they would be taking from her but a child of incest, because she had bedded her brother.

Decision made, she lifted her chin to look at the great bulk of the Liver Buildings and the fat birds atop it. Those birds were loved by sailors returning to port – could be seen for miles down river.

Yet before Kip saw them again, it might all be over with; she might even have been called for her medical for the ATS. She might, if the SS *Bellis* was delayed, be in uniform and far away. She hoped so with all her aching heart.

Sorry, Mark. Sorry, my darling. I loved you so much . . .

Twenty-One

'*How* much? But I haven't got that kind of money! You're sure, Nell?'

'That's what the woman said. First thing she told me. Don't be wasting the doctor's time – if you can't find twenty-five pounds, then there's no point in bothering.'

'But I've only got fifteen. I wouldn't have thought twenty-five . . .' Meg whispered, shocked.

'He's safe, I believe. And you get chloroform. And like the woman said, there's the risk – not to the patient, but to the doctor. Been struck off, see. If he's caught obliging, then it's prison for him. Ten years.'

'Safe, you said? I – I suppose he must know what he's doing, but why did he get struck off?' Meg persisted, still apprehensive.

'I asked the same question. Nothing medical, was all I was told. Messin' about with women patients, if you ask me. An' I'm only telling you what happened. I said I'd make enquiries, and I have. The rest is up to you.'

'I haven't got twenty-five pounds,' Meg said flatly.

'Well, I can't help. I've got sod all.'

'Then that's it.' Meg pulled her tongue round suddenly dry lips. 'Like the woman said, forget it.'

'There's two ways open to you.' Nell looked down at her hands. 'You either go on the game – heard it said the going rate on Lime Street is thirty shillings. Mind, if you haven't a room to take them back to and it's got to be standin' up, then happen it'll be less. No?' she asked, on seeing Meg's horror. 'Thought not. The other way, then, is to sell that clock.' She nodded towards the mantelpiece and the heavy brass timepiece that stood out against the ordinariness of the room.

'Ma's clock! But it's the only thing she ever had that was anything decent. Was given it when the last war was over; a memento, I think.

All she ever said about it was that she'd been given it at Candlefold. All the staff got something.'

'Well, you'll raise ten quid on that, which should just about see you in the clear. Take it to Ralphy Levy in Scotty Road. If you tell him you want it back you'll not get so much for it, but he'll keep it two months for you.'

'And how would I get ten pounds to buy it back?'

'Ten, plus interest. Well, you'd be able to work, wouldn't you? Or you could borrow to get it back, then pay the tallyman bit by bit.' Nell was used to juggling money.

'No. It isn't on. Ten pounds is a lot to owe. I'd never be out of debt.'

'All right, then. Don't have it done. Have the baby. Like I said, it's your choice, Meg. I'm not advising you one way or the other. All I said was that I'd make enquiries.'

'Well, just supposing I had it done. I'd be called up, then – I volunteered for the ATS, don't forget – so how would I be able to pay back ten pounds out of my Army pay? I wouldn't get much. Fourteen shillings a week and your keep, I think it is. Might even be less.'

'You don't want to get rid, do you? Deep down, you want to keep that baby. Is that what it boils down to, Meg?'

'I'd like to keep it – yes. I'd like Mark to do the decent thing and marry me. But it isn't possible so I've got no option. And don't think I'm not scared to death, 'cause I am!'

'Then take it a step at a time? Get the money together, then get it over and done with. That's the most important thing. And must you buy the clock back? Wouldn't it be better, since it came from Candlefold, to forget it – leave it with Ralphy? Best you forget that place, girl.'

'Best I should . . .'

Forget Candlefold and the long, sweet summer of '41? Forget Mark, and the willow pool? Never in a million years! Not even if she wanted to. But best not remind herself.

'This woman, Nell? How did you come to know her?'

'I didn't. Someone who'd been to the doctor told me that was how you got in touch. A sort of go-between. Got to be careful, I suppose, who you tell.'

'So where did you meet and and what's her name?'

'Questions, questions! She works as a barmaid in a pub on the Dock Road. You ask for Mrs Smith.'

'Smith. Yes, it would be . . . And then, if you want to go on with it, what happens?'

'I suppose you get in touch with her again at the pub – if you've got the money, that is. Strewth, Meg, I couldn't find a lot out. Women don't blab when they've had that sort of thing done. All I knew was someone let slip to me she'd had rid. She was the one told me about Mrs Smith and where she hung out. And all I got to know – confidential, like – is that he's safe, you don't feel anything and it's twenty-five quid. Your choice, Meg girl.'

'If – if I got the money, would you come with me, Nell? Too scared to go on my own.'

'Only natural. Some folks is scared having a tooth out. But I told your ma I'd look out for you, and I will. Besides, you'll want someone with you.'

'Yes. Thanks. But how do I go about selling the clock? Do I ask for more than ten pounds, and bargain a bit?'

'No. You take what Ralphy gives you, so let's hope it'll raise ten. But I think I'd better do it. I've been in his shop before. He'll deal straight with me – not sell me short. With you, it might be different.'

'All right, then.' Meg took the clock, rubbing the domed top with her cupped hand, as if she were saying goodbye to it. 'I wouldn't like to part with it if there was a chance of getting it back, so could you tell him that – see what he offers, first?'

'I'll do that.' Nell got to her feet. 'Have you got something strong to put it in? I'll take it right away. You can make up your mind when you see what he offers. Now, you're sure, Meg? You want ten for it?'

'I'm not sure about anything, Nell, except sure I don't have much choice. I'll get you a bag. And I'm grateful – you not preaching, I mean. And let's hope when the time comes that I can go through with it. I did hear it's a risky thing.'

'Only with backstreet biddies. The doctor must know what he's doing. He's the feller to see if you've got to have it done.'

'And I've got to, haven't I?' Meg whispered.

'Nobody's *got* to do anything – you know that. But since you are askin', then I reckon you should. And after all, there's a risk in everything – even having a tooth pulled.'

'OK. So go now, will you, then see Mrs Smith tonight? Best it's done before I get cold feet, uh?'

'Best it is. Won't be long, an' then we can have another talk – all right?'

'Sorry I was so long.' Nell had been gone an hour. 'It's all right.' She laid the empty bag on the table top, then took two five-pound notes and two pound notes from her purse.

'You got twelve!'

'I did. Ralphy can be a sly little sod, but he's never dealt me down. Is that kettle boiling?'

'Yes. There's tea in the caddy – wet your own, will you? So what happens now, Nell?'

'Well, you takes stock. Twenty-seven pounds you got altogether, so that's one thing less to worry over.'

'There's nearly ten shillings left in Ma's post office book, an' all. Think I'll get it out – close the account.'

'So you'll have a couple of quid to see you over – plus your dole money. You should be just about all right till they call you up. Daft of you, wasn't it, to go volunteering?'

'Suppose so. But I didn't think it mattered at the time. I told the lady at the Labour I thought I was expecting, but she said she couldn't do anything without a doctor's note. Said she'd proceed as normal, and if I was expecting like I thought, then the ATS wouldn't want me. Nothing to lose, I thought at the time. And I was pretty fed up, an' all. Suppose I'll have to go through with it now.'

'Do you fancy bein' in uniform? After all, you'll be able to keep your pay for spends. They clothe you and feed you and give you a bed to sleep on – can't be bad.'

'Suppose not. And you get a week's leave every three months with a travel voucher thrown in – at least Davie and Mark did.'

'I thought we were goin' to forget about them people.'

'Yes. We are. Only wouldn't it be awful, Nell, me putting my name down for a driver, then meeting up with Mark or even Davie again?'

'Awful? It'd be a bluddy tragedy. But aren't those two goin' overseas?

'Davie is, and Mark expects to go pretty soon. So I won't be meeting either of them, will I?'

Of course she wouldn't. But she would live each day hoping that just around the next corner she would bump into Mark, or even to see him in the distance would be pretty marvellous. Yet to see him and let him walk away, not knowing how near they had been? Oh, no!

'What are you looking to pained about, Meg Blundell? Getting cold feet, then?'

'No. But scared, Nell. Can you go see Mrs Smith tonight – get it over with?'

'I'll do that.' Nell filled her cup again, glad the girl was seeing sense, though it must be rotten having the child of the man you loved taken out of you. 'The sooner the better, then we can get back to normal – till you get called up, that is. Ar, hey. Takes all sorts, dunnit, to make a world?'

'November is a bluddy awful month,' Nell hissed. 'I hate it!'

'And tonight would've been bonfire night, if things had been normal.'

'Well, they aren't normal. Bonfires after dark is illegal; light a bonfire and the ARP would be round before you could say wet-nelly, and you'd end up fined, or in prison.'

Nell was not best pleased. Firework night had been a laugh, once, with street bonfires an excuse for a cheap get-together. But the war had put paid to that, like it had put paid to ciggies, food, cosmetics and the gin she had been partial to. And the Government did exactly what it wanted; sent young men to their deaths and young girls away from home and put you in jail if you showed so much as a chink of light from a window.

'This blackout is a swine tonight. Give us your arm, Meg, and keep hold of your handbag. Trip over and drop it and we'll never find it again!'

It was eight o'clock, and fires had been damped down for economy's sake with a mixing of coal dust and dead leaves, and the result was a belching of foul black smoke that hung on the air to make the darkness even more dense.

'You know where it is, Nell?'

'The pub on the Dock Road? Course I do. But take it easy, girl, or we'll be walking into a lamppost, or sumthin', and we've enough on our plate without black eyes!'

Lampposts were ringed round with white paint as were the edges of kerbs, but on nights such as this the paint offered no warning until you had slammed into one.

'And will she tell us where to go? Will it be far away?'

'She'll take us, like as not. Wouldn't do for her to give us the address. Probably she'll take us there the back way – down jiggers, an' entries, so we wouldn't be able to find it again. I mean, what she's doing is illegal, innit?'

'And what I'm doing is illegal an' all, Nell.'

'Gettin' cold feet, then, 'cause we're here now so it's make-your-mind-up time.'

They stood listening to the sound of laughing and singing and loud voices – the unmistakable noise of a Liverpool ale house.

'You stand there, girl. I'll see if Mrs Smith is in yet. If any fellers try to get fresh, nip inside.' She felt with the toe of her shoe for the steps leading to the door, knowing already there were three. 'Won't be a tick, and keep tight hold of that money!'

Oh Ma, Meg thought despairingly, please understand? There's no other way out for me. I couldn't go through what you did; couldn't scrub floors and take in washing to feed and clothe a kid like me. I don't have a choice, see?

She sighed in a gesture of surrender, because Ma couldn't hear her. Ma had died nine months ago on a cold, dark night such as this, and gone to a heaven called Candlefold and was beside the pump trough, like as not, where the happy photograph had been taken. Not right to call her back to this filthy hole, all bleak and foggy. Leave her be, why didn't she, and get on with her own life as best she could? Do what Ma had done; strighten her shoulders and stick out her chin and take what life threw at her; take what had been written down in her Book of Life the day she was born.

The door swung open and she turned sharply. 'Nell?'

'In here, girl. We're to go to the back. Make as if we're goin' out to the lavvy in the yard. She'll be waiting there. Now, follow me and keep your eyes down – all right?'

The noise of the room hit her as the blackout curtain swung-to behind her. Through the smoke haze she saw men and woman laughing and drinking; men in uniform and two street women leaning against the bar rail. In the corner beside the far door were two men – oldies who had come in for warmth and company, maybe, and who had to make a glass of ale last a long time.

A great shout of laughter went up from one of the tables – all of them obviously seamen – and Meg wondered how anyone could laugh at a time like this, and what it was they had to laugh about. She clutched her bag tightly and made for the sign marked 'LADIES Mind your step', following Nell, who had a hand on the doorknob.

'Watch the blackout, Meg,' she whispered. 'An' there's five steps down. Hold on to the rail . . .'

A pinpoint of torchlight touched the stone steps, guiding them down; a voice warned them to be careful then said, 'This way. Out of the gate and to your right. We'll take a short cut.'

And short cuts, Meg thought, was a roundabout journey in and out of jiggers, meant to confuse anyone who might try to find the house when daylight came.

'Are we expected?' Nell asked nervously.

'Yes. Eight fifteen. Got the money with you?'

'Yes,' Meg whispered.

'Down the next entry. The woman swung her torch. 'And mind your step. It's full of potholes. Feel your way along the wall. Now wait there. I'll tell them you're here. And only one of you goes in. The other waits in the back yard – understood?'

'I'll wait,' Nell whispered. 'Will it take long?'

'No. And don't try knocking on the door, or anything. Just keep quiet and out of sight if a scuffer walks down 'ere, with a flashlight.'

'Course I will! What the hell do you think I'll be doin', then – a song and a dance? We don't want to be here, so button your lip, lady, and stop givin' your orders!' She reached for Meg, then, grasping her arm, holding her tightly, gave her a comforting pat. 'Now off you go, girl. You'll be all right. Soon be over. I'll be waitin'.'

'Yes,' Meg whispered. 'Thanks.' It was all she could think of to say; all she was able to say without bursting into tears and begging to be taken home. 'See you, Nell.'

'Ta-ra, queen. Chin up!'

The woman who called herself Mrs Smith knocked on the door then said, 'There you are, then. You're expected. I'm off – all right?'

'Yes.'

The door was quickly opened, then just as quickly closed. A hand reached for the heavy curtain that hung there, pulling it across.

Meg pulled in a shuddering breath at the finality of that swishing curtain. It cut her off from Nell, cut off her escape had she decided to run for it.

'Come with me, please.'

The woman was well-spoken and well-dressed. Nothing flashy about her pleated skirt and blouse, Meg thought. Her shoes were not utility, but similar to the kind Mrs John wore.

'The doctor is ready for you. Have you got the money?'

Unspeaking, Meg clicked open her handbag, taking out a fold of notes.

'Thank you.' The woman pushed it in the pocket of her blouse without counting it. 'And I must warn you that your visit here tonight must never be talked about – must be forgotten completely.'

'Yes.' Meg's mouth was dry and it was difficult to speak. 'Forgotten.'

'Follow me. Nothing to be afraid of. All over in less than half an hour. You won't feel anything. I will give you an anaesthetic and don't worry. I am a trained midwife.'

'And the doctor . . . ?' Fear screamed through Meg.

'He is my husband.' She said it firmly and finally, as if no more questions would be answered. 'Now – this way. Are your shoes clean?'

Meg looked down at the rich carpet and nodded, clinging to the heavy banister as she followed upstairs, watching mesmerized the swinging pleats of the woman's skirt, wondering how so grand a house could be so near to the road that ran alongside the docks to the north of the city.

She counted twenty-four steps and four half-landings. The stair lights seemed to have been deliberately shaded and she stumbled as the woman stopped to open a small door, leading on to a narrow passage.

Meg looked down at a linoleum-covered floor, saw the black-painted skylight, the sloping ceiling. It was going to be done, she thought wildly, in an attic.

'Come in, please.' A man in a white coat stood there. Most of his face was already covered by a mask, on his head he wore a surgical cap. He slipped a rubber apron over his head, and tied it behind him.

Got himself well-covered, Meg thought. Meet him in the street and you could walk past him any day of the week. She watched fascinated as he clicked a switch by the door then looked around her at white walls, a trolley covered with a white cloth, a high bed, covered in white sheeting.

Clean, Meg thought. No rusty knitting needles hidden on the trolley. The doctor knew what he was doing – oh, *please*, he did?

'Go behind the screen and take off your clothes – up to your waist, please.' The woman had put on a smock and was snapping on rubber gloves. One of her fingernails was bruised purple, but her hands were clean. It would be all right. It *would* be. In less than half an hour, there would be no baby, no incest child.

'Get on the table, please. Lay back. Relax.' Someone was guiding her knees into a bending position, now. 'Slip your feet into the stirrups.'

Stirrups. God, she was trapped! She slid her eyes to her right. The woman had a gauze mask in her left hand. In her right hand was a brown glass bottle. Meg knew it was chloroform. The woman held the bottle at arm's length, then sprinkled liquid on the mask.

'I want you to breath in as deeply as you can, through your nose. You'll feel floaty, but you'll be all right.'

Meg felt the mask touch her face. All she had to do was breathe the stuff into her lungs and when she awoke it would be all over.

'No! Leave me be!'

The stuff was making her head swim, giving her hallucinations. There was a baby floating in the corner of the room. It was small and dead; covered with the dust of bomb rubble. Soon, someone would reach for it and lay it on the pavement; turn their backs on it as they carried on digging. And now they were going to kill her baby! Hers and Mark's!

'Hold her!'

Dimly she heard the man's voice as she made one last despairing effort, lashing out with her arm, covering her mouth and nose.

'No! Get away from me!'

She struggled into a sitting position, watching bemused as the woman retrieved the brown bottle from the floor.

'Stupid little bitch! Get her out of here!'

Hands pulled her from the table, guided her to the door. Someone was taking her arm, telling her to get dressed. Her head felt better now, though she could still smell the stuff in the brown bottle, and her top lip felt cold and sore.

'I want to go! I've changed my mind!'

'All right! All right! Just put your shoes on and get outside!'

'My handbag! Where is it? And my money . . . ?'

'Oh, no! You've seen the last of that, young lady! Not our fault if you changed your mind! Now pull yourself together. I want you out of here!'

'I'm goin', but not without my money!' Her head was clearing, and the dizzy feeling had gone.

'Now listen to me. I want you down those stairs and out of that door! *Now!* You're not getting your money back because it'll pay for the doctor's wasted time and the chloroform you spilled. Lucky we weren't all out for the count! Now come on!'

Meg stumbled downstairs unsteadily, needing to reach the door and breathe in cold air; fill her lungs with it, then gasp out the acrid smell. She wanted arms around her, needed Nell to shush and cluck and tell her it was all right, that she hadn't seen a dead baby, nor been in the white room and that no one had tried to give her chloroform.

She heard the swish of the curtain, the half opening of a door, and then she was out in the swirling darkness, blinking her eyes, taking in gulps of air.

'Meg? That you, girl?'

'Nell! Oh, take me away. Run, Nell . . .'

A hand took hers in the darkness and she twined her fingers in Nell's, sobbing now with fear and relief and disbelief.

'They didn't hurt you?'

'No. They didn't do it, Nell. I wouldn't let them. All at once I couldn't. I saw a baby, floating it was. Remember the dead baby on the pavement, Nell – the May blitz?'

'There was no baby. It was them, trying to put you out. Where's the money? You didn't pay them?'

'She wouldn't give it back!'

'She *what*? Oh, but we'll see about that!'

Nell marched up to the door, banging it with an angry fist, but the door remained closed.

'Right! If that's the way they want it!' She hooked Meg's arm in hers. 'Come on, girl! I got the measure of this place while you were in there. I know where the front door is! Can you manage? I'm not leaving without that money!'

They found the front door at the head of a flight of stone steps and Nell charged up them, huffing and snorting, lifting the knocker, calling through the letter box. But the front door was not opened either.

'All right! They've had their chips! I'm goin' to the Bridewell! Dirty swines, doing abortions! The police'll have to be told about them!'

'No, Nell! No! Let's go home? I'm tired and I feel sick. And we couldn't tell the police or you'd be in trouble. It was you told me about it, remember? You'd be up to the eyes in it, too! And the woman in the pub on the Dock Road!'

'An' so she should be. No better than a pimp. She'll be on a cut, y'know.'

'Nell – let's go home? It was awful. I just want to forget it.'

'Forget it? An' you still in the club? Won't be able to forget it, will you, when you're as big as the back of a bus!'

'OK. I'm still pregnant and so fed up I could jump in the river!'

'Could you now? Takes guts to jump.'

'I could turn on the gas . . .'

'Oh, for God's sake, stop it! You're pregnant, the father's no good to you, all your money's gone and poor Doll's clock, an' all. But that's no excuse to talk stupid. You're not the first around these parts to land up in trouble and you won't be the last. So let's get you home so we can think what's to be done.'

'Done?' Meg's voice was thick with tears. 'What can be done? It's like I'm living in a nightmare! How did Ma put up with it, will you tell me?'

'I don't know. Happen she had more backbone than you! So are we goin' to stand here all night arguing the toss, or what? And tomorrow's another day, and nothing is ever as bad as you think it's goin' to be.

You think you're badly done to? In Leningrad they're eating cats and dogs! So give us a hug and a kiss, eh? We'll manage!'

They had closed the door at number 1 Tippet's Yard, and were looking dismally at a dead fire, when Tommy walked in.

'Kip's home, Meg. Was here looking for you. Said to tell you he'd call tomorrow.'

'Kip,' Meg said flatly. It was all she needed – Kip asking her again to marry him and she not wanting to hurt him by saying no. Kip deserved better. 'Thanks, Tommy. Ah well, don't think I'll bother lighting the fire again. I'm for bed, Nell.'

'Ar. I'll just nip up to the Tarleton. You never know, there might still be a few ciggies under the counter. Sure you're all right? I'll look in later, eh?'

'No, Nell. Like you said, tomorrow's another day. See you. Good night, and thanks a lot. Sorry I messed it up. The story of my life, eh? See you in the morning.'

The kitchen seemed bleak, and damply cold. Nothing else for it but to fill a hot-water bottle, try to get warm in bed. And try not to let herself think that although tomorrow was another day, she would still be pregnant – and penniless. And before long she would have to see a doctor and that would cost money too. Five shillings for a visit apart from the note she needed, which would be extra.

She filled the kettle and lit the gas, hoping the shilling hadn't run out, glancing gratefully at the meter as the gas plopped and flamed. A cup of cocoa was what she needed and a slice of bread and jam to stop the churning in her stomach. Then bed with the clothes pulled over her head to shut out the miserable night. And she would try not to think about anything at all, and especially about Mark, who had said he loved her. Nor would she think about the child still inside her and how she was to live on seven and six dole money and provide for the child. In May, it would be. A summer baby, born in the home for unmarried mothers.

That's it! No more thoughts tonight, Meg Blundell, and no tears either. Tonight she could hide from the world outside. Tomorrow would come soon enough. Tomorrow she would worry – and maybe cry her eyes out.

She was measuring cocoa and saccharin into a cup when a knock came on the door. She stood very still, spoon poised. She didn't want Nell – nor anyone – now she was calmer and in a mood to try to sleep.

The letter box rattled. Through it a voice called, 'Meg? It's Kip . . .'

Reluctantly she drew back the bolts.

'Lo, girl. Saw Nell in the Tarleton. She said you weren't so good.' He stood there, concern in his eyes.

'I'm OK. Just filling a bottle. Early night . . .'

'You don't look OK. Want to tell me, Meg?'

'It's nothing. Good of you to bother, though. I'll be fine in the morning.'

Dammit, why was she weeping? No tears, hadn't she said?

'Look – you're shaking with cold. Slip your coat on and I'll light a fire. And I'll make you a cup of tea.'

'No! I – I've got cocoa in the mug . . .'

'All right, then.' Already he was raking out the ashes. 'Got any wood?'

'There's kindling in the side oven and I really was going to bed, Kip. There's no need to bother.'

'I think there is. Something's up, isn't it – and where has the clock gone?

'Sold it.'

'So you can't get work? Money? Is that it?'

'Yes – and no.' Oh, to hell with. He'd got to know, some time, and anyway, soon she would be showing, and there'd be no getting away from it. 'I'm having a baby, Kip. That's what's up. Nell knows, no one else, so keep it to yourself?'

She was really shaking now, with cold and shame; Kip didn't deserve this – not straight between the eyes.

'Here. Put on your coat.' He handed her into it, then buttoned it as if she were a child; like he was buying time, maybe, to think how to talk himself out of her life. 'And the kettle's boiling. Wet that cocoa. Fire won't be long.'

'Leave it, Kip. No point. This doesn't concern you. You'll be wanting to go now.'

'Sorry, but it very much concerns me.'

His back was turned from her so she couldn't see his face. She was glad about that, and wiped away the tears, stirring the drink, adding milk, saying nothing because there really wasn't anything to say.

'You wrote me that there was a man you were in love with – it's his, isn't it Meg?'

The fire was crackling alight now, and he got to his feet to face her.

'Yes.'

'So why isn't he doing the right thing by you? What did he say when you told him?'

Kip's face was pale, his eyes narrowed in an anger rare for him.

'He doesn't know. No point telling him. He can't marry me.'

'Can't? Or won't? Is he married, Meg? Around Candleford, did you meet him? Where is he now?'

'Back with his unit. And it's Mark Kenworthy.'

'*The son!* Then he'll have to know – pay his way. Dammit, he's had his fun!'

'Kip – *he must not be told!*'

'Why? Tell me why not!' His cheeks had flushed red, and his words were sharp.

'Oh, if only you knew. It's the most bloody awful mess. Tonight I went to – to –' She stuck out her chin defiantly. 'I went to a doctor who – who gets rid for you. Does it in his attic for twenty-five pounds. That's where the clock went, and my savings.'

'An abortion!' His voice was low with disbelief. 'How could you even think of such a thing? It's filthy and it's wrong!'

'Maybe to you it is, Kip, but it seemed the only way out.' She took a gulp of cocoa and it burned her tongue.

'It's taking life! It's a mortal sin.'

'Yes. To Father O'Flaherty it is, but not when you're desperate! It was my choice!'

'And the child? What kind of a choice did it have?'

'Oh, Kip – I don't want a sermon. Don't go on at me? I didn't do it – couldn't go through with it, if you must know! And she wouldn't give me my money back either! So are you happy now?'

'Yes. No one has the right to destroy a child.'

'That's your opinion, Kip, but I'm not a Cathlick!'

'*No one*, Meg!'

'Look – I've had enough for one night. Just go, Kip? And don't say anything just yet, please? I was scared half out of my life tonight. I don't know what I'm saying, never mind what I'm going to do!'

Tears threatened again and she sucked in air in great despairing gulps, closing her eyes tightly.

'Do? You're going to tell me about it – see what we can work out.' His voice was gentler now, and his eyes kind again. 'I'll help all I can. I want to.'

'There's nuthin' to be done and no one can help me. I'm nearly three months gone – that's all I'm prepared to say.'

'Oh, no! First you're to tell me where you went. I'm getting the money back off that dirty bastard!'

'No! And anyway, you'll be away again, soon – back to sea.'

'Not this time. We're in for three weeks – going into dock – getting guns fitted.'

'Guns? But the *Bellis* is a merchant ship.'

'Well, she'll have a couple of guns soon. We usually sail without escort, so they'll come in handy. And that's not to be talked about, mind. But it means I'll be around a bit longer this time, so I'll be able to help straighten you out, Meg Blundell.'

'You really want to help, don't you? Why are you so bloody good, will you tell me?'

'I'm not good. Spitting mad, at first, but what kind of a bloke do you think I am? Walk out on a friend in trouble, would I?'

'No, Kip. Not you. Look – make yourself a pot of tea. Can't stand the stuff – makes me sick. And if you really want to help, and if you'll swear you'll not say one word, then I'll tell you, Kip, so you'll understand.'

'Swear to God . . .' he said softly.

'Then put some more coal on, 'cause it's going to take a bit of explaining.'

Then, mind made up, and because Kip deserved to know, she opened the cupboard door and took out the attaché case.

'It's all in here. Was a bit of a shock to me when I found out.' She sat at the table and motioned to him to sit beside her. 'Ma never told me much about anything. As far as I was concerned, I had no grandparents and no father. I used to wonder who he was – sinner or saint. Suppose Ma had made up her mind to tell me when I came of age. Anyway, this explains a lot.' She laid her birth certificate on the table top. 'Read it.'

'Father Unknown? She chose not to name him,' Kip frowned. 'And you were born at Candlefold. Did you know that?'

'No. Ma always said I was born here, and I don't know why. She was happy bein' a housemaid there. Always when she talked about it, her eyes would light up. It was as if life began for her there. She never told me one word about her life before she went to work there. I'd ask her if she'd had cruel parents or if she'd been brought up in an orphanage, but it got me nowhere.'

'No shame if she had been. Not her fault. Me and Amy were reared by the nuns.'

'Yes. Well, anyway, there are photographs I'll show you of her and the other servants. She was always smiling and happy when they were taken. Such a bonny girl, Kip. But then I read this, and when you've seen it you'll understand why I had to go and get a look at Candlefold, because I'd got it into my head that that was where I'd find the link.' She took the packet of deeds. 'Read what it says there.'

It seemed a long time before Kip said, 'It would seem the man your mother worked for gave her shelter while she was having you, then provided her with a house. Decent man. So you got lucky – got yourself a job there?'

'Didn't mean to.' Meg explained about the advertisement in the post office.

'But you got the job – why didn't they tell you about your mother – who your father was? Surely they above all people would know?'

'Because I didn't ask. A couple of times my mother's name was mentioned in the conversation and I told them she'd been called Hilda and that she worked in a tobacco factory. And I said my father was a seaman and he'd died when I was little. Y'see, all at once it didn't seem important. I just didn't want to know who my father was or why Ma's employer gave her this house. I was happy there – it was sheer heaven after the bombing – and they treated me more as a friend than a home help. Why worry, I decided.'

'And then you met the son?'

'Yes. And it's his baby I'm having.'

'So why can't he be told? Has he got a young lady? Just having a bit of fun, was he?'

'No. I think it was serious for us both. It was after Polly's wedding that Nanny Boag told me.'

'The daft old girl in the attic, you mean?'

'In the nursery – and she wasn't daft. Sly, more like and bad-minded. She pretended she couldn't get about, but she went through my case, put two and two together – found out who I was.'

'And she told you?'

'Oh my word, yes! It was why I left. Just went without a word. No point telling Mark about the baby and, anyway, I didn't know I was expecting when I shoved off.'

'So if what I'm thinking is true . . . ?' Kip shrugged, looking down at his hands.

'Say it. See if you've worked out what I was too stupid to see – or even to think about.'

'Was the father unknown the man who gave your mother this house?'

'That's what Nanny Boag said. Just threw it at me. Bedded my own brother was the way she put it.'

'And you didn't query it – didn't ask the lady you worked for if it was true?'

'Why should I, Kip? It all added up, anyway. And Mrs John – the wife – needn't have known about her husband and Ma. Just accepted that her housemaid had got herself into trouble. Ma was probably told to say nothing and he'd see her all right.'

'That woman seems like a saint to me . . .'

'She is. She's lovely. They were all lovely to me, 'cept Nanny.'

'And the son got you pregnant, Meg – history repeating itself, I'd say, only you got nothing out of it. And you've never heard from them? They never came looking for you, nor sent a letter?'

'They wouldn't know where to look. I told them I lived in Lyra Street – number 6.'

'But six is bombed. You really didn't want them to know who you were, did you? Why, for pity's sake?'

'Don't know.' She rose to fill an iron kettle, soot blackened, and set it on the fire. 'Maybe I just wanted to be as happy there as Ma had been. Or as she said she'd been. I only had till I was twenty, I figured, and then I'd have to leave Candlefold anyway. I volunteered for the Army, would you believe, when they sent for me to register. They'll find out about the baby when I go for my medical. Save me the price of a doctor . . .'

'But that mightn't be for ages, Meg, and what'll you do meantime? You should have a green ration book, like Amy gets.'

'Oh, yes. The one expectant mothers are given with vitamins and orange juice and extra milk on it? Tell anyone who sees it I'm expecting? No thanks!'

'I'll see you later.' He was folding the papers, pushing them back in envelopes, as if that was the end of the matter. 'First, you've got to get your money back. Where was it, the place you went?'

'I don't know. It was dark. Nell might have an idea – she went with me. But it isn't your business, Kip. I've told you everything, but it doesn't concern you. I just wanted you to understand, that's all. But you should leave it – walk away. It's my mess. I'll get out of it.'

'Well, I've made it my business, Meg Blundell. You've been treated rotten and you're not facing it alone. I'll nip up to the pub – Nell will still be there – and I'll see what she can tell me.'

'No! Don't do that, Kip! Nell meant well. She'll tell you nothing if she thinks you're looking for trouble. It was Nell, see, who told me about the woman in the pub on the Dock Road; the one behind the bar who knows where you can go to –'

'To get rid?' His face showed anger again. 'Well, she's going to tell me, Meg. She will, if I say I'll keep her out of it. But I'll get your money back – and that'll only be for starters.'

'Starters? What can you do, Kip? You've only got three weeks.'

'I can see you get yourself to a doctor and get the green ration book. Amy goes to the clinic for her orange juice and pills.'

'And gives her green coupons to the milkman, eh?'

'The milkie won't care whether you're married or not. His business is to sell milk. You've got to start looking after yourself.'

'Don't want to. Can't eat, anyway. I'm sick all the time, now – not just mornings. Tea, cigarette smoke – even walking past the chippy makes me want to throw up.'

'It'll pass after about three months. Amy's does.'

'An' she should know!' Meg hissed. 'Look, it's different for her! She's respectably married.'

'And you aren't. Does that make the baby less important, then? Hasn't it once occurred to you, Meg Blundell, that that child needs a chance in life, or have you labelled it unwanted and illegitimate already?'

'Put like that, I suppose I have.'

'Then don't be so bloody selfish, girl. That kid didn't ask to be got, but it's a fact of life, now, so face up to it!'

'So you've sorted out a doctor and vitamin pills and you're going to see Nell? She won't tell you anything, Kip. I've said goodbye to my money.'

'Look – just get yourself into bed and let me do the worrying, OK? I'll see Nell. She'll tell me, no messing, then we'll see what's to be done.'

He reached for her, cradling her close and she closed her eyes against the kiss she expected. But he only held her briefly, laying his cheek against hers, telling her he would make it all come right.

'You won't go tearing off to Candlefold, Kip? Please say you won't? Mrs John was good to me – seems she was good to Ma, an' all. Stay away from the Kenworthys?'

'Candlefold is in the past as far as I'm concerned. It's now, and the next six months I'm more concerned about. So lock the door behind me, Meg, and get yourself to bed. I'll see you in the morning – all right?'

'The morning. And go easy, Kip? Don't get into any trouble because of me? I'm not worth it,' she whispered.

'That's for me to decide. I'll be off, now. G'night.'

''Night, Kip. Thanks . . .'

She stood, ear to the door, heard him knock at number 2 then walk away, in search of Nell. But it would be useless. Nell hadn't survived alone more than twenty years because she was a fool. She would tell him nothing. But best do as he said – get herself off to bed.

She filled a hot-water bottle from the kettle on the fire then placed the guard over the coals, reluctant to leave the warmth of the kitchen.

She glanced in the mirror over the mantel. Tonight had happened, all right. There was a pink mark over her top lip where the chloroform mask had been pressed. The struck-off doctor in the white attic room had not been a dream; she was still carrying Mark's child. It would still be there in the morning when she awoke, but Kip would not. Kip, if he had one iota of sense in his head, would get out of her life and stay out of it. The trouble she was in she had made for herself, and only she could sort it out. It was as simple as that. She was an unmarried mother and she would have to learn to live with the shame as Ma had done. And like Ma, do her best for the child – Mark's child – with 'Father Unknown' on its birth certificate.

'Ma,' she whispered to the space on the mantel where the clock had stood, 'I miss you and I want you here with me.'

But Ma had died and gone to a heaven called Candlefold. Selfish to call her back . . .

Twenty-Two

Meg awoke at seven, amazed she had slept so soundly – that she had slept at all. But maybe telling Kip had helped, though he wouldn't be back, she knew it. Beneath all the concern, he must have felt disgust at what she had tried to do because he was a Catholic, and good Catholics didn't have backstreet abortions.

She hoped he wouldn't tell Amy. There was a coldness about Kip's sister, perhaps because she was so taken up rearing children on her own. And that, Meg thought, was how it would be for herself, only with no seaman's pay cheque sent regularly from her husband's shipping line.

She could, she supposed, go to the home for unmarried mothers when her time came. It wasn't as if she had no roof over her head; merely that she would need somewhere to have the baby and a midwife to help. It would cost nothing. The homes who took in women who got pregnant out of wedlock were run by charities who then found homes for the babies left behind for adoption.

But would a respectable couple want her child? Meg frowned. Might it be abnormal? Yet the tiny thing inside her was Mark's and hers, and got in love, and no woman was getting it. Ma hadn't given her love child up for adoption and neither would Meg Blundell.

She opened the curtains briefly. Still dark and miserable outside, but it would be early summer when the baby was born. Probably in May. She wasn't quite sure. There had been a terrible blitz here, last May, and the need to get away from the desolation had sent her in search of Candlefold, she thought sadly, digging in her purse for a shilling for the meter, setting the tin kettle to boil. She felt an ache inside her; a kind of rumbling emptiness that made her long to eat, yet afraid to, because of the sickness.

She went in search of cocoa and a dry water biscuit. Being sick mornings didn't hurt so much if there was something inside you to throw up, Nell said.

'Open up, girl!' The letter box rattled and Meg unbolted the door.

'Might have know you'd be here the minute I lit the gas, Nell Shaw.'

'Saw you open the curtain. Lighting the fire, are you?'

'Not yet.' Coal cost money and her heap in the coalhouse was almost gone. 'Why are you here, Nell?'

'You know why. I saw Kip Lewis last night. What made you tell him, then?'

'Oh – because he's a decent sort, I suppose, and because he knew something was the matter. He didn't lecture me – well, only for going to that doctor.'

'Hm. He wants your twenty-five quid back.'

'I know, and I told him not to. There could be trouble, Nell.'

'You can't blame him for trying. I told him where – as far as I knew, that was. Reckon I can find the place in the daylight. I'm goin' with him. The least I can do, girl.'

'Please, Nell – *no*! They won't open the door to you, let alone part with the money. They'd deny I'd ever been there. And it's no concern of yours. Keep out of it, eh?'

'I'm goin' to. Just tell him where the house is, then I'll shove off.'

'And what's he goin' to do then – kick the door down, get himself arrested? Oh, it's such a mess, Nell. And all the time I've been thinking about myself – never given a thought to how I'm going to bring up a child, get work . . .'

'Doll managed. So will you. Mind, it was workin' too much and eating too little that was the death of her. Too weak to fight off the TB, when she caught it. But she did right by you, girl, though when you come to think of the money them Kenworthys must have, they could have done more to help her – moneywise, I mean. But she was a proud one, was your ma. Never lost her dignity an' you'll have to be the same, Meg Blundell. So let's hope Kip gets your money back, 'cause you're goin' to need it!'

'It would be a help if he could, especially now it's winter. But that doctor's wife was a hard-faced one and toffee-nosed, with it. Y'know, I wouldn't blame Kip if he never came to this house again.'

'No. I wouldn't either, not after the way you've treated him. But the lad just might be lucky.'

Yet Meg knew he would not, and who could blame him if he turned his back on the whole sordid affair? She had seen the last of Kip, decent though he was. From now on she was on her own. Ma had managed and so would she. Somehow, the two of them would muddle through. *The two of them* it was now, and for the first time she wondered if the baby she carried was a boy or a girl. A boy, she hoped. Like his father. Tall and fair and so very good to look at.

Then she put a hand over her mouth, flung wide the door and made for the lavatory. Hell! How long was this being sick lark going to last?

She had been right. Kip was not coming. Twelve o'clock, and no sign of him, Meg thought dully. He had either decided to steer clear of trouble, or got himself into it. No sign of Nell either, but Nell, having found the house with Kip, was like as not on the hunt for cigarettes or in a food queue somewhere.

Her stomach began to ache again, urging her it was time to eat. She poured a small amount of milk into a cup. Milk did not make her sick and it made her think again about the special green ration book that would allow her a whole pint of milk a day. Then quickly, she dismissed the tell-tale book from her mind.

What she would really like – would have stolen, even – was a crisp, crunchy green apple, and there would be no apples in the shops until next summer, when the English crop was harvested.

'Trust you, Meg Blundell, to crave something you can't have,' she whispered to the pale-faced girl in the mirror.

But wanting something she could not have had become the story of her life. She wanted not to be pregnant – even with Mark's child – wanted to be back at Candlefold, wanted to see Mark for one last goodbye. She couldn't have any of those things; only a cold, dark winter to face with bleakness in her heart and a baby growing inside her. And wanting Mark. Always, for the rest of time, wanting Mark. And never seeing him again.

Kip came at one o'clock. Meg heard his whistling and ran to open the door, relief singing through her.

'Hi!' he grinned. 'Think I wasn't coming?'

'I wouldn't have blamed you if you'd decided to give Tippet's Yard a miss.'

'Pressie for you.' He placed a brown-paper carrier bag on the table.

'Kip! Oh! You got it!' Cheeks flushed, she took out the clock.

'Well, put it where it belongs,' he laughed. 'Looks well, doesn't it? Bet Ralphy intended to sell it on – he'd given it a good polish.'

'But how much did you pay?'

'A couple of pounds over the odds – but worth it. And I got this for you.' He handed her a fold of white five-pound notes.

'You got it back? They gave you the money, Kip? But I didn't think – not even for a minute – you'd manage it. Let me pay you for the clock – *please*?' Sudden tears filled her eyes and she let them trickle unhindered down her cheeks. 'And this money is your own, isn't it? You didn't get it back from that doctor.'

'So help me God, I did!' He was still grinning.

'But how? Oh, I'm sorry, Kip, but it's all too much,' she sobbed. 'Why are you so bloody decent? I don't deserve it – not after what I did to you.'

'Hey – come here.' He laid an arm around her shoulder, offering his handkerchief. 'Had anything to eat, lately?'

'Yes, thanks.' The milk had stayed down. 'Have you?'

'I have, but I could do with a pint. Come with me to the Tarleton and I'll tell you all about it. It'll make your day, girl, I promise.'

'You didn't have to do anything awful to get it? I'm sorry, Kip, but I just didn't think they were the sort of people to part with that kind of money.'

'I'll admit it took a bit of doing, but get your coat on and we'll find a quiet table in the pub and you'll have the story from first to last. How'll that be, eh?'

'Fine.' She dabbed her eyes and forced a smile to her lips. 'And I didn't say thanks, did I?'

'No thanks required. I enjoyed it, as a matter of fact.'

He held out his hand and she took it, thinking how warm and safe it felt, feeling a fresh flush of shame for the way she had treated him.

'OK. Ready.' She locked the door, then pulled up her coat collar against a wind that whipped up the entry and hit her full in the face.

'And will you put this money in your pocket, please – keep it safe till I can put in my bankbook?'

Dear, kind Kip. She wished she could love him the way he wanted to be loved, but it was not possible. She was Mark's. She always would be.

Kip lifted his glass. 'Well – here's to justice!'

'I'll drink to that.' She took a sip of lemonade. 'And thanks again.'

'No. *Real* justice, I'm talking about – not your money, Meg. But I'll start at the beginning, shall I? Keep you in suspense? Best I start when Nell was sure as she could be that we'd got the right house. That was when I told her to make herself scarce and marched up the steps bold as brass and rang the bell.

'No reply, of course. Reckon I hadn't expected one, so I kept on ringing and banging, then I shoved open the letter box and yelled, "ARP. Open up, please!" in my best air-raid warden's voice. And would you believe it, a woman came to the door and I knew I'd got the right place. Her fingernail – it was bruised, like you said.

'"What is it?" she said, all toffee-nosed. "I'm sure we haven't been showing a light." And I told her that as far as I was concerned, they hadn't. What I really wanted was twenty-five pounds, I said, and I'd go away quietly. Mind, I'd got my foot in the door by then, so she knew to expect trouble.

'"You'll get nothing here," she said, so I said, all quiet like – that maybe the two scuffers walking down the street might help convince her that she owed my friend money she'd paid for an abortion last night, then decided against having.'

'And there really were police in the street, Kip?'

'Oh, yes. A sergeant and a constable, walking the beat. Couldn't have timed it better. The woman took a quick look out of the door, then told me to come inside. Then she called for her husband and got him in on the act. He wasn't a very big feller – no problem, I thought. So I told him what I'd told her – that I wasn't leaving without twenty-five pounds and that if I had to, I'd shake it out of him.'

'And he gave you it? Without any bother? Are you sure you didn't hit him, Kip?'

'Sure I'm sure. He paid up without a word – just told me to get out and not come back. Which I did, of course.'

'And you're sure that was all that happened?'

He looked, Meg thought, far too cheerful. There was more to come, she knew it.

'We-e-ll, when they'd slammed the door on me I saw the coppers. They'd got to the top of the street and were walking back, real slow. Gave me time to wonder what I could do about those two inside. I mean – rubbish like them should be stopped. Remember the rockery at the side of the house?'

'No. I went in at the back door. It was dark – I didn't see anything.'

'Well, it was more a pile of stones with a few scraggy plants in it. Anyway, I picked up a big round cobble and when the coppers were just a couple of yards away from the front gate, I threw it at the window – made one hell of a noise. They didn't half shift. "What the 'ell do you think you're doing, then?" said the sergeant and the other one got me by the arms.'

'Kip! Why did you do it? Their kind of people aren't worth it! Now you'll land up in court!'

'I won't! I told the sergeant that if they wanted to nick an abortionist all they had to do was knock on the door. But by that time the two of them had come out wondering who'd put their window in, I shouldn't wonder.

'"Those two," I said to the cops, "they do abortions for twenty-five pounds. In the attic. Go and see for yourself!"'

'So you smashed the window so the coppers would come? Wasn't that a bit risky, Kip?'

'No. I'm a quick thinker, see. I had to get that doctor to the front door and the cops as well. It worked. They asked to see upstairs; said if they had nothing to hide, they'd be in the clear and they could charge me with breaking their window. The toffee-nosed woman said they weren't going anywhere in her house without a warrant, and that did it! The sergeant asked them both to accompany him to the alleged attic – he didn't seem worried by the woman's blustering. The other copper stayed outside and took my name and address. I showed him my seaman's book and the number in it and told him I'd be ashore for three weeks, if they wanted me for anything.'

'Nothing about breaking the front-room window, Kip?'

'No. I think they were more interested in the doctor. The constable said they knew about him; only wanted someone to come forward. Seems women who have illegal abortions usually want to keep quiet about it. I didn't give them your name, Meg, but would you give the police a statement? You could ask them to keep your name out of it, if they could. Would you, Meg?'

'It would be in the *Echo*. Everybody would know.'

'Up to you, love . . .'

Then she remembered the dead baby on the pavement; thought that maybe if she did that one thing, the baby would be all right – laid to rest with its parents and maybe in heaven now. Well, in the heaven Polly believed in. She pushed Polly from her mind, took a steadying breath then said, 'Yes. I'd give a statement.' For the dead baby's sake, she would do it.

'Good girl. That doctor could get ten years inside, the cop told me, as well as a bit added on for practising whilst being struck off the medical register. He told me to push off, then, and wait till they got in touch. Y'know what, Meg? I enjoyed every minute of it!'

'Then you're a fool, Kip Lewis! You could have ended up in Walton Gaol!'

'Could have,' he grinned, 'but instead I'm goin' to be the star witness when those two end up in court. And they will!'

'You're very pleased with yourself, aren't you? Didn't you just once stop to think that if anything had gone wrong –'

'But it didn't go wrong and that couple will be out of circulation for a long time. Wish I'd hung around, though, to see them driven off in the police van.'

'Kip Lewis! What are you, eh?' she smiled.

'Your friend, I hope.' All at once he was serious. 'You know I'll do anything I can to help, Meg. Only wish I could take care of you properly. God knows, you need looking after.'

'I'll manage. I'll get everything straight in my mind before long. I panicked, see? Getting rid seemed the only way, especially as – as –'

'As you and the father couldn't marry,' he finished for her.

'The father! Say his name, Kip! It's Mark. And it was as much my fault as his. I didn't say no!'

'All right! You're still carrying a torch for the man, but you're going to have to forget him, Meg. He's blood kin. Once you can accept that, things might get a bit easier for you.'

'So you know all about it, Kip – what's best for me and how I feel?' She said it angrily, because he was lecturing her and she could do without it, grateful though she was.

'I know about accepting what you can't have. I had to, Meg, when I got your letter. I know a bit about how you feel.'

'Yes. Sorry. And sorry I lost my rag. I shouldn't have. Not after what you've done for me today.'

She was grateful that at that moment the landlord of the Tarleton called time, draping towels over pumps, grumbling that his beer allocation was almost gone and that Hitler had a lot to answer for.

'OK. Friends again – but before we go . . .' Kip fished down the neck of his jersey, hooking out the chain on which hung his red identity disc, the St Christopher medallion he always wore – and a sapphire and diamond ring. 'This is still yours if you want it.'

'Kip! I said you'd done enough!' She felt her cheeks burn hotly and was glad she had the grace to blush. 'Sell it. You'll get a good price for it. Rings like that don't exist in the shops any more. Just ones with diamond chippings in them. Anyone would be glad to buy something like that secondhand.'

'I wasn't offering it to you to cash in on it. I'm asking you again if you'd wear it for me.' He threw up his hands as she drew in breath to speak. 'And don't say no right away. Think about it, won't you?'

'There's nothing to think about. You're askin' me to marry you, aren't you, Kip? After all that's happened, you still want me? Shop soiled and pregnant with another man's child? Well, I'm sorry, but the answer has still got to be no. It wouldn't be fair to you, now would it?'

'That's for me to decide.'

'No, Kip. For me. Look – just take me home, will you?'

'OK. If that's what you want. We can talk there. Because I'm not giving up, Meg. I've thought about nothing else since you told me. I've even seen Father O'Flaherty about it.'

'You did! When?'

'Just before I came to see you – on my way back from the pawnshop. But let's go back to yours – and please hear me out, Meg? I shouldn't have sprung it on you like I did, but I've had a whole day to think about it. Can't you an' me just talk; talk quietly with no slanging, no recrims?'

'If that's what you want – yes, at least I owe you that. But you won't make me change my mind.'

'We'll talk about it at your place.' he said stubbornly, guiding her towards the door. They walked down Lyra Street and into Tippet's Yard without speaking. Only when the door of number 1 was closed behind them did Kip say, 'Right. I'll get the fire going. You put the kettle on. We need a hot drink.'

'Bossy with it, aren't you? Do make yourself at home, Mr Lewis,' she said hotly, all at once on the defensive. 'Act like the place is your own!'

'That's my girl,' he teased. 'More like the Meg I know! So fill the kettle, eh?'

'It won't work,' she sighed. 'It really won't, Kip.'

'OK. But you can't blame me for trying.'

'No, though you'll have to accept when you've tried your best, that the answer will still be no. I can't wear your ring, Kip.'

'Why not?'

'Because apart from the obvious, there's the religion, for a start. When you saw Father O'Flaherty, I'll bet the first thing he said was that the baby must be brought up a Catholic.'

'Well, he didn't, though I suppose he assumed it would be, me being the father, that is.'

'You! The father! You told him that?'

'Why not? If the baby is born in wedlock, then it takes my name. Look, Meg, that little one shouldn't have Father Unknown on its birth certificate. I don't know who my parents were and you didn't know who your father was till that old woman told you. Me and Amy weren't told anything by the nuns. They never tell you. I wish they had. I've worked it out in my mind, see, that my father was killed in the last war and my mother just couldn't cope. Or maybe she died in the flu epidemic they had in 1919. Sometimes I want her to be alive so one day I might just find her. But I think she's dead.'

'Kip, I'm sorry. I hadn't thought, you see, about –'

'About Amy and me? Why should you have? But what I'm trying to tell you is that your baby could be born with a mother and a father, Meg, if you'd say yes, and it wouldn't ever be told otherwise.'

'But, Kip, you're only home for a while – less than three weeks now. And you wouldn't be married anywhere but in your church. So had you thought I'd have to have instruction, first, me being a Protty? And that takes weeks. A girl where I worked at Edmund and Sons had a whole rigmarole to go through, her not bein' a Catholic.'

'Well, you'll have to go through it too, Meg, but I told Father that I was goin' to marry you first at the Registry Office – to make it legal, that is. It won't take me long to set it up.'

'You did *what*? And what's your Amy goin' to say about that, you not being married by a priest?'

'Amy isn't marrying you. I will be – I hope.'

'So you'd do that for me, Kip? Marry outside your Church?'

'Yes. But we'd get married at St Joseph's next time I dock, when you'd had your instruction. Then it would be legal *and* moral.'

'Oh, but you've got it all worked out, haven't you?' She sat down heavily at the table.

'Yes. I want you to be my legal wife before I sail. We'll get the Church's blessing later. Drink your cocoa.'

'Cocoa, he says! You'll be gone three months! At least! I can't stand in front of the altar seven months pregnant.'

'It wouldn't be in front of the altar. That's for Catholics,' he grinned. 'With us, it would be at the side of the church – but moral, for all that. And Father O'Flaherty has married a few well-pregnant brides. I'd take bets on it.'

'Look, Kip,' Meg went to sit beside him at the fire, holding her hands to its warmth, looking into the flames as though what she should say would be there, for her to read, 'I loved Mark, loved him so much that I got his baby.'

'Yes, and you probably still do and always will. And you won't forget him because the child will remind you. But there are all kinds of loving. Mark Kenworthy was your first love; ours – yours and mine

– would be different. And there's one thing I'll promise you, Meg. I won't touch you until you want to; wouldn't force myself on you. I've loved you a long time – I can wait for as long as it takes.'

'Oh, Kip Lewis!' She jumped to her feet and went to the window to stare at the yard outside, winter-drab and soot-stained; stared at the lavatory wall against which her mother had died less than a year ago. But it was just a lavvy wall, she thought. Ma wasn't there, so it wasn't any use asking her what she should do. Ma had gone, and Candlefold must never be thought of nor spoken about again, if she could help it. Candlefold would be a memory, golden bright; one that maybe, just sometimes, she could call back, when things got too much to bear. 'Oh,' she said again, turning to face him.

'Oh, what, Meg love?'

'Oh, I don't know. Don't know what to do, I mean, about sayin' yes. You deserve better than me – a girl who loves you, for a start. And you'd be better off with a wife who was the same religion as you are – not one who doesn't believe in God! And one you'll never be sure about – even if we got around to making love you'd never be sure if the woman in your arms was thinking about another man! I can't marry you, Kip. It wouldn't be fair.'

'And if that's a risk I'm prepared to take?'

'Then you're a flippin' saint, Kip Lewis, that's all I can say!'

'You're wrong. I want you to marry me. I want your baby to be born in wedlock, even if I'm thousands of miles away and can't be with you when it happens. And yes, I do hope that one day things will turn out right for us and that you and I will have children, and bring them up in Australia. I still want to go there, Meg, when this lot is over – turn my back on England.'

'It's half a world away, isn't it?'

'Yes. Would you be homesick?'

'What? For this place? For Tippet's Yard that should've been knocked down years ago? Not likely would I miss it!'

'And Candlefold?'

'Ah, well –' She hesitated, because she hadn't been ready for so direct a question. 'I – I think that *if* I said I'd marry you and was willin' to go with you to Australia and never come back to England again – *if*, mind – then Candlefold would be special to me, even from all those miles away, just as it was special to Ma. It was her shining place, see, and I'm as sure as I can be that it will always be mine too. But *if* is a little word with a big meaning. It's *if* I marry you, Kip, 'cause like I said, you wouldn't be getting much of a bargain if you took me.'

'I'd be getting the girl I want – I'll risk the rest. But you've got to think it out on your own, Meg. Don't go asking Nell 'cause she'd tell you yes, grab the chance while you can. When you give me an answer, love, I want it to be your own.'

'And it will be, Kip, and I'll think about it tonight, when you've gone home. I'll think real hard, and thank you,' she whispered chokily, 'for being such a decent man. Whatever happens you'll always be that, to me.'

'Right! So shall we go into town – see a flick – get something to eat, act like we're two friends on a date?'

'Yes. I'd like that, Kip. But not fish 'n' chips, eh?'

And they laughed, as friends do, and she knew in her heart that when he asked her again to marry him, she would say yes, because all the fight had gone out of her and she couldn't cope as Ma had done; hadn't the backbone to be an unmarried mother in a world where unmarried mothers were no better than they need be.

Sorry, Mark, she whispered in her heart. And take care, my love, wherever you are . . . ?

Twenty-Three

They were married on the last Saturday in November on a damp day, bleak and cold, with a wind off the river whipping the city streets. It was a far cry, Meg thought, from that early September day when Polly and Davie had married. Fields grass green or pale gold with wheat stubble; the sky clear and blue, and everywhere trees and flowers and happiness.

She straightened her shoulders and walked to the registry office door, where Kip waited. He wore his best uniform and an expression of relief, Meg thought, to see her there with Nell and Tommy.

She tried not, when the time came to stand at the desk and repeat her marriage promises, to think of All Saints and Michaelmas daisies in the font and Hugh Rushton smiling a blessing. And she tried so hard, when it was all over and they went to the Adelphi Hotel and sat in the lounge having afternoon tea, not to think of Mrs Seed and the big, borrowed teapots and trays of sandwiches and a sponge cake dredged with icing sugar. They were lucky, sniffed the waitress at the Adelphi, to get a scone apiece and jam, too, rationing being what it was, these days.

Nell, in her best costume and navy-blue felt hat, poured tea from a silver-plated pot, then toasted the bride and groom, cup high, little finger stiff. And Meg and Kip smiled, and thanked her and said that one day they would have a real reception – a knife-and-fork high tea and wine for toasts. And because there was no best man to make a speech, Kip had said quietly. 'Thank you both for being witnesses. And I'll see Meg all right for money if you two will keep an eye on her when I've gone.'

They had lit the fire in the kitchen, afterwards, and Kip piled it high with coal, drawing the curtains against the November night, putting the iron kettle to boil.

'Like an old married couple,' he smiled.

'Which we are, though I can't believe it.'

Yet now she wore her mother's worn wedding ring and one of sapphires and diamonds and her left hand felt weighted down and awkward.

'I've seen them at the office; made over half my pay to you. You'll be all right financially. The shipping line will pay you at the end of each month – so here's ten pounds to see you through until then – because it'll be the end of December till your first pay cheque.'

'Kip, it's far too much. I could live well on half that.'

She felt bad about it; about the wedding – about everything. She still felt as if none of it had happened until the left-handed feeling reminded her it had. She was Mrs Kipling Lewis now. Three months gone, but respectably married. And when she had changed her ration book and identity card to her new name, she could visit the doctor – which she could now afford – and be given a signed note that would put paid to joining the Auxiliary Territorial Service, and entitle her to a green, expectant mother's ration book.

Yet the feeling of unreality persisted and she gazed into the fire as if words were written there that said none of today had happened and she had never got pregnant and everything was all right because Candlefold wasn't all that far away and she only had to get a bus and a train to be back there, arranging Polly's long satin train at the top of the aisle.

'What is it, girl – feeling sick?' Kip placed a cup of cocoa at her side.

'No. I'm fine, thanks. Just can't believe it's happened.'

'Well, it has and we'll be married again next time I'm home.'

'By Father O'Flaherty.'

'That's it. You'll have had your instruction by then. And do something for me when I'm gone?' He placed a Cellophane-wrapped packet of cigarettes and three florins on the mantelpiece beside the clock. 'They're for Father – the old devil's always moaning about the shortage of ciggies. Tell him to mind where he smokes them – they're marked HM Forces Only. He'll be chuffed to have them. You can arrange when you go to the manse then – an introduction, sort of, to break the ice. He isn't a bad old stick and he doesn't hate Protties like you think.'

'And the money, Kip?'

'That's for Amy's three, for their money boxes, tell her.'

'She wasn't at the wedding . . .'

'No. Difficult getting away, with three young children.' He looked into the fire because she knew he didn't want to meet her eyes.

'And it was a registry office wedding, which she wouldn't be seen dead at. Why doesn't she like me, Kip?'

'Well, she's your sister-in-law now so maybe things will be different. Like I said, it'll give you something to do when I'm back at sea. Want to come with me when I say goodbye to her?'

'I'd rather you went on your own, Kip. I promise I'll call with the money for the kids, but I think it'll be better without me there – y'know, brother and sister together. She's going to miss you tonight.'

'She won't. She'll be glad to have my bed space. They always have to hutch up when I'm ashore. I'll be getting my head down here, in future. And whilst we're talking about sleeping, Meg. I meant what I said. I know you aren't ready for *that* yet, and I won't bother you.'

'So where do you want to sleep?' Meg swallowed hard. 'Y'see, when Ma died, they came from the Health and took away her mattress and all the bedding. And my bed's only a single and . . .'

Her voice trembled to a stop as she swallowed hard on tears.

'Listen!' He knelt at her side, taking her hands in his. 'The sofa will suit me fine! Don't get yourself upset, love. I'll tuck you in when you go to bed, kiss you good night, and I'll be as right as rain down here. We can talk about – well, you know – when we're properly married in church and the baby's been born. OK?'

'Why are you so decent, Kip?' Tears flooded her eyes and ran down her cheeks. 'Most men wouldn't wait – would want their rights . . .'

'Well, I happen to think you are worth waiting for. It'll come right for us, I promise it will. We're married now and it's legal. The church wedding will tie the knot a bit tighter, that's all. So trust me, Meg? I will make you happy, if you'll go halfway towards letting me. There's no one can point a finger now, at you or the baby, don't forget. And I'll be back before you know it – before the end of February, if all goes well.'

'Australia again, will it be?' She dabbed her eyes and took a deep shuddering breath.

'Yes. We'll be sailing Monday. The guns are fitted, there's nothing to keep us, now the DEMS gunners have arrived.'

'You're a dear man, Kip. I will try to be a good wife to you. Only give me time to get used to the way it is? Please?'

'All the time in the world, Mrs Lewis,' he said softly, cupping her face in his hands, kissing her softly. 'You've got my word on it. And I found a tin of corned beef in my case when I was packing my things at Amy's. Feel up to making us a few sarnies? You won't be sick?'

'Touch wood, I haven't been sick all day – well, only this morning when I got up. Maybe it's starting to get better, like Nell said. Maybe it really does stop when you're three months. So why don't you nip off to the Tarleton, have a quick pint? I'll have them ready for when you get back.'

'You're sure? I wouldn't say no to a drink. You don't want to come?'

'No. Get yourself off – and don't be late back!'

'Nagging me already, are you?' he laughed, hand on the doorknob. 'Oh, and put that money in your purse, will you?'

She looked down at the pound notes she had been clutching. Lucky, she was. Twenty-five pounds in the bank to buy things for the baby, and money to come every month-end. Dead lucky. She should be grateful for the way things had turned out and she was, really. It was just that today, more than ever, she had thought about Candlefold and it wouldn't do, because she was Kip's wife now. And Candlefold and everything remotely connected to it must be forgotten absolutely, or this unreal marriage of theirs wouldn't have the ghost of a chance.

'Don't come with me to the dockyard,' Kip had said, that Monday morning. 'I don't like being seen off. Just say ta-ra and wish me good luck, eh, when I go?'

'If that's what you want. But I'd like to –'

'No. I don't like goodbyes and I don't want you to say it either. Say see you, or so long, but not goodbye. A superstition, see, with seamen. And once I've gone I won't be turning round for one last wave – OK?'

'OK. And since you've said your piece about leaving. Kip Lewis, mind if I have my say, an' all? I'm grateful to you for what you've done and I will try to be a good wife to you and go with you Down Under if that's where you're set on going. I'll try my hardest, Kip . . .'

'And I'm glad I got you, in the end. Maybe not fair and square and courted like it should have been, and maybe I took advantage of you whilst you were in shock from what had happened, but I promise I'll do all I can to look after you and make you happy, Meg. One day, you'll love me. Differently, I know, but it'll come right for us.'

'Yes – well that's it, then. You've got everything? Kitbag packed?'

'Yes. Just my small case for bits and bobs. Now tell me what you've got to do?'

'Change my name on my ration books and identity card, see the doctor and call in on Amy. Anything else?'

'Yes. The most important thing, and you've forgotten it. Take care of yourself, and the babe. Drink your milk every day and don't forget the vitamin pills. Nell said she'd keep an eye out for you if there's an air raid, or anything, and her and Tommy are only across the yard, if you should want them. So have I missed anything out? No? Then I'll have a wash and a shave and get into my good togs. Then I'll be off. I'm always restless for the off when the time comes. You'll get used to it, girl.'

It had been an hour later that he'd kissed her on the doorstep and told her he loved her, and she had held him close, cheek on his chest and told him she loved him too and that she would write every day so there would always be letters for him when the *Bellis* docked.

Then he'd lifted his hand to Tommy and Nell, who'd been standing at their doors, and disappeared under the archway without another word or a backward glance.

'Well, God go with you, Kip Lewis,' Nell whispered as his footsteps faded. 'And may He see you safe home.'

And little Limping Tommy said, 'Aye. Amen to that.'

But Meg closed her door with a bang that said, 'Don't be knocking, you two,' and sat in the chair beside the fire and sobbed as if her heart was about to break. Because she was alone again with a child inside her to nurture; alone for at least three months until Kip docked again. Three months to while away. Thirteen long weeks in this hole where everything around her was down-at-the-heel and mucky, when all she wanted was Candlefold's safeness to keep the war out, and the pump trough where Ma was; wanted her white bedroom with the blue-flowered bedspread and the bed where she and Mark had been lovers and made a child. And she couldn't have any of it; must forget it because she was Kip's wife now. For all time.

'Will you come inside, Mrs Lewis? You'll have come about the talks we'll be havin' about you understanding our Catholic ways. You'll not mind the kitchen? Coal is so short that we rarely light a fire in the parlour these days. Sit you down.'

'Thank you, Father. And I haven't come about the instruction – not really. I'm here because Kip left you a few ciggies. They can get them on the ship a lot easier than us civilians can, and twenty at a time, an' all.' Smiling, she took them from her pocket.

'Kip's away, then?' The elderly priest fondled the Cellophane wrapping as if putting off the moment when he broke it, and the scent of tobacco wafted up to tantalize his senses. 'You'll be wanting me to remember him in my prayers, then? We pray every day for our fighting men and women, you know. I hope you'll come to accept the power of prayer, as you come to understand our Catholic beliefs.'

'I hope so, Father. But I've got to be honest, right from the start, because I don't believe in God.'

'Don't believe in God!' His cheeks reddened, his eyes opened wide. 'Then who, in heaven's name, do you pray to?'

'I don't pray, Father. I'm a fatalist, I suppose. I think that what is to be will be; that it's all mapped out for us the day we first draw breath. An' I'm sorry to say such things, an' I hope they won't be held against me, 'cause Kip really does want us to be married in church next time he's ashore. Quietly, like.'

'It'll have to be quietly if what he tells me is true. But with luck, the child will be born in holy wedlock, and that's all that matters. What did you say your name was?'

'Used to be Blundell. Margaret Mary Blundell. Tippet's Yard.'

'They're good Catholic names. Margaret Mary, and Blundell too. You're sure you've got no Catholic kin?'

'No relations at all, Father. There was just me and Ma. Da died at sea, before Ma came to Tippet's Yard.'

And lying to a priest was a fine start, she thought, looking down at the table top. But she wasn't telling him about Father Unknown or he'd think that sort of thing ran in the family – which it did, if she were to be honest.

'Ah well, you'll soon have a family of your own around you and you've got young Kipling. He's a good man. Kind of him to send the ciggies. Would you mind if I had one, Mrs Lewis? Terrible tempting, they are.'

'Not at all. As long as you don't blow smoke in my face, Father. Cigarette smoke makes me sick, you see.'

'Then shall we meet up again tomorrow maybe, at about three? We can start our talks then – and I'll promise I won't try to convert you, child. Just as long as you understand Kip's beliefs, and that your children will be reared in their father's faith.'

'Convert me? I'd be a hard nut to crack, Father!' Meg laughed, getting to her feet.

'Hard indeed, but what a challenge, eh? What a triumph a convert such as you would be. But away with you for now. I'll pray for your man – and I'll pray for you too, Margaret Mary Lewis. An' see you tomorrow at three?'

It hadn't been so awful, Meg thought. Father O'Flaherty wasn't a bad old stick, in spite of his blunt ways. And, fair play, he'd let Protties into St Joseph's crypt when the raids had been on. She hoped she would have as much luck with Amy Rigby, who wouldn't give a Protty the time of day if she could help it!

But she had promised Kip she would call. He'd given her the money for the children so she would have to and she would try, she really would try, to make friends with his narrow-minded sister.

All at once apprehsive, she made her way to the house at the bottom of Lyra Street, thinking of Kip instead. He would be in the open sea now, with no convoy to wait for, heading for the Azores, with two new guns for protection. The *Bellis* was fast as the *Queen Mary*: could outsail any submarine. Kip would be all right. Father O'Flaherty would pray for him, if prayers were what you believed in.

She lifted the knocker of number 8, then stood anxiously to await the opening of the door, and Amy Rigby's hostility.

'Oh, so it's you. I'm busy.' Kip's sister stood there, a child on her hip. From inside, Meg could hear crying.

'I'll not keep you. Just wanted to call with this.' She held out the three two-shilling pieces. 'Kip left them, for the money boxes.'

'Thank you, I'm sure, but like I said, I'm busy. In fact I'm always busy.'

'Well, I'll call again.' Kip's sister looked older than her years, Meg thought; as if a good night's sleep would do her no harm. 'Maybe there'll be some shopping I can do for you – or I could push the little one out in his pram, give you an hour.'

'No thanks. And don't call. I meant it when I said I'm always busy.'

'Why, Amy? You and I hardly know each other. What have I done to offend you so much?' Meg whispered.

'If you want to know, you've made a fool of my brother. You foisted that child on him, and it isn't his!'

'I see,' Meg said softly. 'He told you, did he?'

'No, he didn't, more fool him. But why else would he wed you? And in the registry office! And don't try to make me think otherwise, 'cause he did say when the baby's due – in May – and that means you got pregnant in late August or early September. I've had three kids – I know how long it takes. And Kip was nowhere near you, then! So don't call again, eh?'

The door was slammed shut and Meg stood stupified, gazing at the peeling paint, and the brass knocker tarnished to green. Her heart thudded and she wanted to face her accuser, tell her that what she said was true, but for Kip's sake, did she have to say anything? But she walked away, feeling all at once sick – a different, despairing sickness. Then she heard the opening of a door, and turned. Amy stood outside, hand on hip.

'There's sumthin' I forgot!'

'Yes?' Meg walked towards her.

'There was a letter for you – registered – and addressed next door. Miss M. M. Blundell, no mistaking it. The postie asked me if I knew where next door had gone and I said I thought the woman who lived there had joined up. So when did you leave Tippet's Yard, then, to live in a bombed house? What have you been up to, giving a wrong address? Thievin', have you?'

'No. And I had my reasons, Amy, though you wouldn't believe me if I told you.'

'Dead right, I wouldn't! Just thought you should know, that's all.'

'And did you see who had sent it?' She would know, Meg thought; would have had a good look at the envelope.

'As a matter of fact, I did. Can't remember the address, but I can remember the name, all right. It was from M. E. Sumner. But it was weeks ago. Told the postie to send it back where it came from. Oh, if my brother could only know what he'd let himself for!'

The door was slammed again, almost in triumph, Meg thought, pushing her shaking hands into her pockets, clenching her fingers into fists.

M. E. Sumner. Mary Eleanor Kenworthy. Polly had written, weeks ago; had cared enough to try to find her.

All at once Meg was glad that her identity card and ration book had borne a false address. And Nanny Boag would not have told Polly otherwise, not said that a letter to Tippet's Yard would find her. Nanny Boag would have let them think the worst of the girl they had taken in and treated as one of their own. Nanny would have suggested they even count the knives and forks!

But Polly had written, Meg thought as she walked home. Polly had cared. Tears brimmed in her eyes and she brushed them impatiently away, sniffing loudly. She was done with tears! She was Kip's wife now, for all time, and never must she forget it, nor that the child she carried was his, too.

There was a letter waiting when she opened the door of number 1. Kip had written – probably posted it in the dockyard before he went on board. Dear, caring Kip whom she must try to love.

Dearest wife,

This will be the last letter for a couple of weeks at least. I will write every day and think of you all the time. This letter is by way of a promise. I will love you always, and the baby, too, and neither of you will want for a thing. And like I said, I will wait for your love until you are ready to give it. You are worth waiting for, Meg Lewis.

Take care of yourself and I will pray for you and think of you every night before I go to sleep.

Always. Your Kip.

'Oh, Kip,' she whispered. 'What's to become of us? How will I ever love you as you deserve to be loved?'

She folded the page and replaced it in the envelope. Her husband's first letter. Her husband's! She must say the word and think the word and look at the rings on her left hand so she never forgot she was Kip's now. Kip Lewis, who deserved better than secondhand!

She was glad that she had slipped a picture postcard of Liverpool waterfront inside the pocket of his donkey jacket, with the words,

> Next time you see the Liver Birds you'll be safe home and I will be waiting. Take care of yourself. Meg

He would find it, she thought, when he put on his working clothes and went on deck for his first watch and it would please him, even though she had not written that she loved him.

She bent to light the fire laid ready this morning. Now she could afford her weekly bag of coal, and paraffin for the stove she had put in her bedroom. Paraffin was not rationed, but hard to come by. Once she had her green ration book she could walk to the top of any queue she liked; it was unwritten law that green books had priority, and no one grumbled.

She filled the iron kettle ready to set on the hob when the fire got red, and when it did, she would make toast and use the last of her jam on it. And tomorrow she would have a cheap but filling meal at the British Restaurant. A shilling it would cost, but she could afford it now.

She sat in the fireside chair, watching the flames licking up, catching hold. Soon the room would be warm and she could take off her coat and scarf and listen to the news and maybe find some dance music on the Forces wavelength. She would be all right if she could accept that this was to be her life from now until the baby was born – filling the days as best she could, waiting for letters, writing letters, going to the shops, standing in food queues.

The dark of winter was on them now: short, cold days; long, blacked-out foggy nights. She closed her eyes and ached for Candlefold and the sun hot on the old stones and roses that climbed the walls and daylight until well past ten at night. And she ached for Polly and Mrs John and Gran. And for Mark.

She clucked, jumping impatiently to her feet, taking pen and ink bottle from the drawer. She must write to her husband as she had promised. At least he deserved a letter a day from her, even if she were hard put to it to find something to say that wasn't I love you and miss you and need you. She couldn't give of herself, but she would try to meet him halfway because sadly, that was all she could do. It was rotten of her and cheapened her in her own eyes, but Kip had known that, hadn't he; was willing to wait.

Dearest Kip,

Thank you for your letter, posted before you sailed, and thank you for all the kind things you said in it. I will try my best to make ours a good marriage because you above all deserve it. Things will work out for us. I know it.

She laid down the pen, closing her eyes, willing herself to accept that it would all come right; that she would come to love him. Love him differently that was, and in her own way, because there really were all kinds of loving. Kip would be her last love and if she tried hard enough, she might be able to accept the fire and passion of her first love and look at the child that had come of it without an ache in her heart.

I called in on Father O'Flaherty and gave him the cigarettes. He was glad to have them. I don't think he's had twenty all at once for ages. He told me, when I left, that he will pray for you and for me too. Like you said, he isn't a bad old stick. I arranged to start my instruction, though I told him I was a hard case. He just laughed.

Then I went to see Amy and gave her the money for the children. She said to thank you, but I didn't expect to be asked in because the baby was crying in the back room. I will call on her again.

And have the door slammed in my face again, like as not, she thought, reading back what she had written. Amy Rigby had no time for a Protty who foisted another man's child on her brother. Flamin' Norah. Three kids in four years! No wonder she was always snappy. And no help with them, either! A year older than himself, Kip had said, yet today, pale-faced and bitter, she could have passed for his mother.

> The weather is very cold here. Soon it will be time to do the blackout. Yet you are sailing towards the sun and blue skies. Will you catch a sunbeam for me and tuck it into a letter?
>
> You said that where you are going you can buy knitting wool without coupons. If you can will you get me some white wool. Tell them it is to knit into vests for a baby and they'll know what you want. Five ounces would make three little vests.

She would not ask him for anything for herself; not even a crunchy green apple.

> I have only been sick once today. I really do think I am getting better. Perhaps it is because I am not worried any more: perhaps because I have a husband to care for me. I am a lucky woman.
>
> I will go to the Food Office tomorrow and have my new name put on my ration books and identity card. Then I will call at the lady doctor's surgery and get a note from her for my green ration book. Like I promised, I will take care of myself and the baby too.

Dear, sweet heaven! What a letter! What a bloody awful letter for a bride to write to her man! Full of passion and longing and the need to be in his arms!

> I will write again tomorrow and let you know how I got on. And in the meantime, look after yourself, Kip. I care for you deeply and I will think about you all the time, and wish you well and a safe voyage home.

She signed it, *All my love, Meg*. It was the best she could do, but she resolved that tomorrow's letter would be more wifely, more loving.

Carefully she addressed the envelope, writing the figure 1 on the back, wondering how many she would have written before a hint between the lines told her he was on his way home, and to send no more.

She was glad, as she crossed the yard, returning from posting the letter that Nell opened her door to call, 'Got a pan of scouse nearly done. Can I finish it off on yours?'

'What's the matter, Nell, shilling run out?' Meg smiled, glad of company.

'Yes, an' me bleedin' coal, an' all. Got nuthin' to burn till the coalie comes tomorrow.'

'Then come to mine, Nell. You'll be welcome. Didn't fancy a night on my own.'

'God bless yer, girl. An' if you feel up to it, there's enough for two. Not much meat, mind, but there's plenty of taties and onions and carrots, and juice to mop up with yer bread. Sorry there isn't a trifle for afters!'

'I'd settle for an apple, Nell. I've got an urge to crunch on something. You couldn't oblige?'

'Apples? You've got to be jokin'. But if it you want sumthin' to crunch on, there's a carrot goin' begging in my pantry.'

She disappeared to return with a pan, a hot-water bottle and, in her pinafore pocket, a large carrot.

'Here we are then, girl! Pity to waste your fire. An' you'd better put a couple of plates to warm. If I can use a penn'orth of your gas, it'll be ready in twenty minutes. An' I've run out of tea, would you believe, and all because of bluddy Hitler! Never mind, eh? It'll get better. It'll have to, won't it, 'cause it can't get any worse!'

She shook with laughter and Meg found herself laughing with her and refusing to ask what about London, then, that was taking more than its fair share of bombing. And hoping Hitler's bombers would leave Liverpool alone.

'Mind if I have one?' Nell took a cigarette from her pocket. 'I'll blow the smoke up the chimney.'

'Nell – you've got no money for the gas, yet you spend it on ciggies! What's to do with you?'

'Ar, well, first things first. Ciggies are a necessity of life. They soothe your nerves and stop your stomach rumbling when your rations are gone.'

She drew on the cigarette deeply, inhaling the smoke then blowing it comically from the side of her mouth in the direction of the fireplace.

'Oh, Nell! What am I to do with you?' Meg laughed. 'And I think I'll scrape that carrot now.'

And Nell said that a good crunch was just what Meg was in need of, then laughed some more, because Nell Shaw would laugh if her roof fell in on top of her.

'Amy knows about the baby, Nell – that it isn't Kip's,' Meg said softly, not meeting the other woman's eyes.

'Well, more fool you! What made you tell her, then?'

'I didn't. She worked it out for herself, even though Kip said it was his. It'll be the talk of Liverpool before long.'

'Nah! She wouldn't bad-mouth her own brother. And it's her word against yours, innit?'

'I hope she doesn't tell Father O'Flaherty. I went to see him today, take him a packet of ciggies Kip left for him. He was ever so grateful. He looked at them all tender, like.'

'Ar. Suppose even priests are human, girl.'

'Maybe. Wouldn't know. What I do know is that life isn't half funny – funny-peculiar, I mean.'

'Oh, life isn't so bad.' Nell hitched her skirt above her knees, opening wide her legs to show suspendered stocking tops, as if she were trying to warm the whole of her body through her knicker gusset, Meg thought.

'So tell me, Nell, what's good about it?'

'We-e-ll, you'll be fillin' my hot-water bottle for me in exchange for a plate of scouse.' The lid of the pan lifted, lazily, letting out a savoury smell. 'And there's you, chomping on a carrot and me with my knees halfway up your fire back. Things are lookin' up in Tippet's Yard.'

'Suppose so.'

But that didn't, Meg brooded, explain away the unreal feeling that hung around her like a curtain; a curtain she longed to swish aside. She wondered if she should tell Nell about Polly's letter, then decided against it.

'Where's Tommy?' she asked, for want of something to say.

'Said he was savin' coal and electric, in the library. A real one for readin' the papers, that one. Then said he was going to the chippy for his supper. I suppose you couldn't,' she said, hitching her skirt even higher, 'lend us a silver shillin' till tomorrer?'

And Meg smiled, and said she could, and that since she hadn't been drinking it lately, she could spare a couple of spoonsful of tea. And thought that in some aspects at least, things were almost back to normal in Tippet's Yard.

Sunday morning. Meg lay, propped on pillows, sipping cocoa, thinking about her life – her unreal life – and how things were shaping.

She had seen the doctor, who confirmed her pregnancy and gave her two handwritten medical certificates. Meg had paid her seven shillings and gone to exchange one of the certificates for an expectant mother's green ration book, to be told by a helpful clerk that the vitamins and orange juice she could get from the antenatal clinic, and where also she could consult with the resident midwife regarding her pregnancy.

And did she know, the helpful clerk continued, that on sight of her green ration book, the Board of Trade would give her an allowance of coupons to provide necessities for the baby until it was born – whereon it would have clothing coupons in its own right? And did she know she was entitled to Board of Trade dockets which would enable her to buy a cot and bedding, though she should be advised to get the cot docket as soon as she could, since there was a long waiting list for such things.

It made a difference, Meg thought, having a wedding ring on your finger; gave you respectability. It was why, she supposed, Ma had spent money she couldn't afford on one.

So she had thanked the clerk and gone to the Board of Trade offices in the city centre, had filled in forms in triplicate, then been told she would hear from them when the necessary dockets had been sanctioned. Meantime, an allowance of clothing coupons for nappies and baby clothes would be in the post by the end of the week, they being a little behindhand with things because of the war, she would understand? And Meg had wondered at the unrealness of what she was doing, because she could not accept yet that she was Kip's wife, nor even, apart from the sickness, that she was having a child. Because though her breasts had become a little tender, nothing else about her had changed.

At eleven, she got dizzily out of bed, wincing at the coldness of the linoleum, feeling with her toe for her slippers. Then she had shrugged into her dressing gown, tied it tightly, and walked downstairs.

The yard was silent. Doubtless Nell and Tommy were in the best place for a December morning: in bed, blankets high. But she would light a fire, then wash and dress in front of it and, when it glowed red, would toast bread and spread it with butter. Butter, kept as her Sunday morning treat.

She allowed herself a small smile. Right on time, the minute she had the doctor's note in her hand, came the official buff-coloured envelope with On His Majesty's Service on the top, addressed to Miss M. M. Blundell, who was to report to Room 21, 2nd Floor, Royal Liver Buildings at 2.30 p.m. on Thursday, 4 December for a medical examination prior to entry into the Auxiliary Territorial Service. If, for any reason, the letter had gone on to advise, that particular date was not convenient, she should inform them as soon as possible, using the enclosed stamped addressed envelope for her reply.

She had replied promptly. There would be no career in the women's army for her; no marching and saluting nor learning to drive, nor turning corners hopefully to see Mark walking towards her. Goodbye, ATS. And anyway, joining up had been as unreal to her as her life had now become.

At noon she ate buttered toast, then wished she had a carrot to crunch. She had not yet been sick. It was an amazing feeling. Kip should be the first to know.

Sunday, 7 December '41

My dear Kip.

Today, so far, I have not been sick! I can't believe it! Maybe it really is going to stop.

I have now got my green ration book you'll be pleased to know, and am taking vitamins and orange juice and drinking extra milk. I had a talk with the lady at the clinic, who is going to keep an eye on me.

I have applied for a docket to get a cot. They take ages to come through: also prams. Waiting lists for both.

The weather is cold. Nell seems to be spending the day in bed – her coal ration has run out till tomorrow – so I think I'll get a tram to the Pierhead, watch the ships. Or maybe I'll go to Sefton Park – get some fresh air in my lungs.

I want to thank you, Kip, for all you have done for me. I still can't believe I am a married woman: I only know I am safe from snide looks and gossip, and more important, I need not worry about money. How grateful I am, you'll never know.

Once I get a letter from you I shall be able to work out where you are but it is so difficult to write a letter and not mention names or places or times.

Take good care of yourself. I look forward to hearing from you soon. I am beginning to feel well again, so you must not worry.

With sincerest love.

She read through the letter. She wished it could have been more passionate; that it was not so matter-of-fact and more yearny. But sincerest love sounded quite nice, she thought, and should please him. And he would be glad she was feeling better and that she had the green ration book and the pills.

There was a knocking on her door and Nell stood there, wearing coat and scarf and woolly knitted gloves, her cheeks pinched with cold.

'Ar, hey! I've had just about enough! That house is freezin'. I tell you, if I could get my hands on bluddy Hitler I'd tar and feather the little sod!'

'Come in, Nell. Get yourself warm, though you can borrow a couple of shovels off my pile if you want.'

'Nah. Only to be paid back. I'll be fine, tomorrer when the coalie's been. But I'm so cold my bones ache.'

'The kettle's on the hob. Make yourself a hot drink. I'm going to the post with one for Kip. Won't be a tick.'

And Nell smiled gratefully and told her she was a jewel and to wrap up warm 'cause the wind had changed and it was blowing up from the river and a river wind always brought rain.

'Damn. I'd thought of going to the Pierhead.'

'Well don't, girl, or you'll get blown inside out!'

'What say we ask Tommy in, eh?' Nell said later. 'I know he got sausages from the butcher yesterday. How about us pooling what we've got, and making a decent Sunday dinner? I've got potatoes and carrots and a bit of stewing beef.'

'And I've got a chop and a tin of peaches Kip brought home.'

'And if Tommy brings his sausages and you can spare an Oxo for a drop of gravy it'll be like old times again, the three of us having a meal together. And we can all sit round the same fire. You'll not mind the smell of cooking, Meg?'

And Meg said she rather thought she wouldn't, and when they'd eaten it they could all listen to the six o'clock news then maybe some nice music on the wireless.

But the news, when they switched on to listen to the bland tones of the announcer, was something none of them had bargained for.

> '. . . News is coming in of an attack on the American fleet at Pearl Harbour, in Hawaii, by Japanese aircraft. As yet, all that can be ascertained is that the attack took place at 7.55 a.m. local time.
>
> It is feared many ships were sunk and that a great many men have lost their lives. It is hoped the BBC will be able to supply further news on our nine o'clock bulletin.'

'The Japs!' Nell gasped. 'What'd they want to do a thing like that for?' Her face was white, her jaw sagged.

''Cause they're Nips, aren't they?' Tommy said mournfully. 'Funny little buggers and all of them wear glasses. Can't see a thing beyond the ends of their noses.'

'Do you think it's true?' Meg found her voice. 'I mean – they could have got it wrong.'

'Not the BBC. They alus get it right. Better than the newspapers at gettin' it right. Well – I'll be buggered! Sounds as if they'd done it sneaky.'

'They must've,' Tommy shook his head. 'They shouldn't have done a thing like that without declaring war first. My, but them Yanks are goin' to be hopping mad about it – if it's true, that is.'

They decided to wash the supper dishes, then go to the Tarleton to see if anyone else had heard it – and wondered how much of a difference it would make to our war, though Tommy said it was between America and Japan, and as far as he was concerned, our Government should mind its own business and let them get on with it. Enough on our plate already, hadn't we?

The landlord of the Tarleton public house was as mystified as anyone about the goings-on half a world away, but thought it shouldn't affect his beer allocation, so until it did, he would give an opinion when he'd heard what the man on the news had to say at nine.

Obligingly, he brought his portable wireless and set it on the bar counter, thus discouraging paying customers from leaving to listen to their own sets.

'Now, 'ave yer all got yer glasses full, 'cause I'm switchin' on now!' he said dramatically, glancing round the parlour with an air of authority.

First came the time signal from Greenwich, then the minute of silence that was always kept, Sunday nights, so people could think their own thoughts before the announcer began to speak.

> 'This is the BBC Home Service. Here is the nine o'clock news, and this is Stuart Hibberd reading it.
>
> Following an attack on the United States Fleet at Pearl Harbour, Japan has tonight declared war on Great Britain and the United States of America.'

In a disbelieving silence, they listened to an account of the loss of ships and men and that the American military in Hawaii had quickly recovered after so unprecedented an attack, and that Japanese warships had been engaged by British and American naval units in the Western Pacific.

'That's it! Don't want to hear no more!' The landlord switched off the set. 'If youse lot wants to know more, then you'll have to get a paper in the morning!'

And because everyone was so shocked and afraid, no one protested, but sat there, wondering how this country was going to fight another war when we'd hardly got the measure of the one we were in!

'Them Jairmains,' said Tommy, 'are goin' to be hand in glove with the Nips. They'll join forces and God knows what's going to happen then.'

'The whole world's at war,' Meg whispered. 'Everybody is fighting! And what have we done to the Japs to make them declare war on us?'

'People like them Japs don't need an excuse for nuthin'.' Nell took a swig at her beer, wishing it were gin. 'They're just the same as them Nazis. They do what they want, 'cause they've got bigger armies than we have, and more planes and ships.'

'Surely they haven't got more than America?' Meg was still shocked.

'Well, seems we're all in it together now. And it mightn't be a bad thing – America has come in, now.'

'Oh, sure, Tommy! But they'll be fightin' them Japs, not sending men here to help us with Hitler,' Nell snapped.

But Meg said nothing because the unreal feeling had all at once left her, and she was afraid. Japan was half a world away, but not from Australia and not from British bases at Hong Kong and Singapore. And our warships had already been in action against the Japanese navy in the West Pacific, hadn't the announcer said? True, the Pacific was a very big ocean, but it was towards it that Kip's ship was steaming, and Pacific waters, it would seem, were no longer safe for British merchantmen.

'I – I'm tired.' She got to her feet. 'Think I'll go home.'

'You all right, girl?'

'Yes, Tommy. Fine. Just want out of here – the – the cigarette smoke.' She said the first thing that came to mind.

'Well, don't go bumping into anything in the dark,' Nell warned. 'I'll just finish my drink and then I'll be leavin' an' all. Watch how you go, girl. I'll call in on you – see you're all right.'

Meg stood outside the Tarleton, breathing in the cold night air, blinking rapidly, standing the customary fifteen seconds to allow her eyes to adjust before moving away. It was very dark. There was neither moon nor stars, and nothing stirred. She stood still for a moment, making out the bulk of St Joseph's church to her right, standing even darker against the blackness, and all at once she wished she knew how to pray.

She turned into Lyra Street, wondering if she should call on Amy, who would have heard the news. Amy's husband was in Far Eastern waters. She would be worried.

But Meg walked on, knowing that even if she knocked, the door would not be opened to her or to anybody; knowing she dare not risk another snub nor face the scorn in her sister-in-law's eyes.

'Kip,' she whispered into the cold, uncaring night, 'take care of yourself? Now, more than ever, take care?'

Twenty-Four

Meg lay in bed, waiting for midnight and the sound of the ships in the Mersey, heralding another year. Always on the stroke of midnight, they let go with sirens and hooters, making such a din that, if the wind blew in from the river, she would hear it here, in Tippet's Yard.

Very soon would come a new year and promises of new beginnings, new hopes. She lay, wide awake, not wanting to be at the Tarleton with Nell and Tommy, needing to think back on the year that was fading – 1941. So much had happened. In February, Ma's death; her slipping away with never a goodbye. And opening the attaché case; finding the deeds to Tippet's Yard and her birth certificate and where she had been born. And tonight, because it was New Year's Eve, she would allow herself to think about an enchanted, sun-kissed summer.

She would not think of Mark, but of Nanny instead, and discovering who she really was and, unknowing or not, that she had bedded her own brother. Such terrible words to fling in her face. They had burned themselves into her mind so she would never be free of them. Then running away; back to Tippet's Yard where she belonged, finding she was pregnant. And marrying Kip, so the baby would be respectable.

Not a good year, if she forgot about Candlefold – which she should. A year to let pass into history because the war was still not going well for the Allies. Mind, America was in it now with us. After the shock of Pearl Harbour, young Americans had rushed, white with fury, to volunteer for the armed forces; show the Japs they had taken on a formidable nation, bent on revenge.

Not long after, news had been released by the Ministry of Information of the sinking of two of our warships in the South China Sea. There had been nearly a hundred Japanese aircraft in the attack; too near to Australia, Meg thought, and Kip's ship, because two guns would give little protection against torpedoes fired from the air.

She burrowed into the warmth of the bed, hugging her hot-water bottle to her, telling herself she was lucky compared to the people in Leningrad, who had no heating, and water frozen solid in taps and wells. And them mixing sawdust with flour to make into bread – if they could find heat enough to bake it.

At least, on Christmas Day, there had been warmth and food and laughter here in Tippet's Yard, with Tommy and Nell and herself combining their meat coupons to buy a small joint of lamb. The smell of the roasting meat had been heady and, best of all, had not made her want to be sick. Indeed, if she were looking for blessings to count, she was feeling well again.

Yet on that Christmas Day, when for a little while the war had seemed not so near, had come the news of the surrender of our garrison at Hong Kong. So terrible a loss which served to prove, if ever there had been doubt, that now the Japanese were bent on taking over the Far East, just as Hitler wanted to dominate Europe – yes, and Russia too. And he'd have been in Moscow now, Meg thought fearfully, had it not been for a winter his soldiers were not able to face. Tanks frozen solid; men unable to resist the vicious cold. It had given Stalingrad and Leningrad and Moscow the chance to see to their defences and hold out for just that bit longer.

So count your blessings, Meg Blundell, she thought fiercely. And it was Meg Lewis now, and she had heat and food enough, and money in the bank and a pay cheque from Kip's shipping line. Oh, she was lucky, all right.

Faintly, she heard the river noise and got out of bed, opening the window to hear that another year had begun; wishing Kip well, thinking as she hurried back to bed that soon he would dock in Sydney. Once, she had thought that reaching the Panama Canal ensured his safety. Now nowhere was safe. The whole world was at war and gone mad. She whispered, 'Happy New Year, Kip. Take care of yourself,' then closed her eyes and tried her hardest not to think about Candlefold – or that Polly had tried to find her.

On 2 January three letters from Kip arrived and Meg knew that about ten days ago, mail bound for home must have been put ashore at Panama. Which meant, she supposed, that now the *Bellis* would have the protection of the New Zealand Navy and ships of the Australian fleet. Those Japanese submarine commanders would not have it all their own way, because now the war had grown to threaten both those countries and more than ever their warships would be on the alert. In just a few more days Kip would sail beneath the harbour bridge at Sydney into sunshine and blue seas. It was summer now in Australia. Kip would send some of it home to her in a letter, she hoped, and perhaps bring food back with him, too.

But did it matter? Food or not, what mattered most was that Kip's ship made it safely back to the Western Approaches and the protection of our own navy and the patrols of planes that kept a watch for U-boats. Kip would be fine; Father O'Flaherty would be praying for him and she, his wife, would send warm, protective thoughts to wherever he was. This year had started well, with three letters full of love and concern for her wellbeing; 1942 would be a good year. She would try her hardest to make it so, if only for Kip's sake. Because Kip deserved it.

'You'll be about halfway now,' Nell said matter-if-factly. 'Been workin' it out. You'll be feeling the baby kicking before so very much longer. An' I must say, girl, you're looking a lot better, these days.'

'I feel it. No more being sick, fingers crossed. Once, I couldn't walk past the chippy – the smell of the frying, y'know – but last night I could have gone in there and bought a fish and penn'orth, I was so hungry. So shall we have fish and chips for supper tonight – you, me and Tommy? My treat, and with loads of salt and vinegar on them. Will you, Nell?'

''Course I will, and Tommy won't say no to a free supper either. Funny, innit, the Government not putting fish and chips on the ration? Every blooming thing else is.'

'Maybe it's a concession, sort of; making sure there is at least something for people to eat when their rations have run out. Rationing fish and chips would be like rationing beer – unthinkable. There'd be a riot, if they tried to.'

'You could be right, at that.' Her eyes ranged the mantelpiece. 'Is that a card from Kip?' Nell missed nothing.

'It is. I said that Kip was to catch some sunshine and put it in an envelope for me. He's written it on the back – *Here is the sunshine you wanted.*'

'Hm. And not passed by censor either. How did he manage that?'

'Suppose because he was careful to write nothing censorable on it, even though he must have posted it ashore and not on the ship, as he should. But there is nothing to associate the *Bellis* with Australia on it. Isn't it beautiful, Nell? A view of Palm Beach. Is the sea really that blue? You can't blame him for wanting to live there.'

'And will you go, if he decided to?'

'Won't have much option. A wife's place is beside her husband, don't they say, though I reckon I'll give it a try – forget –' She shrugged. 'Well, it would be a new start, wouldn't it?'

'So you could forget that place and those Kenworthys, you mean? But will you be able to, once the baby is born? It might father itself.'

'Kip will be its father. He wants it to have two parents on its birth certificate. Kip understands.'

'An' you fell on your feet, Meg Blundell, the day you wed him. And I mean Lewis, pardon me. Takes a bit of getting used to, dunnit?'

And Meg laughed, because laughter came a little more easily these days, though remembering came more easily still, especially in bed when she relaxed her mind as she always did before sleep came. That was when the memories flooded back, and if she felt brave, she lived them wholly, with scents and sounds and voices and lips meeting in lovers' kisses. And you couldn't, she always insisted guiltily, have so passionate a love then forget it, to order. It wasn't natural nor normal. Sometimes, she must allow herself the comfort of wishful thought. Just sometimes.

'So will I tell Tommy?' Nell's voice cut across her broodings.

'Sure. A fish supper at number 1 at six thirty. Evenin' dress to be worn,' Meg grinned.

'Hadn't you best leave it a bit later – you'll get yesterday's chips warmed up, if you're too early.'

So Meg said seven was fine. She would write to Kip, post it, then collect their unrationed supper.

'Be blowed to the war, Nell! Had you thought we'll be into February in a week, and soon it'll be light at five o'clock.'

Daylight at five. One of the certain signs that winter would soon be gone and the sun would return and light, warm nights. And then her baby would be born.

Dear husband, *Meg wrote*,

Tonight Tommy and Nell are coming for a fish supper. I really am getting better because not so long ago, just to think of fish and chips made me ill.

Nell was pleased to see the sunshine you sent as I asked you to. Your card is sitting on the mantelpiece beside Ma's clock.

I feel so well these days compared to the sick wife you left behind you. I am taking my vitamins and drinking my orange juice. The midwife at the clinic thinks I should go into the women's hospital to have the little one – it being my first – but that it is entirely up to me. What do you think?

Amy is well. I saw her two days ago, and the children. They are bonny kids: hard work, I shouldn't wonder, but she seems to take it all in her stride.

No need to say she had seen his sister outside the post office and that she had not spoken. Things like that could keep for when Kip was home. Letters to men fighting a war should be happy ones, full of hope, no matter what was going on at home.

I went into town yesterday and played the window-shopping game – to pretend I had a hundred pounds to spend on anything I liked and a hundred clothing coupons. Oh, you should see my fur coat and posh hat and high-heeled shoes (in my dreams)! It passes the time, though, till you are home.

She read through what she had written. If not a loving letter, then certainly a light-hearted one; one he would be pleased to read.

She wondered where he would be when he opened it. Perhaps it would be waiting at Panama on the return trip, for he should be leaving Australia soon, with a cargo of meat. Might already have sailed.

There is not a lot of news, especially news I can write that won't be cut out by the censor. But things are looking up here. I think that soon I shall feel the baby moving and then I will know I have eighteen more weeks to go.

Take good care of yourself, dear Kip. I look forward to seeing you, brown from the sun. This letter comes with all my love.

Yes, a much better letter. More cheerful. With the coming of summer, things would begin to seem better, even summer in bomb-dreary Liverpool and not in –

No! She must *not* think of the old house if she had a grain of sense in her head! Why was she always doing it? Why was Candlefold the yardstick by which she measured all other things? So when, she demanded fiercely of herself, was she going to start growing up and stop crying for the moon, like a sulky child; accept what was not in her power to change?

'Oh, Ma,' she sighed to the clock on the mantelpiece. 'Am I going to be like you? Will I remember Candlefold to my dying day?'

Almost seven o'clock. Meg had called on her way to the pillar box to tell Nell to let herself into number 1 and put plates to warm in the fire oven, and put the iron kettle on the fire hob, if she wouldn't mind.

Now Kip's letter was on its way and the smell of the chip shop hung on the air. She sniffed tentatively, and was relieved to find she felt nothing but hunger.

The day had been gloomy and darkness came early, tonight. No moon, nor stars, and the blackness complete. She turned sharp left then,

'Aaaagh!'

Hell! A lamppost! Walked right into it! Pain shot through her head, red flashes made her blink her eyes rapidly. She was going to fall over!

She took a step and the pavement tilted beneath her. Somewhere out of the darkness came the screeching of brakes. Swaying, she felt the heat, smelled the engine of the car that loomed in front of her. Then pain hit her all over. She called 'Mark!', then the dizziness went and the flashes, and she closed her eyes thankfully against the pain.

* * *

'It's all right, dear.' Gentle fingers touched her cheek. 'Don't worry. You had an accident. You're in hospital.'

Meg blinked open her eyes, then shut them quickly. White everywhere, and bright lights. She hurt all over from her head to her knees. And there were pains low in her back, sharp and vicious.

'Accident?' she whispered. 'Don't remember. Was I out cold?'

'Concussed, yes. Dreadful old blackout. Seems no bones are broken, but you're in pain. I'll give you something to help.'

'Thanks,' Meg whispered croakily. 'Could I have a drink of water?'

She sucked greedily at the cup held to her lips, then took a deep breath before she asked, 'How did I get here?'

'The soldier who was driving the truck brought you. He said you seemed to lurch in front of him. He couldn't see you till it was too late. So dangerous, people being expected to drive without lights. He didn't know the area and someone passing got in with him and directed him here. A young Military policeman – after a deserter, he said.'

'I remember. I walked into a lamppost – such a bang – went dizzy. Must have fallen in front of him. Not his fault.' Oh, but the pain was terrible. 'Can I have that tablet, please? I hurt something awful.'

'Yes, dear. I'll call Sister, tell her you've come to. Maybe she'll give you an injection that'll help you to sleep. Could I just have your name, first? You had no identification on you.'

Meg told her, then closed her eyes with the effort of spelling out Tippet's Yard.

'And your next of kin? Who shall we tell?'

'My husband's at sea. Mrs Shaw next door to me will come. Please – there's such a pain in my back . . .'

'Where in your back, dear?'

'Low down and underneath, sort of.'

'I'll get Sister to have another look at you, then give you something that will help.'

'Well now, Mrs Lewis. At least we know who you are. Nurse said you've got back pain.' Sister was small and plump and had a kind face. 'Shall we have a look?'

'I – I'm sorry, sister. The bed feels wet.'

Sister pulled down the bedclothes, then pulled them quickly back.

'Nurse change the draw-sheet, then put a pad under Mrs Lewis, please,' she said calmly. 'And tell me, might you be pregnant?'

'Yes. About four months.'

'Ah, we didn't take that into account when you came in.'

The soiled sheet was thrown on the floor. Meg raised herself on an elbow to see it was blood-stained, too. Her eyes, wide with fear, met those of the Sister.

'Now don't worry, Mrs Lewis. You're tender all over and your abdomen took the worst of the punishment. I'll have Nurse ring Maternity – ask for a midwife to come and have a look at you – just to be sure.'

'There was blood, Sister. I saw it!'

'You were in an accident – it could have come from anywhere.'

A pain harsh and sharp caused Meg to pull in her breath and she closed her eyes tightly until it was gone.

'Another pain?'

'Yes. But more underneath, sort of.'

'Nurse! Ring Maternity – stat!'

'What's happening?' The pain had gone and Meg lay back, eyes still closed.

'Nothing is happening. We'll see what the midwife says before we worry about anything. And if she says it's all right, I'll give you something to make you sleep. That suit you?'

Meg said it would. She wanted to sleep, wanted the pain in her head to go away and the grinding pain, too. If they put her to sleep she needn't worry, and when Nell came she would tell her it was all right. She felt sorry for the soldier. It hadn't been his fault.

'There now. Here's someone to have a look at you, Mrs Lewis.'

Curtains swished round the bed, enclosing them in a small private space. The Someone from Maternity smiled reassuringly, drew back the bedclothes, then felt Meg's abdomen with warm, gentle hands.

'I think we'll wait for the next pain,' she said matter-of-factly. And when it came, sharp and vicious she said,

'I think we'll have you transferred to Maternity ward, Mrs Lewis. We can keep a better eye on you, there.'

'Is it the baby? Did the accident harm it?'

'Now that I can't be sure about, but we'll soon know. And you're not to worry.'

Her eyes met those of Ward Sister and Meg knew, from the compassion she saw there, that all was not well. Tears filled her eyes and she brushed them impatiently away.

'I want Nell – Mrs Shaw,' she whispered.

And Ward Sister said they had already phoned the nearest police station who were sending someone to tell her. Mrs Shaw would come – tomorrow, if not tonight.

'Your friend will be here. Just lie still and try to be calm, my dear,' the midwife soothed. 'Soon have you in Maternity and we'll have you sorted out in no time.'

Meg, propped up on pillows, watched as Nell walked the length of the ward. She was wearing her best costume and the felt hat she wore at the wedding, Meg thought, pleased and relieved she had come.

'Just fifteen minutes, this morning,' Nurse said. 'You'll be able to stay longer tonight, when it's regular visiting hours. Seven till eight.'

'Well, what's to do with you, then. Gave us a right old scare. Tommy out lookin' for you and me waiting there in case you came back. Then the police coming, saying you were in hospital.' Nell sat down by the bed, handbag clasped firmly. 'Whatever happened, girl?'

'Walked into a lamppost. Such a wallop. I went dizzy – seems I fell on an army truck.'

'Well, you should be glad you fell on top of the bonnet, not under the wheels, or it could have been serious. And you've got a real old black eye! Nasty things, lampposts. Anything broken?'

'No, Nell. But I'm bruised all over, down below. And – and I lost the baby.'

'Yes. They said.' Nell gazed at her hands. 'Asked at the desk for you and they told me you were in Maternity ward. But when I got there they said you were back here. The Sister there told me you'd lost the baby in the night and she thought you'd be better away from a ward full of mothers and babies – might upset you, she said. Are you upset, Meg?'

'I don't know. The baby never seemed real to me. Not even when

I was being so sick. Perhaps if I'd felt it move or even if I'd started to show, it would have felt more like I was having a baby.'

'And how was it, then – painful, eh?'

'Yes. I think, when it was all over, I'd have wanted a baby at the end of it. Miscarriages are nearly as bad as births. I asked if they knew – well, what it would have been – but they said they didn't.'

'Ar. Kinder that way. Now you won't be able to grieve for the son you lost, or the little girl. You'll just have to think of it as a miss – that it was the way nature wanted it.'

'The way I wanted it, the night I went to that doctor. Am I being paid back?'

'No, Meg. You changed your mind, didn't you? Just bad luck. How long'll you be in here, then?'

'Five days, they said. It isn't bad, here. I don't have to think about anything. The lady in the next bed is very nice, though she sleeps a lot – snores.'

'An' what are you goin' to tell Kip? Will you write?'

'No, Nell. Not till he's home. It wasn't his child, but he'll be sad for all that. Best leave it.'

'Ar. Puts you in a funny position, dunnit? I mean – you needn't have got married the way things have turned out. Did you – er – you know . . . ?'

'Did we sleep together, share a bed? No, Nell. Kip was decent about it. Said he would wait.'

'So it wasn't a marriage?'

'Yes, it was. In good faith him and me got wed, Nell. That's the way it's going to stay – if Kip wants to, that is.'

'Yes. If . . .'

'I believe they call it an annulment – if it didn't take place,' Meg whispered, because the lady in the next bed was no longer asleep. 'And I don't want to talk about it, Nell. It's up to Kip and I don't think he'll want an excuse to get out of it.'

'Ar. He's proper gone on you. And you won't find better, Meg Blundell, not if you search for a month of Sundays. An' it looks as if my time's up. The nurse is coming.'

'So will you keep it to yourself, Nell – about the baby, I mean? Don't even tell Tommy, just yet. I don't want it to get around. Apart from you, Kip's got to be the first to be told. And will you take my clothes back with you – give them a brush?'

'Course I can, girl, an' I'll wash your underwear an' bring everythin' in for you, when you know when you're coming out.'

'Thanks. If you feel in the coat pocket there's a ten-shilling note. Took it for the chippy. You're to take your fares out of it when you come to visit, Nell, and get a fish supper for you and Tommy, eh? And sorry you went hungry last night.'

'Last night is over and done with. You've got to look forward now.' Nell bent to kiss her cheek. 'See you, then. And take care, eh?'

Meg watched Nell walk up the ward, lifted a hand to wave as she turned in the doorway. Then she closed her eyes because she didn't want to talk. Just think. Think about the way it was, now. Not a real marriage in the eyes of the law – Kip, if he wanted, could get out of it.

But Kip would not want to. He loved her; cared enough for her to take another man's child as his own, to marry her, give her respectability. Kip deserved to be considered above all else, so she must try hard to love him the way he wanted it to be, between them. Look forward, Nell said. And if Kip was still of a mind to go to Australia after the war, then she would go with him gladly; put half a world between her and what had gone before.

There would be no baby, now. Not Mark's baby. She would not have to look at it and be reminded, always, of the night it had been made nor the love and passion between them. It had been written in her Book of Life that she should miscarry Mark's child. Fate. She would accept it because that was the way life was. She laid gentle hands on her abdomen.

Goodbye, little thing. Best it should be like this. And goodbye, Mark. I loved you so, but I'm Kip's, now and though you did say you loved me in the end, it was already too late. Think of me sometimes; think gladly of the willow pool and Meg Merrilees. And forgive me for not saying goodbye?

Tears filled her eyes, and she began to cry. Reaching beneath her pillow for her handkerchief, she pressed it to her mouth to stifle the sobs that shook her.

'There now. There.' Sister at her bedside, holding her close. 'Let it out, then. Don't bottle it up.'

'I – I'm sorry, Sister. Shouldn't make a fuss . . .' she gulped.

'You're not making a fuss. Only natural you should weep for your baby. See – here's the tea trolley. A nice cup would help, wouldn't it? You had a sad time last night. You need sleep. Will I bring a tablet to help you? Rest is what you need, Mrs Lewis.'

'Thank you, Sister. I'd like that. I am tired . . .'

'Of course you are. But no more tears, just yet? Give yourself a chance.' Ward Sister offered tea, and a tablet. 'Now drink it down, then close your eyes.'

She pulled round the curtains. They shut out the long, narrow ward to make a small, snug place. There were green leaves on the curtains; green all over like the willow pool. Meg closed her eyes and she was standing beside the pump trough, where Ma's place was. And Polly had just walked beneath the far arch, a trug of vegetables in her hand. And the sun was warm, and high in the sky. Her eyes closed and she blinked them open, telling herself that she must never again think about Candlefold. Not ever. She was Meg Lewis, now.

Her eyes closed again, and sleepily she thought of an enchanted summer and, if she were lucky, she would dream about it; dream to her heart's content, and laugh and love and be in love. Just for one last time. And when she awoke, she would be Kip's wife for ever.

She felt a cool hand on her forehead and dimly, above her head, the soft voice of Ward Sister.

'That's right, Mrs Lewis. Have a good sleep. You'll feel the better for it. And you are a strong, healthy young woman. There'll be more children, never fear.'

Twenty-Five

It was past the postman's time. Usually, he called about eight.

'No more letters,' Meg whispered to the face in the overmantel mirror. 'He's on his way back.' Probably there would be no stop at Panama. Just straight through the canal without on-loading cargo, no chance to put letters ashore for the post.

She had been home for three days, weak, still, but glad to be back in familiar surroundings. Tomorrow would be the first Sunday in February and on the first Sunday in February, Ma always said, it should be light enough to have your tea in daylight. Provided you had Sunday tea at five, that was.

Ma seemed even closer to her, now. Not Ma from the pump trough, not the fair-haired, brightly smiling girl, but Ma who was sick, who coughed and coughed. Ma, who knew she had not long to live and refused the charity that might have given her a chance.

There was a knocking on the door; loud and insistent. Perhaps it was the postie with a parcel, maybe, from Kip. She ran to open it.

'Mrs Margaret Lewis?' A man and a woman stood there.

'Y-yes. Er – do you want to come in.'

'Think we better had. Neighbours, and all that . . .'

'Detective Sergeant Brown, CID.' Immediately the door closed behind them, each produced an identity card. 'And Detective Constable Ward. We'll be as brief as possible, Mrs Lewis.'

'If it's about the accident, then I'll be the first to admit it was my fault,' Meg hastened.

'Accident? No, this is about the matter of the house in Mafferty Road.'

'Sorry?'

'The struck-off doctor, Mrs Lewis. Your husband intimated you would both be willing to co-operate.'

'Oh. Yes.' Nervously she ran her tongue round her lips. 'We-e-ll, he's at sea, though I think he'll be home, soon. I – I – Do you want me to help you?'

'Tell me about the accident, will you?'

'I lost the baby,' she said simply.

'Ah! Because of your visit to the doctor, would you say?' All at once, he was alert.

'No. I fell, in the blackout, in front of a truck. That's why I lost it.'

'But did the doctor try? You see, the fact you were there –'

'What we want to establish,' said the woman constable, more gently, 'if whether or not he – well – laid hands on you – tried.'

'No. He didn't. I got there, paid the wife twenty-five pounds, then I changed my mind – thought better of it.'

'So what can you tell us? We've known about that man for a long time, but no one is willing to admit they actually had it done – an abortion.'

'An *illegal* abortion,' the sergeant said sternly.

'Then I'm sorry. I went upstairs, took off some of my clothes – I even got on the table and the wife tried to give me chloroform. But the doctor didn't touch me – only to get hold of me when I tried to get off the table. I'm sorry,' she said again.

'Dammit! Do you suppose, Constable, we could get him for trying to administer noxious substances with intent?'

'We might – but it's his word against hers – against Mrs Lewis's.'

'Then how about possession of a noxious substance? Anything will do, so long as we get the man for something!'

'It's illegal to have chloroform – well, if you're a struck-off doctor.'

'Maybe we could try. We'll see what the inspector has to say about it. And if we could cop him for something medical, then we could get him, an' all, for practising whilst struck off. Be worth a few years, that would!'

'Look – I know how badly you want to arrest the man,' Meg said, 'but I honestly couldn't identify him. His head was covered, an' his face, an' all. I could identify her, though.'

'I want them both,' the sergeant said snappily.

'I think our best bet is the woman in the pub – the procurer. If we leaned on her, Sarge, I'm sure she'd give us a name.'

'A name that would be willing to talk, you mean?'

'It's worth a try . . .'

'I suppose so. I'm determined to have him, Mrs Lewis. Would you be willing to give evidence that you were there, were given chloroform?'

'Yes. But I wouldn't really want to stand up in court.'

'That could be arranged. You could swear a statement on oath – an affidavit. It would keep you out of court. I'll keep in touch. Maybe,' he said to the constable, 'we could try the woman on the Dock Road again.'

'Put the pressure on . . . ?'

'I'll help all I can – but that man didn't actually touch me,' Meg whispered. 'And I'm ashamed I ever went there. But I will help you to stop him, if there's anything I can do.' There was Nell, of course. Nell had been in touch with the woman behind the bar, but no use bringing her into it, maybe landing her in trouble. 'Anything honest, that is.'

'Your husband will be home soon, Mrs Lewis? Tell him there'll be no charges regarding the broken window. Maybe you'd ask him to give me a call.' He offered a printed card. 'I'd do anything to put that man where he belongs. The wife and I were never able to have children, you see, and it don't seem right he should get away with what I know he's doing. Ah, well – bid you good day. And maybe we'll hear from your husband, eventually? Thank you for being so frank with us, ma'am.'

Meg watched them go, then stood there, waiting for Nell's door to open.

'Who was they, then? Looked like scuffers to me.'

'They were, Nell. After that doctor. The house is in Mafferty Road, it seems.'

'What did they want to know?' Nell sat down at the table, eyes anxious.

'If he actually tried – laid hands on me. But he didn't get the chance. I think they're going to have another go at the woman in the pub – a bit of pressure.'

'But it was me what told you about her!'

'Your name wasn't mentioned, Nell. Think I'd land you in it? Anyway, seems I can't help them, though they want Kip to get in touch when he docks. Don't worry,' she urged. 'I don't think anything is going to come of it.' Though for the sake of the dead baby on the pavement, Meg thought sadly, she wished the couple in prison where they deserved to be. 'Like I said, don't worry. And I need advice, Nell. Like how am I to get work?'

'Well, you won't be joining the ATS, will you? You're married and you don't have to join up.'

'No, but I have no children, so they'll expect me to find a job to replace someone who has.'

'Ar. There's jobs aplenty goin' now. Happen if we both go down to the Labour, they'll fix me up with something too.' Something that wasn't scrubbing floors, that was, or taking-in washing and ironing; some better way to eke out her ten-shillings-a-week widow's pension.

'Well, I'll *have* to work. You're all right yet, Nell.'

'Gawd, I should hope so! The war'll be in a sorry state when they start calling up women of my age. But what will you do, girl?'

'They'll tell me, at the Labour. As I'm married they can't make me leave home. There'll be work in Liverpool – what's left of it, that is. I want to keep myself on what I earn, and put Kip's monthly money in the bank. It'll be a tidy sum, if the war goes on as long as the last one did. What say we go down to Leece Street tomorrow; see what's going? They can't make me go on munitions, but the sooner I find a job, the better.'

'I suppose,' Nell said, 'that I can smoke again – you not bein' sick any more. How does it feel to be normal again?' She lit a cigarette.

'I'm not sure. I was sad about the baby, but glad I hadn't felt it inside me. I tell myself it wasn't quite a baby – hadn't moved, or anything. It helps. And it will be better for me and Kip, I suppose – no reminders.'

'You don't want to forget that Mark, do you girl?'

'No. But I'm going to try. I tell myself that miracles don't happen – not to people like me. And it would take a miracle if I could turn the clock back, and Nanny hadn't told me – or that what she told me wasn't true.'

'And had you never thought that it mightn't be – true, that is? She was a wicked old cow; you wasn't good enough for her Mark. She must have wet herself laughing when she found them deeds in your wardrobe. Is there any chance of a miracle?'

'No. It all added up. The one thing that still amazes me, though, is that Mrs John was so decent about it, and the only conclusion I can come to is that she never knew who had got Ma into trouble. Ma being given this house would add up, then.'

'So that's why you didn't challenge what that Nanny said? Because of Mrs John?'

'Yes. She was so lovely, Nell. A real lady. I wouldn't hurt her. She treated me like I was one of the family.'

'Which you was, truth known!'

'Yes, but Mrs John won't ever know it – not from me she won't. But do you expect me to forget Mark entirely? He was my first love, Nell. They say you never forget your first love.'

'Then you're goin' to have to try or there won't be a lot of hope for you and Kip. He'll know he's second best – it'll be up to you, Meg Lewis, to try your hardest to make a go of it.'

'And I will. I can't have Mark. I've accepted that. I'll go with Kip to Australia, make a new start. That far away, I won't be thinking that around the next corner I might bump into Mark. 'Cause that's what I want to happen, Nell. Just to see him once more – even if he doesn't see me. Crazy, aren't I?'

'By the heck, you can say that again, girl! You really got it bad over that feller, didn't you?' She closed her eyes and drew deeply on her cigarette. 'Is any man that marvellous, will you tell me?'

'Mark was. I suppose he always will be – secretly. But I'll be a good wife to Kip. You know I will.'

'Well, don't talk in your sleep when you're in bed with him, eh?'

And Nell laughed till her shoulders shook and Meg laughed with her, because laughter was better than crying for the moon. Come to think of it, she'd have a better chance, crying for the moon than for Mark.

'You say you are used to counter work, Mrs Lewis?' the lady at the labour exchange asked.

'Used to work in Edmund and Sons till it was gutted in the May blitz.'

'And would you be willing to work full time – nine till six? One afternoon a week off, and Sunday?'

'Fine – except, perhaps, when my husband is home.'

'Most employers make allowances for hubands in the armed forces, Mrs Lewis. I'm sure the Bon Marche will.'

'The Bon? Goodness! I always wanted to work there! And there's a job going?'

'Yes, now let me see . . .' She thrumbed through a card index. 'Hm. Canteen assistant – sales assistant – that's the one. Knitwear and blouses. Like to go for an interview?'

'Yes, please. And did you say canteen assistant?'

'I did. Do you know anyone? Labour really is getting hard to find, these days.'

'My friend, over there.' She nodded to where Nell sat, knees firmly together, handbag clutched. 'She wants work, too.'

'Then I'll just give you a card. Ask for the Personnel Department, Mrs Lewis, and if you aren't suited with the pay or hours, just call back and see me again. I'm sure there'll be something else.'

'I think,' Nell beamed, 'that tonight we'll go to the Tarleton for a bit of a celebration. Imagine, you an' me gettin' work at the *same place*! Mind, I'll be dish washing and the like, but who cares? Seems canteens get an allowance of food for the workers, so I'll be able to scrounge sumthin' to eat if I play my cards right. And a shillin' an hour. More'n two quid a week. Oh, my word!'

'The lady in Personnel seemed glad to have us. And to think I used to dream of working there and never thought I had a chance.'

'Well, you're like Doll. She learned to talk proper when she was with them Kenworthys and some of it seems to have rubbed off on you, girl. Quite refined you can speak, when the mood takes you.'

'I'll have to watch it, Nell. They say all the posh types go there – even ladies with titles.'

'Well, I'm happy enough washin' up and wiping down, so let's hope the landlord at the Tarleton has a nip of gin under the counter. Come on! Let's tell Tommy the good news – reckon we'll treat him to a pint, an' all!'

'Things are looking up in Tippet's Yard,' Meg smiled. 'Pity there wasn't a job for Tommy, too.'

'Nah. He's too little and too lame, God love him. And besides, who's goin' to look after Tippet's Yard when you an' me is out at work? Caretaker 'ere, he'll have to be!'

A good day, had been Meg's last conscious thought as her eyes closed that night. But life was like that, she supposed. Nothing lasts, hadn't Ma always said? Neither good times, nor bad.

Well, there were good times on the horizon. There'd been trouble enough, so now they were due for a spot of luck. Swings and roundabouts. Make the most of it, Meg, 'cause you never know the day . . .

'What's this, then?' Meg picked up the small card that lay on the doormat with a letter from Kip.

'Looks like one of them posh business cards. Who is he, then?' Nell frowned. 'Mr J. C. Rogers, Personnel Officer, Holdon Brothers Shippers, Royal Liver Buildings. Doesn't Kip sail for Holdons?'

'Yes. Maybe something to do with the money he allows me. It says I'm to phone him. Well, it'll be too late now. It's half-past six. He'll have shut up shop for the night.' Meg placed the card on the mantelpiece. 'Suppose I can use the staff phone at work – ring him tomorrow. And who's that at the door? Come in, Tommy!' she called.

But it wasn't Tommy Todd who stood on the doorstep but a tall, well-dressed man, who raised his hat and said, very gravely, 'Mrs Lewis? I'm from Holdon Brothers. I thought –'

'I could have rung you tomorrow,' Meg smiled. 'Nothing all that urgent, is it?'

'We-e-ll – I'm afraid it is. And if you wouldn't mind, madam,' he said to Nell, who tried to squeeze past, not wanting to listen in on private business, 'I'd be much obliged if you could stay? I think it would be better if I were to come in, Mrs Lewis. I took a chance – came back. It's better I tell you now.'

'Bad news?' Nell breathed. It had to be bad news. Always travelled fastest, bad news did. 'Kip?'

'Kipling Lewis? Yes. Please sit down, my dear,' he said gently to Meg, 'because you see, there is only one way to say this. I'm afraid your husband has met with an accident.'

'But why wasn't I told before this? How long has the *Bellis* been in?'

'We don't expect *Bellis* for two weeks yet. Your husband had an accident – a serious accident – in Sydney.'

'But – but there's a letter from him . . .'

'Yes, but letters take time to get here. *Bellis* was loading cargo. I don't know exactly what happened – the telegraph message from the Master didn't go into details – but your husband was on deck when a hawser snapped. A steel hawser. I'm afraid it was instantaneous.'

'*Instantaneous!* What was instantaneous?' Meg's voice was little more than a whisper because she knew, oh, she knew what he was going to say next and she didn't want to hear it.

'He didn't suffer, Mrs Lewis. He had a priest, at the end. And he was buried with full rites, as befitted his religious beliefs.'

'Buried!' Nell gasped. 'Young Kip's dead and buried! For God's sake, are you sure?'

'I'm afraid I am. And it distresses me to have to bring you this news. Believe me, Mrs Lewis, if there's anything – anything at all – I can do to help, you've only got to ask. I am so very sorry. And let me assure you that Holdon Brothers will be only too willing to help financially.'

'But Kip wasn't in any pension fund. Why are they doing that?'

'I'll tell you why they're doin' it, girl!' Nell hissed, all at once out of her shock. ''Cause it was their bleedin' fault, that's what! Go on! Admit it, mister! Them shipowners wouldn't be sendin' you now, offerin' the earth, if it hadn't been them to blame!'

'Madam, I'm sorry, but I can't speak precisely. I know so little about it, you see. Perhaps we'll know more in a day or two. It takes time, when there's a war on. I only know the barest details and I'm distressed to have to bring such news. Please bear with me, Mrs Lewis?'

'Oh God!' Meg folded her arms on the tabletop and laid her head on them. She wanted to shut the room out and the man who was telling her that Kip was dead. She didn't want to know. Not when her heart was thumping and there was such a giddiness in her head! Kip couldn't be dead! He was good and kind! Why should it have happened to him? 'Oh, Kip . . .'

She wanted to weep; wanted to pound the table with angry fists, to tell the man to get out of her house, but she could do nothing, because of the thumping and the dizziness. She wanted to scream at the top of her voice, but she couldn't do that either.

'Madam?' He looked imploringly at Nell.

'Shaw. Me name's Mrs Shaw!'

'Then perhaps you would be kind enough, Mrs Shaw, to make a cup of tea? And if you can spare sugar – for the shock? And I always carry something on occasions such as this – er – brandy. Perhaps a little might help Mrs Lewis?' He pulled out a hip flask and for a moment, Nell felt sorry for him. Poor sod. Havin' to do the dirty work for them shipowners. And Kip dead because of them!

'I'll put the kettle on,' she said sharply, 'but I don't know about the brandy. Don't think she's ever had brandy . . .'

She pulled out a chair beside Meg, cradling her in her arms, making hushing sounds.

'There now. Sssssh. Nell knows. Nell's been down the same road, girl. Let it all come out.'

But Meg was incapable of tears because it wasn't true, it really wasn't true that Kip was dead. Not Kip, who was going to Australia to live; him and her having children together and watching them grow strong in a sunny, more kindly country. Kip, who had wanted to be there, was a part of it now. He'd always be there, lying quiet and still.

She drew her hand through her hair, shaking it away from her face, getting to her feet, holding out her hand to the man who stood there, flask poised.

'I won't keep you, Mr Rogers. Perhaps, when there is more to tell, you'll be kind enough to let me know. I appreciate what you have done. It can't have been very nice for you.' She walked to the door, opening it, not caring that light streamed out into the night to pierce the blackout.

'Just a minute,' Nell hissed, holding out an egg cup. 'You can leave some of that brandy, if you don't mind. She's goin' to need it. Far too calm, she is. I'll see she gets it down her.'

Glad of something positive to do, the tall, grave man filled the eggcup, then, picking up his hat, he said, 'I'll be in touch, Mrs Lewis, when I have more positive news. Good night to you both.'

And he was gone, thankful to be away, feeling pity for the girl who had such dignity about her, even in death. He stuffed the flask in his overcoat pocket, wanting desperately to tilt it to his lips, thinking better of it. Oh, damn the war, and thank God he was too old to fight in it!

* * *

'I'll have to tell Kip's sister,' Meg said dully, stirring her tea. 'She was his next of kin till he married me. She should've been the first to know.'

'No, she shouldn't. You're his wife. I'll tell her,' Nell said shortly, knowing there was little love lost between the two women. 'I'll go an' see Amy Rigby in the morning.'

'No! Father O'Flaherty should know, too. I'll go and tell him, Nell – ask him to tell Amy. Would be better, coming from a priest. And I'll ask him to say a Mass for Kip – that's what they do, isn't it? Say Masses for souls?'

'I think so. But are you sure, girl? Have a little sip of this, eh, before you go. Give you a bit of courage, like.'

'I don't want courage, Nell. What I want is to stand in the street and yell and scream and shout my head off. Because it isn't fair. Kip never hurt a soul. There was goodness all through him. Why was it he had to be killed and why wasn't I there when – when –'

'To say a goodbye, when they laid him to rest, eh?'

'Yes! Why wasn't I?' Her voice was harsh with unshed tears and anger blazed through her like a white-hot pain. 'I'll go now, while I've still got a hold of myself, tell Father about it. Maybe when I've told him . . .'

She shrugged into her coat, hugging it around her, walking, head high, into the darkness.

'Gawd,' Nell whispered, 'but you're Dolly's girl all right. You did it just like poor Doll would have done – dignified, like. She'd have been proud of you, Meg Lewis.'

Then she slammed the door shut with all the pent-up anger that was inside her, and hissed, 'And as for bluddy Hitler, may he rot in hell for all the upset and misery he's caused. Damn him! May he never sleep easy again!'

Then she covered her face with her hands and sobbed as she had done the day a telegram had come in another war. Regretting. She didn't know how to pray for Catholics, so instead she whispered, 'God love you, Kip Lewis. Rest quiet, lad . . .'

Like the poem said, the sailor was home from the sea.

* * *

It was best, Nell said, that they go to work; nothing to be gained, sitting at home. And anyway, most war widows could not afford to mourn publicly; had children to feed and clothe, and must get on with life.

Nell and Tommy were kind; careful of what they said, not mentioning Kip's name if it seemed Meg wanted it that way, matching their mood to hers.

Meg was still bewildered and sad, but she had not yet wept for her husband. There was an ache where she supposed her heart to be, which would not give way to tears. Kip was away at sea, she told herself. Soon the *Bellis* would dock, and only when she was absolutely sure he wasn't coming back to her would she believe the nightmare, and weep.

Until then, she did as all bereaved women did: stuck her chin in the air and got on with life, because there was a war on and working helped. Most women who bought blouses from her, she realized, had a man at war. She knew it because they wore their men's badges proudly: the wings of the Royal Air Force, the Royal Navy crown or the regimental badges of soldiers. She wasn't, Meg knew, alone in her grief and she was luckier than some, who had children to rear alone, and could not afford the luxury of self-pity.

And Nell, never far away, washed dishes in the staff canteen and wiped table tops and swept and mopped the floor. She felt guilty because she had money in her pocket – enough money. She had always said she would consider herself rich beyond believing if she could keep a roof over her head, a fire in her grate and food inside her, and still have five shillings left at the end of every week. And now she had, and those five shillings she put into sixpenny saving stamps. And when she had filled a card with them, they could be exchanged for savings certificates to be cashed when the war was over and which, meantime, earned sixpence in the pound interest every year.

Nell Shaw with savings! Who would have thought it! Another week and she would have three certificates. Life would have been good but for Meg, who had turned into another Dolly Blundell: said little and seemed to drift without interest through each day. It worried Nell. The girl should have had a good weep; would have been more natural and normal, if she had.

Oh, she'd seen Father O'Flaherty, had gone into church, even, and prayed for Kip's soul and left money for a Mass to be said. But she had not understood the prayers, nor the lighting of the candle, and had closed her ears and eyes to them, it would seem, and thought of Kip instead. Funny, Nell mused, that Doll had never told her daughter about God, because God was a good person to pray to when you were at the end of your tether and Nell Shaw had had good cause, over the years, to unburden to Higher Authority.

But Doll had been a quiet one; telling nothing, keeping herself to herself and now it seemed her daughter was getting more and more like her. Pity, because she was a lovely girl to look at – would turn any man's head. Could have gone to a dance, Nell thought, and taken her pick of partners and young men willing to walk her home.

But Meg had lost a husband she respected, a lover, and the child of that unwise love that had not lived to be born. Meg was not yet of age, but she had lived out more heartache than some women twice as old. The young ones were taking the brunt of yet another war and it was all down to bluddy Hitler, rot his evil heart! Oh, but they'd give him a fine hanging when this was over and done with!

Two weeks after Mr Roger's visit, Tommy was waiting at his door when Nell and Meg got home from work.

'Been a man lookin' for you, Meg. Said he was off the *Bellis*. I told him you was at work but you had a half-day, tomorrow. He said he'd call at two. That all right, girl?'

'Yes,' Meg nodded. 'It's a fortnight since – since I got to know. I've been expecting someone from the shipping line. Did he say who he was, Tommy? A mate of Kip's, perhaps?'

'Said he was from the Seamen's Union; wanted to be sure you were all right. Said he had Kip's things to give you. He had a couple of cases with him.'

So at two o'clock tomorrow, Meg thought dully, she would have to come to terms with Kip's death; would have to accept, when she saw his things, that he really wasn't coming back.

She felt sick just to think about it. When the man came, it would all be so final; no more hope. Kip would be just another merchant seaman to die in this war as they were dying in their thousands in Atlantic convoys and on the terrible Murmansk run, with arms for the Soviets. Half of every Russian convoy never made port again. She was not alone. There were many widows like her in Liverpool; women who had loved their husbands.

Yet she, Meg reasoned, had loved Kip and admired him too. Given time they would have had a marriage together, one of respect, on her part, and caring. She could never have loved him with the passion Mark had roused in her, but she would have tried. She truly would. And she would have been grateful to him for the rest of her life for his goodness in wanting to father Mark's child. Kip would never know now that the reason for their marriage had slipped away from her in pain and anguish

'So why don't you two come in?' Nell and Tommy were still standing there, anxious-faced. 'Reckon I can spare a spoonful of tea.'

Slab-faced to the end, Nell thought, gratefully accepting the invitation. Proud as Doll had been. That Candlefold place had rubbed off on Meg, an' all. Pity she'd ever gone there. But you couldn't turn back the clock, she sighed, closing the door behind her, pulling out a chair, sitting at Meg's table as she had done so often when Doll, God rest her, had been alive.

'Any news then, Tommy?' she said, if only to break the silence. 'Nuthin' happened while we've been at work?'

'Nah. Went for a bit of a walk, then read the papers in the library. An' there's a notice in the Tarleton window. Ciggies tonight for regulars only.'

'Ar,' Nell nodded. 'So I'll just have me cuppa, then I'll get there straight away. Don't want to miss them. That OK with you, girl? You'll be all right?'

'Fine, Nell. I'll light the fire, then do a bit of housework. Get yourself off for your ciggies.'

And she was all right, she told herself stubbornly. This far, she had managed just fine, though tomorrow at two, she dismissed from her mind. Because tomorrow, at two, Kip would be dead.

At exactly two o'clock Meg opened the door to a tall, thickset man with two cases at his side: Kip's case and the small one he called his ditty box.

'Mrs Lewis?' He took off his cap, offering his hand. 'I'm Malcolm McTay. I'll no' say it's good to meet ye, for this is a sad occasion.'

He spoke with a soft, Scottish accent – an islander perhaps, Meg thought, gravely inclining her head, asking him to come in.

'You are very kind, Mr McTay. I'm grateful to you. Please sit down? The kettle's on the boil, if you would like a drink.'

'Thank you, no ma'am. It's my rule never to take a civilian's rations. And if I may, I'll come straight to the point. I have spoken with the shipowners' representative. They admit responsibility for your husband's death and will be offering you compensation, though I was not told how much. But whatever it is, ask for double. In your condition you have the child to think about.'

'There is no child – not any longer. I was in an accident with an army truck. I miscarried the baby . . .'

'Then I'll not only offer you my condolences on Kip's death, but on losing the child, too. It would have been a consolation . . .'

'How was it, Mr McTay? A steel hawser, I believe, though I don't understand how.'

'Then best I shouldn't explain, ma'am. A steel hawser that snaps has a whiplash to it that would – well, it's no' a nice thing. Best you should know that like as not he knew nothing about it. Sudden, y'see. The priest came – gave him absolution. And your man had a proud funeral ashore.'

'Strange, isn't it, that we had plans to settle there, when the war was over?'

The man dug a hand into his pocket – strong, seaman's hands, Meg thought – and brought out an envelope. He did not look at her when he said, 'I've brought a photo of the grave. I'll leave it on the table when I go. You'll look at it when you're able. With it is the address of a Sydney lady. Her son came to England, she told me – wanted to fly bombers. And his bomber crashed, taking off. They buried him in England which is a long way away. She hopes, one day, to see his grave, but meantime there is a lady, she said, who tends his grave for her. He's buried not far from Cambridge, I was given to understand. And she would like to look after young Kip's grave, she said, as a return kindness. Her son and your man were of an age. Too young to die in anybody's war. Right and fitting there should be someone to care for them.' He slid a scrap of notepaper across the table. 'And this, Mrs Lewis, is the address of our union representative ashore. You're to feel free to consult with him at any time – especially when the shipping line offers you compensation. You'll bear what I've said in mind, ma'am?'

'I will. And you're very kind.'

'No! I'm not. I'm no' used to occasions like this. Oh, I'm a terror when it comes to my men, and their rights. I'm a good shop steward. But things like this – they make me gie sad, for I'm not good at words.'

'Perhaps not, but the words you did say were kind, and a comfort to me. You've brought Kip's kit?'

'Aye. I went through his locker, packed it all up. You'll find an envelope in the little case. The crew had a collection, instead of flowers. A mark of respect, you'll understand. And I'll be away. We're turning *Bellis* round as fast as we can. Urgent cargo – and no' for Sydney, this time.'

'The Atlantic?'

'Not the Atlantic, Mrs Lewis.' He shook his head mournfully.

She didn't say it; sailors didn't say it either, if they could help it. And not one of them wanted to sail in convoy to it. Murmansk, were they making for? To icy seas that never offered survival, and U-boats that hunted in packs and wiped out one merchant ship in two. The Q convoys. The Murmansk run.

'Then I wish you a good journey and a safe landfall, Mr McTay. And bless you for your kindness.'

His embarrassed concern made her want to weep, but tears were not possible. She had not wept for Kip, nor her child. The pain was still there like a cold heavy stone inside her. Was that pain part of her penance; the price she had to pay for not loving Kip as he loved her?

She opened the door, smiling gently. 'Take care,' she said softly, then watched him go, his boots clattering on the cobbles, echoing more loudly as he walked beneath the entry. And Kip went with him; back to a quick turnround, then to join up with a convoy bound for Murmansk or Archangel. Urgent cargo for Russia.

She closed the door and, without so much as a thought, lifted the case to the table, taking out his clothes, laying them carefully over the backs of chairs in a businesslike way. It must be done. No use putting it off. Shoes and seaboots she placed beside the fireplace. They looked right, there. All else she placed in piles, trying to pretend that Kip had not worn them nor touched them; that Kip was in Sydney where he'd wanted to be, and material things did not matter.

And then she came to a carrier bag. Inside it was something soft. Opening it, she found a fluffy little bear – a Koala bear. Lots of them in Australia, Kip had told her. Funny little things. He'd bought a toy one for the baby.

She drew in her breath. Her heart began to thud. And just to make the feeling of desolation worse, with the toy was a packet of wool. Fine, soft wool. Five hanks for little vests. He had remembered; had really cared about the baby!

She held the soft whiteness to her cheek as if it linked her to Kip and gave way to tears; blessed tears she had so long held back. Now, his one last act of goodness, of tenderness, had released them.

'Oh, Kip. I'm so sorry. I would have tried. I would have . . .'

'Well now, what's to do with you, girl?'

Nell Shaw, standing hands on hips in Meg's kitchen; Meg, her face buried in the soft white wool, sobbing as if her heart would never be whole again; tears of contrition and relief.

'I – I asked him, Nell. Five ounces of white wool, I said – for vests for the baby. He remembered . . .'

'Well, of course he'd remember. He wanted that babbie. He'd have been a good father to it. It would never have wanted for a thing. But Kip has gone, and the baby, too.' She reached down to take the wool. 'And would you mind? That stuff costs coupons in England. Kip didn't send it for you to cry all over. Here – blow yer nose and shurrup weepin'.' She thrust a handkerchief into Meg's hand.

'Sorry. I thought I could do it without making a fuss – unpack his things, an' all that – but it was seeing that wool. That's when I broke down.'

'Yes. And a good job you did. Unnatural, you were acting. Not right you shouldn't grieve for him. Oh, I know all about it!' She held up a hand as Meg tried to speak. 'He wasn't first choice, but he'd have made you happy, girl. And I hope you let it go for that baby, an' all. You didn't shed a tear for the poor little thing either!'

'I couldn't, Nell. Not crying was a part of my punishment.'

'Punishment? It wasn't your fault you lost the baby! You didn't get rid of it, did you? What are you talking about?'

'It's a sin to bed your own brother. Nanny Boag said –'

'Nanny Boag! Damn and blast Nanny Boag!' Nell flung. 'I tell you, girl, if I could, I'd shake the living daylights out of that old biddy, so help me! Shake her till her false teeth flew out and bit her! And where's that eggcup of brandy the man left? Didn't throw it out, did you?'

'No. Still on the larder shelf, gathering dust.'

'Then you're to drink it – now.'

'No, Nell. Don't think I'd like the taste of it.'

'Who says you've got to like it? If it's good for you, it won't taste nice, will it? Now you'll drink it, lady. You'll get it down you if I have to hold your nose and make you! And then you'll wash your face and powder your nose and act so's your ma would be proud of you – all right?'

'All right.' Meg forced a small smile. 'But do I have to drink that brandy? I really don't think I'd like it. You have it, eh?'

'We-e-ll, if you're sure?' Nell opened the larder door. 'Pity to let good stuff like that go to waste, 'cause there'll be no more brandy till the French have kicked bluddy Hitler out! Well, cheers, girl. And to you, Kip lad, wherever you are – God bless, eh?'

'Yes,' Meg whispered. 'God bless you, Kip Lewis. And so long . . .'

Twenty-Six

May 1944. Two years since Kip died; three years since the enchanted summer when Mrs Potter had asked, 'Going after the job?'

Month after month had slipped by without protest. Meg still mourned Kip's death, still longed to see Mark – from a distance. It was all she asked. Just once. A glimpse of the tallness of him and the chiselled face, the thick, fair hair. She would be content, then.

There had not been a return of blitzkreig to Liverpool. Its scars were healing. Buildings still stood gaunt, roofless and empty of windows, yet the seasons seemed to have softened their stark outlines and grass had grown on piles of rubble thrown on bomb sites. With summer, poppies and corn daisies and rosebay willowherb would flower there. She knew all the flowers; had learned their names and seasons from Polly and Mr Potter.

Everywhere were couples: soldiers, sailors and airmen with girls on their arms. She envied them, needed to be close to someone special and not a war widow. But Kip was gone and the man she had wanted she could never have, so why cry over what could not be? She had her home, a job amongst nice people. She had money in the bank, deposited by Kip's shipping line. Once, before the war, it would have bought a small house in a decent neighbourhood, yet when the fighting was over, you wouldn't be able to buy a newly built little sunshine-semi with bathroom for under four figures, some said gloomily.

Nell said stuff and nonsense to that. A thousand pounds for an 'ouse! When the war was over it would be the same as last time: unwanted heroes thrown on the streets to beg because there were no jobs for them. Just see if she wasn't right. But this time around she would have her savings certificates to fall back on and maybe, when it was all over and done with, they would let her keep her job as canteen lady. She hoped so, but it was no use bothering, till peace came. And it wasn't coming yet – well, that was Nell's opinion, Meg shrugged.

But we were winning. The Russians had freed Leningrad and Stalingrad from seige. No more eating dogs and cats and sawdust bread. And there had been El Alamein! Oh, that was something! A special broadcast at midnight, and the entire country waiting up to hear that Rommel's armies had been thrashed in North Africa; thousands of prisoners taken and hundreds of tanks and transports and planes captured. It had not, Mr Churchill said on the wireless, been the beginning of the end, but El Alamein *was* the end of the beginning.

Of course, Stalin had agitated then for a second front in Europe to relieve the pressure on Russian troops. He would have to stop his demanding, muttered the man in the street, yet everyone knew there would have to be one. Somewhere. Sometime.

Then the Italian people had kicked out Mussolini. Big, puffed-up Benito! The King of Italy had returned, then, but Hitler refused to leave. So the Allies had landed on the tip of Italy; the second front, maybe?

'No,' Tommy had said. 'When – *if* – it comes, it'll be in France. Stands to reason, dunnit?'

Now Britain waited for that landing, because all at once it was real. The RAF was softening up the entire coastline of France, with Hitler screaming defiance, threatening his secret weapon. And it was accepted that the second front was not if, but when and where.

Meg pushed the war out of her mind. It looked, she thought, like being a fine warm Sunday and where better to spend it than in Sefton Park? Cherry trees would be blossoming there now, and perhaps bluebells and late narcissi. And ducks would be nesting beside the lake and maybe, if she were lucky, she would hear a cuckoo. Cuckoos came in April, she knew, but not to Tippet's Yard. Polly once said there was a wish on your first cuckoo call; would she hear one, in the park; wish for the second front to be over quickly and not, as Gallipoli had been in the last war, another act of folly and wanton killing?

Perhaps, she thought as she cut bread for sandwiches, if all went well the war in Europe could be over by Christmas. Yet there would still be the Japs to beat. We would have to take Hong Kong back, and Singapore, and help the Americans shift them out of the rest of the Far

East. America was helping us in Europe; it was only common decency to help them against the Japanese.

So how long would the war last? Not five years. It couldn't be over by September. But perhaps by next year, Europe would have peace and after that – who knew?

On a whim, she decided against Sefton Park. Too like the country with grass and trees and sky space. Too easy to remember, there. Instead, she would take the tram to the Pierhead and look at the river and out to sea; watch the ferries and, in the distance, convoys of ships waiting to sail on the tide – or to dock.

Since war came, Liverpool was bustling. Docks full of shipping, dockers with all the work they could want. And the city full of uniforms – mostly sailors and Wrens. Liverpool was important to the war effort. Some said there was even a secret headquarters underground from which the war at sea was run.

Meg sliced her sandwiches into quarters, wrapped them in twice-used greaseproof paper, then put them in a crumpled brown paper bag that had seen better days. No use telling Nell she was going out. Nell spent Sunday mornings in bed, recovering from a week of toil, she said.

'I'll go on my own,' she said to the face in the mirror, 'and have a look at the river.' And she would wish those who sailed out to war a safe landfall.

Mind, things were better now in the Atlantic. Mr Churchill had said so. U-boats no longer hunted in packs because our navy had got the better of them; could find them more easily and sink them. No one knew how; no one cared. Sufficient to say that on all fronts, Hitler was taking a battering. And serve him right! It was he who started it!

Thoughts straight in her mind, she locked the door behind her. She was off out for the afternoon and would not think that her baby – hers and Mark's – would have been a year old now. Nor would she think of Kip, in Australia, nor Polly who had cared enough to try to find her.

And she would absolutely not think about Hitler's secret weapon – bombs filled with poison gas, was he threatening? – nor of the second front and when it would be and how many men would die. This afternoon, she would lift her face to the May sunshine and be glad she was alive; would live each day as it came and let tomorrow take care of itself.

It was all she could do, really.

The second front came four weeks later. Because the tides were right, the invasion of Europe began, even though the weather was bad. Rough seas pounded invasion barges; paratroopers landing in occupied France were battered by gales.

'Surely not in weather like this?' said the man in the street, but we were ashore, and holding our own. A foothold, the Ministry of Information announced warily, because the Germans had been caught napping; been fooled into thinking we were landing somewhere else.

So people went to church to say their own private prayers and commend those they loved to the Lord's keeping. Meg did not join them. She didn't know how to pray. Yet she thought about our soldiers all the time at work, and was glad it was her half-day off, because she would switch on the wireless so as not to miss anything important the government might choose to tell them. And if all went well, the war in Europe might be over by Christmas, she thought. Our armies in Italy had captured Rome, the Russians were pushing back the Nazi armies, and now we were in France again.

No longer the second front; now, it was called D-Day. And today was D-Day plus one and we were establishing a bridgehead in Normandy.

Then she closed her eyes and stood stock still because all at once she thought of Mark; not yearningly, but urgently and sharply. He had come into her mind out of nowhere and without her calling him.

Was he then on the beaches of Normandy?

Tomorrow, Meg thought, would be her birthday. On 29 August she would be twenty-four. Married and widowed. All her life in front of her. Yet still the feeling of hopeless acceptance would not leave her, and she wondered what she would do with the rest of her life.

Nell, she frowned, had learned to live a life alone, and she not half as comfortably off. Why, then, should Meg Lewis expect to be different? The country would have many widows before this war was over, she shrugged, and she was but one of them.

Before it was over. Not by Christmas, certainly, but perhaps a year on, Europe would know peace and Hitler, whose threat of a secret weapon had been no idle one, would be hanged as he deserved.

Flying bombs, that weapon had been, launched in fury at London. Small, pilotless planes, dropping with deadly accuracy on a city that had hoped for no more raids, an end to terror from the skies.

The launching sites would be overrun, promised the Government. Already Bomber Command was hunting them out, bombing them, but still Hitler's victory weapons came without warning. Would they, people feared, soon be directed against Birmingham and Coventry and Clydeside – and Liverpool?

Of course they wouldn't! Our armies in France were doing well. Only yesterday Paris had been liberated with American troops marching down the Champs-Elysées to a rapturous welcome – after General de Gaulle, that was, and soldiers of the Free French Army. Soon, the secret launch sites would be found and destroyed. Soon, the entire country would be free from attack from the sky. It would be all right. That the Allies were going to win was no longer in doubt; all to wonder now was *when*?

So count your blessings, girl, she commanded fiercely, silently. Tomorrow was her birthday. She was one of the lucky ones who had lived out a war; was a survivor and she would go on surviving as Ma had done, with her head held high.

And what of today – Polly's birthday? Once, they had shared celebrations, and it had been oh, so lovely. And a week later had been Polly's embarkation-leave wedding, with all Nether Barton there, and the war a hundred years away. That night, Mark came to her room and they had made a child.

Meg closed her eyes. Candlefold was heaven on earth; always would be. Ma had not forgotten it and nor could her daughter. Those four months were there for the remembering when times were bad or lonely or hard. So yes, she would think about Candlefold today and tomorrow and all week, dammit, right up until Polly's wedding. She would wallow in it, live every laugh, every word, every wonderful minute of that week. Why shouldn't she? Four months out of a whole lonely lifetime was all she would ever have to sustain her! Little enough to ask that sometimes she should be allowed to recall them gladly.

'Happy birthday, Polly,' she whispered. 'Take care, eh?'

And remember me tomorrow; just a thought in passing will do, she yearned, *because I miss you all so much that sometimes it's like a toothache inside me.*

It didn't do, she was to think later, to call back the past so fervently; was not right to want it so much that it was there to hit her straight between the eyes. Came back, that was, in the shape of a pencilled note, painstakingly written.

'See here, Meg girl – isn't it that place you worked at? Kenworthy, wasn't it?' Tommy offered the piece of paper. 'Was in the library, lookin' through the deaths in the Daily Post. It seemed to jump out, sort of. The lady behind the desk gave me some paper and I wrote it down for you . . .'

It took several seconds before the writing made sense to her, and then she read the words again, slowly, so there could be no mistake.

> Kenworthy, Peacefully, on 26 August in her 77th year, Eleanor, widow of James, mother of the late John.
>
> Funeral at All Saints, Nether Barton. Wed. 30 August at 2.30 p.m. No flowers, no mourning, please. Enquiries to Candlefold.

'What is it, girl?' Nell frowned. 'You look as if you've seen a ghost.'

'It's Gran – old Mrs Kenworthy. Dead.' Tears filled her eyes. 'I loved her so much, y'know. Call me Gran, she said to me. It was like I belonged to her. At least it was peaceful – in her sleep, I hope.'

'The invalid, wasn't she?'

'Yes. In pain all the time, but she never complained. She liked me to do things for her. Said I had gentle hands.'

'Wonder why they should put it in a Liverpool paper,' Tommy frowned.

'I think because the family had connections here. This house belonged to them, remember. Someone said the family had property left to them by a Liverpool cousin. Anyway, lots of Lancashire people put things in the *Liverpool Post.*' She sat down heavily at the table, fighting tears. 'She gave me a pearl brooch for my birthday, Nell. I left it there, as if it didn't matter – and it did.'

'So don't take on, girl. The poor soul is out of her pain now.

Wipe your eyes.' She glared at Tommy. 'Pity you saw it. You've upset her!'

'No, Tommy. I'm glad you did. I'd have wanted to know – had a right to. She looked on me as a granddaughter. Might as well have two as one, she said.'

'But you're not thinkin' of going on Wednesday? Oh, you wouldn't! It would all come out, then! And maybe you wouldn't be welcome – not after what you did.'

'What was it you did?' Tommy asked softly.

'Oh, left without giving notice. Crept away without saying goodbye.'

'Ar, Meg. Your – er – trouble.'

'That's right, Tommy. But it doesn't stop me wanting to say goodbye to her – in my own way, I mean. I wouldn't go to the service – wouldn't presume. But I shall go on Wednesday – go to the grave when there's no one there. She was my gran, see?'

'Yes. She was, when push comes to shove, though she didn't know it!' Nell's mouth made a round of disapproval. 'And before you say anythin', Tommy Todd, I was only speaking – well, it was hot air, sort of. Forget it – all right?'

And Tommy, who always knew what was best for him, said he would and no more was said about Eleanor Kenworthy until later that night, when Nell called to exchange two sixpences for a shilling for the gas meter.

'I didn't mean what I said – about the old woman bein' your gran. Not nastily, I didn't mean it. I know she was good to you, girl, but if you'll take my advice, you'll keep away from there. It's all water under the bridge, now. Leave it, eh?'

But she knew that Wednesday was Meg's half-day off work and there was nothing to prevent her going back to that place. And likely as not she would.

'Sorry, Nell, but I'm going. They won't see me, I'll make sure of that. I'll keep out of the way until no one's there. What do you take me for – stupid?'

'No. You're anything but that. But you're gettin' over it now. Don't do anything that's going to open up old wounds? What if you see *him* there? Isn't going to do you a lot of good, now is it?'

Him? She hadn't once thought that Mark might be there! Mark was . . . Where was he? In France? In Italy, or could he still be in England?

'I hadn't thought, Nell. Honest to God, I hadn't.'

'Then think – and stay away. If you know what's good for you, that is.'

'Maybe you're right.' Nell was always right, drat her.

But to get off the bus, see the village again; to turn left at the post office and down the lane to the churchyard; to know that somewhere, maybe somewhere near, would be Mark. And that she might see him from a distance, like she'd always wanted. Say goodbye to him in her heart and to Gran, and then forget for all time. Wouldn't it be the most sensible thing to do?

Candlefold called her. Tommy had been meant to see the notice in the *Post*, and Wednesday was her half-day – no need to ask for time off. It would take time to get there; probably by about four. There would be no one in the churchyard by then. And the last bus out of the village was six o'clock – just time enough to do all she needed to do. Say goodbye to Gran, then walk to the stile and cross the field until she saw Candlefold's old, sagging roof ahead. Just to see the roof, know it was still there.

It was as if, all at once, there was some invisible thread attached to her heart; a thread that linked her to Candlefold and had never been broken. And now she felt a gentle tugging on that thread and knew she would go back. And what was more, Nell knew it, too.

Meg ran all the way to Exchange Station, arriving minutes before the one-twenty to Preston left, collapsing in a corner seat, shoulders heaving. She'd made it, would be there in time to catch the three o'clock bus to the village. If the bus times hadn't changed, that was. In more than two years, lots of things could change. She had changed; had been married and widowed and come of age, was legally an adult now. As was Polly.

Dear Polly. Had she and Davie, on their honeymoon, started the baby she so desperately wanted, or did she still work in the kitchen garden with Mr Potter, living from morning to morning when the post came? Where was Davie, now? Where was Mark?

A pulse in her throat began to beat, because the clackety-clack of the wheels was taking her ever nearer to him. Maybe. Or perhaps *They* didn't give a soldier leave for his grandmother's funeral. Perhaps he and Davie were so far away that they couldn't be there, anyway. Perhaps neither of them knew yet.

Mark – please be there? Let me, just one last time, see you. Only see you; not speak nor explain how it was. Just see you from a distance so I can send my love and wish you well and that you come safely home, when the war is over.

Then she pulled in her breath, so sharp was the shock. Why hadn't she thought of it before? Why, in her utter stupidity, had she not realised that Mark could be married? He was attractive; everything a woman could want in a man. Why had she presumed that loving her would shut out all other love – just as it had happened to her? Even married to Kip, she knew she would belong to Mark for all time, but how deep, how enduring had Mark's love for her been?

Dismayed even to think of such a thing, she cleared her head of thoughts, though her heart still thudded dully and the little pulse at her throat wouldn't stop its frantic fluttering.

Eyes closed, she willed him not to be there, a woman at his side. What you didn't know, she thought bitterly, you couldn't worry about. And he wouldn't be there. Common sense told her he wouldn't. It would be all right. Oh, please, it would be?

The fluttering at her throat began again, but for a different reason. Now the bus had stopped at the crossroads that led to Nether Barton to let a passenger alight, and it was from this place, nearly three years ago, that she had heaved her case onto the bus, grateful that no one from the village who might know her was sitting on it.

From these crossroads she had said a silent goodbye to all her heart held dear; to a summer that had been, could she but have realized it, too good to last. And now, in just a few minutes, she would get off at the post office, hoping she would not be seen, and hurry down Church Lane and past the vicarage to where Gran lay.

A cool breeze lifted her hair and she pulled up the collar of her coat; for warmth, was it, or so she might not be recognized so easily? She glanced at the little shop to see with relief that its blinds were pulled down. She might have known. In the country, blinds were always drawn as a mark of respect. Mrs Potter would be at Candlefold, with the rest of the village. Mrs John would have asked them there. It was like that, in Nether Barton. The village always gathered together in sad times or glad times.

Braver, she stopped to read the notice in the shop window. 'Closed owing to bereavement. Open Thurs a.m.' Mrs Potter would not see her. No one would see her. She let go a breath of relief and the fluttering lessened.

Left, now, into the lane and feeling as if almost three years counted for nothing: that she had never been away. The sun came from behind a cloud and Meg was grateful for its warmth, for the welcome it gave her. Yesterday, her birthday, had passed without much ado; she had not wanted, even, to buy a drink in the Tarleton because it was as if the next day was of far more importance. Tomorrow, when she went to Candlefold. In secret. And secretly she would say her goodbyes then turn and walk away and never look back; walk to the crossroads as she had done before because she dare not risk being seen. And then, if she had any sense in her head, she would get on with the rest of her life as if the Candlefold summer had never happened.

She walked quickly past the vicarage, her eyes on the tower of the church and the clock that ticked away the minutes and hours but was not allowed to strike because of the war. She walked on to the far, smaller gate, then entered the graveyard by the back path. It was easy to find where Gran lay. Beside the gravelled path, she was, the grass around trampled down, a mound of earth over her. And on it, just two wreaths and a posy.

Meg bent to read the black-edged cards: *Dearest mother-in-law. From Mary and all your friends in Nether Barton.* And the other card, written in Polly's hand: *Goodbye, our darling Grandmother.*

The posy bore the inscription, *With deepest respect. Emily Boag.* Nanny was still alive! Nearer ninety than eighty, the old woman lived on, safe at the top of the nursery stairs!

Just to think of her set Meg's heart bumping, and she pushed all thoughts of the malicious old woman from her mind because she was standing beside Gran's grave and there must be nothing but love between them.

Mrs Kenworthy, dearest Gran. She directed her thoughts to Polly's wreath. I loved you so much yet I left without telling you and without saying goodbye or thank you for all you did for me. You could have been my real Gran, if I'd had one, and you above all should have known.

She sniffed loudly, and drew an impatient hand over her eyes because she had willed herself not to cry and now here she was, with tears running down her cheeks and her shoulders shaking with the effort just of being there.

I've come to say goodbye, Gran. I said I would never come back. But I know you always believed in God and in prayers and in heaven, so that's where you'll be now. And because I don't suppose there are secrets in your heaven, then you'll know now why I left and who I am, even though I told you Ma's name was Hilda.

Bless you, dear Mrs Kenworthy. You are out of your pain now, and with your God. Look down on Meg Blundell sometimes, and forgive her, if you think she did wrong.

She sank to her knees, not caring about the damp earth beneath her. She did not kneel to pray – she did not know how – but to be nearer to a lady she loved and who had loved her.

'I might just as well have two granddaughters . . .'

Gran had loved her for what she was; a girl from Liverpool with a thick Scouse accent, who tried hard to be like the Kenworthys – as Ma had done. Ladylike, and quietly spoken, and being kind to people because being kind to people came naturally to gentry such as they were.

I have to go, Gran. If I can I'll come again and see you and maybe bring you flowers. Being here today was like coming home. I loved Candlefold so much, maybe perhaps 'cause I had the luck to be born there, even if in sin. But I shall always remember it, and you, darling Gran. Always.

Slowly she got to her knees, dabbing her eyes and her nose, gazing at the flowers for one last time. Roses from Mrs John – the same roses Polly had carried to her wedding; white chrysanthemums from Mark and Polly. Mark could not have been at the funeral, Meg realized, or the card would have been in his handwriting. Mark, and Davie too, were overseas in Italy or in France. Somewhere dangerous. Take care, the two of you . . .

She turned. She would not look back. You didn't look back in wartime. Instead, she gazed at the path ahead and the iron gates and the person who was opening and closing them behind her. That person she knew only too well and she stood stock-still, chin high, watching as she walked towards her.

'Polly.' Her lips moved, but no sound came.

'Meg. So you've come back.'

Polly had not changed. She was still as pretty, still the girl Meg had thought of as a sister, had she had one. There were tears in her eyes, yet she was smiling.

'I – I came to see Gran. Saw it in the paper. I came late so no one would see me.'

Silly words. Cold words. Words strangers used. The two of them standing eye to eye, two feet apart, saying all the wrong things.

'But Hugh Rushton saw you from the vicarage. He phoned us.'

'Oh,' she whispered. 'Was it gentle, for Gran? It said peacefully, in the paper.'

'Yes. In her sleep. Mummy found her . . .'

'Yes. Well . . .'

'Oh, Meg Blundell! Is that it, then? You left without a goodbye and still all you can say is well!'

'I'm sorry. There was a reason. I had to go. Oh, Poll – do you think I wanted to?'

'No, I never did nor ever have. I have willed you back to us and now that you're here . . .'

With a smile she held wide her arms and Meg went into them gladly, and they hugged, not speaking, cheek on cheek, sisters again. And it was as if they were in the blue-flowered bedroom once more, talking and laughing; watching the sun go down over the far arch, and the wood beyond. The time between had never been, and she and Polly were hugging each other because Polly and Davie were going on their honeymoon in Mrs John's little car.

Then they drew apart, wondering a little about the gladness and the sadness of their embrace, and Meg saying, 'We-e-ll – I'll have to go now. Thought I'd walk to the crossroads, pick the bus up there.'

'Oh, no. You're to come home with me!'

'I can't, Polly. The whole village'll be there. I couldn't face them after the way I left. And I can't face your mother, either.'

'No one is there. Mummy still misses you, wonders where you are. Please, Meg, I beg you? Talk to Mummy and me? At least tell us what happened to make you go. And I have so much to tell you!'

'No. I've got to get the six o'clock bus back. And please don't tell Mrs John this, but if I told you the truth of it, then she would be very hurt. There's nothing can change why I went. I didn't want to – truly I didn't!'

'Then why go, you idiot? What was so terrible to make you do a runner? Mark, was it? I'll bet my brother had something to do with it! Well, if it's any satisfaction he was as mystified as the rest of us.'

'It was everything to do with Mark – and nothing that was his fault.'

'So he didn't get fresh with you – try anything on? That wasn't the reason you went? Because Mark was cut up about it. When he rang home Mummy asked him what he'd done to upset you and he said nothing. When she told him you'd gone, he hit the roof – over the phone, that was.'

'Where is Mark now, and Davie?' She had to ask.

'Davie is in Italy. Thank God the fighting is all but over there. Mark is in France, pressing on to Berlin, I suppose. He's fine, if you're interested, that is.'

'Hey! That hurt, Polly!'

'It was meant to. You hurt him. He told me later he'd made up his mind to ask you to marry him.'

'And I would have – but him and me together – well, it isn't on.'

'Look, Meg – this is getting us nowhere. I want you to come back with me and damn the six o'clock bus. Davie and I have a child – I want you to see her. And you owe my mother an explanation as far as I'm concerned, and you owe me one, too! So are you coming home peacefully, or do I have to drag you there?'

Home? Going home, to Candlefold. So sweet a thought. And she wanted to go. There hadn't been a day – not one single day – she had not thought about it and longed for it and for it still to be the day of the wedding and Nanny hadn't told her about –

'Look, Polly, there is a reason why I can't tell you the truth of my leaving. I won't have your mother hurt and she would be if she knew what I found out.'

'Yes! You said! But what did you find out? Surely you can tell me? Maybe I won't think it's as bad as you imagine. And *who* told you?'

'All right. I won't be coming back with you because – oh, hell! Listen, Polly! I *will* tell you but you have to promise you'll never tell your mother!'

'All right. Whatever it is, I won't tell her. But you're to come back with me. Mummy would want you to.'

'Only if you'll agree to tell her that I left because of Mark. I fell heavily for him, we can say, and I shoved off because I didn't think he'd ever want me.'

'Sounds fair enough. Very wrong, though. Mark was devastated when you left. Mummy said to me that she thought you'd been lovers. Had you?'

'Polly! What must your mother have thought of me!'

'So it happened? I'm not surprised. It used to show when the two of you were together. Who did you think you were fooling?'

'What showed?' Meg demanded hotly.

'You and him. *Need*, if you want it in a word. And it didn't bother Mummy. All she thought was that if you had, the pair of you, then you should have got married. She's not so bad about that sort of thing, but she's very keen on marriage.' She linked Meg's arm, and they began to walk. 'So are you going to tell me then?

'OK. Just between you and me. And you're never to tell – especially Mark.'

'God's honour I won't. Word of a Kenworthy.'

'All right.' They were standing at the church gates, now. 'If I told you that Mark and I could never marry because we're related, what would you say?'

'Related? I'd say stuff and nonsense, because you aren't! How can you be?'

'If we both have the same father, that's how.'

'You – you mean my father and your mother? Oh, Meg! Never in a million years! It just isn't possible!'

'It is. My mother worked here, you see. And I was born here – yes, actually born at Candlefold! And I have a birth certificate to prove it! The one thing missing on it is my father's name.'

'You – born here? But how?'

'Because my mother worked for your mother and father. A housemaid she was, and really happy. I have photographs I could show you. Ma was allowed to stay here to have me when she got pregnant, and then your father gave her a house in Liverpool to live in.'

'In – in Lyra Street, was it?' Polly's face had drained of colour. 'Was that the house?'

'No. The house in Lyra Street had been bombed. I gave that address because I thought someone might have recognized my real address. And I said my mother's name was Hilda when Gran once said she remembered a housemaid called Dorothy Blundell. Gran suspected. But I told her Ma had been called Hilda and she'd always worked in a tobacco factory.'

'Oh, my God! But why did you come to Candlefold in the first place, if you knew about your mother and my father?'

'I didn't. Ma never told me anything. After she died, I went through her papers, then most things made sense. She'd always spoken with affection about her years in service – I just wanted to have a look at the place. Y'see, Ma didn't believe in God, and I wanted her to be somewhere nice when she was gone. Candlefold was the best heaven I could think of – where she'd been happy, in the country.'

'So you came to work for us and never told us a thing?'

'That's right. Decided against it – thought that the Father Unknown on my birth certificate wasn't all that important – especially as he'd cleared off and left Ma to it. I didn't think I was being deceitful. I loved Candlefold just as Ma did. Is it so wrong to be happy, really happy, for the first time in your life?'

'No, Meg. And you fitted in so well it was as if you were meant to be with us. But I don't believe my father would do a thing like that, and especially with a housemaid.'

'Oh, so you think he wouldn't stoop so low!' Meg was angry now. 'His sort didn't go for Ma's sort. She wasn't good enough, eh?'

'No! I didn't mean that, and you know it! But my father was a decent man and he and Mummy were in love. He wouldn't have gone off the rails with any woman, I just know it. And Mummy would have known it, too!'

'Well she didn't, it seems. And when men bed their servants they don't usually tell their wives, do they?'

'Meg! How can you say such a thing? Bedding a servant! It's so – so –'

'So Scouse? Rough, like me?' They were arguing. For the first time, there was anger between them. 'Well, that's what Nanny said I had done. "Bedded your own brother," she said!'

'*Nanny*? But how could she have known?'

'Because on the night of your wedding Mark came to my room, and Nanny heard us,' Meg flung, all at once not caring.

'How could she have, from the nursery?'

'Because she came downstairs and listened at the door! Nanny could manage those stairs. It wasn't the first time she'd come down them. She once went through my case with my private things in it – saw the deeds of the house in Tippet's Yard and your father's and my mother's name on them. And she saw my birth certificate! She told me she had been there when I was born, and it made sense. She told me who my father was, and that I could never have Mark and I was to leave!'

'But – but Nanny was as shocked as all of us. Couldn't think of any reason why you should bolt like you did, she said.'

'Then she's a liar! It was her told me. Could hardly keep the grin off her face! Bedded my brother? Don't you think I wasn't shocked, an' all, Polly? I loved Mark and he loved me; he told me so, that night. And then Nanny dirtied it – incest, it's called! I just left. It seemed the only thing to do.'

'Look, Meg, we're getting cross with each other and it won't do. And goodness, when you think of it, you have more right to be at Candlefold than I have, you being born there!'

'No. You were adopted, made legal. I was – *am* – illegitimate. You see, Ma would never talk about my father. I didn't know who he was or where he was. She wore a wedding ring, so I supposed she'd been married. She just used to clam up. Then she died, and I got to see her papers.'

'Yes. I'll grant you that. It would all make sense, but Nanny – are you sure? She hasn't left that room for years.'

'She *can* leave that room. She did, at least twice to my certain knowledge. And the nonsense is all a part of it. She's as sane as you or I, Poll, and dead cunning with it, an' all! She knew what was going on outside, too, and the only way she could have was to look out of the window!'

'But the nursery windows are high up!'

'Yes! So she stood on a chair. What you'd call agile, for an old woman!'

'All right. So Nanny has been mischief-making. You don't have to see her, Meg. Just come and say hello to Mummy.'

'Nanny will know! She'll be on that dratted chair and she'll see me. Well, I hope she falls off it with shock! An' I'll only come and see Mrs John if you promise on your honour to stick to what we agreed. And *if* I come, promise you'll not talk too much about Mark. It still hurts . . .'

'Yes. If it had been Davie and me, I'd have been desolate. But come? Just for a little while. I'll make sure you're on that bus. Please, Meg?'

So they began to walk, and Polly reached for Meg's hand, and not a word was spoken until they came to the stile.

'This is where I came in,' Meg whispered. 'There were lambs in the field, then.'

'Well, there are bullocks, now,' Polly said, much too matter-of-factly.

'Afterwards – after I'd left, I used to daydream about crossing this field to the bottom arch again, but now it's real, it doesn't seem right. I shouldn't be here, Polly. I should never have come back.

'But you did, and over there – look.'

A smiling Mary Kenworthy stood at the couryard archway, her hand lifted in greeting.

'Meg! It *was* you Hugh saw!' She opened wide her arms. 'Where have you been? Why did you go?'

Meg went into her arms and tears began to fall. Mrs John was so good, so kind, and what had happened between her husband and Ma all those years ago wasn't fair.

'I'm sorry, Mrs John,' she choked.

'Hey! No tears, Meg Blundell. Mother-in-law said we would find you one day and here you are. And anyway, we would have looked for you. Mother-in-law left you money in her will. Her way of making sure, I think. Welcome back, my dear.'

'Please don't be so kind. I don't deserve it and I don't deserve Gran's kindness, either. I'm sorry I just upped and went. Mark, you see. I was head over heels about him – knew he'd never marry the likes of me' She looked into Polly's eyes, daring her to contradict.

'Yes. I know now about you and Mark. He told me you were both in love, so there was no need for you to have gone, was there? Why didn't you talk to me first? Mark was very cut up about it.'

'No, Mummy! According to what Meg says, it won't be any use – her and Mark, I mean!' Polly, red-cheeked, chin stubbornly set. 'You should hear what she told *me*!'

'Polly! *No!*'

'She went because Nanny told her that my father was *her* father! Nanny said Meg had bedded her brother!'

'Polly! You said you wouldn't tell! You promised! How could you do such a thing to your own mother?' Meg gasped, horrified.

'Because I don't believe it of my father. I can't remember him, but he was a decent man, and he wouldn't have done such a thing. He loved Mummy, and no one else!'

'So because you can't bear to think I've got Kenworthy blood in my veins and you haven't, you act like a spoiled child! I thought better of you!' Meg flung, white-faced. 'I trusted you!'

'Now, please!' Mary Kenworthy held up her hands. 'Remember that today we laid your gran to rest. Let's not have a shouting match. Close the door, Polly, and Meg, will you please tell me exactly what Nanny said?'

She said it very quietly, but real ladies never shouted, Meg knew, nor blustered. She took a deep breath.

'I'm sorry. I didn't ever want you to know, Mrs John. I loved Mark. The night of Polly's wedding, he came to my room. And you're not to blame him!'

'No. I know it takes two people to make love. But what had it to do with Nanny?'

'You won't believe this, but Nanny could get about just fine. She came to my room – went through my things, found out I'd been born here and that I was Dorothy Blundell's daughter, even though I'd told Gran different.'

'So! Mother-in-law mentioned it to me; pity I doubted her instinct. But even if Nanny could manage the stairs alone, are you sure, Meg? I don't think she would do such a thing.'

'Well, if she didn't, it was either you, Gran, or Polly. And it *was* Nanny who saw my papers. She could climb on a chair and look out of the window, an' all. She wasn't mad. She only acted that way. I found her out, so she turned on me, told me your husband and my mother were – well – close. That's why he gave her the house in Tippet's Yard, – where I really live in Liverpool. And she said you had never known who got Ma pregnant! There! I'm sorry to have said it, but Polly didn't give me much choice!'

'Polly. Meg.' Mary held out her arms. 'Come here, the pair of you. What a stupid way to behave. And what nonsense Nanny had told you, Meg.'

'Nonsense?' Meg gasped. 'But she was so sure about it, and I believed her because it made sense. The way she put it was that I had bedded my brother. She made me feel like a slut. I couldn't wait to get away, I was so ashamed. I went when you took Davie's parents to the station. And I'm truly sorry, Mrs John. It's an awful way to repay your kindness, isn't it? I wish I'd never known Gran had died; wish I hadn't come back to Candlefold!'

'No, you don't. You were meant to come back, and I'm glad you have, because now you can hear the truth. From me! And I'll speak to Nanny later, be sure of that! So will you put the kettle on, my dear, like you used to, and then I will tell you who your father was. And you are married!' She was looking at the rings on Meg's left hand with disbelief. 'Yet you loved Mark so much . . .'

'Married! You didn't tell me,' Polly whispered.

'I would have. Thought you'd have noticed.'

'Who is he, then? So in love with my brother, yet you soon forgot him! Did you marry the faithful Kip?'

'Yes. And I am a widow, Polly. Kip was killed, two years ago. He was a good man, and I respected him. But you were going to tell me who my father is, Mrs John, and I haven't said I'm sorry about Gran. I loved her very much.'

'And she loved you, Meg. And I'm sorry that what happened caused you to go without saying goodbye to her. But I do understand your leaving. It was an unkind, vindictive thing for Nanny to have said, and totally false. But say you will stay with us a little longer? For one night, will you?'

'No, Mrs John. Thanks, but no. I have to work, and besides, I couldn't bear to see Nanny Boag again after the trouble she's caused.'

'You won't have to. Your room is still there. You see, there is so much to tell you – things I want Polly to hear, too.'

'And there are things I must tell you both, an' all. And I asked Polly not to talk about Mark, but here's me wanting to know how he is.'

'He's safe and well, though I worry about them both. And – and Mark is engaged now. Stella, she's called, though no wedding, I believe, till the war is over.'

'I see.' Disbelief hit Meg like a physical blow. Mark, and someone new! But then, she had married Kip, though no one here would ever know why. 'I – I'm glad for him.'

'No you're not, Meg. You look shocked to the core. She's like you, by the way. Dark hair, blue eyes . . .'

'Stop it, Polly!' Mary commanded.

'Well, she is. And more's the pity he ever gave her a ring – especially now it seems my father is off the hook!'

'Don't say any more, *please*. Your father off the hook, indeed! And hadn't you better go and collect Sarah? Four o'clock, you said. Mrs Seed will be wondering where you are!'

'And I must go too, Mrs John,' Meg said softly when they were alone. 'I'd like to see the little one, but I'll miss the bus if I stay any longer.'

'And not know about your father?'

'It doesn't matter. Seems that Mark and I aren't related and I'm sorry I put two and two together and came up with twenty-two.'

'Then have I your permission to tell Mark you were here?'

'If you want to, Mrs John . . .'

'Oh, but I do want to! He should know. So it's Tippet's Yard where you live? We won't let you go, Meg.'

'I don't want you to.' She walked to the door. 'And I'm sorry I believed what Nanny said.'

'You leave Nanny to me! And promise you'll keep in touch?'

'I promise. Soon. Then maybe you'll tell me who my father really was.'

'Your room will always be ready,' Mary smiled, kissing Meg's cheek. 'Now, you've got fifteen minutes before your bus goes. I'll say goodbye to Polly for you, though she'll be sad that you'll miss Sarah. She's a love of a child – so like Davie.'

'I wouldn't miss – Oh, Polly!' They collided as she opened the door; Polly white-faced and breathless. 'What is it?'

Then she saw the envelope in Polly's hand; small and yellow. A telegram.

'I met Mrs Potter – on her way. Said I'd give you it . . .'

The envelope was stamped OHMS. Mrs Potter had delivered such a one before and had willingly relinquished the one she carried to Polly.

'Oh, dear God. . .' Mary Kenworthy's face paled, then she breathed in deeply and held out a hand. 'For me, did she say?'

Mutely, Polly nodded, watching as her mother took out a precisely folded piece of paper.

'It's your brother,' she whispered. 'Wounded. On August the twenty-sixth.'

'Dear God – the day Gran died. They've been a long time, letting us know.'

'Yes, Polly, but we know now . . .'

'But where is he? How serious is it?'

'Read it.' Mary passed the telegram to her daughter.

'*The War Office regrets to inform you that your son, Captain M.C. Kenworthy was wounded in action on 26.8.44. Letter follows,*' Polly whispered. 'They don't tell you much, do they? Is his CO going to write, do you think?'

'Probably. In time. But Mark, thank God, is still alive and by now he'll be in a hospital, let's hope. And commanding officers don't have a lot of time for writing, especially when they're in action. There'll be a letter. Probably from one of the medical people. Let's be glad the news wasn't worse.'

'Here. Drink this.' Meg held a glass to Mary Kenworthy's lips. 'Would you like an aspirin?'

'No, dear. Just a drink of water . . .'

'He'll be all right. He *will*.'

'Yes, Meg. And Polly – you'd better get the child.'

'No. I can't leave you.'

'Off you go, Polly,' Meg whispered. 'I'll stay with your mother. The little one will be wondering where you are. Off you go!' she urged. 'I'll be here when you get back!'

'Your bus, Meg . . . ?'

'There'll be another one – tomorrow.' Gently she laid her arms round the shaking shoulders. 'You've had just about as much as you can take for one day, Mrs John. I'll stay.'

Of course she would. Didn't she love Mark, too – even if now he belonged to someone else? Mark, who had been wounded . . .

She wished with all her heart she knew how to pray!

Twenty-Seven

'She's beautiful.' Meg cradled Polly's baby in her arms. 'So like Davie.'

Davie's auburn hair that curled like Polly's; Davie's eyes and the hint of freckles to come, above a tip-tilted nose.

'I think so too. Davie hasn't seen her, you know. Awful, but there must be a lot of men serving overseas in the same boat.'

'Was she the honeymoon baby you wanted?'

'No, but I got a few days with Davie before he went. I just wanted to be with him every minute I could – Sarah was a happy bonus. Look – can you give her her feed? Nearly fifteen months old and still demands a bottle at bedtime! I'd better see to Nanny's tea. She's been very quiet – no bell-ringing, or anything.'

'She'll know I'm here,' Meg said softly. 'The minute she heard us crossing the courtyard, she'd be on that chair!'

'You always had your suspicions about Nanny, didn't you, Meg? Now it looks as if you were right.'

'She'll deny ever having said it – say I made it up.'

'Then it's going to be a question of who Mummy believes, and I'm sure it'll be you, Meg. But Nanny will have to make do with a boiled egg and a jammed scone. I'm very annoyed with her.'

'Please, Poll – don't say anything? Leave it to your mother?'

'Mother? Mark is master here – it'll be up to him!'

'Mark is in hospital, wounded. Nanny is the least of his worries.'

'At the moment, yes. But he's going to find out, sooner or later. When he realizes she was the cause of your leaving, there'll be ructions! He was really cut up when you went.'

'Do I stop halfway through this bottle – get her wind up?' No more talk about Mark, please?

'No. She just guzzles it down. She can cope with her own wind now. And don't change the subject! Nanny separated you and Mark. He won't forgive that easily.'

'But he's got Stella.'

It hurt, Meg thought; really hurt to think about Stella, who had dark hair and blue eyes.

'Yes. I suppose he has, though he's in no hurry to get married. Be with you in a tick. I'll just take this tray up. Y'know, it's awful going into Gran's room and her not being there. But she knew she'd be well again, once she got to heaven. I suppose you still don't believe, Meg?'

'No. But when that telegram came, I wished like mad I knew how to pray.'

'Talking of praying,' Polly resumed when she returned from the nursery, 'Mummy is a firm believer in it. It's why she's gone to church. She'll be a lot better, when she's had a word with God. And that's the bottle finished – I'll take her up. Since she started walking she tires herself out, toddling all over the place – thank goodness.'

'Please – let me keep her just a little longer? She's so cuddly and snuggly.'

'All right, then. Just this once. Will a boiled egg suit you for supper, Meg? Everything's gone upside down, today.'

'An egg would be wonderful. You can't imagine what on-the-ration eggs are like. One a week, and so dubious you have to break it into a cup and sniff it before you eat it.'

She hugged the baby close, thinking about her own child. It would have been Sarah's age, she thought wonderingly, and it would not have been a child of incest. Meg was glad she had never known if it was a boy, or a girl. Not knowing helped, just a little.

She laid her cheek on the damp curls, smiling to see eyelids droop and the thumb, noisily sucked.

'You are so lucky, Poll. She's beautiful.'

'Yes – well, I deserved a beautiful baby. I was so sick. Meg, that morning sickness is awful! May you never have it! But will you watch the eggs?' She held out her arms for her child. 'Come on, you! Bed! Two more minutes they want and will you slice some bread? And you have forgiven me for snitching on you when I promised not to?'

'Forgiven, soon as asked.'

It had been for the best, Meg thought. Now she knew who her father *wasn't*, it didn't seem so important to discover who he was. How stupid of her not to have asked Mrs John. But you don't, she told herself sternly, say to someone you like and respect, 'Excuse me, but did you know your late husband is my father?' Not to a lovely lady like Polly's ma, you didn't.

She watched the last of the sand run through the egg timer, thinking about Mark, sending her love to him over the miles, wishing him well. And Candlefold wrapped its warmth around her as if she had never been away, and love for it surged through her like a blessing. Home. At this special moment, it was the most wonderful word in all the world.

'There, now!' Mary Kenworthy came briskly into the kitchen. 'I've had a word with Our Lord – put it all into His hands; no more to be done! And I had a look at Gran, too. I seemed to sense she was telling me not to worry too much. And Hugh pointed out that Mark will be safe in hospital now, so that's a blessing to be counted. Now – is Sarah in bed? And has someone thought to take Nanny's tea?'

'Yes, and yes. And Meg and I have eaten too, God bless the hens! Are you hungry, Mummy?'

'Not particularly, but common sense tells me I should eat.'

'I think you should. You'll be awake half the night; no need to add a rumbling tummy to your worries. How about an omelette?'

'That sounds just right. And then we'll light a fire in the sitting room. It was quite chilly, walking home. One more day, and it'll be September.'

'Yes, and one more week then Davie and I will have been married three years! How long is this war going to last? It won't be over in Europe by Christmas, will it?'

'I doubt it, but we're on our way! Won't it be just marvellous? Church bells ringing again; lights shining through windows and no one to shout, "Get that light out!" And our soldiers home . . .' Her voice trembled.

'Listen, darling, you don't have to do the stuff-upper-lip thing. Have a good weep, why don't you? Do you the world of good. Pity we've got no brandy.'

'No. I shall be fine, Polly. Like I said, it's in God's hands – no use both Him and me worrying. And there'll be a letter soon – maybe in the morning – telling us where he is, so we can write to him.'

'Yes, Mrs John, and maybe even a letter from Mark himself. Had you thought of that? So shall I light a fire in the sitting room whilst you get something to eat? Then I'll make up my bed – and yes, I know where the sheets are,' Meg smiled.

'So you do, and before you leave us, I have made up my mind to tell you what I think you ought to know.'

'No. You've had enough upset for one day. Some other time will do. I hope I'm going to be invited again?'

'You don't need an invitation; just come. And as for being upset – maybe what I shall tell you could be more upsetting to you. But I want you to know; you have a right to, and putting the record straight will give me something other than Mark to think about. But it really is up to you, Meg . . .'

'Then if you're willing, so am I. And nothing can ever upset me as much as knowing – *thinking* – Mark and I were related. That was like telling me I was sentenced to death. And I'd like Polly to hear it, if she doesn't mind.'

'Oh, yes. There are things Polly should know, too.'

'Like who my real mother was? Did you ever know, Mummy?'

'An omelette, didn't you say, Mrs Sumner?' Mary smiled. Smiled with her lips, Meg thought, though her eyes remained sad and worried.

Oh, Mark! Meg closed her eyes and sent her love winging. Come home safely.

When licking flames were crackling the logs in the old stone fireplace, and dancing on copper jugs and lightening corners, Mary Kenworthy, with Meg and Polly either side of her, said, 'Ah, now. This is so peaceful. I wonder how many generations have sat at this hearth?'

'And talked and laughed – and worried,' Polly smiled. 'So are you going to tell us?'

'I am. Everything. And it all starts when a girl of fourteen came here to work. I was a new bride, she was a housemaid. Her name was Dorothy Blundell – Dolly. She came to us from a convent. She had been left there as a baby, I was told, with her Christian name and the date of her birth pinned to the blanket she was wrapped in. She was given the name Blundell in honour of a local family who gave a great deal of money for the upkeep of the orphanage.

'She was a solemn little thing, spoke only when she was spoken to – well, for a time, that was. We were lucky to get her. Usually the nuns wanted their girls to go to a Catholic family, but we undertook to see that she went to Mass regularly, and since there was a church near at hand, they let her come to Candlefold.'

'But Ma wasn't religious!' Meg gasped. 'She never once went to church that I remember, and never told me about God!'

'Well, she was a devout little soul when she came to us, rather thin and, like I said, very solemn. And she went regularly to church. We had grooms, then; one or another of them drove her to Mass. Then she began to laugh and fill out. She blossomed into a pretty young woman.'

'Yes. I have photographs of Ma, here. Always smiling.' Meg's voice trembled. 'But – sorry. I'll try not to interrupt.'

'Interrupt all you like, Meg. After all, it's you and Dorothy we are talking about. Anyway, that awful war came – the Great War they called it – and my John volunteered along with all the young men on the estate and in the village. So patriotic, so eager to fight, though some of them hardly understood what it was they'd gone to war for. And just the same as in this war, part of Candlefold was taken by the Government and turned into a convalescent home for wounded soldiers and sailors. And just like now, we Kenworthys moved into the old part.

'Then, just as we began to hope it would all soon be over, John was wounded very badly. In fact, he came home to die. He was in constant pain. Sometimes, God forgive me, I wish he'd been killed. It was pitiful to see his suffering. What I am trying to say is that his injuries took away his – his manhood. He could not have fathered a child, Meg. It was why we adopted Polly. He died when she was two.'

'I'm so sorry, Mrs John,' Meg whispered, eyes on hands. 'If I'd known that, I'd never have believed what Nanny said.'

'Yes, but Nanny must have known,' Polly said hotly, 'that what she told Meg was a pack of lies.'

'Nanny lives in another world, I'm afraid. She can be very mischievous.'

'Mischievous, Mummy? How dare she say such a thing about my father, and she his nanny, too? She must have hated you, Meg.'

'Not me in particular – just any girl she didn't think good enough for Mark. And you can't blame her. I was very badly spoken when I came here. She used to correct me all the time.'

'But that doesn't excuse downright lies!'

'No, Polly, it does not,' Mary said softly, 'and when we get ourselves straightened out, when we know Mark is getting better, I think we should consider what is to be done.'

'She should go!'

'That will be up to your brother, Polly. But shall I go on, or shall we have a milky drink?'

'Go on, please,' Meg whispered. 'We can drink Ovaltine any time, but it isn't every day you get to know about your mother, and who your father was. Ma never told me a thing about her early life. Life, for Ma, began at Candlefold. She talked of it when she was ill, as the heaven she wanted to go to when she died. It was why I came to have a look at where I was sure her soul was. That was when I met Mrs Potter and she pointed me in the direction of a job. But I want to know, now. I thought I didn't care, but I do.'

'Very well.' Mary cleared her throat and took a deep breath. 'We never had a motor at Candlefold until after the war – stuck to horses. We always had two grooms, and when one of them left, we employed a new one from Ireland. Like most of the Irish, he loved horses and did his job well. He had only one fault, in fact. He was a terrible flirt – all the younger staff went giddy over him – except your mother, Meg. She took no notice of his teasing, his blarney, and he didn't like it. He was a handsome fellow – not used to being ignored by a girl. He set his cap at her.'

'And Ma fell for it, in the end?'

'No, she did not. It happened in December. The weather was atrocious, but your mother wouldn't miss church. So didn't the groom see his chance, offer to take her there himself, him being of the same faith? They took the pony and trap, though more snow came down and they sheltered under a Dutch barn at the roadside – a sensible thing to do, I thought at the time.'

'And what was this handsome fellow called, Mummy?

'Padraig O'Flyn – we called him Paddy. Your mother seemed distressed, Meg, and I told her not to worry, that she was safely back and to change her wet clothes. I thought no more of it until next day when we realized that Paddy had gone – bag and baggage – and it was then that Dorothy told us. He had forced himself on her, in the barn. She'd tried to fight him off, but it was no use. She was worried and afraid, said she hoped she hadn't fallen for a child. I told her it very rarely happened the first time.'

'But it did,' Meg whispered. 'Not only am I illegitimate, I'm a rape child.'

'Yes.' Mary Kenworthy's face was serious and pale. 'When your mother found out, she was beside herself. Where was she to go? What would happen to her? Bad girls like her went to the workhouse, she said. I told her that perhaps the nuns would be sympathetic, that they would care for her, but she said, "No! I'm finished with nuns and religion. It was being afraid of missing Mass got me in this state! Don't send me back there!"

'So what could we do? She was our responsibility. We should have taken better care of her. My John said we mustn't turn her out, that she must stay with us, then he would make some provision for her. He was a good man, always mindful of the needs of others, ill as he was.'

'Yet Nanny branded him an adulterer,' Polly flung. 'She's wicked, as well as mad!'

'Leave Nanny to me, Polly. Be sure she'll answer for what she has done. It's Meg we are concerned with now. Are you all right, my dear?'

'I – I think so, Mrs John. I don't think I'm all that much upset, to tell the truth. Only for Ma, that is. She didn't have much of a life, did she? Just the few years she spent in this house. No wonder she thought of it as special. I'd like to think some part of her is still here, and thank you for being good to her. Most would have shown her the door.'

'Like I said, she was our responsibility. She gave up her religion, though; took down the crucifix from over bed and never went to church again. If that was where religion got you, she said, then she'd had enough of it! The other maids were good to her. She carried on working right till the end, and was paid her wages. When her time came she was confined in the brick part of the house. She stayed with us for a month afterwards, then John gave her a house that had been left to him.'

'Number 1 Tippet's Yard,' Meg said softly. 'I used to wonder why the rent man never called. You were good to her; thank you for sticking by her. So I'm half-Irish! I suppose that's where I get my colouring from.'

'Your beauty, Meg. From your handsome father! But we were sad to see Dorothy go. She was such a nice young woman. She cried bitterly when she left. Her friends here wrote to her, but she never replied. It seemed the break was complete.'

'And then, twenty years after, in another war, I turn up. Seems like Ma guided me here, Mrs John.'

'So will you stay with us now?' Polly asked, her eyes misty with sympathetic tears. 'I've missed you so, Meg. You were born here. You belong here.'

'No. I'll be away tomorrow, if that's all right with you, Mrs John? A right upset I've caused on top of all your other worries. But I'm grateful to you for being frank with me, and bless you for not condemning Ma. Ah, well – now it's all in the open, perhaps I will make us that hot drink.'

'If you like, but the story isn't told just yet. Not all. You see, Dorothy had a long, hard labour. We called the doctor. The midwife insisted. All wasn't well, she suspected. One baby had been born – the doctor said there was another to come. We hadn't known. In those days, twins often came as a surprise.'

'Twins! Oh, my goodness,' Polly gasped. 'Poor girl! And it happening just the once. How unfair can life be? But what happened to the other baby? Was it stillborn?'

'No. The first baby was born an hour before midnight; the second one an hour later. One on the twenty-eighth, the other on the twenty-ninth. Of August,' she added softly, 'and why I didn't connect the two birthdays – until now, that is – I'll never know. Maybe because you told us, Meg, your mother was called Hilda and hadn't been a housemaid. Be that as it may, John and I could have no more children, so we adopted one of them . . .'

'*Me?*' Polly whispered, white-faced. 'I was the other baby, wasn't I?'

'The first to be born, though you were not identical twins. One baby was dark, like its father; the other, the midwife said, was going to be fair – like its mother. And as the Kenworthys are mainly a fair family, it seemed sensible to take you, Polly.' She said it gently, then sat quietly, gazing into the fire, waiting for what she had said to be accepted.

Then Polly said, 'Funny, I always felt close to you, Meg, but I never imagined how close. Do you mind it was me they chose?' Her eyes were bright with tears, but she smiled through them.

'No. Do you mind having me for a sister?'

'A *twin*! No, I don't. I really don't. And when I've had time to get used to it, I think I'll like it very much. But how come I didn't know before this, Mummy? Dorothy had two children – why didn't someone on the estate tell me who I really was? You can't keep two babies quiet, can you?'

'Ah, but we did. Whether we were right or wrong to do so, I'll never know. But Dorothy – your birth mother – had a rough labour. No visitors at all, the doctor said, for four days, so no one was allowed to see her. It wasn't unusual, in those days, for such a thing to happen. By the time Dorothy was getting better, we had made up our minds to adopt you. The doctor agreed – and Dorothy, too – that it was for the best. A woman on her own with a child to provide for would be hard enough; with two, her life would have been impossible. So one night, when you were sleeping, Polly, the doctor took you to a foster mother. No one saw him go. A few weeks later, when Dorothy left, we set the adoption in motion.'

'And Ma never told me. I had a sister, and I never knew,' Meg whispered

'Well, it doesn't matter, does it? We've found each other, haven't we?' Polly sniffed. 'But what are we going to tell people? It'll come as a bit of a shock, won't it? They'll think we were a bit sneaky at Candlefold, won't they?'

'It's got nothing to do with *people*,' Meg said softly. 'The doctor and the midwife obviously kept quiet, and as long as Nanny doesn't say anything, does it matter?'

'Nanny will say not one word – if that's what you both want,' Mary said firmly. 'Nanny Boag, I think, has already said enough!'

Meg sat at the wide-open window of the white bedroom with the blue delphiniumed bedcover and curtains. She had never, not even in her dreamings, thought ever to sit there again. Yet she was watching the setting sun throw shadows over Pygons Wood, and slanting through the far archway to mellow the old stones to softest apricot.

'Here's a nightie for you. Want a milky drink?'

'Please, Poll. Is Sarah all right?'

'Fast asleep. Mummy has gone to bed – said to say goodnight to you. I'll take her a drink then I'll bring ours. Like old times again, isn't it,' she said softly.

Exactly like old times, Meg thought, except that Gran had gone and Mark was wounded – and in love with someone else. Yet she would make the most of tonight; think how it had been in the lovely once-upon-a-time. Tomorrow she would go back to Tippet's Yard and the Bon Marche and life in war-scarred Liverpool. Yet it seemed right that this one special night she should spend beneath Candlefold's old, sagging roof; think about all she had learned; that she had a twin. Someone to call her own. Polly who, come to think of it, had always seemed like a sister.

She tucked her legs beneath her on the window seat, not wanting to miss any part of this one precious night, nor the scents nor the sounds. This night, she would store with her golden memories; the special ones to be brought out, and lived again. If only, she yearned, she could know where Mark was and if his wounds had been bad; could know he was being cared for and was safe. She supposed that tomorrow Mrs John would write to Stella, or maybe phone her. Stella would not know. She wasn't Mark's next of kin. Not yet.

Meg closed her eyes as if to shut out Mark's new love; refused to think of his mouth on Stella's and she, maybe, in his arms and giving herself in love.

No! No more thoughts! Meg let go her indrawn breath, relaxing her body. Today she had come secretly to Nether Barton; tonight she was in her room at Candlefold, and when something as wonderful as that happened you made the most of it, and you didn't whinge for something you couldn't have.

'Here we are, then.' Polly, pushing open the door with her toe, a mug in each hand. 'I've just taken Nanny a drink. I didn't want to, but Mummy said I must. So I told Nanny she didn't deserve it; that she had told terrible lies and now she'd been found out. I was just so angry, Meg, it all came out. And would you believe it, she looked at me blankly, as if she really didn't know what she had done.

'So I said, "Meg is here. Meg Blundell. You remember her?" And then her face lit up as if she were pleased and she said, "Of course I remember. Your little friend, come to play. The one whose Nanny is always in the kitchen, gossiping with our cook." I tell you, Meg, she's either stark staring senile, or she's a damn good actress!'

'Leave it, Polly? Let's you and me enjoy tonight? If you'd told me this morning I'd be sitting here, I wouldn't have believed you.'

'And I bet you never thought you'd find a father, and a sister.'

'Never. I don't much care about finding Father Unknown, but I'm glad I've got a twin, and that she's you, Polly. Do you mind very much?'

'No. I knew that somewhere out there was a mother who'd had to give me up, but I'd never thought I'd get to know who she was. I still can't believe it – the way they kept it dark, I mean. Me being smuggled out of the house at dead of night! Sounds like a novel, doesn't it?'

'I never knew I had a twin, y'know. Ma said nothing. I suppose it was to be expected really. She wouldn't feel too badly about giving you up, knowing you were going to be a Kenworthy and brought up at Candlefold. But I'll bet there wasn't a day went by that she didn't think of you, and sometimes wonder how you'd turned out.'

'You think she'd be pleased with me, Meg?'

'I'm sure she would. And real chuffed that you an' me found each other.'

'So we won't lose you? You'll come often, and stay with us? And I can come and stay with you too.'

'Ha! And find out how the other half lives! But let's have our drinks while they're hot and pretend it's old times again – just for tonight?'

'And that Gran is still with us and Mark hasn't been wounded – oh, yes, and that Stella doesn't exist!'

'Fine by me, though I wouldn't mind getting rid of Padraig. You and I have a father out there, yet he doesn't seem real.'

'No, he doesn't. So rot his socks! Who needs him, will you tell me?' Polly said solemnly, then lifting her mug she smiled and said, 'Cheers! Here's looking at you, Sis!'

And that small special moment became precious and golden and never to be forgotten.

'So where have you been, as if I didn't know!' Nell Shaw, home from work, making for the open door of number 1. 'Not stoppin', you said. Go there when they'd all left the cemetery, so no one would see you!'

'Yes, Nell, an' I meant to. But the vicar saw me, and phoned Mrs John. Polly came – insisted I went back with her. I was going to get the last bus, honest I was, but a telegram came while I was there. Mark has been wounded. He's in France . . .'

'Then I'm sorry about that, and I hope it isn't too serious. His mother'll be worried.'

'She is. And she wasn't told how bad it was, just that he'd been wounded and that a letter followed.'

'Ar. They're like that. No consideration.'

'I hoped there'd be something in the post this morning, but there wasn't; not from the War Office nor from Mark.'

'Oh, I told you not to go back there, didn't I, girl? Said you should leave the past where it belongs. No good'll come of it, I said. Anyway, I told them at work that you'd gone to a funeral and you must have missed the last bus home. They were expecting you'd be in this afternoon, though.'

'Well, I didn't feel like going to work. I didn't sleep last night, nor Polly. And Mrs John didn't either. Things kept going through my mind.'

'Well, they would. Him being wounded has brought it all back, hasn't it? But you wouldn't be told, Meg Lewis!'

'But, Nell, I'm glad I went. You see, I know who I am now. I'm not a Kenworthy. Mrs John's husband wasn't my father, but I know who was!'

'Yes?' Nell sat down, eyes wide, lighting a cigarette. 'Who, then?'

'It was a groom who worked there. On the way to church, it happened. He raped Ma, then took off.'

'*Raped* her! The little toe rag! And Doll got you, with just the once?'

'Look, Nell – there's a lot to tell. I'm going to open a tin of soup, and make a cheese sarnie. Want to share it with me? Ma had twins, by the way.'

'Twins! Oh, poor Doll!'

'Yes. The other twin is called Polly Sumner, née Kenworthy, so if you're stopping for a bite . . . ?'

'I'm stoppin',' Nell gasped, flush-faced. 'Though it's goin' to take a bit of gettin' used to. Doll, I mean, having another daughter!'

'Getting used to? It knocked Polly and me for six! Then we thought about it and we both quite like the idea. Put the kettle on, will you, while I cut the bread?'

And Nell, incapable of uttering one more word, did as she was asked, because what was to come, she was quite sure, would be better than going to the pictures! Oh, my word, yes!

Twenty-Eight

Meg sat on the Nether Barton bus, a warm glow inside her – the happiness of homecoming, was it; the way people felt when the place you belonged was just a little way away? They were insistent. She must come to Candlefold for Christmas, if only for two days, Polly had pleaded.

It was early afternoon and not yet dark, but at four, when the short winter day ended, she would be able to see lighted windows. Except for London and along the south coast, the blackout was no more. Curtains must be drawn at night, but windows need no longer be blacked out. Soon, everyone hoped, streetlights would be allowed again, because the threat to the North of air raids no longer existed.

The bus stopped at the Upper Barton crossroads. Just five more minutes and she would be there, with Mrs Potter squinting out to see who got off the bus. Would Polly be waiting to meet her? Meg's heart pumped contentedly just to think of seeing her again. Mind, Nell hadn't been best pleased when told about Christmas.

'So you're going, then,' she had demanded.

'I want to, very much. You and Tommy won't miss me, will you?'

'Be all the same if we did – you're set on it, aren't you?'

'I am, Nell. Christmas at Candlefold will be wonderful. I can travel there on Christmas Eve, it being a Sunday.'

'But will there be buses?'

'I think so. The Preston train is running, that I do know. I'll get there, somehow. And I'll be back in time for work, on the Wednesday.'

'Ar, well – natural you should want to be with family,' Nell relented.

'They aren't family, if you want to split hairs – only Polly.'

'I'll give the girl her due, she's kept in touch. How's her husband?'

'Still fighting in Italy. She still worries . . .'

'And her brother?'

'You mean Mark? It isn't an offence to say his name, Nell. He was in hospital on the south coast – but you knew that. Now they've moved him because of the flying bombs, it seems.'

'Bluddy Hitler! Said he had a secret weapon, but nobody believed him. Now look at the damage them rockets is doing to London.'

'I think the Government knew about them, Nell. They just hoped they'd be able to find the places they were launched from, and bomb them.'

'Ar. But they can move the things about on transports. Not easy to pin down. Hope none of them gets as far north as Liverpool. That May blitz was enough for me! But talking about young Kenworthy – how bad was his wounds? You've never said.'

'I don't rightly know, Nell, and Polly hasn't said much, in her letters. But as far as I can tell, he's got shrapnel wounds. Anyway, he can't write his own letters. Someone has to do it for him. Mrs John went to see him in hospital down south, and that's what she said, when she got back. Shrapnel wounds, and that he was doing nicely. But now that he's been moved to a hospital in Derbyshire, I should think visiting will be easier. They'll tell me more, when I see them.'

'Pity all the wounded can't have leave for Christmas. Lord knows, they deserve it.'

Meg said nothing. Mark home for Christmas, with Stella there too, didn't bear thinking about. But Mark belonged to the past, Meg brooded, to the summer of '41, and now he was going to marry someone else.

She had wanted to write to him. Just a note, wishing him well. But she had decided against it, because when you had walked out on someone you loved without a word of explanation or goodbye, you couldn't expect to take up where you left off – especially when that man was engaged to someone else. Mark, she frowned, must know she had returned to Candlefold. Mrs John would have told him – and that she was now Meg Lewis. Men like Mark Kenworthy did not like having their love thrown back in their face; nor did they forgive easily.

The bus stopped outside the post office, and Polly was there! She was coming home to Candlefold, Meg thought happily and her sister was waiting to meet her. What more, then, could she ask? What more had she the right to ask?

'Meg! It's so good to see you!' Polly's arms were held wide to clasp her, hug her, welcome her back. 'Happy Christmas!'

'And to you, Poll. Oh, it's great to be back!'

'You had a good journey – no delays?'

'Delays? I'm here on time, aren't I?'

'Sorry! Just me, not knowing what to say.' Polly's cheeks flushed. 'Excited too, I suppose. Let me help you with your things. Where are your cases?'

'Here beside me. Only the one, Polly.'

'Oh, good. Then I suppose we'd better make tracks. The field will be wet – we'll go by the lane, shall we?'

'Fine by me. The case isn't heavy.' Meg glanced sideways at her sister, who all at once seemed reluctant to meet her eyes. 'And Poll – is something wrong? Not bad news? Surely not at Christmas?'

'N-no. Not as far as I know. Davie was well, four days ago.' Polly crossed her fingers as she always did when making such a statement. 'In fact, it's good news – well, I suppose it is . . .'

'Look! Something's up, isn't it? Meg set down her case. 'And I'm not walking another step till you tell me! It's Stella, isn't it? She's at Candlefold for Christmas!'

'No, Meg, she isn't. But someone else is.' Polly's eyes were wide, and bright with tears. 'He came yesterday. Mark is home.'

Meg closed her eyes tightly. It was all she could do, because there was a noise in her ears and a giddiness in her head. Mark – just a few hundred yards away. Turn right into the lane, then under the far archway and across the courtyard and there he would be. She had longed for him until sometimes it was unbearable, almost. Now he was so near, and she felt sick with apprehension.

'Polly! Why didn't you tell me?'

'But I just did!'

'Tell me before this, I mean! Give me the chance to –'

'Give you the chance to decide not to come? You can't mean it, Meg?'

'Oh, but I do mean it. I – I feel sick, and I'm shaking. Just look at my hands!'

'Yes, you have gone a bit white. But Mark isn't going to bite you!'

'What have you told him?'

'Now look, it's cold and I'm not going to stand here, arguing the toss. And Mark knows all about you. Mummy told him. Did you expect her not to?'

'And that I'd be here for Christmas?'

'Yes.' Polly picked up the case and began to walk.

'But you never told *me*! And what else have you kept back?'

'All right! Mark had shrapnel wounds to his face and hands, Mummy said. Seemed perfectly reasonable he couldn't write. But his face and hands are fine. His eyes took the worst of it. Mark insisted Mummy didn't tell anyone at all. You see, at first he was blind. They were so long getting him to a dressing station they feared he would lose his sight. But they've taken the shrapnel out of his left eye. It still hasn't healed – very sore and swollen – but he's going to see out of it. He has drops to put in it and he must keep it covered, but there's hope. For the left eye.'

'And the other one?'

'He has to have an operation. Don't know where yet, but soon. When he goes back. There are a lot of wounded, you see – some far worse than Mark. That's why he was allowed home over Christmas.'

'You're sure about his left eye, though?'

'As sure as anyone can be, Meg. Yes. The right eye is going to be more difficult, it seems. There is still shrapnel in it, but the trouble is that it has affected the retina – it may have become detached, which our doctor explained is rather more serious.'

'Polly – his poor eyes. Isn't that terrible enough for him without having to confront me?' She couldn't stop the shaking that had taken her. 'Are you sure he knows I'm coming?'

'I told you so, didn't I? And surely you're both adult enough to behave like civilized human beings? For Pete's sake, it's supposed to be the season of peace and goodwill!'

'All right. But what about Stella?'

'What about her? And look!'

Mary Kenworthy stood at the top of the stone steps. Behind her the door stood wide open as if in welcome.

'Meg. How good to see you! A happy Christmas, my dear. And I can see,' she said softly, 'that Polly has told you.'

'Yes. I can't take it in; don't know whether to laugh or cry. Cry, I suppose. What am I to do, Mrs John?'

'Do you want to see him, Meg?'

'I – I don't know. A shock, you see. I never imagined . . .'

'I asked if you want to see him?' Mary said firmly, and Meg lifted her eyes and saw kindness in those of the older woman.

'Yes. Of course I want to see him! I'd be a liar if I said I didn't. But will Mark want to see me?'

'Mark knows about, well – *everything*. I told him what you had told me. I hope I did the right thing?'

'And what did he say?' Meg pulled her tongue round her lips.

'Very little, as I remember. It was when I went to see him after he came back to England. He was still in shock, I think. And he was bitter about his eyes. He thought then that he'd lost his sight. Anyway, Meg, he knows you're coming today.'

'Then if you're sure he wants to –'

'Of course he wants to see you! He hasn't actually said so, but I know my own son. I must warn you, though. Both his eyes are bandaged, which irritates him. I can see why the hospital gave him a few days' leave – he's a very bad patient, easily upset. I suppose it is as he said. You think it won't happen to you. The other fellow, maybe, but not to you. But have you eaten, Meg?'

'No. But I couldn't, thanks. I'd like to see Mark, though – get it over with.'

'Oh, dear! Surely it isn't going to be all that bad? You sound as if you're going to the dentist for a filling.'

'Bad? I hope not. I just hope he'll meet me halfway – try to see my point of view.'

'Well, if you ever get around to talking to each other, he'll no doubt give you his opinion on the matter.

'So – so where is he, Mrs John?'

'He's in the woodyard.'

'*The woodyard!* He'll be frozen stiff! Why has he gone there? Out of my way?'

'No. Actually, it's quite sheltered there. He got there alone – swinging his stick and swearing every time he got it wrong. But I followed him. He managed it. And don't mention his white stick. He hates it! Go on, then! Off you go. And the very best of luck. He's very tender around the edges at the moment, remember.'

'But don't let him bully you!' Polly warned. 'He's being very prickly and arrogant, as well!'

'Yes – well – I'll go then.'

The shaking was still there and her mouth so dry she found it almost impossible to speak. At the trough, she lifted the pump handle, cupping a hand beneath the spout. The water that gushed out was icy cold and she slaked her thirst with it. Then, back ramrod straight, chin jutting, she walked towards the far archway – and the woodyard. And to Mark.

She stood for a long time, wanting to call out, to laugh or maybe just to stand there and give way to tears. She longed to gentle his bandaged eyes with her lips, kiss her love into them, make them better. But she just stood, drinking in the sight of him, wanting him so much that the familiar pain inside her was back again.

He was sitting on a tree trunk that had been fashioned into a seat. Around his shoulders was his greatcoat. On the ground at his feet lay a white stick.

Love of him surged through her cold shaking body, warming it into life, but still her feet would not move; still she was afraid to make that first gesture, take the first step.

She tried to say his name, but her lips moved without sound. Impatiently, she cleared her throat and saw his head jerk upwards.

There was a small silence, then he said, 'Merrilees?'

'Yes. It's me . . .'

Then all at once she was free and running to his side, calling his name, loving him so much that pain became pleasure. Then, when she could have touched him had she held out her hand, she stopped to spin out the moment, savour it, store it in her heart.

'Long time, no see.' He said it harshly, his face turned away from the sound of her voice; said it without even taking his hands from the pockets of his coat. And all at once she was cold again, and afraid, and the shaking came back.

'I'm sorry, Mark. I'll go, if you want me to, but I thought – *hoped* – we had things to say to each other.'

'*Things!* Like you shoved off without so much as a goodbye! Like you couldn't wait to get down the aisle with some other bloke! Like –'

'Mark!' The sharpness in her voice caused the tirade to stop. 'Let me tell it the way it was?'

'I know how it was. You've been a widow more than two years, it seems you flew straight from my bed to his! Kip. I might have known it!'

'Kip. But I didn't share his bed.'

'And you expect me to believe that? What do you take me for – a fool?'

'No! Norra fool! Just a – a prickly, arrogant feller who hasn't the manners to get to 'is feet when he's talkin' to a lady, nor take his 'ands from his pockets!' She was angry now; much, much too angry to modulate her voice. Her Scouse twang was back in full flow. 'But I might 'ave known you thought nuthink of me. Didn't take yer long to find Stella, did it?'

'Ah, now.' The corners of his mouth tipped briefly into a smile. 'That sounds more like the Merrilees I once knew! And do you blame me for Stella?'

'No. But let me tell you?' Her voice was calm again. 'And might I sit down?'

'Be my guest. And if you're interested, Stella and I are through – finished. She came to see me in hospital and a couple of days later there was a letter, with the ring inside it. Seems she didn't fancy being married to a blind man.'

'Were you upset about it?' She tried to disguise the joy in her voice. 'And – and was she very beautiful, Mark?'

'Upset? No. Dented my pride a bit, but it wouldn't have worked, she and I. And beautiful? I suppose so, but she wasn't you, in my arms.'

'You were lovers?'

'After a fashion.' He shrugged eloquently. 'Like you and Kip.'

'Kip and I *weren't* lovers. He slept on the sofa. Said he would wait.'

'Then he was mad!'

'No, Mark. He was a good man. I was in terrible trouble – didn't know which way to turn. Kip sorted me out. We were married at the registry office just before he sailed. We'd have been married again in his church, next time he was home, but he didn't come back. He said the registry office wedding made it legal.'

'I see. Legally but not morally married?'

'Yes. It had to be that way. I was pregnant, Mark.'

'*Whaaat*?' He flung round to face her. 'Hell – it didn't take you long, did it?'

'Pregnant with *your* child! The night of Polly's wedding. I didn't know, when I left Candlefold. I was desperate. Went for an abortion . . .'

'God, woman! You thought so little of me that you let some biddy scrape our child out of you!' His mouth was traplike; his face white. 'And why wasn't I told?'

'I told your mother and Polly I was married and widowed. No point telling them about the baby. And not a biddy. The man was a doctor, though I didn't have the abortion. Couldn't go through with it. Kip agreed with me. Said he would marry me, bring up the child as his own. I told him why you and me couldn't marry.'

'Decent of him, I suppose.' Mark's voice was gentler now. 'Lost at sea, was he?'

'No. Killed in an accident, loading ship. He's buried in Sydney. Funny, you know – we'd made up our minds to emigrate there, after the war. A new start, sort of.'

'Half a world away? Would you have gone through with it?'

'Yes. I owed it to Kip.'

'And taken my – our – child with you. Do I have a son, or a daughter?'

'There was no child, Mark. I had an accident in the blackout. I miscarried it in hospital. Y'know, Kip shopped that doctor to the police. They couldn't get him for doing illegal abortions, but they charged him with practising medicine whilst struck off. He got five years, and his wife a year. I wish Kip could've known that.'

'Sorry, Merrilees. Shouldn't have said what I did. Seems there have been misunderstandings all round.'

'Seems so. What Nanny Boag said was wicked. I won't ever forgive her.'

'I've sorted Nanny out. Had a word with Hugh Rushton. There's a Church of England home for the elderly; she'll be on her way as soon as there's a vacancy. It isn't only what she told you I find so damned annoying; it was the way she fooled Mother too. Fooled us all. I think she's sick in the head, now – mental. All I ever felt for her is gone.'

'We-e-ll – it's all cleared up now. And I'm sorry for all the upset I caused. If I'd had the sense I was born with, I'd have told your mother what Nanny had said, but it all seemed to fit together. Why upset Mrs John, I thought, when she probably never knew who my father was?'

'I'm sorry too. Shouldn't have lashed out either. Like you said – prickly and arrogant.'

'No. Polly said it first,' she smiled hesitantly. 'But I'm bound to admit it fits you to a T – sometimes.'

'But wouldn't you be just a bit put out, Merrilees, not being able to see anything? Going round, eyes bandaged, with a white stick?'

'But you are going to see again, Mark. You know you are. One eye for sure, Polly says.'

'Yes.' He held out his hands. 'Come here. Let me look at you – make sure you're real.' His voice was soft now, and tender, and he gentled her cheeks, her eyelids, her lips with his fingertips. 'I'm glad your hair is still long. Still the Merrilees I loved.'

'Loved, Mark?' She hardly dare say the words, but say them she must: tell him nothing had changed, for her at least. 'But I still love you. I never stopped. It wasn't fair to Kip, but it was always you.'

She needed, desperately, to hear him say he loved her too. But instead he said, 'Will you give me a hand?'

He had got to his feet, so she helped him into his coat, fastening the buttons, turning up the collar.

'You're cold, Mark. We should be making tracks.'

He didn't love her, she thought dully; had soon forgotten.

'No. Not yet. Take me to the willow pool, Meg? Please?'

'You're sure?' He had called her Meg. 'It – it's starting to get dark.'

'I'm sure. And it's been dark under these bandages for a long time.' He smiled as he said it, and she took courage from it.

'All right. Give me your stick.' She linked her arm in his, then, twining her fingers in his, pushing their hands into his coat pocket. 'Straight ahead, then, till we come to the archway.'

There was hope in her heart again. It was going to be all right; past mistakes forgiven and forgotten, oh, please they would be?

'By the way,' she squeezed his fingers tightly. 'What did you do with Stella's ring? Not important, of course, but –'

'You're right. Not important. Actually, I sold it to the man in the next bed for twenty quid. He had a crush on one of the nurses. And the best of British to him!'

'Ah. Turn right, here. The cow pasture gate is –'

'Just a few steps ahead. I know!'

'Then tell me why you want to go to the willow pool,' she demanded, all at once serious. 'It'll be boggy and cold there now.'

'Well, if you must know, I seem to remember that that was where it started – really started – for you and me.'

Yes. A long time ago. We're both older and wiser, now.'

'True. But you've changed. Your voice – it's different. Where has Merrilees gone?'

'You mean I speak differently? Yes, I suppose I do – 'cept when I get annoyed. It started with a verse, you see – a piece of poetry. Oh, I'd tried to copy your mother and Polly, because Ma spoke nicely too. I reckoned if she could learn to talk proper – properly – then so could I. It was Nell started it. The shipowners Kip sailed for paid me compensation, even though I hadn't asked for it. So I put it in the bank – tried to forget it. It seemed like blood money.

'Then Nell said I ought to spend it on going to Australia when the war was over; finding Kip's grave, and saying a decent goodbye to him. And with the rest of the money, I should put up a headstone for him.'

'I agree. I think you should go, when things get back to normal. But how does the poetry come into it?'

'We-e-ll, Nell said I should have something special on the stone – not your usual RIP, and all that. She said there was poetry, she thought, with the line *Home is the sailor, home from the sea* in it, but she wasn't sure about it. So I went to the library and the lady there knew exactly what I wanted. It was lovely; made me cry.

> 'This be the verse you grave for me:
> "Here he lies where he longed to be;
> Home is the sailor, home from the sea . . ."'

'"And the hunter home from the hill."' Mark finished softly. 'Yes. A good epitaph.'

'Kip really wanted to live there after the war. A good country, he said. It's sad,' she whispered chokily, 'that that's where he is now.' She cleared her throat, and sniffed loudly. 'Anyway, those words were so right, so beautiful, that I started reading poetry – reading it out loud, an' all. And you can't read lovely verses with a Liverpool accent, now can you? I read poetry all the time, now. Part of my education, I reckon, though I've never told anyone about it – not even Nell – till now. I'm reading John Donne, at the moment. There are two lines he might have written especially for me. *I am two fools, I know. For loving, and for saying so* . . . But what the heck!' She drew in a shuddering gulp of air. 'And I was right. This riverbank looks awful, Mark.'

'*How* awful?'

'Well, the river is high – level with the top of the bank. And the water is brown, and fast-flowing. And the grass is wet and soggy and brown too.'

'And the pool?'

'Gone. Full of winter water, level with the river. And the willows are bare.'

'Yes, but it'll be summer again before you know it, and the water will be warm. Will we swim here again when the willows are green, and the pool shallow?'

'Yes. One day, I hope . . .'

They twined fingers again and linked arms and, thighs touching, walked slowly to the archway.

'Cobbles ahead,' Meg whispered. 'They look a bit slippy. Be careful, Mark.'

'Don't fuss, woman!'

'Left a bit.' She pushed him with her hip. 'Pump trough on my right.'

'I know. I've crossed the yard before!'

'So you have, darling.' There was love in her voice.

Ahead of them were the stone steps that led up to the door. It stood wide open, light flooding out in a golden glow. And she could see a fire blazing in the grate, and a Christmas tree, dressed with shimmering glass baubles.

They were beside the pump trough and she trailed her fingertips across its roughness as they walked.

Happy Christmas, Ma, she whispered with her heart.

Then turning to Mark she said, 'When are you going to kiss me? And when are you going to ask me to marry you?'

She closed her eyes and tilted her chin, cupping his face in her hands, guiding his lips to hers. Then she clasped her arms around him and held him closely, and for a time they were in a summer world of green cool shadows and sunlight on water, and the willow pool, beckoning them.

'I love you,' he whispered. 'Don't leave me again – you and Merrilees, both.'

'I love you too, and I'm not going anywhere, ever again, without you.'

'God, darling, I missed you – you'll never know how much!'

'I do know, Mark, truly I do . . .'

'Then you'll marry me?'

'If you're askin',' she laughed.

'I'm askin',' he smiled, kissing her again.

'Then we'd better tell your mother and Polly, hadn't we – make it official, so you can't change your mind. It'll be a bit of a shock, though. Do you think they're ready for it?'

'I rather think,' he smiled as they walked hand in hand up the steps and into the fireglow, 'that they've been waiting to hear it for a long, long time! Happy Christmas, Merrilees.'

'Thanks. And since you're askin',' she teased in her broadest Liverpool accent, 'reckon I *will* marry you! Happy Christmas, Captain Kenworthy, darling. And since I haven't told you for at least a minute, I do so love you.'

And there, beside the glittering tree, they kissed. And kissed again . . .